He had given his word, his pledge on his honour to come for her when the danger of rebellion had passed or been resolved, but she could not grasp hold of a pledge. There was no warmth, no physical comfort, no substance to a few whispered words delivered on a cold, mist-ridden night. She knew she could have been safe and strong if Alex had just trusted her enough to take her back to Achnacarry.

Instead, she had been shipped off to Derby, exiled back to people she no longer felt tied to or cared about; left to hope and pray for the day when her proud rebel husband would ride his enormous black stallion up the drive of Rosewood Hall and reclaim his wife. If he came at all. If he still wanted to come. If he still believed, after her frosty departure, that there was anything worth coming back for.

If he he survived.

THE BLOOD OF ROSES

Other Books by Marsha Canham:

BOUND BY THE HEART
CHINA ROSE
THE WIND AND THE SEA
THE PRIDE OF LIONS

MARSHA CANHAM

KNIGHTSBRIDGE PUBLISHING COMPANY
NEW YORK

This paperback edition of THE BLOOD OF ROSES first published in July 1990 by Knightsbridge Publishing.

Originally published by Severn House Publishers Ltd. by arrangement with PaperJacks Ltd.

Publisher's Note: This novel is a work of fiction. Names, characters, places, and incidents either are the product of the author's imagination or are used fictitiously, and any resemblance to actual persons living or dead, events, or locales is entirely coincidental.

Published in the United States by
Knightsbridge Publishing Company
255 East 49th Street
New York, New York 10017

ISBN: 1-877961-43-4

10 9 8 7 6 5 4 3 2 1

FIRST EDITION

This book is dedicated to the astonishing number of concerned readers who wrote to me demanding to know if I just intended to leave all those loose ends dangling in The Pride of Lions.

Now really, would I do that to you?

'L'audace, et toujours de l'audace!'
—motto of the '45

PROLOGUE

BLACKPOOL, August, 1745

Catherine Ashbrooke Cameron stood before the rain-lashed window, her breath lightly fogging the inner surface of the glass pane. Outside the inn, the streets were all but deserted, the cobbles glistening under the steady downpour, the lights from the cramped, multi-storeyed dwellings reflected in the shimmering puddles and bubbling runs of the gutters.

She had been in Blackpool for four days—an interminable length of time for someone not normally noted for her patience. A crowded seaport, it smelled of fish and offal, of coal dust from the huge shipments exported south to London, of the countless unwashed bodies who laboured tediously, day after day, to earn a few pennies with which to feed and clothe their families: not exactly the type of company the young and beautiful daughter of an English peer of the realm might be expected to keep.

As she stared out the window, Catherine's long slim fingers toyed absently with the enormous gold-and-amethyst ring she wore on her left hand. It was her only solid reminder of the reality of the time lapsed since she had ridden away from her home in Derby five weeks earlier. Five weeks. It might well have been five years. Or five centuries. She had changed so drastically—*things* had changed so drastically: attitudes, circumstances, situations . . .

Where she had once been careless and spoiled, pampered to within a razor's edge of her finely honed temper, she now felt old and wise, experienced and mellowed far beyond her eighteen years. Where once an arrogant snap of her fingers would have brought any young man within a radius of a hundred miles fawning on his knees before her, she now knew that all the begging, pleading, hoping and praying would not bring to her side the one man she ached to see.

Catherine raised a finger and traced a path along the slippery glass, following the bright slither of a raindrop as it meandered down the outside of the pane. She felt numb, detached from the world, as if the events of the past five weeks had never happened. But the sparkle of the amethyst ring was proof that they had. The faint, lingering bruises that still marred the ivory perfection of her body were proof that they had. The tears that filled her eyes and burned at the back of her throat at the slightest provocation were proof that *something* had happened. Her brother Damien, who had arrived in Blackpool that afternoon to escort her the rest of the way home to Derby, had only needed five minutes alone with her to isolate the cause of the drastic difference in her demeanor. However, already plagued with guilt over the part he had played in condemning his sister to what must have been weeks of pure hell, he misread the tension that shivered through the slender body.

"If that bastard, Cameron, forced you to do anything against your will, I'll kill him myself," he announced savagely.

Catherine had opened her mouth to expound on just how dreadfully she had been used and abused—certainly the Catherine Ashbrooke of a few weeks earlier would not have hesitated to capitalize on her brother's guilt, or to use it mercilessly to win his sympathy and pity—but she could not do it.

"No. No, Damien, it isn't what you think. He . . . he did not do anything to me that I did not want him to do. In fact, in the beginning, he did everything he could to avoid me. He treated me like baggage, he ignored me, he rarely spoke to me unless it was absolutely necessary. And I truly believe he would have kept his word to annul our marriage as he had promised, and send me home as soon as he was safely through the border patrols, but . . ."

Damien's hands had tightened on her shoulders, forcing her to look up into his pale blue eyes. "But what?"

"But . . . I would not let him," she cried softly. "I begged, I pleaded with him to let me stay in Scotland but he wouldn't listen."

"You begged . . . ? Good God—" his voice had softened with disbelief. "You have gone and fallen in love with him, haven't you?"

Catherine raised huge, swimming violet eyes to his. It was no use denying it. Hands that could not control their trembling were flung up and around her brother's shoulders and her whole body became wracked with sobs.

"It was not supposed to happen. I don't even know how it happened, or why it had to happen to me, but yes. Oh yes, Damien, I do love him. I love him and I hate him and . . . and . . . he had no right to do this to me! No right at all!"

Damien had been helpless to do more than hold her and soothe her as best he could. Catherine knew there was no earthly way to explain what had happened, how she and Alexander Cameron had progressed from adversaries to lovers in an apparent wink of an eye.

"I love him, Damien. It is a terrible, hurtful, wonderful feeling and I do not understand how it can be all those things at the same time, but it is."

"Does . . . he feel the same way?"

"Yes," she said, a little too quickly, her voice a little too high-pitched. "Yes, he does. But he's stubborn, and he doesn't think I would be as safe in Scotland as I would be with my family in England. There is the best bit of irony, wouldn't you say?" She laughed bitterly and accepted the handkerchief Damien offered, wiping at her streaming eyes and nose. "He didn't seem to care too much about my safety once he knew I'd discovered he was a Scots spy and forced me to travel north with him as his hostage. He was rude and arrogant, and . . . and . . . he kept me so damned angry all of the time, I didn't have much chance to be frightened. But when I was . . . frightened, I mean . . . he was always there, and somehow . . . I wasn't frightened any more. Does that make any sense at all?"

"For you, my dear Kitty?" Damien had smiled. "Perfect sense. And I should have known something like this would happen, dammit. I should have been able to see it that very first night."

"I had no idea you were a romantic, brother dear," she sniffed wetly, "or that you believed in love at first sight."

"I'm not, and I don't. But you had a look on your face that evening when Hamilton Garner confronted the pair of you out in the garden, one that screamed at anyone who cared to listen, that you had never been kissed quite like that before. I dare say it was what prompted the haughty lieutenant into challenging your bold Scotsman into a duel."

Catherine experienced a flood of colour into her cheeks. "Hamilton recovered from his wounds, I presume?"

"He was on his feet within the week; out scouring the countryside with his entire regiment of dragoons, only to discover the mysterious Mr. Montgomery and his newly acquired bride had vanished without a trace. He was well on his way to tearing up the roads between here and London when confirmation of Prince Charles's landing in the Hebrides reached government ears. Colonel Halfyard rushed Garner's captaincy papers through and ordered his regiment north to reinforce the garrison at Edinburgh."

"Edinburgh?" Catherine gasped. "Hamilton is in Scotland?"

"I thought that might tickle your sense of irony further," Damien nodded. "And if the rumours we have been hearing prove to be correct, if the clans are arming and preparing to support Charles Stuart in his quest to reclaim the throne for his father and fight to bring James Francis Stuart out of exile . . ." He paused and sighed expressively. "It could well bring Hamilton Garner and Alexander Cameron face to face over crossed swords again."

Catherine shivered, remembering the twisted look of hatred on Hamilton's patrician face as he had sworn revenge on the man who had not only humiliated him in a duel of honour, but had then married the plum of Derbyshire. Catherine's father, Sir Alfred Ashbrooke, was not only a prominent Whig and elected Member of Parliament, but his circle of friends and acquaintances could have furthered an ambitious man's career to the top of the mountain . . . and if nothing else, Hamilton Garner was an ambitious man.

"A fine pair of scoundrels we Ashbrookes turned out to be," Damien offered mockingly. "You, the daughter of one of Hanover's staunchest supporters in Parliament, wed to the brother of the singlemost influential Jacobite Chief in all of Scotland; me, the vaunted son, learned solicitor, and heir to one of the oldest, richest seats in England—" a slight deprecatory laugh broke the seriousness of the speech "—on the verge of being hustled to the altar under less than auspicious circumstances so that my bride might deliver me a legitimate heir."

Catherine's astonishment had been genuine. "Harriet? Harriet is—?"

"Indeed she is. Rather beautifully so, I might add. But if you thought Father's rage was monumental on the eve of your unexpected nuptials, you should have seen his chins quavering when he learned of his son's indiscretions. He wanted us to marry with all due haste, of course, but Harriet would not hear of it. Not until she had heard some word from you, that is. Now, perhaps, she will consent to unlock her door and emerge from her rooms."

"A baby!" Catherine had cried then.

"A baby," she whispered now, smiling wistfully as the echoes of the conversation faded behind the insistent tattoo of the rain. She should have been stunned, she supposed, to learn of her friend Harriet's condition. Conceiving a child out of wedlock was sufficient grounds to have a young woman banished from her home, treated as a leper in civilized society, and reduced to a beggar's lot in ignominy. Catherine was not as shocked as she might have been two months before, just as she was no longer ignorant of the effects of wild, blissful passion on the otherwise sane and reserved emotions of a well-bred young woman of quality. If anything, she was a little sad—sad and irrationally envious that Harriet was already able to prove to herself, and to everyone else, that her love was real. That it wasn't just a dream. That it wasn't a lapse, or a moment of insanity, and it wouldn't fade away as if it had never been.

Catherine closed her eyes and felt the hot flood of tears well over her lashes. She had no such proof. There was no child, only a hollow ache of loss, of loneliness. Had it all been a dream? Had she just imagined the warm, wonderful sensation of being loved and wanted? Had she only felt so alive and freed from the stifling confines of her own inadequacy because Alexander Cameron had swept into her life like a storm and could not help but leave it in shambles?

Her body knew beyond a doubt that she was no longer an innocent—dear God, she burned with shame and longing just to think of what a single touch could do to her pride. What a few words, whispered in passion, could do to the peace of her mind.

'I love you Catherine. I know you are angry with me now and you may not believe it absolutely, but I do love you. What is more, I swear on that love—and on my life, that I will come for you as soon as I possibly can.'

"Oh Alex," she whispered, pressing her hand and brow against the cold pane of glass. "I want to believe you. With all my heart I want to believe you but . . ."

She closed her eyes against the darkness and the rain, and imagined she could see him standing before her, silhouetted against the purpling haze of a Highland twilight. The wind would be tugging at the unruly locks of thick black hair, his gaze would be distant and unreadable, his mood as brooding and unpredictable as the misted mountain wilderness he called home. When he moved, it would be with the fluid, lethal grace of a panther, his body hard and dangerously deceiving so that one thought instantly of elegance and later, of shocking, explosive power.

He was a loner and a renegade, yes, but his capacity for gentleness and compassion was boundless, as she had discovered. For too many years he had lived with the past locked inside his heart, hardening it like armour against any further intrusions. At the age of seventeen, he had witnessed the brutal rape and murder of his first wife, Annie MacSorley. In revenge, he had killed two nephews of the powerful Duke of Argyle, Chief of Clan Campbell, and for this, had been declared a murderer and forced into a fifteen-year-long exile.

When Catherine had encountered him in the fogged, sun-streaked glade, he had been returning to Scotland, to his family's home at Achnacarry Castle. Denounced as a spy, yes, in the sense that he had kept his eyes and ears open on his journey from France to Scotland. A traitor? He had no pressing, zealous political convictions of his own; rather it was his ingrained code of honour—unbreakable and unbendable—that was carrying him home to stand by the side of his Jacobite brother, Donald Cameron of Lochiel.

Loyalty and family pride: two qualities to which Catherine had not given much thought before Alexander Cameron. Now she thought about them a great deal, for she was a Cameron too. He had made her one, in heart and body.

"Mistress Catherine?"

A soft voice intruded upon Catherine's memories and with a start, she straightened and dashed away the tears she had not been aware of shedding. She had not heard Deirdre come into the room, and her hands trembled icily as she smoothed them down a non-existent wrinkle on her skirt.

Deirdre O'Shea had remained steadfastly loyal throughout the harrowing five-week odyssey and had, at times, been Catherine's only link with sanity. More than just an abigail, Deirdre had become a friend and a confidant, an ally, a fellow conspirator, as well as unwitting victim. For as deeply smitten as Catherine was with Alexander Cameron, she was not blind to the stolen glances exchanged between Deirdre and the only man to whom Alexander would have entrusted their safety during the perilous sea voyage from Scotland to Blackpool: Aluinn MacKail.

Tall and lean, MacKail had the appearance and soft-spoken manners of an academic—indeed, he wrote poetry and could speak four languages fluently. But he was also the only man Catherine had ever seen best Alex with a sword, and the only man whose character and strength had equalled Alex's through fifteen years of shared exile.

"Yes, Deirdre, what is it?"

"Master Damien wishes to know if you will be taking your supper with him belowstairs tonight."

"I'm really not very hungry."

Deirdre frowned, noting the residue of tears on her mistress's cheeks. "You must eat something . . . to keep up your strength."

Catherine saw the concern in the soft brown eyes and attempted a faint smile. "Tell my brother I do not think I would be good company in public tonight. Ask him instead if he will join me in my room and share a small meal. We still have so much to discuss and so little time . . ."

Deirdre reached out and touched her mistress's arm. "You mustn't worry. Master Damien knows what to say and do. You must trust him to know what is best for you."

Catherine's smile faltered as Alexander's voice stirred in her memory.

"I leave it up to you whether you return to Derby as a wife or a widow. In either case, I am forwarding letters and documents to Damien . . ."

"What is best for me?" Catherine murmured and turned to stare out the window again. "To pretend I am returning home for a visit to make amends with my family while my husband is away in the colonies on business . . . or to return as his widow, determined to put the scandal behind me and to get on with the rest of my life? Such generous offers, both of them, complete with estates and bank accounts—" she bit her lip to check the flow of resentment. Not so very long ago she would have crowed with triumph had she been able to present herself before her peers with such enviable riches. During his life masquerading as Raefer Montgomery, Alex had accumulated an admirably healthy fortune—an attribute Catherine would have once deigned of greater importance in making a good marriage than almost anything else. Now, however . . .

Her hand fell to the back of the chair which stood beside her, her fingers caressing the rough length of tartan wool she had carried away from Achnacarry Castle. Having been smuggled out of Scotland in haste, and having arrived in Blackpool with only the clothes on her back, she had spent the greater part of the last three days trailing listlessly behind Aluinn MacKail as he emptied nearly every store and dress shop in Blackpool to replenish her lost wardrobe. The silk gown she wore now was more extravagant than anything she had owned before, but she would gladly have forfeited it along with everything else that filled the six brand new trunks, for the right to openly wear the Cameron plaid.

The soft yellow lamplight reflected off the amethyst ring and Catherine curled her fingers into a fist.

"What will you do now?" she asked Deirdre.

"What will *I* do, mistress?"

Catherine frowned and glanced sidelong at the startled maid. "You do not have to return to Derby with me if you choose to go elsewhere. There is little point in two of us being miserable."

Deirdre's cheeks flared instantly with two hot red spots. "Wh-where else would I go, mistress?"

"Back. With him. With Aluinn." The frown cleared and there were fresh tears threatening the stability of her voice. "Oh Deirdre . . . don't destroy your chance for happiness because of me. Go with him. Go back to Scotland if he asks you."

"He . . . he has not asked," Deirdre whispered quietly. "And I do not think he will. He and Mr. Cameron are very much alike, I'm afraid."

Catherine's expression slipped, the shine in her eyes grew and shimmered in sympathy. "I'm so sorry, Deirdre. Sorry to have dragged you into all of this."

The Irish girl thrust her chin out stubbornly. "I've stood by your side for eight years, mistress. You did not drag me anywhere I would not have gone willingly. And in truth . . . it has been something of an adventure, has it not? I might even be so bold as to suggest that we could well have lived out the rest of our lives in Derby and not seen one tenth of the excitement as we have these past few weeks. I don't regret it, mistress. You shouldn't either."

Regrets? Catherine wondered. How could she possibly regret the wild, passionate weeks she had spent with Alexander Cameron?

Raised by governesses and servants, tolerated by an indifferent father and shunned by a mother who preferred not to see the evidence of her own mounting years, Catherine had learned early what it was like to feel alone in a house crowded with people. Somehow she had coped and adapted. For eighteen years she had carefully built walls around her emotions, impenetrable barriers to protect her inner self.

Those walls and barriers had all been blown through a hole in the wind the moment she had looked into Alexander Cameron's eyes and recognized a similar look of loss and loneliness aching to be set free. He, too, had been locking away his emotions, throwing obstacles in the path of anything soft and vulnerable that threatened his independence. Two proud, stubborn people . . . was it any wonder the heavens had seemed to crack wide apart when they had finally come together?

Should it be any less surprising that the earth had ground to a halt when he had put her on board the *Curlew* and sent her out of his life?

He had given his word, his pledge on his honour to come for her when the danger of rebellion had passed or been resolved, but she could not grasp hold of a pledge. There was no warmth, no physical comfort, no substance to a few whispered words delivered on a cold, mist-ridden night. She knew she could have been safe and strong if Alex had just trusted her enough to take her back to Achnacarry.

Instead, she had been shipped off to Derby, exiled back to people she no longer felt tied to or cared about; left to hope and pray for the day when her proud rebel husband would ride his enormous black stallion up the drive of Rosewood Hall and reclaim his wife. If he came at all. If he still wanted to come. If he still believed, after her frosty departure, that there was anything worth coming back for.

If he survived.

When they had left Scotland, the Cameron clan had been preparing for war. Hundreds of clansmen had responded to the burning cross Donald Cameron of Lochiel had sent throughout Lochaber; hundreds, thousands more would be rallying around the Stuart standard when it was raised at Glenfinnan. The Highlands were mobilizing for a rebellion and it would be men like Lochiel and his brothers Alexander and Archibald who would be in the front ranks of the fighting when and if it came to that.

"Does Aluinn know how you feel?" Catherine asked abruptly, startling a fresh blush into Deirdre's cheeks.

"Mistress?"

"Does he know how you feel about him? Have you told him you love him?"

The girl's flush darkened painfully and Catherine knew Deirdre had not even dared admit it to herself.

"Oh Deirdre . . . go to him," she urged softly. "Tell him how you feel. Throw your pride at his feet if you have to—" she paused and smiled haltingly. "It seems to be the only way to get through a Scotsman's thick hide."

"But . . . Mr. MacKail is—"

"Mr. MacKail is as reckless and foolhardy as Mr. Cameron. The pair seem determined to challenge their destiny each sunrise and laugh at what they have denied the Fates each sunset." In a softer voice she added, "And you are absolutely right when you say our adventures will undoubtedly stay with us the rest of our lives, but don't turn your back on the greatest one of all. Go to him, Deirdre. If you love him, tell him so; it may be your last chance to do so."

Deirdre allowed herself to be led to the door, pausing there a moment to look back at her mistress, to see the sadness that had clouded the normally vibrant sparkle in her eyes. Catherine was so young and so very beautiful; it just wasn't fair she should have to suffer so. In the beginning, Deirdre could admit to reservations about liking or trusting either Alexander Cameron or Aluinn MacKail. Spies, traitors, mercenaries, fugitives . . . what was there to trust? And yet, part of the excitement and the adventure of the past few weeks had been to witness Catherine

Ashbrooke's transformation from a girl to a woman, and to watch a mighty Highland rogue humbled in the process. It was obvious that Catherine and Alexander belonged together.

Could it be any less of a marvel that she, Deirdre O'Shea, would lose her heart to Aluinn MacKail?

Aluinn was alone, caught in the process of changing into a clean, dry shirt when, with only the barest suggestion of a knock, the door to his room was opened and Deirdre presented herself on the threshold.

"Deirdre! Is something wrong? Has something—?"

"I have come to bid you farewell, sir, since it appears we will most likely be departing Blackpool in the morning."

He looked bewildered for a moment, then, aware that his shirt hung open over his chest, he pulled the edges together hastily and started to tuck the hem into the waist of his breeches.

"I'm, ahh, not sure I understand what—"

"It is quite simple, really," she interrupted bluntly. "I was only thinking to spare you the trouble of having to find a moment or two in your busy schedule to say goodbye to us tomorrow."

His hands idled in their task, then stopped altogether, leaving his shirttails half in, half out of his breeches. His smoky gray eyes narrowing perceptively, he asked, "Are you . . . angry about something?"

"Angry?" Her gaze did not waver from his even though she was fighting the urge to turn and flee from the room. "Why should I be angry?"

Aluinn pointed warily to a chair. "Would you like to sit down?"

"No. Thank you. I shouldn't want to take up too much of your valuable time."

He sighed and raked a hand through his sand-coloured hair, shaking from it some of the rainwater that still clung to the darkened curls. "This feels like another one of those early conversations we had when I was introduced to the praiseworthy qualities of your left hook."

"Laugh at me if you will, sir, but—"

"That's twice."

Deirdre's words stumbled together. "—but . . . I beg your pardon?"

"Twice you've called me 'sir' in the past two minutes."

"How else should I address you? I am, after all, only the maid."

"Ahh." He smiled faintly and moved away from the fire. "So, we're back to that, are we? Mistress O'Shea and Master MacKail? The insurmountable barriers of social class, etcetera, etcetera?"

"They are not imaginary barriers," she pointed out quietly.

"No, I suppose they are not. Still, I thought we had risen above them."

"My father was a gameskeeper, my mother worked in a scullery for all but the few weeks leave she took at various times in their marriage to deliver thirteen children." A rush of pride made her avert her eyes for the first time. "It would take a good deal more than soft words and catholic generosity to rise above what I was born into."

"You are shortchanging yourself," he said softly. "And me."

"No." She shook her head and looked him squarely in the eye again. "It is what I am, and I'm not ashamed of it. I've worked hard to improve myself, but in ways that are important to me, not to impress anyone else. I've taught myself to read and write, and I've been a daughter my mother could be proud of, not a trollop who climbs from bed to bed to earn extra pennies in wages. I'm quite happy with who and what I am, and I've no great desire to change to suit someone else's needs to liberate the masses."

Aluinn's grin broadened. "Is that what you think I am doing? Working a little social reform on the lower class?"

Deirdre flushed scarlet and whirled around. His strong hands grasped her by the shoulders, preventing her from reaching the door.

"Let me go! I'll not stand here and be laughed at!"

"I am not laughing at you, Deirdre," he assured her, his lips close to her ear. "If anything, I am laughing at myself, at the perfect master of disguise I have become. You see—" the pressure of his hands increased, forcing her to turn and face him "—if birth is how you judge a man, then there is no part of me worth more than a single hair on your head."

"I . . . don't understand," she stammered, her deep brown eyes burning him with their intensity, and he seemed to falter for a moment, uncertain of how to begin.

"You once told me how noble you thought I was for sacrificing my freedom to go into exile with Alex. But my motives, Mistress O'Shea, were neither noble nor wholly unselfish. While it was true we were raised together as foster brothers, it is also the plain truth that Alex is the son of the clan chief, and I am only the fifth son of a low-born tenant farmer. My mother and Alex's mother happened to give birth to sons a week apart; his mother died, mine was brought in from the fields to be a wetnurse. Because of that, I was accorded all the privileges and comforts of a gentleman's son, and when the time came to choose between giving up those luxuries or fleeing to the Continent with Alex, well . . ."

"But . . . your loyalty to Mr. Cameron, to his family, is not a fabrication."

"No. No, it's real enough, praise God. I would lay down my life for any one of them willingly and maybe . . . just maybe that might be enough to repay them for all the good years."

Deirdre frowned, saying slowly, "I'm sure they do not expect repayment. I'm sure they would not even want to hear you speak this way."

"What way is that, Mistress O'Shea? That I'm not good enough to rise above the class I was born into? That it is just their . . . catholic generosity keeping me by their side?"

Her eyes widened and the breath caught in her throat. He had deftly managed to use her own words against her, to show her how foolish her fears were. Her gaze slipped lower on the handsome face as she felt him angle her mouth up to his. Her fingers unclenched, inching their way up to his shoulders as the gentle contact of his mouth sent a wave of heat washing sluggishly through her body. From somewhere she found the boldness to respond, to part her lips in an invitation for the conciliatory gesture to become something much more.

A shudder rippled through the smooth, steely muscles holding her, and in the next instant, he was pushing her away, bracing her at arm's length as if any further contact might scald him.

"Wh-why are you stopping?" she gasped weakly. "Don't you want me?"

Shock hardened his features briefly. "Not want you? Deirdre . . . dear God, if you only knew how *much* I want you."

"Then . . . why are you stopping?"

"Because . . ." he dragged his eyes away from hers and stared hungrily at the moist softness of her lips. "Because I'm leaving here tomorrow, and because it wouldn't be fair to you if I didn't stop right now . . . while I am still able."

Deirdre tested the resistance in his arms and found them unmoving.

"Will it be any more fair," she asked after a moment, "to simply say farewell and ride away in the morning, leaving me wondering, wishing, dreaming after what might have been?"

"Deirdre—"

"I'm not afraid, Aluinn. You are a good and gentle man and . . . and I am more afraid of *not* loving you. Besides—" her lips trembled into a faint smile, "—after the lovely speech you have just given me, how can you possibly turn me out the door?"

Aluinn raised a visibly unsteady hand to smooth the sable locks of hair back from her cheek. "My greatest fear has been that you would come to me out of some misguided notion of gratitude, or indebtedness. I thought . . . *damn!* For once in my life I thought that by the simple, oh-so-noble act of not touching you, I could prove I wanted more from you than just . . . this."

"But you do have more," she whispered. "You have my heart and my soul, both given most willingly, most lovingly."

"Deirdre—" he stopped again, his passion waging war with his common sense. "If we just had more time."

"But we haven't. We only have here and now, and if you're thinking the risk to your own peace of mind will be more than it's worth to love me, then perhaps they *were* just a lot of pretty words."

She started to pull back, to turn away, but Aluinn's hands were there to stop her. He drew her slowly forward and his lips sought the soft, dark nest of curls at her temple. The caress, like the touch of his hands, was gentle and caring, unhurried even though the tremors that raged through his body were as obvious and urgent as the need flushing through hers.

"I have a feeling," he murmured, "that even if we had a hundred years together, it still would not be enough time."

Deirdre slid her hands under the parted edges of his shirt. "Then don't you think we should take advantage of every minute we have?"

Aluinn's reply, muffled against the arch of her throat, was lost as he swept her into his arms and carried her to the bed.

DERBY, September 1745

The Southern Route of the Jacobite Army

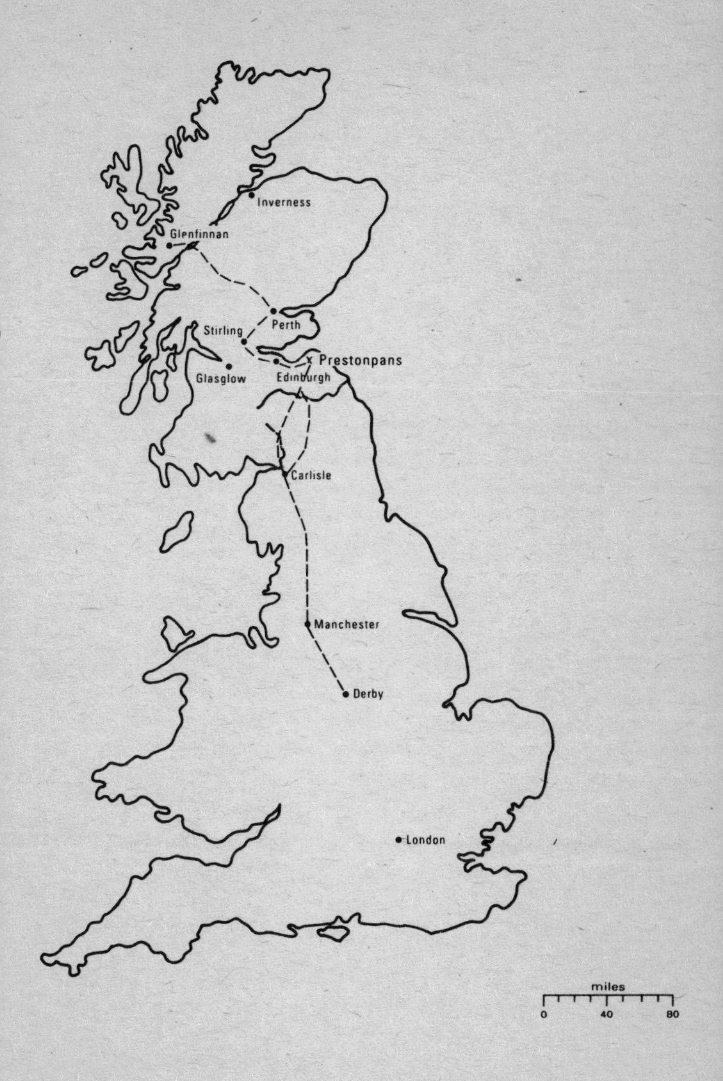

Chapter One

Catherine Ashbrooke Montgomery bowed her lovely blonde head and dabbed a delicately worked lace handkerchief at the wetness that collected persistently along her lashes. No one in the crowded chapel took notice, or if they did, they smiled with understanding. After all, it was not unusual for a girl to shed a tear or two at the marriage of her brother and her best friend. The speed with which the event had progressed from announcement to pronouncement was, on the other hand, ample reason for heads to shake and tongues to wag in disapproval.

Despite the scandalous circumstances, Harriet Chalmers made a glowingly radiant bride. The gown she wore had been her mother's and was made of silvered cream satin, flounced and scalloped with tiers of frothing Mechlin lace. Only an extremely acerbic eye would remark how the sweepingly wide side panniers had been adjusted slightly forward on the hips to minimize any possibility of the quilted petticoats not falling quite flat from the narrow waist. Only the stiffly busked, starchly righteous matrons would criticize the blush of colour in the pale cheeks, or smile slyly at the fact that Harriet's round hazel eyes never once released their intense hold on the groom's face.

Catherine had known Harriet for all their respective eighteen years and was well aware of the distress her friend was suffering, but that was not what kept the shine of tears constant in the violet-blue of her eyes. Should anyone have cared to closely analyse her visible signs of agitation, they might have discovered a young woman floundering in a sea of memories that had little to do with Harriet's wedding, and a great deal to do with her own.

". . . take this woman to be your lawfully wedded wife . . ."

Catherine heard the words as if they echoed through a long tunnel. Her gaze had been drawn upward to the multi-paned stained glass window that framed the altar. Designed to take advantage of the sunlight, the beams streaming through the glass were tinted red, gold, blue, and green. Dust motes, stirred by the guests, swam lazily in the path of the rays, making it appear as if the honoured couple, their heads bowed reverently to receive the final blessings, were kneeling in a coloured pool. The air was thick and sweet with the smell of perfume. A guest coughed discreetly, another snorted at some whispered comment—or was startled awake by some indignant elbow. The minister looked and sounded very pious as he droned the appropriate words and Catherine found herself staring at his long, bony hands, wondering why they seemed to be pushing through water, not air.

". . . pronounce you man and wife."

Damien and Harriet stood and smiled at one another, bathing in the glow of love in each other's eyes. The guests began to stir, to murmur amongst themselves and adjust a wrinkled skirt or smooth a ruffled collar or beribboned bonnet. In a few moments they would file out of the chapel and follow the clinging couple along the sun-washed path to where the coaches waited to transport the party from the village to the Chalmers's estate. To celebrate the wedding of his only child, Wilbert Chalmers had spared no expense in food, entertainment, and lavish decorations. The couple would remain at the estate overnight, then depart for London in the morning, where they would enjoy a brief but undoubtedly blissful holiday before duty called Damien back to his offices.

How different from her own experience, Catherine thought bitterly. A sullen retreat to her rooms to pack for a hasty, furtive departure from Rosewood Hall. Her "blissful" wedding tour had consisted of a two week endurance test in the back of a cramped, airless carriage; bouncing over military roads that had never been designed with elegant coach wheels in mind; dodging patrols of militia; pitting her wits against a husband who seemed determined to make her suffer every miserable step of the way.

"Catherine . . . Catherine, wasn't it simply wonderful?" The new Mrs. Damien Ashbrooke fluttered across the vestibule of the church like a butterfly in flight, her skirts flaring out behind her, a fountain of satin ribbons streaming from her hair like a wind-dragged cloud. Beaming happily, she took up Catherine's gloved hands in her own and lowered her voice dramatically, speaking without moving her lips more than a quiver. "Did you see me almost swoon when the reverend started going on about wifely proprieties and motherhood? I swear I could feel every pair of eyes on me, hear everyone nudge each other and start to whisper at once."

"If they were staring," Catherine assured her, "it was because you made such a ravishing bride. And if they want to whisper, let them. They're just being jealous old cows because you happened to snare the heart of the handsomest bachelor in England."

This last was said with a conspiratorial smile as her brother Damien joined them. He returned her hug and kiss, then with an elaborate flourish, produced five glittering gold sovereigns from the pocket of his white satin waistcoat.

"Never let it be said an Ashbrooke does not honour his debts," he said, presenting the coins to Catherine. "However disputatious the terms of the wager might be."

Catherine and Harriet exchanged a glance.

"Perhaps it comes from the pressure of having to relinquish his freedom," Catherine suggested blithely. "As I recall, he vowed to remain unencumbered until his fortieth birthday."

"Thirty, as *I* recall," Damien corrected her. "And since I am only six years shy of that goal, the pressure, as you call it, is not too dreadfully overwhelming. Nevertheless, it was you who made the grim prediction that I would not be enjoying my bachelorhood much longer, and you who backed the challenge with five gold crowns. To that end, dear Kitty, I concede the wager, and most happily so."

Uncaring of whose eyebrows might be launched skyward, Damien circled his arms around Harriet's waist and drew her into a loving embrace. His kiss left the bride in a deep enough blush to make the smattering of freckles across her nose glow through the layers of rice powder.

Harriet's self-conscious reprimand and Damien's good-natured retort could not help but put a smile on Catherine's face. Their happiness was obvious, their love for each other open and eager and completely devoid of any doubts or hesitation. They suited one another in character. Harriet was shy and unprepossessing, utterly devoted to Damien's wants and needs. Damien was strong and resilient, a caring, gentle and considerate man who would move heaven and earth to ensure his wife's contentment. He had not inherited Lord Ashbrooke's philandering ways. He had certainly sown his share of wild oats, for he was lean and handsome and elegantly suited to delivering lengthy and articulate courtroom dissertations. There had been rumours of a mistress in London and another in Coventry, but to Catherine's knowledge, he had relegated them both to memory the instant he had wakened to the fact that Harriet Chalmers was no longer a braided, freckled brat in pinafores and ruffled pantalets.

Marriage would suit him, Catherine decided. So would fatherhood.

She looked down at the five gold coins nestled against the gray of her kidskin gloves and remembered that there had been a second part to the wager, double or nothing, that she would win a proposal of marriage from Hamilton Garner before the clock had struck twelve to welcome in her nineteenth year. Did it constitute a win, she wondered, that she had found herself married within the required time limit, even if to another man?

Smiling, she pressed the gold coins into Harriet's hand. "For my nephew," she whispered. "Or niece . . . whichever fate allows."

"Fate has nothing to do with it," Damien announced firmly. "I have decided we shall have three sons and three daughters, in that order, and that, by God, is the way it shall be."

"Really?" Catherine mused. "And if your orders should go awry and you are blessed with only daughters?"

"Then we shall name them all Catherine and send them out as a plague upon the world."

Laughing, the girls each took a proffered arm and allowed him to escort them out of the church vestibule and into the crisp autumn air. They were instantly surrounded by well wishers and Catherine, taking advantage of the opportunity, slipped away from the crowd unnoticed. She was in no mood to engage in verbal fencing matches with the staunch-bosomed matrons who circled like vultures, waiting to glean the latest tidbits of gossip and scandal. Back-stabbing had always been the order of the day and Catherine had never felt it so keenly or gleefully directed between her own slender shoulders as she had since her return to Derby six weeks ago. Mistress Ashbrooke had acquired a good many enemies and rivals in her vainglorious climb to the top of the social ladder; they were only too eager to collect their dues now with a vengeance.

That she had dared to show her face in Derby again after being handed over as prize chattel following a duel between two supposed lovers, had shocked the community to its core. That she had returned alone might well have made Catherine the laughingstock of ten counties if not for the fact that she had arrived back at Rosewood Hall in the pomp and luxury of a gleaming new coach-and-four, or that it had required a second coach and six liveried servants to manage the trunks and baggage crammed to overflowing with the wealth and generosity of her absent husband. With Damien steadfastly by her side, Catherine had answered the endless rounds of questions—regardless of how slyly couched in friendliness they might be—with the haughty indifference she had always been able to call upon to cloak her true feelings. Indeed, Raefer Montgomery was a wealthy man. Indeed, he was an extremely successful businessman. He came from a highly respectable family; his name and reputation were lauded in shipping circles and although he might not be well known in London, he had command of the export trade to the colonies. Yes, it was a shame he could not postpone his trip to the colonies, but it had been upon his insistence that Catherine return to Rosewood Hall to dispell any worries her friends and family might have over the suitability of the match.

Sir Alfred's guilt—if he suffered any pangs at all—was erased the instant he saw his daughter alight from the carriage, her person swathed in satin and muffled in a cloak of white ermine. Damien Ashbrooke, forwarned in a letter that had departed Scotland a week before Catherine, had embellished Raefer Montgomery's character and attributes to the point where Sir Alfred had begun to think of his decision that fateful night as nothing less than providentially brilliant. His own reputation would not suffer from obtaining so influential and enterprising a son-in-law, nor would the Ashbrooke fortune, instantly invested in Montgomery Shipping. If anything, it was Catherine who was the more surprised to learn of the extent of her husband's actual wealth; she had assumed it to be as fictitious as his name.

As his widow, Catherine would have been even more attractive to money-hungry suitors than she was before. As his bride, she earned envy and praise from every last one of her peers. It was just one more of the many absurdities she faced being married to Alexander Cameron: having everything she had ever wanted, yet having nothing at all.

It was her sense of isolation that forced her to seek out her own company more and more frequently as the hours bled into days, the days into weeks. She had hoped the wedding would snap her out of her lethargy, but it became apparent early on in the evening that no such miracle would occur. The men, powdered and wigged and prancing about the dancefloor like satin-clad harlequins bored her almost to tears. The women clucked and giggled like a flurry of geese until something in breeches approached. Then it was all simpering smiles and fawning gazes, bosoms heaving against stomachers laced so tightly it was a wonder they could breathe at all. Catherine's patience dwindled proportionately with the champagne in her glass, and, endeavouring to cool the effects of both, she excused herself early from the celebrations to walk alone in the gardens.

The Chalmers's manorhouse was a modest two storeyed affair that could easily have been absorbed into one wing of Rosewood Hall. Far superior, however, were the ornamental gardens; acres upon acres of sprawling, well-manicured, artfully designed sections of thematic landscapes. An avid Greek historian, Wilbert Chalmers had transformed the area sloping away from the wide flagstone walkway of the house into a fairyland of Greek mythology. Here were beds of prized rose bushes and archways blanketted in vines that followed a meandering path through arboretums housing statues and fountains depicting scenes from ancient Greece. One in particular, a marble rendition of a glowering, omnipotent Zeus had always terrified Catherine as a child. Another, the Goddess of Love, Aphrodite, with her flock of stone doves, never failed to infuse her with a sense of tranquility and inner peace.

It was there where Catherine fled, her face aching from the need to smile constantly at the trite conversations of her dinner companions, her feet aching from being trampled upon by over-eager dance partners, her shoulders and back aching from the armour-like inflexibility of her stomacher and stays. Under cover of darkness she surrendered blissfully to the need to scratch at a thigh mercilessly gouged by a too-tight garter.

Half an hour, she decided. She would hide out in the gardens for half an hour and by then the serious flirtations would be well underway, partners targeted and victims ensnared, and no one would miss her if she slipped up the rear staircase to her bedchamber. Both Damien and Harriet would understand and forgive her; anyone else could leap fully clothed into the duck pond for all she cared.

Sighing, she leaned back against the iron bench, relaxing as much as her cumbersome petticoats and wire panniers would allow. The sky overhead was a canvas of black velvet, sprinkled liberally with twinkling chips of starlight. The odd shuffling of a breeze through the overhead boughs played on her senses like the mellow sound of a distant surf; the water splashing from a nearby fountain reminded her of rain pattering lightly on a windowpane.

Servants had hung paper lanterns throughout the gardens but within her particular area, two had been extinguished. The sole remaining source of light was well across the grassed rotunda and cast a miserly opalescent glow over the smooth ivory curves of the gracious Aphrodite. The niche Catherine sat within was blotted in shadows, the bench placed well back beneath a cleverly carved awning of thick boxwood. She was grateful for the shelter and the privacy, never more so than when she heard voices approaching along the path.

It had not escaped the speculation of those who knew Catherine Ashbrooke that her marriage to a relative stranger was more of a convenience than a hindrance. Her mother, Lady Caroline Ashbrooke, was a favorite subject among the gossips; it was rumoured her affairs had begun within days of exchanging vows with the pudgy and opinionated Lord Ashbrooke. Like mother, like daughter? they wondered. Already, not three months into the respectable state of matrimony, Catherine had fielded half a dozen lewd propositions, and could count half a dozen more pursuers panting hopefully in the wings.

It now occurred to her, with a mixture of anger and contempt, that her desire to seek the seclusion of the gardens could well be misinterpreted.

Her first instinct, therefore, was to hurry out of the enclosed arena and make her way back to the house through the maze of clipped rosebushes. Unfortunately, a scalloped ruffle on her sleeve had become unsnared around the delicate ironwork of the bench, and by the time she had freed herself, both the voices and the footsteps had encroached upon her privacy.

Careful not to rustle her petticoat or scrape a slippered foot on the crushed stone, she pressed herself back into the corner of the niche and hoped whoever it was would pass by without noticing her.

To her increased discomfort, not only did they not pass by, they halted beside the marble sweep of Aphrodite's gown and after a long and careful search of the paths ahead and behind, the coarse gravelly voice of Colonel Lawrence Halfyard sent Catherine's heart leaping higher into her throat.

The colonel was her mother's brother-in-law, a brusque, short-tempered pillar of a man who spoke with the blunt authority of twenty-two years of military life. A twitch of the beetling white eyebrows could send a junior adjutant into paroxysms of fear; an equally cryptic stroke of his pen could make or break a rising young officer's ambitions. Hamilton Garner had been one of the colonel's protégés. It was mainly due to her uncle's influence that Garner now found himself a captain of royal dragoons, and that he and his regiment had been among the first detachments of regular troops sent north with General Sir John Cope into Scotland under orders to seek out and destroy the Highland rebels who were daring to answer to Prince Charles Stuart's call to arms.

The Camerons, led by Donald Cameron of Lochiel, had been among the first clans to respond, although Catherine could hardly have volunteered information to that effect. Loyal to the exiled King James, Lochiel had been a leader among the many influential Jacobites committed to finding some way to bring their king back to Scotland, and to terminate the foreign influence in their government. Having fled the country after the failed rebellion of 1715, James Francis Stuart—the Old Pretender, as he was known by the English—had lived the last thirty years in relative ease and luxury in mock courts established in France and Italy. Periodic rumours of uprisings in the Highlands had occurred in the interim years, but rarely earned more than arched brows and yawns in the chambers of Parliament.

To the surprise of both the Hanoverians and the Jacobites, Charles Stuart had sailed from France in mid-July and landed on a remote island in the Hebrides. With what few loyal clans he convinced to join him, the Prince had then proudly declared his intentions of marching south to reclaim the thrones of Scotland and England in his father's name. Unfortunately, neither pride nor loyalty would help his followers combat the military might of the English army. Honour would not shield them against artillery, and the passion that stirred their blood would not prevent it from flowing freely into the ground.

With Cope's arrival in Scotland, news was expected any day of the Prince's capture or surrender—was this what brought Colonel Halfyard and a nervous-looking corporal into the darkest reaches of the garden?

"Damned nuisance, this," the colonel snapped. "It had best be deuced important to interrupt my nephew's wedding."

"Captain Price over at headquarters thought it was, sir," the young man stammered, brushing self-consciously at his dusty tunic. "I've barely been in Derby an hour myself."

"Well, out with it then. Plain terms, boy. No fancy dressings."

Catherine, concealed by the shadows, had no particular wish to be discovered eavesdropping, but it was already too late to make her presence known.

"As you are aware, sir," the corporal was saying, "General Cope's orders were to march north, to intercept and destroy the rebel army before their numbers became unmanageable."

"Unmanageable? Hmphf! Bare-chested shepherds and box-tongued buffoons! How many of them did the general consider to be manageable? Nevermind, boy. Go on. Go on!"

"W-well sir, the general set out from Edinburgh with every good intention of acting upon his orders, but . . . but he was met by Captain Swettenham on the road to Fort Augustus and—"

"Swettenham?" Colonel Halfyard tore the soggy end of his cigar out of his mouth and glared at the hapless officer. "Who the deuce is Swettenham?"

"Captain Swettenham, sir. He was with Colonel Guise's regiment when they were attacked and overpowered in a skirmish with the rebels outside of Fort William."

"Over . . . powered?"

The adjutant blanched. "They were outnumbered ten to one, sir. They were caught in an ambush, and . . . and . . ." The colonel's face was as immobile as a rock and the corporal finished the report on a quavering note. "The captain and his men were held for a week, then released on their own parole. It was he who reported on the gathering of the clans at Glenfinnan."

Catherine, frozen against the prickly boxwood shrubbery, had a sudden image of her uncle grinding his teeth to chalkdust.

"He was at Glenfinnan? As a guest or a participant?"

"According to the captain, sir, they had a grave fear for their lives in the beginning. They were ambushed by a group of MacDonalds, who might well have allowed their enthusiasm to overtake them if not for the timely arrival of another clan—Camerons, I believe, led by their chief, Donald Cameron of Lochiel. These new clansmen assumed charge of the prisoners and escorted them to Glenfinnan."

Catherine, her heart pounding at the mention of the Cameron name, was not the least surprised to hear that Donald Cameron had interceded on behalf of the prisoners' welfare. It was in his character, as a gentle and honourable man, to offer the British soldiers his protection until such time as they could be escorted safely out of harm's reach. Had he not welcomed Catherine, an Englishwoman—a *Sassenach*—into his family and home without question or hesitation?

"The captain was quite impressed with his treatment in the hands of the enemy," the corporal was saying. "He said as how his captors asked if he might be curious to witness the raising of the Young Pretender's standard, and, thinking his observations would be of considerable value, the captain accepted. He has since identified many of the participants: The Camerons, of course, and Clan Donald led by Keppoch and Glencoe; and—"

"Yes, yes," the colonel snarled impatiently. "You've no need to impress me with the condiments, corporal. What I desire is the meat."

"B-beg pardon, sir?"

"Get on with it, blast you! Cope! Where the devil was he while his fellow officers were being held and interrogated?"

"Interrogated, sir? But they were treated like—"

"Like guests? With the utmost civility? And I'll wager this paragon of virtue, this Donald Cameron of Lochiel, knew more about Cope's plans than the general did himself when he was finished wining and dining his 'guests.' Any fool knows you catch more flies with honey than with vinegar!"

"Y-yessir. Well, sir, as I said, the general met up with Captain Swettenham, who estimated at least two thousand clansmen had been present at Glenfinnan, and he had seen more joining the Pretender's army almost hourly since then. The Prince had also been informed of the general's departure from Edinburgh and it was Captain Swettenham's belief that an ambush was being planned to catch the general when he marched through the pass at Corriarick. You would have to see the pass, sir, to appreciate the gravity of the news. It is a narrow, winding trail that cuts between two impassable mountain ranges, fraught with cliffs and overhangs, and the mist so thick in places a man cannot see his horse's nose. An armed force of a few hundred rebels could easily conceal themselves and make quick work of several thousand troops. The general held council with his officers and it was decided to turn north-east and make for Inverness."

Colonel Halfyard started in disbelief. "He left the road to Edinburgh free?"

"N-not exactly, sir," the younger man quailed, melting under the colonel's heated stare. "Perth still housed a sizeable garrison of troops and the general had posted the 13th Dragoons at Stirling and the 14th before Edinburgh. And then, of course, there were the forces garrisoned within Edinburgh Castle—some five hundred seasoned veterans."

Colonel Halfyard inflated his lungs with an obvious effort aimed at controlling his temper. "Go on."

"The general assumed the Pretender would split his forces and send the majority of his troops chasing after them to Inverness—which any military strategist would have done without delay, if only to protect his own flank."

"The Pretender is no strategist," the colonel said with ominous calm. "He is a romantic gaylord who lives and dreams in the past. Any fool worth his oats would know he would make first for Edinburgh, for Holyrood. The entire purpose of this misguided exercise is to reclaim the royal court of his ancestors, and that, my good man, means winning Edinburgh. Always a holy city for the Stuarts, and militarily the key to winning over the Highlands. Go ahead, boy: Tell me I'm wrong."

The corporal swallowed, his adam's apple bobbing like a chestnut on a string. "Y-you are absolute right, sir. The rebels advanced through Dunkeld to Perth, taking both cities within forty-eight hours. Their army remained in Perth only long enough to resupply, then marched for Edinburgh."

"Cope?"

"He was in Inverness, sir. And as soon as he realized the rebels had not split their forces, he arranged for transports to carry his troops and equipment to Edinburgh by sea."

"And?"

"And . . . the rebels crossed the Forth just to the west of Stirling—"

"Where they were halted by the 13th Dragoons?"

"N-not exactly, sir. The officer in command—Captain Hamilton Garner—knew a single regiment could not hope to contain an army of several thousand men."

The colonel's knuckles were white and rigid as he removed the abused cigar from between the slash of his mouth. "Are you telling me that Captain Garner retreated before the enemy?"

"He thought it best to *regroup*, sir. To join forces with the 14th and hold the road until support could arrive from the fort at Edinburgh."

Colonel Halfyard brooded silently. He did not like the taste of the word retreat, however flavoured it might be with rationalizations. He knew it was an act abhorrent to Hamilton Garner as well, and would not have been entertained if there had been any other option available.

"They chose the last bridge before the city outskirts from which to make their stand," the corporal continued, his increasing nervousness now causing him to shuffle his weight from foot to foot. "But apparently Colonel Guest, in command of the garrison at Edinburgh, suffered some delay in responding to the request for support. Either that, or they underestimated how rapidly the Pretender's army was advancing. In any case, the vanguard of the rebel army rushed the bridge and . . ."

"Well? Out with it, damn you!"

The corporal flinched. "It was said later that the rebels were led by the Devil himself: a tall, black-haired spectre mounted on a coal black destry fully twice the height and breadth of any other mortal beast on the field. Even Captain Garner was so struck by the hellish sight, his senses deserted him for a time and the captain of the 14th had to knock him down to keep him from charging the bridge singlehandedly."

"God's teeth! What did the captain of the 14th expect him to do . . . *run*?"

"Apparently—" there was a moment's hesitation before the truth was blurted out "—that's *exactly* what happened, sir. Both regiments broke rank and fled. By the time the officers realized what was happening, the men were halfway back to Edinburgh. To their further disgrace, sir, the men kept running, even though the rebels drew up at the far side of Colt's Bridge and gave no pursuit. Edinburgh fell the next day, the 17th."

"The castle?" Colonel Halfyard gaped. "The entire garrison?"

"No sir! Not the castle. When I left, it was still in the hands of Colonel Guest—eighty years if he's a day, sir, and vowing to see the city levelled by his own guns before he'll surrender a single man."

"A little late for such histrionics, wouldn't you say? And where the blasted bejesus was Cope while all of this was going on? Has he abandoned his wits entirely?"

"General Cope was landing his troops at Dunbar even as I was receiving my orders to ride south with the news of Edinburgh's fall. He has with him sixteen hundred infantry and six hundred horse, whereas the rebels have had to distribute their forces between Perth, Stirling and Edinburgh to consolidate their position. At last report, there were no more than fifteen hundred troops occupying the capital city. I would stake my career, sir, on another rider arriving within the week to bring news of the complete and utter defeat of the Pretender's army."

The colonel's brows crushed together in an expression of disgust as he pondered the corporal's zealous ignorance. Edinburgh would not have fallen by whim or fancy, nor would Stirling or Perth. A crucial mistake in any war was to underestimate the strength and convictions of the enemy; more than one battle had been fought and won on courage alone. Cope had nearly twenty-five hundred men to put into the field, but they were green and raw, suffering from too much righteousness and not enough initiative. The news of the more experienced, seasoned veterans of the 13th and 14th Dragoons breaking and running could be a bigger weapon in the hands of the rebels than all the fine, shiny new artillery the government army could boast.

As he thought of Hamilton Garner and the brilliant young officer's reaction to the sight of his men running like cowards, Colonel Halfyard's stubby fingers closed around his cigar and crushed it to shreds. The corporal stared at the mangled remains then looked up into the coldest, deadliest eyes he had ever seen.

"If I hear one single word of what you have told me here repeated . . . your career will be the least thing you put at risk, Corporal."

"I . . . I was ordered to report to you and you alone, sir. My word is my bond."

"See that it remains so. And see that your Captain Price is fully aware of the consequences as well. Now . . . get out of my sight. I need time to think."

"Yessir. On my way, sir."

The corporal saluted smartly and hastened back through the arbour, relieved to be able to be walking away under his own power. The colonel remained by the statue, his stance and expression equally stonelike as he studied the northern sky. After several long minutes of hard contemplation, he turned on his heel and strode away into the darkness, his footsteps echoing like gunshots in the silence.

Catherine released a breath and felt a chilly trickle of sweat slither down the cleft between her breasts. Edinburgh had fallen September 17th. Today was the 20th. If General Cope's army had been but a day's march from the city, then it was quite possible the battle had already been fought and the outcome decided.

What had the corporal said about a tall, black-haired devil astride an enormous black stallion? It could not have been Alexander . . . could it? Catherine had a sudden image of Alex cantering through the dawn mists on the back of his magnificent Arabian, Shadow. The combined effect of the mighty black beast and the savage splendor of his rider was indeed enough to conjure pictures of the Devil. And if Hamilton Garner had seen and recognized the pair, it was no wonder his senses had temporarily deserted him. What else would stir him to such a blind rage he would charge against the enemy singlehandedly?

"Dear God, Alex," she cried softly. A fresh wave of fear tore at her heart as she lifted her blurred gaze to the serene, compassionate features of the goddess Aphrodite. "Please don't let it be true. Please keep him safe for me. Please. I could not bear it if . . . if . . ."

Unable to complete the horrible thought, Catherine covered her face with her hands and ran from the secluded rotunda, too blinded by tears to notice the second shadowy figure who stepped quickly back between the rows of ornamental shrubs as she fled past.

He, too, had overheard the report delivered to Colonel Halfyard, although not by accident. He had noted the dusty messenger's arrival and had followed the pair into the gardens, the risk of drawing unwanted attention to himself far outweighed by the need to know the latest news from Scotland. His own sources were becoming unreliable, few and far between. The border patrols had been more attentive of late and several of his best couriers had either been caught or killed trying to sneak through. Arrests throughout the country were increasing at an alarming rate; anyone even suspected of harbouring Jacobite sympathies was summarily tossed in jail without overt concern for their guilt or innocence.

Like so many others, Damien Ashbrooke had been swept up in the romance of the Stuart dream. From secret meetings in darkened back rooms to the secretive toast of passing a wineglass over water before drinking—a token of homage to the exiled king over the sea—Damien had been intrigued. He had been raised, like most young Englishmen, believing the "barbarians" who inhabited Scotland, were bare-chested, skirted warlords who were determined to overthrow the government and force the country back into the dark ages of a feudal society.

What he discovered instead were men of courage and conviction. Twice before there had been major uprisings north of the border: the first time in 1689 when James VII had been deposed in favour of William of Orange, the second in 1715 when William's daughter, Queen Anne, had died without heirs and parliament had chosen to ignore the Catholic James Francis Stuart in favour of the Protestant George of Hanover. Electing the German-born and mainly German-speaking king had not only been taken as an insult by the Scots who retained the faith of their kings, but by other influential men who took it as a blatant rebuff to the royal bloodlines of Scotland.

Poorly led, the Jacobite armies had suffered defeat both times, yet here they were again, ignoring the disarming acts that forbade them to bear weapons of any kind, plotting and scheming with the French to send an invading army to support their cause, once again facing the spectre of exile, transportation to penal colonies, even death. Nineteen Scottish peerages had been abolished after the last rebellion. Fortunes had been confiscated, families broken or destroyed, and many brave men cast from their homes and forced into a penniless exile in foreign lands. Some of these men still languished in abject poverty thirty years later simply because they chose to honour the vows of allegiance they had given their rightful king. A chance meeting with one of them, John Cameron of Loch Eil, a Scottish laird living in Italy with the court of King James, had been followed by an introduction to his youngest son, Alexander, and Damien's inclusion had been complete.

The embodiment of the very words "romance" and "passion", Alexander Cameron had both awed and fascinated Damien Ashbrooke. Having spent the greater portion of his life with his nose thrust between the musty pages of law books, meeting a soldier of fortune, a man who had spent most of his adult life fighting wars, dodging assassins, embarking on adventures dangerous enough to make a book-bound lawyer's blood curdle . . . well, it was also enough to make a man take a good long look at himself and his tepid existence. There was more: a vitality he felt just being in the presence of men like Cameron and MacKail; an energy in his blood that came with the realization that he too could face danger and survive. He did not possess the physical prowess or fighting instincts of a soldier, but he could and did contribute talents in other, equally important areas.

He arranged for the funding and purchasing of weapons and supplies to be smuggled into Scotland. He organized and contributed to a system of information-gathering that kept the Jacobites aware of any troop movements, naval deployments, or political maneuverings that might be to their aid or detriment. Conversely, through underground news sheets and words whispered into the right ears, the English Jacobites were kept informed about goings-on north of the border that would otherwise be kept under wraps by the Hanover government. The fall of Edinburgh would definitely be one secret the government would prefer to keep.

Stepping onto the moon-washed path, Damien started back toward the house. He had already announced his intentions to travel to London in the morning. Accompanied by his new bride, he would attract no undue suspicion if he made more frequent stops along the route than were necessary. He would have to see his contacts and ensure that all of England knew of the Jacobite victories at Perth, Stirling, and now Edinburgh—hopefully before the English could counteract with news of a subsequent victory on the misty moorlands outside of Dunbar.

Glancing up at the velvet sky, Damien said a silent prayer of his own. A bright tracer of light etched an arc against the blackness and, as he watched the falling star, he hoped with all his heart it was not an omen of things to come.

PRESTONPANS

Chapter Two

At almost the same instant when Damien and Catherine were directing their prayers toward the heavens, an equally impassioned plea was ringing out across a glistening, dew-laden moor more than two hundred miles away. With Alexander Cameron's darkly chiselled features looming before her, Lauren Cameron curled her fingers deeper into the glossy black shanks of his hair and guided his mouth down over the taut and straining peak of her breast. Her body arched and writhed into the eager boldness of his caresses. Her limbs felt gorged with blood, leaden and useless against sensations she had no means of controlling.

"Oh God, Alasdair," she gasped. "God . . ."

With a grunt of urgency, his body slid forward, impaling her on a thrust of flesh so hot and turgid the air that had hissed through her teeth was drawn sharply inward again. Her lips trembled open and her eyes quivered shut. Her whole body became engulfed in flames of crimson ecstasy and when he began to move within her, it was all she could do to claw her hands into the rock-hard flesh of his buttocks and pray she could retain consciousness. A single mass of pulsating nerves, she groaned in awe and braced herself against the quickening thrusts, plunging headlong into wave after wave of intense, searing rapture. Her head thrashed side to side, further scattering the cloud of titian hair beneath them. Her lips moved, but no sounds came forth, and her hands slid on his gleaming flanks as she strained to take more of him, take all of him, unmindful that each shocking impact sent her skidding on the wet deergrass.

With an echoing groan of mindless pleasure, he arched his magnificent torso upward, no longer concerned with fighting his conscience as a rush of ecstasy burst from his loins. A cry rattled deep in his throat, the shape of it unintelligible as Lauren began to convulse beneath him. So violent were her spasms and so desperate was his own need for release that barely had his senses recovered from one onslaught then he could feel the juices rising in him again . . . and again . . . each shuddering eruption prolonged for what seemed an eternity.

Finally, when the tumult subsided and he collapsed, panting and sweating within her welcoming arms, there were tears of joy and triumph welling hotly along her lashes.

"I knew ye would come tae me, Alasdair. I knew ye would."

The day had begun long before the sun had risen, long before the stars had lost any of their brightness and could still be seen through the lazy mist that cloaked the land. The Highland forces were camped on a field surrounding the small village of Duddington, directly east of Edinburgh. Less than four miles away, near the coastal town of Prestonpans, General Sir John Cope and his government troops were bedding down to a comfortable and refreshing night's sleep, no doubt chuckling over the fancy display of rebel footwork they had witnessed that day.

Cope had chosen his position well. He had the sea at his back, a wide clear plain on either flank—ably protected by rows of silently ominous artillery pieces—and an impenetrable morass of mud and swampland guarding against any manner of frontal attack. The rebel army, bristling for a confrontation, had tested Cope's defenses that day, appearing at first light on his left flank, only to find themselves staring into the black maws of primed and waiting cannon. They had circled back to re-form on his right, a maneuver which had taken three hours to execute and Cope only minutes to swivel his guns to defend.

Prince Charles had grudgingly but wisely ordered his army back to Duddington where he had then convened his chiefs and generals for a hasty council of war.

"Gentlemen," he said loudly, over-riding several heated arguments that were in progress over the day's events. "There must be some way of dislodging General Cope from that plain!"

"Cope is a seasoned campaigner," advised Lord George Murray, the Prince's field general. "He knows he holds the advantage of ground and knows he can sit there until the heavens rain solid gold sovereigns if he chooses. He is in no hurry to bring the battle to us, not with reinforcements on the way from London. On the contrary. The longer he sits the stronger his position becomes and the more confidence his men gain—another factor weighing heavily on his mind, I'm sure, for most of his troops are drawn from militias and have never seen battle before."

Lord George Murray was a tall, elegant man in his early fifties, one to whom soldiering came by instinct. He had joined the Prince's army at Perth and, like many of his peers, had staked everything in this venture, but was quite prepared to lose it for the sake of his king and country. He was not prepared to lose it through incompetence, however, or overeagerness—two qualities he had been much dismayed to find in his prince. Charles, being a much younger man, was prepared to acknowledge and follow sound military logic when it was presented to him. But finding himself on Scottish soil, at the command of an army of volatile Highlanders proved too great a temptation for his sensibilities. He was all for charging straight ahead, taking himself onto the battlefield on his tall white gelding and leading the men to triumph and glory. It had come as a great shock when the clan chiefs had insisted on the appointment of commanding generals, more so when they had specified the need for military experience over zeal.

Lord George Murray had been enlisted in the government army in the days of Queen Anne's rule. Even though he had not seen active duty since the ill-fated rebellion of 1715, the chiefs trusted him implicitly because he was one of them, and because he quickly proved to be a brilliant tactician and canny strategist. The Prince, no fool when it came to pleasing his chiefs, appointed Lord George to command the army on the field, and Lord John Drummond, the deposed Duke of Perth as his lieutenant general. The Duke of Perth was openly candid about his lack of real experience and acknowledged his appointment had been more for political reasons rather than for any burning military genius he could bring to the field. Lord George, however, took his job seriously, and, being a blunt and outspoken man, was not adverse to ruffling anyone's feathers, even if they happened to be princely. He spoke to the Prince sometimes as he would a child, explaining why it was not to the army's advantage to stage a frontal attack, or why they had to be extremely wary of artillery placements.

"Cope knows we must and will carry the battle to him," Lord George said evenly, disregarding the faint lines of tension etched around the Prince's lips. "And when we do, his cannon will cut us to pieces before we have covered half the distance on that wide, flat plain."

"Your trust in our gallant men is inspiring," came the moist, nasal twang of William O'Sullivan. He was an Irishman, one of the Prince's friends and advisors, and, having presumed the post of commander would have been his through patronage rather than experience, attempted to discredit and embarrass Lord George at every turn. He had wasted no time in pointing out to the Prince that Lord George's brother was a prominent Whig and that Lord George himself had been approached by the government and offered a high commission in the Hanover army. He even went so far as to suggest Lord George had secretly accepted, and was only serving the Prince in order to betray their cause from within.

"Your faith in their ability," he continued blithely, "leaves me . . . quite frankly . . . breathless."

"I have the utmost faith and trust in the courage and ability of our Highlanders," Lord George retorted. "As it happens, however, I place a higher premium on their lives."

"Battles have been fought on plains before," the Irishman sighed. "I fail to see the dilemma now."

"The dilemma, sir, is that we are neither trained nor equipped to meet a disciplined army on their terms. Indeed, battles have been fought on open plains before; battles between evenly matched forces who respect and adhere to the standard codes of warfare. They fire their cannon at each other, then, after their cavalries have made their gallant and impressive contributions, march their infantry out in precision lines, five ranks deep. Have you ever encountered a solid wall of musketfire? A wall that moves slowly, incessantly forward, with the front rank discharging their weapons, falling back to reload at a relatively leisurely pace, while the other four ranks advance and fire in turn. Our army has no cannon, no cavalry to speak of, and pitifully few men who even know how to fire a musket, let alone possess one to carry into battle. Our ranks are comprised of shepherds and tacksmen, many of whom will take to the field armed with only a knife or scythe, or a rusted *clai' mór* that has lain buried in the ground for the past thirty years. Any weapons they do come by will be taken from their own dead who have fallen before them—the chiefs, lairds, and officers of the clans who, by right of honour and tradition, occupy the front ranks and who, by that same code of honour and tradition, prefer to test their courage and mettle by the blade of a broadsword rather than the more modern efficiency of a pistol. But in order to test that courage and mettle, gentlemen, those same chiefs, lairds, and officers will have to charge across an open field facing cannonfire and sharpshooters, across a distance which they cannot possibly hope to survive, should God grant them wings! And once the chiefs and leaders of the clans have fallen, I have no doubt the shepherds and tacksmen will continue the charge bravely and courageously—but to what end? Even supposing they survive the wall of unrelenting fire, without leaders what will they be fighting for?"

A round of grimly supportive "ayes" came from the chiefs, none of whom would consider altering the composition of the ranks, but all of whom could recognize the logic of Lord George's observations.

"Oor strength has always been oor ability tae strike hard an' fast," said the crusty old MacDonald of Keppoch, "tae fall doon out o' the hills an' glens an' raid oor enemies afore they raid us. We're nae match f'ae cannon an' fancy *Sassenach* musketry, but I've yet tae see a neat, straight line o' English sojers hald their water against a Heeland charge when it comes at them out o' thin air. We need hills. We need cover. We need room tae wield oor swords an' cut them tae mince afore they ken we're on them."

"I must agree," Lochiel said worriedly. "Put our men on an open field, wi' nae cover and nae chance tae fight the way God intended men tae fight, an' aye, we'd see a slaughter."

The Prince endured the tense silence that followed the chiefs' remarks, knowing they were speaking through experience, knowing he could only lose more credibility in arguing openly with his general. He ignored a whining whisper from O'Sullivan and laid the problem squarely in

Lord George's lap. "Well then, General, how do you suggest we go about ridding ourselves of General Cope's presence? Is there something we are not seeing, perhaps? Some way to use the moorland to our advantage?"

Lord George, relieved to have been presented with an opportunity to salve his prince's damaged pride, quickly agreed. "My thought exactly, Highness. As I recall, this afternoon you suggested scouting the moor more closely with an eye to finding some way to utilize what is, in all probability, a blind spot."

"Why yes . . . yes, I did," the Prince said, not recalling at all.

"Donald—?" Lord George turned his angular face toward the chief of Clan Cameron. "I believe your men undertook the task. Is there any possibility of moving an army through that morass?"

Lochiel resisted the urge to glance first at Prince Charles before lifting his cornflower blue eyes to Lord George. The Camerons, under Lochiel's able leadership had played a major role in every skirmish and victory of the rebellion so far. They had been first into Perth, first into Stirling; they had been wholly responsible for driving the government dragoons away from Colt's Bridge the week before, and it had been a regiment of Camerons who had duped the guards on the gates of the city and entered Edinburgh without firing a single shot.

Since leaving Glenfinnan, many of the chiefs had shed their country gentleman airs and hardened into their roles as leaders of a rebellion. Donald Cameron was no exception, yet his moods were still governed more by concern than zeal, his passion still tempered by logic and reason, his decisions dictated by common sense rather than politics. He wanted his prince to succeed, yet he loathed the very idea of the blood and violence necessary to accomplish that end.

"Ma brither Alexander scouted the land himself," Lochiel said slowly. "He found the slime waist deep in places, tangled wi' weeds and water snakes and the like. He estimated it would take four, five hours tae cross it, and then only by makin' enough noise tae waken half o' Edinburgh. Mairover, once we were caught in the muck, it wouldna take mair'n a handful o' Cope's men tae hold us off. We'd have naewhere tae run, forward nor back. We'd be caught like ducks in a pond."

"*If* we were found out," the Prince reiterated. "But what of the road that cuts through the bog? Not the main thoroughfare that runs parallel to the plain, but the one that cuts through the middle of the swamp?"

"Aye, there is a road," Lochiel nodded grudgingly. "And they took a good look at that as well. But its condition is barely less deplorable than the moor itself. Nor is it in the middle, but mair toward the end o' the plain further frae Cope."

"But still a good deal closer than if we simply formed up along the end of the field," Charles insisted. "And it does provide a degree of cover, does it not?"

"Aye, it runs out o' the moor and onto a cornfield. But the corn's been harvested, the stalks half torn down."

"Still, it's better than nothing at all," the Prince said harshly. "And while, as Lord George has so painstakingly explained, Cope may well be able to afford the time to remain entrenched on that plain until it is our grandchildren he faces, *we cannot*. We must have a victory, and we must have it soon. Aside from the reinforcements being mustered in London, we have received reports that the Dutch are preparing to honour their treaty with the English and send troops across the Channel to help defend England's border. We understand that my cousin William, Duke of Cumberland, has also been advised of his father's growing concern and is considering withdrawing his troops from Flanders and returning home. Worst of all, however, if we show weakness or indecisiveness now, we could lose all that we have gained thus far, not the least of which is the growing support of those who may have shown reluctance to join us in the past, not only here in Scotland, but throughout England and Wales. I am assured that a victory now against our oppressors will have all of England singing our praises, and tens of thousands of loyal Jacobites rushing to join us and carry the victory to the very gates of London!"

The Prince's bright gaze touched upon each man in turn and was met with a mixture of pride and wariness. The chiefs present were undeniably proud to be counted among those who had not shown any hesitation or reluctance to commit themselves and their fortunes to the Prince's cause. Yet they were wary because of the many important men—among them The MacLeod of MacLeod and Sir Alexander MacDonald of Sleat—who had not only broken promises to their sovereign by refusing to lend their support, but who looked suspiciously as if they might even offer men and arms to the Hanover government.

It could not be denied that a victory now against trained, disciplined men who fought behind Hanover colours would undoubtedly give the Jacobites a much needed edge. Defeating Cope would effectively make Charles Edward Stuart master of Scotland, and give them the badly needed time to consolidate their position, reinforce their border, and possibly open negotiations for a peaceful resolution with England. The two countries had existed side by side under different rulers for centuries; they could do so again, as allies, not enemies. The majority of the Scots only wanted what was theirs by right: their country and their king.

"Well gentlemen?" Lord George took command of the council again, retrieving everyone's thoughts from the realm of the possible and redirecting them toward the probable. "We have two choices, as I see it: the plain, or the moor. Since neither, on its own, offers any guarantee of success, I suggest we plan a strategy that uses both. We can split our forces and put the majority on the road through the moor, with an eye toward being in position before sunrise. To avoid or delay detection as long as possible, a second diversionary force will make their presence known on the field flanking Cope to the east. By the time he realizes it is a diversion, with luck and God's grace, we will be across that blasted field."

"An excellent plan, by heaven," the Prince said eagerly, pounding his fist on the table for emphasis. "We agree wholeheartedly and without reservations!"

Lord George did not dismiss the opinions of the chiefs so readily. "Any questions? Further comments? Propositions?"

When there were none forthcoming, Lord George directed his gaze to the opposite end of the long table where the Prince sat sandwiched between O'Sullivan and the other major thorn in the general's side, Murray of Broughton. John Murray, no relation to the general, had acted as liaison between the Scottish lairds and King James since 1737, and had been primarily responsible for encouraging the Prince to embark on this untimely and hazardous foray to Scotland. Also disappointed at being passed over for a command, he was only slightly mollified with his appointment as Secretary of State and, like O'Sullivan, allowed his bitterness to shadow his judgement where Lord George's loyalty was concerned. It had been Murray of Broughton who had first hinted at the general's ulterior motives, and it was Murray of Broughton who kept the rumours and whispers of betrayal alive despite the overwhelming evidence to the contrary. If Lord George had wished to betray the Prince, he could have done so in a score of different ways by now, not the least of which would have been to allow the Prince to follow through with his original plan of a frontal attack.

"If there is no further discussion, Highness, I will excuse myself in order to draft the final details for the attack."

"Certainly, General," said Prince Charles, triggering a harsh scraping of twenty other chairs as he rose to his feet. "I shall expect to hear from you within the hour?"

"Within the hour," Lord George agreed, bowing respectfully and retiring from the cottage, his sheaf of crumpled maps thrust into the crook of his arm. Most of the clan chiefs took advantage of the general's departure to excuse themselves as well, and within a few moments, word was spreading through the rebel camp like a wild bushfire that they were to attack Cope's position at dawn.

Alexander Cameron and Aluinn MacKail listened in silence as Lochiel recounted the details of the council meeting. It was obvious to both men that the Cameron chief was not as enthusiastic about the plan of attack as he might have been, but like Lochiel, neither man could offer a viable alternative. The moor road was the only route that did not leave the rebel army completely vulnerable to the destructive power of Cope's artillery.

Aluinn was dispatched at once to alert the other officers of Clan Cameron. They were to have the men rested and prepared to march out of camp at four A.M. Alex set out with a similar purpose in mind, but somehow found himself standing on a shallow rise of land, his darkly handsome face and brooding thoughts aimed—as they often were—in a southerly direction.

It came as a constant and disconcerting surprise to him that, in moments of tension and anxiety, Catherine's image came to him so strongly it was as if he could reach out and touch her. The faintest breeze came laden with the fragrance of her skin and hair. Even the pale, blue-white moon that hung swollen and glistening above the moor brought to mind the luminous quality of her eyes. She came unbidden into his thoughts when he wakened each morning; the delicate oval of her face was the last swimming link with reality before exhaustion drugged him to sleep each night.

There were times, more often than he cared to admit, when the ache to see her or feel her eager body pressed next to his was so powerful he found himself staring at the wagons that formed their own spirited circle of activity beside the rebel camp. They were filled with nameless, faceless women who were more than willing to pretend they were wives, mistresses, lovers to any man with a few coins to spare. And a man facing battle, possibly death on the next sunrise, could hardly be blamed for wanting, needing, a few moments respite from the tensions.

In the past, Alex had never hesitated to take advantage of such opportunities as they presented themselves. He had even, in a moment of inexplicable truthfulness, confessed to Catherine the existence of several mistresses in his former life, women chosen carefully for salving the needs of his body, not his soul. He had never wanted to feel responsible for another human life again, never wanted his emotions held captive by any one single soft body. He had never wanted to see that *look* in a woman's eye again—the look that was a combination of hope, trust, uncertainty, and yearning. He had seen it in Catherine's heather-blue eyes almost from the instant they'd met. Worse still, he had felt it in his own, each and every time he saw her in a spill of sunlight, or caught a glimpse of her in the soft shadows of a glowing fire, or lay beside her in the utter, complete blackness of night.

He hadn't wanted it to happen, hadn't asked for it to happen, certainly hadn't expected it to happen, not when he had spent most of his adult life perfecting his image of a cold-hearted, arrogant bastard of few, if any, scruples. Women had always been attracted to him because he remained aloof and unattainable—*free*, goddammit—unencumbered by sentimentality or responsibility. He had liked it that way, had fully intended to keep it that way . . . right up until the night at Achnacarry Castle when he had seen that look in Catherine's eyes and knew he wanted to keep it there always.

But that had been then and this was now, when a stray thought or misguided emotion could well affect the way he acted, the way his instincts responded, the choices he made and the subsequent consequences on the lives of the clansmen who trusted his leadership. A man going into battle with distractions churning around in his brain might as well save the enemy's lead and put his own gun to his temple.

No, he had not wanted or asked for any of this. He had sent her out of Scotland for her own safety—that had been an honest enough motive—but maybe there had been other reasons lurking at the back of his mind. Maybe, when she was back among her own kind—the rich, the pompous, the women who spared little thought for anything other than pampering their vanity, the men who strutted around reciting poetry and smelling of lavender pomade—maybe she would begin to see their marriage as a mistake. It was certain she had been swept up in the danger and intrigue. The savage beauty of the land, the naked violence of the people, even the weathered, sombre battlements of Achnacarry Castle had been a complete contrast to everything she had ever known in her sedate, orderly existence. Everything he, himself, loathed about the so-called civilized society.

They had been together less than five weeks—long enough to discover and unleash an undeniable passion, but had they only duped themselves into believing two such opposite lives could meld together as one? Alex knew with complete certainty he could never tolerate a lengthy commitment to the style of life Catherine had been accustomed to; his restlessness in the guise of Raefer Montgomery had been proof enough. And he did not think, despite Catherine's fervent vows to the contrary, she would find absolute happiness in the rugged wildness of the Highlands.

Alex drew a deep, cleansing breath of Highland air. Maybe it was time to sweep away the rose petals and take a good hard look at what he really wanted out of this miserable life.

A drink, for one thing. Company for another. And in his present mood, something to counter the envy he felt as he watched the shadowy figures moving to and from the outer circle of clustered wagons.

Lauren Cameron sighed and slowly, slowly untwined her legs from around her lover's waist. She let them slide languidly down onto the cool grass, vaguely aware of the discomfort caused by the tiny stones and pebbles that had abraded her back. Scratches and bruises were a paltry price to pay for the warm and slippery flood of pleasure between her thighs; the feel of cool wet grass against her naked flesh only heightened the sensations and proved that Alasdair's needs had been as urgent as her own. And still are, she mused dreamily. She could feel him pulsating softly within her, as reluctant to take his leave of the sweet haven as she was to relinquish him.

Extraordinarily sensitive to the slightest impression, she allowed her thighs to flirt subtly with the rough texture of his long, muscled legs, and savoured each breath that caused the dense mat of hair on his chest to chafe erotically against her breasts. His head was pressed into the curve of her throat and, smiling, she combed her fingers through the damp raven locks, scarcely able to believe she had finally won.

How many nights had she lain awake hoping, dreaming, *willing* Alexander Cameron into her arms? Why else had she continued to endure the cold and dampness, the endless jarring miles of road that passed beneath the wheels of her cart? She had been scheming and plotting and conniving for a means to affect her escape from Achnacarry Castle—her home and prison for the past eight years. When Lochiel had raised the clan for Prince Charles, she had been first in line to plead for permission to accompany the clan on its adventure. Her primary motive had been escape and indeed, her heart had soared with joy and triumph as she had ridden through the streets of Edinburgh in the Prince's procession. She had been born and raised the first twelve years of her life within the walls of the royal city and had sworn, at whatever the cost, to return one day to the bustle and excitement.

Well, she had returned. And the price she had paid was steep, drenched in blood and betrayal. But somehow, now that freedom was within her grasp, simply returning to her former life in Edinburgh was not enough. She wanted more. She wanted that life to be shared by someone as volatile and exciting as Alexander Cameron.

She wanted Alexander Cameron.

The desire was not new. If anything, it had increased with each mile that took them away from Achnacarry, away from the memory of his violet-eyed *Sassenach* wife. Lauren had hated the English beauty on sight, just as she had known, when her gaze had first alighted on Alasdair's magnificent form, that he was the lover she had envisioned in her every fantasy. She had heard stories of his dangerous exploits during his long years of exile; she had studied his portrait in the castle gallery and spent many a restless night wondering about the man they called the *Camshroinaich Dubh*—the Dark Cameron. Hearing that Lochiel had finally recalled his brother from Europe had seemed to give her long and tedious years at Achnacarry a reason, a purpose, and she had awaited his arrival the way a bride awaits a groom on their wedding night.

No one at the castle, least of all Lauren Cameron, had been forwarned of the existence of the yellow-haired *Sassenach* who had accompanied him home. And no one had been more pleased or relieved to learn that he had acquired her reluctantly, that the marriage had been forced upon them both, and he had used her as hostage and camouflage to make his way safely into Scotland. Of course he had bedded her, but out of contempt, not passion. He surely did not love her; any fool could see how perfectly mismatched the two of them were, how disastrous such a union would be.

Admittedly, Lauren might have presented herself a little too prematurely into his bed that first night at Achnacarry, and admittedly she might have overreacted—just a tad—to his caustic rejection. But arranging to have his troublesome new bride kidnapped by the Campbells seemed to be a logical solution to the problem—ideal, as it turned out, since Alasdair immediately set her on a ship bound for England after the dramatic rescue. Would a man who loved his wife send her out of his life? Would a man who obviously had enormous needs and healthy appetites settle for a bed on the hard, cold ground with only the length of his wool tartan to keep him warm?

Hadn't she caught Alasdair staring often and openly at her ripe, hourglass figure these past few weeks? Hadn't she nearly melted with anticipation on more than one occasion when his dark, probing eyes had visually stripped the layers of clothing from her body one by one, revealing the voluptuous perfection of her breasts, the incredibly tiny span of her waist, the long and lanky stretch of her nubile legs? Melted indeed. She had felt those bottomless eyes on her naked flesh once before, and experienced the calloused heat of his hands exploring her flesh. The weeks had not dimmed the memory, nor had the roughness of his initial rejection dulled the ache of her desire.

She should not have been surprised that he had been watching her wagon, or that he had followed her out onto the grassy moor. She had sensed something wondrous and devastating would happen tonight, and it had. It had.

Sighing, Lauren shifted slightly, and suggestively, and felt the slow brush of long black lashes opening against her throat.

"I'm glad ye came tae me tonight, Alasdair," she whispered. "I was beginnin' tae despair o' ever seein' this day, ever feelin' yer airms round me, or us bein' togither as it were meant tae be."

"We couldna be mair togither than this, lass," he murmured, nuzzling his lips against her throat.

Lauren wriggled to acknowledge the virile pressure swelling within her, but the echo of his words struck her and her amber eyes flew open in shock.

"What . . . what did ye say?" she gasped.

He chuckled lustily. "I didna have tae say aught, lassie. Can ye no' *feel* what I mean?"

The broad Scots was as thick as dust in a hay stack and, with a cry of horror, Lauren laid her hands flat on his shoulders and pushed upward with all her might. The Highlander had not been prepared for such a swift and perfunctory ejection and cursed angrily as he found himself face down on the wet grass.

"What the hell —?"

Lauren scrambled to her knees and this time, when she clawed her fingers into the thick waves of his hair, it was in order to angle his face upward into the dim wash of moonlight. What she saw stopped her heart cold. Like Alasdair's, his hair was long and shaggy, his eyes dark and deepset under a slash of jet black brows. The jaw was even remarkably similar—square and strong, with a hint of a cleft splitting it in two. The body was as well proportioned, evidently as well endowed, although now, as she studied him with a growing fury, she could see his shoulders were not quite as broad, nor the sculpting of the muscles on his chest as well defined.

"Ye bastard," she hissed. *"Ye bluidy bastard!"*

"Heigh now, halt a blink, wee missy —"

Snarling, Lauren flung herself at him, raking the sharp points of her nails down his cheeks and throat. She felt some measure of satisfaction as the peeled skin collected beneath the tips, and even more when she heard his bellow of pain.

"Ye bastard! Ye bluidy bastard!" she screamed again, flailing at him with her fists, gouging him with her nails, sinking her teeth around a mouthful of flesh when he tried to catch her wrists and bring her to ground.

A second, voracious curse sent the back of his hand slashing sideways into a violent meeting with her cheek. Lauren's head jerked to one side with the force of the blow, affording him the break he needed to toss her onto her back and pin her under the weight of his body. She continued to fight him like a wildcat, hissing and spitting obscenities, wriggling and squirming to free an arm or a leg to vent her rage. The Highlander merely tightened his grip and guarded his more vulnerable target areas while he waited for her strength to wane.

With a frustrated curse, her writhings slowed and finally heaved to a halt. Her breasts laboured under a fresh sheen of sweat and her beautifully angry face was all but hidden by her flying hair.

"Have ye calmed yersel', then?" he asked matter-of-factly.

"Get off o' me, ye great hair-legged lummox!"

"That wisna what ye were beggin' me tae dae ten minutes gaun."

"Ten minutes gaun, I thought ye were —" Lauren stopped and bit her enraged admission into silence. God, how could she have been so blind? So stupid? How could she have mistaken this . . . this *lout* for Alasdair?

"Ye thought I were someone else," the Highlander chuckled. "Lucky bastard, this Alasdair o' yourn."

"Ye *knew*?" she gasped furiously. "Ye knew an' ye still . . . ye still —!"

"By the time ye were bleatin' his name intae ma ear, I couldna care if ye thought I were the pope himsel'. It would ha' taken a far better man than me tae be able tae stop, I can tell ye."

Lauren gained control of her temper. "Ye must have known afore . . . afore it went that far, that I'd mistook ye f'ae someone else. Why did ye just stan' there, gawpin' like a fool an' sayin' nothing?"

"I thought I were dreamin'," he murmured honestly. "I saw ye walk out frae them bushes an' next thing I knew, ye were half out o' yer claythes an' tearin' at mines. What would ye expect a man tae dae? Slap ye on the wrist an' tell ye tae go hame?"

Lauren drew a deep breath. Grudgingly, she conceded the point. She hadn't exactly seen the need for words between them; she had just seen him and assumed . . .

"Well, I suppose it's doun," she said bitterly.

"Aye, that it is, lass," he agreed, smoothing the web of hair off her face. Seeing the glint of moonlight reflected in the almond-shaped eyes, his gaze strayed lower, to the sensuously full pouting lips. They were still swollen and bruised-looking from his avid attentions, and at one corner, a thin thread of blood trickled onto the whiteness of her chin. His own cheeks stung from the missing ribbons of flesh, as did his buttocks, where her nails had wrought similar damage during the throes of passion.

Lauren stared up at the shadowed outline of the face poised above her, seeing nothing but the vague impressions of features. The sudden, renewed tension in his body was more readily identifiable and for some reason, it removed the last of her anger and prompted a similarly bold response in her loins.

When he dipped his head and sent his tongue tracing gently along her lip to capture the blood he had caused to be shed, she did not flinch away or resume her struggle. Nor did she do anything to deter him as his tongue continued down along the arch of her throat, swirling a river of warm sensations into the valley between her breasts.

"Dae ye think I've forgiven ye then?" she asked, conscious of his lower body shifting deftly between her parted thighs.

"The harm's doun, as ye said. Where's the use o' gratin' at one anither?" His tongue arrived at a nipple and toyed with it a moment before hungry lips closed around the bud and suckled a tender mouthful of flesh.

No, she thought, squirming for altogether different reasons now, he wasn't Alasdair. But he was a virile answer for all those long, cold nights when she had lain awake, half mad to feel the vigorous thrust of male flesh within her. Struan MacSorley had been her lover at Achnacarry, but even he had seemed to abandon her, whether out of deference for Lochiel, or a growing suspicion over the role she had played in Catherine's kidnapping, she did not know. She did know she had gone too long playing the part of the innocent, wide-eyed virgin, especially when, during those same long cold nights, she could clearly hear the squeaking and creaking of wagon axles all around her.

Lauren arched sinuously against the greedy lips, her great amber eyes fluttering closed through a shudder of purely avaricious delight. She parted her thighs wider and slid her hands up and around his buttocks, urging the hot stab of flesh to plunge where it was needed most.

Thus preoccupied, neither one of the lovers heard or saw the three crouched figures moving stealthily toward them through the waves of long, silvery deergrass. All three wore red broadcloth tunics and blue breeches; all three exchanged cautious handsignals as they began to close the circle around the naked, writhing couple.

The leader of the three grinned lewdly as he heard the unabashed lust in the woman's groans as she pumped her hips into each grunted pelvic thrust. She was probably not what the captain had had in mind when he dispatched them on this foolhardy expedition, but no doubt he would find some way to make use of her, regardless of whether she provided them with military information or not.

A final gesture for silence and caution had the corporal withdrawing his knife from its leather sheath. He carefully laid his musket aside, not wanting to risk an accidental misfire that could alert the entire rebel army, then crept the final ten paces before raising the knife and plunging it ruthlessly between the Highlander's sweat-slicked shoulder blades.

Alexander heard the shrill scream of a night creature somewhere out over the darkened moorland and paused momentarily to try to pinpoint its source. He had forced himself to take three complete circuits of the sprawling encampment and thankfully, felt the better for it. His body was no longer behaving as if it was stretched on an invisible rack; his nerves no longer scraped against a jagged edge of steel. He was thinking clearly again and knew that to keep doing so, he must not think of Catherine.

His third circuit of the camp, therefore, was undertaken with an eye toward the military action due for the morning. He was in full agreement with Lochiel's assessment of the situation: If Cope had any warning whatsoever of the rebel's presence in the morass, their hopes for a victory were slim. The crossing had to be made in stealth and darkness and completed before the English general had time to realign his damned artillery. Surprise was the key. Surprise and speed, both of which were the mainstay of the Highlanders' methods of warfare.

If only there was some way to unseat the general's confidence in his position. If only there was some way to shatter the iron-fast discipline of his officers and infantrymen, to bring about a repeat of their startling performance at Colt's Bridge.

Recalling the incident, Alexander's dark eyes narrowed against a gust of smoke-laden breeze. He had been leading a small party of Camerons along the road to Edinburgh, intending only to scout the route and determine where the English would be most likely to stage a defense. His men had been spoiling for action ever since leaving Glenfinnan; apart from one or two minor encounters with government patrols, hardly a sword or pistol had been drawn in anger. His men would have gladly, enthusiastically hurled themselves into a skirmish with the two regiments of dragoons they'd encountered at the bridge, had Alex given the order to do so. But before they had even warmed themselves by hurling insults and jeers first, the dragoons had balked and wheeled their horses away from the opposite river bank, leaving the Highlanders staring at each other in complete astonishment.

Knowing they had been vastly outnumbered and outgunned, Alex had shared his men's surprise. Common sense had forbade him from over-extending his distance from the main body of the army, but, as he later found out, the dragoons had maintained their retreat all the way to Leith, several miles beyond the city of Edinburgh, before realizing the Highlanders had not pursued.

Only one officer had appeared ready to stand his ground at the bridge, and he had been as outraged by the cowardly behaviour of his men as he had been to recognize the tall, black-haired figure who sat in similar stone-cold silence observing him from across the bridge.

Hamilton Garner.

There had been no mistaking the lean and arrogant features, the ramrod stiff posture, the uniform impeccably laid on with every brass button and gold braid arranged in military precision. Jade-green eyes, as frigid as arctic ice, had stared across the river with the same piercing fury they had lashed at Alex months before over the span of crossed swordblades. The hatred they emanated was seething and malevolent, almost a tangible thing as it strove to provoke a similar response in Alex.

Lord Ashbrooke, Catherine's father, had said the wound Garner received during the duel had not been fatal. Even so, Alex had not expected to see the haughty lieutenant—now apparently promoted to captain—fully healed and preparing to defend a bridge hundreds of miles from Derby. Damien Ashbrooke had sent word via his couriers that Garner had launched an intensive search for Raefer Montgomery and his new bride. His inability to find any clue as to their whereabouts had rooted an unhealthy obsession in Garner's mind; he had vowed to find both Montgomery and Catherine and exact revenge for his humiliation if it took his dying breath to do so.

With the rest of his regiment, officers and dragoons alike, scrambling for the safety of the forest, Hamilton Garner had drawn his sword and kicked his horse forward toward the stone arch of the bridge. Had the self-righteous fool been about to cross the river and challenge Alexander to a rematch? Cameron had no way of knowing, for within moments of Garner's men interpreting his intentions, they had surrounded him and literally dragged him into the retreat.

Alex frowned over the memory and looked down at the smooth pebble he had been rolling between his fingers. His fist clenched around it as he remembered his own disturbing pang of disappointment that day. He would have welcomed the chance to test his steel against Hamilton Garner again, if only to rectify the mistake he had made in not delivering the *coup de grâce* the first time. And why hadn't he? God only knew, it was not out of respect or admiration for the man. Perhaps it had been because of the flash of pale blonde hair he had seen on the fringe of the crowd of horrified spectators.

Alex tensed and let the pebble slip through his fingers and fall to the ground, forgotten. With a slight, almost imperceptible move of his arm, he closed his hand around the steel-clawed butt of the pistol he wore tucked into his belt. He let the shiver of cool anticipation clear his mind of all thoughts as he concentrated his instincts on the nearby rustle of a carefully placed footfall.

Whoever was walking up behind him was no more than ten feet away, his approach too furtive to be a friendly clansman. Alex was quite alone on the dark rim of the encampment, a situation he was not permitted to enjoy too often these days. Lochiel had detached Struan MacSorley as captain of his own personal guard and ordered him to watch out for Alexander's back instead. Word had reached the chief of the Camerons that the Duke of Argyle, Alexander's mortal enemy, had not received the news of the *Camshroinaich Dubh*'s safe arrival at Achnacarry with any humour, nor had he accepted the subsequent death of his nephew, Malcolm Campbell, at Alexander's hands, with peals of delight. The failure of Argyle's elaborate plan to capture Alexander and see him hang from a noose at Inverary Castle had prompted the Duke to double the long-standing reward of ten thousand pounds for his capture. Also, Aluinn MacKail had learned of the hiring of an assassin, a man known in such specialized circles as The Frenchman, who boasted a success rate of one hundred percent. Alex had shrugged aside the threat with his customary indifference—after all, he had spent most of his fifteen-year exile dodging Argyle's bloodhounds. But Lochiel had not welcomed the reports so blandly, nor had Aluinn MacKail or Struan MacSorley, either of whom, or both, were usually with Alex at all times.

Neither of them would exhibit the poor sense to creep up on him in the dark of night.

"Beggin' yer pardon, laird —"

Alex dropped into a crouch and whirled around, pivoting on the balls of his feet and drawing his pistol at the same time. The old, poorly clad clansman threw his hands up before his face and stumbled back several paces, squawking pleas and petitions in Gaelic when he saw the fully cocked pistol levelled at his chest.

Cursing with equal fluency, Alex sprang to his feet and in a single long stride, grasped the visibly shaken clansman by a fistful of tartan and lifted him onto the tips of his toes.

"You goddamned blithering fool! What were you thinking, stalking a man in the dead of night?"

"I . . . I wisna stalkin', laird," the man stammered, clawing at the vise that gripped his throat. "I didna *mean* tae stalk, laird. I walked normal, but quiet-like so as nae tae distairb ye. I could see ye were thinkin' rare hard an' I didna want tae distairb ye till ye were through!"

Still suffering the effects of an adrenalin rush, Alex lowered the weight of the man slowly, then released his grip on the bunched folds of tartan. With a further effort, he refrained from railing the old man into a quivering mass of witlessness, which would have been easy enough to do since the old fool was already well along in that direction.

The clansman scrabbled cautiously back out of range of the long, powerful arms and watched frog-eyed as the flintlock on the pistol was stepped down and the gun re-sheathed in the leather belt.

"What the devil is so important you risked getting your head blown off?" Alex demanded harshly.

The old man swallowed noisily and lowered his hands, a signal for the rest of his scrawny body to relax out of its cringed stance, uncrumpling like a folded piece of parchment.

"Ma name is Anderson, laird. Robert Anderson, an' I ken the night is short an' ye've a mout o' work tae dae —"

Alex raised his head and the look in the obsidian eyes was enough to cause another spasm in the old man's colon.

"— but when I heard the orders f'ae the morn's mornin', it come at me that I should speak at ye right the way."

"Speak at me —" Alex paused and took a breath. "Speak to me about what, Robert Anderson?"

"Me an' ma three sons live a ways benorth o' Preston, we dae. Raise sheep an' the like, wi' ma brither Lachlan. We've anither brither, Colla, wha' runs a wee cobble alang the coast atween Aberdeen an' Auld Reekie."

"You've a brother who smuggles goods from Aberdeen to Edinburgh? What of it?"

"Weel . . . these sheep o' ours sometimes fetch it in their heids tae wander doon tae the Forth an' romp in the salt water. Fairst few times they doun it—faith, but it took all the blessit day an' night tae tromp round the moor tae fetch them hame again. Then one time, they doun it when Colla were stoppit by tae visit our mam, an' s'trowth, if he didna blow a snirtle up his sleeve an' show us a way straight across the skinkin' muck."

Alex, who had been reconsidering his earlier generosity in sparing the man a tongue lashing, stiffened and felt the hairs across the nape of his neck stand to attention.

"Are you trying to tell me there is another way through the swamp? A way not marked on the maps?"

"Ach, I dinna ken it be markit on any skrint o' paper, only that ma brither Lachlan an' me, we livit here all our lives an' didna ken there were aught but the one way across it." The shepherd spread his hands and twitched his eyebrows upward. "I'm na sayin' it's mair than a bawk atween two bogs o' weed an' mire, but I can tell ye it's a mout sight cleaner an' quicker than sinkin' up tae yer pintel in slime."

Alex tried to calm his racing thoughts. Was it possible: another way across the morass that no one but the local smugglers knew about?

"If I showed you a map, Anderson, could you point out exactly where this balk is located?"

The clansman sucked thoughtfully at his cheek and scratched a few sparse clumps of red hair that prickled over the crown of his head. "Aye. I could dae. I could show ye better, but."

"My friend, if you're right about there being another way across that moor, and if Lord George likes what you show him on the map, you might just end up leading the whole damned army through."

Robert Anderson grinned and jammed his tattered blue bonnet on his head as Alex hastened him back through the labyrinth of campfires and snoring bodies. The general's mood was no better than Alexander's had been at first, but he was soon bristling with cautious excitement at the end of Anderson's story. He sent Alex out at once to verify the existence of the hidden balk and in the meantime, went himself to rouse the Prince. The council of chiefs was re-called; a tentative new plan was proposed and instantly accepted. By two in the morning Alex had returned and, less than an hour later, the entire Highland army was poised on the edge of the black and mist-shrouded morass.

Chapter Three

A lone sentry, standing guard on the border of the harvested cornfield was jerked out of his drowse by a sound that brought to mind a swarm of bees approaching a hive. The buzz receded almost at once, carried away by the drifting banks of salt-tanged fog that scudded up from the sea. Thin and wisped in places like a witch's veil, the mist thickened noticeably when it reached the edge of the bog. There, it lay shoulder high, white as cream, forming a solid mass that constantly shifted, like some undulating globule of foam.

Private James Wallace did not care overmuch for this particular duty. His skin had remained wet and clammy throughout the long night; he had imagined noises coming at once from everywhere and nowhere. And the dismal little fire he had managed to keep alive with bits of twigs and dried cornstalks did nothing to alleviate his sense of unease. If anything, it accentuated the grotesque shadows caused by the broken mist—a mist that was thinning more and more now that the sun was struggling toward the horizon. Already it was light enough to see snatches of the main encampment, less than five hundred yards away. Soon the rolling hills beyond Edinburgh would reveal themselves to the golden cap of dawn, and soon the waters of the Forth would be changing from inky black to gun-metal blue.

The smell from early cook fires was triggering a response in Private Wallace's stomach as well. It rumbled like a small volcano as his nostrils flared to the scent of woodsmoke and frying biscuits. Yawning, he scratched absently at his crotch and, as an afterthought, set his musket aside and unfastened the flap of his codpiece. With a satisfied grunt of relief, he watched the hot yellow stream send its own squirts of steam rising off the broken stalks of corn. The steam blended acridly with the mist and as his eye followed the dispersing puffs, his gaze strayed to the increasing lightness overhead. The clouds were pulling away from the horizon, stretching thin bands of pink and gold into the deep royal of the sky. Towns and villages throughout the countryside would be stirring to life. Early morning vendors would be dragging their laden carts along the roads, hoping to be among the first arrivals when the huge gates of Edinburgh swung open. Cloaked in gray clinging mists by night, the royal city would be emerging, tower by tower, spire by sparkling spire, as the sunlight crept above the gnarled crust of the earth. All around him life was proceeding as usual, the sentry thought glumly, and there he was standing guard over a bloody swamp.

Another annoying wave of buzzing washed past him, louder this time, and he squinted to see through the rapidly lifting fog. Identifying what looked to be a low black hedge bristling along the verge of the cornfield, he frowned and knuckled his fists into the corners of his eyes. He could not remember seeing a hedge there before. But even as he stared and craned his neck forward to get a better view, the hedge shifted, seeming to curl into the cornfield like some great black wave of molasses.

The sentry's jaw gaped slowly open. It wasn't a hedge at all! It was men! Hundreds of them! Thousands of them emerging from the swamp and mists like black twisting creatures from hell.

"Rebels," he croaked. "Bluddy hell, it's rebels!"

Spinning around, he groped for his trusty Brown Bess but the musket was not where he had left it. In its stead stood an enormous grinning spectre of a man, his trunk-like arms and legs blackened with mud, his wheat-coloured mane of hair and beard spattered with grime. As the sentry watched in horrified awe, the giant held up the appropriated musket and offered a companionable wink.

"Lookin' f'ae this, were ye?" inquired Struan MacSorley.

Private Wallace nodded stupidly and reached forward to accept the offered weapon. When his hand was around the cold metal of the barrel, he felt the giant's huge paw close over his wrist and start to squeeze. Tighter and tighter, the pressure increased until he could actually hear the bones being crushed like so much dry kindling. He opened his mouth to scream, but the ice-cold shiver of metal that slashed across his throat prevented anything more than the hiss and bubble of escaping air. With his free hand, Wallace clutched the severed edges of flesh and cartiledge, and felt the warm spray of blood gushing through his fingers. He hardly felt the pain in his shattered wrist; his only concern as he was tossed aside into the sharp, stabbing stalks of corn, was to keep his head from splitting completely away from his shoulders and rolling into the swamp.

MacSorley wiped the blade of his dirk on the dead soldier's waistcoat before he turned and beckoned to the half dozen men crouched behind him.

"Only the one," he snarled contemptuously. "Smug bastards, are they na? Where's the challenge?"

Alexander Cameron laid a hand on MacSorley's arm and grinned humourlessly. "I'm sure you'll have plenty of opportunities to test your mettle over the next few hours."

Raising his arm, he windmilled it once to signal the all-clear and saw the gesture repeated at intervals all along the edge of the morass. Only in one position did there appear to be trouble. The Highlander had been seen and before he could deal efficiently with the sentry, a warning shot popped in the silence.

Lord George Murray used it as the signal to release his contingent of Athollmen. The air swelled instantly with the screeching wail of bagpipes, the swell spreading and rippling along the length of the field until it was a cacophony of rousing, defiant *piob'rachds* that called the men to charge. All but the rear guard were clear of the swamp and within seconds, the ground thundered with the percussion of thousands of running feet. Those who possessed muskets or pistols discharged them in the general direction of the low white tents that pimpled the far side of the field, then, in no frame of mind to dally over reaming, loading, ramming and refiring, flung the emptied weapons aside and swung their heavy broadswords into the air. Others, wanting nothing to hinder their speed or entrap their sword arms, unbelted the six yards of tartan wool that comprised the pleated and folded swath of their kilts and cast their garments aside, hurling themselves into the charge half-naked.

A tidal wave of raised, glittering broadswords surged across the cornfield and swept toward the enemy camp. Cope's troops, stumbling from their orderly rows of low-slung tents, stared at the boiling mass of screaming humanity and as one, experienced a burning clutch of liquid fear in their bowels. They scattered before the onslaught, running in a frenzy of screaming confusion. They grabbed for the neatly stacked pyramids of muskets only to cast them aside unfired. Horses loosely tethered reared free and bolted riderless into the midst of the growing chaos; some were chased and caught by the dragoons who, scarcely recovered from their shameful performance at Colt's Bridge, took the initiative again and began a panicked retreat to the coastal road and safety.

Seeing the dragoons flee before them, the common foot soldiers veered like a school of fish and streaked after them. They sheered off again as a second wave of screaming rebels rose up out of the cornfield and began hacking and slashing at the forerunners. Those brave enough or foolhardy enough to stand and meet their attackers were slaughtered where they stood, their shiny thin bayonets no match for the five-foot lengths of raw steel that showed no mercy in parting limbs from torsos, or paring flesh from bones.

As each clan engaged a pocket of the enemy, they roared the ancient battle cries of their warrior ancestors. The air was torn asunder by the screams of men, the screams of the bagpipes, the screams of those who found themselves standing ankle deep in a sea of weltering gore.

Only at the farthest edge of the camp was there a visible attempt underway to rally an offense. The fearsome and well deserved reputation of the captain in command of the field artillery was sufficient to stem the spread of panic among his men. With cool efficiency they responded to his orders and turned the massive bronze cannons in their caissons, preparing them to fire upon the encroaching storm of charging Highlanders.

Alexander Cameron saw the guns being rolled into firing position and swerved toward them. Struan MacSorley and Aluinn MacKail were close on his heels, leading their regiment of Camerons straight into the gaping black maws of the cannon. Better than a hundred yards from their goal, Alex swung his broadsword high above his head, feeling its raw strength pour down to infuse his body with the bloody savagery of his ancestors. Pride swelled his heart and pumped through his veins, and from somewhere out of a dim and terrifying memory he heard his own voice roaring the Cameron *cath-ghairm*: "Sons of dogs come hither; come hither and eat flesh!"

Through a haze of rage and vengeance, he heard the command to fire, saw the smoldering linstocks lowered to the powder-filled touch holes of the cannons. A searing flare of hot orange flame burst upward, sparking its way into the wadded breech of each gun, where the larger charge of gunpowder exploded, propelling twelve-pound canisters of razor-sharp grapeshot out of the muzzles in an eruption of smoke and burned wadding.

The volley tore through the front rank of Highlanders, obliterating some to eternity, lifting others and catapulting them through the air in bloody cartwheels of shredded flesh. Alex was close enough to feel the scorching lash of heat and to be jarred temporarily off balance by the concussion of twenty guns discharging simultaneously. The pressure caused by the explosions sucked the air from his lungs and left him briefly blinded and deaf, but his arms were driven independently by instinct, already swinging the broadsword into the solid wall of flesh and arrogance that stood before him.

Vaulting between two smoking guns, he brought the mighty blade slicing down across the path of an artilleryman, the weight and force of the two-handed stroke ripping the officer's shiny steel sabre aside, tearing it from numbed fingers so that it flew in a graceful, curving arc and vanished in the clouds of yellow smoke. The officer saw his death mirrored in the primitive ferocity of Alex's eyes and braced himself as the broadsword slashed back and carved a bloody swath through the stretched tendons and muscles of his chest. The soldier spun away, the gouting blood leaving a fine spray of crimson droplets along Alex's arms.

A second defender was able to parry the deadly thrust of Alex's sword, but sagged against the sharp, biting steel of the dirk that was plunged hilt-deep into the unprotected hollow of his raised arm. On Cameron's left, the blurr that was Aluinn MacKail skewered one gunner on the point of his broadsword and, still compensating for the dead weight on one arm, calmly fired his pistol point blank into the chest of another soldier. Struan MacSorley, having slashed his way into a semi-circle of government troops, dealt with each one in turn, churning the ground into red mud beneath his feet. The unexpected insult of steel scratching along his arm had him whirling around, propelled on the wind of a roared Gaelic oath. The soldier who had dared to violate the inviolate, stumbled back in horror as Struan straightened to his full, terrifying height of six-and-a-half-feet of brawn and fury. Both men stared for a moment at the string of scarlet pearls beading on the hairy forearm before Struan reached out, lifted the soldier by the loose folds of flesh beneath his chin and hurled him up and over the spine of a cannon. There, he landed with enough of an impact to split his skull like a ripe melon. The corpse remained balanced across the gun for a long moment, then slid limply, wetly onto the spattered grass.

Alex, pausing to catch his breath, wiped a sleeve across his streaming brow and wondered absently if the blood that came away belonged to himself or his victims.

Still in the grips of the killing madness that had overridden his senses, he stared at his hands, and the pleasure he experienced in seeing them clenched around the blood-slicked hilt of his sword was almost sensual. He felt alive and vigorous. The urges that flowed from the darker regions of his soul made him feel as if he could do anything, conquer any obstacle, overcome any threat that stood between him and his destiny. He wanted to throw back his head and cry a challenge to the fates who professed to know better than he how to govern his future. He wanted to cry out his triumph over the demons who had haunted his past, who had reared their bloodied heads time and time again to taunt him, torment him with thoughts of hatred and revenge. For years he had wandered aimlessly, fighting and killing for the wrong reasons.

He was fighting for Scotland now. For his home, for his family, for the blood and honour of his ancestors. He was fighting for himself too, for his right to live where he chose, and with whom he chose. He was fighting for Catherine, and his right to love her. Catherine . . .

"Alex! Behind you!"

Cameron reacted an instant too late. He turned in time to see the pistol, only inches from his face. He saw the outthrust scarlet arm and the finger that was already tightening on the scrolled trigger.

But that was all he saw. A tremendous clap of thunder shattered the air and exploded within his brain, the force of it carrying him backward and smashing him against the spoked wheel of a cannon. A raw, shearing agony in his temple distorted sight and sound; the hot taste of scorched flesh and black powder robbed him of the scantest mouthful of air.

Slumping against the body of a dead soldier, he thought he recognized Aluinn's face bending quickly over him, but he could not hear the words being shouted at him and, in the next instant, he was sucked into a deep, descending blackness.

General Sir John Cope was in shock. The rebels had erupted out of nowhere, had shattered the nerve and backbone of the government forces as violently and as completely as they had destroyed the misty morning silence. They had charged Cope's camp like a torrent bursting through a dam; had obliterated the army's defenses and left a writhing, red-gored field of broken, mutilated bodies in their wake. The dragoons had scattered and fled. Colonel Whiteford's artillerymen had managed to fire only a single volley before they had been overrun and slaughtered at their posts.

Cope, assisted by his Colonels Home and Loudoun, made a desperate attempt to rally the fleeing horse and foot soldiers, going so far as to fire upon their own men in order to discourage the retreat. But the attempt failed and the officers had been swept along in the panicked stream of men, stopping only when they had gained the high ground at the farthest edge of the plain.

Not all of his men had cowered before the onslaught, Cope realized, as he fought the stinging tears of recrimination. Whiteford, Scott, Loftus, Cane, Simmonds . . . they had all spurred their men into action. Captain Hamilton Garner, whose dragoons had shamed him yet again, had valiantly gathered a body of foot soldiers around him and, though his efforts were obviously futile, he still held steadfast to his pocket of the field.

In other areas, the men were throwing down their guns and swords, and throwing up their hands to plead for mercy. They collected in small, quaking groups, or fell unabashedly to their knees before the advancing waves of rebels. Hundreds of them, the whole damned lot of them, Cope observed with burning mortification. His whole army defeated and surrendered! All but a few feckless cowards who had taken to their mounts and ridden away at the first screech of the bagpipes.

The inefficiency of his own ill-trained, poorly disciplined troops aside, Cope could not help but admire the sheer audacity and cunning of the man who commanded the rebel forces. Lord George Murray had planned and executed his attack flawlessly, brilliantly, affecting complete and total surprise on an enemy that had been too self-assured and contemptuous to look for deviousness. He had himself scorned the need for a full picket of sentries along the fringe of the moor. Who but a madman or genius would attempt to cross such a wide open stretch of swampland under the hindrance of an unfriendly Highland night? And the sight of thousands of screaming, sword-wielding savages charging out of the morass with such vigor and confidence would doubtless have rendered far braver and more seasoned veterans paralysed with fear.

Cope had only heard of the terrifying swiftness and bloody vehemence of a Highland charge; he had never witnessed one before. Truth be known, he prayed God he would never have to witness it again, for as experienced a field soldier as he was, he had felt a distinct and unpleasant lurching in his belly as he had seen the gouting blood and severed limbs scattered in the wake of the advancing rebels.

"Sir! Down there!"

Cope drew sharply on the reins of his horse and turned in the direction of his adjutant's pointed finger. A large, beautifully mottled gray stallion was thundering across the plain at the head of a small group of armed Highlanders. The rider was hatless, his clothing unidentifiable from that distance as more than a splash of royal blue for a jacket and bright red tartan for a kilt. Behind him, in the midst of cheering, arm-waving riders, was the standard bearer who raised the enormous red and white silk flag to support the Stuart triumph.

"We'd best make for Edinburgh, sir," his adjutant urged, "before their cavalry takes it in their heads to pursue."

"Do you see any cavalry, Corporal?" Cope asked bitterly. "Do you see any artillery? Any superior weaponry of any kind?"

The corporal looked back down the field.

"An academic question, of course," Cope continued without waiting for an answer. "Because they now have *our* artillery, *our* weapons, *our* ammunition, *our* stores and supplies . . . not to mention nearly two thousand of our men."

The corporal endured the disdainful recitation with a flush. "Yessir. But their victory today was a fluke. A cruel and undeserved fluke and surely you shall make them pay twofold for the insult when next you face them."

"The *next* time?" Cope directed his red and angry eyes at the solemn collection of officers who remained nervously by his side. "You delude yourselves, gentlemen, if you think a general who delivers the news of his own defeat will be allowed to repeat his mistakes again. As for this victory being a fluke . . . those were, I believe, almost the exact words used to describe the debacle at Colt's Bridge, then again when it was learned that Charles Edward Stuart was making his bed at Holyrood House. The only cruel and undeserved *fluke* I see before me, sirs, is that I should find myself in command of inept yokels on horseback who turn and break water at the first hint of battle. The only *fluke*, sirs, is that I probably will not live to see every last one of these brave dragoons bound and staked on posts along the border, there to be first among those who must now address this plague before it spreads into England!"

"Surely the Pretender would not be lunatic enough to march into England," Colonel Loudoun protested, blanching at the horrible possibility.

"And why not, sir?" Cope demanded. "If you were Lord George Murray, and you had won as resounding a victory as they have won themselves this day—what, indeed, would stop you? Are you suggesting good sportsmanship will prompt Lord George to wait until an experienced English army is recalled from Flanders? Or that the usurper prince will wait until King George opens his eyes and realizes his throne is in true jeopardy?

"The real lunacy, gentlemen, is in our own arrogance in assuming we are invincible. Take a good look at what our presumptions have cost us. Imagine what the cost could well be in the days and weeks to come, when our enemies discover what a handful of bearded farmers have accomplished using nothing more than swords and scythes. Scythes, gentlemen, against the military might of a nation!"

Shaken and demoralized, the outrage faded from Cope's eyes, rendering them a dull, listless brown. His features, normally sharp and animated, seemed to grow aged and haggard even as his shoulders slumped and his hands slackened their grip on the leather reins. His officers, wary of renewed activity on the road behind them, formed a protective circle around the general and urged him toward the coast road and Edinburgh.

Alex was aware of pain along his arms. The muscles were stretched and bruised, his wrists burned from the tightness of the twine ropes that cut into his flesh. For a moment he could not remember where he was. He shook his head to clear the fog from his brain and heard, from somewhere in the darkness nearby, harsh grunts and coarse laughter, snuffling noises in the hay, and the damp cruel thud of flesh slapping flesh.

The pain in his wrists was almost as unbearable as the agony in his temples as he strained to loosen the bonds that were holding him. His ears, his head, his chest pounded and throbbed with the sound of his own heartbeat. He was deafened by it, dying from it, for it was the sound of his life being torn from his chest, thrown onto a bed of hay and raped before his wild, disbelieving eyes.

He was screaming her name, but Annie was already beyond hearing him. The animals had done their work well, clawing her soft white skin, ravaging the sweet flesh until she was a mass of blood and bruises. Dear God in heaven, the blood! It was on her thighs and staining the hay beneath her. It was on her arms, her belly; each slap of plunging male flesh produced more, produced a thin, agonized wail from between the drawn, battered lips.

Annie!

The name grated from Alex's throat as he strained against the ropes that held him, supported him so that he might watch the fun they were having with his young bride. Three of them: Colin, Malcolm, and Dughall Campbell. Blood enemies since before birth, before memory, but invited to Achnacarry as a gesture of peace and goodwill to celebrate the marriage of their cousin Maura to Donald Cameron, Chief of Clan Cameron. They had kept their hatred concealed behind sly smiles and rage-hot eyes, cleverly biding their time until the youngest and most volatile scion had unwisely ignored all precautions and slipped away from the crowds to be alone with his betrothed. They had followed, creeping up on the lovers like jackals and catching them unawares.

Alex screamed again, maddened by the sight of Malcolm Campbell's bulbous figure stiffening, twisting tautly through a rush of carnal ecstasy. Annie, responding more to Alex's torment than her own humiliation, found the strength from somewhere to raise the chunk of serrated stone she had discovered buried in the hay and slammed it into Campbell's sweating temple. She struck again and again, her soft green eyes blazing with pain and loathing. She dragged the edge of the stone down the fleshy jowls and peeled a layer of meat from his cheek and throat, exposing the veins beneath.

Campbell screamed and flung himself to one side, his hands clapping over the bloodied mash of an eye. He struck the rock out of Annie's hand and smashed his fist across her face, striking with enough force to snap her head sideways—enough force that she did not move again.

Alex lunged to his feet, the last few bloody threads of rope parting in a sting of pain that cleared his head of any human thought and reduced him to the same low level of consciousness that fuelled the three animals before him. He grabbed the sword—the ancient *clai'mór* he had boastfully taken out of its hiding place to show Annie, and even though its weight was more than anything his arms had ever wielded before, he grasped the thickly encrusted silver hilt in both hands and swung it high above his head.

Dughall, crouched by Malcolm's side, looked up as he heard the faint whisper of steel. The shock of seeing Alexander Cameron on his feet, armed and charging out of the filthy stall, paled beside the horror of seeing the *clai'mór* streak down and carve deeply into the unguarded back of his brother Colin. The sound of the spine breaking in two and the scream of agony ripping out of his brother's throat, brought Dughall to his feet only seconds before the tremendous power of the *clai'mór* came at him out of the gloom. He dodged the first cut and, arming himself with only seconds to spare, blocked the second with the shrill clash of steel on steel.

He was senior to the seventeen-year-old Cameron by eight years; he should have been able to fend the boy off easily. But there was something unholy burning in the depths of the midnight blue eyes, something ancient and mystic, bloodless and merciless and as cold as death itself. The sour taste of fear turned Dughall's defiant cries into pleas for help as he was forced to retreat into a corner of the stable, to duck and brace his sword in both hands to counter the astonishing power of each attacking stroke.

Malcolm staggered to his feet, but he was too slow in retrieving his sword, too late to forestall the lunging thrust that split his brother open from belly to throat. Alex recovered his stance and swung on the remaining Campbell brother in the same smooth, fluid motion. The light from the lantern flared off the blood-streaked steel like a sheet of flame as he brought it down, angled it sideways over the rat-like face and squared shoulders. Malcolm was able to rear back, to cheat death on a stroke that should have cleaved him cleanly in two, but instead, left him a screaming mass of raw, severed muscle and tissue.

And then there was only Annie filling Alex's sights and senses. It took only one glance at the pale and broken figure lying a few paces away for all of the rage and fury to drain from Alexander's arms. Dropping the ancient *clai' mór*, he stumbled forward, falling on his knees beside the only woman he had ever loved. The only woman he would ever love . . .

But, as he gently lifted back the bright curls of hair that clouded her features, it was not Annie MacSorley's face he saw, but Catherine's. Annie's auburn hair had faded to silver-blonde, her sea green eyes had changed to the colour of a Highland dusk. And, after a long, breathless moment, there was a warm stirring in his arms and it was Catherine's hands, Catherine's lips that were reaching up for him. He bowed his head desperately, tasting love and sweetness and peace in her loving caress.

"The nightmare is over," she whispered. "You can sleep now and never have it again."

"Don't go," he gasped. "Don't leave me."

"I'll never leave you, Alex. Alex . . . ?"

"Alex? Alex, can ye hear me lad?"

Another voice, too fuzzy and clotted to identify broke into his dream. "Do you think there is any permanent damage?"

"Pairmanent? Ach, who's tae say when it comes tae such things. See here? There's still bluid in his ears—" the voice paused while gentle fingers wiped at something wet that was trickling down his neck. "It's common enough tae see bluid if a mon's had his brains stirred like he has. I wouldna work yersel's intae a rupture till he wakens, though. He's the only one who'll ken if he can hear or na."

More fingers, equally gentle, probed through the dark waves of his hair.

"Damned lucky," Archibald muttered, nodding at a hovering Struan MacSorley to hold the bloodied shanks of hair away from the wound so that he could reach it with a needle and threaded catgut. "See here? Anither . . . *paugh* . . . an arse hair's width deeper an' we'd be plantin' him under a cairn come the morn's mornin'."

With swift, precise stitches, the gaping slash was closed, given a final inspection, then left to Aluinn's capable hands to bandage while Dr. Archibald Cameron wiped his bloodied fingers on the front of his tartan and moved to the next man in line.

"If he starts tae puke, tairn his heid so he disna choke," came the last bit of sage advice. "He'll most likely sleep till the morns anyway, but if ye need it, there's a pint o' ma private, medicinal *uisque* that'll dull his pains. Couple o' pints, if the pair o' ye feel ye could use it too."

"A . . . fine . . . idea . . ." Alex managed to utter between clenched teeth. With a massive effort, he accomplished a squint, then a slow, steady raising of both eyelids.

Aluinn's grinning face loomed instantly into view. "Alex?" Then, glancing over his shoulder, he called to Archibald. "I think he's coming around."

"Bah! I tald ye his skull was thick as iron. An' I warrant he's only comin' round on account o' I mentioned the magic word: *uisque*. Come tae think on it, I could use a wee drop masel', if ye're gaun that way."

Bracing himself against the pain, Alex turned his head an infinitesimal fraction of an inch, regretting the rash action at once as a hoard of frenzied demons began crushing his skull with spiked bats. Before he corrected the angle and closed his eyes again, he caught an impression of canvas tarpaulins stretched overhead to cut the glare of sunlight. Rows of bodies were stretched out beneath, sprawled in every conceivable position, wounded in every imaginable manner. Flies had moved in, swarming in black clouds to gorge on blood and leaking eviscera.

"Alex?"

He worked at opening his eyes again, no easy task with lead weights anchoring his lashes.

"In case you were wondering . . . we won."

He hadn't been wondering. Won what? Oh yes, the battle. The battle. The last chilling images of the past faded and he concentrated on thinking through the waves of pain.

"Donald?" he rasped. "The Prince? The . . . others?"

Aluinn grinned again. "The Prince is somewhat out of sorts with Lord George, as usual. It seems the general assigned His Highness command of the rear guard to ensure against any spilling of royal blood, but by the time the rear guard made it through the moor and across the field, the battle was over. Donald is fine. A few scratches, but otherwise fine. I'm sure our contingent suffered the heaviest casualties, what with taking on the entire artillery, but I don't think you'll see the smile off Donald's face long enough to hear a lecture on rash theatrics."

"I didn't order anyone to follow me," Alex muttered thickly, his tongue dragging over his lips. "How many did we lose?"

MacKail shrugged. "We don't have an exact count yet, but I'd say . . . no more than half a hundred dead or wounded. Altogether."

"Half a hundred?"

"Aye, lad," Struan said, beaming. "As soon as the lobsterbacks saw their precious guns puit tae the sword, those who werna on the road already, runnin' as if auld Clootie was breathin' fire on their heels, threw down their weapons an' grated f'ae mercy like wee snivellin' bairns."

"Surrendered," Aluinn added. "Nearly two thousand of the bastards, and too many dead to guess offhand. Archie's had to send to Edinburgh for all the physicians the city can spare."

"Fifteen minutes, lad, an' it were over. Too fast f'ae them tae take aught but the claythes on their backs. We've all their wagons, tents, stores, weepons, powder, even those great hulkin' bastard guns we thought tae take on wi' our swords. No' that I ken what guid they'll dae us, wi' none o' these jack-a-napes knowin' spit about how tae shoot one. A fine morn's work, none the less."

"How long . . . have I been out?"

"Ye been seein' angels f'ae the best part o' the day," MacSorley said. "If ye can smell at all, those are supper fires ye're snorkin'. Sun's got anither hour, nae much mair."

"What . . . happened?"

"You nearly swallowed a few ounces of lead, that's what happened," Aluinn said, finishing his job with the relatively clean strip of linen he was using for a bandage. "The officer who had designs on removing your head had his aim thrown off with . . . an arse hair's width to spare, to use a familial quote. The shot still managed to tear a healthy chunk out of your scalp, and to leave the side of your face looking Moorish. But it could have been worse; you could have lost your ear. As it is Archie wasn't too sure if you'd be able to hear properly or not."

"I can hear," Alex grumbled. "If someone would just kill whoever is pounding those damned bells."

"You'll probably have a hell of a headache for a few days, too."

"I have a hell of a headache now. And I think I'm beginning to hallucinate—"

Aluinn followed the direction of the glance Alex shot past his shoulder. A figure in scarlet satin breeches, purple waistcoat, and deep maroon frockcoat was coming toward them. His tricorn hat was edged in gold braid and plumed with dyed ostrich feathers. The jewelled pin at his throat contained one of the largest emeralds either man had ever seen, nestled artfully in a jabot of rich Spanish lace.

"Tell me I've lost my mind," Alex whispered, trying to blink, but finding the effort too costly and the nausea too threatening.

"No indeed," Aluinn replied glibly. "You're looking at the man who saved it for you."

Alex rolled his dark eyes toward MacKail.

"Honestly. It seems he was standing behind the officer taking aim, and was able to deflect the shot just in time. His name is Fanducci. Count Giovanni Alphonso Fanducci, and he is most anxious to meet the great *Camshroinaich Dubh*."

"You're enjoying this, aren't you?"

"Immensely."

Alex curled his lip in what passed for a scowl and returned his attention to the Italian. Seeing that Alex was conscious, the tricorn was removed with a sweeping flourish and a bow executed with the grace of a courtier.

"Ahh! *Signore Camerone*! All is-a well with you, then? I was-a worried perhaps I was-a too late in my efforts."

Alex stared. Previously shadowed by the brim of the tricorn, the count's features did nothing to discourage the impression forming in Alex's mind. The long, thin nose quivered delicately about the nostrils. A thin and angular chin sported a precisely trimmed and manicured goatee; his wig was dusted blue-gray and flowed over his shoulders in descending rolls of glossy curls.

"But of course, allow me to introduce-a myself. Count Giovanni Alphonso Fanducci at-a you service. You have-a no idea, *signore*, how absolutely thrilled I am to finally meet-a the great Dark Camerone. So many stories, *signore*. So many praises I'm-a hear sung. Such a privilege to humble myself before you."

Out of the corner of one bloodshot eye, Alex saw Aluinn lower his head to shield a smile. Struan was less subtle. The grin that began at the corners of his mouth stretched sideways until it touched each ear.

Alex set his teeth and narrowed his eyes to see past the throbbing pinwheels of light. "Count . . . Fanducci? . . . I understand I owe you a debt of gratitude for saving my life."

"No, no, no, no! No debts, *signore*. We just consider it a . . . mmm . . . *comma si dicci* . . . an exchange. *Sì*. An exchange. One favour to another."

"Favour? What manner of favour can I do for you? And how the devil did you get onto the battlefield?"

"Ahh, *signore*! Not-a by choice, believe me. I was-a pressed into joining those thugs. I was-a on board a ship —the *Tuscany*—bound for Inverness when the Inglaz-y come up from-a nowhere and blow her out of the water. The crew, was-a made prisoner; I too was-a thrown in the bilges, but when the captain found out-a who I was, he released me on-a my own parole. Not so these *bastardos*! They find-a me on the road and *blam*! I'm-a made to work for them, or they take-a me out and shoot me! Me! Giovanni Fanducci! Shot like a common gutter-snipe."

There had to be a clue here somewhere, Alex surmised. And a means of keeping his sanity. "You say you worked for them? Doing what?"

The Italian's brows arched and a slim-fingered hand clutched the lower tier of lace of his jabot. "*Signore*! I'm-a Count Giovanni Alphonso Fanducci. To the Inglaz-y, I'm-a the representation from Roma. The neutral. But they choose to ignore-a this. To them, I'm-a also the threat, because I'm-a come to Scotland to offer my services to Prince Charles."

"And these . . . er . . . services?"

The count smiled wanly. "I make-a the guns, *signore*. I make-a the finest guns this side of-a the ocean . . . perhaps the whole world!"

Alex felt his head take another spin downward and his stomach lurch upward. A master gunmaker from Italy? Fanducci looked like he would be more at home tuning the strings of a harp in a bordello.

"You do not-a believe me, *signore*?" the count asked, visibly offended by the lack of response.

I haven't wakened from the nightmare, Alex decided. The ache in his head was getting bad enough that his entire body felt numb, and he was about to ask Struan for that pint of whisky Archie had mentioned when he vaguely saw both MacKail and MacSorley stiffen to attention. They reached instinctively for their swords, but the Italian was that much quicker, freezing their intentions with two distinctive metallic clicks.

The handsome pair of snaphaunce pistols he held had appeared from nowhere and were unlike anything the Highlanders had ever seen before. The wooden stocks were filigreed with fine threads of silver wire, woven in patterns so minute and intricate as to flatter the hands of royalty. Each pistol had over-and-under barrels inlaid with gold; each barrel had its own flintlock mechanism operated by triggers positioned in sequence within the guard. Four shots could be fired almost simultaneously and would, regardless of aim, obliterate the greater portion of a man's chest at close range.

The bright azure eyes that gleamed straight along the barrels were no longer dancing with good humour. The features surrounding them were no longer foppish or dandified, and the hands balancing the heavy weapons were rock hard and taut with sinew. They had not wavered a breath.

"Signores," the count said quietly, looking from Struan's glowering might to Aluinn's deadly calm. A deft flick of both thumbs released the tension in the mainsprings and the locks of the pistols were adjusted into a safety position. "My handiwork, if you please?"

Another graceful flip of his wrists and the pistols were reversed so that the butts were presented for inspection. Taken aback by the foreigner's speed and evident skill with the guns, Aluinn and Struan exchanged a wary glance before each accepted one of the snaphaunces.

"My family," the count explained casually, "makes-a the guns now . . . mmm . . . eighty years. We make-a the fine guns for all the nobility of Europe. On board the *Tuscany*, we put two thousand guns—no, not so fine as-a these, but still the best-a guns money could buy. All I'm-a have left to show are these two, and . . . mmm . . . three, four more not so fancy. My . . . molds and chisels and files went-a down with the *Tuscany*, so—" he spread his hands apologetically "—all-a you get is me, but, I could perhaps be of some assistance to your own gun-a-makers, no?"

Aluinn fingered the exquisite tooling on the pistol, turning it over to examine the gilded grotesque on the butt. He sighted along the upper barrel, noting the fine weight and balance, the clever way the serpentine heads of the flintlocks curved into a circle through which to align a target. The lockplate bore the maker's name, *Fanducci*, set into a relief of the family crest; below it, the year *1742*.

"A remarkable piece of workmanship," Aluinn murmured, returning the gun to Fanducci. "Unfortunately, we have no gunmakers of comparable skill travelling with us . . . none at all, to be absolutely truthful. You would find your talents sorely wasted."

The count looked crestfallen. "But . . . I'm-a come the long way, *signore*. I would do anything to help in this venture. In Italy, we have-a the big respect for your King-a James. He fights the . . . mmm . . . big odds, no? So does his son?"

"Big odds, yes," Aluinn smiled. He glanced down to see what Alex's reaction to all this had been, but the heavy black lashes were closed, his lips slightly parted, his breathing deep and even. Seeing the bandages on Alex's head, a thought occurred to MacKail.

"You say you were pressed into service with the English, but you never did elaborate as to what capacity."

The Italian smiled wryly. "Bah! The Inglaz-y think that because Giovanni Fanducci makes-a the pistols, he also knows how to make-a the big *bastardos* shoot farther, straighter."

"The big *bastardos*? You mean the cannon?"

"*Sí, sí*. The cannon."

"And? Do you?"

The count caught a glimpse of eagerness in Aluinn's gray eyes and his frown melted into a conspiratorial smile. "But of course, *signore*. To make-a the small gun shoot farther, straighter, it is . . . mmm . . . prudent to know how the big *bastardos* shoot."

"Do you think you could teach a handful of jackanapes how to load and fire the artillery pieces we've captured?"

"*Signore* MacKail." The Italian drew himself to his full, bejewelled height. "I, Giovanni Alphonso Fanducci could-a teach the birds how to swim if that was-a what the Prince asked of me."

"Just a few basics on cannonry will do," Aluinn said dryly. "Enough to justify hauling them farther than the nearest sink-hole."

"Sink hole?"

"Bog," Struan provided. "Quagmire."

"Ahhh, such the waste, *signores*. No, no, no, no, I'm-a teach."

"In that case," Aluinn stretched out his hand. "Welcome to the army. You will have to meet with Lord George Murray first, but I'm sure he will be pleased to have you join us."

"Aye," Struan growled amiably, handing back the snaphaunce with an obvious show of reluctance. "Calls f'ae a toast, by my mind. MacKail?"

"Save me a few drams, I'll be along directly."

Which probably meant he would remain here the whole night through, Struan thought, glancing down at Alexander. "Aye, well, I'll bring ye a keg here afore I go tae check on the men. Fanducci? Ye're welcome tae join me if ye're belly's keen on seein' the inside o' yer throat."

"*Scusa, signore,*" the count objected delicately, "but my family also makes-a the best wine in all Italia. Fanducci bambinos are weaned from the breast to the grape, then back-a to the breast again as-a full-grown men. I think . . .

mmm . . . it would be fair to say *you* would have the disadvantage."

MacSorley's grin spread across his face and his nostrils flared with the scent of easy prey. "Ye wouldna care tae puit a wee wager on that, now would ye laddie?"

The count's brows crooked upward. "Wager, *signore*?"

"Aye. That fine brace o' pistols ye're wearin', f'ae instance."

Fanducci's hand instinctively caressed the butt of one snaphaunce. "And-a you, *Signore* Struan? You have-a something to wager of comparable value?"

Struan's white teeth flashed through the parted wire bush of his beard. "I've a handsomer, deadlier weepon tae wager in Ringle-Eyed Rita."

"Ahh . . . Struan . . ."

MacSorley held up a hand to stop Aluinn's objection and the count looked from one man to the other.

"Might I ask-a what kind of weapon this rink-a-lied rita is?"

MacSorley chuckled bawdily. "The kind o' weepon, laddie, what tairns a grown man's knees tae water. The kind what takes shiny breeks like yourn an stiffens them tae leather afore ye even ken there's sum'mit doun there."

"*Bene, bene,*" Fanducci said softly. "She's-a the woman. In that-a case, *signore*—" he bowed elegantly "—I accept."

"Last man standin' takes all?"

The count nodded graciously.

The bloodied, mud-streaked Highlander laughed, startling many of the dozing wounded awake. He wrapped a trunk-like arm around the Italian's immaculate shoulders and, as they walked toward the open air, he cast a wink back in Aluinn's direction.

"This shouldna take too lang, MacKail. I'll be back in a blink tae keep ye company."

"I'm not sure whether to feel slighted at being left out of the wagering," Aluinn murmured, "or relieved."

"With Rita as part of the stakes?" Alex said, opening his eyes a slit. "How about just plain lucky?"

DERBY, December 1745

Chapter Four

Catherine led her horse slowly along the sun-gilded pathway, her footsteps crunching lightly on the brittle crust of hoarfrost that coated the forest floor. The trees were naked, stripped of their summer greenery and fullness. The bared branches left great gaps of crystal blue sky overhead, the colour so intense it hurt the eyes to stare upward too long. The sun on her back was warm, turning what might have been another dismal winter morning into a brief escape from the gloom and silence of her rooms at Rosewood Hall.

The air was clean and crisp, faintly tinged with woodsmoke. In league with the sun and fresh air, the brisk canter which had brought Catherine across the fields and into the forest had left her cheeks touched with a blush of pale rose. Her hair, never known for its willingness to respect the orderly confines of combs and pins, trailed here and there over her shoulders in shiny wisps, clinging to the lavender velvet of her riding suit like a fine spray of water. The suit was tailored snugly from shoulder to waist, falling from there in deep, rich folds of velvet to within an inch of the ground. An abundance of cream-coloured lace was gathered in dainty scallops at her throat and wrists, and as she walked, a hint of similarly adorned petticoats splashed up over the toes of her Moroccan leather boots.

Catherine hated the winter months. Hated the month of December in particular when the constant dripping, drizzling chill out-of-doors made it too drafty and damp to feel comfortable indoors. The brilliant colours of fall had all faded, burned dull and lifeless by the frost. Days were short, gray, and dreary; evenings were long, lonely, and miserable, and by necessity, spent before a stifling hot fire.

An even worse prospect looming in the skies was snow. Catherine knew this happy little interlude of sunshine was only a cruel prelude to the heavy, wet, mushy stuff that melted and seeped into clothing, ruined shoes, and generally sent her mood spinning into an abyss of bad temper. She had never enjoyed winter, not even as a child. Never felt the urge or the inclination to don bulky layers of clothing and feign throes of rapture while slogging and sledding through the wretched business. Thankfully, there had been but a few brief flurries in Derbyshire so far this season, none of which had survived on the ground more than an hour or so. She had heard reports of heavier snowfalls farther north, of cruel winds and cutting storms of sleet and hail, hindered by banks of fog that froze into solid walls of ice.

Weather, so she heard, was being made the convenient scapegoat in affording the army excuses as to why it had been unable to prevent the army of Charles Edward Stuart from crossing the border from Scotland into England unmolested. Three battalions of Guards and seven regiments of government infantry had been pinned at Newcastle by the snow and fog, effectively stopping Field Marshal George Wade from marching out to meet the invading army.

Taking advantage of the weather, the Prince's forces had crossed into England on November 8, half by a westerly route over the River Tweed, half by an easterly cut across the River Esk. By the next day, the entire rebel force—reputed to be upwards of twenty thousand men

—had rendezvoused unchallenged at the outskirts of Carlisle and, after placing the town and castle under seige, received its unconditional surrender on the fourteenth. On the fifteenth, Charles Edward Stuart had ridden triumphantly into the English city to proclaim his father King and himself regent in the presence of the Lord Mayor and the entire cheering population.

Incredible as it seemed, until then no one in Parliament had taken the threat of invasion seriously; no one had even taken the necessary steps to block the main roads into England. The handful of token patrols that had been dispatched to guard the border and report on any untoward activity, had either been swept up by the avalanche of marching Highlanders, or had fled with all due haste, not troubling themselves to take notice of the numbers or whereabouts of the attacking forces. At the time of the defeat of the army at Prestonpans, there had been fewer than six thousand regular troops available in England. Following the astonishing news of the Prince's victory, a hasty appeal was sent to Holland for troops to honour their treaty with England. William, Duke of Cumberland, was also recalled from Europe, and Admiral Vernon was ordered to abandon his patrols of the Mediterranean and concentrate his navy in the Channel and along the English coast.

It took time to move armies and equipment from the Continent, however, and the Jacobite army had begun its advance southward on November 20, marching boldly through Lancaster to Preston. Marshal Wade, aware of the relatively small number of Highlanders who had achieved the staggering defeat of Cope's army, was loathe to risk his inadequate forces without reinforcements, and made only one attempt to harass the rebels from Newcastle before hurriedly retreating behind the city's defenses again.

Catherine, her loyalties torn, did not know whether to applaud or dread each report she heard. She could not deny the pride she felt upon first learning of the audacious victory at Prestonpans, knowing Alexander and his clansmen would have played a vital role in the events. Yet she had been raised in a Whig household. Her father was a staunch Hanover supporter as were most of their friends, neighbours, and acquaintances. She herself had been presented at court, and had met the pudgy German king on more than one occasion.

With the fall of Edinburgh and the defeat of Cope's army at Prestonpans, Scotland belonged to the Stuarts. Why could they not have been content with that? Only the castle at Edinburgh, two small garrisoned forts—Fort William and Fort Augustus—and the city of Inverness remained in Hanover hands. Probably . . . *possibly*, if the Scots had kept to their own borders and taken immediate steps to bring about a peaceful alliance with England, they could have avoided any further bloodshed. Instead, they had invaded England's sovereign territory. To add to the insult, they did so after deliberately and openly allying themselves with England's hereditary enemies, France and Spain. That alone would ensure the emnity of the military, regardless of any political or social sympathies toward the Stuarts. The three nations had fought too many wars for England to simply sit by and watch their enemies obtain a foothold on their Isles.

Certainly, it was all the fashion to speak at dinner parties of the Prince's charm and the tragically romantic history of the Stuarts. But more, Catherine suspected, with an eye toward what might well lay ahead if his army reached London, than out of any true sense of affection for the dynasty. Outside the gaily tolerant parlour discussions, the country militias were being brought up to strength. Several noblemen were raising regiments of cavalry and infantry at their own expense; the city of York alone had armed four hundred men for its defense, and even the fox-hunting gentlemen of the area had formed themselves into a colourful regiment of hussars.

Cities that lay directly south of Preston and Manchester began to empty of their more weak-hearted citizens who defended their actions with rumours of the Highlanders' unbridled savagery. The inevitable tales of assault and rape had black-busked matrons swooning by the droves. Parlour conversations often ended abruptly in a crush of silks and satins as the women fainted *en masse* over ill-timed and graphic descriptions of how the Highlanders offered live sacrifices to their Celtic druids.

Catherine, who had been to Scotland and seen the gentle honesty of Lochiel and his clansmen, wanted to scream at the absurdity of the lies, and had to constantly remind herself that her husband was supposed to be an English businessman away seeing to his enterprises in the North American colonies. She had to hold her tongue and resist the urge to contradict the stories, regardless of how outlandish or ridiculous they became. It was difficult and draining, especially since many of the fleeing refugees found themselves the centre of attraction at so many luncheons and parties, that they fled no further south than Derby.

Lady Caroline Ashbrooke, not to be outdone by any of her peers, managed to score a brilliant coup in the acquisition of Captain John Lovat-Spence as a houseguest. Wounded at Prestonpans, he had been on his way home to recuperate and had stopped in at Rosewood Hall to pay his respects to Lord Ashbrooke. Ten years Lady Caroline's junior, and unable to resist her porcelain beauty and soft, violet-gray eyes, the captain had been in residence ever since. His understandable reluctance to disclose too many details of the battle fell easy prey to Lady Caroline's powers of persuasion and, at her behest, he stunned selected audiences with eye-witness accounts of the surprise attack.

Catherine had initially avoided his company, preferring the solitude of her own rooms to the silly squeals and heaving bosoms of the gossip sessions. She had further cause to resent Lovat-Spence upon noting his early morning departure from her mother's bedroom the day after his arrival. But her curiosity won the better of her and she found herself drawn to the parlour, hoping there might be some mention made of a tall, black-haired spectre taking to the field astride a midnight black destry.

The Highlanders had fought like demons from hell, Lovat-Spence assured the avid audiences, descending from nowhere and leaving a charnel house of screaming, limbless bodies, writhing in a sea of their own blood. The screeching wail of the rebel pipes had haunted his every waking and sleeping hour since that fateful day, as had the memory of their gleaming, blood-smeared bodies, charging out of the morning mists.

Nothing, the captain confided passionately, could ever equal the sheer terror he had felt that morning. He had fought, but to this day could not recall actual details of how he had earned his wound (a dramatic pressing of a hand against his upper thigh had sent two abigails fluttering after their mistresses with unstoppered bottles of smelling salts) but only that he had been collected up with the others and placed in a hospital tent.

To his amazement (and additional agonies of delight for the ladies), the Stuart Prince himself had visited the wounded men, enquiring after their needs. With grudging respect, the captain related how the Prince had not taken a scrap of food or refreshment until such time as the last wound had been cleaned and bound, and each man assured a comfortable night's sleep. Neither had his officers shown a lack of concern. Lord George Murray had billeted himself with the captured English officers in a house nearby, remaining with them throughout the night, sharing a bale of hay for a bed, so that his presence would deter any thoughts of mischief the celebrating rebels might have had.

Many, if not all of the prisoners—over seventeen hundred—had been released within a few days, or permitted to escape. There had simply been too many for the rebels to attempt to feed and confine. The officers had been released on their own parole after swearing an oath not to actively participate in any further military encounters against the Prince.

"An honourable and generous release," he conceded, "although there were some who only took the gesture as a further insult and were no sooner away from the Pretender's camp than they beat a straight path for the nearest government garrison."

The captain had paused during this particular dissertation to glance at Catherine.

"A former acquaintance of yours, Mrs. Montgomery, was one of the officers who did not consider a promise made to a rebel to be one worth keeping."

Catherine had felt the colour seep into her cheeks and the owlish eyes of everyone present in the drawing room turned to her in breathless expectation.

"Captain Hamilton Garner was *not* pleased with the cowardly way his men behaved. Why, after his dragoons fled, he fought with the infantry, urging them to continue alongside him until every last man but himself was slain."

He paused so the ladies could gasp in wonder at the brave captain's demonstration of courage and, again, Catherine felt their gazes upon her—most of them scorning her for having summarily dallied with Hamilton's affections.

"At the first opportunity, Captain Garner and several others broke out of the compound where they were being held and made for Edinburgh Castle, which as you know, is still in the capable hands of General Joshua Guest. A stout old soldier," Lovat-Spence remarked with a smile. "Well over eighty years of age and quite adamant about the castle remaining in the proper hands. Since the Prince does not possess any heavy siege equipment he can do little against the well-provisioned garrison; any attempts to blockade the castle instantly bring the guns firing down upon the open city. I should think Captain Garner will find a kindred spirit in the general. It was rumoured—unconfirmed to my express knowledge, but quite possible—that the captain has already been promoted to the rank of major in recognition of his outstanding valour on the field."

The captain had regaled the small crowd for another two hours of selected memories, but Catherine had barely heard any of them. The descriptions had remained vivid in her mind long after she had retired and that night, like so many others that had gone before, she dreamed of a battlefield. Dreamed she was *on* the battlefield, hearing the screams, running on ground that had been trampled red with blood. She dreamed she had run past the splayed bodies, through the muck and tangled grasses, past fighting men locked in mortal combat and panicked horses trembling in a sweat of sour white foam.

It was always the same. The same dream, the same battlefield. Each time she had it, the sequences seemed to grow longer, although she never seemed to get any further than a screamed warning, a glimpse of someone high on a hill surrounded by a glittering ring of raised swords. Alexander was always just starting to turn, his dark sapphire eyes searching for the source of the scream . . . when she wakened, drenched in sweat, utterly drained and shaken as if she had indeed been running for miles on end.

It had been because of an almost desperate need to feel the sunlight on her face, to smell the crisp, clean air, and to escape to the haunting beauty of the still, silent forest that she had ridden away from Rosewood Hall that morning as if the devil was snapping at her heels.

Somewhat calmer now, she led her horse along the dappled pathway, the only sound the hoarfrost crunching underfoot. Why she found solace and comfort in retracing the steps that had led to her initial meeting with

Alexander Cameron, she did not know. Was it because, secretly, she hoped to see him in the clearing? Or that by some miracle he had come back to her and was waiting to carry her away just as he had promised?

No. If that was what she thought and hoped, then she was dreaming again.

Her heart and thoughts heavy, she rounded the final copse of evergreens and stood at the outer rim of the clearing, almost in the exact spot she had halted the first time she had seen Alexander. The pond where he had been bathing was crusted with a thin rime of ice, the mossy banks were frozen and coated brown with fallen leaves. Even though it was winter and the trees were stripped to their bare branches, the sunlight was still mottled where it touched the ground, the beams broken and striped with shadows.

Catherine could still feel his presence. She could still recall with startling clarity every detail of their first encounter—her shock at seeing a half-naked man bathing by the pool; the first riveting moment when their eyes had met; the seemingly endless eternity before her heart had commenced beating again. In her confusion and foolishness, she had accused him of trespassing, poaching . . . anything that came to mind in the heady rush of excitement. It had been a defensive measure, taken against an intoxication the likes of which she had never felt before, and doubted she ever would again.

Catherine closed her eyes, reliving the sensation of his hands stroking down her body, of his mouth winning her capitulation. He had possessed her completely, body and soul, flesh and spirit, and branded her forever a woman. *His* woman. Even if he never came back into her life, he had spoiled her for all others. His passion, his strength, his tenderness could have no equal. Never.

"Catherine?"

She opened her eyes slowly, not daring to move or breathe. It was a trick of the wind, it had to be—a torturous murmur of frosted air that carried the echo of a voice, nothing more.

"Catherine?"

She gasped and whirled around. Louder this time, the voice had not been a trick of the wind nor a taunt of her imagination. It was real. It belonged to a real person!

"Alex," she whispered.

"Catherine, are you here?"

With a sob she stumbled past the obstacle of her grazing horse and ran back along the path. She saw a cloaked figure standing partially concealed behind two tightly interwoven evergreens and hesitated the merest fraction of a second before flinging herself into his outstretched arms.

"Damien! Oh Damien, it's you! You've come home! You've come home!"

"Good heavens," her brother murmured, cradling the sobbing bundle to his chest. "For a greeting like this I would make a point of coming back to Derby every other day. Here now, what's all this? I know it's been almost two months since I removed myself to London, but—"

Catherine lifted her tear-streaked face from his shoulder. Disappointment at his not being Alexander was almost as acute as her happiness at seeing her brother again after such a long absence, but she could do nothing more than stare.

"Kitty? What is it? Is something wrong?"

She sobbed pitifully and collapsed against his shoulder again. For a long moment, Damien's frown remained fixed and his confusion was genuine, but then, looking around, he guessed at the reason for her outburst.

"Damn, Kitty. I'm sorry. I should have waited and called at the house, but I wasn't thinking. I saw you ride out of the stables and wanted to see you alone, without Mother or Father badgering me with endless questions, and, well, I guess I just didn't think."

Catherine sniffled loudly and wetly. Having brought no handkerchief with her, she patted Damien's breast pocket and relieved him of his. She held the snowy white linen to her nose and blew, looking up into her brother's face and nearly gasping aloud as she did so. He looked dreadful! His complexion was sallow and unhealthy, his eyes were clouded with fatigue that could not be the mere result of a hurried trip from London.

"Dear God," she cried. "Something has happened to Harriet!" Reaching out, she clutched his arm, nearly tearing the seam of his cloak in her anxiety. "Is she ill? Has something happened to the baby?"

"No! No, Harriet is fine. Honestly. She's fine. A little plumper around the middle, but otherwise shamelessly content."

Catherine swallowed a deep gulp of air to regain her composure. "Then what is it? Why are you sneaking about the woods like a thief?"

Damien arched a brow wryly. "I think I prefer your first greeting, thank you. Since when is it a crime to seek out the bosom of one's own family, on one's own land?"

"Damien Ashbrooke, the only bosom you have cared to seek out for the past three months has belonged to Harriet." She finished wiping away the streaks of tears from her cheeks and glared up at him accusingly. "And what leads you to believe Father would badger you with anything less than a trowel after the argument the two of you had following the wedding? You have been carved up and served *in absentia* for dinner more often than a joint of mutton."

"So. He's still angry with my decision to take permanent residence in London? It never seemed to bother him before I was married."

"Before you were married, and while you were sowing your wild oats all over hell and gone, he was perfectly content to keep you and your scandals in London. But, may I remind you, you are his only son and heir. You are respectably—if somewhat imprudently—married with a possible son and heir of your own on its way. He assumes there is just as much law to be practised in Derby as in London, and as much determination in your soul to preserve the fortunes of Rosewood Hall as there was in the souls of twelve preceeding generations of Ashbrookes."

"Kitty," he sighed. "I am abandoning neither my heritage nor my duty. I am twenty-four years old, hardly the age to consider retiring into dotage. I have a thriving practice in London which I am not prepared to forfeit just yet. I am fully aware of my responsibilities as an Ashbrooke—good Lord, they have been drummed into me since birth—but I am also concerned with my responsibilities to myself and my wife."

"Bravo," Catherine smiled. "Well said, my brave and beautiful brother. And said well in the seclusion of the forest."

"I have said the exact same thing to Father's face."

"Indeed you have. Unfortunately, he isn't nearly as astute or sympathetic as the trees, nor as perceptive as your little sister. There is something more going on behind all this skullduggery, and if you don't out with it soon, I shall go after you with a trowel of my own."

Damien laughed softly. "Obviously, my concerns for your welfare have been unfounded; you haven't lost the edge to your wit yet. Has all been forgiven, or have you just managed to stay out of Father's way?"

It was Catherine's turn to sigh. "He has been so damned civil since you confided the extent of the absent Mr. Montgomery's wealth that one would think he had orchestrated the whole affair himself. Hearing him wax profound on his new son-in-law even has me listening in awe sometimes and wishing I could meet the fellow myself."

"Better that than the alternative," Damien said. "Father can be a self-righteous swine when he wants to be."

"Tell me about it. Swine, is hardly the word I would use to describe a man who forces his only daughter into marrying a complete stranger. He should just *dare* to lecture me on *my* behaviour."

"Meaning . . . what?"

She glared up at him again. "I haven't been following in dear Mother's footsteps, if that's what you are asking. Although, sometimes I wonder."

"It never even occurred to me that you might. And what could you possibly have to wonder about that would cause such an unhappy frown on such a lovely face?"

"Tell me something I have to smile about," she said in exasperation.

"You have Alex," he pointed out quietly.

"Do I? Where?" She looked around angrily. "Are you seeing someone I am not?"

"Kitty—"

"Don't *Kitty* me. And don't patronize me either. I haven't seen Alex, haven't heard one single word from him in over three months."

"He hasn't exactly been languishing on his laurels all this time. If you love him—"

"If I love him? *If* I love him?" She averted her face for a moment, and clasped her hands tightly together in frustration. "You have no idea how many times I have asked myself the same question. Do I love him? Do I even know him? I spent less than five weeks with the man—half of the time plotting how to turn him over to the authorities and collect the reward! The rest of the time . . ." she faced Damien again and shook her head slowly, "the rest of the time, I was so frightened I think I could have convinced myself I loved Attila the Hun."

"Kitty . . you don't mean that."

"Don't I? Maybe you're right. Maybe I don't know anything anymore. Who is to say I would not have been just as happy—or as miserable—married to Hamilton Garner? At least I would know where he was, and know what he was doing all these miles from home. Good God, how I would know. Every time I turn around someone is talking about Hamilton Garner. Lo—the brave hero! Did you know he was promoted to major? I could have been the wife of a respected army officer, boasting night after endless night of my husband's accomplishments. Instead, I find myself spending so much time in my rooms I have begun to tat cobwebs into lace. Have I spent one moment that wasn't plagued with doubts and fears? Is he alive? Is he dead? Did everything happen the way I remember it, or am I seeing things, believing things that are just not true; not even real? Does he think about me? Does he wonder how I spend my days and nights? If I have enough food to eat? If I'm warm or cold? Am I one *tenth* as important to him as . . . as . . ."

"As he is to you?" Damien provided softly.

She looked up at him through the shine of fresh tears. "Do not put words in my mouth, either, Damien Ashbrooke. Especially when you cannot possibly be sure of what they are."

He sighed expressively. "Very well. I guess I was wrong. I guess I should not have told him you wanted to see him."

Catherine grew very still. It came together, like two tin pans crashing in the silence, why Damien had followed her into the woods instead of meeting her at the house; why he looked so tired, so haggard . . . so worried!

"It's Alex, isn't it?" she asked tautly. "You've seen him. Something has happened to him . . . he's been hurt!"

"No! I mean, yes, I've seen him; no, he hasn't been hurt. Well, not that you'd notice, at any rate. He was wounded at Prestonpans, but—"

A roaring filled Catherine's ears. The roaring was Damien's voice and she could see his lips moving but the words were blended together in a melee of distorted sounds and echoes. She swayed forward slightly and

Damien had to reach out and catch her about the waist to prevent her from falling. He led her to a nearby tree stump and made her sit down. Watching the colour come and go in her cheeks, he searched beneath the frilly jabot at her throat until he found and unfastened the top three buttons of her velvet jacket.

"Wounded?" she gasped. "You said he was wounded?"

"He has a few new scars to show you. Nothing serious. Nothing missing, nothing broken, nothing twisted out of shape or disfigured. My word of honour, Kitty. He's fine."

"Where . . . where did you see him?"

"He showed up in London a few days ago. Completely unannounced, of course, and walking bold as brass through Picadilly Square as if he owned the place. He stayed a few hours, gave me a list of errands as long as your arm to run, then vanished again, him and that great bloody stallion of his."

"Alex was in London?" she repeated slowly, her heart hammering against the confines of her tightly laced stomacher. To reach London, he would have had to have passed by Derby . . . wouldn't he?

"His business was urgent," Damien said, reading the question in Catherine's eyes. "He could not afford to stop or delay on the way there. However—"

"He is coming here on his way back?" she cried.

"That, er, was his intention. Until I, in a more rational state of mind, managed to dissuade him."

"You did *what*?"

"Well, for one thing, there is the trifling matter of the two companies of militia Father has so generously invited to encamp on our grounds." The point, well made, was also well coated in sarcasm. At the first suggestion of the Pretender's intent to march south, Lord Alfred Ashbrooke had run, wig askew, to Colonel Halfyard's headquarters and demanded armed protection for his property. "A tinker cannot get close to the house without running a gauntlet of questions and accusations. I was stopped four times in the final mile."

"I could meet him," she gasped. "Anywhere!"

"Anywhere and everywhere is swarming with soldiers. And I wasn't the only one who followed you away from the stables. A rather priggish-looking lieutenant stopped me at the edge of the forest and would have run me through with his sabre if I hadn't been able to convince him I was your brother. And if you don't believe me, look behind you . . . *carefully*! You can just catch a glimpse of a red tunic here and there through the trees. Lord help both of us if we don't walk away from here arm and arm singing praises to the king."

Catherine felt a surge of anger. "Father! How dare he have me followed!"

"Undoubtedly for your own protection," Damien said placatingly. "But a distinct nuisance, none the less."

"A damned nuisance," she retorted, jumping to her feet. "And one that shall end here and now."

"Frankly, I wouldn't say anything about it, if I were you. The old Catherine Ashbrooke we all knew and loved would probably have demanded an entire regiment to escort her on a walk through the gardens. You wouldn't want to lapse too much out of character now, would you?"

Catherine opened her mouth to toss back a retort, but thought better of it and sank back down onto her seat on the log.

"Was I really so obvious?" she asked, chewing her lip.

"You were just young and foolish and more in love with the reflection in the mirror than you were with reality."

"A sage observation, brother dear. Considerate of you not to mention it before now."

Damien shrugged. "I had hopes it would pass. And I can see by the look in your eyes, every time you say your husband's name, it has."

"Alex," she whispered. "Oh Damien, I have to see him. I just have to!"

"He'll be relieved to hear it. I gather he was not altogether certain what to expect by way of a reception. He seemed to dwell particularly upon the chilliness of a certain young lady's departure from Scotland and her reluctance to acknowledge even the tiniest bit of good judgement on his part for taking such swift action to see to her safety."

"He thinks I am still angry?"

"In truth, I think the two of you have more in common than you realize. He paced a rut in my floorboards telling me how it would be better for all concerned if he'd never taken you out of England, never accepted the challenge from Hamilton, never so much as spoken to you, let alone touched you. I told him he was absolutely right, of course."

Catherine's heart missed a beat. Her chest, her shoulders were suddenly so heavy under the weight of her emotions, that she felt doubled over. "Is that why he did not come here first? Is that why he went straight to London?"

"Actually . . . he wasn't sure you were here."

"Not here? Where would I be?"

"Considering half the shires are evacuating before the descending hoards, it was not an altogether unreasonable concern." He paused and tilted Catherine's chin higher so that she was forced to meet the rarefied blue of his eyes. "He wasn't even sure if you were living here as a widow, or as the wife of an absentee businessman."

"He didn't know? All this time and . . . *he didn't know*!"

"How could he, Kitty? He has been fighting a war, remember?"

"But . . . he should have known," she said, the tears swelling along her lashes. "He promised. He gave me his word of honour. He should have known I would have waited for him. Damien please . . . you must take me to him. You must!"

"I can't do that—" he held up his hand and pressed a fingertip over the arguments forming on her lips "—not because I don't want to, but because I don't know where he is."

"Then how—?"

"He, on the other hand, knows where I will be staying tomorrow night—"

"Tomorrow!"

"We have allowed a day for Father's trowel and Mother's appetite for gossip. Anyway, he knows where I will be staying, and that is where he will go in search of your answer."

"Answer? Answer to what?"

"To this—" Catherine stared, her eyes rounded with disbelief as her brother reached to an inside pocket of his frockcoat and withdrew a folded, sealed sheet of paper. She gaped at the letter, then up into his handsome face, and his smile faded under the hot flare of violet sparks that burned in her eyes.

"Do you mean to tell me you have been sitting here for ten minutes with this in your pocket!"

Without waiting for a reply, she snatched the letter out of his hand and pressed it to her bosom for a long, breathless moment before daring to break the wax seal. Her hands were shaking as she unfolded the single sheet and she had to read the opening salutation twice before her eyes would focus properly.

My dearest Catherine,

She stopped, clutched the letter to her breast again and felt Damien's arm circle her shoulders.

"I'm alright," she whispered.

He bent over and kissed her tenderly on the forehead, then stood up from the log and walked a few paces away to give her some privacy.

My dearest Catherine,

I pray Damien has found you well and in good spirits. We had heard most of the gentry were relocating and so I did not hold much hope of seeing you. I was happy enough and relieved just to hear that Mrs. Montgomery was visiting at Rosewood Hall while her husband is out of the country.

Somehow, a piece of paper seems hopelessly inadequate for expressing what I want to say. I should have had Aluinn's talent for poetry to know how to properly tell you what is in my heart. Instead, I shall simply have to be content with the truth, blunt as it may be. Not one single hour of one single day has gone by wherein I have not thought of you. I sometimes find myself wondering if it was all a dream, if I only conjured you out of a desperate need to feel something warm and loving in my life again. If I am dreaming, I pray I never wake up. If I am awake, I pray you dream me into your arms and, one night soon, God willing, we shall waken together.

Your devoted servant, A.C.

Catherine's lips trembled. "Damien . . . Damien, I must go to him. Take me with you when you leave tomorrow. We can take precautions, we can—"

"Kitty, I can't do that. It isn't safe."

"I don't care! I am going back with you and there is nothing you can say or do to prevent it. I listened to logic and reason and concerns over my safety once before, and see where it has gotten me?"

"If you won't think of your safety, then think about his," Damien implored, recognizing the determined set to her jaw. "Kitty—" he took her hands into his "—I have had more inquiries in the past two months as to the whereabouts of the mysterious Raefer Montgomery than I could tally on five pairs of hands."

"Good gracious, what has that to do with—"

"Some were just the usual curiosity seekers, those who had heard about the duel and wanted the gory details. But there were others, not the least bit interested in the duel, but damned persistent when it came to questions about his current and past affiliations—including his lovely new wife. At the same time, I'm hearing another name discussed in the coffee houses and men's clubs—Alexander Cameron—complete with questions and curiosities."

Catherine felt the warmth drain out of her face. "What do you mean?"

"The Camerons are a large and important clan. Without The Cameron of Lochiel backing his cause, the Prince might not have found himself ten men willing to support a rebellion, let alone thousands. As for Alex's importance, well, it might interest you to know that your husband has won himself a great deal of attention. He and his men were responsible for sending our valiant dragoons cantering away from Colt's Bridge; they were instrumental in taking Perth, Stirling, and Edinburgh. At Prestonpans, it is said he led a charge against heavy artillery and instead of being blown to hell and gone like any other mortal, he captured more Hanover cannon than they have men knowledgeable enough to shoot them. Shall I go on?"

"You seem to be quite well informed about what goes on in the Jacobite army," she said tersely.

"It is my luck to be privy to information London prefers to keep close to its breast, including the stories and rumours of a certain legendary figure who is quickly assuming the title 'invincible'. The result, my dear sister, is that any lobsterback worth his salt ration would trade his first-born son for the honour of capturing or killing Alexander Cameron."

"I still don't see what it has to do with me."

"Frankly, I'm worried that it may have a good deal to do with you. And Alex was worried as far back as August, when he sent you out of the country in hopes of throwing the hounds off the scent."

"Damien, for heaven's sake, will you stop talking in riddles!"

"You are a clever girl, Catherine, figure it out. You married a tall, strappingly handsome, black-haired rogue whose skill with a sword was sufficient to win honours from the Master of His Majesty's Royal Dragoons. Moreover, after the much celebrated duel and much gossiped about nuptials, the pair of you disappear without a trace for over a month. Coincidentally, during the same four-week period, Alexander Cameron—another tall, strappingly handsome, black-haired rogue, reappears in the Scottish Highlands after a prolonged absence on the Continent. Once there, does he keep his presence low-keyed and unremarkable? Heavens no. He acts out a fifteen-year-old vendetta against the nephew of one of the most powerful Hanover chiefs in Scotland, doing so while in the act of rescuing his beautiful, golden-haired English bride."

"Damien . . . *you* know all the details, and *I* know all the details, but who on earth is going to take the trouble to run back and forth between Scotland and England to link the two stories?"

"You met some of the Duke of Argyle's kinfolk," Damien said bluntly. "And you still require an answer to that question?"

"But . . . it was a personal matter, between Alex and Malcolm Campbell. Campbell is dead now; that should be the end of it."

"Should be," Damien agreed. "Would be, if we were talking about proper English gentlemen here, but we're not. We're talking about a race of people who were born fighting. Highlanders take their honour very seriously; an insult to a fourth cousin twice removed is still an insult to the clan chief. When Alex killed Dughall and Colin Campbell fifteen years ago, the Duke had enough influence to run him out of the country and keep him out. He posted a steep enough reward to entice a constant flow of Campbell clansmen to the Continent to try their hands at collecting it. Now, with the demise of the third Campbell nephew, the insult has doubled and so has the reward. He's worth twenty thousand gold sovereigns to any man with enough guts or cunning to creep up on him in the dark of night and stick a knife in his back.

"And if that weren't enough, I'm hearing nasty rumours, laced with words like 'assassin' and 'paid killer,' and if that is the case, you can bet they'll be probing for any obvious weaknesses in our valiant friend's armour."

"Meaning me?"

"Meaning *any* weakness. You just happen to be foremost in my mind, for obvious reasons. Which is why I am here—despite the freezing weather and its possibly detrimental effects on my future abilities to add to my family—acting the role of matchmaker, secret agent, buffoon . . ."

Catherine threw her arms around her brother's neck and hugged him fiercely. "Never the buffoon, Damien, never. I know how truly worried you must be. It worries me just as much, but—" she eased herself to arm's length "—you know I must see him. I must, Damien. Even if it is only from a distance and only for a few brief moments."

"Strange. He said almost the exact same thing . . . and I did not believe him either."

She flushed softly and lowered her arms from around his shoulders. "Well then, big brother, what do you suggest we do?"

"*We* do nothing. *You* return to the house and go on about your business as if nothing untoward has happened. You take no more long and lonely walks through the woods and you do not stray more than a hundred yards from the main house without someone keeping you in sight at all times."

"But—"

"I, in due course, shall meet with your husband as per his instructions, and together we shall decide the best and safest way to arrange a meeting. I want your promise on this, Kitty, I want your word that you will not try anything foolish, like following me, or venturing out on your own. Rumours of other unpleasantries aside, there is still an army headed this way, and it isn't just the gentry fleeing before them. Cutpurses and thieves are flocking south in droves, hoping to loot the empty houses before the rebels get there. I would not want to have to go through all of this trouble just to see you ending up in a gutter somewhere, with your throat slit ear to ear."

"Spoken with true, tender sentiment," she mused.

"Spoken by a man who knows his sister well enough to be wary of any promises given too lightly." Again he tilted her face upward, his hand as firm and uncompromising as the stern set to his jaw. "I told you once before, regardless of the name he used, Alex was my friend long before politics came into the question, and long before you managed to work your feminine wiles on his sensibilities. He knows what he is doing. If he thinks there is too much danger, he won't send for you. But we both know if there is any chance in hell of him getting you alone for five minutes, he will."

"It's so hard," she said, her chin quivering slightly. "Knowing he is close by, yet knowing I may not see him."

"Oh . . . I think you'll see him. It is just a question of whether you see him on his own, or riding into Derby at the head of the rebel army."

Chapter Five

"We shall have to evacuate," Sir Alfred declared, thumping an authoritative fist on the mantlepiece.

Lady Caroline Ashbrooke, seated on the opposite side of the drawing room, noted the proximity of his fist to a delicate porcelain figurine, and smiled tightly. "Now why on earth would we want to leave Rosewood Hall?" she asked calmly.

"Leave? Of course we must leave! If what Colonel Kelly says is correct, we could be overrun any day now. Manchester has fallen, by God! Not a whimper, not a whinny. Not a single shot fired! Why, the snivelling cowards had the utter gall to ring the church bells in welcome. Cheered and rang the church bells, by Jove, and some say there were men lining the streets waiting to join the Pretender's scurrilous pack of Jacobite dogs!"

Sir Alfred, spitting profusely in his vexation, paused to empty the contents of a glass of raw spirits. The ladies present took up their fans, their eyes darting from one face to the next, uncertain as to how they should react to the news. The men looked plainly uncomfortable.

"Manchester," Sir Alfred continued, wiping at an annoying dribble of liquor on his chin, "is less than fifty miles from here. What steps are being taken to ensure the safety of our homes and families?"

The question was directed to one of the three officers present, representatives of the two companies of militia camped on Ashbrooke property. The commander, Colonel Braen Kelly, was a compact, square-faced man given to serious breaches in attentiveness when positioned anywhere near a well-endowed guest of the opposite sex. Aiding the colonel in his daily task of recruiting and organizing the local populace into a defensive force, were two regular infantry officers, Lieutenants Goodwin and Temple. Lieutenant Temple was innocuous enough to blend in with the furnishings. He rarely spoke, rarely wore any expression other than that of acute boredom. His counterpart was Lieutenant Derek Goodwin, a sensation with the ladies despite the overly tarnished reputation which had followed him out of London.

Since Colonel Kelly was, at the moment, preoccupied with adjusting the angle of his overview into Mistress Pickthall's cleavage, Lieutenant Goodwin elected to offer an answer to the irate squire.

"I assure you, Sir Alfred, every possible step is being taken to guarantee the safety of all families and properties in the shire. There have been rumours of looting and mischief, but on the whole, we have no real reason to believe the rebels wish to cause harm. One of the Pretender's greatest axioms is his intent to win the English people to his cause. He could not possibly hope to do so if he went about burning homes and stripping warehouses to the bare walls." The lieutenant paused and added silkily, "Not that I believe he has a chance of winning so much as an English flea to his cause."

A round of appreciative giggles rewarded his humour and the lieutenant glanced at Catherine to see if she had noticed.

"Hang the fleas!" Sir Alfred trumpeted. "Look around you, man. What of my valuables? What can you possibly do to guarantee this . . . this candlestick, for instance."

He picked it up from a nearby trestle table and raised it in his clenched fist, shaking it so the flames leaped and the wax splashed onto the floor. "Who is to say it will not capture the eye of some Highland brigand and end up in a wagon bound for Inverness? For that matter, hang the gewgaws! I have a cellar full of vintage wines and brandies that have been collected over generations. The Scots can sniff out spirits like a dog sniffs after a bitch! The work of generations, I say. Gone in a sniff!"

"Now Alfred," Lady Caroline murmured. "You mustn't work yourself into a state over a few musty barrels and a rack of old green bottles. It would probably improve your spleen immeasurably to have your cellar emptied for you."

"There you are," Lord Ashbrooke declared in disgust. "Women have no sense in these matters. Had I used the example of Paris gowns instead of fine liquors . . . well, we should undoubtedly have heard quite a different sentiment!"

"Why naturally, my dear," Lady Caroline smiled. "Gowns are works of art. Quite irreplaceable, especially now that you men have insisted upon this silly blockade of the coast."

"Silly blockade?" Sir Alfred knocked his temple, setting his wig at a slight angle in the process. "You see what I must endure? *Silly blockade*, madam? You would prefer the French to land on our shores and drape you in the *fleur-de-lys*?"

"If it would mean a fresh and ample supply of silk, I should be most happy to greet our foreign cousins."

Another round of repressed titters left Sir Alfred red-faced and spluttering. Lady Caroline returned to her conversation with one of the ladies seated in her small group, sparing an occasional glance toward the pianoforte where the lean figure of Captain Lovat-Spence stood.

Catherine saw the tiny sparks of silent communication pass between her mother and the captain. She lowered her lashes at once, puzzled that she should no longer feel as much resentment as sadness. Was this her mother's way of enduring a loveless marriage? At one time Caroline Penrith must have been as spirited and gay as her beauty and easy laughter intimated. An arranged union between two families had robbed her of any chance to follow her heart, and certainly, Sir Alfred could not have been an easy man to live with all these years.

Flushing at the ungenerous thought, Catherine sipped her wine and tried not to compare her mother's loveless union with Sir Alfred, with her own passionate union to Alexander Cameron. Was that the reason behind her mother's constant parade of lovers? Was she searching for passion?

You are being a harsh judge, said the tiny voice of her conscience. *Especially since you think of little else yourself these days.*

Catherine's cheeks grew warmer. Since her meeting two days ago with her brother, she had been in an agony of suspense—waiting, watching the road for signs of a messenger. In two days, there must have been a hundred callers at the door. The sound of each hoofbeat on the gravel carriage path sent her flying to the window; each knock on the heavy oak doors found her poised on the landing, her hands clutched around a railing bannister as if to crush it.

Alex was nearby. He wanted, needed to see her as desperately as she wanted and needed to see him. How many times had she read and re-read his letter? How many hours had she stood at her bedroom window and imagined herself back in the tower room of Achnacarry Castle ensconced in the enormous tester bed with her husband? Certainly there was more to love than passion, but dear God, how wonderful it would be to feel his arms around her, to hear his voice ragged with desire, to know the tremors in her body were shared by an equal longing in his.

How does one love someone desperately? he had once asked her, mocking the use of the word and the sentiment, even as he had shown an unusual curiosity over both. He had used the same word in his letter: desperate. Was he asking her, or reminding her? And did she remember her answer from that day so many lifetimes ago?

"With one's whole heart and soul," she whispered.

"I beg your pardon?"

Catherine glanced up, startled. Lieutenant Derek Goodwin was standing by her side, his mouth arranged in a smile that suggested he knew exactly what she had been thinking about.

"I . . . was merely agreeing with my father . . . wishing . . . with my whole heart and soul, that these troubles were behind us."

"A needless plea," he assured her warmly, "for I shall consider it my sworn duty in life to see that not a single strand of your hair falls victim to more trouble than a noisome breeze."

Catherine managed a smile and leaned away from the intimacy of his murmured pledge. She had not even been aware she had spoken out loud, much less that anyone had been standing near enough to overhear her. So near, in fact, she could smell the pungent, stale odour of an overpowdered wig.

"Your glass is empty; may I refill it for you?"

"Oh. No, no thank you, Lieutenant. I'm afraid I haven't much of a head for strong spirits tonight."

"On the contrary, Mrs. Montgomery, I find you hold your spirits very well indeed. I should think any other young and . . . highly desirable beauty such as yourself would be all but crushed by the loneliness of having a husband abandon her so soon after the nuptials."

"I was hardly abandoned, Lieutenant," she replied evenly. "My husband is a businessman. He could not ignore his business ventures for pleasure."

The slick smile widened. "One cannot imagine the proceeds of any business being half so rewarding, nor the labours half so fruitful—" his eyes slid to the dusky cleft of her breasts "—as those ventured within your arms."

Amazed and annoyed by his boldness, Catherine's eyes sparkled a warning. "I assure you my husband's energies are limitless. I have not felt shortchanged, at any rate."

"Not even on these cool, wintry nights when your only source of excitement is found within the pages of a penny novel?"

"Penny novels can be extremely exciting, Lieutenant. More so than some of the company I find myself enduring."

Lieutenant Goodwin warmed to the repartee. He had accepted his posting to Derby with something less than enthusiasm, knowing it was a punishment for having dallied with the affections of his former commandant's nubile young wife. Nubile young wives were a particular hobby of his. He collected them the way some men collected weapons after a skirmish, to remind them of battles fought and won. Wives were never screaming virgins. There was never any danger of being set before an altar after the fact, and they rarely reported their misdeeds to their husbands, not even when his methods of persuasion were . . . less than conventional.

Goodwin's disposition toward his present posting had altered considerably the instant he had laid eyes upon Catherine Montgomery. Blonde and willowy, in possession of a body that was made to burn a man's honourable intentions to cinders—she was not the kind of woman who should remain four days, let alone four months without the vigorous attentions of a man. She was also, if the stories he had heard about her were true, married to a man she hardly knew and held no particular affection for. Her reputation as a coquette belied the calm, serene beauty who stood before him now. He could well imagine a similar stance—eyes slightly downcast, lips forming a moist pout, fingers drumming a silent tattoo on the stem of an ivory fan as she stood watching two men duel for the privilege of claiming her as prize. Was that it? Did she enjoy playing games? Had she ridden into the forest the other morning fully intending someone to follow her? If so, then she must have been just as annoyed as he had been to see her brother in hot pursuit.

If it was games she wanted, she was about to discover she had met her match.

Who did he think he was? Catherine wondered. Did they all assume, because Lady Caroline had no qualms about cuckholding her husband in open company, the daughter would behave in a similar fashion? It struck her suddenly, and unpleasantly, that Derek Goodwin was very much like Hamilton Garner—arrogant and self-confident, ignorant of any emotion having to do with anything or anyone other than himself. There were at least three pairs of watery eyes following the good lieutenant's every move. Why could he not go bother one of them?

Stupid men, stupid women, she thought angrily. Had she really striven most of her life to be accepted and admired by such foolish, shallow people?

Snapping her fan open, she fluttered it once and looked up into the lieutenant's hard gaze. "I find the air has grown a trifle stifling. You will excuse me?"

"Allow me," he said, and tucked his hand beneath the crook of her arm to steer her toward the door. The cool, vaulted silence of the hallway was a welcome relief from the noise and press of warm bodies and Catherine could almost feel the tension being expelled on her first breath.

"Thank you for escorting me, Lieutenant," she said, turning so that his grip on her arm was subtly broken. "It has been a very long day and I suddenly find myself extremely tired."

"You are leaving the party?"

"I am retiring for the night, yes."

"But I thought we might continue our conversation in private."

Catherine cast a cool glance down to where his fingers had curled around her wrist. "Whereas I was quite convinced our conversation was over. Now, if you do not mind—"

"I do mind," he interrupted. "I mind very much, Mrs. Montgomery, wasting my time on a flirt and a tease."

The anger in Catherine's eyes flared anew. "Then by all means, Lieutenant, waste no more. You will find the taverns and brothels in Derby teeming with whores willing enough to give you fair exchange for your valuable time."

"Why would I travel so far on such a cold night, when your bedroom is only up the stairs?"

Outrage flooded Catherine's cheeks a dull, throbbing red, but before her hand could lash out and strike the sly grin from his face, the doors to the drawing room swung open and several laughing guests swept into the hallway. One of them, a young corporal by the name of Jeffrey Peters veered instantly toward the lieutenant.

"Oh, I say sir. Colonel Kelly sent me to fetch you. He says we mustn't wear out our welcome." He stopped beside Catherine and bowed gallantly. "A perfectly splendid evening, Mrs. Montgomery, as usual."

Catherine extricated her wrist from the lieutenant's cutting fingers. "You are always welcome, Corporal Peters. No more so than tonight."

The corporal's animated features flushed crimson at the thought of such a lovely and worldly creature even noticing him, much less looking forward to his company. In an agony of embarrassment, he turned to the lieutenant for some clue as to how to unstick his tongue from the roof of his mouth, and was instead nearly induced to swallow it from the sheer force of the hatred emanating from the icy hazel eyes.

"Thank you, Corporal," Goodwin said tautly. "You were dispatched to find me and so you have. You may return to Colonel Kelly and inform him I shall rejoin him directly."

Corporal Peters started to turn away when Catherine reached out and laid a hand on his arm. "I shall bid you good night now, Corporal, since I am feeling the effects of an aggravatingly long day and probably will not return to the drawing room."

The corporal bowed and smiled. "Good night, Mrs. Montgomery. I trust you will feel better in the morning."

"I am sure I will. Good night to you as well, Lieutenant. And better luck elsewhere."

Goodwin stared after Catherine as she walked away, his body still reacting to the fragrance of her skin, the imagined feel of her warm, naked skin rubbing up against his. She obviously liked playing the fox, leading the hunters on a merry chase, smug in the knowledge that she could retreat into her lair at any time. Well, this hunter knew exactly where the lair was, knew her rooms were isolated at the far end of one wing of the house with nothing but empty chambers on either side.

Run and hide, my luscious little fox. Stoke the fires and warm the sheets, for you'll not be spending another cold night alone.

"Beautiful, isn't she, sir?"

"What?" Goodwin whirled around, surprised to see the corporal still beside him. "What the devil did you say?"

"I . . . I w-was merely complimenting M-Mrs. M-Montgomery's beauty, s-sir." The corporal strained over each word, cursing the impediment that made him stutter at the least sign of pressure. "I m-meant no offense."

Goodwin raked his gaze along the corporal's thin, lanky body. "And just what would you know about women, beautiful or otherwise? I thought pretty little things like yourself gravitated toward your own kind?"

Corporal Peters paled. After a long moment, and with a visible effort, he drew himself to attention.

"The c-colonel is waiting," he said tersely. "Sir."

Goodwin laughed and, adjusting the lower edge of his red woolen tunic, he strode toward the door of the drawing room. Corporal Peters lingered long enough to force his fists to unclench, then followed.

"Deirdre, if something doesn't happen soon, I shall go completely mad."

The slender, dark-haired maid smiled solemnly and dragged the brush through the long, shiny mass of her mistress's hair. "You will hear something from Mr. Cameron soon, I'm sure of it."

"But it has been two whole days! Why would he have sent Damien so soon unless he was confident of being able to make arrangements right away? Something has happened. Something dreadful. I just know it."

"Nothing has happened," Deirdre insisted and set the brush aside. "You have said yourself, a dozen times, he is too clever to be taken by surprise."

"Damien is not so clever," Catherine remarked dryly. "Suppose he was followed and watched?"

"Why would anyone follow Master Damien?"

Catherine's only answer was a sigh.

"Indeed," Deirdre said, "something may have gone wrong with their plan. After all, there are troops moving every which way across the country. Perhaps their original arrangements had to be delayed or amended."

"Or abandoned altogether," Catherine said miserably. "My husband is far too impatient to let such a trifling thing as a wife delay his return to the battlefront." Her sarcasm was not as believable as the sigh that drew her forward onto her elbows. "Did I tell you what Damien said about him? The risks, the chances, the foolish . . . brave exploits he has taken upon himself to perform?"

"Several times, mistress. And with more pride shining in your eyes with each telling."

Catherine glared at the maid's reflection, then rose from her seat before the dressing table. "Pride indeed. How proud can a widow be?"

Pacing over to the long double French windows, she opened them on a sudden impulse and strolled out onto the narrow stone balcony. The air was cold, the breeze scraping an instant chill into her flesh as she gazed out over the moon-washed courtyard.

"Come inside, mistress, before you catch your death!"

"He's out there somewhere, Deirdre. I can feel it."

"As surely as you'll feel a fever in your brow by morning if you don't come back by the fire at once!"

Catherine scanned the twinkling darkness of the landscape one last time before surrendering to Deirdre's orders and returning to the hearthside. Scolding under her breath, the maid closed and securely latched the windows, then, as if the cold air had had time to sabotage her earlier efforts with the warming pan, she scooped fresh coals into the covered copper pot and passed it slowly between the bedsheets.

"Shall I braid your hair, mistress?"

Catherine's gaze went from the hypnotic flames in the grate to the gilt-edged cheval mirror. She was wearing a voluminous muslin dressing gown, the sleeves of which were long and full, ruffled with tiers of lace. The collar was high under her chin, trimmed with tiny satin bows and chains of delicately embroidered flowers. Her hair, brushed full and glossy, spilled over her shoulders in a golden cascade which stopped a scant inch shy of the wide satin sash that circled her waist.

"A vestal virgin could not look so pure," she grimaced. "I should think Lieutenant Goodwin would have enjoyed sacrificing me tonight."

"Goodwin? What has that wretched man to do with you?"

"You know him?"

"I know *of* him," Deirdre said with a frown. "The first day he was here he strutted into the servant's quarters and looked the women over as if he was making his selection. A couple of the younger girls who were fetched from the village to help the regular staff were plainly smitten by his looks and his uniform, and I suspect he has had his merry way with more than one of them. Has he dared try his bold ways with you, my lady? If so, Sir Alfred should be told at once! I don't trust his sly ways or his cold clammy hands."

"I am confident it will not be necessary to call upon my father's . . . paternal indignation. I was not too gentle on the good lieutenant's vanity this evening; he may think twice before accosting me again. Do you think I should cut it?"

Deirdre, her thoughts chasing after Lieutenant Goodwin, momentarily lost the drift of conversation. "Excuse me, mistress? Cut what?"

"My hair." She gathered handfuls at the nape of her neck and piled it high on the crown. "Harriet writes it is all the rage in London. Cap curls, she calls it."

"Hmph. And if the plague visits the city again and everyone has to shave their heads bald, will that become the rage as well?"

"It was just a thought," Catherine said meekly. "Ahh well, I suppose vestal virgins must maintain their image."

"Vestal virgin," Deirdre muttered, and was there in an instant to take the robe from her mistress's shoulders as Catherine slipped the sash from around her waist. The wry comment turned into an instant gasp of disbelief as the nightgown worn beneath was revealed. *"Miss Catherine!"*

The gown was silk, so luminous it might have been woven from liquid moonlight, so sheer where it flowed over breasts and thighs it silhouetted the curves and planes like silver stardust. It was definitely not the gown of a vestal virgin, and certainly not the modest lawn negligee Deirdre had laid out earlier.

"Mistress Catherine! Wherever did you find such a . . . a . . ."

"Shameful, wanton piece of frippery?" Catherine supplied, executing a graceful pirouette before the mirror. "I borrowed it from my mother's wardrobe, where else."

"Lady *Caroline*?"

"She has scores just like it. I borrowed two, in fact, and I doubt she'll miss either one."

"But . . . surely you don't intend to actually . . . I mean, what if someone should see you in it? It isn't even . . . why, it isn't *decent*, mistress."

Two thin slivers of silk passing over the bare shoulders were all that held the filmy garment in place—not that it mattered. The brazen display of pale ivory flesh and contrasting rose-tipped breasts showing through the translucent fabric was enough to send a faint-hearted Deirdre to the window again to draw the curtains tightly together.

"Who, in heaven's name, is going to see me?" Catherine demanded wearily. "We're two full storeys above the ground, and the only man I would want to see me is goodness knows where. I just . . . I don't know. I just wanted to feel . . . different tonight. Special."

"Well, you certainly look that. As special as any doxy plying her wares on a waterfront brothel."

"Are you insinuating my mother does her shopping there?" Catherine inquired, smiling as Deirdre flushed uncomfortably. "I thought a higher class of bordello, at least."

"Into bed with you now, mistress, or you'll catch your death for sure."

Obediently, Catherine removed her dainty satin slippers and lifted the cloud of silk so that it floated down around her as she settled against the pillows. Stretching her arms and legs, she savoured the erotic texture of the material where it brushed her skin, sighing as she envisioned what further erotic sensations a pair of broad, masculine hands might make. She reached beneath the pillows and retrieved the much-read, fully memorized letter Alexander had sent her and, after reading it again, pressed it next to her heart and smiled up at Deirdre through a wavering shine of tears.

"If I could just see him. Just for a moment. If I could just be certain . . ."

"Certain of what, mistress? That he loves you?" Deirdre's soft brown eyes filled with compassion. "You worry needlessly. Of course he loves you. And he'll send for you soon, I know he will."

Catherine blinked away her tears and grasped Deirdre's cool hand. "How selfish I must sound, carrying on so, when you must be suffering equally without Aluinn MacKail."

"Tis true, I . . . I miss him," Deirdre admitted in the barest of whispers.

"Perhaps they are together," Catherine said encouragingly. "Lord knows they are never more than a stone's throw apart, especially when there is any chance of adventure."

"Perhaps," Deirdre agreed, not sounding the least convinced. She returned the faint pressure of Catherine's hand before releasing it and moving away from the bed. As she snuffed the candles one by one, her thoughts wandered here and there, distracting her, stretching a chore that should have taken seconds into several minutes. By the time she had added a final log to the fire and returned the brushes and combs to their proper place in the dressing room, Catherine was fast asleep, the letter still held possessively to her breast.

The fire was little more than a sporadic ripple of flames at the ends of the half-charred log when a faint scratching noise disturbed the silence. The blade of an infantry bayonet intruded its way between the panes of the French doors and crept slowly upward, pausing when it found its way blocked by the brass latch. See-sawing carefully against the bolt, it managed to raise the brass bar from its seat and scrape it upward so that when the handle turned, the door opened without protest. The serrated knife was resheathed in its pocket on the wide leather belt before the door opened further and a cool gust of wind accompanied a shadowy figure into the bedchamber. Securing the panes behind him, he stood for a moment, concealed by the floor-length velvet draperies, listening for any sign that his entry had been detected.

Satisfied, he lifted aside the curtain and stepped into the muted light cast by the fire. The red wool of his tunic glowed like fresh spilled blood; his white crossbelts and tall black leather boots reflected the shine of the night lamp, as did the dark, narrowed eyes. Still wary of a misplaced footfall, he moved cautiously to the door leading to the outer hall and, after listening for any sounds from without, coaxed the key around in a full circle until a faint click told him it was locked. Stealthily, he removed the key and slotted it into a pocket of his tunic.

The ease with which his mission had been accomplished put a smile on his face as he made his way back to the foot of the bed. He stood and stared down at Catherine's sleeping form where she lay nestled against a soft bank of pillows, her blonde hair loose and spread beneath her in a pool of molten gold. The covers had been partially displaced, leaving the pale curve of a slender shoulder bared to his hungry gaze.

At first glance, he had thought her to be naked and his heart had thudded so loudly in his ears he felt sure the sound would waken her. A second, more devastating scrutiny caught the sheen of silk molded around the breathtaking perfection of a breast, and his mouth went dry; his senses wavered and threatened to abandon him to the urgent needs building in his body.

His hands trembled noticeably as he unfastened the row of ornate brass buttons that ran down the stiff red wool of his jacket. Slipping his arms free, he shrugged the garment to the floor, where it was joined moments later by his belts and sash, the high collared scarlet waistcoat, and white powdered periwig. He pulled the tails of his shirt free of the tight-fitting uniform breeches and, unwinding the starched ties from around his neck, lifted it up and over his head in a motion which caused the muscles across his chest and shoulders to flex in the gleam of firelight.

Catherine stirred and made a soft purring sound deep in her throat as she sought a warmer hollow in the mattress. The covers slipped further and she dreamed of searching fingertips skimming over the taut peak of her nipple, of naked, heated flesh pressing against hers, and of long skillful fingers stroking deftly into the aching junction of her thighs.

She knew the dream would not last and a small frown of dismay formed across her brow. All the craven sensations, so long denied, were flooding into her loins and curling upward like a wave of thick, rich cream. There was pressure where she longed most to feel it and she moaned, parting her thighs willingly, undulating against the insistent, probing tension until the sheer layer of silk was wet and slippery with her need.

The pressure was so real . . . the pleasure so intense, she cried out and pushed herself closer to the new source of warmth, and for as long as it took her to realize it was *not* a dream, she was *not* alone in the bed, her body continued to respond, to urge a deeper intimacy. The violet-blue eyes snapped open. The very real presence of muscle and bone and hard male sinew brought a jarring halt to all sensations in her body and a scream of pure terror bubbling to her lips.

The scream was stifled before it was fully formed. The same hand that bore the faint musk of her arousal was clamped firmly over her mouth, while a naked, muscular leg was thrown overtop her own before she could thrash herself free. Blinded by fear, knowing only that she had to escape, Catherine struck out with her fists, pushing and writhing against the great wall of muscle that threatened to crush her. She managed to land a solid blow to his temple and was gathering steam for another when she heard a softly muttered Gaelic oath.

Her fist froze in mid-air and her eyes widened. Certain her mind was playing some dreadful hoax, her body tensed and her heart skipped several beats.

"A hell of a greeting for a wife to give her husband," Alex murmured, his hand still in place over her mouth, but easing slightly so that it was almost a caress. Indeed, as she continued to stare up at him in shock, the hand slid around to cradle the side of her neck and the pressure of his lean fingers was replaced by the possessive warmth of his lips.

"Alex?" she gasped. "Oh God . . . *Alex*?"

"You were expecting someone else, perhaps?" He leaned back and let the firelight play havoc with the glimmering wash of silk. "Come to think of it, you certainly look as if you were expecting someone."

"N-no. No! No, I . . . I . . ." Her hands trembled up to his cheeks as if to confirm he was real flesh and blood. "Please . . . tell me I'm not dreaming."

"You are not dreaming," he assured her, kissing each disbelieving eyelid with a gentleness that caused a sob to catch in her throat. "I'm here. I'm real."

"But . . . how did you get here? I thought . . . I mean, Damien said it would be too dangerous for you to come here . . . that I was to wait for a message . . ."

Alexander's hands moved down her body compulsively, as if he could not stop their actions now that she was finally in his arms.

"When Damien impressed upon me the fragile nature of your patience—" his palm encircled the heavy softness of her breast "—I found my own condition to be rather indelicate as well. Far too indelicate to bother with cloak-and-dagger nonsense."

"But the soldiers . . . the militia . . ."

Alex's gaze followed his hand. His thumb stroked the velvety crown of her nipple and he watched it grow taut and rigid beneath its veil of silk. Catherine's eyes were fixed unwaveringly on his face, on the square, rugged jawline, the dark slash of eyebrows, the twin crescents of long black lashes. She felt the motion of his thumb and she felt the pressure from each individual finger against her breast. Icy shivers of anticipation raced across the surface of her flesh, growing more and more insistent at each slow circuit of his thumb.

Suddenly, the obsidian eyes were gazing deeply into hers. The muscles in his arms were tense and unyielding, his body seemed strained to the limit of his composure. Was it her imagination, or had the months of rigorous army life added even more strength, developed even more formidable breadth to his shoulders and chest, whittled a lean new hardness to his waist and hips? His hair was as long and unruly as she remembered it and, responding to an impulse, her fingers released the thin black ribbon binding it and let the glossy waves spill free and curl forward over his shoulders.

His hands had not been idle. They had roved lower on the smooth, silk-clad outline of her hips and thighs, and returned with the captured hem of the nightdress. He drew it above her waist and left a shimmering crumple under her arms while he sent his fingers skimming back down into the soft golden thatch below her belly. Catherine endured the first light, delicious strokes in silence, awed by the sweet, sharp ache of shameless pleasure. But as the incursions became deeper and more determined, she rose against him, arched against the shivering torment with a need she could neither deny nor conceal.

"Easy, love," he whispered. "Easy."

"I . . . I can't," she gasped, a shudder wracking her limbs. "It's been so long. I didn't know if you were alive or dead. I didn't know if I would ever see you again, if you would ever come back to me. I began to wonder if I had imagined it all . . . everything . . . Achnacarry . . . everything."

A sob of sheer ecstasy was torn from her throat as he lowered his dark head to her breast. His lips claimed the tightly crinkled nipple, drawing the succulent flesh into the heated well of his mouth where it was taunted and ravaged with the same deliberate thoroughness his fingers were displaying elsewhere. A breath away from releasing her tensions, his hand withdrew and his mouth covered hers, smothering her harsh groan of disappointment. His tongue plunged repeatedly over and around hers, teasing, tormenting gasps of pleasure from within, the sensations coiling downward and inward until she felt like a molten sheet of flame.

Leaving her lips moist and tenderly chafed, Alex's mouth blazed a trail of fire from the underside of her chin down past the labouring rise and fall of her breasts. From there, his tongue swirled onto the fluttering plateau of her belly and into the seductive little indent of her navel. Restlessly, he travelled lower, prompting shocked reverberations that weakened each limb as he eased them apart. His hands curved beneath her hips and braced her as he explored the silkiness of her inner thighs. Holding her firmly, his mouth probed the tender pink junction, his tongue lashing over and over again at the remaining shreds of her modesty. She reached down with frantic, disbelieving hands to claw her fingers into the raven mane of his hair, intending to plead an end to the stunning indelicacy, but they only encouraged him to lead her deeper and deeper into the shuddering, rhythmic wonders of her body.

Beneath his skillful tutelage, she opened and blossomed. She pressed her head back into the linens and stretched her arms out on either side to clench at twisted fistfuls of bedding. Her lips drew back over soundless cries as hot, shivering spirals of pleasure whorled through her loins. Tasting them, delving for them, his tongue set wave upon wave of fiery convolutions rippling through her body, turning her into one continuous ribbon of ecstasy.

With a groan that mocked his own self-restraint, Alex rose above her, his muscles gleaming under a sheen of sweat. His hands still cradled her hips and he used them to draw her forward, to angle her upward so that when the searing heat of his flesh began to fill her, there was not a single nerve between them that was left untouched. Catherine felt the delicious ache of his power and strength stretch within her, burying his love so deep she could not determine where her body ended and his began. Her cries were soft, raw whispers as he began to move within her. She locked her arms around him, locked her legs around him and heard him groan, for as deep as he was inside her, she tautened around him more, transforming the captor into the captive.

Helpless to forestall the white-hot tide of rapture that was sweeping through her, Catherine surrendered to the thrusting demands of his body. Alex, dimly aware of her ragged cries, gloried in the sleek friction of their bodies moving in perfect unity and, with one last mighty thrust, he let the spasms tear free, the ecstasy grip him and hurl him through one raging crest of mindless pleasure after another.

Dazed, they clung together, straining and writhing with an insatiable need to savour each prolonged tremor until it shimmered into memory. Only then did pent-up breaths find a release; only then did the shivering, quaking tension drain away to leave the two damp, entwined bodies collapsed and gasping together. From somewhere, Alex found the strength to raise his streaming brow from her shoulder and kiss her—a kiss as honest and naked in its emotion as she would ever live to experience.

"I did not think a man could miss his wife as much as I have missed you," he admitted shakily. "A mistress, aye. I could more easily understand the mystery and fascination there, but a wife? Perhaps it is just that I still cannot believe you are mine, that you will always be mine . . ."

His lips descended hungrily again, carrying a murmured pledge of his love from her mouth to the tiny pulsing vein below her ear. Catherine's eyes opened slowly; two pools of violet, swimming with unshed tears of happiness. Her arms were still draped around the broad slabs of muscle that formed his back, and they tightened reflexively, as did her limbs, when she felt him stir and start to lift himself away.

"Please don't," she said on a rushed breath. "Don't leave me just yet."

"I have no intentions of leaving you. I just thought—"

"Don't think. Don't do anything . . . just hold me. As close as you can."

Alex wrapped his arms around her, and, conscious of his superior weight, compromised by gently rolling with her onto his side. Catherine buried her face in his shoulder, the inner tumult of her emotions giving way to an irrational urge to cry. She bit down savagely on her lips to hide her sudden weakness, but he could feel it quivering through the slender body.

"Catherine—" he pressed his lips to her temple "I never meant for you to worry or be afraid. If there had been any other way to ensure your safety, I never would have let you out of my sight, you must know that."

"Sometimes . . . I think I would rather risk any danger on earth than suffer such loneliness as I have these past months."

His arms hugged her closer.

"The rest of the time—" she caught her lip between her teeth and angled her head upward so that she could see his face. "The rest of the time," she sighed, "has been spent contemplating divorce, revenge . . . even murder. Three months, Alex. Three months and you never once wrote to me. Not a note, not a letter, not one single paltry word to let me know you were still alive."

"I wrote hundreds of them . . . thousands. In my head. Every day."

"As if anyone could ever read what was in your head," she countered on a damp sniffle.

"Can't you?" He cradled her chin in his hand. "Look again."

Catherine did indeed look, and they were all there. The hundreds and thousands of words and feelings he had been unable to commit to paper were flickering poignantly in the dark depths of his eyes.

"Oh Alex," she cried, burrowing against his shoulder again. "It isn't the same."

"I guess it isn't. But I didn't exactly see a flood of mail coming from the other direction."

Catherine pushed herself upright. She stared into his face a long moment before turning and climbing down from the bed. With the gossamer folds of her nightdress flowing out behind her, she snatched up the lamp from the night table and disappeared inside the dressing room. The loud scrape and bang of a drawer signalled her return before the murky yellow glow of the light, and she re-entered the chamber, her arm full of unposted letters.

Dumping them unceremoniously on the bed beside him, she set the lamp aside and planted her hands on her hips. "I did not know where to send them."

Alex dragged his eyes down from her face and scanned the impressive pile of letters. Most were several pages long, folded into thick wads that required several seals to close.

He reached a tentative hand out to select one, but with an angry gesture, Catherine brushed them all to the floor.

"No. What's in them doesn't matter any more. They were . . . a way of passing the time."

"Catherine, I am sorry. But your husband is supposed to be away in the colonies," he reminded her gently. "How would you go about explaining letters and notes that arrived regularly from northern England? Or suppose they were intercepted and opened? I doubt if even your quick wit could produce an adequate excuse for being in receipt of letters from a captain in the Jacobite army. Especially if they contained anything half as inflammatory as most thoughts I have about you."

"Don't try to wriggle out of it by being logical and rational."

"Alright, I won't." His arms snaked out and curled around her waist, pulling her back down onto the bed in a flurry of silk. "I'll make it up to you instead, by being perverse and avaricious."

His mouth made good on the threat, and when the kiss ended, she was flushed and laughing as she clung to his broad shoulders. She was also naked, the nightdress flung up and away somewhere in the shadows.

"How did you get in here tonight? The militiamen have the manor surrounded."

"One of them was generous enough to loan me the use of his uniform."

She frowned and raised her head, peering at the door. "You just walked into the house and came up the stairs to my room?"

"I came in the same way any lusty Romeo would think to come—by way of a very obliging trellis which leads straight from the ground up to heaven. Remind me to show you how to keep those doors locked from now on; that latch isn't worth a damn."

"It wasn't meant to keep out intruders, only drafts."

"Nevertheless, I want you to keep it locked tightly when you are in here alone."

"And when I'm not? Alone, I mean."

The dark sapphire eyes narrowed consideringly. "By all means, leave the doors unlatched. But choose your lovers carefully, madam, with an eye towards swiftness and an ability to fly, for if I ever paid a visit unannounced and found some addlebrained Lothario trespassing on territory I have clearly staked as my own . . ."

A growl defined the consequences and Catherine welcomed the roughness of his kiss, as well as the distinct stirrings elsewhere in his body. Unfortunately, another fit of muffled laughter brought an unwanted end to both intimacies.

"You find the prospect of infidelity amusing?" he demanded with a frown.

"Only the sudden image of my vaunted lord and husband chasing some hapless scoundrel about the room at the tip of his sword."

"Your own pretty buttocks would find nothing to smile about, I assure you."

"They have nothing to fear," she said and pressed a chaste, tender kiss over his lips. "For the situation will never arise. You are lover enough for me in this lifetime . . . indeed, ten lifetimes."

Snorting contentedly, Alex shifted his weight lower on the bed and rested his head between the firm white mounds of her breasts. He kept one arm curled around her waist and a muscular leg hooked over hers so that it was impossible for her not to be aware of the masculine texture of his body. She traced her fingertips over the hard-surfaced flesh of his shoulders, marvelling that she did not suffer the least pangs of immodesty. Six months ago she would have died from shame had anyone glimpsed a bare ankle, and the thought of lying naked with a man—even a husband—would have mortified her to the very core. Yet here she was, very happily naked, cradling a magnificently naked man to her breast and wishing with all her heart his mouth was a scant inch or two more to the right.

In an effort to exhibit some measure of restraint, she turned her thoughts to safer subjects.

"Have you had any word from Achnacarry? Is everyone well? Lady Maura, Jeannie, dear Auntie Rose?"

"The news is erratic, naturally, but the last we heard, everyone was fine. I imagine Maura has her hands full keeping the household running smoothly. Rose had a bout of the ague—it seems to settle in her bones every fall—but she's coping. And Jeannie . . . well, Jeannie is Jeannie. She was fit to be tied when both Donald and Archibald forbade her to accompany the army, and I don't expect she is making anyone's life a joy as a result."

"Jeannie wanted to march to war with you?"

"Scots women are a strong breed, didn't you know? Some take up the sword and fight right alongside their men. Others . . . well, they leave the fighting to the men, but contribute their, er, services in other equally vital areas."

"Such as?"

"Oh . . . cooking and tending the wounded." He nuzzled his mouth against the plump swell of flesh beneath his cheek. "Tending the needs of the healthy."

Catherine tilted her head forward, the better to see the angular planes of his face. "Dare I ask what that entails?"

"There is always a certain degree of tension in a camp full of men—especially before a battle. It makes sense practically and militarily to provide some sort of outlet."

"Mmmm. Are you justifying their presence . . . or confessing to something?"

"As a matter of fact," he raised his head briefly and smiled. "It so happens I have been the flattered recipient of several interesting offers since the army began its march."

"Have you now," she said dryly.

"Yes, indeed. And I considered each one quite seriously; weighed the advantages and disadvantages—warm nights versus cold, the young and energetic volunteer versus the older, more experienced veterans—that sort of thing, you know."

"And?" she demanded.

He smiled and settled his head comfortably again.

"Naturally you chose the young and energetic ones. It would be more in keeping with your character."

"Would it?" He frowned, as if debating the notion. Helping him mull it over, his hand slid upward and began toying with the button of the nipple that loomed in his direct line of view. "Am I as flawed as all that?"

"Flawed," she agreed, trying to ignore the immediate, tingling response that coursed through her veins. "Unconscionable. Brutish. My first mistake was in not obeying my own well-bred instincts to have you shot as a poacher the first time we met."

"Your *first* mistake?" He wet the tip of his finger and touched it upon her breast, making the outthrust nub sparkle in the firelight. "You mean you are admitting to having committed more than one mistake in your lifetime?"

"The second was trusting the word of a spy and womanizer when he vowed to return me to the bosom of my family as chaste and pure as the day I was stolen away."

"Chaste *and* pure?" he mused, widening the ring he painted on her flesh. Catherine's hands, clenched into fists, uncurled and twisted around the tiny hillocks of sheeting which had served her previously. "I might argue that eighteen-year-old virgins, pure of intent, chaste of deed, do not wear gowns that erode a man's sanity. The night of your birthday party, when you lured me out into the garden with your wily feminine ways, it was all I could do to keep my eyes above the level of your pretty neck . . . and my hands to myself."

"As I recall," she countered evenly, "you failed miserably at both."

"Ahh, yes," he murmured. "But I wanted to do so much more. And very nearly did, as *I* recall, that night in Wakefield. Now there was a test no healthy man should have to endure: legally wed, abroad for the first night of wedded bliss, a lusciously naked woman swooning in his arms . . . *damnation*! I should apply for sainthood."

"If I was swooning, sir, it was because I was terrified for my life. Being chased through the woods at night, half drowned in a raging river, then *forcibly* stripped naked by a man known for his perversions rather than for his gentility . . . it hardly creates a mood for romance."

His mouth, having succumbed to the sweet temptation of a nipple, relinquished it again with a loud, wet *thwick*!

"Perversions, madam? Me? Do you not call it more perverse for a young woman of quality to intrude upon a man when he is attempting to bathe the grime of a difficult journey from his person? Not only intrude, but parade before him in a gown sheer enough to read the pages of a book through." He glanced upward at the silk nightdress which had ended up draped over the headboard of the bed. "Not quite sheer as this fine piece of nothing, I grant you, but equally debilitating on the senses of a man who had not seen anything half so lovely in some time."

Catherine gripped the sheets again as the hungry tug of his lips descended to her breast once more.

"There is no defense you can offer in excuse of your behaviour that night at Achnacarry. You took advantage of me, sir. You admitted it yourself the next morning."

"You wanted to be taken advantage of," he insisted, his thigh intruding between hers in such a way as to make the hairs across the nape of her neck prickle to attention. "And your body admitted it repeatedly all through the night."

"I was . . . acting under the influence of Archibald's wine."

"Whereas I was drunk on your beauty, your spirit—" he tilted his head up and his teeth flashed in a rakish grin, "—your willingness to learn. And such a willingness it was, as I recall. How could any mortal ignore such academic inclinations?"

"You are ignoring them now," she whispered, pressing unabashedly against the firm presence of his thigh.

His expression grew speculative as he contemplated the lush moistness of her mouth. Shifting his position on the bed again, he rolled onto his back and gently carried her with him so that she ended up lying atop his body. Smiling, he drew her knees higher, positioning them on either side of his waist.

Catherine pushed herself upright, sitting motionlessly astride him and wondering what wickedness he was after. While she wondered, she studied the molded bands of muscle that formed his rugged torso, and could not resist stroking her hands along his arms, up to his shoulders, down through the dense mat of curling black hairs that clouded his chest. Discovering the hard bead of a nipple, she leaned forward and razed it with her teeth and tongue, tormenting it with the same deliberation he had used against her earlier. She pounced hungrily on its twin and felt his fingers curl into her hair; she heard the thundering beat of his heart and felt his need rise up beneath her with growing impatience.

She was glad she had refrained from braiding her hair earlier on in the evening. It streamed over her shoulders, gilded by the firelight into a bright silver cascade that clung to the weathered surface of his body like finespun webbing. It also hid her face from view as she slid lower on his body, leaving the precise mechanics of her assault to his imagination. As it was, he gasped her name on a shiver of incredulity, his body arching and writhing uncontrollably, his soul groaning in an agony of pleasure.

While he still had hold of his faculties, he drew her forward and, blinded by the veil of her own hair, Catherine felt his hands slide down to her waist and lift her onto the virile strain of his flesh.

Her lips trembled apart and the breath became trapped somewhere in her throat. His hands remained firmly in place, coaxing her hips slowly to and fro, each stroke taking the solid, throbbing penetration deeper than she would have believed possible.

"A lesson worth remembering," he said huskily. "Never challenge the teacher."

Catherine's lips moved, but somewhere along the way she had lost the ability to produce sound. She could sense his eyes on her, watching her through the glimmering waves of her hair, his lips thinned to a calculated smile.

A shudder, like a powerful current, sent her head arching back against a rush of heat so exquisitely pure Alex had to brace himself to counter the stunning effects.

"Do you . . . have any idea . . . how that feels?" she gasped.

"No. Tell me."

She arched again and this time Alex removed his hands from around her waist, setting her free to move at her own pace and rhythm. He caught up her breasts in the palm of his hands and caused another cry to break from her throat.

"Tell me," he urged again, conscious of the heat pouring over and into his own loins.

"It feels . . . oh Alex, it feels the way I have wanted it to feel every night and day we've been apart. Is it wrong of me to say that? Is it wicked of me to think and want such things?"

"If it is," he murmured shakily, "then we are both condemned to moral hellfire, my love, and at the moment, I can think of no happier fate to share."

Catherine gasped, concentrating her every thought and sensation around the rich, sliding heat of his flesh. All the weeks of separation vanished as if they had never been; the doubts, the fears, the worries fled with each driving thrust. She groaned as Alex's hands circled her hips again, holding her, steadying her so that her pleasure was intense and protracted.

Catherine reached forward, her hands leaving the slick surface of his chest to claw for support against the wall of cushions behind him. She began to push herself greedily into the encroaching waves of ecstasy, crying out hoarsely as a shower of erotic sparks signalled the end of reason. Alex might have delayed her yet again, but she shook off his good intentions and pleaded instead for him to hold her, to help her, to share in the rising tumult of pleasure.

Shattered by the wildness in her eyes and foiled by the stunning demands of her body, Alex relinquished the slender threads of command and wrapped his arms around her. With a coarse and triumphant cry of his own, he surrendered to the drenching heat and, in moments, there was no air left to breathe, no sound left to hear, no motion in the universe beyond their clenched, shuddering bodies.

Chapter Six

Catherine levered an eyelid slowly. Sunlight was pouring through the window, bathing the room in the warm, bright glow of mid-morning. The clock on the mantlepiece was ticking away the final few minutes before the tenth hour, the curtains were drifting faintly with a breeze that carried faint sounds from the gardens and stables. The French door stood open barely an inch. There were no clothes lying on the floor, no breeches, boots, coat, shirt . . . even the letters she had scattered onto the carpet were gone.

"Alex!" she gasped and sat bolt upright. She whirled, dreading the sight of an empty bed beside her and was so shocked to see a pair of bold indigo eyes calmly watching her, she gasped again and sent both hands up to cover her trembling lips. "You're still here!"

He lazily arched a black brow. "You sound disappointed."

"No! Oh no, no . . . I just thought . . . I mean, I saw the open door and . . . and—" she stopped and bit down hard on her lower lip. She had been too afraid to ask during the night how long or short their time together would be. She was afraid to ask now.

"In all honesty," he said, stretching to flex the corded muscles in his arms, "I only meant to stay a few hours. However, due to the devious machinations of an incredibly energetic young woman, I found myself too drained to take advantage of the brief hour before dawn when the night was at its blackest. Curse my luck as well, it turns out to be a gloriously sunny day—far too sunny to attempt to dash across an open field in plain sight of a militia encampment, despite the borrowed uniform."

Catherine could scarcely believe her ears. "You mean—"

"In simple terms, madam? I am your prisoner. At the whim of your mercy—or devilment—for the remainder of the day and the better part of the night . . . er, assuming you desire my company, that is."

"Desire your company?" She flung herself into his arms with a small cry. "If I thought it would keep you here, I would burn your clothes and tie you hand and foot to the bed."

"An interesting proposition," he mused. "Perhaps when all of this is over, we might explore it more thoroughly."

Catherine snuggled against him, conscious of the heady, masculine scent of his skin and the total incongruity of his raw animalism surrounded by frilled and feminine furnishings.

"I wish it was over now," she said fervently. "I wish all this dreadfulness would just *end*. I wish I'd never let you put me on that ship out of Scotland. I wish you would have believed me when I said I did not care about the danger or the risks, that I just wanted to stay at Achnacarry where I belonged."

Alexander touched his lips to her forehead. "Catherine, Achnacarry is less than twenty miles from one of the strongest English garrisons in the Highlands. With Fort William so close, I could not have left you there alone."

"But I wouldn't have *been* alone. I would have been as safe as Lady Maura and Jeannie—"

"We have already been through this," he sighed. "Maura, Jeannie—even Rose all know what to expect.

They were weaned on bloodshed and violence and for them, living behind fortified castle walls is a way of life. Jeannie comes from the mountains; she could disappear into them again and survive in the caves for months on end, if the need arose."

"You talk as if Achnacarry is being held under siege. The Prince has won the Highlands. His army is in control of Scotland. What possible threat could there yet be from a couple of small English garrisons?"

Alex threaded his fingers into the silky skeins of her hair and drew her mouth up to his. "My beautiful innocent. Possession of the Highlands means nothing so long as the Prince is here, in England. The tables could turn so easily, so quickly—how could I live with myself knowing I had gambled the life of a lamb into the clutches of wolves? No. You are safe here and here is where you will stay, by God, until this affair is resolved one way or another."

"But—"

"No buts, madam. And no further arguments. I believe I told you once before I would have nothing to do with a nagging, disobedient wife."

Catherine slumped back down onto his chest again, but her hands curled into a fist and her voice was tart with sarcasm. "Yes, my all-powerful, all-knowing husband. If you think me so weak and helpless that I cannot draw a breath without your wisdom and protection, then by all means, it must be so."

Alex frowned. "I have no doubt you could go back to Achnacarry and cope with whatever might occur, whether it be a raid by the Argyle Campbells, or a siege by government troops. I'm sure you could learn how to help repel an attack on the castle walls, or how to cauterize an open wound, or sew a man's intestines back into his belly, or even to slit his throat to give him a swift and merciful death instead of a slow, agonized one." He paused to let the ugly reality of his words sink in. "I'm sure you could do all that and more besides, but the simple truth of it is—" he tucked a finger under her chin and forced her to look up into his face, "I don't want you to. There isn't any need for you to see the pain and ugliness of life's harsher realities."

"Only a need for me to be available for a little rough and tumble whenever you happen to be in the mood, or in the neighbourhood?"

Alex was silent a long moment. "If that was all I wanted, I could have had it from anyone, any time, and not gone through the bother of taking on a wife."

"Then tell me: What do you want? You say you love me, you say you want to protect me and keep me safe—and heaven knows, I do feel safe and warm and loved when I'm in your arms—but there has to be more to a marriage than possession and protection. I want to feel that you trust me, that you want to share . . . not only your life with me, but your thoughts, your hopes, your fears. I want to know that what you say to me and confide in me isn't just what you think I want to hear or should hear—*I* could have had *that* from a dozen Hamilton Garners, anytime, anywhere. I want more, Alex. I want to know what makes you happy, what makes you sad; what worries you, what angers you."

She reached up and tenderly brushed aside a heavy lock of raven hair. "I know you love me, Alex. The proof is in the way you look at me and touch me and . . . and I hear it in your voice even though the words are sometimes strange and forced. You said yourself you weren't a poet, but if you will recall, I did not fall in love with one. I fell in love with a man who was blunt and honest, caustic and infuriating, and so absolutely sure of himself he puts the rest of the world to shame. That was the man I fell in love with, and that, my lord, is the man I want to spend the rest of my life with. If I wanted something else—a philanthropist or a gallant who only wanted to set me on a safe little shelf and protect me from reality, I would have cringed away from you as if you were a carrier of the plague. I certainly never would have defied you to the point where you had no choice but to take me to Scotland with you."

The dark eyes gleamed. "You say that as if you planned the whole thing."

"Good God, no," she exclaimed, then flushed at the profanity. "I did not plan any of it . . . well . . . maybe just at the very beginning, when I thought I could use you to make Hamilton jealous."

"You succeeded," he said quietly.

She bowed her head to recoup her train of thought. "What I am trying to say, is maybe I did not know it consciously at the time, and maybe I fought against it because I knew you represented the end of everything orderly and predictable in my life." She raised huge, shining eyes to his. "But you also made me come alive, Alexander Cameron. You swept away all of the pretentions and . . . and the deadness.

"You showed me exactly how empty my life had been without you, how false my values were, how little self-esteem I had. I was Catherine Ashbrooke—rich, spoiled, and selfish, and I had everything, yet I had nothing. The Catherine Cameron who spent two wonderful days locked in a damp stone cottage on the edge of a Highland moor had nothing, yet it felt as if the whole world was spread out before us. I could have stayed there with you, quite happily, for the rest of my life. Because we shared, Alex. We shared the truth, the pain, the reality. You may have a dangerous and unpredictable temperament; you are certainly stubborn and proud, and make me want to scream sometimes just because you are who and what you are. But you are also honest to a fault, direct, loyal, gentle and compassionate—and I do not think you would want a wife who was afraid to be all of those things herself."

Alex remained silent for so long, Catherine imagined she could hear the actual voices warring back and forth within his conscience. If she was wrong, if he only wanted a pretty parlour dressing and a soft and willing body in his bed—then she had lost him. If he patted her on the head and smiled his way through a heart-warming accolade, then she might as well have lost him.

His hands were the first thing that moved. They slid up from where they had been resting on her shoulders and gently, thoughtfully cradled her face between them. His gaze was somber and guarded, as unreadable as always, yet she thought she saw a glimmer of self-effacing humour as he angled his mouth down over hers. The kiss had none of the passion or urgency as those he had caressed her with during the night. Rather, it was a simple, basic affirmation of his love.

"Are you absolutely certain there isn't Scots blood in you somewhere?" he murmured. "You show remarkable skill with a verbal blade."

Catherine bit down on her lip and waited.

"You are right, of course," he admitted with a sigh. "I wasn't sure what to do with you once I had you. I wasn't sure if you had just been carried along in something new and adventurous, or if you could actually love me enough to willingly turn your back on all of this. I sent you out of Scotland for your own safety, make no mistake about that. But I guess . . . in a way, I was also testing you. Testing myself as well."

"And?"

"And—" he smoothed his thumbs lightly along the curve of her cheeks "—I think I should consider myself a lucky bastard to have a wife who knows my faults and isn't afraid to stand up to me, rather than one who ignores my faults and learns to live with them. Mind you," a quick downstroke brought both thumbs to rest against her parted lips, "I would naturally expect the same rights and privileges."

"Naturally," she whispered.

"I know I have not been much of a husband to you in the past few months, and I may not make much of a domesticated creature in the years ahead . . . but by God," he mused, "I'd like to try. I'd like to grow old with you. In fact, I want to grow old and portly and contented —just like my brother. I always thought Donald's love for Maura was his one great weakness, but I can see now, it is his strength."

Catherine tried to match his smile, but the quivering in her chin and the sudden scalding of tears in her eyes did not permit much success. Alex gathered her close and wrapped warm, wonderful arms around her, and for a few moments, that was enough.

"Actually . . . there was another reason why I sent you out of Scotland," he said huskily, pressing a kiss into the crown of her hair.

"Another reason?"

"Mmmm. If I'd taken you back to Achnacarry, you would still be there and I would be here, and . . . if the Prince has his way, a month from now he'll be marching through the gates of London and we would have been that much farther apart." His teeth flashed a smile and his hands stroked down through the tousle of her hair to settle over the rounded softness of her buttocks. "Rather clever of me to have planned to have you here, wasn't it?"

"Very clever," she murmured dryly. "And I don't believe a word of it."

Melting into the sensation of his roving lips, she allowed herself to be gently guided deeper beneath the warm cocoon of blankets, to be loved and caressed by his hands, his lips, his superbly honed body. And for a time, she almost forgot there was a war going on outside their isolated sanctuary of happiness. She almost forgot that, in a few hours, he would be gone again and the fear would begin its process of erosion all over again.

"Alex?"

"Mmmm?"

"Are you asleep?"

He stirred and she could feel the lingering dampness that still clung to his chest and shoulders.

"Sleep?" he asked on a yawn. "What's that?"

"I'm sorry," she said guiltily. "Forget I said anything. Go back to sleep."

He took a deep breath and his body tautened through a stretch that brought his head sliding up from its resting place on her belly. He snuggled into the crook of her shoulder, his arms enfolding her more securely, a long leg nestling more intimately between hers. In a few moments, his breathing was deep and even, his body completely relaxed.

"Alex?"

". . . mmm . . . ?"

"Are you really going to sleep?"

The dark eyes opened slowly. "Apparently not. Why?"

"I have been thinking about what you said—about me being here and you being in London. Is it true? Is Charles Stuart really planning to march his army all the way to London?"

Alex knuckled the weariness from his eyes and stretched again. "I don't know. He has his army and his intentions aimed that way."

"Can he do it? Can he reach London?"

"Well, no one thought he could get this far, including some of his closest advisors, but he has."

A very neat way to avoid answering the question, she thought.

"Father says the Young Pretender will have to meet and destroy the king's army before he advances much further."

"He says that, does he?"

"And more besides. He says that even if the Prince does reach London, he will never hold the city against the guns of the Royal Navy. He says Admiral Vernon will never serve under a Stuart monarchy, and with five hundred ships under his command, he will have the firepower to prove his point."

"Your father is very perceptive. Has he any insights as to how the government will react?"

"He is certain Parliament would collapse, and all but certain the nobility would band together and form their own army to march against the Stuarts."

"He is talking civil war," Alex remarked calmly.

"And then there is the church. Canterbury will never tolerate a return of the papacy to England, and there are simply not enough Catholics in the country strong enough to wrest the power away from the Anglican Bishops."

"For someone who professes to dislike politics and talk of war, you seem remarkably well informed."

"I have eyes and ears."

"So you do," he mused, gazing thoughtfully at both. "Beautiful eyes and perfectly charming ears."

"You haven't answered my question," she reminded him firmly.

The dark eyes flicked down to the naked opulence of her breasts. "The mood is hardly what you might call conducive to talk of armies and political strategies."

"Nor is it, evidently, very fertile for truth and simple honesty . . . or is this how you mean to share your thoughts with me: by changing the subject when it pleases you, or avoiding unpleasant topics when the mood is not upon you?"

The black lashes lifted slowly and, after a careful scrutiny of the clear, direct expression on her face, he sighed and pushed himself higher on the pillows, propping them comfortably behind his back and crossing his arms over his chest.

"Very well. If it is the truth you want, it is the truth you shall have. Ask me whatever you want to know."

Catherine noted the prick of irritation in his voice, but softened her own enough to undermine it. "Is it true? Will the Prince march on to London?"

"If the decision is his to make: yes."

"Is his army strong enough to meet and defeat King George's troops?"

"If Cumberland's ships sink in the Channel and the Dutch have a change of heart, I'd give us an even chance. In spirit, I would even go so far as to say our Highlanders could win hell from the Devil, if they set their minds to it."

"In spirit? Are you saying they are lacking elsewhere?"

"The English don't seem to think so. Not after General Cope was so obliging at Prestonpans by leaving behind his artillery, his stores and equipment."

Catherine's attention was distracted briefly to the fresh scar above her husband's left ear. He hadn't mentioned the wound, or how he had earned it, and she had not asked, but she did not have to be a doctor or a breather of doom to see how close he had come to losing his ear, his eye, or his life.

Unwittingly, her eyes travelled higher to the opposite temple, to the thin white furrow of scar tissue that marked the cut Hamilton Garner's sword had dealt him in the duel. He bore another on his thigh from that same encounter, and she had a sudden, clear image of how he had looked standing in the parlour, fresh from the duel, the sweat still glistening in his hair, the blood still leaking over the top of his tall black boots as he repeated his marriage vows. He had worn the same impenetrable mask over his features then as he did now and, wary of his mastery over words as well as emotions, Catherine proceeded cautiously.

"Father credited the loss at Prestonpans to inexperience. Even Uncle Lawrence admitted General Cope was ill-supported and the troops were mainly new recruits with few having seen battle before."

"True enough," Alexander agreed. "But the bulk of the Prince's army consisted then, and now, of farmers and shepherds who had never seen a musket before Prestonpans, much less faced or fired one. Cope's troops, on the other hand, even though they lacked the seasoning, were trained and drilled, well equipped with not only muskets and shot, but enough artillery to pepper the countryside full of holes."

"It was also said your army took them by complete surprise."

"Cope had the advantage of choosing the field. He had his back to the sea, a wide open plain on either flank and a morass of filthy swampland guarding his front door. A schoolboy with a handful of stones should have been able to defend that position. Cope deserved to be humiliated, and he was."

He was testing her desire to learn the truth, Catherine suspected. Telling her something . . . but what?

"Cope had barely three thousand men," she said slowly. "The Prince reportedly had four times that number."

"Scraping the barrel for excuses, are we?" A black brow arched in wry amusement. "Rather creatively, too. Four times as many, you say? The last I heard it was only three."

Thrust and counterthrust.

"You said if it was the Prince's decision to make, there would be no question of marching against London. Does that mean there are those among you who might prefer another strategy?"

"Some of the clan chiefs have been against the idea of invasion from the outset," Alex admitted candidly. "Others were willing enough to make the attempt, providing there was some show of support from the English Jacobites."

"And? Has there been?"

"Not so that you'd notice," he said dryly.

"Does that mean the Prince is losing support from within his own ranks?"

"Even a blind man knows when to turn away from a stone wall."

"A stone wall? Must you speak in riddles?"

Alex sighed. "A stone wall—figuratively speaking. In reality, what the chiefs are beginning to see, and quite clearly, is an army of Highland sheep farmers marching boldly along a main road of a country that has not had an army invade this deeply into its heart since the days of William the Conqueror. On their left flank, they see Marshal Wade lurking with his army of five thousand men, all of whom would dearly love to avenge their fallen comrades at Prestonpans, but who are wary of a similar fate befalling them should they act in too much haste. On the right flank is Sir John Ligonier's army of seven thousand, equally eager, equally prudent. And now we hear the news that King George's son, the Duke of Cumberland, is speeding back across the Channel with several thousand well-blooded veterans who are most perturbed at having to abandon their jolly little war in Flanders just to deal with a horde of skirted insurgents at home.

"Last but not least, is the stalwart brigade of a few thousand dragoons and assorted royal guardsmen who stand poised at Finchley Commons, not too pleased at the prospect of standing alone to defend the city against the descending hordes, but nobly willing to die for king and country should the Duke not arrive home in time to fortify the ranks. I was in the city when King George delivered a rousing speech intended to bolster the courage of his brave guards—at the same time he was discreetly loading his valuables on a ship anchored in the Thames. He obviously has more faith in the Prince's loyal followers than he does in his own."

Catherine did some quick mental arithmetic. "Discounting Admiral Vernon's navy, and discounting the pockets of local militia throughout the countryside, the government only has about twenty thousand men to pit against the Prince's army. No wonder the King has reservations."

There was a strange glint in Alexander's eyes. "The odds are considerably more in his favour than they were in ours at Prestonpans, yet we held no such . . . reservations."

"I'm not sure I follow you."

He smiled faintly. "Despite what you heard, we put less than two thousand men on the field that day; Cope had closer to three. One of the main reasons why we had to release most of the prisoners was due to the fact that there were more of them than there were of us."

"But . . . why would the Prince only send two thousand men into his first engagement with the English army? Wasn't he taking a terrible risk with their lives?"

"He had no choice. Two thousand was all he could spare. The rest—a few hundred here and there, were needed at Perth and Edinburgh to hold on to what we had already captured."

"A few *hundred*? But we heard there were upwards of ten thousand at Prestonpans, with more joining the rebel army every day!"

Alex uncrossed an arm and ran a blunted fingertip along the curve of her cheek. "Catherine," he said softly, "if we had ten thousand Highlanders in our army, we could capture not only London, but all the capitals of Europe as well. There have never been more than five thousand following the Prince's standard at any one time."

Catherine's look of total disbelief mirrored his own of less than a month ago, when Donald Cameron had informed his officers of the Prince's decision not to winter in Scotland, but to push on with the invasion without delay.

"Charles Stuart has invaded England with five thousand men?" she asked incredulously. "Five thousand against . . . against a *modest* estimate of twenty thousand? Surely you are joking!"

"I wish I were," he replied tautly. "Well? What do you think of the truth so far?"

"So far?" she whispered. "Does the Prince realize the odds he is facing?"

"Amazingly enough, he does. He is quite well informed, whereas—and here we only have Lord George's brilliance at deception to credit—his enemies are completely ignorant of the most basic information: namely, the numbers and exact whereabouts of our forces."

"How does he justify marching so few against so many?"

"Our Bonnie Prince *Tearlach* is obsessed with the justness of his cause," Alex said simply. "He is also convinced, beyond a doubt, that not only will the common people rise in support of his father, King James, but every English soldier bearing arms against him will lay their weapons aside and welcome the restored Stuart monarchy with rose petals and accolades."

"He's mad," Catherine gasped.

"We are all a little mad," Alex said with a sad smile, "or we would not be where we are today."

"And tomorrow? Don't you care what will happen to you tomorrow if Wade and Ligonier and the Duke of Cumberland join forces? Or if even one of their armies discovers the ruse?"

"Of course I care," he said gently, bending his lips to the glowing softness of her shoulder. "But what would you have me do—desert?"

"Yes!" she cried promptly. Then, "No." And after yet another miserable pause: "I don't know!"

"You've about covered every option," he remarked. "And it gives you some idea of the prevailing mood of the Prince's nightly councils."

"Your brother: What does Donald think?"

Alex raked a hand through the thick black waves of his hair and sighed. "Donald has been pleading for caution for so long, the Prince only listens with one ear. He pretends to listen raptly, of course, for he knows if he loses Lochiel's Camerons then he loses a third of his army—and that doesn't include the clans who have been feeling the shroud tightening around them since we crossed the River Esk. They would only have to smell a hint of a mutiny in the air and they would be back across the border before the Prince knew they were missing."

"But what hold does the Prince have on them? What possible arguments could he use to persuade a man like your brother against truth and logic? Sweet merciful heavens, why is Donald remaining with him if he sees little hope of success? And please, dear God, don't tell me about Scottish pride and honour and loyalty, or I shall scream, I swear it!"

"Alright, I won't tell you about pride or honour, or loyalty," he said considerately. "I'll tell you about consequences instead. Each and every man who rallied at Glenfinnan knew there could be no compromises, no turning back. Either we would win it all this time, or lose everything. You said earlier we had gained Scotland back from the English and asked what possible threat a few garrisons of Hanover troops could prove? Well, it's true, we won Scotland fairly and cleanly, and I suppose the logical move would have been to spend the next six months or so, fortifying our borders, strengthening our defenses, arming ourselves against the counterattack that would be sure to come. And there would have been a retaliatory strike against us, no doubt about it. England could not possibly sit back and accept such an insult to her imperialistic pride. How would it look to the rest of her budding empire if she could not even hold on to a barren stretch of rock and moorland that adjoined her own border? The North American colonies would surely sit up and take note. So would her enemies—Spain and

France—both of whom are vying with the British for trading footholds in the West Indies and Persia. King George would have had to send his army north, to fight us for possession of Scotland whether he wanted it or not. *England's* pride would be at stake, not ours."

"But at least you would have bought the time to build your army," Catherine argued.

"Aye, and maybe had twenty or thirty thousand men willing to fight for their freedom instead of the five or six we have now. But there again, we would have given England more time as well. The English would not waste the same six months idling in ignorance; they would call in all their markers from allies abroad, they would train and drill their army so that a fiasco like Prestonpans would never happen again, they would utilize their naval power *first* and strangle us to death with a blockade so tight the fish would be screaming. There would be no more mistakes, no more inefficiency, no more second-rate generals being sent to deal with a minor disturbance. England would throw everything she had against us, and it would be a bloodbath on both sides."

Alex saw her worried frown and took her small, cold hands into his. "In the end, you could be sure they would have left us with nothing. The English would have conquered us and destroyed us once and for all, if only to use us as an example to any other colony that might be getting ideas. But instead of five thousand misguided fools to punish for their audacity, there would be thirty thousand, all with wives and families and properties. Everything we had would be confiscated or destroyed. There would be no more Scotland."

He brooded a long moment over the thought and Catherine used the time and the morning sunlight to study the hard lines of his face. There were shadows circling his eyes that had not been there before, lines etched across his wide brow and carved alongside the stern set of his mouth which had not been there when she had thought him to be merely a spy and murderer . . . when he had claimed not to have had a conscience, and she had believed him.

"I love you, Alexander Cameron," she said evenly. "I will love you regardless of the life we must share; if we live in a castle or a cottage."

"We Camerons may not even have a cottage or a *clachan* to call our own if the rebellion is lost and the leaders penalized into forfeiture."

"Donald could lose Achnacarry?"

"It almost happened once before, after the rebellion of 1715, when our father led the clan into the uprising for the Stuarts. The leaders were given the choice of the hangman's noose, or exile if they refused to swear allegiance to King George. In most cases, where the chief was stubborn or adamant, there was a son or brother he could order to pay lip service to the government's demands, and in that way, save the lands and titles even though he himself would have to accept banishment."

"Your father is still in France, is he not?"

"Italy, with King James. There were many chiefs who later petitioned for pardons, with the Stuart king's permission, and returned to Scotland, but we Cameron men are a stubborn lot, as you might already have guessed. Old Lochiel remains in exile and declares he will continue to do so until there is a Stuart king on the throne again."

"The pride of lions," Catherine murmured, winning a curious glance from her husband. "It was something Lady Maura told me: An affliction most Scots seem to possess."

"Aye, well, this time there may not be any cubs to retain title of the lands if it comes to that. No sons or brothers untainted by Young Lochiel's actions."

"But isn't there a brother who refused to join the Prince? Your brother John?"

"John is not a zealous Jacobite," Alexander said guardedly. "Nor has he ever displayed any overt support for the Hanover government. If the wind changes, however, it is conceivable he could protect himself by sending a few men to fight against us, but if he does, he would lose all credibility within the clan. They would never accept him as chief."

"Would they accept Archibald, or you?"

The dark eyes glowered briefly. "Neither Archie or myself would ever consider holding the title as long as Donald was alive—not that we would ever have to make such a decision. If we are forced to retreat back to Scotland in defeat, we would be returning for a very short time only. Forfeiture, exile, prison . . . even the noose are probabilities too real for my liking."

"They cannot hang everyone who has participated in the fighting!"

"Cut off the head and the body dies. They only have to hang the leaders to see the whole clan system collapse."

Catherine shivered and sought comfort within the warm circle of his arms.

"Here now, cheer up," he said, soothingly. "We Camerons should not be left entirely destitute. Not unless the lovely Mrs. Montgomery has been imprudent with her husband's life savings."

"She has squandered every penny," Catherine replied morosely, burying her face deeper into his shoulder. "I'm sure Damien told you everything in great detail."

"As a matter of fact, your brother tells me you have not drawn a single ha'penny. Master Montgomery would not be pleased to think of his wife doing without."

"The only comfort Mrs. Montgomery has lacked and craved was the presence of the errant Master Montgomery by her side."

"He is here now," Alex said softly. "And has been doing his utmost to make up for everything you may have lacked and craved."

His hands skimmed up her naked body, running up beneath the tousled gleam of her hair until they were situated one at the nape of her neck, one beneath the delicate curve of her chin. They held her through a stunningly passionate kiss, but when he would have sent them roving further afield, she broke free and pushed herself upright.

"What is it?" he asked. "Have I said something wrong?"

In silence, she shook her head, her eyes very large and deeply hued—a storm warning he had seen often enough to be placed on his guard.

"Have I done something wrong?"

Catherine's lips put an abrupt end to his speculation. The kiss was bold, as aggressively thorough as his had been, and had the fine hairs on his forearms rising on tiny bumps by the time she was sated and drew away.

"Forgive my ignorance, madam," he said haltingly. "But have I missed something here?"

"A question, Sir Rogue. One which you neatly refrained from answering."

"To win such a reprimand, I should gladly avoid it again."

She dug her fingers savagely into the tender flesh over his ribs. "The offers of comfort you were so flattered to receive—you failed to mention if they were also too appealing to resist."

His gaze fastened on the seductive pout of her lips. "Suppose I said I accepted every one of them?"

"I should call you a liar and a braggart," she retorted evenly. "As well as a perverted, lustful beast."

"Perverted *and* lustful?" There was a wry crook to one dark eyebrow. "Just because I have not been able to keep my hands off you for more than a few minutes at a time, does not necessarily mean I am always desperate for such attention."

"Not necessarily?"

"On the other hand, I have it on good authority that to deprive myself of physical relief could result in seriously harmful effects. Count Giovanni Fanducci is a living example of the restorative and beneficial powers of a good woman's attention. When we first encountered him, our inclination was to keep all the pretty young lads hidden from his sight. A few nights with Ringle-Eyed Rita however and—"

"*Who* is Count Giovanni Fanducci, and *what* is a Ringle-Eyed Rita?" Catherine demanded.

"The count is a volunteer. He joined us after Prestonpans and made an immediate impression on the majority of the Prince's army by drinking Struan MacSorley into a stupor that lasted three days. Conversely, the count was not only able to put our golden-haired friend under the table, he was seen and heard shortly thereafter, collecting his wager in the arms of a certain Ringle-Eyed Rita—so named because of her knack of being able to—"

"Nevermind! There is no need to elaborate."

"Not that I have personal knowledge of her talents, you understand."

"Of course not."

"Or the opportunity. Not since our Italian friend has found his way onto the scene at any rate—much to Struan's displeasure."

"I thought Struan MacSorley and dear Lauren had an . . . understanding."

Alex's smile faded slightly. "Aye, we all thought so. Especially when she insisted on accompanying the clan when we left Achnacarry."

Catherine stiffened, all traces of humour vanishing at once. "Lauren is travelling with the army? She's travelling with you?"

"She was," he admitted, wary of the feline sparks snapping to life in Catherine's eyes. "But only as far as Edinburgh. She was born there and made no secret about wanting to return. As near as anyone can recollect, she slipped out of camp the eve before the battle at Prestonpans and has not been seen or heard from since."

Good riddance, Catherine thought. Somewhat mollified she allowed herself to be drawn back into her husband's arms, but a sudden, clear image of Lauren Cameron kept her from enjoying the comfortable haven. Wild titian red hair, a complexion warmed by the sun and weather, eyes the color of amber—there had been a distinct and open challenge in the way Lauren Cameron had presented herself as a sultry rival for Alexander's attention. Memories of her voluptuous body and brazen sensuality had not been the least of Catherine's worries over the past few months.

"Is that a jealous scowl I detect misshaping your pretty face, or is it some aftereffect of your last night's meal repeating itself in your spleen?"

"Jealous? Me? Of that . . . that . . ."

Alex laughed and muffled her stammerings beneath his lips. "You may believe this or not as you see fit, but I scarcely even noticed Lauren—or anyone else for that matter. There, you see what you have done to me? Gelded me. Deprived me of one of man's most basic and revered instincts."

"Good. As long as you remain deprived, we shall have no quarrels."

"Does that order extend to include food and drink as well? Half a dozen buckets full of hot soapy water would not go unappreciated either, unless of course you are bent on keeping me earthy and well-sweated to discourage outside interests."

"How thoughtless of me!" she cried, pushing herself upright. "You must be starving!"

"I *was* starving; now I am merely ravenous. Aside from being here with you, there are three things I fantasize about the most: a hindquarter of beef dripping with gravy, blackberry pies fresh from the oven, and being able to bathe in something other than ice-cold river water."

"You shall have all three," Catherine declared, leaning down to bestow a fleeting kiss on his cheek. Naked, she jumped down from the bed and padded barefoot to the dressing room, her long golden hair swinging on each step, the curls dancing brightly as she passed through a streamer of sunlight. Alex propped his head on his folded arms and openly admired the luscious curves and gazelle-like grace of his wife's body; she was intelligence, beauty, and passion combined—how could he ever have contemplated giving her up?

He had spoken the truth earlier when he'd said he only meant to stay a few hours. He had been gone nearly a week from the Prince's camp and it was inexcusable for him to be delaying his return for purely selfish reasons. But when he had held Catherine in his arms and heard the need trembling in her voice, the thought of leaving, the idea of rushing back to a cold bedroll on the hard ground, and the company of men snoring and coughing and breaking wind loudly enough to bring down the walls of Jericho . . . well, it suddenly was not important anymore. Lochiel could manage without him for another twelve hours. Or fourteen.

"Do you intend to lay there grinning, sir, or do you think it possible you could bestir yourself to help in some small way?"

Catherine was glaring at him, her eyebrow raised inquisitively. Alex swung his long legs over the side of the bed and joined her before the dressing room, following her pointed finger to where the large copper and enamel bathtub was pushed into the far corner.

"If you will place it before the hearth, my lord, and see to building up the fire, I shall find Deirdre and enlist her assistance in fetching those buckets and buckets of steaming hot water."

"Deirdre?" Alex frowned as if he had never heard the name before. "Damnation! I knew there was something else I was forgetting."

He walked back around to the far side of the bed and retrieved the scarlet tunic from the chair. Patting the inner pockets, he found what he was looking for and produced them with a flourish. "Aluinn's threat of violence was uncommonly graphic in the event I neglected to deliver these to Deirdre."

"These" proved to be letters, almost as thick a packet as those Catherine had flung on the bed the previous evening.

Alex had the grace to flush sheepishly when he saw the look on his wife's face.

"Aluinn MacKail has never been at a loss for words, regardless of the situation. They flow from his pen in torrents, more so now that he is in love."

"Perhaps he could give you lessons," she said quietly, staring enviously at the twine-bound bundle. In the next instant, she was regretting the petty outburst. She was married to a man who loved her, something not one woman in ten could boast with any truth these days, regardless if she had volumes of letters and sonnets in her possession.

Setting aside the jar of bathsalts she had been holding, she went to Alex and ran her hands up around his neck and pressed her soft body up to his with a message as clear and urgent as the one in her eyes. The letters fell forgotten onto the floor as his arms went around her, and he was about to scoop her up and carry her back to the bed when a brusque tapping on the chamber door brought an abrupt and breathless halt to the embrace.

"Deirdre," Catherine gasped. "I shall send her to the kitchens for food and hot water."

"Tell her not to hurry," he murmured, his voice sending a liquid thrill down her spine.

"I thought you were ravenous."

"I am."

The second knock was not as subtle, nor as easy to ignore.

"Y-yes? Deirdre?"

"It is your father," replied a gruff male voice. "I must speak to you at once."

The latch on the door rattled impatiently, sending Catherine's heart up into her throat. Alex was already in motion, gathering up his clothing, boots, and swordbelt, and carrying them into the dressing room. He tossed Catherine the key to the door as he passed, then vanished into the tiny antechamber.

The latch rattled again. "Daughter?"

"J-Just a moment, Father," she cried, smoothing back her hair with one hand while she snatched up her robe with the other. A glance into the cheval mirror nearly caused her to swoon: Her lips were lush and swollen, her hair so tangled it would require a solid hour of brushing to tame. And . . . oh sweet merciful heaven! The bed looked as if a war had been waged beneath its scalloped canopy—linens, blankets, and pillows were tossed every which way. Sir Alfred was no fool. Even as she dashed madly from one side of the bed to the other, attempting to restore some semblance of order, she knew it was futile. He had noted Lieutenant Goodwin's attentiveness last night and would undoubtedly draw his own conclusions as to why she had withdrawn from the parlour early.

Catherine yanked the satin sash painfully tight about her waist as she approached the door. Her hand was trembling so badly it took two attempts before the key fitted into the slot, and when she finally managed to open the door, her smile was as brittle and unnatural as her high-pitched voice.

"Father," she shrilled. "What a surprise."

Sir Alfred's complexion was ruddier than usual, his stride brisk with agitation as he propelled himself through the doorway. His frizzed gray wig was set on a slightly unbalanced angle on his otherwise bald head; his shirt, waistcoat, and breeches were the ones he had worn last night and looked as if they had been slept in.

He barged straight past Catherine without seeming to have seen her, and came to an abrupt halt in the middle of the room. His back remained to her long enough for Catherine to pat a few more strands of hair into place but she quickly whipped her hand down by her side as he turned to confront her.

"I trust I am not disturbing you? I know the hour is early yet."

"N-No. No, you are not disturbing me, Father. I was awake. I was, er, just about to take a bath."

"Mmmm. Good. Good."

Catherine moved slowly away from the door. She could never, in all her years, recall Sir Alfred paying a visit to her rooms. Nor, for that matter, could she remember him ever apologizing for disturbing anyone.

"Father . . . is something wrong? Is something troubling you?"

"Wrong? Trouble?" He stared, frowning as if he could not recollect what had brought him here. "Trouble," he said again and this time paced to the foot of the bed.

Catherine's composure was shattered a second time when she noticed the neatly bound packet of letters lying on the floor not two inches from the toe of Sir Alfred's buckled shoe.

"There could very well be trouble," he bellowed, jerking his daughter's gaze back up to his face. "Word arrived late last night that the rebel army has moved out of Manchester and is headed this way. Moreover, it is rumoured that over fifteen hundred erstwhile loyal citizens actually joined the papist locusts and have taken up arms against King George! It is inconceivable such a thing could have happened—worse still, that it could possibly happen here!"

"Here, Father? You believe the rebels will come here, to Derby?"

"What is to stop them?" he demanded, in a rage. "The army has deserted us, the militia is folding camp and retreating before them with such haste they are uprooting whole trees from the gardens!"

"Father, there is no point in bringing a fit down upon yourself. Here, sit down, and—"

"A fit? A *fit*? Why the deuce should I not suffer fits? That papist princeling has left a wasteland behind him; a veritable wasteland, I tell you. He has caused whole towns and villages to be razed to the ground and he has driven the decent citizens into hiding for mortal fear of their lives. I warned them. I warned them all what they could expect from thieves and savages, but did anyone listen? Parties, teas, luncheons—that is what they threw instead of cannon balls. Now, we must all pay for their ignorance and pay dearly!"

"Father, I have heard the stories . . . the rumours your so-called authorities seem determined to spread and frankly, I find them not only hard to believe, but downright contradictory. Why should a city welcome the Prince's army with bells if it anticipates chaos? Why should the citizens join his army if they burn and level everything behind them? If the stories were true, would we not see more evacuees fleeing for their lives instead of just the rich transporting their gold and silver to safety?"

Sir Alfred glared caustically at his daughter. "You have learned bold lessons from your brother on the art of arguing, I see."

"I am not arguing, Father. I am merely questioning your sources."

"Sources be damned! The reality, daughter, is that my Lord Cavendish, the Duke of Devonshire, is insisting upon a full evacuation of Derby—a decision with which I wholeheartedly concur. I have spent the better part of the morning arranging my affairs so that we might take our leave with all due haste."

"Leave!" Catherine gasped, glancing at the closed doors of the dressing room. The thought of riding away, of being torn from Alex's side a second time against her will was so abhorrent she scarcely heard the first few words of her father's renewed tirade.

"—only to encounter a most stubborn form of opposition from—of all people—your mother! Scorned me, she did. Called me a spineless worm and said she has no intentions of budging one foot off the estate. God's teeth, I do not know what has come over her. Not even when I pointed out the possibility of her being grossly abused, or that Rosewood Hall could well be burned down about her ears—not even then would she relent! I have come to you, daughter, in the very real hope that you can persuade her to come to her senses."

Sweating profusely, he withdrew a large square of linen and began mopping his face and throat.

"Ungrateful," he muttered. "That's what she is. Twenty-five years of boundless privileges have affected her sense of obligation. She no longer remembers who she *is* or who she *was* before my generosity saved her from a life of ignominy and shame. This . . . this *leave-taking* of her senses has clearly made her forget her most solemn vow of obedience. How will it look to my Lord Cavendish if she defies my orders? How will they regard me in Parliament if it is seen that I cannot even control the whims of my own wife? She must be made to obey. I am relying on you, daughter, to show her the error of her ways."

Catherine temporarily forgot the listener in the dressing room as she smiled at her father. "Me? A model of obedience?"

"You have not been too great a disappointment," Sir Alfred allowed. "You married this chap Montgomery, did you not? As violent a tantrum as you threw when I put the matter before you, and as ardently as you professed to hate him and every other human being who walked the face of the earth that particular evening, you still acknowledged my sound judgement in the matter and married him. What is more, you followed him dutifully to

London and accepted your responsibilities with the grace and humility women were bred to assume."

Catherine drew a controlled breath, her temper crackling with the swiftness of a lightning strike. But before she could add to her mother's fine assessment of Sir Alfred's character, she watched him bend over and pick up the letters he had narrowly missed treading upon.

"Women were not put upon this earth to rebel and contradict," he continued in his best parliamentary mein. "Certainly not to dictate to a man what he should or should not do to protect his best interests. If women had been given brains large enough to accommodate such matters, they should also have been given the brawn and fortitude to see them through. Knowledge of how to paint one's fingernails and preen before a mirror for two and three blessed hours a day is hardly a prerequisite for understanding the intricacies of politics and military strategy." He slapped the bundle of letters against the palm of his hand and pursed his lips in thoughtful repose as he glanced down at the boldly scripted name on the top envelope. "I must insist you speak with her at once, Catherine. She must be made to recognize her obligations to the Ashbrooke name."

Catherine's gaze was frozen on the letters, her mind racing ahead for a plausible explanation as to why she would have letters addressed to Deirdre in her possession.

A further bubble of panic swelled when she saw Sir Alfred's attention begin to wander toward the glorious dishevellment of the bed. Shining at her, like the beacon atop a lighthouse roof, was the pooled silk of the nightdress which still hung draped over the headboard.

"I'm not sure what influence I could bring to bear," she said hastily. "Especially since I am not altogether convinced Mother is wrong."

Sir Alfred's head swivelled around. "What? What is that you say?"

"I said—" she paused and drew a breath, "I think I rather agree with Mother's viewpoint. I see no reason to evacuate, no need to run away with our tails tucked up between our legs. In fact, if she wants the company, I shall most happily remain here at Rosewood Hall with her."

Sir Alfred spluttered incoherently. "Have you lost your mind, child? Do you understand what you are saying? Do you understand what I have been telling you these past few minutes? The rebel army is on its way to Derby. It could well be here in a few hours! The militia is withdrawing; the servants, groundskeepers, even that addled boy who gathers cow droppings for the gardens has fled. You will be completely alone and unprotected here, entirely at the mercy of uncouth louts and barbarians."

"I'm sure we will be quite safe, Father. The reports *I* have heard all suggest the Prince is a perfect gentleman and quite the congenial houseguest."

"Houseguest!" Sir Alfred's multi-level presentation of chins and jowls shivered with outrage. "You would extend the hospitality of Rosewood Hall to that . . . that French usurper?"

"I shall even endeavour to keep an accounting of the number of bottles of your fine Burgundy he appropriates."

Lord Ashbrooke flushed crimson. He flung the bundle of letters aside in a gesture of utter disgust and walked stiffly to the bedroom door. "It is clear to me now that neither you nor your mother is in full command of your faculties. I shall therefore instruct the housemen to come up the stairs at once and collect you both—using force, if necessary."

"Then by force shall they be met," Catherine retorted evenly, her fists balling by her sides. "I might remind you we are both of the age of majority; we are neither of us bound by writs of slavery or serfdom, and are therefore free to decide whether we wish to remain in our home or run into the woods like frightened children."

"You will obey me!" Sir Alfred roared indignantly.

"I will obey my own conscience," Catherine declared calmly.

Sir Alfred's astonishment was complete. Confronted by this further defection from his circle of authority, he launched himself out the door and ran headlong into Deirdre O'Shea. The tray of tea and biscuits she had balanced precariously in one hand, flew up and smashed against the wall in a shower of broken crockery and steaming liquid. Sir Alfred's wig was carried away on the edge of the platter and landed like a splayed dustmop in the centre of the spilled tea.

An even more voluminously roared curse sent the shocked maid scurrying to retrieve the headpiece as Lord Ashbrooke cast a scathing glance back at his daughter. "My carriage will be departing at the stroke of noon! If your sanity returns before then, you may beg leave to accompany me. If not—" he snatched the wig out of Deirdre's hand and gestured scornfully, spattering the adjoining walls with a spray of tea "—you may beg your leave of whichever libertine, thief, or cutthroat takes your fancy!"

Catherine watched her father storm off down the hall, but even before he had turned a corner out of sight, she was dragging Deirdre inside her room.

"Mercy, but I begin to understand why Mother has been compelled to turn elsewhere for companionship."

"Mistress?"

"Nothing. It doesn't matter. Just shut and bolt the door."

"But the mess—"

"Leave it. It's not important."

Deirdre's brown eyes, keener by far than Sir Alfred's, gaped at the results of the minor hurricane that had passed through Catherine's bedchamber. Where there would normally hardly be a crease to show where her mistress had slept in the wide feather bed, there was now an eruption of sheets and bedding. Where her mistress was uncommonly fastidious and neat when it came to her appearance, she now looked like a virago, all flying curls and mottled blushes.

Her first thought—outlandish as it seemed—was that father and daughter had resorted to fisticuffs. Her second, arrived at when her eyes focussed on the hanging beacon of silk, was that she had not been mistaken when she had thought she heard someone creeping about in the hallways last night.

Restless for some reason and unable to sleep, Deirdre had been returning from the scullery with warmed milk and honey when she had caught a glimpse of someone lurking in the shadows outside Catherine's room. The door to the servants' stairwell was situated at the far end of the corridor; also, it swung on hinges that sounded like the wail of a lovesick banshee. By the time Deirdre had set aside her cup of milk and hurried along the hallway to investigate, there was no one there. The door to Catherine's room, when she tried the handle, was locked and, apart from the muted crackle of the fire, there were no sounds coming from within.

Deirdre's sense of unease had remained with her as she had mounted the narrow steps to her own room, and had increased considerably when she had chanced to look out her window and had seen Lieutenant Derek Goodwin momentarily trapped in a spill of moonlight. He had been crossing the cobbled courtyard and had paused to glare up in the direction of the second-storey windows. Even through the gloom and distance, Deirdre had seen the fury on his face. He was gone a moment later, swallowed into the darker shadows by the stables, but the impression of his anger had lingered for some time.

Now, equally disturbing, was the sight of her young mistress running to the dressing room and flinging the doors wide, laughing as she threw herself into the arms of a tall, half-naked man whose face was briefly hidden behind a cloud of soft blonde hair.

"Mistress Catherine!" Deirdre gasped. And then, when Catherine turned and her lover's face was unveiled, the maid's hands flew to her mouth to stifle a further shocked cry. "Mr. Cameron!"

"Mistress O'Shea. A pleasure to see you again." Alex kept his arms wrapped securely around Catherine as he grinned at the maid. He had hurriedly donned his breeches during Sir Alfred's visit, and shrugged his shirt over his head, but the latter hung carelessly open over the rugged expanse of his chest. Deirdre looked from one glowing face to the other and needed no further explanation for the condition of the chamber or its occupant.

"A pleasure to see you, my lord. And a fine time indeed you've chosen to visit us."

"Is it true?" Catherine asked. "Is what my father said true? Has the rebel army left Manchester?"

"It's as true as when I heard it this morning," Deirdre nodded. "I came up to the room to waken you, but the door was still locked and I . . ." the wide brown eyes strayed back to Alexander's sun-bronzed features. "I'm happy to see you are safe and well, sir, what with all the stories we've been hearing. Surely . . . surely you did not cross through such dangerous country alone?"

"I am sorry to say I did. Aluinn sends his love, however. He could not be spared from my brother's services, but—" his gaze settled on the foot of the bed where the bundle of letters had been tossed. Leaving Catherine's side, he fetched the packet and put them into Deirdre's hands with a smile. "Perhaps these can tide you over until he appears here in the flesh—which could be sooner than any of us realizes if he is clever enough to put himself in the advance guard."

Deirdre stared at the bounty in her hands. Her father, a poor and uneducated Irish gameskeeper had not seen the value or purpose of sending his daughters to school to learn to read or write, but Deirdre had stubbornly plagued one of her brothers to teach her the basic rudiments. Once, during the long trek north into Scotland when fear and anger had kept her wary of Aluinn MacKail, she had seen him writing in a small leather-bound journal and she had envied his ability to set his thoughts down in such clear, precise script, seemingly without any real effort or concentration. Knowing she held pages and pages of those thoughts, written expressly for her, to her, set her pulse racing and her cheeks burning with nervous excitement.

"What shall I do?" she asked in a whisper.

"Find a quiet corner and read them," Catherine insisted.

"But . . . I should fetch more tea—"

"I am not completely helpless when it comes to finding the kitchen," said her mistress with mock indignation. "Now, away with you. I shall tend to myself and my husband, and I do not expect to see you again until you can quote every single word from every single page by heart."

Deirdre beamed her thanks and turned back toward the door, but halted after only a few steps and glanced back. "Is he well, my lord?"

"Aluinn? Fitter than I've seen him in years, benefiting immeasurably from the lack of rich foods and soft beds."

Deirdre bit her lip. "His shoulder—"

"Fully healed. My word on it. The scoundrel even managed to best me with a sword last time we practised—and won ten pounds from me in the process."

The maid flashed a misty smile and executed a quick curtsy before leaving Alex and Catherine alone again. When the door closed behind her, Alex's smile took a wry twist as he planted a kiss on the frosty blonde crown of Catherine's head. "It is truly a sad state of affairs to think what you English wenches have done to us. Although, in

Aluinn's case, I can only say it serves him right for being so damned cocksure about my own fallibility."

"Does that mean you have no regrets?" she asked, tilting her head up to bask in the warmth of his love.

"A wise old warrior once told me the only regrets we should have are for the things we have not done."

Catherine's eyes sparkled. "Your grandfather, Sir Ewen?"

"Yes. How did you know?"

"Lady Maura told me Sir Ewen Cameron was a rather remarkable old fox. She said he defied life and logic, and shamelessly took advantage of men, women, and children alike. There was something else, something about dark gods riding on his shoulders?"

"Ahh yes, the druids." Alex winked conspiratorily. "According to the story, Sir Ewen went up into the mountains one day when he was hardly more than a gillie of fifteen. A sudden storm forced him to spend the night in a cave and when he went back down the mountain, he found he had been gone a month, not a day. His clothes were torn and bloodied, though there was not a scratch to be found on him anywhere. And the sword he carried, when it was examined closely, was discovered to be nearly five hundred years old and the original property of a shadowy ancestor known only as the *Camshroinaich Dubh*—the Dark Cameron. Sir Ewen had no idea how the ancient *clai' mór* had come to be in his possession, but as the legend goes, it was said to be charmed, forged from the same steel the druids had used to make Excalibur. It was also said that no man taking the sword into battle would ever suffer personal defeat, and whether it was the sword or the legend that worked for him, the wily old fox never returned to Achnacarry anything but the victor."

"Where is it now?"

"The sword? I buried it with Sir Ewen fifteen years ago, after I used it to kill Colin and Dughall Campbell."

The statement, quietly made, sent a shiver trickling icily through Catherine's limbs. It was the first time he had ever made reference to the horrific events of that night. Had it not been for Lady Maura painfully recounting the story of Annie MacSorley's death, Catherine might never have known the origins of the demons Alex had carried around locked inside him. Unfortunately, it also gave birth to some demons of her own, namely, how to combat the memory of a woman Alex had loved with a passion as wild and boundless as his love for the Highlands themselves? There were ways of fighting the Lauren Camerons of the world, but how was one supposed to fight a ghost?

Probing for the reason behind the softly out-of-focus stare, Alexander tipped her face up to his.

"My love for Annie was special," he told her. "As special as only youth and innocence and a first stolen kiss can be. My love for you is a man's love, Catherine. You are a part of me and nothing—no man, no king, no war, no ghost—can ever come between us."

Catherine's arms went up and around his shoulders and she clung to his warmth and virility, thrilling to the feel of his lips, his hands, his heartbeat thundering against hers.

You are so right, my love, she thought in wild despair. No man, no king, no ghost is strong enough to come between us; only the indominable splendor of your honour, your pride and your passion can accomplish that.

Lochiel would remain with Charles Stuart until the end because he was a gentle and honourable man who had pledged his word to his king. Archibald Cameron would stay because he *was* a Cameron, and because his pride in his name and his clan was paramount, even to life itself. Alexander's motives were equally pure, potentially as self-destructive. He would stay with his brothers out of loyalty, fight alongside his clansmen out of pride, but if he died, it would be for Scotland, for his love of the barren, windswept moors and jagged corries he had been unable to call home for so many years and wanted so desperately to call home again. His passion was his strength, but it was also his greatest weakness.

The wolves were circling, wary of the might and presence of the kingly beasts who dared to challenge possession of the crown and so far, the lions had proved to be invincible. But should they drop their guard for an instant, or should the scavengers discover the quixotic virtue of their armour, all of the honour, pride, and passion in the world would not save them. It would, instead, cause their ultimate downfall.

Chapter Seven

It became apparent, a short while later, that Deirdre had not obeyed Catherine's orders to sequester herself with Aluinn MacKail's letters. A second knock on the bedchamber door sent the lovers scrambling again, this time to admit three burly servants, one burdened under a heavy tray of cheese, meat, and freshly baked biscuits; the other two carrying large buckets full of steaming hot water. After filling the enamel tub—careful to avoid staring too closely at the bed or the dishevelled state of the young mistress—the servants departed again. Catherine had not finished turning the key in the lock before Alex was out of the dressing room and attacking the tray of food. While he ate, she completed her own toilette, including a vigorous battle with a hairbrush, and, leaving him soaking blissfully behind a cloud of steam, she ventured out of the room to satisfy her curiosity as to exactly how many desertions had occurred amongst the staff and family.

Sir Alfred's coach had churned down the drive in a swirl of dust and gravel precisely at noon. Of the thirty-odd maids and manservants who normally accounted for the invisible workings of the manorhouse, only a handful remained at their posts. Among the valiant were Walter Brown, the skeletally thin vintner, whose nose and eyes were perpetually as red as the wines he so lovingly made and sampled twenty-four hours a day. He had insisted he would guard the buried casks and locked cellar door with his life, if necessary. Joining him in a toast to their personal bravery was John Simmonds, the head groom and a man not given to crediting humans with half the wits of the meanest plow horse. The two men shuffled awkwardly to their feet when Catherine passed through the kitchens, but she quickly set them at ease by liberating a bottle of Burgundy to take back to her rooms with her.

All the lower apartments were deserted, her footsteps the only sound as they echoed hollowly on the wooden floors. Some of the more valuable paintings and ornaments had either been removed or hidden for safekeeping at Sir Alfred's insistence. The windows were locked and the curtains drawn, as if to say that by not looking out, one could prevent anyone from coming in.

The hallways and upper rooms were quiet, the houseguests having departed along with Sir Alfred. Thinking of one guest in particular, Catherine set the bottle of wine on a credenza and delayed returning to her own chambers in favour of paying a brief visit to Lady Caroline. Her knock was answered by one of two harried maids, both of whom were in the midst of sorting and packing Lady Ashbrooke's belongings into several enormous leather trunks.

Seeing her daughter standing in the doorway and noting the puzzled look on Catherine's face, Lady Caroline dismissed the maids with a curt wave of her hand. When they were gone, she indicated a seat for Catherine on the brocade divan, although she elected to remain standing by one of the full-length windows.

"Your father told me you had refused to leave," she began, her hands nervously toying with a lace handkerchief. "Perhaps you should have reconsidered."

Catherine glanced around at the silk and satin chaos. "You seem to have."

Lady Caroline met the cool sarcasm with a faint smile. "I did not tell Alfred I was refusing to leave Rosewood Hall, only that I was refusing to leave with him."

"I see. And Captain Lovat-Spence?"

"John has ridden to Spence House to fetch a carriage. It seems Alfred needed all of ours to carry away his personal treasures."

"Then you will be leaving with the captain?"

"Yes. I'm leaving Rosewood Hall. I am also leaving your father, Catherine. For good this time."

Catherine could not help staring. Indulging in less than discreet affairs was one thing; leaving her husband and family, running off with a man ten years her junior would be the utter ruin of Caroline Penrith Ashbrooke.

"I presume you have given this careful thought," Catherine said slowly, a comment which caused her mother's brow to arch delicately.

"I have given it twenty-five years of careful thought. It has only just recently occurred to me that I do not have another twenty-five years to squander in a futile search for something I shall never have again."

Catherine looked up and Lady Caroline turned her face into the soft light from the window. She was still a very beautiful woman. Her skin was firm and unlined, her figure as lithe and trim as a young girl's. Only the eyes betrayed the years of indifference and forced laughter, the boredom and loneliness, the sadness that went far deeper than anything Catherine could comprehend.

Outwardly, I will look much the same in twenty years, Catherine thought not unhappily. Except that I will not have lived my life imprisoned in a loveless marriage. I will not have been driven to look elsewhere for affection, and I will not, ever, push my children away from me and give them into the cold hands of servants and nannies to raise. I will teach them about love and happiness by example, and they will never have cause to wonder if they were wanted, or if they were simply unpleasant consequences of marital obligations.

Startled, Catherine became aware of her mother's soft violet-gray eyes contemplating the changing expressions on her face. The smile, when it touched those oh-so-unyielding lips, was even sadder than the one in her eyes.

"We have not been very good friends over the years, have we, Catherine?" Lady Caroline asked quietly—a question which raised an embarrassed flush in her daughter's cheeks even as she lowered her lashes to guard against the unexpected sting of tears. The piece of lace suffered another series of agonized twists and turns before Lady Caroline found the strength to continue. "No. I did not think you would deny it. You may not believe this, Catherine, but I never meant it to be this way. You were my daughter, my own flesh and blood, and I wanted to love you. I wanted to. With all my heart."

Then why didn't you? Catherine wanted to ask. I was lonely, too. Lonelier than you could ever imagine. Confused. Frightened. Sick at heart because I knew you did not want me but I did not know what I had done wrong to make you hate me so! You mourn the lack of friendship? I mourn the lack of something as simple as the touch of a hand against mine.

"I am not asking for your forgiveness, Catherine. I know it is far too late for that. But not, perhaps, for a little understanding?"

"There is nothing to understand. You obviously are not happy here and never have been."

"No. But as much through my own fault as anyone else's. I made some mistakes—bad mistakes—and thought, if I paid a hefty enough price in guilt and misery, it would all balance out in the end. I was wrong. The lies just get bigger, the deceit more complicated and painful, the contempt almost harder to bear than the guilt of the original sin."

Reluctantly, Catherine met her mother's eye. Twenty-five years of confessions were wanting absolution, begging for a sympathetic ear, but did Catherine really want to hear them? Her new life was waiting down the hallway for her. Did she want shades of the old life intruding on her happiness?

Lady Caroline interpreted Catherine's silence as assent. "Please, do not misunderstand me. It is not that Alfred has been cruel or unkind to me over the years. In the beginning, I was very grateful to him for marrying me . . . for giving my son a name and permitting me to retain a respectable position in society. I suppose one of the reasons I have stayed with him this long is gratitude." She paused and gazed out the window again, and there were two soft splashes of colour on her pale cheeks. "He seemed content enough that the child was male and the Ashbrooke name would survive through another generation despite his . . . inadequacy. You see, even though he was able to prove his manhood in half the brothels of London, a disease suffered in his infancy had left Alfred incapable of siring children of his own. It was very important to him not to be the last to bear his family name —important enough that he willingly accepted another man's child as his own."

Catherine felt her face drain of all warmth. Sir Alfred was incapable of fathering children . . . *any* children.

"Damien's real father never knew about my condition. By the time I had worked up the courage to tell him, he had left London, left the country, and by the time his letter of apology reached me, explaining the need for his sudden departure . . . it was too late. My mother had already arranged for my marriage to Sir Alfred. I was here, at Rosewood Hall, and I was Lady Caroline Ashbrooke. The terror of being alone and ostracized was still too fresh in my mind and . . . and I just wasn't strong enough to tell him about me or about his child. Your grandmother Penrith replied to his letters, informing him

I was married and living in the country, and wanted nothing more to do with the wastrel and scoundrel he had become."

Lady Caroline's face tilted upward, her gaze focussed softly on a cloud drifting out across the open fields.

"It was five years before I saw him again, purely by accident." She stopped and smiled suddenly, wistfully. "He'd halted our coach to rob it."

"Rob it!" Catherine gasped. "He was a . . ." She couldn't say it. Could hardly dare to acknowledge it.

"He was wild and handsome," Lady Caroline said. "Free as the wind and possessing the same inability to remain content in one place for any length of time. Being with him was like being blown off the peak of a mountain and not knowing if you were ever going to land, or if you did, whether you would land in one piece. He frightened me with his talk of freedom and his reckless, careless approach to responsibility. How could I possibly have fit into his life? How could he have guaranteed his children a home and a safe future when he could not even assure his own?"

Plural, Catherine thought. "Children?" she asked in a whisper.

"It was wrong of me to do so, I know, but I agreed to meet with him. I . . . couldn't *not* agree," she added helplessly, and the pain in her voice caused the ice around Catherine's heart to melt in a rush. Two lovers reuniting after so many years apart: Her own experience still achingly fresh, Catherine could no more condemn her mother's actions than she could her own.

"He wanted me to leave England with him," Lady Caroline whispered. "Run with me, he said. Be free with me. Our love will keep us safe and warm and happy. But I did not think . . . I still could not tell him about his son . . . and I *had* to think about Damien, about the effect on his life, our life . . . *my* life. I was Lady Caroline Ashbrooke and I had barely managed to survive through one hurricane intact; I did not think I could suffer through the uncertainty of another. The fear turned to anger—anger that he had managed to keep his easy, reckless grasp on life while I . . . I had born the shame and the guilt and the loss alone. In my anger and bitterness I rejected him again. I sent him away. And . . . months later, when I bore him a second child, I transferred my anger and my resentment to her."

Catherine was staring at her mother, shock keeping her outwardly frozen to her seat on the divan, but inwardly, her heart feeling as if it might burst from her chest.

"Alfred, naturally, was outraged. He threatened to expose the whole sordid affair and only an equally contemptuous threat from me, regarding his impotence and the effect a scandal of this magnitude would have on his political aspirations, kept him silent. How long the years seem when they are endured in silence! How endless the days and cold the nights, especially when your body aches and burns with the memory of past passion! Alfred had his politics and his brothels to keep him satisfied; I had an empty house, a son who grew more and more into the image of his father, and a daughter in whom I could not bear to see the same fierce spirit as possessed by the love I had thrown away. I took lovers into my bed, one after another, hoping to dull the pain and dim the memories. The loneliness always came back, however, stronger than before, each time I looked into your eyes and saw in them the woman I might have been."

Her laugh was as raw as the sound of tearing lace. "Imagine my relief when I thought I had finally managed to see you safely wed and out of this house. And imagine the agony of seeing you come back, looking the way a woman can only look when she has found true and utter bliss within herself. You were glowing with the wonder of newfound love, Catherine. It was radiating from you then as it still is now, as if you had just come from your lover's bed an hour ago."

Catherine stood and took two halting steps toward her mother, but before she could speak, or even reach out in a gesture of empathy, Lady Caroline had regained her composure and hardened herself against any pity that might be forthcoming.

"As soon as Captain Spence returns with the carriage, I . . . we will be leaving this place. Arranging his affairs will take several weeks, during which time I shall be a guest at Spence House. He informs me he has land in the colonies—in New England—and seems quite convinced we can be very happy there."

Catherine swallowed past the lump in her throat. "What do you think?"

"I think . . . I think if I do not go this time, I may never have the chance again."

"Do you love him?"

Lady Caroline frowned and dashed at the tears that still streaked her cheeks. "He makes me laugh. He makes me feel . . . wanted."

"But . . . do you love him?" Catherine asked again, softly.

The shining violet-gray eyes turned slowly to hers. "I will only ever love one man, Catherine. Only one."

"Then why not go to him, or at least try to find him?"

Lady Caroline smiled ruefully. "The life expectancy of a highwayman is not exactly encouraging. I do not even know if he is still alive. The last I heard of Jacques St. Cloud, he had returned permanently to France, but even if I knew where to look, or under which name to begin to search for him, catching up to him would be—as the authorities have discovered these many long years—like trying to catch the wind. No, my memories will have to suffice. And who knows—perhaps Captain Spence and I will be able to make some new ones."

"Will I see you again before you sail for the colonies?"

Lady Caroline seemed briefly taken aback. "You would want to see me again? After all I have told you?"

"All you have told me, Mother, is that you are human, and very much in need of a friend. I should like to be that friend, if you will let me."

Trembling, Lady Caroline raised a hand and laid it gently on her daughter's cheek.

Catherine was deep in thought as she made her way along the deserted hallway. She stopped to retrieve the bottle of wine from the table where she had left it, then proceeded to her bedroom, unlocked the door, and entered the room as if she was moving in a trance. She had been given a great deal to absorb in the last half hour. Sir Alfred was not her father. Her blood had not descended through the veins of a dozen generations of Ashbrookes, but from a highwayman and scoundrel who periodically terrorized the English countryside before disappearing back to his lair in France. Jacques St. Cloud. Was he still alive, still playing the roguish bandit as Lady Caroline wanted to believe, or had he died years ago, his neck stretched on a gibbet like a common thief?

"Catherine? Is something wrong?"

She looked over at her husband, a man guilty of treason, murder, and espionage in the eyes of the law. She had more in common with her mother than either of them realized.

"Catherine?"

"What? Oh, no. No, nothing is wrong. I've just come from seeing my mother. She is in the middle of packing . . ."

"Packing?" Alexander relaxed back against the support of the tub and lifted his hand away from the cocked pistol he had placed within easy reach on the table beside him. "I thought she was adamant about staying at Rosewood Hall?"

"She is running away with Captain Lovat-Spence. He has just arrived now with the carriage."

Alex's hand paused mid-way to raising a thin black cigar to his lips. "You don't seem to be too upset at the news."

"I'm sure she will be happy with Captain Lovat-Spence; she says he makes her laugh."

Wary of his glaring lack of understanding as to how a woman's mind functioned, Alex frowned and drew deeply on his cigar. Spying the bottle of wine in Catherine's hand, his face brightened. "Are you just going to stand there tempting me, or did you bring glasses as well?"

"I can see you are feeling much better now that your belly is full and your skin is wrinkled. How long do you plan to stay in that tub?"

"Until I am given a good reason to get out," he said, his gaze roving down to where her breasts strained against the bodice of her robe. "No one thought it odd you were wandering around the house in the middle of the day in your bedclothes?"

"This robe happens to cover more than some of the gowns I own," she countered tartly. "As for anyone noticing, I should think you could rouse more attention by shooting a cannon down the halls, but not much. I counted only five people on the grounds, not including Deirdre or my mother and her maids. You will be happy to know Cook was one of the ones who stayed, although I am not surprised. She has developed such an appreciation of her own talents over the years, she can barely waddle from one room to the next without resting."

"You will hear nothing contradictory from me about her talents," Alex grinned, indicating the tray of food that had been swabbed clean of the tiniest crumb.

Catherine poured out a glassful of wine and handed it to him. "The groom stayed, but there are only two horses in the stables; one of them a mare in foal."

"Mmmm. Would he object to an extra guest for a few days?"

"Shadow?"

Alex nodded. "I left him with a smithy about a mile or two from here, but I don't imagine he is too pleased, or behaving himself very well."

"Then by all means, we should fetch him home." Catherine took a sip of wine before her eyes rose to meet her husband's over the rim of the glass. "Did you say what I think you just said? A few days?"

"Maybe more, depending on how long the Prince decides to accept your father's generous offer of hospitality."

"The Prince? Here? At Rosewood Hall?"

"He has to sleep somewhere, doesn't he? At the very least, his officers will require billetting—" the rest of what he said was muffled under a pair of soft and deliriously overjoyed lips.

He was staying! A day, two days, three days . . . it did not matter exactly how long, only that he was not planning to leave in the next twelve hours, as originally announced. Of course, Sir Alfred would pass a kidney stone when he heard the Jacobites were camped on the grounds of Rosewood Hall. He would pass another when he heard his wife had run off with another man, his daughter was playing hostess to the renegade Stuart Prince, and his son . . . What was his son playing at?

"Alex?" She leaned against the side of the tub and trailed her fingers over the milky surface of the water. "Exactly what part has my brother played in all this? Was he really just Raefer Montgomery's friend, or was—*is* he something more?"

He caught up her hand and kissed the wet fingertips. "What makes you think he is anything more than a friend?"

"The look on your face, for one thing."

The roving lips paused a fraction of a second too long. "Not exactly grounds for a conviction."

"Not the only evidence against him either," she said evenly.

"Do you think you know something, or are you just guessing?"

"Both," she replied, exchanging her wine glass for the bar of soap. "I never did feel absolutely comfortable with his performance that night at Wakefield. Damien would never have ridden away and entrusted me into your hands if he did not know precisely who you were, where you were going, and why you were going there. Moreover, he would have had to have known how important it was for you to reach Achnacarry with the information you had collected for your brother. In order to know that, he would have had to either know what some of the information was, or . . . sympathize with the urgency of seeing it reach the proper hands."

The indigo eyes narrowed as he felt her fingertips, slippery with lather, begin to knead the ridge of muscles across his shoulders. "You realize what you are suggesting?"

"My brother is a Jacobite," she said softly, unsure herself as to how she should react now that the words had finally been spoken out loud. "Furthermore . . . he was involved, if not outright responsible for providing you with the information for Lochiel." Her hands stopped suddenly and she stared at the gleaming wet shanks of black hair before her. "He was the one you came to Derby to see in the first place, wasn't he? He was the mysterious 'Colonel' who gave you the information about the army's state of readiness; the numbers and locations of the troops in England. He is still giving you that information, isn't he? That was why you went to see him in London, and that was how he came to know so much about what had gone on in the rebel camp. He's a spy. A Jacobite spy."

"All this supposition from a look on my face? You are leaping ahead of yourself, aren't you?"

"He called you *Alex.*"

The dark eyes flickered sardonically. "By all means, hang the bastard."

"At the inn in Wakefield," she said shrewdly. "He made you swear to guard my safety with your life—and he called you *Alex*. Rather too familiar for someone who has just discovered the duplicity of a supposed friend he had known only as Raefer Montgomery."

"Very clever, Mistress Sleuth. What else do you think you know?"

Catherine pursed her lips thoughtfully. "Damien said the reward for your capture has been doubled."

"Damien talks too damned much."

"He also believes an assassin has been hired to track you down and kill you."

Alexander drew a deep breath to control his temper. "Your brother is going to have a few very unpleasant moments when I see him again. He had no business frightening you with rumours that so far haven't proved to hold a shred of truth."

"He was only trying to protect you . . . and warn me, I imagine. Hired killers do that sort of thing, don't they—go after the families of the intended victims in order to gain a hostage?"

Alex reached around, cradling her face between his hands and holding her within the intense blue depths of his eyes.

"You are completely safe here. No one in Lochaber knows who you are, or where you came from, much less where you went after I put you on the *Curlew*. In fact, as far as anyone at home is concerned—in particular the Campbells and their ilk—you never left Scotland. You are still at Achnacarry Castle and can be seen frequently enough to prove it."

"I don't understand," she said, puzzled.

"It was Maura's idea. Just a precaution. She suggested we find a local girl who resembled you enough from a distance to fool anyone watching the castle. My 'wife' appears at the windows now and then, in the gardens, on the battlements. She is always under heavy guard, of course, but then, what decent mercenary would expect anything other than absolute protection?" He smoothed his hands down her arms and smiled. "Like I said, it is just a precaution. It isn't you the Campbells are interested in; it's me."

He was lying, Catherine decided. There was something out there that worried both men—she had seen it in Damien's eyes the other day in the woods, she saw in Alexander's now.

"Does this girl know the risk she is taking?"

"She isn't taking any risk," Alex insisted. "She is, on the contrary, enjoying an extravagant vacation away from the cornfields at my expense. She is in no danger, and neither are you—except perhaps from me, if you persist in questioning my good intentions."

Catherine regarded him coolly and resumed gliding her fingers over the sleek, hard surface of his shoulders. She let them trail down onto his chest, onto the glittering wet mat of curling black hair, and the distraction pulled her gaze away from his. Awed that she never failed to uncover something new, some minute detail she had overlooked on her last voyage of discovery, she traced her fingertips over and around a small, crescent-shaped birthmark seated just above his right nipple. Dark strawberry in colour, it was obliterated under a film of soap lather, and reminded her of a Highland moon rendered opaque behind a veil of moorland mist.

Other discoveries had not roused such pleasant images —a new scar over his ribs, another at his waist, a myriad of small healed cuts and scrapes on his arms and legs, and the deep gouge over his left ear . . .

"You have that look of wifely concern on your face again," he chided gently.

Catherine lifted her eyes slowly to meet his. She did not answer, but leaned forward instead to brush her lips over his cleanly shaven cheek. Before she could safely retreat, his hand was firmly around her wrist.

"My concerns, sir, are for the condition of my robe, which has rather more soap and water on it than I would prefer it to have."

His eyes gleamed speculatively at the froth of rich lace which fashioned the collar and deep front plackett.

"Easily enough remedied," he mused, reaching over to unfasten the satin sash. A further gentle tug saw the dressing gown ripple to the floor, and, with a suggestive tilt of his eyebrow, he extended an invitation to join him in the tub.

"There isn't room for two," she said on a breathless laugh.

"Depends how friendly you care to be," he murmured and drew her forward.

"Wait," she pleaded, standing and walking naked to the dressing room. She emerged seconds later, her hair twisted into a golden coil and pinned haphazardly on the crown of her head. Still looking dubious, she stepped into the water and permitted his hands to guide her down so that her back was cushioned comfortably against his chest. His knees made equally passable armrests—wickedly wonderful ones, in fact, especially since the slightest move brought the coarse texture of his thighs in contact with her breasts.

Cupping his hands, Alex carried water up to her shoulders, leaving them sparkling like white marble. The wisps of hair straggling down her neck turned the colour of dark honey and clung to her skin in slithery ribbons. His lips planted a row of kisses across her nape, his tongue triggered shivers of sensation from her shoulders to the delicate pink lobes of her ears.

With soap in hand, Alex worked up a rich lather and began massaging it over the smooth flesh, taking deliberate care to seek out the nooks and hollows he knew to be the most susceptible to the warm, slippery strokes. He lavished attention on each supple arm, attended each nerveless finger with a fastidiousness that soon turned her breathing shallow and dry.

Anticipating where his hands would venture next, Catherine braced herself for the shock of feeling the long, tapered fingers glide up along her ribcage and mold themselves around the sleek fullness of her breasts. The dark fingers on her skin were a bold contrast, the strength of them seeming to promise pain rather than arouse pleasure, but how delicate he touched, stroked, teased, caressed . . . as if his hands were made of velvet.

She gripped the edges of the tub as the tangled knot of desire tightened within her; her nipples swelled and tautened and rose like tiny mountain peaks through the foaming whitecaps of soap. The tension began to build and coil, to twist inward and outward, settling finally and insistently as a throbbing tremor between her thighs. Despite the obvious temptation to pursue those tremors, Alex lingered over the round, plump mounds of her breasts, ignoring the convulsive shivers that wracked her slender body until they became violent enough to disrupt the placid surface of the water.

Adjusting their positions slightly, Alex dipped his hands lower, moving them with delicious precision from her breasts to her waist to her hips, then sliding them soapily around to the soft triangle of tawny blonde curls. Catherine tensed as his fingers traced slow, languid circles on her inner thighs; she shivered and gasped for breath each time a thumb rasped with cat-like stealth over flesh almost too sensitive to bear the torment.

"You are splashing water all over the floor," Alex chided, his lips pressed to her ear. "What *will* the servants think?"

Before she could form an answer, his fingers curled into the quivering petals of flesh, bringing her head arching back against his shoulder. His questing strokes became more intimate, more determined as his fingers probed and darted between the silky creases, touching, testing, manipulating her to within a breath of release, only to retreat and leave her trembling on the brink of ecstasy.

Catherine did not know where to look, what to do with her hands, what further torment her body could endure without bursting and splintering into a thousand fragments. She was afloat in a dark world of flesh, aware of every touch and stroke, feeling every soft vibration within and without. She wanted to laugh, she wanted to cry. She wanted to plunge over the precipice and experience the spiralling pleasure of sensual madness, but she was at the mercy of his fingertips, and they had learned their skills from the Devil himself.

Again and again he probed and taunted, withdrawing when it seemed she was but a tremor away from oblivion, returning again when the immediate danger passed. Water sloshed over the enamel lip of the tub, some of it spattering as far as the logs burning brightly in the grate. The crackle and hiss of exploding droplets found a sympathetic response in Catherine as her passion grew hotter and more volatile, threatening to turn the water to steam where it lapped against her scorched flesh.

Bold and hungry, Alex's own need strained against the pliant roundness of her buttocks, his condition not alleviated in the least by the erotic motion of her hips and thighs rubbing against him. He wanted desperately to lift her from the restrictive confines of the tub—his own damned idea, he recalled with chagrin—to share the pleasure he could feel tearing her apart, but it was already far too late.

Cursing softly, he ran his fingers into the warm, sleek haven he had prepared so well, groaning as he felt the throbbing tightness close around him like the lash of a silken whip. His free hand slid up to her breasts, but they were still coated with a film of soap and the nipples slipped and slithered out of his fingers like well-oiled pearls.

For Catherine, the combined sensations were too much to bear. A moan rushed from her lips and a sheet of water was startled out over the carpet and floor as she writhed and gasped and twisted in an agony of pleasure. The pressure of his fingertips chased each shiver, isolated each spasm, prolonged each eruptive contraction until it convulsed into the next and the next. He urged her through wave after wave of consuming ecstasy as if he was there inside, sharing her exaltation, and when her cries began to diminish to whimpers, he continued to hold her, to ease her gently through the successive little tremors that brought her drifting back to reality.

Was it minutes or hours before she could think or see clearly again? She was dimly aware of his lips nuzzling the curve of her shoulder, of his hands rinsing the last traces of soap from her skin. Her breasts were still flushed and rosy, her limbs weak, her belly fluttering, quaking from the force and power of the tumult he had released within her. She could feel the pounding of his heart against her back and she could see his hands were not as steady as they might be.

"How," she demanded in a dry rasp, "am I supposed to ever look at a bed or a bathtub again without dying of absolute mortification?"

"That was the idea," he murmured. "And we still have the floors, the walls, the tables—" A soft gust of laughter tickled her nape. "And I know this delicious little trick of painting warmed brandy on—"

"Nevermind," she croaked, and reached a wobbly hand for her wine glass. She drained it thirstily, the wine feeling smooth and mellow as it travelled down her throat, sweet and regenerative as it sent a blush of warmth through her veins. Too weak to bother setting the glass back on the low footstool, she let it dangle limply from her fingers as she leaned back against the wall of muscle, her lips parting on a deep-felt sigh of contentment.

Alex steered her chin around and angled her mouth up to his. The kiss was bold and firm, and she suspected his own needs were still far from satisfied. Her eyes opened slowly, dreamily, and after a moment, when he became aware of their scrutiny, he gave her lips a final, lavish caress, and released them.

"There it is again," he commented wryly. "The look of wifely concern."

"Oh Alex, laugh at me if you like, but how I wish I could keep you locked in this room and never let you go. I wish . . . I wish—" her eyes widened, the violet darkening and coming alive with a sudden flare of excitement. "Alex . . . why can't you take me with you? You said there were women in the camp; wives, lovers—"

"No," he said, cutting her off abruptly. "Absolutely not."

"But *why* not? You said you missed me dreadfully and worried about me constantly. Lord knows, I have missed you and been half out of my mind wondering if I would ever see you again. If I was with you—"

"No."

"If I was with you," she continued emphatically, splashing more water over the rim of the tub as she half-turned to face him, "I could at least see you occasionally and know you were safe. I would not have to live with this terrible fear of losing you."

"You are not going to lose me," he said firmly. "And you are not going to change my mind, no matter what weapons you bring into play against me."

He was referring to the bright film of tears collecting on her lashes, and, confronted by his implacably cold eyes, Catherine's shoulders slumped in dejection.

"Do you really think me such a helpless weakling?" she asked miserably.

"I don't know where you got that idea. You are neither weak, nor helpless. Stubborn, perhaps, but not helpless."

"I'm not stubborn," she said stubbornly. "I'm just tired of feeling useless. Besides, you are my husband; I should be with you."

"No."

"You still think I would fall apart if I had to forgo the silks and satins and comfortable feather beds . . . but I wouldn't. I would not miss any of this for a moment, not if I was with you. I would not complain either. Not ever."

Alex said nothing, but it was easy enough to read the disbelief etched into his humourless smile.

"The dreams would stop too," she whispered. "I know they would."

"What dreams?"

Catherine bit down on her lip. She had not meant to tell him about her recurring nightmare, certainly not like this when he would assume it was merely another ploy to win his sympathy.

"Just . . . dreams," she said, and put her hands on the edge of the tub in order to stand up.

"What dreams?" he asked again, tilting her chin toward him, forcing her to meet his gaze once more.

"Terrible dreams," she admitted with a shiver. "Horrible dreams. I have them and I wake up crying . . . frightened half to death . . . screaming sometimes. They are always the same, they never change—not in the way they begin, anyway. Only the endings get longer and longer; I see more and more each time and I can't stop it. I can't wake myself up or change the way anything happens."

She shivered again and Alex wrapped his arms around her. Feeling the chill sweeping through her body, he stood and lifted her out of the cooling water, bundling her in one of the huge, thirsty towels that had been left to warm before the fire. Her skin had turned the colour of ashes and he rubbed vigorously, trying to chafe some heat into her flesh. All the while, she stood mute and docile, her eyes downcast, her hands balled into tight, defensive little fists.

When he had dried her and wrapped her in a fresh towel, he settled her into a large wing chair, which he dragged to the hearth. He added a handful of kindling and two enormous logs to the fire and within moments it was blazing, causing the moisture on his own skin to steam dry. Satisfied with his efforts, he brushed the wood scraps off his hands and scooped Catherine into his arms once again, taking her place on the chair and keeping her cradled, towel and all, in his lap.

"Now, tell me about these dreams."

Catherine shook her head and buried her face against the curve of his shoulder.

"It is not uncommon for wives to have nightmares when their husbands are away fighting a war," he said soothingly. "But that's all they are: nightmares."

"No." She shook her head again vigorously and clasped her hands around his neck, her voice so muffled he could barely decipher the words. "It started before I even knew there was a chance of you going off to fight. It started before I even knew I would *care* about you going off to fight. Do you remember the day we stopped by the gorge? The day we were attacked by the Black Watch and Aluinn was shot by Gordon Ross Campbell? Well . . . that was the first time it happened. We were having our lunch and the sun was shining and the day was warm and peaceful and there was so much beauty around us—" she lifted her head from his shoulder and Alex experienced a genuine jolt of alarm when he saw her eyes. They were dark and shimmering, seeming to stare straight through him, the centres enlarged so that barely more than a rim of violet remained. "It was only a brief flash—like someone lifting a curtain and allowing a glimpse into another room. I did not even know what I was seeing, or who I was seeing, but it was so real. I cut my finger on a knife . . . do you remember?"

"I remember," he said, feeling a tickle, like the dragging filament of a spider's web, across the nape of his neck. He was not a superstitious man, nor had he ever given credence to the old crones and ancients said to possess the *sicht*. Alexander Cameron did not believe in visions or omens, did not believe in any power but that of his own making. He was about to say as much to Catherine when she began to speak again, her voice low and inky, as if being drawn from a deep, dark well.

"I'm standing in the middle of a field. A huge field, littered with bodies. Hundreds of bodies! There are men fighting all around me, blocking my way, and I am trying to push my way through them, but they cannot see me. It's as if I'm not really there, yet I *am* there, and I am running. I run and I run but . . . I'm not moving. Everything else is—the clouds of mist and smoke, the trees . . . horses . . . men . . . even the ground is shaking because of the cannon shells. And . . . there is blood everywhere." Her voice faltered to a whisper and she slowly withdrew her hands from around his neck and stared at them in horror. "My hands are covered with it. It is raining and the blood is pink on my skin, but it won't wash away—there is too much of it."

"Catherine, stop. It's alright. You're here with me now; it's alright."

"No. No, I have to find you. I have to tell you—" she drew a sharp breath and sucked the terror inward. She stared at the bright flare of light coming in through the bedroom window, but the horror she was seeing was too shocking to put into words. "There," she gasped. "On the hill. You're fighting the soldiers—ten, twelve, maybe more, I don't know, but they are all around you, closing in a circle and they have their swords raised! I scream and you look around . . . but it's too late! You try to fight them off, but there are too many, and your arm . . . oh God, Alex, *your arm*!"

Alex struck her, swiftly and sharply across the cheek, cutting off a shrill scream of hysteria. She gasped and flinched from the quick sting of pain, and for a moment, looked as if she might strike back in rage. In the next instant, she seemed to grasp hold of the reality that she was not on the battlefield, and she crumpled into Alex's arms, the sobs wracking her slender body with great, heaving convulsions. Alexander held her desperately close, sick at heart for having raised a hand against her, stunned in mind and body over the extent of her fear.

"Alex please . . . please take me with you!"

He closed his eyes. "Catherine—"

"If you leave me, I know I will never see you again. You will never come back. Everything will happen, just like in the dream, only I won't be there to warn you!"

"Nothing is going to happen!" he declared fiercely. "It's a dream, Catherine, a nightmare! Nothing is going to happen to me, nothing is going to happen to you!"

"But . . . it is so real," she cried, her eyes round and wet, her lips trembling beneath the hail of kisses he assaulted her with in order to try to calm her.

"It only *seems* real," he insisted. "Because you're worried about me. And I love you for worrying about me, only . . ." he took her face into his hands and there was as much desperation in his eyes as there was fear in hers. "Only please don't ask me to do something I can't do. If I took you back with me and something—*anything* happened to you, however trivial or small: a cut, a scrape, a *hangnail*, by God! I would never forgive myself. Can you understand that, Catherine? Can you understand how important it is for me to know you are safe, regardless of the madness going on in the rest of the world?"

Catherine allowed herself to be drawn forward, allowed her lips, her very breath to be plundered by the savagery of his embrace. His hands raked up into her hair, scattering the steel pins as he freed the golden cascade and brought it streaming forward over her shoulders. Strong, determined arms lifted her then and carried her to the bed where she was not permitted to speak again, not permitted a single thought beyond the ecstasy of their union.

And when, at last, they drifted together into a passion-drugged sleep, Alex held her molded against his body, refusing to surrender to his own exhaustion until he was assured of her calm and easy breathing.

"Just a dream," he muttered thickly, as if to purge her sleeping form of any final, lingering doubt. Yet despite his own firm denials of any basis for her fears, he found himself dreaming of a battlefield, of men screaming and dying all around him, and of a woman with bright yellow hair running toward him . . .

Chapter Eight

If asked, Deirdre O'Shea would not have admitted to believing in omens or incidents of precognition either, but privately she crossed herself and spat over her shoulder if a black cat strayed across her path, and she was equally quick to recite an ancient Celtic homily if the wind was heard to whisper certain words. She was Irish and the caution was in her blood. That was why, as she stood before the fireplace, she found herself staring at an ominous configuration formed by a chance spill of charred wood and ash.

The image of a man's and woman's bodies twined together —not in life but in death—was dismissed in the wink of an eye as Catherine emerged from her dressing room, her arms burdened under a shiny mountain of rich, lustrous satin.

"Oh mistress, I . . . I couldn't possibly—"

"Nonsense. You can wear it and you will. The gown was purchased with a wedding in mind, and I can think of no one else I would rather see wear it."

Earlier in the day, the unearthly silence that had enveloped Rosewood Hall for two days, had been shattered when a group of armed Highlanders had ridden up the packed-earth lane. Alex had been expecting them. When he and Catherine had gone to retrieve Shadow, they had learned the Prince's vanguard was less than five miles out of Derby. Alex had escorted Catherine back to the Ashbrooke estate, and then had immediately ridden out to meet the advancing rebel column to extend their invitation of hospitality to the Cameron contingent. Many of the neighbouring estates were being visited by emissaries from the rebel army and told they could expect to provide quarters for large contingents of men. It would not draw an inordinate amount of suspicion for Rosewood Hall, as one of the largest estates in the parish, to play host to one of the largest rebel clans.

The Prince would be taking quarters in Derby itself, in a house belonging to Lord Exeter. The townspeople for the most part, had respected the orders of the powerful Cavendish family and had evacuated to the country, leaving hardly anyone to bear witness to Charles Stuart's triumphant march into the city on the fourth day of December.

Determined to make Alex proud of her, Catherine wore one of her best gowns and served her father's best cordials to the blustery group of Highlanders who gathered in the formal parlour of Rosewood Hall. She was genuinely pleased to greet her brothers-in-law again. To Donald Cameron, the Chief of Clan Cameron, she had at first offered a reserved welcome, but his honest pleasure at seeing her again soon put her at ease and she ended up hugging him with as much enthusiasm as her tightly laced stomacher would allow. Dr. Archibald Cameron, looking strangely disoriented without Jeannie, his firebrand of a wife by his side, completed the crushing damage to Catherine's ribs, leaving her barely enough breath to greet the friendly faces of Aluinn MacKail and Struan MacSorley.

Aluinn, in turn, scarcely waited for Lochiel to brush the dust of the road off his clothes before he was presenting himself and Deirdre to the Chief with a formal request.

"Ye're askin' ma permission tae marry, are ye?" Lochiel had asked, his pale blue eyes twinkling merrily as he regarded the solemn couple standing before him. "Aye, MacKail, I can see ye have the fever on ye. But what about ye, lass? Can ye no' think o' anither lad ye'd rather spend the rest o' yer days and nights with?"

Deirdre had managed to tear her gaze away from the imposing, tartan-clad chieftain long enough to exchange a searching glance with Aluinn.

"No, my lord. In truth, I could not think of another single soul who could make me happier."

Donald Cameron of Lochiel had stepped forward then and taken their hands into his. "In that case, ye have ma most hearty blessing, happily given. Aye, and what's mair," he added with a wink, "ye should see tae it soon, f'ae I've a notion the Irish and Scots blood, once mixed, will show an impatience tae bring fine, healthy bairns intae the world."

Deirdre's blush had darkened furiously when Lochiel's comment prompted both Alexander and Archibald Cameron to suggest a minister be fetched that very day to make the vows legal. Catherine had agreed and, meeting with no objections from either party, had whisked Deirdre out of the parlour and led her up the stairs to her bedchamber.

Now, Deirdre stood nervously watching her mistress return again and again from the dressing room, her arms laden with silk stockings, chemises, and frilly underpinnings that, as a maid, Deirdre had felt privileged just to touch, let alone wear. Bewildered, she saw the bounty pile up on the bed, and, stunned, she obeyed Catherine's crisp orders to strip out of her own drab black gabardine frock and indulge in a hot, perfumed bath.

After Deirdre had dried herself before the fire, Catherine took it upon herself to heat the curling irons and crimping tongs and set about coaxing the chestnut waves into corkscrew side-curls, heavy ringlets, and a becoming fringe of dark twists to frame the heart-shaped face. Impressed with her own proficiency, Catherine added tiny silk flowerets, irreverently plucked from the flounces of one of her other gowns and woven here and there among the shiny curls. A discreet amount of khol was applied to highlight Deirdre's already large and expressive eyes; ash and charcoal were brushed onto her lashes to darken and thicken them.

Tolerant of the girl's need to halt after every addition and study her reflection in the mirror, Catherine acted the part of maid, helping Deirdre into sheer white stockings, silk chemise, and a lace underbodice with a regal spill of scalloped falling cuffs. A stiffened buckram stomacher was laced tightly around Deirdre's midsection, altering her figure into the fashionable hour-glass shape, further emphasized by the addition of wire panniers that sat on the hips like overturned baskets. Three billowing layers of fine linen petticoats were fitted over the panniers, the top one quilted and embroidered with tiny seed pearls where it would show through the opened vee of the skirt. Over the stomacher, the snug, busked bodice molded to the shape of Deirdre's waist like a pearlized outer skin; the cloud of silvered satin that was the skirt settled into place with a shimmering sigh.

"Oh," was all Deirdre could manage to say as she stood before the cheval mirror, transfixed by the fairytale image. "I never dreamed . . ."

"A girl's wedding day should be remembered the rest of her life," Catherine said, biting back regrets about her own hastily conducted service. What she had been denied, however, she was determined to provide for Deirdre in a display of selflessness that most surely would have baffled her six months ago. Dressing an abigail in silk and satin, turning her home upside down for a clan of rebelling Scotsmen, rushing here and there like a headless chicken to see to everyone's needs but her own . . .

A knock interrupted Catherine's thoughts just as she was about to grip the newel post of the bed for her turn at the corset stays.

"May I come in?"

It was Alexander's voice, and it earned a muttered oath from Catherine before she answered.

"Yes, but if you have come to complain, or to seek my help in tying your cravat, I . . ." She stopped, her gaze fixed upon the resplendent figure standing in the doorway.

Once before, the very first time she had had occasion to see Alexander Cameron in full Highland dress, she had been stunned speechless. The hairs on her neck had stood on end and her belly had gone all weak and fluttery, as if her insides were dissolving down to her knees. The same melting weakness came over her now as she straightened from the bedpost and stared at her husband.

The black, windswept mane had been tamed by shears and fettered with a narrow velvet ribbon. A shock of white lace at his throat underlined the ruggedness of his chiselled features and made a mockery of the pale-skinned, powdered dandies who had, until their exodus a few days ago, graced the corridors of Rosewood Hall. A long-skirted waistcoat of purple satin hugged his massive upper torso, topped by a frockcoat of hunting green velvet, the deep cuffs and lapels banded and embroidered in gold. From his waist hung the gathered and pleated folds of the crimson-and-black tartan that formed the short breacan kilt. A length of plaid was draped crosswise over his chest, pinned at the shoulder with an enormous brooch studded with topazes. A sporan—a pouch made of soft animal hide—hung from his waist; a wide leather belt, chased with gold and silver ornamentation, held his rapier, the tip of which fell to within an inch of the floor. His calves were encased in hose of dark scarlet fretting, his brogues were leather, buckled in steel; his smile, when it stole across the saturnine face, was pure vintage rogue.

"A fetching outfit, I must say," he mused, his teeth flashing whitely as his eyes—so dark a blue as to be almost black—raked up and down his wife's scantily clad body. "But a tad shy on decorum, wouldn't you say?"

"Beast," Catherine muttered, glancing down at her skimpy chemise, corset, and stockings. "I am not even the one you should be looking at."

"Since when?"

"Since—" she had to give Deirdre a slight shove to stir the girl out from behind the obstructing view of the curtains on the tester bed. "Since Mistress O'Shea finished dressing."

Deirdre stood for what felt like an eternity, a hot blush colouring her cheeks as she stared steadfastly down at the floor. Only when she saw the toes of Alexander's shoes come into her line of view, and felt the pressure of his hand beneath her chin, did she dare look up.

"It is no wonder the man has been driven to writing volumes of poetry lately," he said softly. "You look absolutely beautiful, Deirdre. Aluinn is a very lucky man."

"Thank you, my lord," she whispered. "It was all Mistress Catherine's doing."

The knowing eyes flicked over to his wife and Catherine felt the skin tauten across her breasts. His gaze released her after a long moment and returned to Deirdre.

"Why don't you go to him? The poor bastard is pacing up and down the halls like a caged tiger."

"Absolutely not!" Catherine cried, countermanding the suggestion. "She is to wait in the winter parlour until just before the ceremony. I'll not have all my hard work undone by an overeager groom. Deirdre . . . to the winter parlour. I shall join you there in a few minutes."

"Yes, my lady," Deirdre said, smiling as she presented a curtsy to Alex and went gliding past him out the door.

"A very few minutes, I hope," Alex mused, moving in congenially to take up the task of lacing his wife's stomacher. "A crueller torture could not be imagined, madam, than to toy with the olfactory senses of men who have had little more than oatcakes and salted porridge for the past few weeks. Archibald has already mounted one attack on the kitchens and was, reportedly, driven off at knifepoint. He is arming himself with reinforcements as we speak, and I fear a full scale assault within the hour. On the other hand—" he considered the smooth white expanse of her shoulder for a moment before lowering his mouth for a closer sampling, "a lesson in patience would do them all good."

It was difficult enough to hold one's breath and concentrate on sucking every rib and excess ounce of flesh inward while one was being girdled into the latest tortures of fashion. It proved to be impossible with the added pressure of a hungry pair of lips exploring the nape of her neck.

"Alex . . . I must get dressed."

"I like you the way you are," he murmured, flicking the tip of his tongue into the delicate pink curl of her ear.

"Alex," she moaned softly. "Stop. Your brother—"

"My brother is a most understanding man."

She batted his hands away as he began pulling the steel pins and combs from her hair, but he persisted, eventually spinning her around and gathering her into his arms for a kiss that seemed to never end. When it did, she gaped up at him, dazed and gasping, her pulse racing and her heart beating a tattoo against her ribs.

"There," he mused, dropping the last of the troublesome pins to the floor and combing his fingers through the silky tangle of her hair. "This is much better. More like the wild and wanton temptress I've been keeping company with these past few days. Besides, I'll be double damned if I let Aluinn win all the envy tonight."

"You are incorrigible," Catherine laughed.

"So you keep insisting." His hands slipped lower, easing the shoulders of her chemise halfway down her arms as they went. But before his lips could erode her senses any further, Catherine wriggled out of his embrace and moved a safer distance away, beyond the long reach of his arms.

"You would not want to be late for your best friend's wedding, would you?"

His smile suggested he might.

"I suppose I should have inquired as to the number of guests Donald has invited. I hope there will be enough food."

"From what I managed to see over Archibald's shoulder—" he paused and grinned sheepishly "—there appears to be enough food to feed the entire army for a month."

"I told you Cook was thorough."

"Yes," he murmured. "You did."

His dark gaze had not left her face and Catherine felt the flush rise self-consciously in her cheeks. Two days and nights of lovemaking should have left them both with a stronger sense of self control—at the very least, exhausted—but if anything, the opposite appeared to be true. A touch or a smile could set the heat churning in her loins; a thought of the weeks, perhaps months of separation that lay ahead heightened the urgency in her blood and made her feel continually on the edge of arousal.

Alex read all of that and more in the hauntingly lovely violet of her eyes. He would take the memory of those eyes to his grave, he knew. Eyes, lips, hands, body . . .

Indeed, he had damned well better turn his mind to other things, or they would never leave this room again.

"Donald has had a temporary lapse, it seems, in remembering my wife is supposed to be back at Achnacarry."

"Oh?"

"Yes, oh. And to answer your question as to whom he has invited: anyone and everyone above the rank of captain. He's filling the role of brother-in-law well, making himself right at home in your father's library. We must remember to leave a note complimenting Sir Alfred on his fine brandy; he had every right to be concerned for its longevity. The Prince, for one, is most impressed with—"

"The Prince! Prince Charles? He's here?"

"Naturally. It would have been the height of bad manners not to have invited him."

"Oh, but . . . ! My hair! My dress! My—!"

"My goodness," he said with a dry smile. "Is this a note of panic I detect? Over a rebel princeling you declared you would never look upon twice, thank you very much?"

Catherine ignored his sarcasm and ran to stand in front of the cheval mirror. "Oh Lord, look at me!"

Alex's grin broadened. "If I look any harder, you will have no clothes left at all."

Scowling at him, she ran into the dressing room. The blue silk gown she had originally decided to wear was instantly dismissed as being far too plain for entertaining royalty—dubious though the title might be. The red brocade was too flamboyant, the russet muslin too prim. She briefly debated over the pink satin sacque dress, but concluded the pleated train would make her look too matronly. She was left with a midnight blue velvet gown, or a splendidly worked creation of gold brocade.

"Velvet . . . or brocade?" she pondered aloud.

"Velvet," Alexander suggested, watching her over the flame of the candle he was using to light his cigar.

Catherine ripped the heavily embroidered brocade off its holder and flung it onto the back of a chair. She returned to the dressing room and emerged with an armful of petticoats which she struggled into unassisted, despite Alex's willing offer of help. She grudgingly requested his strong—and suspiciously skillful hands—to lace her into the brocade bodice, and, after attaching the wide, bell-shaped skirt, she stood moaning before the mirror again, this time decrying the scattered tumble of blonde curls. Wild and wanton, they did absolutely nothing to compliment the elegant lines of the brocade.

"I believe I did suggest the velvet," Alex reminded her smugly.

Catherine spun around, her eyes flashing hotly. She knew it would take the better part of another hour to repair the damage he had wrought to her coiffure. He knew it too, the bounder.

Struggling with laces and stays again, she stripped out of the brocade and retrieved the blue velvet from the wardrobe. Alex had the good sense to conceal his smile as he assisted with the fastenings, but a glance up into his eyes was all the mirror she required to know the results of the change. They were smoldering with approval, full of dark promises as they followed the plunging neckline to where her breasts plumped warm and soft against the bodice. Her temper was somewhat defused by his bold stare, and she retreated to the dressing table to work with the brush a frantic few minutes to regain her edge.

With the help of two pearl-encrusted silver combs she managed to tame the golden cascade so it spilled softly from the crown of her head. Satisfied she would draw an eye or two in admiration despite her husband's mischief, she slipped the amethyst ring on her finger and snatched up an ivory fan.

"Very well, Sir Rogue," she announced. "I am ready."

"Almost," he agreed, tossing his half-smoked cigar into the fire. He reached into a pocket of his coat and withdrew a small parcel wrapped in a square of red silk, bound by a thin satin ribbon. Catherine accepted it with a curious frown, balancing it thoughtfully in her palm for a moment or two before removing the wrapper.

It was a brooch, oval in design, the silver filigreed border presenting an amethyst as large as a gull's egg, the stone perfectly matched to the one she wore on her finger. Surrounding the huge centre stone was a fiery halo of diamonds, each more than a carat in size, each of a cut and clarity to rival those in the crown jewels.

"Alex," she gasped. "It's lovely!"

"I was hoping it might make up for a few letters I neglected to post." He lifted the brooch from her palm and pinned it over the deep vee of her bodice. The warmth of his fingers, combined with the flush of love and pride she experienced, sent her up on her tiptoes to press her lips, soft and trembling against his.

"I shall never let it out of my sight," she whispered. "Nor, my lord, will I ever let you out of my sight once this wretched business is over."

His hand caressed her cheek as he returned the kiss, then with a brusque clearing of his throat, he offered his arm to escort her to the guests waiting below.

"Before I really do change my mind," he advised.

Suspended on a cloud of happiness, Catherine floated beside him along the tapestry-lined hallway. At the top of the main staircase, she paused and gazed down over the vast, open foyer and vaulted recess of the great hall. It felt odd hearing the strains of a piper warming his instrument somewhere within the echoing chambers; odder still to hear the thick Gaelic brogue spoken in rooms accustomed to hosting the cream of the English gentry.

Acknowledging the subtle pressure on her arm, Catherine followed Alexander down the first short run of steps, her skirts swaying in a crush of velvet and lace as they turned on the landing and descended the second tier. At the bottom, she braced herself and held fast to Alex's arm as he escorted her through the arch of the great hall and into the throng of suddenly hushed Highlanders. Catherine recognized a handful of clan chiefs from her brief stay at Achnacarry, among them the MacDonalds—Keppoch and Glencoe—Cluny of MacPherson, and the stout and gnarled Stewart of Ardshiel. Dr. Archibald Cameron, bewigged and formally attired, bustled forward without waiting on ceremony and spun her in a graceful pirouette.

"Ach, such a sicht f'ae sour eyes," he beamed, his grin as bold as his chuckle as he eyed the trimness of her waist. "Enjoy it while ye can, lass. Frae what we hear tell, wee Alasdair's been dain his best tae make cairtain ye'll no' fit these pretty frocks much longer."

Rescuing her from a fit of embarrassed flushes, Alexander steered her toward the group of men which included his brother Donald and Lord George Murray. Donald's compliments were far more subdued, as were those of the lean and articulate commander of the Prince's army. By far, her biggest surprise came when Alex took her by the hand and introduced her formally to Charles Edward Stuart, self-proclaimed Regent of Scotland, England, Ireland and Wales.

Startled, for she had seen no one in the group of men to fit the dark and lusty image of the Stuart prince she had formed in her mind, she found herself staring into large, sombre brown eyes that were painfully shy of any manner of outward pretentiousness. He was twenty-four, but looked much younger, so tall and slender he might almost have been termed pretty with his fair complexion and pale gold hair. He wore a tartan shortcoat and red velvet breeches, his only ornament the jewel of the Order of the Thistle, pinned to his left breast.

Catherine hastily offered a curtsy, which he acknowledged with a slight flush and a wide smile.

"This is indeed a pleasure, Lady Cameron," Charles said, his voice softly modulated to suit his unprepossessing frame. "Your husband has been one of our most valuable assets both on and off the field of battle, although I now see why he was in such a hurry to bring our army south. I must also thank you for your generous hospitality in offering your home so that we might celebrate the good fortune of yet another gallant officer."

"Aluinn MacKail," Lochiel announced with a grin. "Unless his legs have tairned tae straw and he's tucked himself away in hiding."

Aluinn stepped forward to join the celebrated group, returning Catherine's smile with an apologetic nod as Archibald roared to have everyone's glass filled to the brim for a pre-nuptial toast.

"Leeze me on thee, John Barleycorn," he wheezed jovially, raising his glass. "Thou king o' grain. Lang life an' happiness tae our brither Aluinn, f'ae he is that: a true an' proper brither. Aye, an' help him swally the lot in one gulp, doon an' guid, f'ae it's the last taste o' freedom he'll have, if I ken the Irish."

"The last I'll want," Aluinn said, catching Alex's eye. "Believe me."

The toasting concluded, the minister stepped forward and asked for the principals to be brought before him. Catherine excused herself and went to the winter parlour where a very nervous bride was waiting and causing irreparable damage to one of the sprigs of flowerets which had come loose from her hair. Catherine fussed and fretted over the folds of the satin skirt for several moments, then with a kiss and a smile of encouragement, she led the way back to the great hall.

The ceremony, conducted by a Presbyterian minister who belonged to the Cameron clan, was delivered in Gaelic for the benefit of the audience, but there was no misinterpreting the shine of happiness in the bride's eyes, or the proud tremor in the groom's hands as he slipped a thin gold band around her finger. The crowd was hushed, apart from the occasional rustle of tartan and clank of steel, but when the vows had been exchanged and the couple were pronounced man and wife, the expected eruption of cheering and applause did not occur.

Instead, the smiling bride and groom stepped to one side and the minister crooked an inquisitive brow in Alexander's direction.

"Is the second couple ready?"

Catherine froze as all eyes in the room turned toward them. Startled, she looked up at Alexander, whose hand tightened on hers as he raised it to his lips.

"I thought we were a little rushed last time, and somewhat lacking in enthusiasm. You don't mind, do you?"

"Mind?" she said on a gasp. "Oh Alex . . . I don't know what to say."

"There's the beauty of it," he whispered. "You just have to say 'I do.' "

Chapter Nine

"Where are you going?" Catherine asked drowsily, stifling a yawn with the corner of a pillow.

"Donald wants me to ride into Derby with him," Alex explained, and smoothed a curl of hair back off her temple. He planted a kiss in its stead and smiled. "Go back to sleep."

"Mmmm. What time is it?"

"A little past five."

"My God," she groaned, snuggling deeper into the nest of warm blankets. "Why does it feel as if I've barely closed my eyes?"

"Possibly because you just have, my insatiable young minx. I should have remembered what effect Archibald's company had on your tolerance for wine."

A pale violet eye slitted open accusingly. "It was not the wine that kept me awake, sir. It was the brandy."

He glanced up from tucking his shirttails into his breeches and grinned wolfishly. "Perhaps next time, we should try drinking it out of glasses."

"Perverted and lustful," she grumbled crossly. "That's what you are. And far too knowledgeable of things decent men and women would never dream of doing in their most wicked fantasies."

"Is that a complaint?" he asked, leaning over the bed again.

"Yes." She opened both eyes and stretched her arms up to slide them around his neck. "Of course you could always come back to bed and try to convince me otherwise."

He kissed her, leisurely and deeply, and while the moan was still forming in her throat, he bowed his head to her breasts, suckling from each, the last, lingering traces of brandy. When he lifted his head again, the nipples were dark and erect, puckered tautly with arousal.

"Shameless," he murmured, "for a woman twice married."

Catherine smiled and drew him down for another clinging kiss. "Thank you. And thank you for knowing how much it would mean to me to be married properly, with a smile on my face."

"I am not completely without sentiment, madam."

"Only scruples," she countered, stretching provocatively so that the blankets slipped down around her waist.

Alex cursed softly and planted a moist kiss on the delicate indentation of her navel. "Keep everything warm for me. I won't be gone long."

"I'll have more brandy waiting," she promised and rolled sleepily onto her side. "Perhaps a hot bath, as well . . . ?"

Alexander's gaze kept wandering back to his wife as he finished dressing, but there was no further sound or movement from beneath the bundle of quilts. He truly hoped this meeting concerned something of momentous importance to justify leaving such a warm and friendly bed.

He was still frowning irritably when he joined Lochiel outside in the courtyard. Shadow was already saddled and waiting impatiently alongside a dozen other mounted clansmen who formed Donald's personal guard.

"I'm surprised that beast let the groom near him," Lochiel said, watching as Alex lovingly stroked the stallion's neck and fed him an apple he'd pinched from a basket of fruit on his way out.

"He'll let almost anyone near him. Just don't ever try to climb into the saddle."

Tossing a greeting to Struan MacSorley and Archibald —whose eyes were red-raw from the effects of the long night of celebrations—Alex swung himself up onto the stallion's back and felt an instant surge of energy pump through his system. Also plainly anxious to be away from the claustrophobic confines of the stables, Shadow snorted an indignant reminder to his master that Alex had not paid him much attention since arriving at Rosewood Hall.

As indifferent to the rules of propriety as his rider, the coal black stallion reared and danced out of the cobbled courtyard without waiting for any signal. Once clear of the outbuildings, Alex gave him his head and for the next few miles, the pair tore across the countryside as if searching for a hole in the wind. Joining in the chase, Struan MacSorley's sturdy horse was at a distinct disadvantage from the amount of weight he carried, but the race was still invigorating, and ended with both men grinning through wind-burned creases.

"By the Christ, I'm gonny find masel' a match f'ae that wee beast o' yourn one o' these days," Struan scowled goodnaturedly, knowing full well it would never happen. Shadow stood easy, his head arched high as if even he disdained the lathered, blown condition of MacSorley's mount.

"I'm glad we have a few moments alone," said Alex, glancing back along the road. "Has something happened in camp the two weeks I've been away? Lord George and the Prince barely exchanged a civil word last night; the tension was so thick between them you could cut it with a knife."

Struan scratched a hand through his leonine mane of tawny hair and cursed as he realized the wind had torn his blue woolen bonnet from his head. "Lochiel hasna told ye?"

"Told me what?"

Again the burly Highlander scratched, this time with a distinct look of discomfort crumpling his face.

"I'm sure I'll find out eventually," Alex said. "But I would rather hear it from someone I know than to walk into a situation blind."

"Aye. Well, ye're right there, lad. No' that I'm sayin' I ken the whole story."

Alex waited patiently. Struan rarely entered into any discussions, and damn few that required giving an opinion or taking sides. However, big as he was, hardly anyone took notice of him in his capacity as Lochiel's captain of the guard, and, as a result, he usually knew more about what went on in camp than any of the principles.

"It started even afore we crossed the border intae this soddin' country," the Highlander growled. "The Prince an' his fancy gray-haired gillies—them two what are always whisperin' an' gratin' in his ears—" (Alex did not need a poke in the eye to recognize O'Sullivan and Murray of Broughton) "—came tae be he were listenin' tae them mair'n he were listenin' tae the guid common sense o' Lord George. Aye, an' it seems the general took enough o' their blither-blather about how he were secretly an agent f'ae the *Sassenachs*, an' how he had plans tae deliver the Prince intae the hans o' his enemies. It all come tae a heid in Carlisle, when the general gave the Prince his resignation an' the Prince actually took it!"

"He *what*?"

"Aye, aye. I ken how ye feel about the general. Same as we all dae, I warrant. Well, he werena resigned mair'n two, three days when the Prince were struck by a bolt o' lightnin' an' realized as how it were the general the men followed an' trusted, an' the general the men respected as far as foolin' the *Sassenachs* an' holdin' this band o' rabble togither. It galled him tae the quick tae admit it, but he doun it an' asked Lord George tae take up command again."

Alex swore inwardly, wondering why everything seemed to be conspiring against their success—even, it seemed, the Prince himself.

Struan barely let him digest this information before he was dealing another blow. "Dae ye ken the Council voted tae retreat at Manchester?"

"I suspected it was coming," Alexander replied cautiously. "Long overdue too, by my way of thinking."

"Aye. Yourn an' just about everyone else's."

"So what the devil are they doing in Derby? Surely the Prince still can't be hoping for English support?"

Struan reacted uncomfortably to the sarcasm. He was, after all, in this rebellion of his own free will, unlike many who had merely obeyed the command of their chief to join.

"In Manchester, while the lairds were lookin' over their shoulders an' wonderin' if the roads ahind were bein' blocked by lobsterbacks, the bonnie wee laddie were dreamin' o' his victory march intae London. It were Lord George, much as that Irish bastard wouldna admit it, wha' talked the lairds intae gi'in the *Sassenachs* one last chance tae keep their promises. At the same time, he swore by Derby if there werena any sign o' support, he would tairn the men 'round whether the Prince agreed or na."

Christ, Alex thought savagely. This, then, must be the purpose of the early morning meeting of the Council. When he asked as much of the brawny Highlander, Struan only shrugged noncomittally.

"I wouldna take wagers against it. We had but two hunnerd men join in Manchester; less than twenny outside Derby."

Not even enough, Alex reflected bitterly, to make up for the loss of men who—like himself—had been convinced long ago of the folly of invading England with an army less than equal in numbers to what King George's supporters could put in the field. Unlike him, many of those men had simply melted out of camp by twos and threes and returned to Scotland, more than willing to fight to defend their own border if the need arose, but not to fight, and very likely die, for the possession of a country that obviously did not want liberating.

"What would you have me do—" he had asked Catherine. *"Desert?"*

"Yes . . . no . . . I don't know . . ."

Alex did not know either. He had committed himself to stay and fight to the end, but suddenly, there were more urgent reasons for wanting to fight for a new beginning.

"Gentlemen, you cannot be serious." Prince Charles appeared genuinely surprised when the suggestion of a retreat was put before him. "How can you even contemplate such a thing when we have accomplished so much, come so far, and have so little to conquer ahead of us?"

Lord George Murray seemed all alone as he stood at the far end of the table. None of the other chiefs could bring themselves to meet the Stuart prince eye to eye; none of them could believe him to be so deluded as to think they could reach London on their own resources.

"Sire," the general began, "The Duke of Cumberland—"

"Yes, yes, I know. My esteemed, warmonging cousin has returned to England and has ridden in haste to take command of Ligonier's army . . . but only because his own troops are battle-weary and must endure several days' hard march to bring them anywhere within striking distance. In that same proscribed time, we could be in London."

"We have also confirmed the reports that Field Marshal Wade has removed himself from Newcastle-on-

Tyne and is preparing to swing his army around and intercept us at Leicester." Lord George paused for emphasis. "If he does, it will effectively place two sizeable bodies of men on the road between here and London, with a third speeding to provide reinforcements. Our army, on the other hand, is hardly sizeable, nor do we have any reinforcements speeding anywhere."

James Drummond, the Duke of Perth, hastened to interject, "We do, however, have confirmation that my uncle, Lord John Drummond, has arrived in Scotland with his regiment of Royal Scots, and several contingents of French volunteers. A second army of Highlanders is being formed in Perth at this very moment."

"Therefore," Lord George added quickly, seeing the flush darken in the Prince's cheeks, "if we returned to Scotland now, we would have shown our strength without actually having to play any cards. We could winter in Edinburgh *as originally planned*, and strengthen our ranks sufficiently to launch a second invasion in the spring. At that time, we would know what had to be done. We would harbour no illusions as to how much support the English would be providing . . . or not providing, as the case may be."

"You believe our Highlanders alone cannot defeat the army of a Cumberland or a Wade?" Charles Stuart demanded. "Have you so little faith in your own brave countrymen?"

"Faith in our men and our country is what has brought us all this far," Lord George stated flatly. "Faith in their courage and their fighting ability leaves me no doubt we could face either one of those armies and win—but at what cost? There would surely be a horrendous loss of valuable lives, and with no hope of replacements, how then could we expect to confront a second, or a third force?"

A grumbled chorus of "ayes" circled the table to indicate the chiefs were in complete agreement with Lord

George's assessment. There was no question they would fight Cumberland's army if presented with the challenge, but there was also no faith on earth that could make them visualize their meager army emerging victorious over a combined force of over twenty thousand Englishmen.

The young prince looked at each face seated around the table, his complexion white as chalk save for two bright stains high on his cheeks. His voice, when he managed to fling out the words, stung with a sense of betrayal.

"Is there no one among you who will support your prince in his hour of need? Is there none among you who believe, as I do, that our cause is just; that it will, it *must* prevail?"

The room echoed with the silence of men who had marched hundreds of miles from their homes and families, risking everything, guaranteed of nothing in return. The MacDonalds of Keppoch, Lochgarry, and Glencoe were represented; Lochiel and his Camerons, Ardshiel and his Appin Stewarts; the MacLachlans, the MacPhersons, the MacLeans, MacLarens, and Robertsons; the Grants of Glenmoriston, Lord George Murray's Athollmen; the regiments of the Duke of Perth, Lord Ogilvy, Glenbucket, and Colonel John Roy Stewart; the Lords Elcho, Balmerino, Pitsligo, Kilmarnock; the MacKinnons, the MacGregors, Clanranald . . .

"Gentlemen," Charles Stuart rose to his feet slowly, his mouth pinched into a tight white line. "We are less than one hundred and fifty miles from London. Raise your noses in the air and you can smell the filth of the Thames. Worse, you can hear the laughter of George of Hanover as he mocks our cowardice for stopping mere feet from his front door! Did you not just hear, with those same ears, of Lord John Drummond's triumphant arrival from France? Did you not also hear of the treaty signed at Fontainebleau which ensures us the military assistance of the King of France?"

"We heard it," Lord George said bluntly. "We have been hearing it for months, but where are the men? Where are the guns Louis had promised time and time again?"

"I have it on good authority that there are thirty thousand men amassed at Calais, waiting to embark on a moment's notice!"

"The moment has long been and gone, Highness. Even a dozen ships with a few thousand men could have been put to good use preventing Cumberland and his troops from crossing the Channel. A blockade could have held them in Flanders indefinitely. No, Sire, we can no longer count upon the French, nor trust their hollow pledges and treaties. They have proven to be as illusionary as the thousands of loyal English Jacobites we were assured would rise and join us the moment we stepped foot across the border."

"They will join us! They will!" Flushing an angry red, the Prince pounded his fist on the table. "This is what defeats us, this lack of faith! This . . . this lack of willingness to believe in what we have accomplished, what we might yet accomplish if only our hearts were steadfast enough. Sweet God in heaven, we cannot give up now! The city of London, the throne of England is within our grasp! If we turn back now it will all have been for nothing!"

"Not f'ae nothing, Sire," Lochiel said calmly. "We've won Scotland. We've won the right tae bring our King James—yer faither—hame again."

"Home to what? The shame of seeing his army in retreat? The laughter and scorn of the English who will know we had victory within our sights and gave it up in a moment of senseless panic?"

"It was resolved by the Council in Manchester to begin the retreat homeward should there be no further evidence of support by the English."

"*You* resolved it, sir!" the Prince shouted at Lord George. "Your prince did not! Instead, he finds himself begging for a single voice of support for a venture he was assured would be carried by their unflagging faith to the very end. He finds himself facing betrayal and mutiny, arguments, lies, deceit, dissention—all from men in whom he had placed his utmost trust and confidence; men in whom his father, their most righteous sovereign king, had placed his hope for redemption! Where is that loyalty we were most solemnly pledged? Where is the courage we saw displayed so brilliantly at Prestonpans? *Where is your pride?*"

Complete silence engulfed the room. From his position standing at the back of the table behind Lochiel, Alex regarded the circle of taut faces, seeing the conflicting emotions in each man's eyes. The Prince had struck for the quick, as he had done so many times before to good success, for a challenge to a Highlander's pride and honour was as good as a gauntlet slapped in his face. Some sat motionless, stiff with indignation. Some faltered visibly and began looking to each other, groping for reasonable alternatives.

"We could withdraw into Wales," the Duke of Perth suggested reluctantly. "Sir Watkins-Wynn has offered the help of his Welshmen should we first be able to secure their border from the English."

"And you trust his offer?" Lord George said with icy disdain.

"Aye," Ardshiel grunted. "Who's tae say he'll keep his word an' march anywhere wi' us, let alone tae London? Who's tae say how lang it would take tae secure his bluidy borthers, an' wha's tae say Cumberland couldna offer him a sweeter deal, or use the time equal well in formin' up his armies tae catch us comin' back? Trapped in Wales, by the Christ, we could well end up like chicks in a cavie."

Most of the chiefs nodded in agreement. One or two voices rose in argument, but these were halfhearted and evidently meant only to impress the Prince with a semblance of loyalty. These men, Alexander noted with a surge of resentment, were mainly the foreigners—O'Sullivan prime among them—officers who held French commissions and were soldiers of fortune rather than rebels against the crown. As such, they could argue and debate points of strategy from a military standpoint, without thought of the consequences to their homes and families. They did not face the risk of execution for treason if taken prisoner. They had no personal stake in the country, no property to forfeit, no wives or children to see thrown out of their homes and reduced to a beggar's lot. It was not that they lacked dedication, or merely mouthed loyalty to the Prince's cause: They were simply men who had nothing to lose by advocating a bolder course of strategy.

The Highland chiefs, on the other hand, knew they had everything to lose in this venture and knew, from past experience, they stood to lose it all should the Prince fail. They argued passionately in favour of retreat, for there was no dishonour in questioning the senseless, needless waste of good men's lives—and so far there had been nothing in word or deed to suggest such a terrible waste could be avoided. Yet they also knew they would fight to a man if this was the decision of the Council; they were not afraid of fighting or dying, only of doing so ignominiously.

"Gentlemen," Charles had calmed himself, the anger in his voice had relented, and his soft brown eyes held a look of desperation. "I implore you to think carefully on the matter. Search your hearts, discuss it among yourselves and if . . . if you are adamant in this course . . . if you can foresee no possibility of success, then . . . then surely I must . . . I must accede to your wishes. But, I beg you—" a bright flicker of hope sparked in his eyes—"walk among your men. Listen to their voices raised in song and spirit. They have the will to fight, indeed they are impatient to be about it! They have the courage and the hunger to win it all, if we will but let them! Have faith in your men. Have faith in yourselves!"

A final bright stare circled the table before the Prince straightened and walked stiffly toward the door. O'Sullivan was quick to follow, almost overturning his chair in haste, as was Sheridan and John Murray of Broughton. Their departure was noted with derision, for it was sure they would be anxious to convince the Prince that, although they had not spoken out against the retreat, they privately shared his sentiments. And all, undoubtedly, at Lord George's expense.

"It does not matter," the general said wearily, when the supposition was stated openly and bluntly by Lochiel. "Nothing matters but that we salvage what we can while there is still time. If he means to continue the march, we must do so at once to take advantage of Cumberland's lack of preparation. If we are to retreat, we must commence the action at once, before Wade draws too close." He paused a moment and for the first time allowed his bitterness toward the Prince's unfounded suspicions rise to the surface. "In the event of a march forward, my men and I will form the vanguard. If the decision falls to retreat—and I pray God he sees the wisdom of such action—I and my Athollmen will be the last to march along the road, protecting the brave men who go before us. There will be no arguments, no discussions on this point. The decision is mine to make and I have made it."

Alex, standing behind Lochiel, caught the general's eye over the silence.

"In either case, sir, it would seem to me imperative to know exactly where the government troops are and where they might conceivably be twenty-four hours from now."

Lord George smiled appreciatively. "And have you someone in mind foolish enough to volunteer for such a task?"

"Two fools, actually. MacKail and I could be on our way within the hour. Give us a dozen or so men from the Manchester Regiment—Englishmen who could move quickly and inobtrusively through territory familiar to them, and we will gather all the information you need."

"You understand the consequences if you are caught?"

"I understand the greater consequences if we try to move blindly in one direction or the other without knowing what is out there. As for your holding the rearguard position, sir, I have at least five dozen men under my personal command who march very slowly indeed. We would consider it a personal favour if you could incorporate us into your own brigade—at least until we reach the border."

Lord George regarded the tall, black-haired Highlander with a mixture of humour and regret. He suspected that if he'd had a thousand men like Alexander Cameron at his disposal, the question of retreat would never have entered his mind.

"Take as many men as you require, and . . . ahh, extend my heartfelt apologies to Captain MacKail. I'm sure he had better things planned for today than riding about the countryside peeking through hedgebrush."

With a nod in Lochiel's direction, Alex slipped quietly out of the crowded, noisy room. A second glance was exchanged almost immediately and Struan MacSorley, acknowledging the silent command from his chief, followed Alex out into the cold, damp air.

Aluinn traced a strong, lean finger along his wife's lower lip and smiled, if for no other reason than to keep himself from shouting his happiness out loud. Deirdre's eyes were closed, her lashes still dewy with spent tears of wonderment; the skin across her brow and temples was still moist and slightly flushed from her exertions; the wet, clinging tendrils of hair glistened in the mid-morning light.

A commotion of horses hooves out in the courtyard caused a brief distraction, but it passed, and his attention easily reverted to the moist and supple lips he so adored. Leaning forward, he kissed them tenderly and earned a soft, husky sigh in return.

Deirdre could feel the smoky gray eyes studying her intently. Her body still tingled, inwardly and outwardly with the effects of his lovemaking, and she could barely muster the strength to lift a hand and stroke it gently against his cheek.

"Do you have any idea how happy you have made me?" he asked, his lips turning into the palm of her hand. "I keep thinking I will waken any moment and find myself rolled in a cold, coarse length of tartan on the hard ground."

Deirdre smiled. She could hardly believe she deserved, let alone had won the love of a man like Aluinn MacKail. Despite his confession in Blackpool—it seemed like years ago—she could never think of him as a tenant farmer. He had travelled half the world with Alexander Cameron, had visited with kings and queens, lived among the nobility of Europe.

Catching the glitter of the gold band on her finger, Deirdre stretched her arm to its full length to admire the acquisition. "When I saw Mr. Cameron in my mistress's room the other day, I could not believe it. And when I saw you riding up the drive yesterday, I felt sure my heart would fly straight out of my breast." Her arm was lowered again, curling possessively around Aluinn's shoulders. "I love you, Aluinn MacKail. I will always love you, as long as there is breath in my body."

"My love," he murmured, his lips molding to hers. "And now my life."

Deirdre moaned softly with the realization that he was still warm and hard within her.

"You didn't think you'd get rid of me that easily, did you?" he chuckled, moving his hips in a gentle, languid rhythm.

Deirdre moaned again and shook her head in disbelief. It just wasn't possible for a body to feel such happiness! It wasn't possible to feel so fulfilled, so complete, so much a part of someone else.

"There?" he asked on a whisper.

"Yes . . . oh . . . !"

She shuddered against the deep, repeated thrusts of his flesh, and felt the fever rising within her again. Another impossibility, and yet the tremors were building, the flashes of heat and cold were closing together, one upon the other, tightening muscles, nerves, reactions until she was gasping his name, over and over, rising and falling on waves of rapture that came upon her so swiftly, and so sharply she could do nothing to temper them, nothing but ride the crests and swells and pray she would someday learn to give her husband one tenth the pleasure he gave her!

Had she not been too shy to ask, she would have known she had already accomplished her wish. She would have known that each sheet of fiery passion that engulfed her, sheathed him in its grip as well, and left him just as awed, just as dazed, just as determined not to fail her as a lover.

Gasping and sweat-slicked, they collapsed in a tangle of arms and legs, and it was only a soft, urgent tapping on the door that kept them from slipping into a pleasure-induced sleep.

"MacKail?" came a familiar baritone. "Are you awake?"

Aluinn took a deep breath and swung his legs over the side of the bed. It took several moments for the room to stop swaying, several more for him to curse through a stubbed toe and limp his way to the door. After a quick glance back at the giggling figure hurriedly covering herself with the bedsheets, he opened it a crack and glared out into the hallway.

Another round of curses was forming in his mind when he saw Alex's broad back, but when Cameron turned around and Aluinn saw the expression on the rigid features, he became instantly alert.

"How long?"

"Five minutes. Christ, I'm sorry," Alex said. "But I wouldn't disturb you if it wasn't absolutely necessary."

Aluinn nodded. "I'll be ready."

Alex glanced along the hall toward Catherine's bedchamber and Aluinn was shaken away from thoughts of his own interrupted bliss by the look of complete helplessness on his friend's face.

"What is it? What's wrong?"

"I don't know what to say to her, Aluinn. I don't even know if I can walk into that room and walk out again without her."

Aluinn heard a rustle of linen sheets behind him and a moment later, felt Deirdre's cool hand on his arm. She gazed somberly up into her husband's eyes before looking past his bare shoulder to where Alex stood.

"Deirdre . . . I'm sorry," he began.

"It's alright." She tightened her grip on Aluinn's arm. "It had to happen sooner or later. Will . . . will you be coming back?"

"I don't know," Alex said. "I honestly don't know."

"I see." Her face lost a shade of colour before she spoke again. "Have you been to see my lady yet?"

"No. No, I . . . I was just . . ."

"I'll tell her if you like," she offered in a whisper. "It might be easier that way . . . for both of you."

"I can't just leave without saying goodbye. She would never forgive me."

Deirdre saw the naked pain on his face and felt it beginning to tear at her own heart.

"No. My lady *would* forgive you. She'll be angry at first—furious, I warrant—but then she'll calm down and she'll realize it was for the best. In the meantime, her anger will see her through the worst of it. Please sir, she's been so happy. Let her remember that as a parting."

What about me? Alex thought savagely. How can I leave without seeing her, touching her one last time?

In the end, he nodded his agreement. "The longer you leave it, the better. Who knows, we might be back later tonight—" He caught himself from saying more, knowing the chances of their returning to Rosewood Hall were negligible. Aluinn had disappeared back inside to dress and Alex wanted to give them a few moments alone, but before he could leave, he took Deirdre's icy hands into his. "When you do speak to her, tell her . . . tell her I will be back. I will come back for her, on my honour."

"I'll tell her," Deirdre promised, the tears bright in her eyes. The door opened wider and Aluinn joined them at the threshold, still pulling on the last of his clothes and buckling his sword around his waist.

With a small cry, she turned to him and buried her face against his breast. Aluinn held her close, his own emotions stretched to their limit, and he knew if he did not leave quickly, he would not be able to leave at all.

"I love you," he said tersely. "And I'll be back for you just as soon as I can."

"Take care of yourself," she pleaded. "Take care of each other."

Her lips were wet with tears as he kissed her; the sweetness and the bitterness lingered on his senses long after he and Alex had ridden away from Rosewood Hall.

Chapter Ten

Catherine slept through most of the day. She wakened, briefly, when she heard the sound of someone moving about the room stoking the fire in the hearth, but when no warm body joined her between the covers, she merely sighed and drifted back to sleep. Deirdre, who had cursed her own clumsiness in dropping a log, waited on tenterhooks for Catherine to sit up and begin asking questions, so she was relieved to see her mistress fall back asleep. She was hoping against hope that their husbands would return before there was any need to break Catherine's heart with the news of their departure.

Twice again, during the evening and late at night, Catherine bestirred herself from bed. Once, answering the grumbles of a very empty stomach, she ventured out of her room and went below to the kitchens. The house was dark and quiet—almost too quiet, she would remember later—and she raided the pantry of biscuits, cheese, and several thick slices of cold goose before retreating back to the cozier atmosphere of her room. After eating, she debated taking a long hot bath, but the thought of finding someone to heat and carry water up to fill the tub defeated her and she settled for a cursory wash in a foot tub.

She tried to settle herself by reading, but the adventures of *Joseph Andrews* seemed boring by comparison to her own and she found herself yawning and skimming past every other paragraph. Periodically, she wandered to the French doors and gazed out over the courtyard and gardens. The Highlanders had constructed a small town of ridgepoles and sailcloth on the lower parkland; by daylight, resembling whitecaps on a rolling green sea, by night, a cluster of twinkling campfires. There was very little movement that she could see from this distance, and hardly any noise from the camp or the stables.

Finally, out of sheer boredom, she tidied the main bedchamber and affected some order out of the hurricane of discarded clothing that littered the floor of the dressing room. Several articles belonged to Alex—including the uniform he had worn the night he had first stolen up to her room. As she hung each garment on the racks, she ran her hands lovingly over the fabric, imagining she could still feel the warmth from his body. One of his oversized shirts quickly found an appreciative new owner as she shed her frilly nightdress and donned the plain, soft cambric. The sleeves fell well below her fingertips and the hem was almost to her knees, but his scent was in the fabric and it stayed with her everywhere she went.

His tartan amused her for several more minutes. Fascinated at the ease with which he could spread the six yards of it flat, gather the better part into pleats, roll himself into it and stand up belted and fully dressed within seconds, she became tangled in the folds of crimson wool, looking more like a sack of old potatoes than a Highland border lord.

It was well past midnight when she ran out of things to do. She debated searching for Deirdre until she recalled where the bride was, who she was with, and what they were celebrating. With no other options remaining, she tackled Henry Fielding again and, although she had no intentions of doing so, curled off to sleep within minutes.

The sunlight was bright and hot where it poured through the open curtains. Catherine pushed herself upright, at first mystified, then disappointed, then annoyed to find she was still alone in the tester bed. A sudden, icy prickle of alarm sent her jumping off the bed and running into the dressing room, but Alex's tartan and other belongings still hung where she had left them. Chiding herself for her unwarranted suspicions, she completed the briefest of morning ablutions and emerged a few moments later, having hastily pulled a satin robe overtop the cambric shirt.

This time she was determined to disturb Deirdre, honeymoon or not.

Halfway across the room, another oddity struck her: The house was completely silent, inside and out. There were no faint clangs of steel out in the courtyard, no thickly accented voices shouting orders out in the field, no distant skirling pipers assisting the clansmen through their morning drills.

Frowning, Catherine veered toward the window, but before she went more than a step, the familiar, heavy fall of boots out in the corridor drew both her gaze and her smile to the bedroom door as it was flung open.

Standing there, a startling clash of bright scarlet broadcloth and high white buttoned gaiters, was Lieutenant Derek Goodwin.

For a full minute they stared at one another without moving, without speaking.

"Lieutenant," Catherine managed at last. "What on earth are you doing here? How . . . how did you get in?"

"Why, Mrs. Montgomery: What a perfectly dismal greeting. Especially since I have come all this way, risking peril to life and limb to rescue you!"

"Rescue me?"

"Of course. You do require rescuing, do you not? After all, your house has been used by the rebels for the past two days, has it not? And you have been kept here as their hostage, have you not?"

Clasping her hands tightly together, Catherine tried to keep her voice calm. "How did you get in here? Where have you come from?"

"I've come from the forest," he replied blandly. "I had, at first, thought the house to be as deserted as the countryside, but . . . what luck I came and checked up here."

"Deserted?" Catherine went very still. "What do you mean, deserted?"

"Didn't you know? The Pretender has moved his army out of Derby. Decamped. Scuttled. Retreated. And in such haste and stealth we could hardly believe it ourselves until the sun came fully over the horizon. They must have left some time during the night, which would put them . . . oh, ten, fifteen miles back along the road to Manchester by now."

"I don't believe you," Catherine gasped, running to the long, elegant French doors. She opened them and burst out into the cold winter air, her breasts heaving against the tightness of the robe as she searched wildly for proof of the lieutenant's lies. But the courtyard below was deserted. No laughter, no footsteps, no smell of cooking fires tinged the chilly air. The silence she had noticed earlier was almost deafening as she stood staring out at the barren landscape. The parkland was a muddy green again; there were no tents, no pyramids of muskets, no staked picket lines for the horses.

"When our company withdrew," said the lieutenant, joining Catherine on the narrow balcony, "we only moved about a mile or so down the road. We have been keeping an eye on things, so to speak; watching the comings and goings with a great deal of interest, as you can imagine. Tsk tsk, but Sir Alfred will *not* be pleased to know his house has been used by Jacobite officers . . . and their whores."

The emphasis on the last word was so subtle, Catherine missed it. She was, in truth, barely aware of the lieutenant's presence beside her—something which could not be said for Derek Goodwin. He was very much affected by the proximity of her soft woman's body, the ripe swell of her breasts, the telltale effects of the cool breeze constricting her skin and offering tautened little nipples for his approval. Lower still, the clinging satin defined the exact shape of her long, slender limbs, molding around and caressing each curve like liquid silver.

"Retreated?" Catherine whispered. "Gone? Without a word?"

Goodwin's eyes climbed leisurely up to her face again. "What were you expecting? Did you think they should ask your permission to depart?"

A retort to his sarcasm was very near the tip of her tongue. She wisely checked it, however, when she saw the gleam of watchfulness in his eyes.

"I think it would have been civil of them to tell me when they planned on vacating my home, yes. They invaded my privacy, assumed possession of my father's house and made free use of his storehouses, his cellars. I dare say they have drunk the wine reserves to the bare walls."

"No doubt, they caused you immeasurable discomfort," he mused.

"It was inconvenient, having a houseful of ignorant, loutish Scotsmen under one's feet day and night, although I must say they behaved quite decently, all told."

"I'm told the Pretender fancies himself quite the ladies' man. I've heard some women will follow him between the sheets after hardly more than a courteous nod."

"Some women," she countered frostily, "will follow any man between the sheets, whether they find him to be amiable or not. But to respond to your supposition, I found the Stuart Prince to be generally shy and mannerly, and, as far as I could ascertain, too engrossed in the business of winning a country over to his plight to give much thought to dalliances. He is very serious and very earnest in his beliefs, and, I dare say, would do nothing to provoke ill feelings amongst the people he is striving to impress."

"These . . . serious and earnest beliefs, do they hold true for his officers? Some of them looked brutish enough to dispense with formalities of any kind and just take what they wanted."

Catherine stiffened as she felt his watery gaze slither down the front of her robe. "If you are asking, Lieutenant Goodwin, in your own subtle manner if either myself or my maidservants were molested in any way, the answer is no. As I have already told you, the Prince was a perfect gentleman, and set an example followed by his officers and general staff."

"Ah . . . then your participation was voluntary."

"Participation? In what, pray tell?"

"In whatever it was that went on in your room and kept the lights burning twenty-four hours a day."

A flood of shocked disbelief surged into Catherine's cheeks. "How dare you! How dare you speak to me in such a way! How dare you even enter my chambers without being announced. Get out! Get out of my sight at once before I report this affront to your commanding officer!"

Goodwin smiled lazily. "Oh, I don't think you will report anything. Nothing, at any rate, that might prompt me to issue a countercharge of aiding and abetting the enemy . . . or should I say, *abedding* the enemy?"

Catherine's delicate blonde beauty gave the impression of fragility and weakness, but there was nothing fragile or weak in the powerful swing that sent her hand up to slap the leering smirk off the lieutenant's face. Her palm caught him squarely on the cheek, and with such force, she felt the sting from the shadow of beard stubble scrape her fingers. His head jerked to one side and he was taken sufficiently off guard to falter back half a step.

"Now get out," she hissed. "Get out of my sight, get out of my house! If I so much as glimpse you on my property again, I shall order you shot!"

Goodwin had kept his face partially averted as he absorbed both the shock of the slap and the tirade. When he slowly straightened, the imprint of her hand stood out a vivid red against the pinched white anger of his complexion. Without a further word, he turned and strode back through the French doors.

Catherine did not realize she was holding her breath until she heard the distinct slam of the bedroom door. Releasing the pent-up air, she sent a trembling hand to her brow. Where had he found the nerve to simply barge into her house, into her bedroom, and demand . . . demand what? An accounting of her behaviour? It was none of his damned business what she did or who she entertained in her rooms. None of his business if she chose to cavort naked in the streets of Derby with a dozen lusty stableboys!

And how the devil had he just walked into the house, climbed the stairs, and forced himself into her room? Good heavens, someone should have seen him and questioned his boldness. Surely, she had not been left completely on her own! Surely, Deirdre would have stayed with her, or at the very least, come to say goodbye if she had gone with Aluinn.

Gone! If she had gone! If Alex had truly gone without saying a word!

Shivering with the cold, Catherine peered cautiously through the French doors. Her view of the room was partially obstructed by the billowing lace curtains, but she continued inching forward until lapses in the breeze settled the sheer fabric and she could see into every nook and corner. He was gone, the room was empty. She had the presence of mind to glance into the dressing room, but the doors stood wide open and revealed no unwanted surprises.

The brass doorkey was sitting in the lock and, with her heart lodged firmly in her throat, Catherine dashed across the room and gave it a resounding twist. When she heard the locking mechanism ratchet into place, she withdrew the key and clutched it gratefully to her bosom.

Feeling safer, she pushed the heavy fall of her hair back from her face and edged away from the door. A cool gust of wind from the windows sent a spray of gooseflesh crawling along her arms and she quickly crossed the room again to close and latch the two glass doors. A movement from behind the lace curtains, just above where her hand grasped the wooden frame, caught her eye and sent a shudder rippling through her body like a cold current. The face was just a blur, the features distorted through the glass and lace, but there was no mistaking the grin or the strong, masculine hand that snaked out and grabbed her around the wrist. Catherine had a split second to realize the lieutenant had only gone through the motions of storming through the bedroom and slamming his way out the door. He had obviously doubled back and concealed himself behind the heavy, green velvet draperies.

She opened her mouth to scream, but the sound was bitten off into a sharp cry of pain as her wrist was wrenched back and twisted around into the small of her back. Swinging her against the wall, Goodwin crowded her roughly between the plaster and the smothering press of his body. Before she could overcome the pain or gather her wits to scream again, his free hand was around her throat, the fingers digging cruelly into the tender flesh beneath her chin.

"Go ahead, Mrs. Montgomery. Scream, if it makes you feel better. There's no one to hear you; no one who'll give a damn, that is. Only my own men—twenty-two healthy young studs who would be only too eager to come up and see what all the fuss was about. Twenty-two, Mrs. Montgomery. That would keep the lights burning for quite a few hours, wouldn't it?"

His breath was hot and sour against her face. The hand forcing her neck into a painful arch was also cutting across her windpipe so that her every scant gasp was a minor victory. The arm he held twisted behind her back felt as if it would pop from the shoulder socket at any moment, or snap at the wrist from the pressure he was applying. As the waves of agony and desperation grew, the need to breathe slowly overcame the instinctive need to fight, and Goodwin smiled as he saw the blazing hatred in the wide violet eyes turn to helpless submission. It was her only means of communication and she was begging him, pleading with him to show mercy, to release her and stop the pain.

Enjoying a powerful boost to his sense of dominance, Goodwin ground himself against the softness of her belly, his lips parting on an oath of appreciation as he felt the distinct and urgent throbbing surge into his loins.

"There, you see? I only want some of what you've been giving your Jacobite houseguests." He pressed his body closer, using her frantic squirmings to add to his arousal. "But if you want to fight me, I don't mind. In fact, I prefer my women to show a little spirit."

He released her arm and relaxed the vise-like grip on her throat just enough to keep her from blacking out. He stroked the rounded swell of her breast, savouring the way the firm, ripe little orbs filled his hand without sagging or mushing flat under pressure. Her heart was pounding beneath his fingertips; the cold chill of fear was keeping her nipples erect and pebble-hard. He rolled one of them between a thumb and forefinger and his grin broadened when he felt the shudder race the length of her body.

"You really shouldn't pretend you don't enjoy this," he murmured, his hand pushing beneath the lace collar to reach the silky hotness of her skin. "Just like you and your lover shouldn't have stood before the window, night after night. Trees are good for more than decoration, you know; they're good for climbing and for offering a vantage point. Better than seats in the opera house, some nights, especially with the help of a spyglass."

Catherine's attempt to lunge to one side to avoid the probing fingers brought the crushing force back against her throat, and she was, once again, too preoccupied with the need to survive to notice or care what his other hand was doing.

The knot of her belt gave way after several frustrated tugs, and the hand intruded beneath the satin again, this time to stroke and knead her flesh through the layer of cambric. Catherine was choking, her lips were blue and her eyes beginning to cloud when he released her and used both hands to grasp the front of the shirt and rip it wide open.

Dimly, she was aware of his hands intruding everywhere, and lips clamping savagely over her breast, tormenting the nipple as if he meant to chew the flesh from her body. A wave of excruciating pain helped to clear her senses, to jolt her back to the reality of violation. She flailed at his neck and shoulders, somehow managing to tear the ridge of his ear on the amethyst ring. He flinched back with a snarl, and Catherine wrenched free, stumbling past him as she grabbed at one of the heavy panels of the French doors. She swung it back as hard as she could, but, with neither pain nor tears to blind him, the lieutenant blocked the glass before it could smash into his face.

Catherine ran for the door. She pulled and yanked and screamed at the brass latch to turn, forgetting she had locked it herself only minutes ago. She heard a husky laugh behind her and whirled around in time to see Lieutenant Goodwin bend over and pluck something off the rug.

"Well now, I hadn't planned on offering you anything in exchange for your services, Mrs. Montgomery, but perhaps you would be more receptive if you had some form of motivation." He dangled the key before her frantic eyes and his smile was almost charming. "In other words, my dear Catherine: if you want this, you'll have to earn it."

"Please," she gasped. "Please . . . unlock the door. I don't know why you are doing this, but if you let me go, I swear I won't say anything to anyone."

Goodwin's long fingers caressed the brass stem of the key suggestively. "I will be more than happy to unlock the door . . . once we have settled our account."

She saw where his eyes went and she clutched at the torn halves of the shirt to shield her nakedness. "You're wrong . . . about what you saw . . ."

"Wrong?" He arched an eyebrow and paused long enough to turn and bolt the French doors closed behind him. "My dear Mrs. Montgomery, I am neither blind nor deaf. I knew the kind of games you enjoyed playing the night I stood outside your room and listened to you and another of your lovers rutting as if there would be no tomorrow."

"Oh God," Catherine moaned, closing her eyes against a flood of hot tears. "He wasn't my lover. He—" How could she explain the man had been her husband?

"Yes? He what? Was an old family friend?"

"Please . . . you don't understand."

Pocketing the key, Goodwin started unfastening the row of buttons down the front of his tunic. "I understand perfectly. It is you who seems to be having trouble understanding that I do not intend to leave here until I get what I came for. And what I came for is so much more enjoyable naked, so if you don't mind—?"

Catherine dashed the tears from her face. There was no other way out of the room, no adjoining chambers other than the dressing room and *garde robe*. There was only the balcony, but even if she could get past Goodwin, she doubted whether she had the speed or the presence of mind to clamber over the banister and down the trellis.

Her gaze flicked around the room, stopped, and flew back to the fireplace. Leaning against one sculpted marble caryatid was a black iron poker, its head molded into the bust of an eagle, complete with viciously hooked beak. With a cry, she lunged for it, but her intentions had been so transparent, Goodwin laughed as he stretched out a long leg, tripping her onto her knees halfway there.

"Tut, tut," he scolded mockingly. "You're not thinking hospitable thoughts. And you wouldn't want *me* to start mulling over the possibilities of how to put such an interestingly shaped poker to use . . . would you?"

Catherine sobbed and scrambled to her feet, veering away from the fireplace. She ran into the dressing room and slammed the double doors behind her, sealing them with the ridiculously delicate privacy bolt. There was more husky laughter from the outer chamber and she knew she had bought only a few seconds' reprieve, no more.

"Come out, kitty, kitty," he crooned, scratching his nails down the outside of the door.

Catherine recoiled from the sound, her nerves screaming, her skin shrinking in terror.

"If you are very good to me, I won't tell the others—twenty-two of them, remember? I'll keep you all to myself even though I promised they could each have a turn."

Catherine bit the back of her knuckles to keep from screaming aloud. There was no escape this time, she had trapped herself. There was nothing she could use as a weapon amid the clutter on the top of her dressing table—bottles of perfume, hairbrushes, bathsalts, combs . . .

"Kitty, kitty, kitty," Goodwin hissed. "I'm counting to five—"

He took a step back, raised his foot, and sent his booted heel crashing into the seam of the doors. The lock sprang from the wood and flew across the narrow room, barely missing Catherine's cheek. She had pressed herself as far back against the wardrobe as she could go, and as she watched him stalk slowly, triumphantly through the doorway, her face blanched as white as the marble cherubs on the fireplace.

"I gave you every opportunity to make this easy and pleasurable," he said in a low voice, his eyes glittering malevolently as they raked down her trembling form. She was standing with her hands behind her back, unaware that the edges of her robe and shirt hung open, baring the whiteness of her skin to his hungry gaze. Her hair was flung about her shoulders like a veil, her lips parted against quick, dry gasps of air that caused her breasts to rise and fall invitingly between the torn fabric. Staring at those lips prompted such a strong image of pleasure in Goodwin's mind, he experienced a premature spurt of ecstasy within the stretched confines of his breeches.

"Come over here," he commanded harshly. "Now."

Catherine remained motionless, unable to react, unable to think of anything other than the open door looming beyond his shoulders.

Goodwin advanced a step. He was sweating lightly; the heat in his groin was flaring upward, engulfing his chest and sending the blood hammering up into his temples.

"I said . . . come here. You don't want to make me any angrier, Catherine. You don't want to make me have to punish you before I—"

Catherine lunged unexpectedly, launching herself across the narrow gap that separated them. Goodwin saw the blur of her hands swinging up from her sides and realized too late they held a flash of silver. He dodged, quickly enough to avoid one of the ornate silver and steel hair combs, but not both of them. He felt the razor-like edge tear into the skin just above his ear, then carve downward through the flesh of his cheek and throat until it sank into the ridge of tendons that joined his neck and collarbone.

Goodwin roared out in pain and struck Catherine's hand aside. Blood was beginning to streak hotly down the side of his face and spatter onto the stark whiteness of his shirt and waistcoat. It slicked his hands, causing his fingers to skid on the fantail of the comb twice before he was able to fix a firm grip and pull the shiny steel ornament free. He stared at the dagger-like point of the comb for a long moment, then turned to Catherine like a maddened pit bull, grabbing for her just as she regained her balance and was trying to dash past him.

The sound of tearing satin was louder than the pitiful scream her bruised throat was able to produce as she was flung back against the wardrobe. Pain exploded in her head as his fist drove into the side of her face, and she would have fallen if not for the bloodied claw that caught her, dragged her upright, and braced her for a second obliterating blow. Stunned, she reeled sideways and thought at first the hot spray of blood that splashed across her chest was from some horrendous injury he had dealt her with the comb. But it wasn't. He had dropped the steel ornament and kicked it out of reach; the blood was gouting from the wound in his throat, splashing her on each pass of his fists.

She staggered back, flailing out blindly with her fists, dodging one way, then the next, but always being driven further back into the corner. Catapulted by yet another solid blow to her jaw, she sprawled, arms outstretched against the bright row of gowns, her hands smearing ribbons of blood on the expensive silks, brocades and velvets. Sobbing, she clawed upward and began clearing the upper shelves of missiles. Hatboxes, shoeboxes, shawls, gloves, flimsy clouds of silk and lace were flung at the lieutenant to hamper his progress, but as quickly as she was able to toss an obstacle before him, he kicked it aside or swept it out of his way with a bellowed curse.

Catherine's fist closed around a familiar shape and she brought it slashing around in an arc just as the bloody talons of his hands reached out for her. Again and again she flayed the slim leather riding crop into his face, his arms, his bloodied shoulders, to no effect. His madness had carried him beyond all pain. He grabbed hold of the lower edge of her robe and began to reel her in, hand over fist, hauling her toward him, and she could do nothing but scream and continue to crack the leather whip, over and over.

From somewhere beyond the charnel terror of the dressing room, came the sound of fists pounding frantically on the outer door. Someone was out in the hallway. Someone had finally heard the commotion and had come to investigate . . . but the door was locked and the lieutenant had the only key!

The moment of Catherine's distraction was all Goodwin needed to haul in the final few inches of satin and bring her crashing to the floor. She rolled and thrashed against the bloodied hands, managing to get onto her knees and crawl only a few inches before her ankles were hooked and dragged back beneath him. He threw his weight on top of her, his breath rattling against her throat as he groped and tore the shreds of her clothing aside. Catherine's body stiffened into an arch of pure agony as the blunt tips of his nails gouged four bloodied stripes from her breast to her belly, the agony blinding her to everything but the colour red. It was everywhere! Scarlet brighter than his tunic, twice as deep and vibrant where it streaked the whiteness of her skin, smeared the floor, the wall, the clothing. She continued to writhe and struggle against the mauling weight, but she knew it was no use. His hands were jerking her thighs wider apart, his fingers were scratching viciously at the tender junction, ramming their way into her softness and bringing scream after scream of pain to her lips.

Her screams turned to pleas as she began to beg for an end to the horror. For death. Mercifully, she saw a spectre of blackness loom before her eyes, and she sobbed a final, desperate plea for oblivion to claim her. But it was not the shrill pitch of her own voice she heard. Through the tears and blood and the pain she saw the blackness descend, only to rise again, descend and rise in a rhythm matching the sickening thud of pounding wet flesh.

Dazed and gasping for air, Catherine wondered why there were no further bursts of pain. He had withdrawn his hand from between her thighs, but there was still the menacing presence of thicker flesh there, freed from the woolen breeches, pushing eagerly against her. His whole body was twitching and jerking; she could hear the repetitive thud, thud, thud, and feel the warm splashes of fresh blood trickling down her flesh.

She managed to free an arm and reached feverishly into the empty air. The thudding stopped almost at once and a cry brought Deirdre falling to her knees beside her mistress.

"You're alive! Oh dear God . . . dear God, you're still alive! I thought he . . . I thought . . . !"

"Deirdre," Catherine sobbed weakly. "Please—"

Together, pushing and pulling, they rolled the lieutenant's dead weight off Catherine's body. When she was clear, Catherine threw herself into Deirdre's arms and clung to her for dear life.

"Are you hurt?" Deirdre asked, shocked by the amount of blood on her mistress's arms and legs, fearing the worst. "Did he cut you, or . . . or . . . ?"

"No," she rasped. "T-tried to. T-tried to!"

Rage, dark and ugly boiled to the surface, temporarily burning away the fear. Catherine raised her head and started to look around, but Deirdre's hands were there at once to prevent it.

"Mistress—you mustn't look. You must stand up—I'll help you—and you must walk straight into the other room. You mustn't look back. You mustn't look down. You mustn't look anywhere but straight ahead."

Catherine would have questioned the orders, would have balked at being treated like a child, if her gaze had not strayed to where the iron poker lay at their feet. The skillfully crafted eagle's head and fearsomely hooked beak were red with blood, some of the etched detailing clogged with bits of flesh and tufts of hair. She remembered the dull metallic thuds and the jerked spasms that had torn choked grunts from the lieutenant's throat—not out of lust as she had supposed, but out of frenzied pain.

"Dear God . . . Deirdre . . ."

"Just promise me you will not look," came the whispered plea. "I won't look either and perhaps, that way, we can both walk out of here with our sanity."

Catherine nodded. She was again shaking so badly the maid had to practically lift her and carry her out of the dressing room. When they were clear of the double doors, Deirdre reached back and slammed them shut. Backing away, she wiped her hands down the front of her dress as if the door latch had been crawling with maggots. She started to say something reassuring to Catherine, but the added shock of seeing her young mistress in the harsh beam of sunlight was enough to cram the words back into her throat.

The silvery cascade of gleaming blonde hair was threaded with streaks of blood. The satin robe hung limp from her shoulders, one sleeve torn open to the elbow, the whole of the skirt looking as if it had been used to mop the floor of a slaughterhouse. The cambric shirt beneath was in shreds and where the pale ivory flesh showed through, it was scratched raw in places, bruised everywhere else.

"Dear Lord," she cried softly. "Dear Lord. Dear God in heaven, help us."

The prayer was not in vain, she realized, for was there not a dead British officer in the anteroom? Catherine, still numb from the violence, could easily succumb to shock in the next few minutes and be of no use to anyone, including herself.

"Mistress . . . take off those clothes. Hurry now, we must get you cleaned up before . . . before you catch your death of a chill. Look how your teeth are chattering already!"

Catherine held out her arms obediently as Deirdre peeled away the sodden, ruined garments and threw them into a heap before the fireplace. She bundled Catherine into a bedsheet and sat her on the edge of the bed with strict orders not to move so much as an inch. The command was unnecessary. Terror, horror, anger, panic . . . they had all taken a toll on Catherine's strength and she could not have moved had she wanted to.

Deirdre returned with an enamel washbowl and two full jugs of water. The latter was icy cold and Catherine's teeth were visibly dancing a flamenco long before the blood had been sponged and rinsed from her body. Two more full jugs were required to wash the gory residue from her hair, and a good many minutes of vigorous rubbing with towels were necessary to restore any degree of warmth or comfort.

Again she was bundled into the bedsheet while Deirdre —who would not venture near the dressing room—went in search of clean, warm clothing. She returned with two complete outfits of men's garments: breeches, stockings, shirts, and waistcoats, as well as thick woolen cloaks for travelling.

"It should not raise quite so many eyebrows for two men to be seen riding along the road," Deirdre explained. "These are Master Damien's things; I don't imagine he will mind if we borrow them. Quickly now, mistress. We must not dawdle. We must be changed and away from here before any more soldiers come to Rosewood Hall."

"Soldiers?" Catherine frowned over the word as if it should mean something. With a gasp, she remembered and grabbed Deirdre's arm. "He said there were more! He said there were twenty more men downstairs and that . . . that . . ." she stopped, her chin quivering, her mouth moving but unable to form words or sound.

Deirdre took a firm grip on her mistress's shoulders. "He was lying. He was no doubt saying it just to frighten you. There is no one down the stairs. No one, do you hear me? Not a soldier, not a servant, not even a mouse, I warrant, for they were all driven off these past few days by the smell of Scottish cooking."

Catherine's sad attempt at a smile wrenched at Deirdre's heart and forced her to note the further damage to her beautiful young mistress. The left side of her face was beginning to swell out of proportion. Beneath her chin, stretching ear to ear, were dark purpling bruises that would become much worse before the day was through, as would the multitude of cuts and welts on her arms, her legs, and . . . dear God . . . there were four deep scratches down her midsection, from breast to belly, that made it look as if she had been savaged by a mountain cat. Deirdre could feel the fury rising in her again, the rage she had felt when she had seen the animal climbing over her mistress, beating her. Deirdre had not even been aware of running back to fetch the poker, or of striking him again and again until she had turned the back of his head and shoulders into a mash of crushed bone and tissue.

"Deirdre? What is it? What is wrong?"

The maid swallowed the lump of revulsion rising in her throat and forced a calm reply. "As soon as we have dressed, we will have to leave the house and make our separate ways. You will have to go to Lady Caroline at Spence House—she'll know what to do. She'll know how to protect you."

"Protect me? From what? H-he was assaulting me . . . t-trying to rape me."

Deirdre frowned. "Above all, you must make it very clear to anyone who asks—including your mother—that I was the one who did the killing. In fact, you had best say it was me involved in the attack and you were hurt trying to stop him. Yes. Yes, that would be much better . . . much safer."

"But, why would I tell anyone such a thing? Defending oneself against rape is hardly a crime."

Deirdre faced her squarely. "British officers do not go about forcing themselves upon married ladies of quality, not without exceptional cause. If it became known the lieutenant was intent upon raping *you*, the authorities would naturally wonder why; what you had done to provoke such a thing. There would be an inquiry and endless rounds of questions. Don't forget you have just finished playing hostess to enemies of the crown. There would be doubts and aspersions cast upon your character, your loyalties. Why, you might very well end up being the one regarded as the criminal. A maid, on the other hand, is another matter entirely. The gentry *expect* us to be of loose moral fibre, to service their filthy needs wherever and whenever the mood comes upon them. I doubt anyone would even consider it an act of rape . . . more likely a miscalculation on the lieutenant's part."

Catherine's voice trembled with concern. "But . . . where will you go? What will you do? The roads to London will all be blocked, you would never make it through."

Deirdre glanced toward the window. "I shan't be heading south, mistress."

"But Damien is in London! He is a lawyer, he will know how to straighten this whole ugly mess out!"

"Indeed, Master Damien is a fine lawyer, and no doubt he would fight to see justice done, but it could take months—months I could spend being much happier and much safer elsewhere."

Catherine stared. "You are going to follow the rebel army! Oh Deirdre . . . you can't! If what the lieutenant said is true and Prince Charles is in retreat—"

"Then I shall retreat also. They will be bound for the border, for Scotland. It is my husband's home and will be mine as well, sooner now than later, is all."

"But—"

"Please, mistress, we must hurry. We must be dressed and gone from this place before any soldiers do take it in their heads to visit."

Catherine responded slowly, stiffly, her mind and body too battered to fully grasp what was happening. She had been set upon by a swaggering, bestial officer of her majesty's services; had been beaten, nearly raped, and only saved from almost certain death by Deirdre's timely intervention. Now, she was being forced to flee from her house, from the very authorities she had been raised to believe were beyond reproach. Men like her uncle, Colonel Lawrence Halfyard—surely, he would not condemn her for acting in self-defense? Even a man like Hamilton Garner would never have condoned such brutish behaviour in a fellow officer—would he?

And what would happen to Deirdre?

Catherine's hands faltered midway into buttoning the front closure of the warm, quilted waistcoat the maid had provided.

Deirdre was prepared to take the blame, to have the questions and accusations, and ultimate reprisals brought down around her own head rather than see Catherine suffer further abuse. Catherine Ashbrooke would most certainly have allowed it, would have grasped at any avenue of escape regardless of the right or wrong of it—but would, *could* Catherine Ashbrooke Cameron?

"The lieutenant said the rebel army withdrew well before dawn," she said, her bruised throat unable to produce much more than a whisper. "We will need fast horses if we hope to catch up to them. Spirited ones too, I should think, for there are bound to be government troops and patrols aplenty."

Deirdre looked up, her hands freezing on her neck ties. "Did you say 'we', mistress?"

"I think—" Catherine paused to moisten her lips, "—after all we have been through together, you needn't address me as 'mistress' or 'my lady' anymore. Criminals are all equal in the eyes of the law, for one thing. For another, I would greatly appreciate being considered more your friend than your employer."

Deirdre's large, solemn brown eyes followed the motion of Catherine's scraped hands as they resumed the painful task of buttoning the waistcoat. Damien Ashbrooke was lean and not too much taller than his sister so the clothing was not comically oversized. Still, the gathered cuffs of the shirt covered each girl's fingertips and the waist of the breeches had to be rolled twice and secured with belts.

"I think it would be rash for you to make any decision before consulting with Lady Caroline."

Catherine sighed and brushed away a persistent tear. "My mother will have more than enough difficulties of her own to overcome in the next few weeks, nevermind being burdened with mine. As for Damien—" she sighed again and gave up on the bottom two tiny pearlized studs, the shaking in her fingers simply too much to control. "He is a Jacobite, Deirdre. He will undoubtedly be worried after his own safety and the safety of his wife and unborn child. I could never knowingly put them in further danger. Not Damien. Not Harriet. Not you," she added quietly.

"But . . . the lieutenant died by my hand. *I* wielded the poker. *I* killed him."

"For that, I shall be everlastingly in your debt. However, even though I may not know much about doctoring, I suspect there was far too much blood leaking from his neck to have been caused by a simple scratch. You may have hastened the good lieutenant along the road to hell, but, I dare say, he was already well on his way."

"But—"

"And if you think me so weak and utterly lacking in character that I would permit you to suffer the consequences for an act which I, myself, committed, well then—" she straightened and faced Deirdre sternly. "Well then, we shall indeed be travelling alone, despite a similar destination, and despite the hope we truly could become good friends."

"Similar destination?" Deirdre's jaw slackened. "Oh no, mistress, it is far too dangerous. Your husband would never allow it!"

"Whereas your husband would?" She saw the consternation on Deirdre's face and was actually able to smile. "Come now, Deirdre. We have just done murder; surely, we are capable of dealing with the wrath of two self-righteous Scotsmen? Believe me, I appreciate what you are trying to do, and I will even go so far as to admit that a very large part of me wants desperately to run to Spence House and live out the rest of my days with my head buried in the sand. Unfortunately, there is another part of me—the part I would have to live with the rest of those same days, that tells me I would never be able to look myself in the eye again." She paused and her smile turned wistful. "I am guilty of murder and I desperately need and want my husband's protection right now—can you think of any better reason for leaving Derby far behind?"

"No," came a low male voice from the bedchamber door. "But I can give you at least one thousand armed reasons why you would not get very far."

Both women gasped and whirled around. Standing in the doorway, his musket primed and cocked for business, was Corporal Jeffrey Peters, the grimness of his expression erasing any and all hint of youthfulness and inexperience from his face.

RETREAT

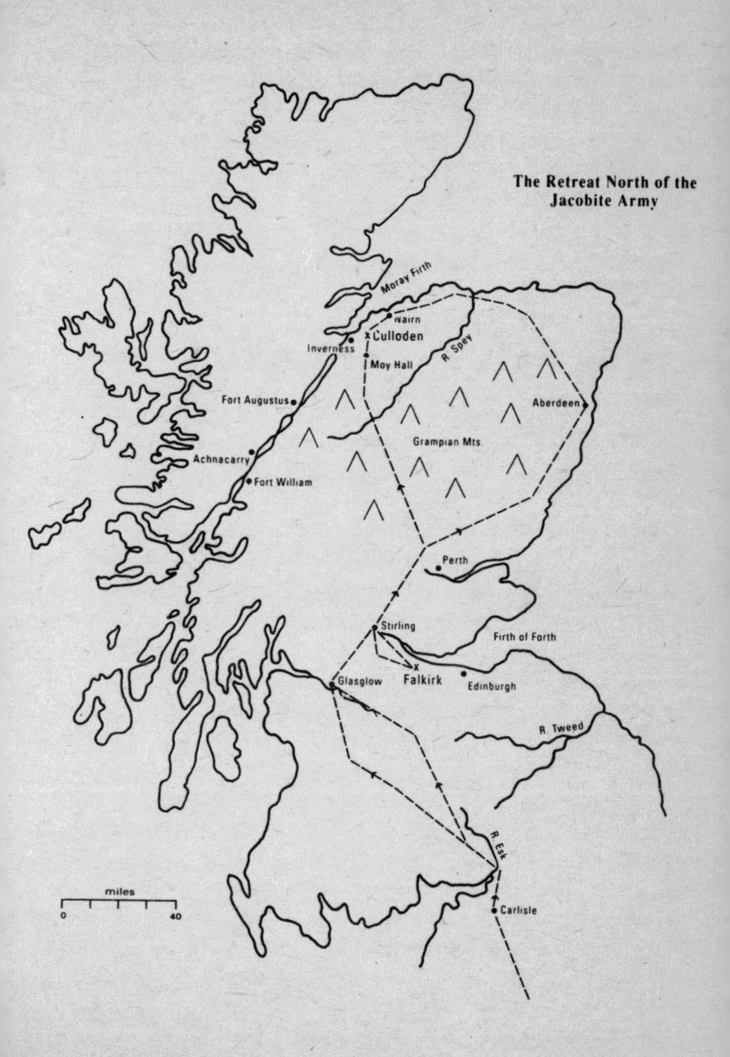
The Retreat North of the Jacobite Army
Moray Firth
Nairn
Culloden
Inverness
Moy Hall
R. Spey
Fort Augustus
Aberdeen
Grampian Mts.
Achnacarry
Fort William
Perth
Stirling
Firth of Forth
Falkirk
Glasglow
Edinburgh
R. Tweed
R. Esk
Carlisle
miles
0
40

Chapter Eleven

In less than twenty-four hours, the attitude of the Jacobite army had undergone a complete and potentially disastrous turn-about. In Derby, poised to march the remaining one-hundred-and-fifty victorious miles to London, the clansmen had tackled their daily routines with a strength of purpose few men could not help but admire. Hundreds of miles from home, suffering from a constant lack of adequate provisions and shelter, regarded with open contempt and hostility by the English people, they still sang to cover the rumble of empty bellies, danced around the campfires to keep the numbing winter chill out of their bones, kept their weapons honed and their outlooks keen for a confrontation with the Hanover army.

That was why, when the order to retreat was finally delivered, it was decided only the chiefs and their senior officers were to know their destination beforehand. The army was to be roused before dawn and settled into a brisk pace before the sun betrayed in which direction they marched. If asked, the officers were to imply they were marching out to a meeting with either Wade's forces, or Cumberland.

It was not until a few discerning eyes recognized landmarks they had passed only two days previous, that rumours began to spread throughout the clans that they were on retreat. The rumours were met at first with disbelief, then outrage, and finally, bitter disillusionment. The common soldiers, had not been aware of the doubts and fears plaguing their chiefs; they had seen only victory thus far and could not fathom why they were turning away so close to their goal. The pace of the march slowed. Arguments broke out within the ranks, and, for the first time since crossing the border into England, the chiefs were regarded with mistrust and suspicion. Why had they been brought so many miles from home only to retreat with victory within their grasp? Where was the pride, the honour, the glory of fighting behind the Stuart standard when it could be so easily turned and blown back into the wind? Where was the passion and confidence that had led them to an astounding triumph at Prestonpans against odds no sane man could willingly entertain? And where was their prince? Where was the man whose heartfelt pleas and unshaking faith had swept them to victory in Scotland and convinced them of similar possibilities in England?

Prince Charles Edward Stuart did not make an appearance all day. Acting the part of a man who had lost not only his heart but his courage, he behaved as if the army was no longer his to command, as if their loyalty had been stripped from him by men who wished only to see him humiliated by betrayal and defeat. On the march south to Derby, he had risen each morning at dawn and walked all day on foot alongside the men, suffering the same effects of weather, hunger, and exhaustion. For the first twelve hours of the retreat, he rode in a small covered cart, weeping disconsolately and searching for comfort at the bottom of several bottles of whisky. His attitude was contagious and a pall settled over the clans; by nightfall, the men had become quiet, morose, and too ill at heart to do more than curl themselves in their tartans and lie, staring into the fires.

In those few short hours the Prince had changed from conqueror to fugitive, his army no longer the hunters, but the hunted.

Lord George Murray's greatest concern in those same twelve hours, was the opposite effect the news of their retreat would have on the English forces. Those who had elected to keep a prudent distance from the advancing Highlanders, would now have the scent of the kill to infuse them with new courage and purpose. Alexander Cameron's reconnaissance had established Cumberland's army at Conventry, Wade's at Doncaster. Less than forty miles separated the two armies. They were on familiar ground, well suited to their artillery and cavalry; as soon as word of the retreat reached them, they would undoubtedly strive with all haste to join forces and intercept the Highlanders before they could effect an escape across the border. Cumberland, although several months younger than his Stuart cousin, Charles Edward, was an experienced commander, a soldier known for his relentless pursuit of his enemies.

True to Lord George Murray's promise, he and his Athollmen had taken up the position of highest risk at the rearguard of the army, travelling only as fast as the slowest clan contingent. Alexander Cameron, true to his word, joined his forces with the Athol Brigade and had, in turn, assumed the role of scout and liaison officer between the clans. He had been fielding reports of government sightings all day long, riding out to check the greater percentage of them personally. His mood, therefore, as midnight came and went and still found him pouring over maps and charts of the territory they would be passing through come daylight, was not exactly sterling. His seemingly endless reserves of strength and patience were rapidly dwindling; he had scarcely spoken a dozen words to anyone all day that were not laced with acid.

When he heard a muffled disturbance approaching his tent, the expression on his face should have sent any man fleeing who valued his neck—any man, except Struan MacSorley.

"I ken ye've had a lang day," the Highlander said, poking his head beneath the canvas tent flap, "but I thought ye mout be interested in seein' what the picketts foun' prancin' alang the road a wee while ago."

Alex leaned back in his chair and scowled blackly. "Unless it is the Duke of Cumberland and he has come to present a flag of surrender, absolutely nothing could interest me at the moment."

Struan arched a golden brow. "Aye, an' if that's true, I'll toss them back soon enough. I'm o' a mind they've a rare tale tae tell, but. Couldna hairt tae listen."

Alex swore irritably and knuckled his eyes to rub away the sand and fatigue. "Alright. What the hell, I've nothing better planned but a few hours sleep."

"Aye, an' growin' fewer." With that cryptic comment, MacSorley caught up the tent flap again and raised it to the height of his shoulder. A nod brought three grimy figures into the small space, two dressed in civilian clothes, the third wearing the uniform of a junior officer in the government infantry. Of the three, only the soldier dared to raise his face to the yellowish lantern light—as much for the hint of warmth it offered as for illumination. The other two kept their heads lowered and their eyes downcast so that their features were cloaked in the shadow of their tricorns.

"Well, well. So this is the vanguard of Cumberland's army, is it? Or perhaps a delegation from King George asking when we might be wanting the keys to the palace?"

MacSorley snorted humorlessly and reached over to casually lift away the two tricorns. It took a full minute for the recognition to cut through Alex's weariness, but when it did, when he saw the thick, glossy braid of blonde hair snake down over the slender shoulders, his expression darkened like a thundercloud about to erupt. It was only with an almost superhuman effort that he was able to control his reaction and keep his voice smooth and level, his hands flat and steady on the table.

"I trust there is a bloody good explanation for this," he said through his teeth.

The soldier, his face flushed and his brow beginning to dot with moisture, snapped to attention at once. "Corporal Jeffrey Peters, sir, at your service. These two ladies are—"

"I know damn well who these two *ladies* are, boy. What I want to know is what the bloody Christ they're doing here?"

"W-well, sir, they—"

"And I would prefer to hear it from them, if you don't mind!" Alex snarled, glancing at Struan, who only had to rest a ham-like hand on the corporal's shoulder to intimidate him into instant silence.

Alexander glared at Deirdre and Catherine in turn, his eyes black with fury, his temper stretched on a thin thread. "Well?"

Deirdre was the first to meet the Scotsman's challenge. "We have left Derby, my lord, not by choice, but out of necessity. We were hoping we might be allowed to travel north with you."

Alex stared. When the seconds ticked away and there was still no response, the silence became so oppressive, it started a loud humming in the girls' ears. Catherine clutched Deirdre's hand tightly for courage; she was shaking so badly, she was disrupting the folds of her cloak. To Deirdre's credit, she withstood the chilling effects of Alexander's stony gaze, only showing visible signs of faltering when the obsidian eyes flicked over to Struan.

"I think you had best find MacKail," Alex said evenly. "He should be privy to this, don't you agree?"

"Aye. Shall I fetch this ane wi' me?"

Alex spared a shrivelling glance for the corporal. "God no. He has come this far, driven no doubt by some misguided sense of chivalry. He should at least be here to make the grand offer of having his backside flayed to strips in place of theirs'."

The corporal swallowed reflexively. Struan ducked back out of the tent and Alex, who had not moved a muscle up to this point, tipped his chair back on the rear two legs and crossed his arms over his chest.

"I had honestly expected better from you, Mistress O'Shea," he remarked dryly. "I had thought the Irish had a stronger sense of self-preservation."

"It is exactly because of a sense of self-preservation we thought to find our best protection with you, sir," Deirdre answered defiantly.

"Protection? From what?" he demanded. "The clans have taken advantage of the hospitality of countless estates and homes belonging to you English, with no repercussions to date. If this is some kind of ploy, madam, I'll warn you both now, it will not work."

Although Catherine could not yet bring herself to meet her husband's eyes, she could feel their probing effect on her knees, which were turning rapidly to butter, and on her stomach, which was beginning a slow, unobstructed slide toward her feet. Their angry heat relented only when the sound of running feet brought Aluinn MacKail's sand-brown head of hair thrusting under the tent flap.

"Deirdre!" he gasped. "Good God, it *is* you!"

He pushed all the way inside the tent, followed closely by MacSorley and a third man neither of the women had met before—a lean, tall, elegantly middle-aged gentleman dressed incongruously in courtly garb. At the sight of the ladies, Count Fanducci removed his plumed tricorn at once. At the sight of MacKail, Deirdre's nerve collapsed and she turned into his embrace, her arms thrown about his neck as if she might smother him in her need. Aluinn started to respond in a similar fashion, but a single glance in Alexander's direction halted the movement of his arms and instead, he reached up and gently pried her wrists down from around his neck.

"Deirdre . . . what are you doing here?" he asked, his tone less threatening than Cameron's, but cool enough to produce a shine of tears in Deirdre's eyes. "How did you get here? Don't you know the whole of Cumberland's army is breathing down our necks?"

"Th-that's not entirely true, sir," Corporal Peters ventured to say. "The main body of his army is still en route to London, to reinforce the guard at Finchley Commons and to act upon rumours of an impending invasion by the French. The Duke has but a thousand cavalrymen at his disposal, and they, in turn, are riding to a rendezvous with Marshal Wade. Sir."

Aluinn's gray eyes narrowed as they went from Corporal Peters to Alex. "Who the devil is he?"

"Corporal Jeffrey Peters," Alex drawled belligerently. "At our service. Rather, it might be said, at the service of these two—" he paused and searched a moment for an appropriate word "—adventuresses."

"Corporal Peters helped us out of an extremely unpleasant situation," Deirdre said defensively. "Furthermore, he escorted us here at great personal risk. If it had not been for Mr. MacSorley taking the time to recognize us, there is no telling what your brutish guards might have done to the corporal—or to us."

"You should not feel so assured of your safety just yet," Alex warned silkily. "And I am still waiting to hear an explanation as to why you are here. Catherine? It astounds me you have managed to hold your silence this long—is this supposed to be for dramatic effect?"

Deirdre blanched and pushed angrily away from Aluinn. "She's not said anything yet, sir, because it would be extremely painful for her to do so. If it is drama you want, I suggest you use your eyes to look at the bruises and cuts on her face rather than to show us how cold and heartless you can be by frightening us half to death."

She caught a trembling lip between her teeth and watched as Alexander's gaze turned slowly away from hers to his wife. After another long, heart-thudding moment of tension, he rose from the chair, his eyes never wavering from Catherine's down-turned face as he advanced around the table toward her. He stopped within arm's reach, halted by the shock of realizing the darker shadows on his wife's face were not a result of the angled lantern light. Bracing himself, he tucked a finger beneath her chin and tilted her head upward, turning it slightly so that both the purple bruise on her cheek and the partial swelling of her eye had the full benefit of the sepia glow. Even before his senses had absorbed this new shock, his eyes were drawn lower, to where the pleats of her neckerchief had been dislodged and revealed the ugly black and broken-veined contusions on her throat.

"Jesus Christ," Aluinn whispered, moving to stand by Alex's side. "What the hell happened?"

Catherine's eyes swam behind a film of tears as she opened them slowly and looked up at her husband.

"When we woke this morning," Deirdre said, "the house was deserted. Most of the servants had left, either to spread gossip or to run away and hide before anyone else decided to commandeer the house and property. There was a British officer . . . one from the company of militia who had been camped on the grounds prior to your arrival, and he . . . he was the first to come back after your men left. He must have guessed the house would be deserted for a while . . . at any rate, he . . . he took advantage of the fact that my lady was alone and . . . and . . ."

Catherine felt a tremor shudder through the hand that still supported her chin. She had seen anger in Alexander's eyes before—cool, dispassionate anger used to turn an enemy's soul to ice. But she had never seen anything comparable to the naked, consuming rage she saw now —a fury focussed as much inwardly as it throbbed outwardly, commanding every tautly held muscle in his body, rasping on every short, dry breath.

"Struan: Have Shadow saddled and ready to ride in five minutes."

"Aye. An' ye'll be takin' me alang tae see the job's doun right."

"No," Deirdre cried, grabbing MacSorley's arm and literally being dragged several steps toward the tent door before making him aware of her clinging presence. "No, there isn't any need to go back!"

"I want his name," Alex said quietly. "Aluinn—?"

MacKail gripped Deirdre by the shoulders and turned her abruptly toward him. "His name, Deirdre; do you know the bastard's name?"

She stared up in disbelief. The face of her tender and loving husband had hardened. The same primitive violence that had flared to life on Alexander Cameron's face had molded Aluinn's into something unrecognizable— something she did not wish to acknowledge or to see again, for a very long time.

"Please," Catherine gasped, the word hardly more than a pain-filled breath of air. She clutched one hand around Alex's arm, another around Aluinn, and cast a frightened, imploring glance toward Struan. "He's already dead. The one who did it is dead."

"Dead?" Aluinn asked. "How? By whose hand?"

Catherine looked up into her husband's face. "We killed him, Deirdre and I. We had no choice . . . it was self-defense!"

Alexander's composure cracked visibly. "What? What did you just say?"

"It's true, sir," Corporal Peters stammered. "I c-couldn't believe it either, n-not at first. But it's t-true. S-so help me God, it's true!"

"What do you know about this?" Alex snarled, rounding on the corporal as if in search of some victim for his anger . . . a victim wearing the uniform of the British army.

"I was l-looking for Lieutenant Goodwin, s-sir. That was his n-name: Goodwin. I w-was supposed to relay the orders from our colonel as to h-how and wh-where we were to join up with C-Cumberland's army. I had seen the w-way Goodwin had behaved in Mrs. Montgomery's presence on s-several other occasions and I . . . I had my suspicions as to wh-where he might have gone as s-soon as he heard that the Reb . . . er, the Jacobite army had withdrawn. B-by the time I got to the house, sir, it was all over. The ladies had managed to overpower him and—" His voice wavered, his eyes glazed with the memory of walking into the dressing room, of holding a light over what had once been the head of Lieutenant Goodwin, and of having to go through the motions of checking for any sign of life. "I sh-should never live to see another man as d-dead as he was, sir. I swear to God. I'm only sorry I did not arrive in time to deal with him p-personally. But when I saw and heard what he had done to Mrs. Montgomery . . . well, had it been the king himself, I would gladly have killed him!"

Alex did not miss the fiery earnestness in the young corporal's eyes that said: yes, and I will kill you too if necessary.

"Go on, Corporal."

"Well, sir, when I heard their story, I knew they could not remain at the manor or risk facing a tribunal. I tried to convince them to go elsewhere—*anywhere*—Mrs. Montgomery has a brother in London, I believe—but they would have none of it. They insisted on being brought here, and from here to make their way under your protection to Blackpool, where they hoped to meet up with Mrs. Montgomery's husband. It was all *I* could do to insist they accept my services as escort this far."

"I'm sorry, Alex," Catherine cried softly. "We didn't know what else to do, where else to go to feel safe again."

Alex drew her gently into his arms. Safe? He could have cursed the word for mocking him so. *Safe?*

"Corporal Peters—" his eyes sought the young officer over the top of Catherine's head. "For what you have risked, and everything you have done for my wife and for Mrs. MacKail, you have my deepest thanks and my humblest apologies. If there is anything—anything I can do to repay you, please let me know."

"Your . . . wife, sir? But—" Peters frowned and some of the rigid army discipline deserted him. "B-but I thought . . . I mean, they told me Mr. Montgomery was a merchant . . . ?"

Catherine disengaged herself from Alex's arms and turned to the bewildered corporal. "I'm sorry for lying to you, after all you have done. I just was not sure what your reaction would be if you knew my husband's true identity."

Corporal Peters returned her weak smile and was about to offer the same to Alex when he seemed to notice for the first time, the jet black hair, the massive shoulders, the power and authority rippling through every muscle, echoing in every word. "Jesus H. Christ on a stick," he muttered slowly. "You're him, aren't you! You're the one they call the Dark Cameron!"

"Alexander will do. Alex, if you prefer," the reluctant legend said wryly. Wrapping an arm protectively around Catherine's waist, Alex thrust his other hand out toward the corporal. It took an additional moment or two for Peters to acknowledge the gesture, then to wipe the dampness from his palm and accept the offered handshake.

"I'm honoured, sir. And indeed, there is something you can do for me: You can honour me further by personally accepting my sword in surrender."

Alex started to protest, but the corporal's grin cut him short. "Please, sir. My father has been drinking secret toasts to the 'king over the water' for the past forty years. I guess I just didn't think I had the guts to join you before, but . . . well, now that I'm here, and . . . and . . . well . . ."

Alex put the corporal at ease with a smile. "In case you haven't been listening to your own dispatches, Corporal, we're in retreat. You may be picking the wrong time to change sides."

"I don't think so, sir. If Mrs. Mon—Mrs. Cameron has enough faith in you to join you, I cannot see any mistakes being made at all."

Alex's smile slipped. He glanced down at Catherine and felt a resurgence of anger boil into his blood again, only this time, it was solely for his own inadequacy as a husband and protector. She was standing firm, putting up a brave enough front, but most of her weight was trusted to the arm he had around her waist. Her head was leaning gratefully on his shoulder and she seemed unaware of the people around her.

"Alex?" Aluinn dragged his attention away. "Do you want me to find Archibald?"

"What?"

"Archibald," Aluinn repeated the question gently. "Do you want me to fetch him?"

Alex suffered another severe jolt to his equanimity as his focus reverted to the bruises on Catherine's cheek and throat. Those were only the ones he could see; there were sure to be others, possibly even more devastating.

"Deirdre?"

She could read the question and the fear in the dark sapphire eyes and she shook her head. "No sir, he didn't hurt her . . . not that way. I think she'll be alright, now that she's here with you. She's exhausted, to be sure, and I don't know how she managed to stay in a saddle as long as she did, but a few good hours of sleep should work wonders."

Alex nodded and smiled his thanks. It was the Italian, Count Fanducci, a silent observer up until now, who took a cue from the way Alex tightened his arm around his wife, and who stepped out of the shadows to deliver a devastatingly well executed bow in Catherine's honour.

"*Signora Camerone*! A very brave-a lady. If there is anything I, Giovanni Alphonso Fanducci can do for either of you beautiful ladies, you joost-a snap-a you fingers, *sí*? But for now, we leave-a you alone. Come, come!" He flicked his hands to indicate everyone should share his fine sense of timing and vacate the tent. "I'm-a personally posting the guard outside so no one is disturbed, *sí*?"

Aluinn did not need to be told twice to take his tearful wife into his arms and lead her out of the tent to seek their own. MacSorley crammed his blue woolen bonnet on his head and offered a final, muttered curse to the British army, then clamped an almost friendly hand on the corporal's shoulder and ushered him out into the crisp, dark night air, the Count following close on their heels.

Alone, Alex surrendered to the overwhelming need to circle his arms around his wife and bury his lips in the damp fragrance of her hair. He held her as closely as he dared, aware of the tiny shudders of pain she was doing her best to conceal. Not so easily contained were the tears that began on a stifled sob, swelled in volume and substance until she was crying openly, her fingers clutching the lapels of his coat, her body shaking against his like a leaf in a storm.

"It's alright," he murmured. "You're safe now. You're with me, Catherine. You're safe . . . *safe*."

"Alex—" her eyes swam before him, two enormous pools of glimmering violet and blue and deepest, darkest black. "Please don't send me away again. Please. I know you are angry with us for coming here, but we had nowhere else to go. Please, Alex, please, I—"

Caused by the bruised chords of her throat, her whispers drove cleanly through his heart like steel spikes. He silenced them beneath his lips and felt a scalding sensation flood his own eyes. "I am not letting you out of my sight again, Catherine, you may count on it. I only hope you can forgive me—"

Once before he had sworn to keep her safe, to keep her sheltered and protected and loved, and a spectre by the name of Malcolm Campbell had nearly destroyed them. Alex had sent her to Derby, again to be safe, sheltered, protected, and loved . . . and God only knew what horrors had been stamped on her mind and body this time. All because of him. *Because of him!*

"Alex—this wasn't your fault," she cried weakly, her hands reaching up to cradle the bronzed cheeks. "None of it was your fault, you mustn't blame yourself."

"I am your husband," he rasped. "Who else should I hold to blame for not shielding you against all of this?"

"Alex . . . it would have happened, regardless of whom I loved and whom I married. It would have happened to anyone who crossed paths with the lieutenant . . . Deirdre, me, anyone!"

It was a weak platitude at best and it brought his dark head bending forward, his lips desperately seeking hers. "I am truly damned if I know why you love me, Catherine. I seem to cause you nothing but pain, show you nothing but ugliness and fear and death where you should only be surrounded by beauty and happiness. If I'd known . . . if I'd had any idea at the outset that any of this was possible, let alone that it could happen—" he shook his head and Catherine's fingers were there, pressing over the stern lines of his mouth.

"What would you have done about it? Changed who you are? Changed what you believe in? Or perhaps you would have walked away and left me to Hamilton

Garner? I asked you once to run away with me, to take me to France, or Italy—anywhere as long as we were safe and together. But I doubt I would have loved you a fraction as much if you had turned into a parlour dandy—nor you me, for taking you away from your family, your loyalty, your honour. I believe our love is quite inevitable, my lord, and I give thanks for every moment we are together. You are my love and my life, and I am resigned to accepting whatever that entails, my darling. Quite, quite happily so."

The long speech drained both her strength and her remaining ability to speak through the wall of pain in her throat. She gave herself to the clouds of darkness swirling gently around her, aware of Alex's arms there to catch her, to hold her close as he carried her to the narrow cot. The aches and stiffness in her body melted away, taking with them the last traces of the pampered Mistress Catherine Ashbrooke, and leaving behind the confident and deserving Lady Catherine Cameron.

Chapter Twelve

Each town and city the rebels passed through on the retreat was far less friendly than it had been during the advance. The good citizens of Manchester, for one, gathered in mobs and threw stones. In lieu of having his men return fire, the Prince levied a hefty fine on the city, although with Cumberland's vanguard closing fast, there was not enough time to collect it. The pursuing forces entered the English town of Preston less than four hours after the Jacobites had cleared it, and at Lancaster, Cumberland was so close, Lord George Murray rode out with Lochiel and Alexander to choose ground advantageous for a battle. The threat was subsequently postponed when a hand-picked Jacobite detachment of the Manchester Regiment, dressed in captured government uniforms, brazenly circled around behind the Duke's army and delivered an urgent message to the effect that the French had landed in force on the south coast. Cumberland halted at once and spent three days waiting impatiently for couriers to travel back to London for new orders.

Temporarily gaining an advantage of time, the Prince seemed to rally some of his former spirit. He no longer rode in the covered cart, but marched alongside the clansmen once again. Lord George Murray maintained his vigilance in guarding the rear of the retreating army, with various regiments spelling the Athollmen from their dangerous and active position. Losing Cumberland for a time provided a much needed breathing space, but the Duke's task of harassment was enthusiastically taken up by companies of local militia. So keen were they to prove their newfound boldness, Lord George found himself organizing frequent skirmishes to scatter the militiamen back into the trees. They always came back, like an itch that could not be scratched, and valuable time was lost in minor raids.

On December 18, the rearguard of the Highland army reached the village of Clifton and were once again alerted to Cumberland's presence on their flank. Lord George Murray sent ahead for reinforcements from the main column, but the Prince, unaware that the Duke was less than a mile from the rebel guard, decided to march on to Carlisle and make a stand there. By the time Lord George received the order not to confront Cumberland, but to retreat with his men to Carlisle, members of the King's Own Regiment of Dragoons and Kingston's Horse were forming for the attack. With Alexander Cameron riding by his side and fewer than eight hundred men at their command, Lord George drew his broadsword and led half of his forces into a charge. The other half were split in two, positioned along either flank of the advancing government forces and ordered to make enough noise and flying dust to convince the English the entire Jacobite army was waiting in the wings to attack. The ploy worked. The dragoons were put to flight and the bulk of Cumberland's forces retreated a discreet distance from the field. When it became apparent that the English general was in no haste to attack again, Lord George recalled his men to Penrith, then to Carlisle, where he rejoined the Prince.

Freshly invigorated by the victory, however minor, Lord George was at first shocked, then outraged to learn that Charles Stuart, against the advice of his council and without troubling to consult with his general, had made the decision to leave a garrison of men at Carlisle to delay Cumberland's advance rather than having to march with one eye constantly over their shoulders. Lord George argued passionately that it was a suicidal detail; four hundred weary men could not possibly hold off three times their number of fresh, seasoned troops. Furthermore, it was the Prince's choice to designate the Manchester Regiment for the post of dubious honour, and, being Englishmen, if captured, they would be treated doubly harshly as both rebels and traitors.

Unable to convince the Prince of his folly, Lord George then volunteered himself and his Athollmen for the hazardous duty. It did his heart good to see Lochiel, Keppoch, Ardshiel and a dozen other chiefs instantly volunteer themselves and their clansmen to share the burden, but in the end the gestures were made in vain. Despite the ever increasing animosity between them, Charles Stuart knew he could not afford to sacrifice his only general and Lord George's orders were countermanded.

On December 20, suffering with the guilt of knowing that they could never hope to return to Carlisle in time to relieve or save the four hundred brave men, Lord George led his dispirited troops to the banks of the river Esk. It was the Prince's twenty-fifth birthday, but there was no time for celebrations. The recent rains and heavy snowfalls had swelled the waters to such a depth the men could only stand and stare in horror at the swift, raging currents that marked the border between England and Scotland.

Two men, attempting to ford the river at its narrowest point, were swept off their horses and carried several hundred yards downstream. Unable to wait out the floods, both directions of the bank were scouted and, after holding a brief council with Lord George, Alexander selected the men riding the tallest, stoutest horses to follow himself and Shadow into the icy waters above the ford, forming a living dam to break the force and speed of the currents. Lord George was the first to wade into the river. Even with the dam, the water was so deep that only the heads and shoulders of the men rose above the surface. Shorter men were helped or carried by their comrades. Struan MacSorley, looking like a maypole, walked across with men hanging off his arms and clinging to ropes slung through his belt. The Prince, Lord George, and the Duke of Perth made countless trips, back and forth, ferrying men and women on horseback. Many of the supply wagons had to be abandoned, the supplies carried across on the men's backs. To Count Fanducci's overwhelming distress, the cannon—those same guns captured at Prestonpans and nursed faithfully by the energetic Italian all the way to Derby and back—had to be spiked and abandoned.

Catherine was, for once, thankful not to be sharing Shadow's saddle with her husband, and rode across the inky, rushing waters, balanced securely on Struan's broad shoulders. Her first steps on Scottish soil in four months were not taken without some misgivings. She stared back across the raging river, knowing for certain her choice had been made, irrevocably so, and she might not ever be free to cross back into England again. Behind her, the pipers played and the men danced reels to warm and dry themselves, but Catherine could only think of Rosewood Hall, of her mother, and of the sheltered, socially regimented life she had once lived which was completely foreign to her now. She had forfeited it willingly, knowing her life and future belonged to Alexander Cameron, but there were still some sad memories: She had left Harriet behind, and Damien. Her mother was sailing for the colonies, and it might be years before she ever heard word from her again . . .

Such thoughts were quickly pushed to the back of Catherine's mind, for there was still a great deal in the present to be concerned with. In less than a fortnight, an army consisting mainly of infantry had withdrawn nearly two hundred miles, chased every step of the way by cavalry and still threatened by Wade's army of regulars garrisoned at Newcastle. The weather conditions were deplorable. When it was not snowing, they were buffeted by high winds, rain, and sleet. The men were cold, hungry and tired; many had worn through their shoes and marched barefoot through icy puddles and drifting banks of snow.

Once into Scotland, the army divided into two columns, Lord George taking one by the low roads toward Glasgow, Prince Charles and the Duke of Perth marching by the high route through Peebles. They arrived at the port city a day apart and, like the people of Manchester, the Glaswegians reacted with open opposition and hostility. Tempers were so worn on both sides, that only Lochiel's intervention prevented the city from being sacked and razed in retaliation. Again the Prince sought to levy a fine, this time collecting it from the merchants in the form of clothing, blankets and warm footwear to refit the ragged Highlanders.

For the first time, no attempt was made to conceal or exaggerate the size of the army which had marched to within striking distance of England's capital city. Hoping their audacity would have inspired support from home, both Lord George and the Prince were surprised to learn the opposite had occurred. In mid-October, the Earl of Loudoun had travelled by sea to Inverness and had taken command of a sizeable force of troops recruited by the Lord President, Duncan Forbes. Forbes had commissioned officers from the clans loyal to the House of Hanover, and had also threatened, bribed, and extorted some of the most influential Jacobite chiefs to ignore the increasingly desperate pleas from their prince. Moreover, the entire territory controlled by the Argyle Campbells was firmly in support of the government—lands which stretched from the lowland border to Lochaber. Territory north of Inverness was committed to Hanover; the western Highlands of Skye were firmly held in the hands of Sir Alexander MacDonald of Sleat and The MacLeod of MacLeod—both of whom had initially supported the Prince, but who now led companies in the service of Lord Loudoun.

In the Prince's absence, Edinburgh had received reinforcements by sea and the city's population—those same throngs who had turned out in cheering and waving crowds to greet the Stuart prince—now cheered as long and hard for the new Commander-in-Chief in Scotland, General Henry Hawley. A seasoned campaigner who had fought with Cumberland at Dettingen and Fontenoy, Hawley was supremely contemptuous of the Prince's army, and was determined to make his mark as the general who had defeated and disbanded the rebels for all time. As soon as word reached Edinburgh that Charles Stuart had returned, Hawley prepared his army to march.

The news was not all bad. A second Highland army numbering upwards of thirty-four hundred men had been forming in Aberdeen, and upon word of the Prince's arrival in Scotland, marched to Stirling, effectively doubling the size of the forces at the regent's command. Among them was Lord John Drummond, the Duke of Perth's brother, newly arrived from France with eight hundred men. Declaring himself and his Royal Scots official representatives of King Louis, Lord Drummond sent a dispatch at once to the commander of the Dutch forces who had sailed to England to support King George, reminding him of the terms of a recent treaty between the Dutch and the French, wherein, the Dutch had pledged not to fight against them again until after 1747. The seven thousand troops Cumberland had counted upon to bolster his forces, had no choice but to embark for home again without having completely dried the salt spray from their tunics.

On January 13, Lord George made a routine foray to Linlithgow to intercept supplies intended for Hawley's troops and learned that the government army had departed Edinburgh and was half a day's march down the road. With less than two hundred men at his disposal, Lord George prudently withdrew to Falkirk, then to Bannockburn where the Prince immediately made plans to lure Hawley into battle.

For two days, Hawley remained camped at Falkirk, the Prince, at Bannockburn. Aware of the importance the Jacobites placed on Bannockburn, where one of Scotland's greatest warrior kings, Robert the Bruce, had won a resounding victory in 1311, Hawley was not about to budge from his position to carry the battle to the Prince. Annoyed, but not daunted, Charles Stuart marched his clans onto the high ground overlooking Falkirk, the move such a complete surprise to Hawley, that the general was not even present in the camp. He had been invited to dinner with the enchanting and curvaceous Lady Kilmarnock (whose husband was, at the same time, forming his clansmen alongside the Prince). Stunned to hear of the rebel's presence on the moor, Hawley rushed back to the field, his dinner napkin still tucked into the collar of his shirt. He arrived breathless, hatless, and in time to see his touted cavalry charging uphill against the sea of Highlanders blanketing the far slope . . . then fleeing straight back down into the face of their own advancing infantry.

On the age-old cry of *claymore*, the Highlanders were unleashed, pouring down the slope and onto the level plain like a screaming tidal wave. Torrential rains had rendered the government's firelocks ineffectual, and, unable to fire their muskets, the red-coated infantry had little defence against the glittering wall of broadswords. Unfortunately, the rain also worked against the rebels, for instead of pursuing the routed, scattering English as they should have done, they chose to plunder the deserted camp instead, considering food, wine, and clean clothing preferable to a wild chase in the streaming downpour.

Even when the weather cleared, the Prince preferred to celebrate his victory, rather than send his army in pursuit of the disorganized government troops. He ignored missive after missive forwarded by Lord George, and seemed to see no urgent need to march right away to recapture the city of Edinburgh. The urgency became quite clear a week later when it was learned that Hawley had safely returned to the capital city, and that William, Duke of Cumberland, had sailed unmolested up the Firth of Forth and assumed personal command of the garrison at Edinburgh Castle.

Enraged over the Prince's lack of decisive action, and knowing they had lost a major advantage by not following up on their victory at Falkirk, the Chiefs were faced with a similar situation as the one they had encountered in Derby. Cumberland's army was en route to Edinburgh, and General Wade's forces were massing along the border. This time, they refused to even listen to any of the Prince's pretty speeches or impassioned pleas and issued the order to retreat again, to the Highlands. Safely in the rugged terrain of their own lands, they were confident they could hold against whatever forces the English dared send after them. They firmly believed Cumberland would never venture into the mountains, where his vaunted cavalry, infantry, and artillery would be at the Highlanders' mercy.

On February 1st, the Jacobite army began a northward retreat. News of his enemy's escape both astonished and angered Cumberland, who had begun to look upon his cousin, the Prince's, erratic behaviour as an insult to his own military intelligence.

"I am told the rebels simply packed up their gear and

walked out of Falkirk with their noses in the air!" Cumberland declared, his corpulent figure dominating the head of a long dining table. Gathered about him and hanging warily on every word and gesture, were the principal officers of the fourteen battalions of infantry and dragoons currently holding command of Edinburgh. General Hawley, conspicuously silent throughout most of the meeting so far, was seated well along the table in a humbling position of demoted importance. Conversely, officers who had distinguished themselves by meeting their enemies bravely and refusing to give ground or flee, sat favourably close to the Duke. On his immediate right was crusty old Colonel Guest, who had steadfastly held Edinburgh Castle through a lengthy siege by the Jacobites, and on the colonel's right, one of the few dragoon officers who had distinguished himself at Prestonpans—Major Hamilton Armbruth Garner.

"You may well understand our surprise when we marched to Falkirk intending to engage our cousin," the Duke continued in a droll voice, "only to find the town deserted, the camp in shambles, and, from the few hearty souls who had been left behind to sleep off their drunken stupors, to learn of their successful retreat across the waters of the Forth."

Possessing a very long thin nose, the Duke sighted along it now, narrowing his frog-like eyes against the haze of pipe and cigar smoke, the better to fix his stare on the bewigged and formally attired company of king's officers.

"Opinions, gentlemen?"

In the nervous silence that ensued, Hamilton Garner's jade green eyes made contact with the general's and were one of the few that did not instantly flash away. "I should think, my lord Duke, they have lost heart. Why else should they have chosen flight over pursuit? It cannot be denied they held the immediate advantage following the battle at Falkirk."

"They also held it before and during, as I understand it," the Duke remarked. "Since their methods of fighting are not in the least affected by inclement weather, they had no call to worry after the dampness of their powder, or the mud splashing up to soil their pretty white gaiters."

"They fight like devils from hell," one of the junior officers commented with a shudder. "They come out of nowhere, cloaked in mist and mud, screaming like banshees, and swinging those great bloody broadswords of theirs like farmers scything a corn field."

"Primitive methods, to be sure, but most effective, would you not agree?"

"Our men are trained in musketry and artillery tactics," Hawley declared. "Our fighting forces are second to none in discipline and skill."

The Duke's feral gaze settled on the disgraced general. "But in order to demonstrate this vast superiority, must we wait for temperate weather and extend specific invitations as to time and place, so as not to inconvenience our palates?"

Hawley's face throbbed a dull, mottled red. "The Lady Kilmarnock was alarmed. She was requesting our protection for her lands. The hour grew late and—".

"And her bosoms undoubtedly grew more and more attractive," the Duke snapped. "I must make a point of meeting this paragon of virtue myself; perhaps you could arrange an introduction?"

When Hawley's lips compressed to a thin smear of outrage, Major Garner provided a response. "The, er, *lady* in question has withdrawn, Sire. It seems she found better company with her husband and his Jacobite clansmen."

The Duke drummed the squared stubs of his fingertips on the table. "Indeed. Weather, women . . . what other seemingly harmless weapons do the rebels manage to use to astonishing advantage? Our own fear, for one thing. Four thousand of them marched to within a hare's leap of my father's throne. Not the thirty thousand we had been duped into believing had swarmed across our borders, but four thousand. *Four*, gentlemen, against a combined force easily five times their number. And when we do find the courage to venture out against them, do they trouble themselves to consult a rule book to see how the war games should be properly acted out? Zounds, no! Why should they, when they have caught us fumbling about with our breeches down around our knees every single time? As for their methods, gentlemen, they are neither demons nor hounds from hell. They are mortal men, made of flesh and blood; they cut, bleed, and die just as easily as we do."

"But their weapons, Sire—"

"Weapons!" Cumberland pushed himself to his feet, glaring along the table. "Archaic steel swords, too heavy to wield with anything but the minimum range of accuracy, too long to be effective against anything but turned and fleeing backsides! Hughes!"

A young adjutant came running at the barked command and fitted a captured Highland broadsword into the Duke's hand. Five feet long, made from double-edged steel four inches wide across the blade, and capped by an ornately wrought iron hilt clasped from behind a protective basket-shaped guard, it was an impressive weapon. Memories of its devastating capabilities were reflected on the faces of the men, some of whom looked away, others mentally comparing it to the slim steel sabres belted at their waists.

Cumberland lifted the sword, swinging it to and fro, to test the weight and balance. Once again, his attention was caught by a pair of intense green eyes and he paused, signalling Major Garner to join him.

"You were, I believe, Master of the Sword for your regiment?" the Duke asked. "You have also seen the rebels in action, witnessed the charge and the ensuing slaughter of our ill-countenanced men?"

Garner begged permission and unsheathed his own sword. "I suggest, my lord Duke, it is not so much that our men are ill-countenanced, as they are ill-trained in ways of countering a Highland charge."

"Explain."

"Well, Your Grace, in the first place, as you are no doubt aware, the broadsword is an extremely heavy, ungainly weapon, almost impossible to use effectively in a traditional duelling stance of thrust and parry. Instead, it must be grasped in both hands, in most cases, and swung in broad, windmilling strokes, at which time, the momentum alone is enough to carry even the most experienced swordsman slightly off balance. It also—if I may be so bold as to request a demonstration—leaves the swordsman highly vulnerable in one particular area while he is recouping his stroke."

Cumberland appeared intrigued as he raised the sword and drew it back as if to slash it in Garner's direction. The Duke was squat and stout, with more than enough weight behind him to wield the broadsword with considerable power and control, but the major's point was well taken. For a moment or two, when the arc of the sword was at its maximum distance from the Duke's body, his right arm was fully extended and his entire right side was exposed and vulnerable. Garner made the observation even more graphic when, on the Duke's second swing, he stepped forward and simulated driving the tip of his sabre into the armpit and straight through for the heart.

"Even in the pouring rain, my lord, with muskets unable to fire, I suggest our bayonets could do as much, if not more damage in close quarters—assuming we can retrain our men to aim for the enemy on his right and trust his comrade-in-arms to do the same, thus dealing with the rebel directly in front of him."

"I want this looked into at once," Cumberland said excitedly. "But could so simple a tactic be the solution to overcoming the men's fears?"

"We have Highland regiments fighting under our command, Sire," Garner said. "The Argyle Campbells, for one, would be able to stage a mock charge so that we could more carefully observe any other weaknesses and possible countermeasures."

"Excellent!" The Duke handed the broadsword back to his adjutant and clapped a hand on Garner's shoulder. "I shall put you in command of the exercise, Major, and, should it prove promising, you will have my full support in retraining the men as you see fit. I want this myth of invincibility crushed, by God. I want our men convinced they have nothing more to fear from these blasted mountain warlords, and when that happens, we can be on about the business of destroying them once and for all."

"What if the rumours we have heard are true?" asked an elderly colonel, his face bloated and veined from a life of debauchery. "What if the Prince's army is disbanding even as it retreats? What if they reach their mountain lairs and deem it more prudent to retire in safety than meet us on the battlefield?"

The Duke pursed his lips distastefully as he considered Colonel Putnam's question. "An obvious and tempting supposition to draw, but I am more inclined to believe these Scots are a stubborn and belligerent breed of rebel. They have been testing the throne's leniency for fifty years now, fading away into their hills when the smell of defeat becomes too pungent, only to reappear ten, twenty years later when they fancy some new insult to their pride, or find themselves some new idiot to rally around. If we allow them to escape again, unscathed, and to return to their farms as if all is forgotten and forgiven, how many more years will pass before they will use the victories they have gained thus far in this campaign—and which have so far gone unchecked—to rally the passions of the next generation of dissidents and traitors?

"No, gentlemen," he went on. "It is my considered opinion that we cannot accept anything short of the complete destruction and eradication of the rebellious factions. If it takes a sword to affect this result, then so be it. If it takes the death of every so-called Jacobite—man, woman, and child—then so be it. They must be absolutely stripped of power and utterly discouraged from ever harbouring a thought of rising against us again."

He paused and regarded the gnarled faces of his seasoned officers. "These are not to be considered honourable enemies we face, gentlemen. They are traitors, insurgents—vermin who would see our rightful sovereign, King George, swing from a common gibbet while an old and syphilitic papist king watches on in amusement. You have seen the unholy pleasure they take from slaughtering our brave men where they stand. Should we now reach out with a severed limb and offer an olive branch in the hopes they will not rise against us again for another thirty years? Shall we explain to the wives and mothers of the men who drowned in their own blood at Prestonpans and Falkirk, that we were content just to chase the treacherous murderers into the hills, there to return to their rich and prosperous lives unmolested?"

Hamilton Garner drew a calculated breath before raising his fist in anger. "No! No, by God! We will not let them get away with it!"

"No!" The chorus of harsh, gutteral nays sped around the table, accompanied by the pounding of fists and the scraping of chairs against the floor as, one by one, the officers stood in support of Cumberland's policy. Major Garner took the gesture to completion by snatching his half-filled glass of wine off the table and lifting it high in a salute.

"To William, Duke of Cumberland!" he roared. "To his victory over those who would dare rise in arms against the throne, and to all of us who vow to see the victory swift and complete!"

"To Cumberland!" came the enthused, passionate echo. "To victory!"

Chapter Thirteen

Hamilton Garner weaved his way along the musty castle corridors toward his own quarters, his patrician face flushed from the combined effects of many toasts and the zealous pride he felt in being singled out by the Duke to take personal command of retraining the troops. It had been a risk, bringing himself to the general's attention like that, but it had worked! Cumberland had last been seen talking with Colonel Guest, and it was Hamilton's bet that, by morning, he would be permanently assigned to the Duke's personal staff!

Arriving at his rooms, he kicked the outer door open and stood a moment on the threshold, his green eyes gleaming as he drank in the luxurious accommodations he had won for himself by proving both his loyalty and worth to General Cope and Colonel Guest. The cold masonry walls were draped in rich tapestries, the massive armoire and dressers were made of cherrywood, warm and lush on the senses. The bed was four-posted, perched on a platform two feet high, canopied in velvet, piled high with satin coverlets and quilts stuffed with goose-down. Underfoot were Persian carpets and, should his boots track mud upon them, either of his two personal valets would be on their knees in an instant, restoring the pile to perfection. The fireplace was Corinthian marble, the multitude of candelabra cast in solid silver, the very air he breathed redolent with exotic spices and perfumes supplied for and used lavishly by the silk-encased figure, who lounged against the nest of pillows on the bed.

He kicked the door shut with the same indifferent boot and approached the bed. Smiling crookedly, he reached down and lifted a lock of hair from the girl's shoulder and slid it through his fingers. She scarcely glanced up.

Hamilton's fingers twisted slowly around the shank of hair, taking up the slack and forcing her to tilt her face up to his.

"Such a warm welcome," he murmured. "One might almost think you were not happy to see me."

"I'm that happy, I can hardly control masel'," she replied indolently, jerking her head to free it from his grasp.

Garner gave her the moment. Waiting until her attention had returned to the box of bonbons, he took up a fistful of hair and yanked it so savagely, the chocolates scattered and the girl scrambled onto her knees, yelping in pain. Garner's mouth was greedy and voracious as it plunged over hers, his hands brutal as he grabbed two fistfuls of silk and ripped the flimsy gown she was wearing from neckline to knee in one tearing sweep. A graphic oath of contempt broke from the full pouting lips and she raised her hands, beating them ineffectually against the wall of his chest.

Garner only laughed and caught her wrists before the sharp little nails could wreak any real damage to his face and throat. "Ahh, my sweet Maggie. A pleasure as always to find you in such an accommodating mood!"

"Let go o' me, ye bastard!" she hissed. "Ye reek o' sweat an' piss, an' I'll no' have ye crawlin' on me this night, ye can be sure."

Garner laughed again and wrenched her hands down and around into the small of her back. Bending forward, he sank his teeth into the soft white flesh of one exposed breast, not the least surprised to feel the nipple harden into a stiff little button at the first flick of his tongue.

Another benefit of being held in favour, he mused. He had his choice of any bed in Edinburgh, any woman, any whore, any milkmaid who happened to take his fancy. This one had come into his hands a few short weeks ago, as fiery and fiesty a she-cat as he'd ever sought to tame, but well worth the effort and the expense to do so. She had come highly recommended from Colonel Putnam, who had lost her on a roll of the dice and sought him out later, offering twice the price to buy her back. Intrigued, Garner had naturally tried her out for himself and, well, she had been in his bed ever since.

Maggie MacLaren was a local girl, and as such, never submitted without a show of resistance. However, once she had been dutifully "conquered," she was not the least adverse to employing any and all of her considerable talents to ensure there was always some extra token of esteem left on the nightstand each morning.

Grinning, his mouth still clamped to her breast, Garner pushed her down onto the mattress and without further preamble, unfastened the codpiece of his breeches and thrust himself between her thighs. His groan was genuine; she was hot and slick and tight as a leather glove. She offered the usual show of defiance, struggling to unseat him for all of a minute, her hair flying, her teeth bared, her feet kicking and gouging and digging into the bedding for traction. But just as suddenly, her curses became moans and her efforts to bar his driving thrusts became violent surges to grind him as close as humanly possible. Her hands fought his restraining grip until he released them, then they were flung up and around his shoulders, clawing and tearing into him until their frenetic activity nearly sent them lurching off the side of the bed.

As it was, Hamilton thought she might never let him go. The long, energetic legs were locked tightly around him, holding him in place until every last possible shiver of ecstasy had run its course. When she released him, Hamilton collapsed limply on the mattress beside her, his flesh throbbing with aftershocks. The sweat rolled off his brow, soaking a wide damp patch on the satin coverlet; his wig had been torn off his head and cast aside to land precariously close to the flame of a burning candle.

"Thank Christ the rebels never thought to use you as a weapon," he gasped. "They could have had the rebellion won by now."

Maggie's head was tilted forward, her brows crumpled in dismay as she inspected the damage brought about by his brass buttons, leather belts, and starched lapels. Her breasts, large enough to satisfy any man's wildest fantasies, were chafed as red as the dye in Hamilton's woolen tunic; her inner thighs were pink and itching from the friction of the nankeen breeches. All in all, however, she supposed the discomfort was worth the price of seeing her *Sassenach* lover quiveringly depleted. He was insufferably vain, obsessed with his own self image, and ambitious enough to be a cunningly dangerous man.

Tall and lean and undeniably handsome, the flaxen-haired officer exercised daily to keep his body in peak condition. He also duelled with fellow officers at the hint of an insult, mainly to dispute any taint of cowardice which might have clung to him following his former command of the 13th Dragoons. Immediately after the fiasco at Colt's Bridge, it was said he ordered his two junior officers shot for cowardice and hung twenty men from the rank and file as an example. Following a repeat of their performance at Prestonpans, Garner's regiment had only managed to come away with their lives upon the intercession of General Cope himself, who had wisely counselled that to have them all shot or hung would serve no purpose other than to delight their enemies.

Garner's approach to women was as cool and arrogant as his personality. He was an adequate lover—not the best she had had by any means, but energetic.

"If tha's how ye judge yer weaponry, *Sassenach*," she said sardonically, eyeing the limp digit of flesh that flopped out from beneath his codpiece, "I'd still be wary o' yer chances against ma kin."

The jade eyes opened slowly. "One of these fine days, my rebel minx, I might begin to think your tongue is growing a measure too sharp for my liking."

"As long as it's only ma tongue," she laughed, "then ye've nae worries."

Garner contemplated the swollen moistness of her lips a moment, then let a smile curve across his own. Until recently, he had shown little interest in her background. Other than noting the fact she was Scottish and possessed exemplary skills between the sheets, he had barely paid any attention to her. Winning her on the toss of a die was not exactly a challenge to his manly powers of seduction, but where most women were easily captivated and made slaves to his blond, virile dominance—and in turn, quickly boring him—Maggie MacLaren was proving to be the exception. Only one other woman had shown the same combination of fire and ice. Catherine Ashbrooke had been the embodiment of passion and desire; it had raged in every sultry glance, glowed from every luminous curve of soft white flesh. Yet she had held herself aloof, as if she hadn't cared a wit if he were alive or if he dropped dead at her feet.

The image of dropping dead—or wounded, as it were—at her feet, caused Hamilton's face to harden perceptibly. Wealthy, refined, spoiled and beautiful, Catherine Ashbrooke had come the closest to winning an honest proposal of marriage from him. Instead, she had played him for a fool, manipulating herself between two lovers and selling herself to the victor. The humiliation he had suffered in losing the duel to Montgomery had been nothing compared to the mortification of discovering she had not sought an annulment for their marriage, had not left the black-haired merchant at the nearest inn as she had promised, had not even deigned to leave a note telling of her change of heart so that he, Hamilton Garner, might be spared the nudges and exchanged winks of his men as he chased up and down the length of England searching for her.

"Was she pretty, *Sassenach*?"

"What?" he asked, startled out of his reverie. "Who?"

"Whoever ye're thinkin' about wha's makin' the drool hang down yer lip an' wee willie there spring back tae life like as if he'd been stung by a bee."

Hamilton glared at her and sat upright, the flush in his cheeks betraying more than the distant gleam in his eye. More than enough to provide Maggie with a fistful of barbs.

"Dae I remind ye o' her?"

"Not likely," he snapped, cursing as a button on his waistcoat became snarled around a loose thread. Maggie, sniffing some profit to be made, rose to her knees before him, her nimble fingers taking over the task of unfastening belts and buckles, buttons and laces.

"Was she beautiful?"

The muscles in Hamilton's jaw flexed. Beauty was relative, was it not? Compared to spun gold, Catherine's hair was indeed beautiful. Compared to sunlight and moonlight her face was more radiant, her body more ethereal. Compared to nectar, her lips were sweeter.

"She was a bitch, actually," Hamilton sighed wanly. "A yellow-haired, blue-eyed bitch. But she came with a very impressive pedigree and could have set me up quite nicely for the rest of my life."

"*Could* have? Ye mean ye lost her?"

"The duel was rigged," he blurted angrily. "The contest was hardly fair, what with her and—" He stopped, noting the gleam of interest in the golden eyes. He had answered more than she had asked, had told her far more than he had ever intended to let her know. She was studying him closely, speculatively, as she loosened his shirt and ran her fingertips down over the smooth bulge of muscles across his chest. Lower still and she encountered the hard ridge of scar tissue over his ribs—the only blemish of ugliness on an otherwise classically perfect body.

"So," she mused. "Ye fought a duel f'ae her an' lost."

The jade eyes flared and his hands grasped her shoulders so tightly his nails gouged her flesh. "No one has ever bested me with a sword," he hissed, jerking her forward. "No one!"

Her eyes glowed maliciously. "Ye have the scars tae prove someone did."

"The duel was supposed to be to the death. I drew first blood, by God, and was about to finish him off when the coward balked and turned away, his sword tip lowered as if to concede. And when I, suffering some delusion of mercy, thought to grant him his life, he attacked. I lay near death for days and when I regained consciousness, I learned the bastard had run away. Both of them had run away. Oh, she lied so sweetly. Lied to me as I lay bleeding in my humiliation, but I should have guessed the two were in collusion all along."

Releasing the pressure on Maggie's shoulders, he clenched his fists on his lap and ground the heels of his palms into his knees as he continued. "When I was fit, I followed them. I spent weeks combing the inns and posting houses, hoping to pick up their trail and deliver them both their just rewards. But they were gone. Vanished. I could not believe it at first—they were hardly an invisible couple. But everywhere I asked after a slender blonde-haired woman and a tall, black-haired, black-eyed bastard from hell, I was shrugged aside."

Maggie was engrossed in watching the remarkable shades of fury that coloured his expression, but at the description of the errant lovers, her eyes grew larger and rounder, the breath quickened in her throat and an unwitting rush of excitement caused the skin around her nipples to pucker and darken in anticipation.

"Having found them nowhere, I gave up and returned to my regiment just as the news of Charles Stuart's arrival reached London. I have not forgotten nor forgiven either one of them, though, and sometimes . . . the image is so clear, the desire to win my revenge is so strong, I see his face on the enemy—in taverns, in crowded streets, even once riding at the head of an enemy patrol. It wasn't him, of course. It couldn't be. Montgomery and his whore-bitch are hundreds of miles away, crawled back into their London snakehole, or more likely, somewhere on the Continent, laughing over what a fine fool they made of me. Dearest Catherine. Dearest, sweetest Catherine . . . how I do hope we meet again someday."

Turning his attention back to the girl, Garner saw that her hands were lying quite motionless in her lap, and her complexion had turned pale around the large, amber tiger-eyes that now seemed to have widened to encompass her whole face.

"Maggie? What is it? You look as if you've seen a ghost."

"Did ye say . . . Catherine?"

"Catherine Ashbrooke: Why do you ask?"

"An' his name? Ye said it was Montgomery?"

"Raefer Montgomery. *Why?*"

Maggie's hands dropped away completely and she sat back on her heels. It couldn't be! It just couldn't be!

"Guid lord," she muttered. "O' course it could! She said once as how her fiancé were an officer wi' the dragoons."

Hamilton's frown deepened as a low, throaty laugh burst from her lips. She tried to stifle it. She covered her mouth with her hands and rocked back, but it was no use; the laughter came harder, the irony of it all producing tears of mirth that streamed all the faster, the angrier the major became.

"What the devil are you on about?" he demanded. "*Who* said her fiancé was an officer in the dragoons?"

"Catherine," Maggie managed to choke out over a new peal of laughter. "Aye, it were dear, sweet Catherine. A yellow-haired, blue-eyed *Sassenach* bitch what come tae Achnacarry . . . oh . . . seven, eight months gaun. Newly wed too. Tae him. Tae the black-haired devil himsel': the *Camshroinaich Dubh*!"

Far from sharing the girl's amusement, Hamilton gripped her arms tightly again, shaking her so brusquely her titian-red hair flew around her shoulders in a shiny tumble.

"Will you stop and tell me what the hell you are talking about!" he shouted.

"I tald ye!" she gasped. "It were him! It were him an' it were her at Achnacarry! Only his name isna Montgomery, ye daft bastard. It's Cameron! Alasdair Cameron! An' when ye thought ye saw him across the field leadin' a rebel patrol, ye most likely *did* see him! He's Alasdair . . . Alexander Cameron, brither tae Donald Cameron o' Lochiel!"

"How do you know?" Garner rasped. "How do you know it is the same man?"

"There couldna be two like him in the whole world. Besides—" She brought her laughter under control and wiped at the moisture streaking down her cheeks, "—I should ken ma ain cousin, should I na?"

"Your . . . *cousin*?"

"Aye." The amber eyes lifted to his, the irony still sparkling brightly in their depths. "Cousin tae the grand *Camshroinaich Dubh*, I am. Cousin tae his brither Lochiel as well, and tae Dr. Archibald—"

"Donald Cameron of Lochiel . . . the chief of Clan Cameron . . . you are related to him?"

"Gie's ye a wee shiver, daes it?"

"And . . . Raefer Montgomery—" Hamilton moistened his lips and adjusted the suddenly damp grip on the girl's shoulders "—you're absolutely certain he's . . ."

"The *Camshroinaich Dubh*? Aye, I'm certain. He boasted o' duelin' a sour-faced redcoat *Sassenach* f'ae the privilege o' marryin' his yellow-haired bride. Aye, it comes back tae me now; Alasdair mentionin' he'd used the name Montgomery tae start a shippin' business out o' France."

Hamilton was only partially listening. His head was reeling—not from the amount of wine he had consumed earlier, but because he had just learned the man he had fought his duel with seven months ago was none other than Alexander Cameron—the man reputed to be the greatest swordsman in all of Britain, possibly in all of the civilized world! Catherine's involvement hardly merited a passing thought. Hamilton had studied with the great masters of Europe and had heard the whispered rumours surrounding the legendary Dark Cameron, the Scottish warlord living in exile. To think he had actually fought Cameron . . . and damned near bested him!

"Where is he?" Hamilton demanded eagerly. "Do you know where I can find him?"

"Well, unless he's taken a likin' tae wearin' red," she snorted, "he's still wi' the Prince."

Garner cursed inwardly. Of course, he knew that. *Calm yourself! He's out there somewhere and he's not a ghost anymore. He's real, by God. Real!*

"Maggie, listen to me—"

"Lauren," she said, interrupting.

"What?"

"Ma name's no' Maggie . . . it's Lauren. Lauren Cameron, an' if ye dinna stop squeezin' ma airms, I'll have nae bluid left in ma fingers."

Hamilton's hands sprang open. He stared at the livid marks he had left on her skin for a moment, collecting his thoughts before he reached for her again, this time by two clenched handfuls of thick, curling hair.

"Catherine," he said suddenly. "What do you know about Catherine?"

"Nae mair than what I want tae know. Only that she didna gladden too many hearts by comin' tae Achnacarry, hangin' on Alasdair's airm, lookin' at us all as if we were scullery maids."

Her words struck him like a wet cloth. "He brought Catherine to Scotland!"

"That's what I said, did I na? He brung her tae Achnacarry—a *Sassenach*, nae less. Auld Sir Ewen must have tairned in his grave."

"Is she . . . still there?"

Lauren narrowed her eyes consideringly. If she said the bitch was back in England, would he go tearing off to find her? Losing Alasdair to her had been a bad enough blow to her vanity; losing her gilded *Sassenach* major would just be too much to tolerate. Lauren was far from finished with him. He shared some of her main qualities—greed and ambition—and she was not about to give him up until a better prospect came along.

"Aye," she said coolly. "He left her at Achnacarry wi' the rest o' the simperin' lot."

"Where is this Achnacarry? How do I get there?"

"Achnacarry?" Lauren scoffed openly. "Ye *must* be daft. Naebody just *goes* tae Achnacarry Castle. Even if ye could get through the fifty miles o' cold, black forest an' scaled the dozen corries atween here an' there, ye'd never get through the wall o' clansmen wha' dae naught all the blessed day long but look f'ae *Sassenachs* an' Campbells. Achnacarry's no' had an uninvited guest since . . . since auld King MacBeth took the keep by siege. An' he only held it a day or so afore fleein' f'ae his life. If ye dinna believe me, ask yer friend, the Duke o' Argyle. He's been tryin' tae get inside Achnacarry's walls f'ae years. Aye, an' he's also been tryin' tae put a hangman's noose roun Alasdair's throat f'ae the past fifteen years, but never come so close as tae catch sight o' him. If it's revenge ye're wantin', ye'll have tae stand in line ahind about five thousand men."

Hamilton flung her aside with a curse and stood up from the bed. He paced to the far side of the room, standing at the heavily curtained window for several minutes until a faint tinkle of laughter drew his gaze back to the bed.

"Surely ye still dinna want the bitch?" she asked, uncurling her long feline body and standing up. "No' after what she's doun tae ye."

"I want . . . explanations," he said carefully. "I have heard of this Dark Cameron, and of the various crimes he has committed. Perhaps he forced her—"

"Forced?" Lauren scorned the word and the idea. "I didna see her bein' forced tae rut wi' him day an' night in every room an' cavie in the castle. Fact is, she'd drag him away frae the table afore he'd half finished a meal, an' leave a trail o' torn claythes tae the nearest bed."

Garner was in motion before she could scramble out of the way. The slap echoed in the silence like a whiplash, the force of it spinning her back to sprawl across the bed. She screamed as he caught a fistful of hair and arched her head back.

"Bitch! What do you know about it!"

"I know what I saw!" she insisted, the rage in her voice causing it to tremble. "She couldna keep her hands off him, nor keep frae keenin' an' bleatin' her pleasure loud enough f'ae the whole castle tae hear!"

"Liar!" he roared, striking the small white face again. This time she came up fighting, her nails bared and raking at his chest, her teeth flashing whitely through the crimson slash of a split lip. Lunging at him, she was caught in mid-air, but the sheer violence of her attack threw them both off balance and they crashed together on the floor. Hamilton was on top of her in an instant, rolling the weight of his body over hers to restrict the wild thrashings. He felt her nails carve into his shoulder and he grunted as a well-placed knee came crushingly close to its target. He struck her again, smearing the fiery red mane of hair across the carpet, aroused despite his anger as he felt himself pressed up against her heat and wetness.

He thrust his mouth down over hers, smothering the stream of lurid Gaelic oaths under lips that were brutal and unrelenting. Lauren's rage turned quickly to pain as his teeth sawed back and forth across her torn lip, then into something else again as the hot stab of his flesh plunged into her. On a gasp, she stopped fighting him. On a coarse, gutteral moan, she twined her legs around his waist and challenged his supremacy over each feverish thrust.

And as she clutched at him and shuddered within herself, Hamilton Garner squeezed his eyes tightly shut as he had done so many times before, knowing if he opened them too soon it would not be Catherine's face he saw, glazing with passion beneath him, and not Catherine's body hurling him into the mindless, primitive realm of ecstasy.

Lauren pried her eyes open slowly. She was alone on the bed, her body flung sideways across the mattress, her limbs splayed inelegantly on the crumpled and stained satin covers. The shreds of her gown were gone. Her breasts throbbed and her thighs ached; it felt as if she had been used by ten maniacal men, all at the one time.

Her head wobbling drunkenly, she tilted it forward. The major was standing by the fireplace, his hand propped on the mantelpiece, his face profiled against the orange and bronzed light. A faint groan settled her head back onto the cloud of her own scattered hair, and a half-formed thought of modesty had her fold her legs together in a graceful tuck.

"What the bluidy Christ happened? Dinna tell me I fainted."

"Alright. I won't tell you."

Lauren frowned and stared at the canopy overhead. He was lying, of course. Or gloating. She had never fainted beneath a man before in her life—not even Struan MacSorley, and he had a well-deserved reputation for putting several women in a swoon in a single night.

She turned her head slightly, testing the ache at the back of her skull and prodding gently at the puffed lip, the bruised tenderness along her jaw. It was no wonder she had fainted, if indeed she had done so: the bastard had hit her hard enough to have scrambled her brains for a month of Sundays.

Something else you'll be paying for, *Sassenach*, she thought bitterly.

"Christ, but," she muttered, levering herself inch by cautious inch into a sitting position. "Is there anything ye didna dae tae me? Anywhere ye didna poke an' prod me wi' tha' bird-beak ye call yer manhood?"

Garner turned from the fire. He was still naked, his body, lean and smooth, glowing handsomely in the firelight. He was a bonnie bastard, she had to admit. Far bonnier than the lava-faced Colonel Putnam she had first been delivered to. Garner's obsessions with being the best at everything made him a fool as well as an insufferable peacock as far as Lauren was concerned, but as long as she never catered to his vanities or let him believe he had the upper hand, her position as his mistress was quite safe. And quite comfortable.

When the soldiers had stolen her off the moor at Prestonpans, her first thought was that she would die—or at least, be slated to die. She had been taken to Colonel Putnam and questioned, but it became clear within the first few moments that the colonel was more interested in what lay beneath the gaping fabric of her bodice than any information she might or might not have had about the rebel camp. She had passed herself off as a local girl, put up a few groans of resistance, then kept the *Sassenach* colonel salivating at her feet for almost a month. In that time, she demanded and received the luxuries she had only dreamt about. Silks and satins, maids to tend her baths, to crimp her hair, to trim her toenails when her lover complained of too many scratchmarks. She amassed quite an impressive purseful of gold coins as well—not as impressive as the one she was filling at Hamilton Garner's expense, but the combined sum was already more than enough to set her up in a comfortable house in Edinburgh. Not nearly enough for what she wanted, of course, but it was a good start.

Sighing expressively, she slipped down off the bed and padded barefoot to the full-length cheval mirror, scowling as she inspected the cuts and bruises that marred her face. She flashed a look of disgust over her shoulder as Garner came quietly up behind her.

"If ye treated yer sweet Catherine as gently as ye treat me," she sneered, "it's nae wonder she left ye f'ae Alasdair."

Garner smiled blandly, the barb falling harmlessly to the wayside. "Considering the way you looked when Colonel Putnam's men brought you into camp, a minor bruise or two should not distress you overmuch."

"Ye saw me in camp?"

"I saw *something* in camp. A good deal of filth and scratches, hair like a clump of brambleweed, and skin as brown and tough as leather." He allowed a hand to trail a lazy path from her shoulder to the bursting ripeness of her full breasts. "Frankly, that was why I could not work myself into too much of a delirium when I won you from the good colonel."

A finely shaped auburn brow ached delicately. "An' now?"

"Now . . ." his fingers lingered over the wine-red crest of her nipple, his smile tugged wider as he watched the skin pucker and crinkle together on each stroke. "Now I can at least understand why Reginald wanted you back so desperately. I'm told he has been through every whorehouse and brothel in Edinburgh searching for a replacement. If he doesn't find one soon—" Hamilton sighed and leaned forward, pressing his lips onto the ivory curve of her shoulder "—I fear he may be foolish enough to challenge me to a duel."

The amber eyes narrowed. "Ye'd fight a duel f'ae me?"

"What is mine, is mine," he said simply. "What I have, I keep, and what I want, I usually get, regardless of the cost, regardless of the method, regardless of the time involved. You would do well to remember that, my dear."

"Ye dinna *own* me, *Sassenach*," she said evenly.

Garner backed away a pace and spread his hands wide. "You're free to leave anytime you please. But keep in mind what I said: What is mine, is mine, and you'll not find a man within a hundred miles willing to contest the point, nor a nest half so comfortable as the one you have here."

With a toss of her bright red hair, Lauren turned and faced him squarely. "Ye'll no' be here in Edinburgh forever, *Sassenach*. I can afford tae bide ma time."

"Ahhh, yes. Your services have not come cheaply over the past few months, neither for myself or Colonel Putnam. I suppose if you had invested your ill gains wisely, you might well have been an independent force by now. Unfortunately, little woolen socks do not make the best of banks."

Lauren stiffened, her eyes growing rounder and darker as they flicked across the room to the tall armoire. She broke past him and ran to the cabinet, flinging the doors wide and dropping onto her knees before it. Oaths were hurled over her shoulder in as colourful a profusion as the scarves, shawls, stockings, ribbons, and smallclothes that were cleared from the lower shelves. She found what she was searching for and stared at the empty red stocking aghast, her expression passing through shades of disbelief, anger, shock and disgust.

Two months! Two months of having to endure the sweaty gropings of an impotent buffoon and an arrogant tyrant . . . gone!

"Where is ma money?" she demanded, barely able to hiss the words through clenched teeth.

"Safe."

She rounded on him. "Safe *where*, ye liver-lipped, sour-bellied excuse f'ae a man? Ye had nae right tae touch it! It were mine; I earned it!"

"Many times over, I'm sure. And it *is* quite safe, you'll get it all back—with interest, if you play your cards right."

"Play ma cards? Ye want me tae play cards?" she shrieked.

He grimaced wryly. "Only a figure of speech, my dear —you Scots take everything so literally! It's no wonder you've been feuding for generations. What I meant to say, in plainer terms, is that if you help me, I will be more than happy to restore your paltry little nest egg to its cozy hiding place, and give you a good deal more besides."

"How much mair? An' what dae I have tae dae?"

"How much depends entirely upon how greedy you are—enough to transform you into a queen, if you wish, drowning in furs, jewels, gowns . . . villas in Spain, chateaux in France . . . anything is possible when you've been introduced into the proper circle of friends."

Lauren's fist uncurled from around the crushed red stocking and she managed to temper some of the snapping fury in her eyes. "*Your* friends, I suppose?"

"I have . . . connections."

"Aye, an' mayhap I already have what I want, *Sassenach*."

"You're content with being a whore? A plaything passed from bed to bed on the roll of a die?"

Something glimmered angrily in the depths of her eyes, but she controlled it and glared up at him. "Ye still havena tald me what ye want me tae dae in exchange f'ae all this . . . generosity."

"Nothing that would not bring you as much satisfaction as it would bring me—unless of course, I have completely misinterpreted the cause for your trifling display of feminine outrage a short while ago. Something tells me, however, that we both want the same thing: to see your cousin Alexander Cameron cut down a peg or two—perhaps see him taught a lesson in humility?"

"Who's gonny dae that—*you*? Ye've already fought him the once an' had yer guts skewered; what makes ye think a second time will be any different?"

Hamilton flushed. "I told you: The first time, he won by trickery. I was caught off guard. This time, I will be prepared."

"Aye," she smirked. "An' I tald ye, ye'll have tae stand in line ahind a few thousand Argyleshire Campbells, an' a few thousand mair *Sassenach* sojers afore ye'd even get a tairn at him."

"Not if I have you to guide me to the front of the line."

"An' just how would I dae that?"

"Simple. You rejoin your kinsmen. You retreat to the Highlands with them, and when you judge the time to be right, you get word to me when and where to find the grand Dark Cameron."

Lauren gaped as if she had not quite heard his words clearly. "*Rejoin* them? *Retreat* wi' them? After eight long years o' schemin' tae find a way *out* o' the bluidy Highlands . . . ye want me just tae walk back *in*?"

"Actually—" he rubbed his smooth-shaven jaw thoughtfully "—you would require a cart and a fairly fast horse; there's about a week's hard ride ahead of you."

"Ye're mad," she laughed. "Stark an' starved mad! I wouldna dae that f'ae ye, nor f'ae anyone else. No' even if the heavens opened wide an' poured solid gold raindrops on ma heid every step o' the way."

She pushed herself to her feet, shaking her head and scoffing under her breath at the very notion of going back with the rebel camp. Go back to the Highlands? Go back to Achnacarry?

"There is a reward of twenty thousand gold sovereigns for the capture of Alexander Cameron," he reminded her mildly.

Lauren laughed again. "Aye, there's been a reward f'ae fifteen years, an' naebody's come close enough tae sniff it."

"Forty thousand might sharpen the scent somewhat."

"Forty?"

"Twenty from Argyle, twenty from me. With an extra something besides, if your initiative provides me with both Alexander Cameron and his yellow-haired bride."

Lauren's gaze remained locked steadily on his, and Garner had to suppress the urge to smile as he contemplated the almond-shaped eyes, the mouth formed in a perpetual, sinfully suggestive pout, the body designed to inspire and provide unimaginable delights. He was not fooled for a moment by her pretended disdain; she enjoyed what they did in bed together, and enjoyed it even more when she knew any extra efforts on her part would be rewarded with more coins. She was the ultimate whore, both in body and in spirit, and greed emanated from her as strongly as the musk of passion.

"An' all I'd have tae dae is arrange a meeting atween ye an' Alasdair? That's all? Ye dinna want the Prince or his army thrown in as well, so Cumberland can make ye general o' the world?"

It was Hamilton's turn to stare. He had been so absorbed with the idea of winning his revenge with Alexander Cameron, he had completely forgotten Lauren's relationship to Donald Cameron of Lochiel—who in turn, was one of Charles Stuart's closest and most trusted advisors.

"Naturally," he said slowly, "I would be most interested in hearing anything you might learn about the Prince's plans and movements in the upcoming weeks. If we were to have advance knowledge of where and when he plans to make a stand against us, it would certainly be to the government's advantage."

"Mine as well?"

Garner hesitated. "Actually, we already have a man working for us who has been successful in ingratiating himself with the rebels. He has, of course, been promised any rewards forthcoming from his efforts, but, on the other hand, half of something is far more appealing than all of nothing."

Lauren's eyes narrowed. "If ye already have a man planted in the rebel camp, why dae ye have need o' me at all?"

"Because you, my amoral vixen, being one of their kinsmen, will be privy to far more lucrative information. Our man, however he may have proven his loyalties to date, is still an outsider. Moreover, since he has appeared to have changed sides once already, he is bound to be held in suspicion by some. There is also the language barrier. You speak the Gaelic; he does not."

"Who is he? How will I ken him?"

Garner studied the lushly seductive features for an additional moment before allowing a slight grin. "I think perhaps I should keep his identity my secret for the time being. I shall tell him all about you, however, and arrange a signal for later, when you have something to pass on. A ribbon, perhaps?" He lifted a handful of silky red hair and let it slither through his fingers. "A red ribbon. When he sees you wearing it, he'll know you have information to pass on, and when he deems it safe, he'll make contact."

"Ye dinna trust me, *Sassenach*?"

Garner edged closer, raising both hands to cradle her long, slender neck. "No," he said softly. "I *dinna* trust you. But I am hoping you are clever enough to realize that if you betray me, or doublecross me in any way—" his thumbs stroked down the length of her throat and came to rest briefly over her windpipe "—I will find you, and kill you . . . very, very unpleasantly."

"Nae mair unpleasantly than Lochiel if he lairns I've come tae betray the clan."

"Gentle Lochiel?" he murmured cynically. "The diplomat and arbitrator who saved Glasgow from a sacking?"

"Gentle Lochiel," she countered, "who threatened tae have the heids cut frae the shoulders o' any clansman who didna join ahind the Stuart standard."

"In that case, you had better not get caught," he suggested. "You had better not even give them a reason to be suspicious."

"Scots are born suspicious," she said, conscious of the rippling effect the motion of his thumbs was producing elsewhere in her body. "They're born fools as well, though, an' will welcome me back intae the fold like as if I were a wee lamb gaun astray an' found ma way home again."

"No questions? They will not wonder where you have been or what you have been doing for the past two months?"

"I was born in Edinburgh," she said, leaning into the pressure of his fingers as they stroked lower. "It wisna any secret I wanted tae go back."

"I see. And no one will question your change of heart?"

"A Highlander's heart is his honour. Question his heart, ye question his honour, an' that, a Highlander would never dae. Besides," she inched closer and ran her hands up and around his shoulders, "*ye're* gonny tell *me* some secrets, *Sassenach*. Enough tae convince them ma loyalties never swayed frae true. Nothin' they wouldna be able tae find out on their ain, o' course—I wouldna want ye thinkin' I'm after betrayin' ye already."

"The notion would never have occurred to me," he said dryly, fascinated by the way her entire body seemed to envelope his even though they were barely touching. His bold and immediate response elicited a brief but savage assault on his mouth, after which her lips, tongue, and cuttingly sharp teeth descended to the hairless expanse of his chest.

"A rare pity," she mused, nipping and suckling the flesh over his breast. "Ye sendin' me away just when we were comin' tae understand each ither so well."

Garner locked his jaws against an answer until he was reasonably certain his nipples had escaped a bloodletting. "I somehow do not think I will be forgetting you too soon, my dear, nor remaining too patient until your return."

"I know ye willna, *Sassenach.* See how wee willie perks right up when he kens I'm comin' his way? He's gonny remember me f'ae a long, long time. Longer than he will any yellow-haired, purple-eyed bitch ye mout find hidin' in the glens."

Sweat beaded across Hamilton's brow as he watched her sink down onto her knees before him. His muscles tensed into slabs of marble and the blood thundered through his veins, pumped to a racing fever by a heart that beat against the walls of his chest like a hammer.

He acknowledged the thin, disbelieving grunts of air as having their origin somewhere deep in his own throat, but there was nothing he could do to control them; he could only stare and gasp and hope he retained some shred of a grip on his sanity. Not surprisingly, he did not retain the ability to remain standing. The tug and pull of her lips brought him quaking to his knees, then prone and splayed before the hearth like a sacrifice. With the voracious greed of a thief, she continued to plunder his flesh, robbing him, stripping him of all sense and sensibility.

When Hamilton Garner was able to rouse himself again, she was gone. A hint of light seeping through the velvet curtains let him surmise it was after dawn. He was still lying on the floor by the fireplace, although the last of the glowing embers had long since flaked to ash. Recalling only vague snatches of their final hours together, he swallowed tremulously and reached an unsteady hand down to his groin. Relieved, yet awed there could be anything left to offer sensation, he let his hand slump limply back onto the floor, and was instantly asleep again.

INVERNESS, February 1746

Chapter Fourteen

The 11th day of February began innocently enough, with the sun shaking off its mantle of gray sodden clouds long enough to allow a vibrant display of pink and gold streamers to break over the mountains. Too cold for fog, the ground had been covered in a light crust of frozen dew, which glittered like a blanket of broken glass underfoot.

After leaving Falkirk and passing through Stirling, the Jacobite army had once again divided into two columns, the Prince leading the majority of clan regiments by the Highland route north through Blair Atholl, Dalnacardoch, and Dalwhinnie. Lord George Murray had taken the slower moving column by the lowland route through Angus to Aberdeen, the master plan being to reunite the two forces near Inverness and rout the government troops garrisoned there.

Two days into the mountains, a blinding storm had struck the Prince's column, causing the easily exciteable Count Giovanni Fanducci much wringing of hands and gnashing of teeth as they were forced, yet again, to abandon the heavy artillery they had captured at Falkirk. The roads through the Grampians were not much better than cow tracks at the best of times, but with high winds, drifting snow, and sleet storms, it proved impossible to haul anything but essential equipment and supplies from one glen to the next. The men, happy to see the last of the bronze monsters hurl barrel-down over a steep precipice, tried to cheer the morose Italian gunmaker by drawing him into a stirring rendition of "My Highland Laddie," but with a dramatic swirling of a multi-caped greatcoat, the count stalked away into the curtain of snow, and sought more tangible succour in the arms of Ringle-Eyed Rita.

Struan MacSorley, discovering the cause of the bouncing wagon springs and high-pitched shrieks of rapture, would have slain the pair of them at the height of their exuberant release if not for Aluinn MacKail's timely arrival on the scene. He managed, with the assistance of four other clansmen, to disarm the golden-maned giant and persuade him to vent his fury by cleaving firewood instead of skulls.

Although the maps he was carrying were slightly crumpled, Aluinn left the axe-wielding Highlander under several pairs of watchful eyes and continued on his way to a consultation in Alexander's tent. When he thrust the thin canvas flap aside and poked his head into the tent, after giving a cheerful hallo, he found a very pale, visibly distressed Catherine Cameron doubled over a shallow metal basin and grappling with the shuddering after-effects of nausea.

He stared at her for several long moments before entering all the way into the tent. The worst of the spasms had passed and there was nothing he could do to help other than steady her back onto a seat on the cot and empty the contents of the basin. When he returned, she appeared to have calmed considerably, although her lips were still tinged blue and her hand trembled as she held a dampened cloth to her brow.

"Are you ill?" he asked, knowing the answer already, dreading its confirmation.

Catherine looked him straight in the eye and admitted, "I'm pregnant. I'm going to have Alexander's child."

Aluinn's gaze slid involuntarily to the bulky layers of woolen clothing she wore to ward off the chilling effects of the mountain air. "How long have you known?"

"Are you asking how pregnant I am? I cannot say for certain. At most, two months; at the very least, two hours."

Aluinn's cheeks reddened. "I'm sorry. I guess the question was a little blunt. I didn't mean to pry, I just—"

Catherine's shoulders slumped. "I know, Aluinn. I'm sorry, too. I didn't mean to snap. I'm told women in my condition suffer irrational moods and tempers, but it doesn't mean they should take out those moods on friends. Forgive me?"

He sighed and moved over to the cot, then sat beside her and took one of her ice-cold hands into his. "Does Alex know?"

"No. I wasn't exactly sure myself until a few days ago and since then, well, I haven't quite found the right time or means of telling him. He has been so busy seeing to everyone else's problems, I didn't think he needed this one just yet."

Aluinn raked a hand through his sandy brown hair. "If it were me, if it were my wife and child, I would want to know, Catherine. Right away."

"I have every intention of telling him. I'm not as brave as all that, you know; it isn't something I want to keep to myself or deal with alone."

He smiled. "You are not exactly alone. I can count at least a thousand men off the top of my head who would move heaven and earth to see that nothing ever hurt or frightened you again. And I'm not even talking immediate family. When Alex told Lochiel and Archibald about what had happened to you in Derby, they were all for turning the whole army around and wiping out every last English militiaman in the county. I can't say I wouldn't have been right up there in the vanguard myself."

A tear shone in the corner of Catherine's eye as she leaned her head on Aluinn's shoulder. "Deirdre is a very lucky lady."

"I am a very lucky man. So is Alex. But then, I told him so at the very outset; he's just a stubborn bastard, in case you haven't noticed."

"I've noticed," she murmured, twisting and worrying the edges of the handkerchief she was holding. "He'll want to send me away again, won't he?"

Aluinn circled an arm gently around her shoulders. "He'll want to guarantee your safety. He'll want to protect you and your child; can you fault him for that?"

"No," she whispered. "It's just . . . I've been so happy. He's been happy too, I know he has, but we've had so little *real* time together."

"You will have the rest of your lives," he promised sincerely. "This can't go on much longer; it will have to be resolved, one way or the other, and soon. We just don't have the momentum any more. It was there for a while and we accomplished more than anyone thought we could or would in their wildest dreams, but now the men want to go home. They all have wives and families and farms that have been neglected too long and crops that have to be planted soon if the whole country isn't to starve over next winter. Men are drifting away by twos and threes every day, still as loyal and willing to fight as they were in the beginning, but knowing as I think we all do, that there just isn't anywhere left for us to retreat. Even if the Prince takes Inverness, there isn't much he can do with it. The English navy has the entire coast blockaded; we can't get anything in or out, whereas Cumberland has fresh supplies and troops landing almost hourly."

Catherine looked up. "You think Charles Stuart should surrender?"

"If you are asking me if a surrender now would spare the Highlands, my answer would be yes: It is possibly the only thing that will keep Cumberland from razing us to the ground. If you are asking if Charles Stuart will see it that way, the answer is no. He likes the role he is playing too much to surrender it. He has been prince and regent and commander of a crusading army for almost six months now—an army that has not really tasted defeat, only suffered disappointment. If he gives up now, if he admits his dream can never be realized, even after the tremendous victories we have won, he knows he will never have the chance again. He knows he will never have as much power and glory as he has right now. Ignominy is a difficult fate to accept after you have captured the hearts and hopes of the world with your audacity."

"The same could be said about Alex," she pointed out softly. "After the life he has lived, the adventures he has experienced—"

"Is that what worries you?" Aluinn tucked a finger under her chin and tilted her face up to meet his. "Are you afraid Alex will not be content after settling down and forfeiting the role of legendary hero? Catherine . . . that's foolish!"

"Is it? Look at him, Aluinn: He's strong and vital and glowing with energy. He thrives on danger and excitement. He's afraid of nothing; he lives and breathes pure undiluted passion. He became a legend at seventeen and hasn't looked back or slowed down since. Do *you* really think he would be content as a fat and lazy country squire? Do you really think he wants a wife and ten drooling children hanging on his coattails?"

Aluinn was silent for a full minute, his gray eyes intent on hers, the muscles along his jaw tensing as if the words were there but he lacked the means or courage to shape them.

"Do you want the truth?" he asked finally. "Will you believe it and not hold it against me if I tell you the blunt and honest truth?"

Catherine held her breath and nodded.

"Very well then," he said on a sigh, "I think you are almost as big a fool as he is. A lot prettier, to be sure, but every bit as blind and stubborn, pig-headed, and insecure as the man you profess to love."

"Profess to—"

"Don't interrupt. Just nod your head when I ask a question. Do you love him?"

"Of course—!"

"Just nod!"

She nodded.

"Do you want him more than anything else in the world? More than the life you left behind? More than any guarantees of safety or comfort or wealth or social acceptance? More than you have ever wanted anything or anyone before in your entire life?"

Tears were flooding the drowning-pools of her eyes as she nodded, and nodded, and nodded again.

"Then why, in heaven's name, can't you believe he could feel the same way? Why can't you believe he loves and wants you whether you come alone or with a passle of—what?—'drooling children?' He is not blind, you know. He can see what you have given up for him, and what it is costing you in peace of mind to be here right now."

"But . . . I don't want him to feel he has to give up anything for me."

"Rather selfish of you, isn't it?"

"Selfish?" she whispered.

"Has it never occurred to you that Alex is tired of being the legend other people have made him out to be? Or the possibility that circumstances, not personal preferences, keep throwing him into this role he is playing? I have been with him for thirty years, Catherine. A lot of his restlessness, over the past dozen or so years, stemmed from his not knowing what he wanted, not caring. Now he does. While he has never actually confessed it in so many words, I truly believe he initially came back to Scotland because he was tired of being a rogue and a loner. He wanted a home and a family, and a chance to find out the meaning of the word peace. If he seems more energetic and vigorous and impatient lately, it is because he wants this damned war to be over, and if it means donning the guise of the Dark Cameron one more time to speed things on their way, then by God, that's what he's doing. He would like nothing more than to give it all up for you. Don't make him think he has to keep playing this role, or that you'll stop loving him if he turns into that fat country squire."

When Catherine made no response, he smiled and plucked the handkerchief out of her hands, using it to blot up the residue of tears on her cheeks.

"Of course, if I'm wrong, just tell me. If you will miss all of this when the rebellion is over—?"

"No!" she gasped. "No, I just . . ."

"You just have to learn to trust your instincts. I trust mine: implicitly. They told me Deirdre was the best thing ever to come into my sorry excuse for a wastrel life, and did I question them? Did I give one moment's thought to the trail of shattered hearts that will no doubt tumble all across the Continent and parts beyond?"

She looked up sidelong from under the wet fringe of her lashes and giggled. "Those were rhetorical questions, I hope?"

"Absolutely," he agreed, frowning.

"Oh Aluinn," she cried, flinging her arms around him. "You are a dear, dear friend. It doesn't seem fair you should have to listen to everyone's problems and solve them, too."

He laughed. "Perhaps I've missed my calling. I should have been a father confessor. No matter . . . as long as I have helped to solve them?"

Smiling, she nodded vigorously, then startled and pleased him further by planting a warm, affectionate kiss on his cheek. He was blushing and she was laughing harder when they heard a familiar baritone.

"I trust I am not interrupting anything here?" Alex scowled from the doorway of the tent. "If I am, if you would like another hour or so alone, I would be only too happy to oblige."

Aluinn loosened his arms from around Catherine's waist, but held her gaze long enough for a quick glance downward and a silently mouthed smile of congratulation.

"What do you think?" he asked aloud. "Will an hour be enough?"

"Mmmm—" Catherine tilted her head. "I don't know. Maybe two. We would not want to have to rush through anything."

"Quite right, how thoughtless of me." He turned to Alex and held up two fingers. "Two hours, if you are certain you won't mind."

"I won't mind," Alex said evenly. "But how will Deirdre feel about wearing widow's weeds so soon after becoming a bride?"

"Ahh." The two fingers were hastily withdrawn. "I see your point. In that case, Catherine, I shall have to withdraw the offer. Perhaps another candidate might suit your needs? MacSorley, for instance—he's honest, stalwart, and damned comforting on a cold winter night, or so I have been told. Or Fanducci? There is a man who could keep you from becoming bored."

"He is rather handsome," Catherine agreed. "Witty, too. Charming. A very elegant dresser—he reminds me of someone, I cannot quite think who at the moment—but yes, he certainly has the manners and civility of a man who would gladly cater to a woman's every whim. I shall give the matter serious thought."

"How serious?" Alex demanded.

Catherine stood up, walked over to where her husband was glowering by the centre tent pole, and wrapped her arms around his neck. The kiss was long and meaningful enough to cause a distinct stirring beneath the folds of his kilt.

"About that serious," she murmured, conscious of the increased pace of her own heartbeat. Alex was about to bend his mouth to hers again when Aluinn cleared his throat and collected up his maps from the cot.

"If you two would rather *I* leave you alone for another hour or so . . . ?"

Alexander grinned and released Catherine with a quick, chaste kiss on the temple. "Work before pleasure, unfortunately. I take it those are the charts Colonel Anne drew up for us last night?"

"Aye. She swears they are accurate down to the last stand of trees. One of her men was also allotted the privilege of spending some time in a prison cell at Fort George, and has returned the favour by providing us with detailed sketches of the interior buildings and armory."

It never failed to surprise Catherine how quickly their mood of light banter could be transformed into one of deadly earnest. Sighing, she unwound her hands from Alex's neck and planted them on her hips instead.

"Colonel Anne, Colonel Anne, Colonel Anne . . . her name is all I have heard lately. Should I be jealous?"

"No more so than I," Alex replied lightly, "walking into my own tent, finding my wife clutched in the embrace of my best friend."

"We were hardly clutching," she said dryly. "We were . . . commiserating: over the multitude of broken hearts we have left behind." She paused and reached for her cloak. "But perhaps I, too, could put my experiences to good purpose and petition some of the men like Colonel Anne did. I'm sure I could win a hundred signatures from a hundred clansmen willing to march behind me in battle."

"They would not march very far with broken legs," Alex advised blandly.

Catherine wrinkled her nose at the threat. "Did she really do that? Did she really go against her husband's wishes by bringing her clan here to join the Prince?"

"Considering her husband, Angus Moy, is a commissioned officer in the Hanover army, I would say she went against his wishes, aye."

"She has a great deal of courage," Catherine decided, lifting her chin so Alex could help button her cloak warmly around her neck.

"I doubt if Angus Moy sees it as courage. He is a very honest and conscientious man, and takes his responsibilities as Chief of Clan Chattan very seriously. His father was a Jacobite and he lost two uncles in the last rebellion. It had to have been a hard decision for him to make to turn his back on us now—harder still, when he hears his wife has thumbed her nose at his authority."

"I still think she is brave."

"Because she followed her heart and not her head? If we all did that, where would we be?"

"Probably right where we are now," she said impertinently, rising on tiptoes to kiss him.

Alexander's scowl returned. "You think rather highly of your own cleverness, don't you?"

"Uh-huh. And I have the perfect example to follow in you, my lord husband."

"Then, perhaps, I should keep the surprise to myself a while longer, to see if you are clever enough to discover it for yourself."

"Surprise?" she asked, her interest piqued at once. "What surprise?"

"Oh . . . just something I stumbled across early this morning. But the more I think on it, the less deserving you appear to be. Besides," he scratched pensively at the stubble of black beard on his jaw. "You may not be all that pleased to see him."

"See him? See who?" she demanded.

Alex stepped back and slowly raised the flap of the tent. A man stood a few feet away, his hands cupped over the lower half of his face, the gaps between the reddened fingers venting steam as he tried to warm them with his breath. The colour ebbed from Catherine's face for a moment, then was restored to a full flush as she ran past Alex with a joyous cry.

"Damien! My God, Damien!"

Damien Ashbrooke spread his arms wide to catch his sister, spinning her around in a half-circle as he did. When they came to a halt, they hugged each other fiercely, laughing, crying, trying to speak simultaneously.

"What are you doing here—?"

"Where did you come from—?"

"Harriet—?"

"In London, she's fine—"

Catherine waved her hands for order. "Damien . . . what are you doing here? Where is Harriet? How did you get here?"

"Harriet is in London," he laughed. "And I almost didn't get here in one piece. And what the devil are *you* doing here? Half the haystacks in Derby have been overturned, looking for you."

"I . . . had to leave. I had to come here with Alex. Damien . . . you've left Harriet alone in London? Does she know where you are? Does she know *what* you are, what you are doing?" She frowned suddenly and held him at arm's length. "What *are* you doing? Why are you here in Scotland?"

"I'm doing what I should have done long ago, and yes, Harriet knows what I am doing, and why I have to do it. She sends her love to you, as well as a haversack full of letters which I had to promise you would open one by one and answer in order. Imagine my surprise when I stopped off at Rosewood Hall to deliver them and confess my terrible, traitorous inclinations . . . only to be informed that my sweet, innocent sister was being sought to answer questions of treason, collaboration, and *murder*!"

Catherine's smile vanished. "You heard about Lieutenant Goodwin?"

"Heard about him? You thought you were the gossips' delight following your marriage to the elusive Raefer Montgomery? It is a wonder your ears have not been singed to nubs even at this distance. What the deuce happened?"

"It was self-defense. We had no choice."

"We?"

"Deirdre and I. We were alone in the house, and . . . and . . ." Her eyes burned with the remembered horror, and Damien did not need to see the warning look on Alexander's face to quickly change the subject.

"Not only did I arrive at Rosewood Hall to find my sister had vacated the premises, but did you know, Mother has fled to greener pastures? Taken it into her head to abscond with a chap by the name of—"

"Lovat-Spence," Catherine nodded. "Yes. I know. We spoke together before she left, and she seems content with the decision. She probably should have done it long ago, if you ask me, but I gave her both our blessings and told her I would explain everything to you when I saw you."

Damien's look of incredulity deepened. "Either the air is thinner here in the mountains and my mind has been affected, or you and I are in dire need of a long, uninterrupted conversation."

"Your mind has been affected for years, brother mine," she said mockingly and slipped her hand into his. "But I shall attempt to straighten it out for you . . . assuming you are free to join Deirdre and me in our little cart. It's not exactly a coach-and-four, but it's cozy. Alex—?"

"By all means, spend as much time as you like together—" A solemn gleam in the indigo eyes promised Damien a private conversation between the two of them later. "We haven't anything more troublesome than a mountain pass to conquer today."

Catherine ran back and gave him a quick hug. "Thank you for the wonderful surprise."

"You're quite welcome. I'll collect my reward later."

"Indeed you will," she agreed huskily.

Alex watched them walk away, hand in hand, following a path worn in the rutted snow and frozen peaks of mud.

"Where the hell did you find him?" Aluinn asked casually and moved forward to stand at Cameron's side.

"A better question might be, how the hell did he find us?"

Startled, Aluinn glanced over, but there was no hint of what was lying behind the question—curiosity, or suspicion.

An hour later, Aluinn and Alex were still pouring over the maps Colonel Anne Moy had provided. The topmost one was a diagram of the city of Inverness, complete with roads feeding in and out of the town, the location of bridges and rivers, rough estimates of distances between local landmarks: Fort George, Culloden House, Moy Hall.

"Culloden House," Alex mused. "I don't imagine we'll find the Lord President in residence when we get there."

"Colonel Anne seems to think Duncan Forbes would be feeling a good deal safer behind the battlements of Fort George. Loudoun is holed up there already with about two thousand troops, armed and supplied for a siege."

"A siege?" Alex snorted. "We can only hope that by failing to take Stirling Castle after three weeks of useless and pointless stalemate, the Prince has learned his lesson."

"Aye, and hopefully he'll not be so quick to trust O'Sullivan with bombarding anything bigger than a beehive."

"Lord George seems to think our regent was simply testing his powers of command. Hell of a way to do it: throw away a potential rout at Falkirk, then waste time, manpower, and ammunition trying to assault a fortification that could hold out against them for a hundred years, if it had to. Conversely, he thinks nothing of leaving a handful of men to hold off the entire might of Cumberland's army."

Alex did not bother to check the bitterness in his voice, nor was Aluinn surprised to hear it. They had received word only the night before that the men they had left behind to hold the garrison at Carlisle had finally signed a capitulation, after holding out against the government forces for nine days. From the two officers who had escaped to carry the news, it was learned the entire contingent of prisoners had been thrown in chains and were slated for execution. Four dragoons who had deserted to the Prince after Prestonpans, and who had volunteered to join the Manchester Regiment, had been hung on the spot, cut down while still alive, their bellies and joints slit open and their bodies torn into quarters, by way of an example of Cumberland's policy toward traitors.

"We should reach Invernesshire sometime in the next two days, weather permitting," Alex said. "We will have to take the city if we are to have any hope of holding on to the Highlands over winter. We need the food and supplies in her warehouses and we need to keep at least one damned port open on the offchance a ship from France manages to break through the Royal Navy's blockade. If only we had retaken Edinburgh . . ."

"It is the 'if onlys' of the world that choke a man to death," Aluinn declared sagely. "If only we had done this instead of that; if only we had gone here instead of there; if only I had married ten years ago, I would have been a happy man ten years sooner."

"That isn't what you thought ten years ago. And certainly not what I ever thought I would hear you say, old friend."

"Oh? The voice of wisdom and experience, is it? You were so eager for wedding vows yourself?"

"God no. But at least I wasn't falling in love every five minutes either—or thinking I was in love."

"I like to look back on it as . . . preparatory research. Nothing at all like the real thing, of course, but a more pleasant way to spend the evenings than glowering at shadows. Not as shocking to the equilibrium to give up, either."

"Are you, in your inimitable fashion, making a point here?"

"Heavens no. You appear to have made the transition from rake to respectability without a hitch, as far as I can see. Far better than I might have predicted. You might even excel at it, given a few years of country living."

The dark sapphire eyes searched for an explanation for the poorly concealed smile on MacKail's face and came away frowning.

"What in blazes *were* you and Catherine talking about?"

"Oh . . . the weather, her health."

"Her health? Is there something the matter with her health?"

"Not a thing. I just thought she looked rather glowing these days and decided to mention it to her. A nice change from the way she looked when she first joined us, don't you agree?"

Alex straightened slowly. He still felt the muscles in his belly constrict whenever he thought of what Catherine—and Deirdre—had suffered at the hands of the British. The bruises had taken weeks to fade, the haunted look in her eyes, almost as long.

"You should try complimenting her now and then," Aluinn suggested blithely. "Tell her she looks as good in men's breeches as she ever did in a Paris gown—not that she wouldn't look good in a burlap feedsack if she chose to wear one—but you would be amazed at the small things that twig in a woman's mind. And that, good friend, *is* the voice of experience." He leaned over and began collecting up the maps. "Now, shall we join the others, or should we wait until they collapse the tent over our heads?"

MacKail adjusted the woolen scarf he wore around his neck and led the way out of the tent, grimacing as he looked up into the graying sky. There would be more snow before the day progressed much further—good news, insofar as it meant Cumberland would be locked in at Edinburgh; bad news for the men, who had to march through the blowing, drifting white stuff.

The two men had not walked very far in the direction of their waiting horses, when their attention was drawn to a group of approaching riders. In their lead, sitting proudly astride an enormous dappled gray gelding was the Lady Anne Moy, Colonel Anne of the Clan Chattan regiment. Her husband Angus was The MacKintosh, chief to the clan of that name as well as to the dozens of small clans that had amalgamated to form the powerful Clan of the Cats. Unfortunately, with The MacKintosh serving under Lord Loudoun's Highland regiments, and Lady Anne pledging her support to Prince Charles, the power of Clan Chattan was greatly reduced. What might well have been a contingent of over two thousand men, united behind the single standard of the Cats, was reduced to less than four hundred.

As much courage as it had taken for Lady Anne to go against her husband's orders, it would take a great deal more, should she ever find herself facing her husband and clansmen across a battlefield.

"Ahh, MacKail," she said, greeting the men with a smile and a wave. "Alasdair. I hope the maps prove to be of some use."

"They are excellent, thank you."

Colonel Anne was neither beautiful in the classic sense of the word, nor delicate—two qualities considered essential in women of the aristocracy. She was tall and statuesque, with the steely, long-limbed grace of a Highland lass raised among the heathery moors and wild mountains. She met a man's gaze directly and openly scorned any attempts to patronize her gender; only twenty years of age, she had personally ridden from clan to clan, eliciting support for Prince Charles, falling only three signatures short of the one hundred required by clan law to lead the men into battle herself. As honorary colonel, she had chosen John Alexander MacGillivray for her captain, an equally raw-boned, intelligent and articulate leader. They were usually together, to the delight of the rumourmongers, and this morning was no exception.

"MacGillivray," Alex said, extending his hand to the laird as he and Lady Anne dismounted. "You managed to sober up, I see?"

"Ach, I'll have tae have a wee talk with yer brither," MacGillivray replied, wincing through a handsome grin. "I ken his stillman must be dain somethin' mines is na. Powerful stuff, that. Medicinal, Archie calls it? Mair like pisen f'ae what disna ail ye."

Lady Anne laughed, a delightful sound in the crisp, clear mountain air. "We'll be riding on ahead, Cameron of Loch Eil. The Prince has accepted ma offer to lodge at Moy Hall until the rest of the army arrives in Inverness. Ye shouldna be more than a day or two behind us, and by then, MacGillivray will know how things stand in the city—assuming he sobers enough to see straight."

"You will take no initiative on your own, I trust," Alex cautioned. "The MacLeods and the Grants have reinforced Lord Loudoun's troops and they will have had plenty of warning about our approach."

"MacLeod," she spat derisively. "I canna believe ma own husband would keep company with a soft-gutted traitor like MacLeod. Mind, I still canna believe Angus would ever raise a sword against Bonnie Prince Charlie, so there ye go. It's fair justice we fill Moy Hall with good, honest Jacobites. Ye'll both be joining us with yer wives?

Ye ken ye canna keep a proper lady from a soft bed and a hot bath too long, or she starts to look like me."

"I could think of worse fates," Alex said admiringly, earning a blush and a self-conscious laugh from Anne Moy. Her glance was directed sidelong at John MacGillivray, and Alex could not help but share the speculation as to whether their relationship had progressed further than the chart tables.

Sensing the moment had gone on too long, Lady Anne strode back to her horse and, refusing any assistance, swung herself up into the saddle. "We'll bid ye godspeed, then; a fair wind at yer backs and safe passage through the corries."

"Godspeed," Alex replied, standing to the side of the path as the group of clansmen filed past. He watched them weave their way around a pair of carts and start a slow canter toward the deep, icy fissures that carved a pass through two looming mountain walls. Within minutes, even the brilliant splashes of colour from their tartans would be cloaked and dulled by shadows, their heads would be tilted forward into the whistling wind, and their smiles frozen into determined slashes.

Turning back to scan the tiny, sheltered glen they had camped in overnight, Alex noted with satisfaction that most of the tents had been struck, the carts of provisions loaded and rumbling single-file toward the mouth of the pass. The Prince's tent, marked by the red-and-white silk standard, was still standing, but the regent's horse and guardsmen were gone, indicating he had left with an earlier contingent.

A tiny dot of movement on the opposite slope of the glen caught Alex's eye and he squinted against the glare of the snow to identify it. The dot appeared to be a single cart, led by one mounted rider in front and flanked by three more in the rear. A heavily bearded clansman held the reins of the plodding horse, and beside him sat a lone passenger, swathed in folds of tartan.

As they cleared a ridge of shadow and descended into what passed for brighter daylight, the passenger—sensing they were under observation—reached up and loosened the shawl covering her head. Seeing the unveiled froth of bright red hair, Alex's black brows crooked upward.

"Well I'll be damned. Look what else the wind has brought us."

Alexander, Aluinn MacKail, and Struan MacSorley were all standing in the cart's path as it drew to a rattling halt in the basin of the glen. Lauren Cameron's face was pink and wind-chafed, her eyes downcast and apprehensive as she waited for a reaction from the ominous reception line.

When none seemed to be forthcoming, she shifted uncomfortably on the hard wooden slat that served as a seat and raised her thick auburn lashes.

"Is there none o' ye even willin' tae offer a hello? Four days an' nights I've been on the road tryin' tae catch up wi' ye, an' naught but a lick or two o' melted snow an' a bite o' dry biscuit have I had since leavin' Auld Reekie."

His arms crossed over his chest, Alex stood, legs braced wide apart, raven hair blown forward against his cheeks and throat, giving a very good impression of a warlord of doom.

"I suppose the pertinent question here might be, why," he said casually. "Why did you leave Edinburgh at all?"

Lauren blinked at the harshness in his voice and two splotches of red flowed up into her cheeks. Aluinn MacKail's demeanour was hardly less reassuring and it was with genuine desperation she directed her appeal to the stalwart Struan MacSorley.

"I were wrong. I admit it freely, Struan. I thought . . . I thought I could go back hame an' find everything the way it was when I left . . . but I were wrong. The people were cold an' cruel. They laughed at the way I dressed, the way I spoke, the . . . the way I looked. Oh, there were jobs aplenny f'ae lassies what came tae the city an' were willin' tae make their coin on their backs. There were rooms too, an' taverns filled wi' sojers only too happy tae offer their protection . . . f'ae a night or two . . . till they had what they wanted an' grew bored wi' it. Well, I'm nae whore, Struan MacSorley. Aye, I take pleasure in life an' aye, in the pleasurable things life has tae offer, but I'm nae whore." She stopped and bit the fleshy pulp of her lip. "I wouldna blame ye f'ae holdin' yer anger, Struan. T'was a surly thing I doun, creepin' away in the middle o' the night, tairnin' ma back on ma friends, ma family, ma clan." She bowed her head and the glistening swell of a teardrop rolled slowly down her cheek and dropped onto her tightly clasped hands. "But I'm sorry f'ae it now an' want tae come hame."

"You came alone?" Aluinn asked, noting the accompanying clansmen and identifying them from a patrol he had sent out during the night.

"Aye, alane. Fast as I could too—see?" She held out her red and weather-cracked hands for their inspection. "It were all I could dae tae steal this miserable garron an' cart, let alane find someone tae fetch me. But it didna matter. Naught mattered, as long as I could catch up wi' ye."

A small red hand was dashed across a cheek, smearing tears and grime together. Alex and Aluinn exchanged a glance, but MacSorley's eyes had not wavered from Lauren Cameron.

"If ye dinna think ye can find it in yer hearts tae forgive me, I'll understand," she continued in a whisper. "Truly, I will. But . . . if ye can, if ye dae—" she looked up and fastened huge, gleaming gold eyes on MacSorley, "—I'll work twice as hard as anyone else in camp. I'll cook, an' scrub claythes, an' dae the meanest chores ye can find wi'out a word o' complaint. I swear I will. I swear it by ma ain poor mam's deid soul."

MacSorley approached the cart. "Ye'll have tae speak wi' Lochiel. It's his decision whether ye stay or whether ye go."

"Aye. Aye, I ken that, Struan."

His hazel eyes narrowed piercingly. "It mout go easier on ye if ye had someone willin' tae stand by yer side; someone willin' tae take charge o' ye an' see that ye behave yersel' this time."

"Are . . . are ye offerin' tae dae that f'ae me, Struan?"

"I dinna need a scrubwoman or a cook," he said bluntly. Seeing her blanch under his stare, he relented somewhat and twitched his beard into a crooked smile. "If I take ye back, it'll be as ma wife."

"Yer . . . wife?" she gasped.

"Aye. An' as ma wife, ye'll keep yer eyes straight an' yer skirts doon, or ye'll feel the flat o' ma hand, hard an' often, make nae mistake. As yer husban', I'll see ye never want f'ae aught; I'll keep yer belly full an' yer thighs warm, an' I'll kill any man wha' disna treat ye wi' the proper respect due a MacSorley."

"I dinna desairve it, Struan," she murmured, taken aback by the offer.

"No. Ye dinna," he snorted. "But ye dinna have much choice, either. Take it or leave it, lass; I'll only play the fool once."

Lauren saw the looks on the faces of the other two men and nodded quickly. "Aye, Struan, it's a handsome offer an' I take it gladly. What's mair, I promise ye'll never regret it. Ye'll never even have tae raise yer voice tae me. Never!"

"Enough said then." He stretched up his massive arms and grasped her about the waist, swinging her effortlessly out of the cart. He did not set her on the ground at once, but held her so that her tear-stained face was level with his. Emitting a small, strangled cry, she flung her arms around his neck and kissed him, her lips seemingly as starved for affection as they were for forgiveness.

Struan appeared similarly eager to impart both, but as Alexander watched the impassioned reunion, he could not quite shake the feeling that something was not right. His dark eyes queried MacKail's, but Aluinn could only offer a noncommittal shrug.

Through partially closed eyes, Lauren noted the exchange. Struan was guided by instincts that were centred below the waist, not above the neck, and she had known he would be the easiest to manipulate. Lochiel, as always, would be susceptible to a tearful confession and a humble prostration, and would welcome her back into the fold, as well as giving his hearty blessings to the marriage. Cameron and MacKail were more suspicious by nature and, therefore, would be the most difficult to convince of her reformation.

To that end, Lauren's immediate concern was for the insistent pounding in her breast. It had begun the moment she recognized the tall, black-haired Highlander striding down the path, and had grown in intensity and purpose each heartbeat since. He was still in her blood, despite the months apart and the creditable efforts of Hamilton Garner to wipe her memory clean. It disturbed her to know the ache was still inside her, the desire as strong as it had been the very first time she had laid eyes upon him. Perhaps she should have left Edinburgh long ago. Perhaps the months of separation from his *Sassenach* wife had cleared his senses, or at the very least, made him more vulnerable to a soft word and a woman's ripe musk. Perhaps—

"Alex! Alex, there you are! I was hoping to speak with you before you left. Damien was—" Catherine skidded to a halt, her cheeks flushed from the brief run, her breath frosting out before her. Her eyes sparkled as they went from Alex to Aluinn to Struan, then apologetically scanned the woman standing beside the wagon before returning to her husband. "Damien was wondering if—"

She stopped again, took two measured breaths, and looked back at the figure who was partly concealed by Struan's bulky frame.

An equally rigid, disbelieving Lauren Cameron stared back in shock, the absolute unexpectedness of seeing her yellow-haired nemesis in the rebel camp almost undoing the brilliance of her performance thus far. She was here! The *Sassenach* bitch was here! Not in England, not banished from sight and mind, not removed from Alasdair's presence, as Lauren had supposed her to be. She was here! In Scotland!

Fury, hatred, resentment rose in Lauren's throat, all but choking off her ability to breathe. Struan's arms were still around her waist and she was grateful for their restraint: without them, she might have lunged for the loathesomely sweet and delicate face, tearing it to bloody ribbons, and happily so.

Catherine's emotions were just as much in turmoil. She had been told Lauren had elected to abandon the rebel camp and remain in Edinburgh—where she belonged, as far as Catherine was concerned. For the briefest of instants, before either party had recognized the other, the amber eyes had been fixed on Alexander's face, the envy and scheming hunger as avidly apparent to Catherine as it had been six months ago. She had grown accustomed to women staring at her husband—she stared at him herself truth be known—but most did so out of respect and awe for the Dark Cameron. There was no respect in Lauren's eyes, only lust; the awe translated into desire, as pure and raw as the hatred smoldering in them now.

"Why Lauren Cameron," she managed to say past a brittle smile. "What a pleasant surprise. Wherever did you come from?"

The pits of hell, Lauren wanted to scream, where I'd love to send you, right now!

Instead, she pressed herself deeper into Struan's embrace and smiled brightly. "Why, I've come hame, have I na? Where I belong."

"Aye," Struan said proudly. "Lauren's hame tae stay an' mair's the luck, she's agreed tae share the name MacSorley."

"You are going to marry her?" Catherine gasped, startled again. She felt the subtle pressure of Alex's hand on hers and covered her obvious slip with another smile. "Well, of course I am happy for you, Struan. Happy for both of you."

"Aye. She's a wild enough tigress tae try tae tame," MacSorley said, grinning down at his prospective bride. "But I'll gie it ma best effort."

"It's me who'll dae the tamin', Struan," Lauren murmured suggestively, and with the relish of a hawk swooping down on an unsuspecting victim, Lauren drew MacSorley's lips into a crushing kiss, using every inch and undulation of flesh at her disposal to strip the imagination of any doubts as to the truth behind her promises. Struan's arousal was instantaneous and Herculean; obvious enough to have the three clansmen gaping.

Catherine stared, so long and hard, Alexander had to turn her forcibly around so she had nothing to distract her apart from the humour in his eyes.

"You were looking for me?"

"Looking for you?"

"Something to do with your brother," he prodded gently.

"Oh. Yes. I mean . . . no. No, it's nothing important." She started to angle her head around, to investigate the source of the heated gasps and groans, but a firm hand kept her face averted.

"Let she who is innocent cast the first stone," he murmured, adding unnecessarily, "Reminds me of another reunion a few weeks ago."

Catherine flushed and conceded a smile. "At least ours was private."

"Crowds of spectators wouldn't have stopped me."

Catherine considered the angular features, the gleaming dark eyes and boldly sensual mouth, and knew he spoke the truth.

"You are wicked, sir," she murmured, conscious of his hand straying beneath the shield of her cloak.

"Just a man in love," he said, drawing her forward.

Lauren, out of breath and very much aware of the iron-hard shaft of flesh nearly lifting her off the ground, ended the kiss on a triumphant note. She glanced away from Struan's steamy determination in time to see Alex and Catherine come together in an open-mouthed, affectionately prolonged embrace. Before she could react, her eager groom-to-be was scooping her into his arms and turning the tables on her seductive prank. He carried her to the nearest available tent, bellowing jovially over his shoulder to the grinning audience that there would be a slight delay before he rejoined the column.

"Struan, no!" Lauren gasped, her face beet red with dismay. "We should speak tae Lochiel fairst. Ye said so yersel'!"

His lips muffled her protests, his hands stilled her thrashings. A startled clanswoman, driven out of her tent by the sight of the giant Highlander flinging his tartan and his woman onto the ground, was only one or two sentences into a scathing protest when the choked, high-pitched cries began to bounce and echo off the iced, cavernous valley walls. The sounds sent her scrambling back even further and it was left to Aluinn MacKail, as peacemaker—and the only one who could keep a straight face—to calm the woman and assure her that neither the tent nor her belongings would suffer any damage, and would be returned in due time.

The woman could be thankful she did not wait. An hour later, the tent was still standing, the walls were still flapping and quivering, and renewed choruses of shrill cries were shattering the hollow silence of the glen. The bemused audience had long since melted away, however, as had every other tent, cart, horse and wagon in the valley.

Chapter Fifteen

In the end, it took five full days for the column of men to struggle through the snow-clogged mountain pass and file into the glens surrounding Inverness. The hills fell away sharply, the intense bluish-white of the deep snow giving way to patches of ground that were brown with dead bracken, gray with silvery heather stalks, soggy with peat bogs that never quite froze over. Tiny stone and sod *clachans* marked by pencil-thin spirals of peat smoke huddled against sheltered slopes, dotting the valleys and fields. Their curious occupants ventured only as far as their doorways as the rebel army marched past, then returned to their hearths again, dismissing the intrusion as being of no consequence.

Inverness was the capital city of the Highlands, a small town by comparison to the other major ports of Glasgow and Edinburgh. There were fewer than five hundred houses and three thousand permanent residents, most of them merchants and businessmen, which meant the town was structured around the four main streets that converged in the market square. Export goods and produce from the northern Highlands were brought to Inverness. Likewise, the ships that sailed from London, Paris, and points beyond, all sailed into the Atlantic blue waters of the Moray Firth and offloaded their cargoes at exorbitant profits.

The city was strategically important to both the government and rebel forces. The river that flowed through the centre of town joined the Moray Firth to Loch Ness, which in turn led to a series of smaller lochs and rivers flowing south-east along the length of the Great Glen, past Fort Augustus—the halfway point—to Fort William, slashing through the Highlands on a sharp diagonal and linking the two major shipping ports. The army that controlled Inverness, controlled the Highlands.

Looking south from Inverness, the mountains were piled hill against hill, woods against woods in every shade of blue, black and gray. Crouched to the north across the firth, were the distant hills of Cromarty and Dornoch, and still more remote, the clustered crust of highlands that marked Sutherland territory. Rising above the town, seated on a steep little hill on the south side of the river, was Fort George, old and crumbling, built in a time when the only threat to the Highlands was expected from the sea. Her guns were all pointed out into the firth and, even though there were barracks for six companies, most of the military personnel felt more secure outside the dilapidated walls.

To the east of Inverness, the coast road led to Nairn, passing the grand and spacious home of Duncan Forbes, the Lord President of the Court in Session. Culloden House was four miles outside the city, sitting high on a gentle knoll of land that commanded a view of adjoining parklands, wooded hills, and a wide, sloping plain known by the locals as Drummossie Moor.

Less than five miles to the south of Culloden was the residence of Angus Moy, Chief of Clan Chattan. A large estate by Highland standards, Moy Hall was built of quarried stone that had weathered to a soft gray tint over the years. The surrounding hills were dark with cypress and cedar, alive with deer and wild game, ribboned with burns that bubbled silver with fat, energetic trout.

The road leading to Moy Hall wound its way through forests and tiny glens, flung itself around a shoulder of hills and finally spilled into a wide, sweeping glen, glittering under a thin blanket of snow. A sheep dog, white-muzzled, white-chested but otherwise black as night, sounded the alarm as the Prince's entourage rounded the final bend, and Lady Anne was at the door of the manor to greet him, her tartan trews and belted broadsword traded for immaculately coiffed hair and elegant satin gown.

The main bulk of the Prince's column had spread out, taking quarters in the neighbouring farms and villages, but while Charles Stuart was in residence, Lochiel and his Camerons would make camp in the glen at Moy Hall. Keppoch and his MacDonalds settled to the west of the glen, the Stewarts of Appin guarded the approaches to the east.

Alexander Cameron at first declined Lady Anne's invitation of hospitality in favour of remaining in camp with the men. A second invitation, delivered in person by their adamant hostess, could not be honourably refused—to Catherine's overwhelming delight and relief. She had managed to remain outwardly stoic and silent through the initial decision to refuse lodging, but nearly wept with joy when Alex informed her they would be sleeping under a real roof, in a real bed, between real sheets. Her last intimate meeting with a tub of hot water had been in Glasgow, nearly a month before. The mere thought of a roaring fire sent a feverish flush through her body, one that did not lessen by any degree when she skimmed a hand over the quilted covers of the canopy bed, or ran her fingers along the frilly, softly feminine articles of clothing Lady Anne had thoughtfully provided for her use. Since leaving Derby, both she and Deirdre had elected to remain in men's clothing, finding it far more practical than heavy dragging skirts, and far warmer during the day and night. To that end, she had not felt a silk chemise next to her skin for almost ten weeks, and just the thought of feather pillows and a thick, warm mattress, left her trembling with anticipation.

After so many weeks of hard tent cots and drafty canvas walls, the bedroom Lady Anne had prepared was nothing short of heaven. A large square chamber, it boasted two tall, leaded windows facing east, each with cushioned windowseats and thick velvet draperies to discourage any whispers of wind. Taking up one entire wall was a large stone fireplace with a carved marble mantle. Polished oak floors were covered in Turkish carpets woven in soft patterns of blue, gold, and a touch of rose.

As in most Scottish homes, the furnishings were sparse and functional; on the wall to the left of the fireplace was an enormous wardrobe, on the wall opposite the hearth was a wide feather bed set on a mahogany catafalque, with draperies tied to each post that could be loosened at night to enfold the sleepers in a cozy velvet cocoon. Between the windows, a round, long-legged table held a vase filled with winter roses Lady Anne grew in a sunny garden greenhouse, attached to the breakfast room. By the fireplace was a damask settle and a pair of high-backed wooden chairs.

Absolutely heaven, Catherine thought, nearly speechless with happiness. Left to her own resources while Alex organized the camp, she indulged in a long, steamy bath before a blazing fire, shamelessly calling twice for more heated water. Alex seemed immune to the discomfort of washing in icy streams, but then he was also asleep within minutes of hitting the hard ground, and his body always emitted the heat of a small furnace, whether it was a moderately warm night or howling with a blizzard. Catherine, on the other hand, had been cold since leaving Derby. Her fingers, her toes, the tip of her nose were perpetually pink and chilled, and she had begun to wonder if she would ever feel warm again.

Her moods, of late, had been growing proportionately erratic as well, a condition noticed by everyone but Alex. His days were mostly taken up with army affairs, and by the time he was able to fall into an exhausted sleep at night, Catherine was grateful just to be able to share the heat of his body. Each day, when Aluinn saw her, the question was in his eyes as to whether she'd had a chance to impart her good news to her husband, but there just hadn't been the right combination of time or mood.

She had told Deirdre right away, of course, and the beaming Mrs. MacKail had welcomed the news with smiles, tears, and a frown or two of concern, for good measure. Secretly hoping to find herself in a similar condition before too long, Deirdre was happy for Catherine, and a little envious. But when she began to dwell on the more practical realities of the situation—the long rough hours of travel in deplorable weather, the inevitable sickness that went hand in hand with exhaustion, poor food, and lack of sanitation—she grew more and more concerned, and agreed with Aluinn that Alexander should be told without further delay.

"If I wait much longer," Catherine muttered, inspecting her profile in the mirror (was it her imagination or was her belly developing a distinctly rounded curve to it?) "I shan't have to *tell* him anything at all."

Tonight, she decided. She would tell him tonight, and hang the consequences. If what he had said, all those months ago, about hating children and kicking small dogs was true . . . well, he would just have to grin and bear it. There wasn't much she could do about it, even if she wanted to . . . which she didn't. The mere thought of giving birth to a child terrified her, and would terrify her more as the babe grew and swelled within her. But it was Alex's child, and that made all the difference. She would be strong and brave and . . . and . . .

Something—a tickle of a draft against her shoulder, or perhaps just the instinctive knowledge that she was no longer alone in the room made her turn slowly toward the door.

Having just recently stepped from the bath, she was dressed only in a thin chemise as she stood before the fire brushing her hair dry. Alexander, who had come into the room unobserved, had been standing quietly by the door enjoying the view of his wife's lithe body turning this way and that before the glow of the fire. The chemise had ridden up to bare more of the gently rounded hips and pale buttocks than her modesty might have allowed, but Alex's dark eyes devoured the pale loveliness, relishing the effect she had on his own body.

He had been taking her beauty for granted, he was realizing. The stunningly long, slender legs; skin as white and fine as porcelain, as clear and unblemished as the day he had met her, despite all the hardships she had been through. How long had it been since he had seen her hair out of the thick regimental braid she had taken to wearing? How long since he had seen her trim figure enveloped in anything less than unflatteringly bulky men's clothing? Even making love, lately, had become a furtive, hasty act, accomplished around barely loosened clothing and beneath mounds of scratchy wool blankets.

Perhaps that was why he had not noticed the changes. They were slight, to be sure, but to a man who prided himself on having explored and committed to memory every mole and crease, every curve and supple indentation, her secret was as glaringly obvious as if she wore a sign draped around her belly.

"How long?" he asked calmly.

Catherine held the hairbrush clenched tightly in both hands, the knuckles turning ivory where they gripped the handle.

"I cannot be sure," she answered in a voice that feigned the same cool indifference as his. "But I am praying it happened the night you came to me at Rosewood Hall. I never loved you more than I did that night. Never any less since then, but that was the first night I knew beyond any shred of doubt you were the only man I would ever love. It was the night I knew everything that had gone on before in my life had been meaningless and empty, and anything after—without you—would be without purpose."

He had moved closer while she was speaking. The firelight was bathing his face, gilding his skin, his hair in gold, illuminating every feature, yet unable to penetrate the quiet, brooding intensity of his eyes. She could live to be a thousand and never be able to cipher them completely. Her chin suffered a tremor and her blood felt thick and sluggish. She was standing too close to the fire, she rationalized, and the heat was infusing her limbs, melting her flesh, scalding her senses, and blurring her vision behind a film of tears. Blinded by love, she watched his shimmering outline come almost close enough to touch her. Almost.

"When were you planning to tell me?"

"As soon as I was sure," she admitted in a whisper. "But you were always so busy . . . and . . . and I was afraid . . ." Her voice trailed away and the dark eyes narrowed sharply.

"Afraid? Afraid of what?"

"Of you. Of how you would react. I mean, you did say once that you abhorred the thought of having children. You also said you abhorred the thought of having a wife, and I thought . . . well, I thought you had adjusted to the one shock rather well, but having a second one thrown at you so soon, it . . . it . . ." She stopped, her eyes wide and wet and very deeply hued as she fastened on the smile that was slowly spreading across his lips.

Without speaking or explaining the unsettling grin, his hands cupped her face gently between them and his mouth covered hers, the kiss as deep and passionate as a physical act of love. It left her speechless—as intended—and breathless, awed by the sheer emotional power of that one act of touching. Her awe spread, paralyzing her further as he dropped humbly onto one knee before her, circling his arms around her waist and pressing first his lips, then his bronzed cheek against her belly.

"I am sorry if I frightened you," he murmured hoarsely. "I am truly sorry if I led you to believe I would be anything but . . . overwhelmed and . . . overjoyed at the thought of you loving me enough to bear my child."

Catherine let the brush slip out of her hands and combed her fingers into the thick waves of gleaming black hair. "Oh Alex . . ."

He felt the splash of a hot tear drop from her chin onto his cheek and he took hold of himself, standing again and gathering her into his arms. But neither of them were steady enough to support the other, so he compromised by lifting her and settling onto one of the chairs before the hearth, his body cradling hers against his possessive warmth, his lips laying a path of caresses through the silky fragrance of her hair.

"You did indeed manage to change my opinion of married life, madam," he whispered pensively. "You have managed to work your way into my bloodstream so I cannot draw a breath without thinking of you. Not content to simply have my peace of mind, it seems you must now have my heart, my life, my soul."

"It is only fair, my lord, since you have mine."

He kissed her tremulous smile and gathered her even closer. "I suppose you are also going to tell me you are not the least afraid of bringing a child into the midst of all this?"

"I'm not afraid," she said, pulling back enough to look deeply into his eyes. "I'm not, Alex. There has to be peace soon. The fighting cannot go on much longer, and when it ends, we will be able to return to Achnacarry and live there happily and peaceably ever after."

"Just like in a fairytale?" he chided softly.

"Just like in a *family*," she corrected. "Our family, Alex. You, me, and the beautiful son we have made together."

He said nothing—could say nothing through the incredible, constricting pressure that seemed to grip his every muscle and nerve.

"Alex . . . we will be able to return to Achnacarry, won't we? I mean, we will be safe there . . . won't we?"

The fear in her voice helped ease some of his own. "Of course we will be safe at Achnacarry; why wouldn't we be? Lochaber has been isolated and inviolate for centuries; nothing has happened to change that."

Catherine remembered vividly the miles of winding, endless forest tracts that camouflaged the approach to Achnacarry Castle; the remoteness, the strength of the structure itself, with its hundred-foot-high battlements and mist-drenched parapets. Not even Cromwell had dared venture into the wilds of Lochaber, and Cumberland was half the soldier he'd been and had only a quarter of the armed strength behind him that Cromwell had had.

"Alex?"

She felt his lips move against her temple by way of a response.

"I don't suppose . . . I mean, I've known all along I would not be able to remain with the camp once my . . . our secret was out . . . would I?" When a quick glance up into his face confirmed there would be no argument on earth ever able to persuade him otherwise, she quickly redirected the assault. "In which case, I was hoping I might be able to go on ahead to Achnacarry and wait for you there. I have already discussed it with Deirdre and Aluinn, and they both agree —"

"Aluinn? He knows?"

"He guessed. And he has been breathing down my neck ever since, threatening to tell you himself, if I did not do it soon. But now I have told you and I am asking you—pleading with you—to let me go to Achnacarry."

For another taut moment there was no sound other than the steady beating of his heart within the muscled chamber of his chest. Catherine braced herself for the inevitable arguments: England would be safer, France would be safer, Italy would be safer, a penal colony in Australia would be safer . . .

"Aye, Achnacarry is probably the safest place for you to be in the circumstances."

"Maura will be there to take care of me," she insisted, blurting out her first line of defense without having heard his answer. "Jeannie and Rose will be there too, and Deirdre has said she will —" She paused and two quick breaths brought her head up off the crook of his shoulder again. "What did you just say?"

"I said yes. With Cumberland behind us, it would take more men than the Prince or Lochiel could spare to escort you back to England. Barely one ship in twenty breaks in or out of the blockade, so it would be out of the question to even try to smuggle you out to Europe. Offhand, I cannot think of any safer place for you than Achnacarry."

"Do you mean it?" she gasped, lacing her fingers excitedly around his neck. "Do you really mean it?"

"Yes," he smiled tenderly. "I really mean it. As it happens, the Prince has finally seen the wisdom of removing the government troops who still hold Fort Augustus and Fort William. He has ordered Lochiel and Keppoch to undertake the task with all due haste, and to be perfectly honest —" his smile became rueful "— I was trying to think of some way to suggest you remain at the castle when we passed through Lochaber."

"And then to conveniently forget to retrieve me again when you returned to Inverness?"

"The thought had occurred to me."

"It had, had it?" she scowled, sitting attentively upright and swivelling around on his lap so that she faced him squarely. "What about the promise you made that we should never be apart again?"

Alex skimmed his hands up the naked length of her thighs, running them up beneath the lacy hem of her chemise. "You would prefer to nurture our son in the open fields, in tents and dank stone cottages?"

"You were making your nefarious plots before you knew I was with child," she reminded him, squirming closer, her small oval face level with his.

"Aye, and now that I do," he said, frowning, "I am inclined to think it might be best if you remained here for the next week or so until we clear the garrison out of Fort Augustus. As soon as they're driven out, the route to Achnacarry will be clear and I will be able to come back and escort you with all the pomp and ceremony befitting a princess."

"A week?" she murmured. "When are you leaving?"

Alex hesitated. "Tomorrow."

"Tomorrow! And when were you going to tell me?"

"I only just found out myself. They're still arguing between themselves as it is—neither of the chiefs thinks it is a particularly good idea to leave the area before Lord George arrives, but . . ." His hands moved restlessly and his forehead creased with displeasure. "The Prince has taken command and has assured everyone he is perfectly capable of protecting himself for a few hours."

"Inverness is so close, and the city is full of government soldiers," she began.

"None of whom know the Prince is here," he assured her. "Or that he is alone—which he isn't. Not entirely. Ardshiel's men will close ranks when we leave, and MacGillivray will keep the soldiers in Inverness busy elsewhere. There is absolutely nothing to worry about . . . if there was, would I be willing to leave you?"

"For a week," she reminded him petulantly.

"Lady Anne will be pleased to have the company. And you cannot tell me you would prefer to leave all this —"

he indicated the comfort of the bedchamber with a twist of his eyebrow "— for drafty tents and creaking cots?"

"I have not complained so far, have I?"

"Not in so many words, no. You have been very stoic . . . and made me feel very guilty in the process."

"So you should," she muttered disconsolately. Her hand trailed across the breadth of his shoulder and came to rest over the silver and topaz brooch he wore clasped to the folds of tartan.

"A *week*," she said again, bending her head so that her forehead was touching his chin.

"Do you think you can manage without me for that long?" he asked, his voice gently mocking.

The clasp of the pin gave way under her fingers, releasing the wool so that it slithered down from his shoulder. She looked up at him and smiled coyly.

"I shall sleep as soundly as a child, I warrant. It might even be a welcome change to lie the whole night undisturbed."

Alex made no move to either assist or resist her efforts to unbuckle the belt from around his waist and insinuate herself under the loosened folds of tartan.

"I disturb you, do I?" he mused, his thumbs idling over the smoothless of her skin.

"Mmmm. Sometimes several times a night," was the flippant reply, given while nimble fingers made short work of the buttons down his waistcoat and the laces binding his shirt. "But I am getting used to stealing a few winks of sleep, here and there—as many as I am alotted before a hand strays where it shouldn't."

"Whose hand: Yours or mine?"

Catherine's eyes glinted in the firelight. She pulled herself forward, lifting her hips slightly before settling herself over the vaunted thrust of his flesh. Inch by inch, she lowered herself onto him, angling her body in such a way as to allow the deepest, tightest sheathing. She was smugly pleased to see the shock flare in his eyes, and to feel the tremor ripple through his body as he found her hot as molten silver, sleek as satin.

"Madam, your inventiveness never fails to astound me," he said, his teeth flashing whitely through a grin of avaricious pleasure.

"*My* inventiveness? I believe, sir, it was you who redefined the purpose of bathtubs, fine brandy, and balcony balustrades."

Conceding the point with a smile, his hands slid upward to engulf the heaviness of her breasts and, without troubling himself to remove the skimpy garment she wore, he lowered his mouth to the crest of each upthrust nipple, toying with them through the wet circles of silk until they were peaked and straining for freedom.

Not to be outdone in deviousness, Catherine curved her lower body against his, drawing slowly back and curling forward again in deliberately measured undulations that soon had him cursing softly and holding her immobile against him. He was hard and pulsing vigorously inside her, thudding eagerly against the moist, clinging enclosure.

"Do you want this to end quickly, or slowly?" he asked on a rough breath.

"I want to remember this all week," she murmured brazenly, her lips slanting over his.

"Your wish is my command, madam," he replied huskily, and slipped his hands down from her breasts to her waist, then along her thighs until they were hooked into the fold of her knees.

Catherine dragged her mouth away from his, startled to feel the room lurch beneath her. Another start, brought on by a second lurch and an incredible surge of pressure within her, made her grasp more tightly to him as she realized they were seated on a chair that rocked back and forth on curved runners.

"You are no gentleman, sir," she gasped, drowning in her own heat as he kept rocking evenly, back and forth. "You do not play fair."

"We established a long time ago I was no gentleman," he reminded her with a grin. "And since when does a man have to play fair when his other half obviously has no such qualms?"

Catherine swallowed hard and melted against him. She ran her hands beneath the parted edges of his linen shirt and pressed herself against the crisp black mat of hair, moaning softly as she introduced this new abrasion to her already aching nipples. She folded her arms around his neck, bracing herself for every forward and backward roll of the chair, arching her head back to savour the rich flow of sensations gliding from his body to hers.

Alex drank in the subtle currents of pleasure mirrored on her face. Her hair glowed and swayed like liquid sunlight in the reflection of the fire; the thin, transparent layer of her chemise absorbed the damp fragrance of her skin, teasing his senses like a rare perfume. A parting of soft, moist lips, a quick intake of air and the strained, disbelieving escape of a sigh warned of an imminent drenching elsewhere and he tried to keep his mind detached from his body, tried not to focus on the silken muscles that lured him deeper and deeper, grew hotter and less stable on each completed roll.

Twice, in order to survive his wife's writhing implosions, he had to close his eyes and clench his teeth so hard he thought he would surely snap them off at the gums. And twice, when he could safely catch his breath again, it was expelled on a groan, for as hot and tormenting as Catherine had been up until then, she was now a moving, feverish wraith of sensual torture. His groans came harsher and more frequently, and his hands moved from her knees to her bottom, locking her even closer to his body.

Catherine lost track of time, lost all perceptions of space and surroundings as she crested time and time again, each peak higher, steeper, swifter into the maelstrom than the last, each swooping fall more bittersweet and protracted than any that had gone before. Dimly, she heard him cry out her name, and clung to him more from instinct than ability, only to feel his rushing heat burst within her and send her into yet another steep, aching spiral of ecstasy.

Later, dazed and clinging together in wonderment, Alex's lips sought the damp crook of her neck.

"I sincerely hope, madam," he said shakily, "if we should have a daughter, she will be a tad more self-disciplined than her mother."

"Why?" Catherine demanded, her mouth grasping his for a long moment before she could continue. "You would prefer a lock-kneed spinster who would cost you a small fortune to settle into married life?"

"Spoken with true motherly concern," he noted with a soft laugh. "And here I thought I had married a decorous, genteel lady."

"A pox on decorum," she announced, her lips chasing after a bead of sweat as it trickled from his temple down along the corded column of his neck. "I want her to know what *this* is like. I don't want her to be afraid of love, or of loving a man. I don't want her to faint at the sight of a bare chest, or rush after smelling salts every time she hears or thinks of the word *pleasure*. Mind you—" she raised her tousled, damply curled head and fixed an icy stare on her husband's face, "the debate is purely hypothetical in any case, for I intend to have only sons. Tall and black-haired, as devilishly handsome as their father. As principled, as proud . . . as gentle, loving, and compassionate."

"You neglected to mention skilled and unselfish."

"I neglected to mention humble," she added, her eyes narrowing. "A trait sadly lacking in the father."

"And completely foreign to the mother."

Catherine peered at him for all of three seconds, then sighed languidly and snuggled against his chest.

"What? No rebuttal?"

"I'm too happy to argue," she admitted softly. "And too busy wondering whether or not my legs will ever work properly again."

"Good God—" Alex's handsome face paled and he glanced anxiously down to where they were still joined. "I haven't hurt you, have I? Christ, Catherine, I didn't even think —"

Catherine smothered his concerns under her lips. "You most definitely have not hurt me, my lord," she assured him. "And you were not supposed to think, just act . . . which you did, most magnificently."

After a moment, he relaxed and circled his arms around her again. "Shameless: that is what you are."

"I had a marvellously uninhibited teacher, if you will recall."

"Yes . . . one who does not remember doing anything particularly inventive with balcony balustrades."

"I have no doubt you would have, given time."

And that, there would never be enough of, he thought bleakly. There would never be enough time to give her enough pleasure to make up for the pain she had endured because of him. What had he given her so far, dammit? Dampness and cold, beds fashioned out of planks and canvas, poor food, lonely days and nights filled with fear and uncertainty. She had given up everything for him, and, as if everything were not enough, she was prepared to risk her life in childbirth—a hazardous undertaking, even under the most pristine and comfortable conditions.

"What is it?" she asked, stroking her hand along his jaw. "What are you thinking about to bring on such an unhappy expression?"

He smiled faintly, unaware she had been studying him. "You. And my grandfather."

"Sir Ewen Cameron?"

"Aye. The old *gaisgach liath* would have liked you, I think. It would have amused him and pleased him to no end to see how easily I have been tamed."

"Not tamed, my lord husband. A little softened around the edges, perhaps, but never tamed. I would not want it so. Who would I have to argue with? And who would I have to keep me solidly in line?"

"Ah-hah! You are admitting you are a stubborn piece of baggage, are you?" He leaned forward, lifting her with him as he stood up from the chair and crossed over to the enormous tester bed.

"I'm admitting nothing," she said, welcoming him back into her arms as he stretched out on the bed beside her. "But I do promise you, sir, that my past behaviour will seem positively angelic in comparison to what it will be if you take any unnecessary risks in the coming week, or do anything at all that might keep us apart any longer than it takes to frighten a few redcoats out of a nuisance fort. I expect your promise on this, Alexander Cameron. Your most solemn word of honour."

"Would it stop you from worrying?"

"No," she said after some consideration. "But it would help."

"Very well—" he removed himself from the bed and walked back to where his belt and kilt lay in a crush of tartan beside the rocking chair. He returned to Catherine's side carrying the small steel-and-ebony dirk he always wore sheathed at his waist. "We have a pleasant little custom in this country when a man's most solemn word of honour is demanded. He gives it, sealing his pledge with the full knowledge that if he should break it, or dishonour his word in any way, the blade he kisses will be the one used to take his life."

Alex raised the dirk, pressed the blade to his lips then kissed Catherine with the taint of steel still cool on his mouth. "I give you my word, Catherine, I will do everything in my power to see that I am back with you at Achnacarry, for good and ever, in plenty of time to see our son born."

When there was no visible lessening of the fear that glowed hauntingly in her eyes, he kissed her again. "Are you questioning the oath of a Highlander, madam?"

"No. Not exactly. I mean . . . I don't know how to explain it, but I have this dreadful feeling, deep inside, that something terrible is going to happen."

"Is it your dream again?"

"No. At least, I don't think so. I have not had it since I left Rosewood Hall . . . yet, somehow . . . it feels as if I am living it, or some part of it, anyway."

"I told you before, people have dreams all the time when they're frightened or under stress."

"Yes, I know."

"But . . . ?"

She looked up. "But it was so real."

Alex set aside the dirk and joined Catherine on the bed again, taking her into his arms and holding her close.

"It was still only a dream," he insisted. "Something your mind conjured up because you were overtired, or your defenses were weak . . . or simply because we were not together. But I have never heard of a nightmare that has actually come true and believe me, men have some beauties when they are trying to get some sleep the night before a battle."

"Have you? Had nightmares, I mean?"

Alexander hesitated fractionally, his mind drawn inward on the memory of the chillingly realistic enactments of the night Annie was slain. How many times had he lived through that hell? Too many to recount. Now, the fear was always with him, riding on his shoulder like a satyr, that the same thing might happen again—with

Catherine—as it almost had with the British lieutenant. He tried not to think about it, or dwell upon the possibilities for evil he envisioned whenever he walked away from camp and left Catherine alone for any length of time, but the thoughts were there. The fears were real. He knew the Campbells would not let something as incidental as a rebellion stand in the way of their hunger for revenge. MacKail was still worried about some elusive French assassin he'd heard about—an assassin who had been hired by the Duke of Argyle to hunt Alex down. And there was Hamilton Garner; he was still out there somewhere, obsessed with the need for revenge.

"Alex . . . ?"

"Yes. Yes, I have had nightmares. I have had day-mares too and lived through them—we all have, and we all will again, so there is no use fighting them or worrying about them, for it would be a sure road to madness."

"If you are telling me this to make me feel better," she said glumly, "it isn't working very well."

"I am telling you this to make you stop worrying. I am doing this—" he kissed her and sent his hands down to coax her limbs apart "—to make you feel better."

"In that case," she murmured after due consideration, "it is working very well, indeed."

Chapter Sixteen

Later that evening, Lauren Cameron MacSorley found herself thinking a similar thought to Catherine's: Everything was working out very well indeed, better than she had dared hope. Lochiel had welcomed her back with tears and toasts. Struan had stalked after her like an oversexed bear ever since a minister had blessed their union. But aside from his constant, feverish attentions during the nights, she had been left pretty much to her own inclinations the rest of the time.

Five days and nights of camp life had erased any pangs of doubt or guilt she might have been harbouring. The ice cold nights spent snowbound in the mountains left her moaning—not from Struan's efforts to warm her, but from the memory of the deep, soft, warm feather bed she had left at Edinburgh Castle. The frosted, mist-ridden dawns that arrived in a glorious avalanche of gold and lavender clouds only reminded her of the miles of trudging dampness that lay ahead, the probability that her nose would leak constantly, and her hands and feet turn to blocks of ice before she pitched their sorry little excuse for a tent again. She had seen no beauty in the sheer cliffs and jagged tumble of misshapen boulders that had guarded their passage through the mountains. She had felt no great stirring in her soul as she looked forward, backward, side-to-side, and saw nothing but snow-capped peaks, piled one upon the other.

She was glad to leave them behind, thankful to descend through the densely forested foothills and into the graduated sweep of the glens. Moy Hall was eight miles from Inverness and Inverness was a busy seaport—while it was still under the control of the Hanover government—with ships leaving every day for London and points beyond. The closer the rebel army had come to Inverness, the more eager the clansmen became, anticipating a long-overdue confrontation with the enemy. The closer Lauren came to Inverness, the more urgent it became to do what she had come to do and escape as quickly as possible.

Despite what Hamilton Garner may have thought, there was no sum of money on earth worth her taking the risk of going any deeper into the Highlands. She had been trapped there once already and it had taken twelve years to break out. Now, bearing the yoke of a husband on her back—a husband as dangerous and predatory as a wild beast if he was roused—she could well vanish in those glens and never be seen or heard from again.

She had almost bolted and run when she'd heard the Camerons and MacDonalds were preparing to leave for Lochaber. It was the only time she could recall being thankful for anything Catherine Cameron had caused —her "delicate" condition had had all the men agreeing that the women would remain behind until such time as Fort Augustus was taken and the route made safe for them to travel unmolested to Lochaber.

No one had worried after the women's safety before this, she mused wryly. There had to be half a hundred clanswomen walking around the camps with swollen bellies, lugging heavy armloads of firewood, hauling water, cooking, seeing to the voracious appetites and needs of the men . . . but not sweet Catherine. She was settled into the big house like a queen, her every whim and fancy seen to, no doubt. It was enough to make a lass puke.

As for the proud father—the entire camp was buzzing with good cheer. The pipers were playing their fingers raw, the bards were already composing songs and poems to bring the grand *Camshroinaich Dubh*'s heir good luck and good fortune, not to mention another score of healthy, braw bairns in succession. They would naturally, conveniently neglect to mention sweet Catherine's heritage; that she was a *Sassenach* of weak and impure bloodlines. They would also neglect to mention that the marriage had been conceived in hell, consummated in anger, and the offspring of any such union would undoubtedly be limp of wrist and as pale, and sickly blonde as the mother.

Alasdair deserved *sons*. Highland sons, born and bred of the land. Lauren could have given him such sons. Tall and strong-limbed, with fire in their spirits and passion in their souls. But he had shunned her in favour of his thin, vapid-looking *Sassenach*, and so he deserved whatever he got. Deserved more than ever he bargained for . . . which was why Lauren found herself slogging ankle deep through the slushy snow and mud, picking her way carefully along the forest path with a recently filled bucket of water.

She searched either side of the gloomy path, wary for any sounds or movement that would indicate she had been followed away from the camp. She was obeying the instructions on the crumpled note she had found earlier in the afternoon—the note which had been left in response to the fountain of bright red ribbons she had worn in her hair all morning.

Her teeth chattered from the dampness, her skin felt clammy, and her nerves were rebelling at the sight of the silent stands of tall fir trees that crowded the path from the camp to the stream. Another fifty yards and she would have the comfort of roaring campfires to guide her down the gentle slope, but here, where the trees were thickest and the mist almost opaque, she felt as cut off and isolated from the real world as a child lost in a nightmare.

She stopped dead in her tracks and whirled around.

Nothing.

She could hear herself breathing and feel the steady pounding of her heart, but aside from the constant drip, drip, dripping of the snow melting from the upper branches of the trees, there were no other sounds to explain the alarm swelling in her chest.

Cursing, she expelled her breath in a stream of white vapour. A scream would bring half the camp to her rescue in a matter of seconds, if any were necessary. After all, it was not as if she was meeting an enemy alone, unarmed, unprotected in the middle of a deep, dark, cavernous forest . . . she was meeting the man who would hopefully speed this farce on its way and send her cheerfully back to Edinburgh.

Lauren started walking again, humming under her breath just to prove to whomever might be watching that she could be as calm and proficient at these games as he could. She had barely taken two paces when she heard the distinct rustle of bushes off to one side, followed by the sucking sound of a wet foot stepping onto the path of slush behind her.

She slowed, her chest a wall of ice, the skin on her arms and legs becoming so sensitive she could feel every seam and thread on her clothing.

"Keep walking," a voice hissed. "Don't turn around."

"What dae ye mean, dinna tairn around?" she asked in a normal tone, already halfway into her turn. Before she could complete it and before she could catch a glimpse of his face or form, he had an arm slung around her waist, another locked preventatively under her chin.

Her first impulse was to scream, which she would have done had he not anticipated the reaction and clamped a hand bruisingly over her mouth. Her second instinctive reaction was to drop the heavy bucket and claw behind her for any vulnerable, exposed area of his face.

He only swore at the futile gesture, and, after catching both her wrists and twisting them around to the small of her back, he lifted her bodily off the track and carried her into the deeper shadows behind an outcrop of rock. There, she was shoved roughly against the wet surface of the boulder, pressed against it with enough force to leave her struggling for air.

"If you scream, or make one single sound before I tell you to, I'm going to snap your neck like a piece of kindling. Is that understood?"

Lauren's eyes stung with tears of outrage at being manhandled so brusquely. He was crushing her body, his hand was mashing her lips against her teeth, and he was holding her neck at such an angle it felt as if it would snap without any further help from him.

She managed a jerky nod and slowly, the iron-like fingers unclamped from her mouth.

"Stupid bitch," he snarled. "You think this is some kind of a game?"

She dared not answer, not while he still held her neck arched at an impossibly painful angle.

"You have a message for me?"

Nodding again, she tried to angle her head a bit farther around, but he only tightened his grip and kept her eyes pointed at the slimy rock.

"Well?"

"Leave go o' me fairst. Ye're near breakin' ma bluidy neck."

After another taut moment, he relented. Lauren barely waited for the blood and air to resume normal circulation before she was twisting around like a dervish, her lips drawn back in a snarl, her hands flung up and hungry for a strike.

"Who d'ye think ye are, ye damned heavy-handed bastard! Who d'ye think *I* am ye can just drag me intae the bushes like a sack o' grain!"

One of her fists made contact, but the pleasure was short-lived as he grabbed her and slammed her against the rock again. He curled his fingers around the ribbon-bound shank of her hair and yanked at the thick knot until the scalp was in danger of being ripped from her skull.

"Who do I think you are?" he spat, ignoring her shrill whimpers of pain. "I think you're a cheap little whore who'd spread her legs for anyone with the shavings from a copper penny to shove up your skirts. I, on the other hand, am a man who is taking an incalculable risk by meeting you here like this. I didn't like the idea in the first place, didn't agree with the major's assessment of your . . . special talents, and see no reason why I should have to coddle the vanity of a useless, foul-mouthed trollop. In short, I could walk away from here right now and not give it a second thought. Whereas you—" he tightened his fingers, prompting another thin wail from the swollen lips "—if I do walk away, Mrs. MacSorley, you will be on your own. There will be no one to watch your backside or scrape your pretty butt off the ground if someone finds out the real reason why you came back to camp. And they will find out," he promised ominously. "I'll make damned sure of it."

Too shockingly aware of just how strong this madman was, and just how isolated they were here in the forest, Lauren swallowed back her rage and indignation. She had no idea who he was, only that he was not a Scot. Although he had lowered his voice in order to disguise it, there was no mistaking the cultured accent. She had not needed Hamilton Garner's forewarning to tell her the man was a foreigner, but to a Highlander, a foreigner was anyone born south of the Grampians. There were Frenchmen among the Jacobite rebels, Italians, Irishmen,

Welshmen, even proper English gentlemen who had volunteered their services to the Stuart cause—all of them foreigners, but to an army starved for manpower, they were not required to show much proof of loyalty.

"Shall we try again?" he hissed. "You have a message for Major Garner?"

"Lochiel an' Keppoch are bein sent tae attack Fort Augustus," she said, struggling to keep her voice steady. "They're takin' all their men wi' them, but leavin' the women an' most o' the supplies until they've cleared the route."

"Is that your message?" he demanded incredulously. "You took a risk like this to tell me something every man, woman and child in camp will know by morning?"

"There's mair they dinna ken," she insisted evenly.

"Such as?"

"The Prince. He's stayin' on at Moy Hall. He has a bad chest an' a cough an' disna feel well enough tae move until Lord George comes f'ae him."

A lengthy, tension-filled pause ended with a slight reduction in pressure on her neck. "Where did you hear this?"

"Ma husband was wi' Lochiel an' his brithers all mornin'. He came tae me noontime in a rare foul mood f'ae havin' tae pick extra guards tae stay ahind an' nurse the Prince."

"Are you absolutely certain he said Moy Hall? I thought the Prince was supposed to move to Kilravock Castle tonight."

"Aye, that were the plan, but he changed his mind. He's stayin' here wi' but a han'ful o' guards; twenny, mayhap less, if Lochiel canna spare them."

"Lady MacKintosh has men."

Lauren shook her head as much as she was able. "They've all gaun hame tae wait till the rest o' the army comes up frae Aberdeen."

"I see," he murmured.

"Dae ye now?" she sneered. "An' what will ye dae about it? A *clever* man would get word tae Inverness an' have the Prince snatched frae his bed afore anyone was the wiser. A daft bastard would stall an' blether an' miss his chance f'ae a share o' thirty thousan' pounds reward."

"A share?" he rasped pointedly.

"Aye. Half o' its mines, or the only ither information the *Sassenach* major will get frae me is where tae find yer moulderin' body."

The threat was absorbed and dismissed with a coarse laugh. He would have liked to have called her bluff, but the sound of a cracking twig somewhere near in the fog had him moving her lightning-fast into a deep niche in the rocks. Lauren heard a faint whisper of steel on leather and was startled to feel the presence of a cocked pistol in his hand. Where it had come from and the speed with which he had produced it made the blood sing through her veins and the danger flood her senses with excitement.

The sliding footsteps of two clansmen, returning from sentry duty, passed close to the outcrop of rock before fading in the direction of the camp. Lauren and her companion remained frozen in the shadows for several more long minutes, the latter alert for any further indications of unexpected company. Lauren, conversely, was more aware of the heat of his body where it was pressed up against hers, and of the heady scents of horse-leather, wind and weather that clung to his skin and clothing.

"Ye can leave go o' me now," she murmured huskily. "Unless ye've found somethin' ye like."

Startled, the man moved away, unself-consciously rubbing his hand along his jacket to erase the memory of contact.

"An' what the devil were ye plannin' tae dae wi' the gun?" she asked. "One shot, but, an' ye'd have the whole camp crawlin' down yer throat."

Glancing down, she straightened her shawl and sent a hand up to probe her scalp. Her hair had been torn loose and the ribbon lost somewhere in the mud and slush at their feet. She spared a moment or two in a useless search of the shadows, and when she straightened again, she was alone.

"What the bluidy hell—?"

She whirled, her eyes searching the murky darkness, but there was no sound, no movement of any kind—nothing but cold, empty space where her fellow conspirator had stood only seconds before.

"Bluidy bastard," she exclaimed softly. "Sairves ye right ye didna hear the whole message, then."

With a toss of her frothing, titian hair, she stepped out from behind the rocks and regained the familiarity of the path. She located her bucket—empty, of course—and cursed the need to go back to the stream and fight her way through the crust of ice to refill it.

On second thought, she decided, if MacSorley wanted a wash he could damn well go to the stream himself, or melt snow over the fire. She kicked the bucket under some brush and started back down the path toward the faint sounds of the distant camp. Muttering to herself, and massaging the abused patch of skin at the base of her skull, she rounded the final bend and emerged from the trees, halting abruptly in the swirl of clinging mist that had followed her out of the forest.

Standing less than ten feet down along the slope was Struan MacSorley, his arms crossed over his chest, his massive frame silhouetted against the brighter glow of the camp spread out behind him. He was leaning on a tree stump and when he caught sight of her, he straightened, dropped his arms slowly down by his sides and started walking forward to meet her.

Lauren arranged her face in a smile and started to call out a greeting, but a movement out of the corner of her eye drew her attention farther along the meandering border of trees. With the field of clear snow to define his shape and the brightness of the campfires to dispell most of the distortion of the mist, she had no trouble in identifying the *Sassenach*, Damien Ashbrooke, casually emerging from the forest, whistling softly to himself, and hitching his breeches as if he had just returned from relieving himself.

Aluinn MacKail *had* just relieved himself and was about to mount his horse when he heard the discreet clearing of a throat behind him. Without looking around, he knew who it was and sighed inwardly. Eager, earnest, devoted were all words he could easily use to describe Corporal Jeffrey Peters. In the past few weeks, he had been eager to prove himself a hard worker, earnest about being accepted as one of them despite the distinct shade of gray he had turned upon hearing of the fates of the four hundred men of the Manchester Regiment captured at Carlisle. And there were few, with the exception of Alexander Cameron himself, who were more devoted to Catherine. As Alex, in one of his rare moods of generosity liked to say, his wife had found a stray puppy that night in Derby and it had slavishly followed her home to stay.

The corporal had, by nature, attached himself to the Englishmen who formed their own small contingent of the Prince's army. But every spare moment he had, he was usually dogging Catherine, helping her about the campsite, fetching, carrying, running errands—all for the reward of a smile, which never failed to send him into crimson paroxysms of stuttering rapture. Doubtless, he had heard the women would be remaining behind at Moy Hall and was here to plead his case in the hopes he might be permitted to stay and act as Catherine's bodyguard and champion.

"Mr. MacKail, sir?"

"Corporal Peters." Aluinn clamped a firm restraint on his patience as he half-turned to address the young soldier. "A fine evening for a stroll."

Peters peered up into the misty web of tangled clouds the moon had spun out across the stars. "Yes, sir. I suppose it is."

When several moments passed with no further sign of life from the corporal, Aluinn turned fully around. "You wanted to see me about something, Corporal?"

Peters' head had remained tilted up toward the sky, only his gaze flicked down to MacKail. "Actually, sir, I was hoping to have a private moment to speak to Mr. Cameron, but I haven't managed to catch up to him at all today."

"He has been a little busy. Is it something I can help you with?"

"Well . . . I did want to speak to Mr. Cameron."

"If it's important, I'll see that Alex gets the message tonight."

The corporal bit his lip thoughtfully. "Well . . . the honest truth is . . . I don't know if it's important or not. I mean, I could be wrong, and seeing things that aren't there, and if that's the case, then we would have a fine mess on our hands indeed, and all b-because of me."

Aluinn frowned, stroking absently at the snout of his horse who seemed to be as impatient as he to get away. Aluinn wanted to spend what time he could with Deirdre, not act as a go-between for some nerve-wrought, love-smitten rival for his best friend's wife.

"It has been a very long day, Corporal," MacKail sighed. "I estimate I have, at best, five hours to spend saying goodbye to my wife, so, if whatever this is all about can wait until the morning—"

"Not *what*, sir. *Who*. It has to do with the Count. Count Fanducci? The Italian gentleman who—"

"I know who Count Fanducci is, Corporal," Aluinn cut in, exasperated. "What the devil has he to do with Lady Cameron? If you're looking for someone to act as your second, lad, you have come to the wrong place."

"Excuse me, sir?"

The corporal looked genuinely baffled and Aluinn cursed softly. "Nevermind. It has been an *extremely* long day. What about Fanducci?"

"Yes, well, as I said, sir, I could be seeing something that isn't there. I could be dead wrong in my suspicions, but . . ."

"But," Aluinn prompted irritably.

"But . . . I have reason to believe the Count may not be who he purports to be; that his loyalties may not lie where he would like us to believe they lie."

Mildly taken aback, Aluinn's hand dropped slowly from the horse's snout. "I hope your reasons are damned good, Corporal."

Peters flushed. "That was why I wanted to speak to Mr. Cameron privately. I haven't said anything to anyone else, and have no intentions of d-doing so, sir. I know too well how ill-spoken rumours can d-destroy a man's reputation and career."

MacKail's gray eyes pierced through the gloom. "Say what you have to say, Corporal. What makes you suspect something is not right about Fanducci?"

"Well, sir," the corporal moistened his lips and drew himself to attention as if reporting officially to a senior ranking officer. "I had occasion to observe Count Fanducci when he was unaware of my presence. He was sitting by one of the wagons cleaning and oiling his pistols."

"Not an entirely suspicious act for a gunmaker, I shouldn't think."

"N-no, sir. But the thing is, he was distracted for a moment by one of the men, and as he talked, he reassembled one of the metal fittings on the snaphaunce improperly. I know he did, sir, because after the clansman moved away, he noticed the firelock was not quite seated properly and he had to take it apart and refit it."

Aluinn frowned again. "Forgive me, Corporal, but haven't you ever made a mistake while cleaning and reassembling a gun?"

"Yes, sir. Dozens of times. But I do not profess to be a master gunmaker. One would think a master gunmaker would be able to strip and reassemble the firing mechanism of a gun—a gun he boasted of making—in the dark, blindfolded, and with one hand tied behind his back, the other in a splint."

"One would, indeed," Aluinn agreed quietly.

The corporal looked visibly relieved. "Then you concur with my suspicions, sir?"

"Now hold on, Peters, don't go leaping to conclusions. Just because I agree it seems odd for a gunmaker to make a mistake handling a gun—"

"A *master* gunmaker, sir, handling a gun he supposedly carved, molded and designed himself."

Aluinn gave the points a moment of silent thought. "You have, I trust, taken into consideration the fact that Fanducci is an odd sort to begin with—a little eccentric, a little excitable, and extremely European. Having spent a good many years in Italy myself, I can almost say the Count is, if anything, rather reserved by comparison to some of the population. I rather like him, to be perfectly honest."

"I like him too, sir. Very much so. He's usually so jolly and dramatic and . . . "

"Yes?"

"Well . . . I just wouldn't want anyone to be caught unawares, or to be duped into thinking he was one thing while he was really another."

"A spy, you mean?"

Corporal Peters looked glumly down at his hands. "I know it sounds ridiculous, sir, but with such a mixed bag of patriots in the army, it is possible for one or two of them to have been planted here by the government to watch our movements. And just because the Count looks and sounds and acts the way we expect him to look and sound and act . . . well . . . "

Aluinn's gaze strayed past the corporal's shoulders to the hazy lights of the campfires that dotted the glen.

Ridiculous? As ridiculous as being duped into accepting a man simply because he showed up at the time and place he was supposed to show up at and, yes, because he looked and acted and sounded the way he was supposed to. Seven months ago, both he and Alex had made a near fatal mistake in accepting the man who called himself Iain Cameron of Glengarron, because neither of them had considered the ridiculous. Neither one had suspected the Duke of Argyle of substituting one of his own men for Glengarron, and because of their laxness, Gordon Ross Campbell had not only come damned close to collecting the reward for Alex's capture, but had put a shot in Aluinn MacKail's shoulder—a shot which had missed his heart by mere inches.

"I appreciate your coming to me with this, Corporal, and no, I don't think the notion is the least bit ridiculous that the British have planted spies in our camp. The Count is coming with us when we head out to Fort Augustus—you can be sure I'll keep what you have told me in mind and watch him like the proverbial hawk. In the meantime, you will keep this to yourself?"

"Of course, sir." The corporal came to attention again, only just discouraged from throwing a full salute by the open grimace on Aluinn's face. "May I ask, er, if all the Camerons are departing for Fort Augustus?"

"All the men, yes. With the exception of a few guards we're leaving behind to stay with the women, naturally."

The solemn, puppy-dog eyes were fixed unwaveringly on MacKail's face and Aluinn was hard pressed to confine his smile.

"It occurs to me, Corporal," he said, reaching nonchalantly to untether his horse's reins, "that you could be in a position to do me a great favour . . . not that I have the right to ask it of you, since you have already done me a service I can hardly hope to repay."

"I have, sir?"

Aluinn smiled. “In case you have forgotten, you also escorted *my* wife safely out of Derby with Lady Catherine.”

“Oh.” Corporal Peters flushed again. “Of course, sir. Don’t mention it.”

“My wife and Lady Catherine will both be staying on at Moy Hall as guests of Lady Anne. Frankly speaking, I think both ladies might feel slightly more comfortable being left behind if they had a familiar face around—one who did not speak with a Celtic brogue.”

“Oh! Oh, I would be honoured to stay with Lady Catherine, sir!” gasped the corporal. “Honoured and p-privileged, and . . . and I would guard her with my l-life, sir! I swear I would not sleep a w-wink the whole time you were away, and I w-would never let her out of my sight!”

“Your dedication is commendable, Corporal, although I don’t think you will have to be quite so . . . intense. They are perfectly safe at Moy Hall. Lady Anne’s men are within shouting distance, and Lord George’s column is due to arrive in Inverness sometime in the next twenty-four hours.” Aluinn took up the reins and swung himself up into the saddle. “But I feel better already, knowing I am leaving my wife in your capable hands.”

“Oh. Yes, sir. Naturally I would guard Mrs. MacKail with equal diligence.”

“Naturally,” grinned MacKail. “Goodnight, Corporal.”

“Goodnight, sir. And good luck at Fort Augustus. Give the Philistines hell, sir!”

MacKail laughed and nudged his horse into a brisk canter. The mist was wet against his face, the air chilly, his thoughts as sharp and piercing as the few stalwart stars that managed to penetrate the scudding haze overhead. The corporal’s suspicions about Count Giovanni Fanducci soon erased the lingering remnants of his smile and by the time he drew up at the stable yards of Moy Hall, a deep line of concern was etched deeply across his forehead. The frown, in turn, remained until he had climbed the stairs to the chamber he and Deirdre shared, but his resolve to seek out Alexander Cameron and share this new worry took a decided downgrade in importance when he opened the chamber door and won a sweet and eager greeting from his wife's lips.

Chapter Seventeen

Catherine put on a brave face, as did all the women who were gathered to watch their men leave for Fort Augustus. The pipers winded their instruments, pumping the sheep's bladders and forcing the air out through selected holes in the ebony chanter to produce what, to a Scotsman, was music, and to most anyone else, was suspect.

"How do you know when they are playing an actual, rehearsed tune, from when they are just having a good time?" Catherine had once asked Alex. His answer, laden with frowns and hesitations, was hardly satisfying: "You just know."

Prince Charles, rising from his sickbed, had given a passionate speech of encouragement to the clansmen, ending with a subtle suggestion that their goal should not simply be to rid the two English forts of their garrisons, but to push further south into Argyleshire and deal with the annoying presence of the Campbells. Lochiel managed to hide his shock well enough. The Duke of Argyle had five thousand men to call onto the field at the snap of his fingers; less than a thousand of them had been sent to Edinburgh to answer Cumberland's request for men. The MacDonalds and Camerons combined forces added to only seven hundred and fifty—worse odds than those that had turned the entire army around at Derby.

The slope curving away from the majestic stone facade of Moy Hall glowed with tartans of red, blue, green, black, and gold. Only fifty or so of the highest ranking officers were mounted; the rest of the men marched on foot, with a dozen small carts laden with supplies bringing up the rear.

Damien had elected to stay with Catherine and stood by his sister's side as she watched the men bid their final farewells and form up in their columns. She picked out familiar faces—Lochiel, Keppoch, Archibald, even Count Fanducci—and tried not to think too long and hard on the possibility she might be seeing them for the last time. No one seemed too concerned about the task ahead. By all reports, Fort Augustus had a skeleton posting of less than sixty soldiers, supported by nothing in the way of artillery or cavalry. But they were still soldiers and they knew how to fire muskets, and muskets could kill, even accidentally.

She absolutely refused to think of Fort William, garrisoned by upwards of five hundred men and built on the shores of Loch Linnhe. It could be resupplied daily by sea, if necessary, and a prolonged siege was out of the question. There were heavy guns mounted on the fortified walls and ready access to the four thousand remaining Campbells held champing in reserve less than forty miles to the south.

No, she would not think of Fort William. She wanted them to take Fort Augustus with all due haste so that she could be retrieved from Moy Hall and delivered safely to Achnacarry.

Had it really been seven months since she had first seen the weathered stone masonery and high, buttressed walls of Achnacarry Castle? Was it really seven months ago that she'd walked in the fragrant corridors of the mile-long apple orchard, and sat in the garden under the sun-splashed protection of the gazebo—Lady Maura's pride and joy? Did they think of her—Lady Maura,

Jeannie, Aunt Rose—or had they forgotten her the instant she'd sailed out of their lives? Was it possible these feelings of attachment and home-sickness burning inside her were real, or just born out of a need for something she had never had?

Lady Caroline Ashbrooke had delivered quite a blow to her sensibilities by revealing the circumstances of her birth, and yet the news was not as devastating as it might have been had she been raised in an atmosphere of love and security. Her first introduction to either of those two emotions had come with her marriage to Alexander Cameron. Losing him once had almost destroyed her; losing him again would take away any reason to go on living.

"You are looking terribly intense, Mrs. Cameron," came a warm whisper against her ear. "Can it be you are going to miss your husband after all?"

Smiling, Catherine leaned into his embrace as Alex wrapped his long arms around her. "Is that why you are taking both Struan and Count Fanducci with you? To remove temptation? Well, it won't work, my lord. Lady Anne has offered to provide me with a lusty lover if my needs become uncontrollable."

"She has, has she?"

"And then, of course, I always have Corporal Peters."

"He wouldn't know what to do with you," Alex murmured huskily, his lips nuzzling her throat. "I barely have the strength to keep up."

"In that case, you should make good use of this week and rest well, my husband, for I am already feeling the lack."

Alex released her, turned her slowly around and tilted her mouth up to his for a kiss—one which eventually drew the stares and smiles of every man and woman standing within twenty paces. Aluinn, thinking the idea a fine one, scooped Deirdre into his arms and took up the challenge. Lauren Cameron, her eyes flecked with hot yellow sparks, whirled into Struan's embrace and kissed him so fervently he had difficulty climbing into his saddle when the time came.

"Mad," Archibald Cameron declared summarily. "They've all gaun stark starved mad."

"Aye," Lochiel agreed. "But a fine madness, none the less. Ye canna say ye dinna feel a wee bit envious, brither dear. Or that ye'll have nothin' buzzin' up yer kilt when ye see Jeannie standin' at the gates o' Achnacarry."

"Jeannie? Faugh!" Archibald denied the notion roundly. "That harridan couldna puit a buzz up ma kilt an she had a hive o' bees atween her legs. Come tae think on it, she does have a mout o' somethin' up there, since all I ever come away wi' is an itch the likes o' hellfire!"

Donald threw back his head and laughed, knowing full well that Archibald and Jeannie both left their wickedly barbed wits at the bedroom door, collecting them again when they departed flushed and voraciously satiated. Jeannie was Archibald's mainstay and he could not imagine either one surviving overlong on their own. Just as he could not imagine the sun rising or the heather growing wild and fragrant without some word of approval from his Maura.

Maura. God, how he missed her. As happy as he had been for Alasdair and Catherine these past months, Donald found himself grudging them their time together. Their visible joy only accentuated his own loneliness and he knew, if for no other reason than to see and feel his Maura in his arms again, he would sooner raze Fort Augustus to the ground than waste an unnecessary hour in diplomacy.

Bristling impatiently, he raised his arm to signal the pipers to commence the stirring *piob' rachd.*

"I have to go," said Alex, stroking his fingers softly down Catherine's cheek. The motion was carried lower to bestow a private caress on the gentle roundness of her belly. "Take care of our son."

Catherine nodded, her eyes wide and shining, a more vibrant shade of heather-blue than Alex had ever seen. They were swimming with tears in spite of the smile she forced upon her lips; the wetness brimmed over her lashes and hung suspended in perfect silver droplets until a blink caused them to splash onto the back of his hands.

"A week," he promised. "I swear it. Even if we should come up against the whole of Cumberland's army. I'll be back for you in a week's time."

"I shall hold you to account, Sir Rogue," she whispered valiantly. "You would not want to guess what your son and I have conspired to do in the event you are but a single hour overdrawn."

Smiling, he kissed her one last time, then took up Shadow's reins from the nervous lad who had led the stallion up from the stables. Watching her husband swing easily into the saddle, Catherine's heart swelled with pride. With his wind-blown hair and bottomless blue-black eyes, Alexander was indeed the Dark Cameron. Mounted astride his gleaming, prancing jet black stallion, whose mane and tail flowed like ebony silk on the wind, was it any wonder the pair of them had tongues wagging in awe as far away as London?

Damien stepped up beside her and slipped his arm around her waist, giving her a supportive, brotherly squeeze. "You have managed to find yourself quite a husband, Kitty dear," he sighed, gauging Alex's effect from a man's point of view. "Quite a man, quite a soldier, quite a legend in his own time."

"I will be happy just to have the man come home to me," she said, dashing a hand across her cheeks to chase away her tears.

Shouts, huzzahs, and the skirling of the pipes started the massive flow of humanity along the basin of the glen, heading west toward the road to Inverness. They would steer well clear of the town itself, making use of Wade's military roads—cut some thirty years before with an eye to controlling the Highlands and preventing any further threat of an uprising—to follow the rugged miles along the shore of Loch Ness. There were rumours of monsters lurking in the inky depths of the lake, serpents as thick around as a house and filled with the remains of curious victims.

Alex had recounted the story of the monster with the same degree of solemnity as he had the legend of Sir Ewen Cameron's mystical sword and, in the strong light of day, Catherine was inclined to give both equal credence. Charmed swords, druids, dark gods, and sea monsters—how could such a superstitious race of men also be the possessors of such pure logic and unquestionable honour?

"Hungry?" Damien asked, giving a final wave as the last of the marching men snaked out of sight behind the shoulder of the road.

"I confess, I am still not comfortable looking at food this early in the morning," Catherine admitted. "But I do have a desperate craving for a cup of strong, hot tea—something the Scots appear to regard with the same appeal as arsenic."

Damien laughed. "Your craving is my command. I shall see what I can do about scrounging some for you in Inverness."

"Inverness?" She looked at him with undisguised shock. "You are going into Inverness?"

"Why not? I am as English as the river Thames, and if stopped, have papers identifying me as Damien Ashbrooke, Esquire, Solicitor at Large, son and heir to Sir Alfred Ashbrooke, Honourable Member of the Hanover Parliament. God's boots, who would dare question such references?"

Catherine did not like it, but before she could put forth any convincing arguments, he effectively cut them off at the knee.

"Besides, I have a younger sister wanted for questioning on charges of murder and treason, a brother-in-law who seems bent on defying the laws of survival—it's high time I carved a little niche for myself in this rebellion before all the choice indictments are used up. We wouldn't want the Derby gossips to run short of fuel, now would we?"

"I could care less if they ran short of air to breathe," Catherine replied sincerely. "Just don't do anything foolhardy, like getting yourself arrested for spying."

"Believe me, Kitty dearest, I have no burning desire to inspect a scaffold up close," he murmured, "and absolutely no intentions of being caught."

"I should think we would want to avoid being caught in another fiasco like Falkirk or Prestonpans."

The speaker was Colonel Blakeney, an officious bore of a man with a face as dull as a rainy day. He was newly arrived from Perth, an envoy from the Duke of Cumberland who brought news of the commanding general's decision to weather out the winter in Edinburgh. Seated with him in the damp, cold stone barracks in Fort George were Duncan Forbes, Lord Loudoun, and a scowling representative of the Highland companies under Loudoun's command, Norman MacLeod, Chief of Clan MacLeod.

When news of the approaching rebel army had reached Inverness, the Lord President, Forbes, had prudently moved his family from Culloden House to the fortified citadel at Fort George. Warehouses in the city were ordered emptied into ships and the vessels sent to anchor outside the blockade line of the Royal Navy where their valuable cargoes would be safe from confiscation by the Jacobites. The town itself had no real defenses against an army wishing to occupy it, and the fort's armaments were laughable: only six rusting cannons facing out into the Moray Firth.

"I repeat, gentlemen," said Blakeney, "if there is a chance to end it all here, tonight, then I say we should take it."

"How can we be certain your information is correct?" asked Lord Loudoun. "We have received ten different reports today, alone, which place the Pretender in ten different castles in ten different areas, north and south of the Grampians."

"My source is above reproach, my lord," Blakeney insisted. "He is a loyal subject of King George who has managed to infiltrate the highest levels of confidence and trust within the rebel army. He travels with Lochiel's Camerons and several times, has been no further from the Stuart prince than you are to me now. If he says the Pretender is in residence at Moy Hall, then by God, I would be willing to commit myself and my men to the task of removing him from there."

"Moy Hall," Lord Loudoun murmured. "Is that not the estate of Angus Moy, Chief of Clan Chattan?"

"Indeed it is," said Duncan Forbes, turning from the window with a frown. "The same Angus Moy of Clan MacKintosh who has raised a regiment of his clansmen and holds the rank of captain in King George's army."

"He commands a company o' MacKintosh men, aye," The MacLeod sneered, stepping forward. "But his wife rides at the heid o' anither company—mostly Farquharsons an' MacGillivrays—an wears the white cockade o' the Stuarts."

"You must be joking, sir," Forbes said, clearly astonished by the news. He was in his middle years, cutting a lean and debonair figure in his green-and-yellow tartan. The Lord President presented a dignified contrast to the Earl of Loudoun's military precision, the Colonel's dusty indifference, and The MacLeod's surly belligerence. Forbes had been appointed Lord President by King George's government and held the position with pride and conviction; the Highlands were his home and Culloden his birthright, and he wanted peace at any cost—anything short of more senseless bloodshed.

"I have known the Lady Anne since she was a child," he continued softly. "My wife and I have been guests at Moy Hall, just as Angus and Lady Anne have been guests at Culloden."

"Aye. But until she came tae live fine an' fancy at Moy Hall," The MacLeod reminded them all, "she were hangin' off the kilt o' her great gran'faither, Fearchar Farquharson o' Invercauld."

Forbes sighed and rubbed his temple wearily. "Surely, you do not mean to tell me next that Fearchar of Invercauld is in arms and armour? The man is as old as history itself."

"Aye. One hunnerd an' ten years, if ye can believe the kirk records. One hunnerd an' nine o' them spent spewin' treason an' rebellion. I'm even told it were him wha' put the notion intae Lady Anne's heid tae ride against her husban', Invercauld an' The MacGillivray."

"Regardless of the Lady Anne's affiliations," Colonel Blakeney interjected, "the question before us, gentlemen, is whether or not we can afford to turn a blind eye to this opportunity to remove the thorn from our side. Lord George Murray is still a day's march from Nairn. Lord John Drummond is at Balmoral Castle requisitioning provisions, Brigadier Stapleton has removed himself with Lochiel and Keppoch to Lochaber with all of their men. The Pretender is virtually alone at Moy Hall. I can have fifteen hundred men mustered by nightfall, giving you gentlemen the pleasure and honour of offering the Stuart Pretender the hospitality of the barracks gaol by midnight tonight."

Forbes pursed his lips and studied the drooping afternoon sun outside the window. "And if this informant of yours is wrong? If the Camerons and MacDonalds have not left the vicinity but are, even as we speak, lining the roads in wait of an ambush? You know full well the rebels must take Inverness to maintain any control over the Highlands. Having our men simply march out and place themselves in the rebel hands . . . well, the thought is devastating."

"More devastating than if the Prince escapes and manages to rouse support from the clans we have so far been unable to convert to our cause?" Loudoun asked. "More devastating than if he should find himself another ten thousand men to rally the tide and flood back across the border into England? We all saw what he was able to accomplish with but five thousand men. Imagine those numbers doubled, or trebled!"

Forbes seemed not to have heard; he was staring out across the clustered rooftops of Inverness. Soon enough, the light would fade from the sky and the blues of sea and sky deepen to black; the taverns would be winding up for their usual nighttime revelry, the shopkeepers conducting their last minute trades before rushing home for their evening meals. Farther out, a lone English merchantman could faintly be glimpsed anchored against the sleek pewter sheen of the water, her sails furled, her masts standing bare to the wind.

Somehow he had sensed, even six months ago, when word of the Prince's landing had first blazed across the Highlands, that it would all end here. He had felt a presence, like the hand of fate resting on his shoulder, forewarning him of some terrible event that would shatter, forever, the peace and tranquility of his beloved Caledonia.

"Very well," he said slowly. "If there is the remotest possibility of taking the Prince into custody, of ending the bloodshed and dissention, here and now, then I give it my fullest support. Take your fifteen hundred men, Colonel Blakeney. Bring me back a healthy and unscratched Charles Edward Stuart, and you shall have earned the undying gratitude of the Scottish people."

"There will be no casualties on either side," Lord Loudoun said flatly, glancing pointedly at the colonel and MacLeod. "We are not looking to fight a battle, only to accept an offering from Lady Luck."

Laughlan MacKintosh's eyes bulged until they were round as saucers and twice as shiny. He was not exactly sure what his next move should be, he only knew that luck and perseverence had brought him farther than any other foray to date.

Licking his lips, he angled his head forward, the better to see Cheristine MacDonnell's expression through the closing gloom. It was a shame the light had faded so quickly, but it had taken nearly a full hour just to convince her to allow the laces of her bodice to be unfastened, and goodness only knew how much longer to let him slide her skirt and petticoat up her thigh. The trouble was, now it was getting too damned late. Her mam or one of her brothers would surely be sent out to fetch her soon and Laughlan would have to begin all over again another day.

"Can I kiss ye, Cherry? Would ye mind?"

"Ye've already kissed me intae a rare state, Laughlan MacKintosh," she murmured, adding in a shy whisper, "An' no' just on ma mouth."

He looked down to where his hand still cupped the immature rise of her breast. They were in the stable, out back of her father's tavern, and the hay had made a cozy nest for the fledgling lovers. At fifteen years of age, neither one of them were experienced in such things, but the stirrings in their bodies were genuine and so far, just following their instincts had kept their hearts beating rapidly and their cheeks flushed with the fever of desire. Although her breasts were small and nearly flattened by gravity as she lay back in the hay, there was no mistaking the hard little nub of her nipple where it thrust against his palm. As long as it stayed there, so would his hand.

"Are ye cold?" he asked casually, gaining another cautious inch of territory as he slid his thigh higher over hers.

"Nae," she breathed. "Nae cold; a bit itchy, mind."

"Itchy?" His eyes were all concern as he cast them down to the snowy whiteness of her limbs. "Where?"

"Where a proper lass shouldna mention," she said, squirming guilelessly to part her thighs another innocent measure.

Laughlan swallowed hard and debated whether to relinquish the victory over her breast and launch a skirmish farther afield, or to hold fast and wait until there was a definite breach in her defenses. While he debated, he kissed her, encouraged by the willing way she opened her mouth and darted the tip of her tongue back and forth across his.

Feigning uncontrollable delight—not a difficult pretense to muster at this stage of the war—he shifted again, this time managing to hoist his kilt and her skirt together so that she could not help but become aware of the bold presence nudging her thigh.

"Laughlan," she gasped, breaking her mouth away. "Ye mustna!"

"Mustna what?" he asked, lowering his mouth quickly to her breast. He flicked his tongue over the ripe little bud, knowing it to be the surest way to distract her from any protests elsewhere. He gave the rose-tipped flesh his sincerest effort, and while she squirmed and wriggled with the pleasure, his hand stole past the remaining few inches of obstructing wool and slid into the warm thicket of tight curls guarding the final bastion.

Afraid to move too quickly, he probed with the merest fingertip, finding what he was looking for on the first pass. He had listened attentively to the boastings of the older boys and knew that to rub the taut button of flesh was to drive a lass wild with passion; to rub it with something other than a finger was to guarantee oblivion for both of them.

Testing the first half of the theory, he dragged his finger back and forth through the springing nest of curls, feeling Cherry's body clench spasmodically against him on each stroke. She was breathing oddly too, and the peak of her breast had swelled beyond his best ministrations and hardened like a fruit pit in his mouth. The faster he moved his fingers, the quicker and drier her gasps. The deeper and firmer he pressed into the slippery folds of flesh, the more urgently her hips moved with the rhythm; up and down, faster and faster until it was all he could do to control her thrashings long enough for him to attempt a test of the second half of the theory.

Cheristine, at first too stunned by the showering sparks of pleasure to deny him anything, became aware of something hard and thick that was definitely not attached to his hand venturing intrepidly into the fray. She went cold with shock and managed, just when success was within his grasp, to shove mightily against his shoulders and win his attention.

"Laughlan! No!"

"No? Oh . . . oh, Cherry, love . . . just the once," he pleaded. "I just want tae ken how it feels. I'll nae *dae* anything, I swear it! I'll stop when ye tell me, I promise I will."

"But Laughlan," she wailed softly, "how will I ken tae tell ye tae stop?"

"Ye'll just know," he insisted, fighting the tension in her thighs as well as the tension in her arms. He felt the sweat break out across his forehead and he would swear later his entire life flickered before his eyes as he waited for the pressure in her balled fists to relent.

"Ye promise . . . just a wee bit?" she gasped.

"Aye, love, aye. Oh Lord . . . Cherry—" he pushed forward, sinking himself into the warmth and wetness, shuddering with the vision of eternal glory he saw unfolding before him. "Lord . . . Lord . . . "

Something abruptly intruded across the path of his quest for glory and he drew up short. He took a breath and stabbed again, but the barrier was firmly in place, tight and unyielding, and with a low, snuffling groan, he dropped his forehead onto the curve of her shoulder in defeat.

"Laughlan?"

"Aye?" he croaked.

"Laughlan . . . what are ye dain?"

"Nothing. Nothing, Cherry, honest. Just like I promised."

"Ye must be dain something," she persisted, feeling a hot, dissolving sensation everywhere in her body. "It feels . . . funny."

Funny, he thought miserably. He had heaven within his grasp . . . he could feel himself swelling and throbbing as if to burst . . . and she felt funny.

Gulping noisily at a mouthful of air, he tested himself gingerly against the shield of her maidenhead . . . hoping . . . but it held and he groaned inwardly.

"Laughlan . . . why are ye just settin' there?"

He shook his head and tried not to think of a stallion he had seen once, frustrated from its mare, left hanging in all its splendor while cruel little boys threw sticks and stones at him.

"Laughlan?"

"Ach . . . aye?"

"D'ye love me, Laughlan?"

It was barely a whisper of breath that carried the question to his ears, but he opened his eyes, instantly alert. Was this the sound of heaven's gate about to open before him?

"O' course I love ye, Cherry. Would I be where I am now if I *didna* love ye?"

"An' if I said . . . if I said ye didna have tae stop?"

The lad was beginning to find it difficult to breathe, let alone form sensible answers. "I'd dae it . . . only if ye wanted me tae."

"I wouldna want anyone tae know. I wouldna thank ye f'ae tellin' any o' yer randy friends I let ye spread yer kilt aneath me."

"I swear," he gasped, nearly sobbing in his relief. "Oh Cherry, hold me! Hold me love—"

"Laughlan! Laughlan, wait!" she hissed, tensing even as he braced himself for the 'Ultimate Experience.' "Whisht! Did ye hear something?"

He heard nothing aside from the pounding tempo of the blood surging through his veins. He felt as if he was about to explode, to distend beyond all reasonable proportions and incur permanent damage if the pressure was not eased soon.

And then he heard it, too.

Someone was walking around the outside of the stable, his footsteps stealthy and crunching lightly over the frozen ground.

"Laughlan," she cried in a shrill whisper. "Ma brithers! What are we gonny dae?"

Visions of Cheristine's seven Olympian brothers danced across Laughlan's eyelids as he hastily shoved his kilt down to cover his nakedness. He gestured her to silence and scrambled across the hay to the mouth of the stall, edging no more than a corner of an eye and a hairless cheek around the post of rotted wood. The shadow of a man intruded across the doorway, the profile of his face unfamiliar to MacKintosh, but ominous enough to shrivel any concerns he may have had about permanent damage.

Feeling a tremulous tug on the hem of his kilt, he slinked back and, pressing warning fingers over Cherry's mouth, he drew her back into the deep bank of hay.

"Did anyone see you come here?" a voice demanded harshly, startling the two young hearts into skipping several beats.

"I was careful," a second voice responded. "Well? Are they going to act on the information I gave you?"

"I delivered it personally to Lord Loudoun and he, in turn, helped me convince Forbes to send fifteen hundred men to Moy Hall tonight, under cover of darkness. If the Prince is there, as you say, we will have him trapped in a net so tight he couldn't melt through it."

"You have underestimated his abilities before," the shadowy figure said dryly. "I would not take too many things for granted, nor wait too long to take action."

"It should take no more than an hour or so to move my men out of Inverness, another two to get into position. I suggest you stay away from any open windows to avoid being mistaken for the wrong silhouette . . . if you know what I mean."

"You're going to kill him?"

"Why?" Colonel Blakeney smiled cynically. "Does the thought cause you undue distress?"

The other man shrugged. "If you just wanted him dead, I could have done the job myself weeks ago. I was under the impression Cumberland wanted him alive, if at all possible, to make an example of him to others who might question English supremacy."

"If he comes willingly enough, I will be glad to escort him all the way to London in a princely cage. But if there is the slightest question of complete success, I shall not hesitate to kill the royal regent and anyone else who stands in my way."

The second man looked away for a moment, then glanced back at the colonel's shadowy features. "Lady Anne has another houseguest staying with her. A woman. I don't want her hurt, and I don't want her taken with the others."

"Who is she?"

"No one of any possible interest to you, Colonel, nor of any political threat to the government. She is English, however, and the daughter of a prominent friend to King George who would prefer to have her brought back discreetly to the bosom of her loved ones, not locked in manacles and put on display."

"My main concern is the Prince," Blakeney said. "If this woman is so important to you, I suggest you see to it that she is well away from the house when my men arrive. If she is captured and arrested with the others, I cannot guarantee the salvation of her reputation, not even if she was the daughter of the king himself."

"Fair enough. I should be able to think of some excuse to get her out of the house. And now, I had better be on my way . . . unless there is something else?"

"No. Major Garner will be pleased to hear you are earning your keep. By the way, I had almost forgotten . . . he wanted me to forward this on to you—" Blakeney removed a sealed letter from an inner pocket of his cloak, and then a second, smaller parcel bound in twine. "And here is the tea you wanted. Are things so hellishly barbaric travelling with those rebels?"

"They prefer to brace themselves with whisky rather than water steeped in herbs. The benefits show, don't you agree, in their approach to, and performance during, battle?"

Blakeney scowled at the sarcasm. "As long as your admiration does not spill over into your loyalties, sir. On that note, I leave you with one final word of caution: If anything . . . *unforeseen* should happen tonight, such as an ambush or an obvious entrapment, it will be my pleasure to see every strip of living flesh flayed from your body and fashioned into bloody replicas of the Stuart cockade."

"A charming picture, but uncalled for. You will have the Prince tonight, one way or the other."

Laughlan and Cheristine, huddled against the straw, listened raptly as both sets of footprints moved away from the stable, each going in opposite directions.

"Bluidy hell," Cherry exclaimed on a sigh. "I thought we were deid gaun, I did."

Laughlan crept to the end of the stall, listened intently for any further sounds from outside in the yard, then darted to the entrance of the stable and peered out into the shadowy parade of buildings and cramped stone stores.

"Have they gaun?" Cherry asked, appearing like a ghost over his shoulder.

"Aye. Seems so."

"Did ye see who they were? Did ye recognize them?"

Laughlan shook his head. "I canna be cairtain, but I ken one o' them was the new colonel arrived at the fort—Blackey or Blackeney, or some such thing. The ither—" he shrugged his lack of knowledge.

Cheristine's fingers were busy repairing the damage wrought by Laughlan's earlier fumblings. She laced her bodice prudishly tight and brushed her skirt and sleeves free of clinging bits of straw. Running back to the stall, she found and retrieved her woolen shawl, and, wrapping it securely around her head and shoulders, started out into the yard.

"I must get back afore mam notices how late it is," she said, attempting a normal conversational air. It failed, however, as did her attempt to dash past Laughlan before he could reach out a hand to stop her.

"Laughlan, I must get back—"

"Cherry, love, ye canna just leave me alane! We have tae warn Lady Anne an' the ithers."

"W-warn them?"

"Aye, lass! Did ye na hear what them two men were sayin'? They've laid a trap tae ambush Prince Charlie in his sleep! We're the only ones wha' know, so we're the only ones can warn them."

"Warn them . . . but how?"

"Well . . . I can cut ayont the glen tae Moy Hall. It shouldna take mair'n an hour, if I run all the way. Cherry, love, ye'll have tae find a way tae get word tae The MacGillivray. He'll have men an' guns, an' he'll ken what tae dae. Are ye wi' me in this, lass? Will ye help?"

"Moy Hall? The MacGillivray?" She chewed savagely on a clenched knuckle. "Oh. Oh, Laughlan. I'm afeared o' the sojers. They havena any qualms about arrestin' anyone wha' helps the rebels, an' . . . an' ma faither would throw fits if he even knew I were here wi' ye." She hesitated, swallowed hard at the panic welling in her chest, weighing it against the young but breathtakingly handsome features of Laughlan MacKintosh. She'd had her heart and her head set on winning him from the time he'd pulled her out of a well and saved her life at age three. "Aye. Aye, I'll dae it, Laughlan. I must dae it, must I na? Ye're right, we're the only ones wha' can help Lady Anne an' the ithers. I'll find ma brithers—Duncan an' Jamie—an' they'll ride f'ae The MacGillivray."

"Ach, I knew ye were a bonnie lass, Cherry," he said, kissing her hard and fast on the lips. He drew the ends of his own heavy breacan kilt around his shoulders, and was about to run out into the night when Cheristine's hand stopped him.

"Laughlan?"

"Aye, lass?"

"Dae ye . . . dae ye still love me?" She faltered, drowning in discomfort until he caught up her sweet face between his hands and smiled.

"Aye, lass, I dae. I didna ken how much until just this very minute."

"Godspeed," she whispered, her kiss as lush and mature as the feelings wrapped around her heart.

Grinning, he stole a last kiss and dashed out of the stable, his feet fairly flying over the snow-encrusted ground.

Chapter Eighteen

Lady Anne Moy stretched and offered a delicate yawn toward the fire. Damien, who had just recently joined the ladies in the parlour, noted the yawn and glanced at the clock ticking on the mantel.

"Ten past eight," he said to no one in particular. "Yet it feels like three in the morning."

Catherine looked over and smiled. "Only because you have come to experience the true meaning of the words 'work' and 'commitment', brother mine."

"You were much nicer to me before I gave you your cache of tea leaves," he remarked dryly. "Maybe there is something to be said about avoiding it."

Catherine wrinkled her nose pertly and drained the last of the honey-sweetened brew.

"In any case," Damien said, "now that I have thawed sufficiently, I think I shall see to my last few chores for the evening and then retire. It occurs to me I have gone twelve full hours without writing a letter to Harriet and, regardless if I write ten on the morrow to compensate for the omission, she will somehow know and punish me in some heinous, cruel manner."

"What possible chores could ye have to do this late at night?" Lady Anne inquired. "Ye spent the best part of the day in Inverness—against ma better judgement, I might add—and ye have, indeed, barely been home long enough to warm the chill out of yer claythes."

"I promised Dr. Cameron I would keep an eye on some of his patients. Apart from my mission to find tea leaves for a certain shamefully spoiled young lady, I managed to scrounge some medicines Archibald said were in short supply."

"Is there sickness in the camp?" Lady Anne asked, alarmed.

"Nothing out of the usual," he assured her. "Some fever, some dysentery . . . nothing a good strong dose of liverwort won't cure."

Catherine sighed audibly. "Dose someone suffering from dysentery with liverwort, my fine budding apothecary, and you would see them writhing in agony in no time."

Damien arched a brow. "Since when have you become a physician's apprentice?"

"Since Deirdre and I decided to make ourselves useful around the camp," she replied smartly.

"In that case, perhaps you would care to come along and offer your expert diagnosis and advice?"

"I'll go," Deirdre said, standing at once. "It's much too damp for Catherine to be out this late at night."

"Nonsense," she said, setting aside her teacup. "I could use a few breaths of fresh air."

"No," Damien held up his hand. "Deirdre is right. Alex would have my liver if I let anything happen to you, even to catching a runny nose."

"It is my nose," she insisted. "And since Alex, himself, usually allows me to accompany him on late night strolls around the camp, he can hardly object to you doing the same thing."

"And if I still say no?" he demanded.

"I shall simply follow you anyway."

Damien scowled. "I'm sorry I ever mentioned the matter. Very well, you can tag along, but you are not to go anywhere near the sick tents and you are not—"

A loud, frantic knocking on the manor's front door echoed down the corridor and interrupted Damien's train of thought. Lady Anne glanced around, startled at first by the noise, then puzzled as to its cause.

"Whoever could it be at this hour?" she wondered aloud. "Surely it canna be someone else to see the Prince."

The doors had been knocked upon all day long, for even though the Prince's precise whereabouts were supposed to have been kept a closely guarded secret, some of the local villagers and lairds had caught wind of it, and came to pay their respects. Charles had retired to his chambers several hours ago, accompanied by three of Angus Moy's friendlier wolfhounds and a full bottle of strong, locally brewed spirits. He was nursing an inflammation in his chest, and although his cough and sniffles had vastly improved since coming out of the mountains, he used it as an excuse to keep his own company.

"Pardon, ma lady," came the voice of Robert Hardy, the wizened stewart of Moy Hall. "There's a lad at the door, name o' Laughlan MacKintosh. Seems in a rare state, he daes, an' says he must take a word wi' ye . . . in privat'cy."

"Young Laughlan—Eanruil's son?"

"The same, ma lady." Robert arched a graying brow. "Says he has run all the way frae Inverness wi' a message ye must hear wi' yer ain ears."

Lady Anne smiled. "Then by all means, Robert, show the lad in."

Moments later, Laughlan MacKintosh, his face a glowering red from the long run in the cold misty air, dripped his way into the richly-furnished drawing room, his blue wool bonnet crushed in frozen fingers before his chest, a large bead of moisture hanging from the end of his nose.

Robert Hardy pinched the lad severely on the arm and indicated by way of a frosty glare for him to remove his furskin brogues from the rug to the polished—and thus wipeable—wood floor.

Lady Anne Moy, as regal a hostess to a sweating, quivering fifteen-year-old gillie as she was to the royal prince regent, stood and waved the lad closer to the roaring fire.

"Ma lady," he began. "I'd have a word wi' ye, if ye please."

"Whisht, Laughlan MacKintosh," she interrupted, signaling a disapproving Robert Hardy to pour out a glass of brandy. "Warm yerself first. Yer teeth are chattering so loud I can barely hear anything through them."

Laughlan dragged the sleeve of his coat across his nose and forehead, then accepted and gratefully drained the glass of spirits. "I'd have a word wi' ye alane, ma lady," he insisted, spluttering over the liquor-induced fireball in his throat. "It's fair important, what I have tae say."

"I'm sure it is to have brought ye out on a night like this. But these are ma friends, Laughlan. Ye can say what ye must in front of them."

"Well—" he spared a last glance around the ring of quiet faces before blurting out his story. "The sojers frae Fort George are on their way here, ma lady. They're on their way frae Inverness tae surround the Hall an' take Prince Charles their prisoner."

Damien, leaning interestedly against the pillared column of the fireplace, straightened and set his glass on the mantel. Deirdre and Catherine exchanged worried glances, but Lady Anne only laced her fingers together and smiled calmly.

"Where did ye hear this, Laughlan?" she asked.

"It's the truth, ma lady, I swear it. I haird two men talkin' about a plan tae attack an' kidnap the Prince. One o' them was an officer frae the fort, an' said as how Lord Loudoun had given him fifteen hunnerd sojers an' they were tae march wi'in the hour. The ither one said as how there werena but a few men left at Moy Hall tae guard the Prince; he said as how Lochiel an' Keppoch had left this mornin' an' the Prince were alane until Lord George comes frae Nairn."

"Who was this second man?" Lady Anne asked sharply. "Did ye see his face?"

Laughlan shook his head. "Nae. But he were *Sassenach*—a proper *Sassenach* wi' an accent crisp as toast. I mout ken him again if I seen him by the side an' wi' the same kind o' shadows roun him—or if I heard him talk low-like, in a whisper. I come here quick as I could, ma lady, on account o' they said as how the sojers would have the Prince in gaol afore midnight."

Lady Anne, Catherine, Deirdre and Damien looked at the ticking clock simultaneously.

"If what the boy says is true," Damien stated, loud enough for his cultured Derby accent to win a shocked stare from Laughlan, "then we haven't much time."

"Robert—" Lady Anne took command efficiently. "Ye must go and rouse the Prince at once. Take him warm claythes—a plain kilt and jacket—and tell him to dress quickly; we'll have to hide him somewheres until we find out if it's true or na'."

Laughlan dragged his wary eyes away from Damien, and settled his gaze firmly on Lady Anne. "It's true, ma lady. On ma honour as a MacKintosh, it's true."

For two full seconds there was silence, then Robert cleared his throat. "He could be taken to the caves, ma lady," he suggested.

"Aye. Aye, Robert, we'll have to risk it. We only have but forty or fifty men on hand. *Damn* MacGillivray f'ae choosing today of all days to go home and check on his farms."

"I've already sent a message tae The MacGillivray," Laughlan said with a measure of manly pride. "I knew ye mout be needin' his help."

"Bless ye f'ae that, Laughlan, but it will still be well past midnight before he can call his men together and be of any use. *Robert! Have yer feet grown into the floor?*" She waited until the valet hurried away before she spoke again. "What we have to do is think of some way to stall the soldiers long enough to get the Prince safely away."

"We can begin by rounding up all the men from the camp," Damien said, striding for the door. "If you don't need the boy any more, he can help me by collecting together all the servants, stableboys . . . anyone and everyone who is old enough and willing enough to carry a weapon."

"Deirdre and I qualify on both counts," Catherine declared. "We want to help, too."

"Absolutely not!" Damien growled, halting at the door. "You will both go up to your rooms, lock yourselves inside and wait for me to come back and fetch you. And I warn you, Catherine Ashbrooke Cameron, if you defy me on this, it may be the last bit of willful disobedience you will ever attempt while *in one piece*."

He was gone in a startled blink of an eye, although it did not take long for either woman to redirect an appeal to Lady Anne.

"Please," Catherine cried. "You cannot expect us just to hide away in our rooms and do nothing! There must be some way we can be of help."

Lady Anne, anxious to be away on errands of her own, shook her head after little or no consideration. "No. Your brither is right, Catherine. Ye've nae hand f'ae violence, if it comes to that. Both yer husbands would skin me alive if I allowed either you or Deirdre anywhere near danger. Ye're safest in your rooms, as ye were told. The soldiers wouldna dare enter Moy Hall."

"I thought they would never dare violate Rosewood Hall," Catherine said, stubbornly following Lady Anne out into the hallway and up the stairs, "but they did. As for violence, Deirdre and I have both witnessed our share lately, and regardless of my brother's misguided sense of chivalry or my husband's reputation for vengeance, I insist on helping in some way!"

Robert Hardy chose that opportune moment to appear in the hallway, his arms burdened under yards of plaid, his speech and mannerisms agitated.

"It's the Prince, ma lady. I canna rouse him. He's locked himsel' in his room an'—"

"Christ on a cross!" exclaimed Anne Farquharson Moy, abandoning all pretense at patience. "Break the bluidy door down if ye must! Carry him out over yer shoulder if ye canna get him to move any other way! When I go back down the stairs, Robert Hardy, I dinna want to hear he's still in the house, or I'll have yer nether parts slung around ma neck to wear as a trophy!"

Clearly stunned by his mistress's vehemence, Robert flinched out of her way, flattening himself against the panelled wall as she brushed past. His eyes remained owlish and watery as he swallowed and glanced nervously at the two remaining ladies.

"Break down the door?" he stammered. "Carry him out over ma shoulder?" He paused and gulped again. "But . . . he's The Stuart!"

"Well, I have no qualms about stirring the royal buttocks," Catherine said firmly. "Take us to his rooms, then fetch two more sets of plain, warm clothing. Find Corporal Peters . . . Corporal Jeffrey Peters. He shouldn't be too far if he's heard there is trouble on the way . . . and have him waiting at the front door for us with horses and men to guard the Prince. What are these caves you mentioned?"

Robert stumbled along beside them as he led the way down the hall. The tartan was becoming tangled around his bony legs, the trailing ends flapping this way and that, and he seemed to be having difficulty thinking, talking, and walking at the same time. Deirdre relieved him of the garments, earning a smile of gratitude.

"Aye," he said. "The caves up the glen. There's nae a house nor castle in the Heelands disna have a hidey-hole somewheres, by-the-by."

"Do you know the way? Can you lead us there?"

"Aye. Aye, I could dae."

"Good. Then you'd best fetch some warmer clothes for yourself as well. And weapons. Pistols or muskets . . . even a fowling piece will do. And quickly. We'll take care of the Prince."

Robert left them at the royal chamber and hurried away, repeating his instructions to himself in muttered Gaelic.

"Your Highness?" Catherine rapped sharply on the door. "Are you awake?"

When there was no answer, she tested the latch, not surprised to find it still securely locked.

"Your Highness? This is Lady Catherine. I must see you at once on a matter of great urgency."

"Go away," came the muffled rejoinder. "I'm not well . . ."

Catherine frowned and rattled the latch again. "Your Highness, I do not wish to alarm you, but there are soldiers on their way from Inverness. They have intentions of surrounding Moy Hall and taking you prisoner."

"Have they a reputable physician with them?" quavered the voice. "If they do, I should gladly throw myself upon their mercy."

Catherine looked at Deirdre. "What shall we do?"

"I doubt if we could break the door ourselves," Deirdre said, studying the thick wooden panel skeptically. "We might have to go back down and—"

The key scraped into the lock and a bleary, bloodshot eye appeared in the crack of the door.

"Good God. Lady Catherine, it *is* you." The crack widened and the eye narrowed as if to see through the alcoholic vapours of his own breath. "And Mrs. MacKail.

What manner of mischief brings you clamouring to my rooms at this ungodly hour?"

"Sire. There are soldiers on their way from Inverness."

"So you said. What do they want?"

Catherine held her patience in check. Why was it that all men seemed to revert to infancy when assailed by the slightest sniffle or sneeze? "They most likely want you, your Highness. We must, therefore, take you up into the hills and conceal you before they have a chance to succeed."

"Into the hills?" he exclaimed. "In the abominable damp? I should die of pneumonia long before I so much as saw a hill, never mind climbed one. Here—feel my brow. Does it not cry out for heat and bedrest?"

Without leaving Catherine the choice, he snatched up her hand and pressed it to his forehead. Granted, there was some warmth under her fingertips, but she suspected it was more a result of the empty bottle she saw lying on its side by the bed, than because of any fever he might be nursing.

She pushed her way into the room, wrinkling her nose distastefully at the smell of stale air, whisky, and a lidless chamberpot. The three wolfhounds, cringing in the corner of a room they knew they were forbidden access to, slinked past and bounded down the hall in search of their own kennels. The Prince appeared to be similarly disoriented. The threads of fair reddish-blond hair that poked out from beneath his nightcap were scattered about his ears and temples, too thin and wispy to have retained any curl. His complexion was sallow, his brown eyes ringed with dark smudges. The linen nightshirt he wore reached his ankles and bore large splotches of spilled whisky, food, and other questionable stains.

"Your Highness, we have brought you warm clothes. You must get dressed at once. The soldiers—"

"A pox on the soldiers," he grumbled, weaving his way back to the bed. "Let them come, if they like. I shall sneeze them all to perdition for their insolence."

"There are fifteen hundred armed men on the way, sire," Catherine said sharply. "I seriously doubt a few sneezes will deter them from clapping you in irons and dragging you away to gaol."

Charles staggered to a halt, his eyes screwing to slits as he peered back at Catherine. "How dare you speak to me in such a tone. Who the devil do you think you are?"

"Lady Catherine Cameron, as you well know. And who the devil are you to think you can jeopardize the lives of every single man, woman, and child on this estate simply because you do not feel well enough to stir from your bed?"

He drew back, blinking several times to bring her into better focus. "I beg your pardon, madam?"

"You heard me," she said evenly. "And to think, our husbands almost had us convinced that what they are doing is right and just. They claimed you were an honourable, courageous man willing to continue this fight singlehandedly and to fight to the death, if need be, for the sake of what you believed in." She paused and cast a sardonic glance along his dishevelled form. "In reality, it seems you are not even willing to risk a few hours of mild discomfort in order to save what is left of your army. The soldiers are welcome to you, sir. Perhaps they, too, will take pity on the miserable creature they find before them and continue to let him drown his miseries in fine whisky."

In a swirl of velvet skirts, Catherine started back for the chamber door, and gestured to an astonished Deirdre MacKail to deposit her armload of clothes on a chair and leave the room.

"Wait!" Charles demanded. "Hold up there, damn you!"

Ignoring the outburst, Catherine addressed him coolly. "Mrs. MacKail and I are adjourning to our rooms to change into warmer clothing. In fifteen minutes, we will be outside the front door, mounted on horses, and prepared to leave. You may join us if you wish. If not—"

retrieving a memory of Sir Alfred's more dramatic moments, she spread her hands wide "—you may share the company and hospitality of the manor with whomever you choose."

Ten minutes later, Corporal Peters was waiting nervously by the front doors of Moy Hall, a primed and cocked pistol clutched in his hand. He was alone, and did not appear especially pleased with the thickness of the shadows or the rustling night sounds that suggested an army of bloodthirsty warriors skulking behind every bush. He heard a particularly loud click behind him and spun on the balls of his feet, swallowing his heart back into his chest as he recognized Catherine, Deirdre, and Robert Hardy emerging from the house.

"Thank God," he said, wiping a sleeve across his brow. "I'm h-hearing Cumberland himself at every other turn. Where is the P-Prince?"

Catherine sighed and accepted a pair of reins. "I'm afraid—"

"The Prince is directly behind you," said Charles Edward Stuart, stepping out of the doorway and into the faintly luminous mist. He was dressed, as they all were, in plaid trews—breeches—warm upper clothing, and a long swath of wool tartan draped around his head and shoulders for protection against the elements.

"Where are my guards?" he demanded.

"Th-there's only me, sire," Corporal Peters explained. "The others have been commandeered to w-watch the roads and fields approaching Moy Hall."

"How many are there altogether?"

"Sixty-three, sire, plus another two dozen women who volunteered to help as well. B-but they are expecting The MacGillivray and his men any moment now."

"It is my fault," the Prince murmured soberly, "for being so obstinate. I should have listened to Lochiel and moved to Kilravock as originally planned. Because of me, these good men and women must put themselves in dire jeopardy."

He looked directly at Catherine, and, after a moment, removed his bonnet and approached her. "Forgive me, Lady Catherine. You were perfectly within your right to say what you did, whereas my own behaviour has been unconscionable. I trust you will not hold it against me overlong?"

"It is already forgotten, sire."

Raising her hand, he bowed over it and brushed his lips across the cool fingers. "Your servant, madam. I shall hereafter obey your every command unhesitatingly."

"In that case, sire, choose your mount," she said, pointing to the horses Corporal Peters had brought with him.

After assisting Deirdre and Catherine into their saddles, the Prince and Corporal Peters mounted and the group set off in a brisk canter behind Hardy, who had taken the lead. They rode swiftly across the sweep of the glen, the motion of the horses stirring the trailing fingers of mist out behind them. At the edge of the black, encroaching forest, they looked back to where the fires in the camp had been stoked into tall pyres and would, from a distance, give the impression of providing warmth for hundreds of men.

They entered the forest in single file, forced to walk their horses slowly until they could climb above the mist and use the light from the crescent moon to guide them. The air was damp and cold, chilling them through the heavy layers of clothing and seeping into flesh and bone so that they shivered uncontrollably. Charles Stuart, having sobered up considerably since leaving his rooms, frequently doubled over with bouts of sustained, wracking coughs that he could neither contain nor muffle. He cursed the weakness roundly in gutter Italian each time a spasm gripped him, and apologized profusely each time the echoes faded away. Neither sentiment aided in relieving their growing sense of unease as they climbed higher and higher on the mountain, deeper and deeper into the forest. Catherine's skin was wet and clammy with perspiration. Fear of being followed, fear of an ambush, concern for her brother and the others left behind at Moy Hall, worry over the Prince's health were thoughts enough to keep her glancing constantly back over her shoulder— and an unshakeable sensation she had of being watched.

A light snowfall earlier in the evening had cloaked the fields but had not been able to penetrate the thick overlay of branches in the forest, keeping the paths they followed as black as pitch. Here and there, where there was a clear patch of ground, it shone out of the gloom like a beacon, drawing the riders toward it, casting them adrift again when they passed. There was little wind to bring the surrounding hillside to life; only a gentle whisper of dead leaves and the careful plod, plod, plod of their horses hooves scraping over frozen earth and loose stones.

Conversation between the five riders was minimal. Too many glaring interruptions were brought about by distant, disturbing echoes of sound far below in the glen. Too many whispered speculations made everyone prefer to hunch their shoulders deeper into their tartans and ride with their own private thoughts.

To Robert Hardy's credit, he never seemed to falter when it came to choosing the correct path to take. He had admitted early on that it had been many years since he had sought refuge in the caves. His bones were too old for such nonsense, he claimed, yet he kept them moving at a brisk pace up the mountain and allowed only brief five-minute rests at infrequent intervals.

At the end of an hour, he stopped his horse and tilted his head to one side. The trees had been visibly thinning, the patches of moonlit snow growing wider over ground which bore the solid feel of rock instead of earth beneath them.

"Caves be just ayont," Robert murmured, conscious of how the slightest sound vibrated the nerves along everyone's spine. "They be stocked wi' food an' blankets an' the like."

"A fire?" the Prince asked hopefully, his teeth chattering around the words.

"I shouldn't advise it, sire," Corporal Peters said. "In these hills, in this kind of darkness—" he fell silent a moment, awed by the sight unfolding around them as they rode out of the trees "—the glow from a fire would be visible for miles."

Indeed, once out of the trees, the air was crystal clear, the moon a bright slash of blue-white light set against a backdrop of pure black velvet sky. The path they rode upon climbed steeply for perhaps another dozen yards, then levelled onto a wide, flat plateau, its front and back faced with a sheer, ragged drop of solid rock. Below them, the glen sprawled black and cavernous, the moonlight glowing on the upper surface of the mist, broken here and there by black protrusions of hilltops and ridges.

Hardy had dismounted and seemingly disappeared into a crack in the side of the rock wall. His efforts at scraping tinder and flint were clearly discernible in the eerie silence and in a few moments, the opening of the fissure bloomed with a soft yellow light.

Contemplating the height and width of the opening, Catherine clung to the corporal's helpful hands a moment longer than was necessary as he helped her off the horse.

"Corporal . . . could we not find some way to cover the mouth of the cave?" she asked, her voice a sliver of ice. "See? It is not very wide, not very tall—"

"We could use blankets," Deirdre suggested. "Or cut branches thick enough to cloak it."

"We could certainly try, ladies," Peters conceded. "Especially since the alternative appears to be five frozen blocks of ice come morning."

The Prince succumbed to another bout of ragged coughing, and, in consideration of the others, staggered a few feet farther along the plateau. Hardy reappeared at the mouth of the cave, but his smile was cut short on a shouted warning.

Charles Stuart stumbled back again, the coughing spasm shocked into silence as he realized how close he had come to stepping off the lip of the cliff and falling into the darkness below.

"Good God, man," he gasped as the others rushed to join him. "Is there anything else we should be aware of? Are you certain we're safe here?"

"Safe as in yer ain bed, sire," Roberts assured him. "An' a mout as cozy, too, once we get a fire lit. It's no' so bad a drop, in truth," he added, peering over the edge of the cliff. "Mayhap twenny feet, an' all bush tae the bottom. Come daylight ye'll see f'ae yersel'."

"Thank you, but I shall take your word on it," the Prince said, stopping shy of admitting outright that he was uncomfortable with heights. As for hiding in caves . . . "It's not exactly Holyrood House, is it?" he mused, casting an eye up the sheer rock face.

"But safe," Robert Hardy reiterated. "A flea couldna find us here an' the cave were full o' brayin' hounds."

"Well, we are hardly fleas, Robert," Damien said in a distinctly dry tone as he and another rider nudged their horses out of the shadow of the trees. "Yet we have managed to find you easily enough."

"Damien!" Catherine cried, running along the plateau to greet him. "Where have you come from? And how did you find us?"

"A more pertinent question, Kitty dear, is what the hell are you doing here? I thought I gave you direct orders to remain locked in your room. When I went to collect you there, all I found was a very pretty pile of crushed velvet and wired petticoats."

"Panniers, darling, and they are most uncomfortable when one is contemplating going any distance on horse-back. As for you issuing a direct order and my feeling obliged to obey it, you should have learned by now I have a mind of my own."

"I can attest to that," the Prince said wryly. "But you shouldn't scold her, Damien. She has done us all an inestimable service tonight—one that shall not be soon forgotten."

Catherine's smile held for several seconds as she looked from Charles Stuart to her brother. "You still haven't told us how you managed to find us . . . or was it you I felt breathing on our backs every step of the way?"

"I confess," Damien nodded. "Young Laughlan here had an idea where you might be headed and, well, it seemed a good idea to hang back a little to make sure no one else was following."

"Just in case," Corporal Peters advised, "we should tether the horses somewhere out of sight and tuck ourselves away in the cave."

"Agreed," Damien said at once and half-turned to the silent shadow standing beside him. "Laughlan—do you think you could take those daggers you call eyes out of my back long enough to see to the animals? Hello there? Have you gone suddenly deaf, lad?"

Laughlan MacKintosh had not gone deaf, nor blind. The longer he stared, the more the others became aware of the distant popping sounds that were coming from the glen below. There was no mistaking the sporadic crackle for what it was. In the past few weeks, they had all become acquainted with the sound of musket reports, and too uncomfortably aware of the telltale volleys that marked a skirmish.

Colin Fraser had been a happy man in his former employ as smitty to the tiny village of Moy. More recently, as a recruit to Colonel Anne's contingent of MacKintoshes he had proved himself to be an able leader who found the danger and excitement more stimulating than any threats or entreaties his wife of twenty-two years could provide. He had marched away to join Bonnie Prince Charles against her wishes, and undoubtedly would march back to their small thatched *clachan* when all this was over, against his own.

Roused by the sight of Lady Anne thundering out of the smoky evening mists astride her huge gray gelding, he had quickly taken the eleven men assigned to him and headed off at a run down the forested dirt road. Halting his patrol some three miles from Moy Hall, he had deployed them at intervals along the roadside, then settled himself behind a camouflage of junipers and hunkered down to wait and watch.

He hadn't been hiding a full minute when he felt the hairs at the nape of his neck stand on end as he realized they were not the only ones skulking in the woods. More specifically, he knew he was not the only one who had chosen that particular clump of junipers in which to crouch.

Slowly, sinew by cautious sinew, he stretched his neck to its full length so that just the top of his head and his two bulging eyeballs cleared the awning of evergreen branches. What he saw was another head stretched upwards, another pair of startled eyeballs peering back at him from less than a body length away. Without thinking, and certainly without giving the other fellow a chance to react, he sprang up from the bushes, knife in hand, and launched himself at his enemy.

Four hundred yards down the road, Colonel Blakeney raised his hand and brought his troop of men to a standstill.

"Did you hear something?" he asked his second-in-command.

The younger officer listened, his head cocked to one side, his eyes searching the twisted, vaulting shadows that crowded either side of the road.

"An owl perhaps?"

"Owls do not scream, Lieutenant," Blakeney remarked, his own head swivelling in an attempt to judge their position and guess how much further the forest ran before emptying onto the glen.

"Send back for MacLeod," he ordered. "And for the love of God, do it quietly. Pass the word as you go: I want absolute, blood-still silence among the men. The first sneeze I hear ends in a slit throat."

"Aye sir."

The lieutenant ran noiselessly back along the fidgeting column of infantry, relaying the colonel's command for silence as he went. The men had been nervous to begin with, for they had all heard the rumours of the massive Jacobite encampment in the glen surrounding Moy Hall, and few of them believed it to be truly deserted. The names Cameron and MacDonald reacted on their bladders and bowels more fiercely than the brisk winter air; some of the soldiers had been present at Prestonpans and knew firsthand the fighting savagery of the two clans. Others, who had been at Falkirk, remembered the terror of seeing screaming Highlanders charge out of nowhere, wielding blood and death in their hands.

Fully half of Lord Loudoun's army was English and they hated and feared these bens and glens where no normal soldier could be expected to fight efficiently. The other half consisted of Highland regiments, raised from the clans who supported the Hanover monarchy. Their hearts were not attuned to a pitched battle with their own kinsmen, and because of their own proud blood, they knew that the blind passion carrying the rebels this far would be eradicated by nothing short of death.

"Why have ye stopped the column?" demanded Ranald MacLeod, captain of the company of MacLeods. Like his father, he was short, and blunt of feature, quick to find fault with every tactic suggested by anyone other than a Highlander. Unlike his father, however, he was acutely conscious of the trust the MacLeods had betrayed in refusing to honour their pledge of support for the Prince, and was grudgingly envious of his younger brother Andrew, who had thrown scorn in their father's face and ridden off to join the Jacobites.

"We are nearing one of the junctions marked on the map," Blakeney surmised. "Once through this narrow gorge and over the hill, we will be able to divide the men and spread out in a pincer movement to surround Moy Hall."

"Over this hill there are ten ithers," MacLeod spat derisively. "A better approach would hae been frae the east, where there were moors an' a level field."

"And a greater likelihood of being seen and discovered by our enemies."

MacLeod considered the mist, sniffing it like a hound scenting game. "Nae doubt they've seen us already. Nae doubt the *owls* are soundin' the alarm even as we sit here shiftin' foot tae foot."

Blakeney reddened. "Then I suggest we close ranks and fix bayonets."

"We're under nae orders tae fight the whole blessit rebel army," MacLeod said evenly. "The general were clear on that, bein' as how we're all what stands atween them an' full possession o' the Heelands."

"Is your concern for the welfare of the Highlands . . . or the wellbeing of the MacLeod estates?"

An angry paw of a hand fell to the hilt of a broadsword. "Ye'll take a care in what ye say, Thomas Lobster. Some o' ma men are no' too keen tae be trampled by yer brave sojers should they happen tae catch a glimpse o' the white cockade."

Blakeney's cheeks flushed once again. He managed to tolerate the blatant reference to his men's cowardice, but just barely. His hand dropped to his own sword hilt, itching to test the burly Highlander's mettle, and well he might have, had one of the advance scouts not come tumbling out of the shadows, screaming at the top of his lungs.

"Rebels, sir! Up ahead! In the trees, in the hills . . .!"

"Slow down, man!" Blakeney commanded harshly. "Calm yourself and tell me exactly what you saw."

"Rebels, sir! Half a mile down the road, maybe less by now."

"Damn!" The colonel glared ahead into the darkness and obstructing mist. "How many? An advance guard? A company? A regiment? Speak up, man, what did you see?"

"I dunno how many, sir. They was all around me though, that much I could tell just by listening. They was swarmin' through the trees, thick as bluddy flies in June. Settin' up for an ambush, I'd say. Already killed Jacobs and would have had me too if I'd been a hair slower."

A buzz rippled through the column of men, and *en masse*, they could almost be seen to flinch back a step. Neither their expressions nor their stance altered much when Blakeney wheeled his horse around and lunged to the centre of the road.

"Form up the men! Muskets primed, bayonets fixed! Prepare for attack! *Prepare for attack!*"

Two hundred yards down the road, Colin Fraser heard the order and left his grove of junipers, plunging back through the underbrush to where his men were crouched and waiting. His primary concern now was to find a way to warn the others back at Moy Hall that what looked to be the entire government force posted in Inverness was on the road and about to break through their feeble defenses.

Feeble be damned, he thought! Raising his musket in the air, he fired it, shouting at his men to prepare to attack. In desperation, he not only shouted their names, but the names of every clansman he could think of, and began running from bush to bush, screaming the *caithghairm* of the Camerons, the MacDonalds, the MacGillivrays, the Stewarts, the Chisholms . . . His men quickly grasped the idea and discharged their weapons, reloading as they ran into the trees, roaring orders back and forth, moving constantly to make it seem as if the woods were alive with blood-thirsty Highlanders.

"Christ!" MacLeod shouted, "That's Lochiel himsel'! They were waitin' f'ae us! The bluidy bastards were waitin' f'ae us!"

"Hold your ground!" Blakeney screamed, drawing his sword and raising it in the air.

"They were waitin' f'ae us!" MacLeod raged, drawing his own broadsword. "The whole bluidy lot o' them, waitin' tae take us in our ain trap!"

Blakeney's horse reared as a musketball hissed by his ear and struck a man standing in the front line of the infantry column. Clutching his throat, the soldier gurgled an ear-piercing scream and was jerked back off his feet, the blood spraying the men on either side and behind. Breaking apart, the column started to split out of formation and Blakeney, sensing they would turn and run, regardless of what orders he gave, had no choice but to try to salvage what discipline, if any, remained.

"Retreat!" he shouted. "Fall back! Fire at will into the woods on either side of the road! In God's name don't let them box us in!"

His horse bolted as he dug his bootheels into the quivering flanks. MacLeod was right behind, stopping long enough to pull the wounded man up into his saddle, and long enough to shout a reply to the blood-curdling challenges being hurled at them from the bushes.

Colin Fraser maintained his frenzied shouting and shooting until his supply of powder and shot was exhausted, and his voice was reduced to a dry rasp. Drenched in sweat, knowing he had done all he could to delay the inevitable, he and his men collapsed by the side of the road, astonished they had managed to hold the government troops as long as they had, convinced the reprieve was only temporary before the soldiers would return with a vengeance.

It would not be until morning that they would learn the twelve of them had sent fifteen hundred men scrambling all the way back to Inverness.

"Definitely gunfire," Damien murmured, listening to the distant pop and crackle of musket reports. "Although, the way the sound carries up here, there is no telling where it is coming from or how big a force is involved."

"There's nothing much we can do about it," Corporal Peters said, loudly enough to remind Damien of the women's presence. "I suggest we all move into the cave, where it is warm and dry, and perhaps we can brew up a soothing cup of tea."

"Tea?" Catherine said, startled. "In the middle of nowhere?"

Peters flushed and drew a small parcel out of his coat pocket. "I remembered hearing you say how much you longed for a good cup of strong English tea, and, well, I managed to barter some away from a man in Brigadier Stapleton's regiment."

Half a dozen paces away, Laughlan MacKintosh tugged gently on Damien's coattail to draw his attention. "Sir! Sir, it's him."

"What? What are you talking about?"

"Sir, it's *him*. He's the one I seen outside the stable talkin' wi' the *Sassenach* colonel. I wisna sure until he spoke just then, an' now . . . well, I seen the colonel gie him that wee packet in the stable. It's him, I swear it. The one wha' betrayed the Prince an' Lady Anne."

Damien took a split second too long to absorb the information and react, and by then Corporal Peters, sensing the reason for the alarmed exchange of whispers, had already drawn a brace of pistols from beneath his coat. In an almost gracefully fluid move, he wrapped an arm around Catherine's waist and drew her against his body, the muzzle of a gun thrust up against the underside of her throat.

Catherine's shocked cry was bitten short as she felt the cold metal dig sharply into her flesh.

"I wouldn't try it if I were you, Ashbrooke," Peters grated, halting Damien's reach for his own guns. "Not unless you want to see your sister's brains splattered all over the hillside."

"Corporal!" Deirdre gasped. "What are you doing?"

"My job, madam," he replied calmly, his voice as level and even as a razor blade, and displaying none of his previous hesitancy or stuttering. "Hardy: drop whatever it is you are carrying beneath your tartan and move over with the others where I can see you."

Robert Hardy's hand and arm emerged from the wide swath of his tartan, the pistol he clutched gleaming dully in the moonlight. He did as he was told, laying the gun carefully at his feet before stepping over beside Damien and the boy.

"I implore you, sir, to let Mrs. Cameron go free," said the Prince. "I assume it is me you want, and I will go with you willingly, if you will only let the dear lady go free."

"Very touching," Peters said, aiming the second gun at the Prince. "But what I want you to do, Highness, is move over to the edge of the cliff. I want you standing with your heels at the edge and your arms stretched out in front of you. *Now*, or the lady dies."

Peters waited until the Prince complied, then backed closer to the cliff himself, dragging Catherine with him. He stopped near enough to the Prince that a sudden kick or shove would send the regent backwards over the edge of the rocks, and far enough from the others to have plenty of warning to pull the trigger of either gun should anyone make a move to attack. His eyes darted from face to face, halting finally on Deirdre.

"Moving very slowly and very precisely, Mrs. MacKail, I would like you to gather up all the weapons . . . guns, muskets, knives . . . everything. Throw them over the cliff, if you please."

Deirdre did as she was told, making two trips to the edge of the plateau before all of the weapons were located and disposed of. Only then did Catherine feel a lessening of the pressure on her neck—not much, but enough to allow her to think clearly again, and to see without the exploding starbursts of pain clouding her vision.

"Very obliging of you, Mrs. MacKail," Peters said when the job was done. "If you will go now to my horse, you will find some rope tied to the saddle."

"Why?" she asked, bewildered and stunned by the unexpected turn of events. "Why are you doing this?"

"Why? Come now, Mrs. MacKail. My king and country forevermore—do you really believe ten shillings a month is ample pay for a soldier to risk life and limb?"

"You prefer higher stakes, I gather," Damien snarled.

"Thirty thousand pounds is not to be laughed at," Peters replied, unperturbed. "And fifty thousand should about set me up for life."

Catherine's eyes fluttered half-shut on a stifled cry. "Alex. Dear God, we led you right to him."

"A bit of luck I hadn't planned on," Peters admitted, chuckling dryly in her ear. "A masterful calculation on my part, as it turned out. I had originally been ordered to simply join the Jacobites in Derby, but, as you well know, their hasty departure from the area caught everyone a little by surprise. I was setting out to catch up to them when I stumbled across Lieutenant Goodwin's path, surmised where he was going and what he was planning to do, and followed him to Rosewood Hall. Imagine my astonishment when I found out the innocent lamb I had escorted safely out of the wolf's lair was none other than the wife of Alexander Cameron! The Dark Cameron himself! What better way to ingratiate myself with the rebel leaders and carry out my assignment for Major Garner."

"Hamilton Garner!" Catherine gasped.

"Ahh, I thought the name might stir some hot juices. Oddly enough, I only learned of your connection with the major this afternoon. Communications being what they are, I have only been relaying the pertinent information to my superiors: numbers, locations, disbursements, that sort of thing. I had no idea the local gossip would be of equal importance to the major, or how very much he wanted to reacquaint himself with you and your illustrious husband. Nothing personal, you understand, as far as my part in any of this goes. Although, in these past few weeks, I must admit I have been sorely tempted to dispense with my naive and stammering impersonation of Corporal Milquetoaste and sample some of what has so obviously captivated the Dark Cameron." He paused and the press of the gun against her flesh imitated a hideous caress. His body, which she had assumed to be slender and soft from uncertainty and inexperience, was like steel where it molded against hers; the muscles in his arms were whipcord taut and so well conditioned that not even the awkward balance and position of the heavy pistols had produced a tremor.

"Who knows," he murmured. "After we have rid ourselves of the excess baggage here tonight, and trussed the Prince up good and tight for delivery to his gaolers, you could try to persuade me out of handing you over to the good major. I imagine you must be very good indeed to have brought the mighty Lion of Lochaber to his knees."

The brush of his lips against her temple caused such a shudder of revulsion to course through Catherine's body, she staggered against a violent wave of nausea.

Both Robert Hardy and Damien moved simultaneously, but Peters, his view briefly blocked by Catherine's flying hair, saw only Hardy making his lunge. In a purely reflex action, he shifted the aim of the gun he held at Catherine's neck and squeezed the trigger. The steel hammer tripped forward, striking the flint and causing a minor explosion of smoke and spark as the gunpowder was ignited. The lead ball blasted into Hardy's forehead, smashing through the bone and carrying away the back half of the Scotsman's skull.

Deirdre's scream of horror further distracted Peters, giving Damien the precious extra fraction of a second he needed to propel himself across the plateau. Striking Peters' lanky body from the side, he had no choice but to carry Catherine to the ground with them, and no way to shield her from the second gun except to place his own body between her and Peters. She rolled clear just as the second shot exploded, the flash of powder and spark blinding Damien temporarily, but through sheer luck missing his temple by a margin so close, the lead drew a bluish line across his skin.

The two men struggled together, cursing and grunting as they punched, kicked, and tore at each other's exposed flesh. They rolled perilously close to the edge of the cliff, then back again, straining and writhing to gain control, to land a solid punch that could stun their opponent long enough to gain the advantage. Peters still maintained a grip on one of the pistols, the other having cartwheeled off into the darkness. He whipped it again and again at Damien's head and shoulders, savouring each dull, sickening thud of metal on flesh.

Damien screamed inwardly as each blow struck. For one of the few times in his life, he cursed the affluence and soft living that had left him a poor physical match for the lithe and tough Corporal Peters. The man was trained to fight and to kill with his bare hands, and Damien knew he was quickly losing ground. Literally losing it too, he realized with a lurch of his stomach as the two men rolled and Damien felt his head and shoulders plunge over the side of the cliff. Only Peters' weight across his legs kept him from losing his balance completely, but even as he was shaking the dizziness out of his eyes and trying to reorientate up from down, he saw the flash of reflected moonlight glance off the blade of a raised knife. He thought he heard himself cry out Harriet's name even as he threw up both arms, sucked in his belly, and braced himself for the pain that was yet to come.

When it came, it came not from a slicing wound to his chest, as expected, but from a second-hand bruise caused by the large rock that bounced once off the back of Peters' neck before slamming into Damien's shoulder. He saw the knife spin out of the corporal's hand, saw Peters' body jerk to the side, his mouth gaping wide in agony as young Laughlan MacKintosh's foot caught him squarely in the groin. Dazed by the blow to the neck and seared by the flaring pain in his lower body, Peters rolled to the edge of the rock ledge and, too late to grab hold of any scrub or outcrop to save himself, slid off the lip of serrated stone. He was swallowed into the blackness, his scream ending abruptly in a crunch of broken branches some distance below.

Charles Stuart was the first to move. He ran over to assist Damien, who was coughing and staggering unsteadily onto his knees. No sooner had he pulled Catherine's brother back onto the safety of the plateau, when a second heartrending scream pierced the mountain silence.

Deirdre was on her knees beside Catherine, her hands covered with blood, her face pale and stricken in the moonlight.

"She isn't breathing!" Deirdre cried. "The second bullet . . . help me please! *She isn't breathing!*"

Chapter Nineteen

Exactly two weeks to the day of their departure, a small but heavily armed party of Cameron clansmen were reportedly seen on the outskirts of Inverness. Word of their success in capturing the garrison at Fort Augustus had preceded them by four full days, but the victory had already been overshadowed by the Prince's own daring maneuver against the government troops occupying Inverness. A day after the astonishing rout at Moy Hall, the vanguard of Lord George Murray's column had marched into the glen. Hearing of the Prince's close call with Blakeney's men, the general had whisked Charles Stuart away to Culloden House, there to be surrounded by three thousand of his own men. A few days later, taking advantage of the enemy's loss of credibility, the Prince had boldly advanced on Inverness, chasing Lord Loudoun's troops across the waters of the Moray Firth to Dornoch.

"It is all in the timing," Aluinn remarked wryly. "Had we arrived a week earlier, we would have been heroes. Today? We're just adding another minor feather to the Prince's bonnet."

"Tell that to my wife when you see her," Alex muttered. "The closer we get to Moy, the tighter my collar feels."

"At your age and with your experience, you should know by now not to make rash promises you cannot keep. Especially to a pregnant female. I'm told the condition does something to their sensibilities; increasing the protective, feline instincts or some such thing. And since she has a rare temper to begin with—" he shrugged and let the sentence hang, earning a glare from the indigo eyes.

"You are an absolute font of cheer," Alexander commented, nodding abstractedly to a couple of sombre-faced women who had paused by the roadside to stare at the passing riders. "So is everyone else, for that matter, or am I just imagining all these rousing accolades of welcome?"

Aluinn slowed his horse to match Shadow's pace, both animals drawing to a halt on the crest of a knoll overlooking the glen and parks of Moy Hall. The scene appeared tranquil enough; the camp was off to their right, snuggled at the base of the imposing, forested slope. A dozen or more fires trailed lazy fingers of smoke into the clear air, and there were visible signs of activity in and around the canvas tents. The backdrop of rolling hills marched off toward the horizon like choppy green waves on the ocean, some peaked in foaming white snow, some so distant and faded, they blended into the underbellies of low-lying clouds far to the south.

"Everything seems quiet enough," Aluinn said.

"Too damned quiet, if you ask me."

Struan MacSorley halted his shaggy-maned garron beside them, and next to him, Count Giovanni Fanducci reined into line, his feathered blue tricorn as sweepingly incongruous in the surroundings as usual.

"Maybe we should have-a taken time out to shave," he noted with a disgruntled twitch of an eyebrow. Most out of character was the several days worth of stubble on his cheeks. Angered that the siege of Fort Augustus had taken longer than anticipated, and anxious to return to Moy, Alex had forced his group to ride straight through, stopping no more than an hour at a time to rest the horses and partake of a hasty meal. Despite his unshaven appeareance, the count looked the least ruffled of them all. Both Alex and Aluinn wore full beards, and were coated with the grime and sweat of the long hard ride.

Alex nudged Shadow forward again, his gaze alternating between the regal stone manorhouse and the camp. Half-way down the slope, a familiar figure mounted on a muscular gray gelding came pounding across the turf. Lady Anne Moy, her hair flying loose around her shoulders and her cheeks flushed pink from the exertion, pulled to a rearing halt a few paces away.

"I was told ye were taking the road frae Inverness," she gasped. "I sent men along the way to watch f'ae ye."

"We decided to cut across country," Alex explained, frowning. "We weren't really expecting a reception committee."

Lady Anne's horse pranced impatiently and she cursed under her breath in Gaelic. "Then ye havena heard?"

"Heard what?" Aluinn asked.

Lady Anne's bright green eyes went to Alex. "We had some trouble after ye left. The king's men came in the night, hoping to take the Prince. Catherine was the only one who could rouse the Prince into moving himself up the mountain, to the caves where we thought he'd be safest. There was a fight, an' . . . an' Catherine was hurt—not bad!" she added quickly. "She scared the living bejesus out of her brither, mind. I ken he aged ten years bringing her back down the mountain again. But the doctor says she's fine. She's fine, the bairn's fine; bedrest an'—"

Alex did not wait to hear the rest. He kicked his heels into Shadow's ribs, startling the beast into a gallop that carried him the rest of the way through the glen and up to the front door of Moy Hall. Horse and rider came to a flying halt, and with cloak and tartan swirling around his massive frame, Alex vaulted to the ground and launched himself through the double doors. He took the stairs to the second storey, two at a time, and was at his wife's rooms before the other riders in the group had even gained the front yard.

Catherine did not hear the sound of his boots in the outer hallway; she was laughing too hard. She was not even aware of the impending storm until the door to her chamber blew open and a tall, caped, and heavily bearded intruder filled the doorway. The laughter died in her throat as she recognized the windblown figure; her instinctive cry of pleasure met a similar fate as she saw his expression change from concern to anger with startling rapidity.

Deirdre, seated by the bedside, dropped the bit of lace she was mending and added her stare to Catherine's. Damien, lounging in a chair by the fire, was cut short mid-way through the passage he was reading and abandoned the comedy as quickly as his smile when he, too, saw the look on Alex's face.

The implacable dark eyes slashed through the relaxed atmosphere with the sharpness of an axe. Catherine's cheeks bloomed under their intense scrutiny and even though his gaze remained fixed on her face, she could feel his concern probing beneath the layers of linen and lace she wore, stripping back the plumped satin coverlets and examining her from head to toe.

Temporarily assured her health was in no immediate danger, some of the tension eased from his stance, but only someone who knew him as intimately as a siamese twin might have been able to perceive the change.

"Alex!" Catherine's indrawn breath escaped on a rush. "You're back!"

"If I am disturbing you, I can come back later," he said in a silky tone which deceived no one. Damien and Deirdre moved simultaneously, fumbling to collect up the book, scraps of lace, wineglass, cups and saucers. Catherine remained quite still. She was not intimidated by her husband's tactics, although she knew enough to be as wary as a sailor becalmed in the eye of a hurricane. She folded her hands daintily and precisely on her lap and offered her sweetest smile.

"Are you going to stand there glowering all afternoon, or are you going to come in and tell us all about your adventure at Fort Augustus?"

Deirdre gaped at her former mistress. Damien held his breath and looked toward the doorway.

Alexander only folded his arms across his chest and leaned indolently against the oak jamb. "It wasn't much of an adventure, really. We met with a bit of resistance, but nothing too daunting. I hear you had some excitement of your own?"

"Mmmm, some." Catherine unclasped a hand briefly and smoothed a wrinkle on the coverlet. "Nothing too daunting, as you say. We simply foiled a kidnapping plot, saved the Prince's life, and scattered the king's army into a panic."

"All in a day's work," he mused, looking deeply into his wife's eyes. He was not fooled by her cool bravado either. Not for a minute. There were still faint shadows beneath her eyes and the flush in her cheeks bore the unnatural brightness of recent fever. The movement of her hand had also drawn attention to the thick wadding of bandages distorting the shape of her shoulder and upper arm; the slight tightening of her lips betrayed the true cost of the nonchalant gesture.

The dark eyes flicked to the two silent observers and his mouth curved up lazily. "Would you mind excusing us? I'm a little tired, a little dusty, and not very promising company at the moment."

Deirdre and Damien Ashbrooke were spurred into motion again, stammering unnecessary apologies and offering the briefest and most perfunctory of salutations before prudently exiting the room.

Out in the hallway, Deirdre spied several grimy, bearded men approaching along the corridor and she broke away from Damien to fling herself into her husband's welcoming arms. Count Fanducci whipped the plumed tricorn off his head and discreetly hung back with Struan MacSorley, while the two embraced.

"What the devil is going on?" Aluinn demanded, prying her away to arm's length after several clinging moments. "We met Lady Anne outside and she said Catherine had been hurt?"

Deirdre nodded, her relief not too overwhelming to prevent her from taking a swift inventory of arms, legs, fingers, ears. Finding no injuries, her gaze returned to the lean, handsome lines of her husband's face and responded to the concern in the soft gray eyes.

"It was not as bad as we first thought. We . . . *I* thought she had been shot dead, but—"

"*Shot?* Catherine was *shot*?"

Deirdre nodded again. "Corporal Peters shot her. There was so much blood and she didn't seem to be breathing, but she was only shot in the arm, as it turned out. Still quite horrible, but—"

"*Only?* How the hell did she *only* get shot in the arm? And what do you mean Corporal Peters shot her? Was it an accident?"

"Oh no. It was quite deliberate. He'd already shot dead the houseman, Robert Hardy, and was planning to shoot all of us as well, I'm sure, and to take the Prince back to Inverness and hand him over to the English army."

"Peters? *Jeffrey* Peters?"

"It was all a pretense, you see," she explained, the words tumbling out in a flurry. "He was really one of them all along. I mean, he didn't actually change loyalties when he rescued Catherine and me from Derby; he only used us so that he might be more convincing in his role. His nervousness was all an act as well, and the stutter—although I warrant his infatuation with my lady was in some part genuine—but he was really just a spy! He was the one who alerted the government troops and told them the Prince was staying here at Moy Hall, but when he saw the army's plan to kidnap Charles Stuart had failed, he went up into the mountains with us, intending to do the job himself."

"I'm-a knew it!" Count Fanducci exploded, smacking the back of his hand against the side of Struan's arm. "I'm-a knew something about that man, she's-a no right!"

"Yes, well," Aluinn said grimly, "he felt the same way about you—or at least he tried to make damn sure any suspicion was directed away from himself."

Fanducci's eyes narrowed. "Soooo. That's-a why you stuck to my back like the flea! He made-a you think *I* was-a the spy!"

Aluinn shrugged apologetically. "He was very convincing, and I was . . . open to suggestion."

"Hmphf!" the count snorted, feigning supreme indignation.

"Back to Peters," Aluinn said, reverting his attention to Deirdre and Damien. "What happened on the mountain?"

"The lad who overheard Peters talking to an officer in Inverness, and who warned us in time to get the Prince away, twigged on to the fact that it *was* Peters," Damien said, picking up the story. "Something about tea leaves . . . I'm not too sure. Anyway, he thought it was me at first, and since he and I did not travel with the others, but followed a few minutes behind, he didn't really get a good look at the corporal until we were up at the caves, miles away from anyone who might have come to the rescue."

"Peters might well have succeeded, too, if it wasn't for Master Damien," Deirdre interjected.

"I only distracted him long enough for Laughlan to crack him a good one over the head with a rock," Damien pleaded modestly. "And a well-placed boot in the . . . er

. . . lower extremities finished the job, sending the corporal over a twenty-foot drop off a cliff."

"Guid bluidy lad," MacSorley growled. "The bastard's deid then?"

"As far as we know," Damien said quietly.

"What do you mean?" asked Aluinn sharply.

"It means, the last we saw of him, he was going off the side of the cliff. I took some men back up the mountain the next morning to collect the bodies and found Robert, exactly where we had laid him, but Peters was gone. From the amount of blood on the rocks and bush below where he landed, it looked as if he had been dragged off for an evening meal by mountain cats."

"You don't sound so sure."

"I don't like loose ends," Damien said. "It's the lawyer's instinct in me. There was a lot of brush growing down the side of the cliff. It isn't likely a man could have survived a drop like that, but it is possible. I've been out almost every day scouring the forest and nearby glens, but so far there hasn't been any trace of him. The whole camp and countryside has been alerted to watch out for him, so even if he did manage to walk away from a twenty-foot fall and a broken head, I doubt he could have gotten very far on his own. Nights have been colder than hell, lately, so you would expect if the cats didn't get him, the frost would."

"But you still have doubts."

Damien rubbed absently at a fading bruise on his neck. "I would just feel better if we had the body."

Aluinn had noticed the bruises and swellings on Damien's face—he almost hadn't recognized Catherine's brother in the first few seconds—and he took a closer look now, mentally picturing how bad they must have been two weeks ago.

"You're alright?"

"You're looking at the worst of it," Damien assured him. "Unfortunately, my reflexes were a few hairs too short to save either Hardy or Catherine."

Deirdre reached out and touched Aluinn's arm. "Tell him he mustn't blame himself for what happened. If he'd done nothing at all, we would all be dead."

Reading the guilt and recriminations in Damien's clouded blue eyes, Aluinn released his arm from around Deirdre's waist and walked over to where Damien stood.

"She's right: You have no reason to hold yourself to blame for anything. In fact, it sounds to me as if we have a great deal to thank you for."

Damien looked up, wondering if he was being handed a platitude, but saw only honest friendship and understanding in Aluinn's eyes.

"Besides," MacKail added with a wry twist, "there won't be enough guilt to go around once Alex collects it all onto his own shoulders."

"Alex? But he was fifty miles away when it happened."

The smoky gray eyes glanced toward the closed bedroom door. "You know that, and I know that . . ."

"You promised you would be back in a week," Catherine said lightly, hoping to break the silence that had taken hold of the room since Damien and Deirdre had vacated it. After the door had closed, Alex had walked over to the window and hadn't budged since, save to push the curtain aside and stare out over the bright afternoon landscape. "As I recall, you even waved your little knife around and—"

The indigo eyes traversed the distance from the window to the bed without warning, freezing the words at the back of her throat. His mouth was pressed into a grim, bloodless line, barely visible through the two week growth of luxuriant blue-black beard. There were other indications he had not wasted time in returning to Moy

Hall. There were thin black crescents of dirt crusted under his fingernails, his hair was lashed roughly into a queue at the nape of his neck and the bits that had escaped were dulled with grime. Her flush deepened proportionately with a wash of guilt and she felt mildly ashamed.

"Aren't you going to say anything to me?" she asked softly. "Aren't you even going to ask me what happened?"

"You foiled an attempt to kidnap the Prince, saved his life in the offing, and sent the king's army running for the hills . . . all singlehandedly, no doubt."

His sarcasm wounded her vanity and Catherine responded in kind. "It must be your influence, my lord. How else should the wife of the great Dark Cameron behave, but to follow her husband's example and try to take on the entire *world* singlehandedly?"

He raised an eyebrow as if in amusement, but she knew him well enough to brace herself for the counterthrust. She bit her lip and waited, wondering how the air could feel so sensually charged and at the same time so cruelly cold. He was obviously very angry—but whether the anger was directed at her, or at himself was difficult to discern.

"I did not deliberately go out looking for trouble," she said quietly. "And I did not deliberately stand in the path of a discharging gun so that I could win anyone's sympathy or admiration."

He took a moment longer to study the tousle of fine blonde silk that lay scattered about the pale, oval face before he dropped the corner of the curtain back across the harsh glare of daylight and slowly turned toward her.

"Very well." His words were clipped, measured. "What happened?"

"Will you sit down first?" she asked, patting the flat of her hand on the mattress beside her.

He took an even longer moment to follow the motion of her hand, to trace a path from the gathered ruff of lace at her wrist, up the fullness of the creamy-yellow lawn nightdress, and finally to give in to the lure of the wide, imploring violet eyes.

"I have been in the saddle nearly forty-eight hours straight—"

"I have seen and smelled worse," she said, patting the mattress again.

Alexander sighed. He debated the sanity of moving within range of the softly feminine body, but in the end, regarded it as a personal challenge and took up the mental gauntlet.

Catherine made room and smoothed the satin quilt as he grudgingly lowered himself onto the edge of the bed.

"Would you like a glass of wine, or ale? I can have someone fetch hot food and drink for you if you—"

Alex leaned forward suddenly, his hand curling around her neck, his mouth claiming hers with a forcefulness that was more reminiscent of an invasion than a kiss. She resisted the brutish intrusion for the span of a few sharp breaths, then just as she was on the verge of relenting, he broke away, leaving her more confused and unsettled than before.

"I thought I should do that," he said obliquely. "Just to get it out of my system. And now, if you don't mind, perhaps you can tell me why it is you always manage to get yourself into trouble the instant I turn my back?"

The tip of Catherine's tongue traced the moistened tenderness of her lips, trying to capture the lingering taste of him.

"Bloodlines?" she offered lamely.

Something flickered in the depths of the dark eyes, but it was brought swiftly and savagely under control behind a steel-edged stare. It was a stare that should have sent her cringing under the covers, but in fact, had the opposite effect. Her eyes held his without evasion, without conceding a single, solitary degree of defiance, and for what it cost her to maintain her composure, her return was twofold in seeing the glacier melt away from around his heart.

"Don't be angry with me," she whispered. "I'm sorry if I frightened you, or gave you cause to worry—"

"I lost ten years of my life running up those stairs—" he interrupted bluntly, "—only to find the three of you reading bad poetry and laughing like jaybirds. How was I supposed to react?"

"You were supposed to react exactly as you did: You were supposed to eject them from the room, take me in your arms, and tell me how proud you were of me and how brave you thought I was."

"I did all that? I must have missed it."

"I didn't," she whispered softly. "I know how to read your letters now, remember?"

For the first time since bursting into the room, the thick black lashes were lowered, as if to save himself from any further betrayals.

"Mind you, you did a very nice job startling Damien and Deirdre out of their skins. They're probably still running."

"I will apologize to them later," he said after a moment.

"Sweet merciful heavens, don't do that. You will lose all of your credibility as a tyrant and warlord, and I'll not be pampered an inch more than my life is worth."

Alex glanced up slowly from beneath his lashes. "It is worth a great deal to me, madam. You might do well to remember that in the future."

"I promise. No more rescuing of princes by moonlight."

His gaze fell to the faint outline of bandages on her shoulder. "Would you care to tell me what happened now?"

"Are you sufficiently calmed down?"

He closed his eyes briefly, a smile firmly in place when he opened them again and leaned forward to bestow the gentlest of kisses on her lips.

"Reasonably so," he said. "But don't test me just yet."

"Fair enough," she agreed, detecting the first true shiver of menace underlying his tone. She began relating the events as she remembered them happening, from the knock on the manor door, through Laughlan MacKintosh's urgent warning, to her confrontation with the Prince and his subsequent appearance in the front courtyard. She took him up the side of the mountain onto the moon-washed plateau, and she saw him share her surprise and shock at Jeffrey Peters' treachery, the horror of seeing Robert Hardy die, and the sensation of being kicked sharply in the shoulder as the second gun went off.

"It did not feel anything like I expected it to feel. More as if someone had punched, rather than shot me. But then I felt something warm and wet running down my arm and I knew. I saw the blood and . . . and that was really all I remember apart from a lot of confused images." And pain, she refrained from saying. Sheets of it, pyres of it; great burning conflagrations of pain centred on her shoulder and radiating into her arm and chest, even her legs. She had been semi-conscious through the endless, jostling ride back down the mountain. If Alex had aged ten years running up the stairs to her chamber, poor Damien had aged fifty, trying to get her down the mountain before she bled to death.

"Lady Anne sent for a doctor at once—by then the soldiers had turned around and were running back to Inverness—and I've been here—" she indicated the bedchamber with an airy wave of her hand "—ever since. Pampered shamelessly and loving every minute of it."

Alex caught her hand in his and raised it to his lips. "As soon as you are well enough to travel, you will have a castle full of people pampering you."

Catherine sank back into the nest of cushions. "The doctor says I mustn't exert myself too soon."

"The doctor says that, does he?"

"He says I'm lucky the bullet did not do more damage than it did, but it will still be some time before I can move it without . . . without a great deal of pain."

She looked sincere enough for him to believe she still suffered some discomfort, but far too plaintive for him not to smile.

"I'm sure Archibald will be only too happy to supervise your recovery."

"You want rid of me that badly, do you?" she grimaced.

"I don't want rid of you, at all—God knows what heights you will aspire to the next time I leave you alone —but the plain truth of it is, with the Prince's army in Inverness, Cumberland has no choice now but to come after us. I don't want you anywhere near here when it happens."

"When the time comes, my lord husband," she said quietly, drawing him forward, "I will leave only too willingly. Until then, however, can we not find some better way to spend our time together than arguing?"

Her breath was soft and warm against his skin, her tongue sweet and seductive as it flitted between his lips.

"I thought you were in dire pain?"

"I am. But it's not the dire pain in my shoulder that needs tending at the moment."

Struan MacSorley lingered at the main house only long enough to complete his personal duties and assure himself the *Camshroinaich Dubh* would not be requiring a bodyguard for the rest of the day and evening.

Back in the camp, Struan nodded, smiled, and exchanged greetings and news with those who rushed forward to meet him, all the while searching the crowd anxiously for a familiar shock of bright red hair. As soon as he could break away, he left his pony in the able hands of one of the young gillies and strode purposefully toward the tent he shared with his wife. The ache was urgent and pounding in his loins as he neared the low-slung canvas tent; his need was so great, he could almost taste the sweetness of her flesh on his tongue.

"Wife!" he roared, throwing back the flap of the canvas door. "By the Christ lass, have ye no' heard—"

He stopped, his grin temporarily held in abayence when he found the tent empty. There were signs she had been there recently—clothes strewn into the corners, a dirty mug beside the bed of crushed leaves and quilts, the tantalizing, musky scent of her skin.

A quick search into the neighbouring supply wagon deepened the frown of impatience and he planted his hands on his hips, scowling up at the brooding silence of the forest.

"A hell o' a time tae go f'ae a pee," he muttered under his breath. He paced to the edge of the camp, then back again, stopping when he heard a good-natured jibe behind him.

"Ahhh! Mac-a-Sorley! You look-a like you lose something!"

Struan cursed and turned, laughing heartily when he saw Count Giovanni Fanducci, his peacock-blue tricorn perched askew over the side of his head, being practically dragged under cover of canvas. His clothes were already half undone, his satin breeches were loosened and the grasping pink hand of Ringle-Eyed Rita was lewdly enticing him to leave go of the tent pole and join her inside.

"You wish-a to make the wager again, *Signore* Struan? Not how much whisky this-a time, but how much nectar?"

Ringle-Eyed Rita, her name derived from an affliction which sent her eyes rolling in opposite directions whenever she was caught in the throes of ecstasy, saved Struan the necessity of giving an answer. A second hand was thrust out of the door and into the satin breeches and, with a squawk that sounded like it had come from the throat of a dying chicken, the Count buckled forward and lost his grip on the wood support.

Struan, his loins tingling anew from the images roiling into his mind with the sight of the Count's twitching legs, set off in a thundering stride toward the edge of the forest. He prowled first along the common paths that led to the stream, then spread the search wider to include several smaller arteries. He was contemplating firing an angry shot or two into the gloomy silence to flush Lauren out from wherever she was tending her private needs, when he thought he saw a bold splash of crimson high above on the slope.

"What the devil is she dain up there?" he wondered aloud.

Not waiting for ghostly voices to provide any answers, he veered off the path and started climbing, moving stealthily, and still with some degree of good humour, as he envisioned the look on her face when he sprang up out of the bushes.

After a hundred yards or so, he unstrapped the heavy, clanking broadsword from around his waist, leaving it by a tree stump with the two pistols he wore slung on leather thongs around his neck. Fifty yards further up, he tossed his blue wool bonnet onto a juniper bush and divested himself of the thick and cumbersome leather jerkin he wore.

He halted again after a few more minutes of climbing and darting from bush to bush, a slow, dark frown replacing his smile when he realized she was not alone. There was a man with her—an old man to judge by the way he was bent over and leaning heavily against a thick, gnarled stick of oak. They were perhaps another hundred yards away, moving in the opposite direction, and Struan dropped all pretense of gamesmanship as he straightened to his full height and shouted Lauren's name to catch her attention.

Lauren stopped dead in her tracks, her face blanching white as chalk as she whirled around to locate the source of the shout. Rooted to the spot, she was unable to do more than gape down the hillside at her husband as he commanded her to stand fast while he tramped the rest of the way up through the tangle of junipers and leafless saplings to join her. Beside her, she heard a shuffle of tartan and a distinctive click of metal as Jeffrey Peters cocked the hammer of his steel-butted pistol.

"Dinna be a bluidy fool," she hissed. "Ye fire that bluidy thing, ye'll have the whole glen alive an' up here on the run."

"Then you had best think of something real quick," he snarled. "Because it isn't just my throat he'll be going after, Mrs. MacSorley—or have you forgotten the part you played in all this?"

Lauren had not forgotten. Nor could she believe the thing she had dreaded most could possibly be about to happen!

After the plan to capture the Prince had failed, she had been set to cut her losses and make her way to Inverness before the government troops withdrew. She certainly did not want to linger about until Struan and the others returned, for as soon as the yellow-haired bitch recovered from her evening of adventure, Alasdair would undoubtedly whisk them all away to Achnacarry as intended. It was a shame sweet Catherine had not died outright; equally unfortunate she had not miscarried and bled to death on the side of the mountain!

Fully convinced it had been the other *Sassenach*, Damien Ashbrooke who had accosted her in the woods, Lauren had genuinely been shocked to hear the real culprit identified. She had been even more shocked when, the evening after the botched kidnapping attempt, she had found the broken and bleeding Jeffrey Peters waiting for her in the small cave she had painstakingly provisioned for herself when they had first arrived in the glen. How he had managed to crawl down the mountainside, she would never know. He had badly wrenched an ankle in the fall, broken three ribs, and his skin was crusted with blood from so many cuts and contusions, it looked as if he had run through a hail of broken glass.

Faced with the very real possibility he could be caught and forced to talk, Lauren had found herself with two choices. She could kill him herself and be a heroine in the eyes of the men who were scouring the woods and glens hourly. Or she could nurse him back to health and take him at his word when he promised to see her safely back into the hands of Major Garner.

One choice would leave her on her own, forcing her to make her way to Inverness and rely on the good will and protection of the *Sassenachs* to see she came to no harm. The troops in Inverness were under the command of the English, but they were still mainly Highlanders, recruited locally, and she would be in as much danger from their lunatic ideas of loyalty and betrayed honour as she was in Jacobite hands.

The second choice—to trust Peters—involved a greater immediate risk of being seen going back and forth into the forest, but it also gave her time to think, perhaps to arrive at a third possibility where she would win everything and lose nothing. In the end, revenge for past injuries, the forty thousand pounds Garner promised for the *Camshroinaich Dubh*'s capture, and the gnawing, unresolved insult of the yellow-haired *Sassenach*'s continued good fortune were convincing reasons to stay, despite the risk.

In two weeks, Peters had already improved remarkably, venturing out on longer walks to build up the strength in his legs, wandering further and further from the sight of the concealed cave, yet never anywhere near the normal traffic areas frequented by the men and women in the camp. MacSorley must have stalked the woods like a panther for neither one of them to notice until he was practically on top of them! But by God, she was not about to fall apart now. Not after everything she had been through!

All of this passed through her mind in a split second. With Peters beside her, his finger tightening ominously on the trigger of his gun, she threw off her tartan shawl and started running down the slope.

"Struan!" she shrieked happily. "Struan, is it really you!"

"In the flesh, lass," he roared, catching her as she flung herself into his outstretched arms. He spun her around and around, laughing at her greedy eagerness as she kissed his lips, his cheeks, his throat, finally lashing her tongue into his mouth with such a feverish passion he temporarily forgot himself and returned her ardour thrust for thrust.

A squeal of feminine delight sent his hands down to cup the plumpness of her buttocks, pulling her against the swift and potent response rising in his loins. She tightened her arms around his shoulders and rubbed herself against him—breasts, belly, and thighs—gasping with a pleasure that was not entirely feigned.

"Struan," she moaned. "Struan, Struan, Struan . . . sweet Mither o' Christ, but, I missed ye."

"Missed me, eh?" His eyes narrowed and his teeth flashed through the golden bush of his beard. "Enough tae go walkin' in the woods wi' anither man?"

"Anither . . .?" She laughed heartily and clawed her fingers into his hair, savaging his mouth again before she answered. "He's naught but an' auld daft clootie lives in the caves wi' his sheep. Eighty years, if he's a day, ye randy bastard, an' so crippled wi' damp he canna straighten his back, na' never mind any ither part o' his body. I come here sometimes tae trade f'ae fresh cheese."

Struan tried to glance back over his shoulder but determined hands and lips kept his thoughts pinioned elsewhere.

"He's gaun by now," she whispered huskily. "Yer bellow near caused a rupture in his spleen—mines too, truth be known, but no' f'ae fear."

He swung around anyway, in spite of the wriggling invitation and the hot, moist lips sucking eagerly at his. Indeed, the old man was gone. Struan's keen eyes could just make out a smear of dark tartan well along up the slope, and . . . moving far too nimbly and hastily to be wrapped around the shoulders of an eighty-year-old reclusive shepherd!

The old clutch of suspicion returned without warning, combining evilly with shades of jealousy and unwanted, nagging doubt.

"Cheese, ye say?"

"Aye, husban'," she purred. "But I'll settle f'ae fresh cream . . . if ye have any tae spare."

MacSorley's frown eased into a thoughtful grin as he turned again, backing her up until she was crowded against a fat tree trunk.

"Mayhap I'd have a pint tae spare," he murmured, his hands reaching down to tug at her skirt. "Mayhap two or three."

"Oh . . . oh aye, Struan. Aye . . . but na' here. It's cold an' . . . an' the auld man mout come back. It's only a wee hap-step-an' lowp tae the camp, where it's warm an' there are blankets tae lie down on."

"Ye dinna need blankets, lass. I'll keep ye warm enough. As f'ae lyin' doon—" he inserted a hand between her thighs, his sudden roughness lifting her onto her tiptoes with a gasp. "I've never known ye tae balk at takin' yer pleasure where ye may. Ye did say ye missed me, did ye na?"

"Aye," she said on a forced smile. "Aye, Struan, o' course I missed ye."

"An' ye *have* been faithful tae me, have ye na?"

The amber eyes widened. "Course I have, Struan MacSorley! I tald ye, he were naught but a shepherd! An auld, bent-up shepherd!"

His face loomed closer and his hand curled deeper, the blunt, calloused fingers probing into her flesh like red hot irons. "If ye ever gie me cause tae think ye've gaun back tae yer whorin' ways, lass, ye'll wish ye stayed in Edinburgh, wi' yer *Sassenach* lover."

"Edinburgh!" she cried, recoiling from his cruelty. "Struan! What are ye talkin' about? Ye ken I didna take any lovers in Edinburgh! Especially no' a *Sassenach*!"

"Aye, there's the hell o' it, lass," he said evenly. "I dinna ken any such thing, I only have yer word on it. The night we were wed, ye bleated an' grated an' twisted yersel' intae rare knots tae please me, but when ye cried out yer pleasure, it wisna ma name ye were cryin'."

"Struan!" she gasped, hesitating the slightest fraction of a second too long. "It must be the Devil's work. On ma honour, ye're the only man I've taken tae ma bed since . . ." she searched her memory for a plausible name, knowing full well she had never presented herself to him as a virgin, knowing equally well he had not expected, nor particularly wanted one. In fact, one of the first times she had seen Struan MacSorley, he had been standing on the other side of some bushes, his tongue hanging down to his knees, watching her teach one of Lochiel's nephews a lesson in pleasure.

"Since?"

"Since ye fairst taught me the difference atween a boy an' a man, Struan. On ma honour, it's so."

"Ye shouldna fling yer honour about so carelessly, lass," he cautioned. "T'is a precious thing, tae be guarded wi' yer life."

"Then I'll swear it on ma life, Struan MacSorley," she declared vehemently, becoming almost desperate to squirm out from under the assault of the scraping fingers. "I'll swear it on anything else ye'd have me forfeit as well!"

Her sigh of relief was audible as he removed his hand from under her skirts. His gaze never left her face as he smiled lazily and reached for something sheathed in the belt at his waist.

"Life an' honour go hand in hand, wife. If ye're willin' tae swear one against the ither, an' if the auld dark gods dinna strike us both deid where we stan', then it'll be guid enough f'ae me, an' I'll never question ye again."

Lauren, still stunned by the sudden and unexpected violence as well as the very real fear of MacSorley's jealous rage, felt the press of cold steel in the palm of her hand. As soon as she recognized the shape of the dirk and understood what he wanted, the tension melted out of her spine like a rush of icy water. To a simple lummox like Struan MacSorley, an oath was all that was required to confirm her status in his eyes. He had frightened her half to death, chafed her raw with his suspicions over her activities the past two weeks, when all he needed and wanted was a little manly reassurance. If an oath was what he wanted, an oath was what he would get; the most heart-melting, teary-eyed oath she could produce.

With a shine already formed on the surface of the amber pools, she raised the dirk solemnly and pressed it to her lips.

"Struan MacSorley, I swear by all tha's—" she stopped, her gaze shooting back down to the carved ebony hilt of the knife she held. She had no control over the gasp that parted her lips, or the sinking sensation that drained the blood out of her face, leaving it a pale, gray mask.

The dirk was the same one she had used to silence Doobie Logan, all those months ago. She had last seen it sticking out from between his bony shoulderblades, the day Alasdair's *Sassenach* bride had been stolen from the gardens at Achnacarry Castle.

Logan had been a slimy, treacherous creature who had betrayed the clan's trust for a few miserable gold coins and a moment or two of self-glorification. After the deed had been done, Logan had swilled himself into a drunken stupor—his usual state of mind—and Lauren had feared a loosened tongue might spread stories both true and untrue to aim an accusing finger in her direction. Killing him had seemed to be her safest recourse, for who would suspect her involvement with scum like Logan? Who indeed would believe she could ever have befriended such a Judas, let alone conspired with him to have sweet Catherine delivered into Malcolm Campbell's hands?

Indeed, no one had. Not until now.

But if Struan had carried the knife with him all this time, it meant he had also carried his suspicions, hiding them well, waiting for the right moment to confront her.

Her eyes flicked past his shoulder, glancing in the direction Peters had taken. Struan unwittingly followed her gaze, breaking his concentration just long enough for Lauren to reverse her grip on the dirk and thrust it forward with all her might. At the last possible moment instinct brought one of his hands forward to deflect the aim and he felt the blade slice through his fingers, severing the tendons through to the bones. He managed to twist the blade up and away from its intended target even as his other hand shot up and closed around her wrist, squeezing it so tightly she screamed with the pain. A second hot flaring of agony cut the scream short, ending it on a harsh gasp of incredulity.

Slowly the tiger-eyes widened and she looked down—down to where the blade of the knife had punched through the fabric of her bodice just below her right breast. Little more than half the blade had penetrated, but as she watched, Struan leaned forward and she felt the cold, sharp slash of steel thrust deeper into the cavity of her chest.

"No," she gasped. "No, Struan, I—"

He pushed harder, giving the knife a savage twist as it pierced through the wildly beating muscle of her heart. The small red border marking the entry of the blade burst suddenly into a widening stain across her bodice, and he heard the ugly gurgle and hiss of blood rushing to flood the chest cavity.

"Struan!" Shock turned the amber of her eyes into gold flames. Her lips moved again, but there was no sound. Her jaw went slack and her hands went limp where they clutched at his arms. She slumped forward and Struan caught her, balancing her across his arm until he could lower her gently onto the ground.

"Why?" he asked in an agonized whisper. "Why, damn ye?"

Tears burned at the back of his throat as he straightened. Blood from his damaged fingers dripped steadily, forming a shallow red pool on the frozen ground.

"I could have made ye happy, lass. I could have given ye the love o' ten men, if ye'd only given me half the chance."

Cradling his hand against his chest, he turned and walked back down the mountain.

Chapter Twenty

Catherine's recovery was slow but steady, aided considerably by Alexander's constant attention. At the end of four weeks, there was little more to show for her escapade than a puckered red weal on her upper arm.

By contrast, the Prince's situation was deteriorating almost hourly. His health was restored, but his money was gone and he could no longer buy food or munitions for his army. In desperation, he was pressed to requisition corn and meal from the local farmers, stores and supplies from the well-stocked castles and estates surrounding Inverness. This endeared him to few of the local lairds, most of whom no longer believed the Prince's promises of payment could or would be honoured.

Following the peaceful occupation of Inverness, Charles Stuart's army suffered bad luck in cornering and running its adversaries to ground. In the north, Lord Loudoun was proving to be an irksome fox to hunt. After prudently withdrawing his troops from the city, the English earl had taken himself and his army across the Forth to Dornoch, confiscating all the available boats for his use. He found it childishly easy to evade the Prince's attempts to corner him: Each time, Charles dispatched men to march around the coastline in the hopes of winning a confrontation, the Earl would simply load his men into boats and row them to a safe inlet on the opposite shore.

Fort William, placed under siege by Lochiel and Keppoch, was holding out with the ridiculous ease both chiefs had predicted. The fort was well-manned and well-provisioned and any summons to surrender was met with effective cannonades and strident gunfire.

Lord George Murray, in the meantime, had marched south with seven hundred of his men into his own Atholl country where the Duke of Cumberland's troops were taking unopposed training exercises. In a single, co-ordinated assault, Lord George managed to surprise and recapture thirty Hanover positions, but before he could do much more than send the English troops running back toward Perth, the Prince commanded him to return at once to Inverness. Cumberland, it seemed, was on the move. He had hoped to keep Lord George occupied in Athol while he swung the main body of his army north through Aberdeen. The ruse worked, insofar as the government army advanced almost eighty miles along the coast without encountering any serious resistance—no real surprise, since Lord James Drummond had but a few hundred men to protect the Prince's flank. He did his best to hold his position at bridges, crossroads, and villages until the last possible moment, but in many cases, the rearguard of the Jacobite column was retreating from one end of the town, while Cumberland's forces were entering the other.

"Tomorrow morning?" Catherine said softly. "But that's—"

"That's giving us ten more hours together than if I strapped you onto the back of a horse and sent you on your way right now. And the only reason I'm *not* sending you right now, is because it's raining so hard out there, you'd drown before you'd gone a mile."

The anger in Alex's voice caused her to flinch and he cursed inwardly, going instantly to her side and taking her small, cold hands into his.

"Catherine . . . we both knew this would happen. It was your choice, remember, and your promise to leave without question, without argument, the instant I ordered it. Those were the terms you proposed and the terms you bargained for."

"Yes, but I didn't think the time would ever come," she admitted morosely, her violet eyes dark and threatening tears.

"Catherine—" he took her face between his hands and kissed her. "Please don't make this any harder than it is already. There is so much I want to say to you and so little time to say it."

Again his voice was rough with anger. Only two hours ago, the Council had been informed—shocked to hear more likely—that Cumberland's army was not encamped forty miles away at the River Spey, as O'Sullivan's inept scouts had previously reported. They were, in fact, already marching to occupy Nairn, a village less than ten miles from Inverness. The Council's immediate priorities included attempting to recall as many of their scattered forces as possible: The Frasers had returned to Lovat to try to raise more men; the Earl of Cromarty and his fifteen hundred clansmen were still playing cat and mouse with Lord Loudoun across the firth; many of the clans had sent their men home to plant their spring crops, knowing they had to do so now or face the prospect of their families starving, come the fall.

Alexander's first priority was strictly personal: to make the necessary arrangements for getting his wife safely to Achnacarry. With the situation in Inverness growing more critical by the hour, neither he nor Aluinn MacKail could be spared to escort their women themselves, but had instead cajoled, ordered, and finally threatened both Struan MacSorley and Damien Ashbrooke to undertake the urgent mission. One look into Alex's face had told Catherine how reluctant he was to have to entrust her safety into other hands, however capable and fearsomely adequate those calloused hands might be. And even though she was quaking with fears of her own, she knew she could not let Alex see them. Not now. Not when they both needed to know the other was strong enough to go on alone.

"*How can love be frightening?*" she had once asked Lady Maura Cameron.

"*When it consumes you. When it blinds you to all other considerations . . . then it can destroy as easily as it can save.*"

Catherine understood Maura's wisdom now. As strong and indomitable, as brash and fearless as Alexander was in all other respects, he possessed one glaring weakness: his love for her. It could very well blind him to his responsibilities, and it could very well destroy him if he was too preoccupied with her safety to worry about his own.

She *had* to be strong. Now, more than ever before, she had to prove herself worthy of the Cameron name. And she was, by God. She was no longer the frail and helpless Catherine Ashbrooke who had fainted dead away at her first sight of a Highlander. She was no longer the charming, delicate butterfly who had won the hearts of half the men in Derby by proving how utterly helpless she was in the face of all their masculine strengths.

Catherine Ashbrooke Cameron had done murder. She had committed treason and joined a rebellion against her king and country. She had been mauled and beaten, kidnapped and threatened; she had faced danger and flirted with death more times than she could recount, and, as a result of it all, she was strong, vibrant, and healthy, she was loved and wanted by a man who could still take the very breath away from her with a single glance.

Testing that theory, she looked up and their eyes met. A soft smile confirmed the insistent, delicately suggestive tremor that set itself into motion at the pit of her belly as she slid her arms up and around his broad shoulders.

"I refuse to be sad," she decided. "In fact, my lord, for the next . . . ten hours did you say? may we declare, that for the sake of expediency, all the usual warnings have been duly delivered and understood, freeing us to put our time and energies to better use?"

Alex bowed his head and planted a tender kiss on her upturned mouth. "Have you anything special in mind?"

"Special? As in *special* . . . or memorable?"

His tongue traced a thoughtful pattern across her lips, then flickered between them with a husky laugh. "Lady's choice."

She broke her mouth away and regarded him with a long, considering look.

"An intriguing offer," she murmured, "and with so many possibilities to choose from."

"Has your imagination finally run dry?" he challenged, bending his dark head to the crook of her throat. Locating the pulse beneath her ear, he began assailing it with a predator's instinct.

"Excuse me," she said firmly, pushing against the wall of his chest. "But you did say lady's choice."

"Then you had best choose quickly," he advised with a sardonic twist of a black brow. "Or lose your turn."

She moistened her lips, her body swamped with cravings, her senses giddy with conjecture. She forgot her fears, forgot everything but the roguishly gleaming eyes that were waiting for her to take up the challenge.

"A game," she declared breathlessly. "My rules."

"Name them."

"Only one: You are not to move until I tell you you may. Not one hair, not one eyelash."

"Interesting." Alex crossed his arms negligently over his chest. "And what do I win for my trouble?"

"Win?"

"Every game should extend some sort of incentive for winning, don't you agree?"

"Oh. Well, yes, but—"

"If I win," he said, narrowing his eyes boldly, "I want a prize."

"If you win," she countered evenly, "I shall climb up onto the roof of our tower at Achnacarry at nine o'clock every evening and stand there quite naked, thinking lewd and lascivious thoughts about you."

"Creative. And if you win?"

"If I win, I shall still climb up onto the roof every night at nine o'clock, but I shall think only the sweet, celibate thoughts of a virgin, and I shall do so swathed in wools and flannels and thick tartan underpinnings."

His grin spread slowly. "I like the first option better."

"Then I shouldn't move, if I were you," she said, reaching up to unlace the front of his shirt. She brushed the linen slowly back from the broad shoulders, her own blood not as cool as she pretended. Certainly not as cool as she needed to carry off a delicate performance.

Alex did not move. Not even when her nimble fingers unsnapped the buckle at his waist and sent his kilt pooling around his ankles. Not even when those same cool fingers skimmed down the bared plane of his belly and danced into the coarse nest of curling black hair at his groin.

His casual indifference compelled her to further boldness and she cradled the heaviness of his flesh in her hands, feeling it grow lighter and lighter under her ministrations as it was encouraged to stand on its own.

"I presume you took into account the one exception to your rule," he murmured blithely.

"A minor infringement. It is allowed."

Magnificently naked, he stood before her mute and still, although there was a distinct, throbbing tautness in every muscle and sinew of the tall, sculpted body. His long, rough-cut hair framed his face in black silk, his square, chiselled features reflected the gold and umber light from the fire. His skin seemed to drink in the warmth and, in exchange, intoxicate her with the heady, masculine scent of sunshine and heather. Such familiar territory these rugged planes and ridges, these bands of muscle and pelts of soft black hair. Yet, each time she saw him unclothed, or watched him walk from one side of the room to the other gloriously unmindful of his own nudity or the effect it had on her, she blushed as though she were an innocent bride. She was blushing now, hotly and furiously. More so, when she realized he was studying her and enjoying her predicament immensely.

"In a quandary as to what to do next?" he inquired solicitously.

Unaware she had been standing and staring for several unmoving seconds, she swallowed hard and backed off a pace. Her hands rose slowly and converged on the row of tiny seed pearl buttons that fastened the front of her robe. One by one, she slipped the satin loops until the bodice gaped open to the waist. There, she released the wide sash and unbound the folds of the skirt—a simple matter, next, to shrug the garment off her shoulders and banish it to the floor.

Beneath it, she wore a plain nightgown of fine muslin, full in the sleeves and delicately pleated from the top of the modest neckline to the high, gathered waist. A chaste gown by normal standards, it was rendered all but transparent as she stood in the glow of the fire.

A tic in Alexander's cheek shivered to life and he drew a slow, measured breath. "I would really prefer to do the next part myself," he chided, his voice provoking a moist shudder deep within her.

"I know, Sir Rogue. But you have had your own way, far too long."

She pulled the topmost ribbon at her throat, the ends trailing down and leading her fingers to the next in line. His eyes followed every move, still the predator's eyes, biding their time, although the gleam had intensified to the point where it seemed there were tiny blue flames burning at their core. His flesh stood bold and rigid against his belly, the skin stretched smooth and sleek, pulsing gently as a pearlized bead of impatience swelled into existence.

Catherine slipped the last bow free and turned back the opened edges of the bodice, pushing the muslin aside just enough to reveal the contoured vee of soft white flesh. She knew he was holding his breath, knew also that it was one of his favorite endeavours to trace tongue and lips and hands over the enticingly plump, ivory mounds. She impudently reminded him of this pleasure by running her fingertips down into the deep cleft and slowly back again, stroking the edges of muslin farther apart on each pass.

The teasing delay brought the dark eyes flickering back up to hers, the fire in them brighter, warning of imminent danger.

"Not one eyelash," she whispered, sliding the muslin aside.

The dark eyes flew downward again and this time the sensual lips parted on a soundless breath. Her nipples stood firm and proud, so tightly crinkled with expectation they seemed to be crying out to him to end the torment.

The nightdress went the way of the robe and, as if his agony was not yet complete, she tilted her head to one side and began drawing out the steel pins and fine filagreed combs binding her hair. The shining curls spilled over the sloping whiteness of her shoulders like a turbulent waterfall, catching the sheen of the firelight and dazzling his eyes from one spellbinding curve to the next. Desire raged in his blood; she could feel the force of it emanating from his body in waves. His hands had curled into fists, even his toes seemed to be clawing into the pile of the rug for added restraint.

Catherine reached for the decanter of brandy on the trestle table and splashed some into a dainty crystal goblet.

"I prefer mine without the glass," he said, his teeth flashing in a grin that was part wolfish, part bluster.

Catherine glanced over.

"I know that, too," she said cooly, effectively cutting the cocky smile off to a weak grin.

Dipping a finger in the brandy, she watched his reaction as she swirled the amber liquid around and around. She could tell by the sudden hardness in his jaw that he was anticipating her next move, and when the indigo eyes wavered toward the roseate peak of her breast, she smiled. Soaked in brandy, her finger touched the crown of her nipple, leaving a bright, warm droplet glistening on the nub. She smeared the drop, stroking it around and down into the seductive valley, her mouth forming a soft, sultry moue when the trail of brandy ran dry.

The dark eyes were so hooded now as to be almost closed, his tongue arrested in motion midway across his lower lip.

He took a slow, halting breath as her fingers drew a fresh, shimmering path up to the hollow of her throat, exhaling again with a husked groan as a glittering amber pendant was encouraged to trickle down the smooth flesh.

"You will pay dearly for this," he admonished silkily.

Catherine smiled and stepped forward. He did not have to follow the motion of her hand from the glass to his body to know where she was bound with her further devilment. Nor could he have moved if he had wanted to at that particular moment. The shock of feeling the heat of the brandy meet with the flames already searing his flesh stunned him to the very core.

"You see, my lord husband?" she murmured. "I remember all of your wicked lessons."

"I never taught you this one," he said on a clenched whisper.

"Perhaps not this particular adaptation," she conceded, lowering her gaze to the awesomely formidable evidence of his desire. "But you must admit, the results are admirable."

"Admirable, mmm?"

In a shriek of surprise and a swirl of scattered blonde hair, Catherine was swept up into his arms and carried to the bed. The brandy glass was snatched out of her hand as she was deposited on the satin counterpane and, without wasting time on ceremony or finesse, the contents were dribbled in a fiery stream from breasts to belly, then lower, streaking warm and wet into the triangle of pale gold curls.

"You moved," she gasped. "You lose."

The dark eyes scorned hers a brief moment before he bent his mouth to the gleaming valley between her breasts. His tongue chased greedily after the spreading runnels of brandy, licking it eagerly from her flesh, tracking down every last drop and vapour with a thoroughness that left Catherine dizzy and short of breath. He scaled the peaks of her nipples, suckling the sweetness from every ridge and wrinkle, then luring great mouthfuls of opulent flesh to a deeper warmth, exerting a determined suction that caused unending waves of pleasure to radiate through her body.

Smoothing his hand down to her hips and thighs, he ignored her half-hearted protests and sank his fingers into the dampened thatch of tight gold silk. Stroking the brandy deeper into the trembling folds of flesh, his forays were at first light and charitable, the thrusts gauged to match the timbre and rhythm of her quickening gasps. A second finger joined the first, introducing more brandy, more pressure, and Catherine's low-pitched whimpers turned sharply to gusts of raw pleasure. She tensed around each deep stroke, her hips rising and falling in the throes of a growing fever, her whole body wracked by one massive shudder after another. Only when her thrashings became almost frantic, and her nails threatened to tear ribbons of skin from his arms and shoulders, did the weight of his body shift between her thighs. He breached her hard and fast, thrusting himself into the shivering heat with a low and throaty groan.

Catherine stared up into his face, clutching to him with a gasp when she felt the driving shock of his need. She arched her head back into the linens and moaned again, harshly, for his hands were clamped so rigidly to her waist, she could not move to accommodate him, could do nothing but absorb the hard fullness of him and wait his pleasure. He was in no hurry. He refused to surrender to the pounding, primal urge to seek a swift and gratuitous release, refused to even acknowledge the possibility of yielding.

Reeling under the exquisite pressure, Catherine knew, suddenly, why he was waiting, holding back. She turned her head and tensed her body but without the challenge of his eyes to brace her, she could only cry out and cry out again, as the liquid fire of the brandy began to saturate her senses. The heat flared and spread until even the surface of her skin seemed to burn, and when he moved, testing her readiness, it was as if live nerve endings were being chafed with fire and ice. She rose up against him, fighting his efforts to restrict her, arching into his thrusts with a need that went beyond decency, beyond shame, beyond all vestiges of control.

Passion erupted in tiny, shimmering sparks in her eyes. She tightened around him, lashed herself around him, convulsing wildly, fiercely, joyously, and began sending shock upon shock of ravaging pleasure scorching through his body. Each spirited thrust brought an explosion of ecstasy, and as they moved faster and faster together, straining, stretching, arching, twisting in unbelievable joy, the tempest flung them to feverish new heights and sustained them there, their hands, mouths, and limbs fused in a bond of pure sensation.

In a blinding, mindless crush of rapture they clung together, their limbs and loins locked in wondrous desperation, denying the inevitability that they could ever again become two separate beings. Flushed, labouring for breath, they dissolved in a rush of molten heat, the movement of their bodies less frantic, but not yet willing to abandon the riveting little shudders that demanded the last of their reserves. Eventually, there were startled groans of laughter to mark the necessary release of hands clasped too tightly, shy whispers of slippery modesty as positions eased and shifted, limbs untwined, and bodies rolled damp and panting onto the cool coverlet.

"Christ Almighty, woman," he gasped after a few moments. "What was that?"

Her head lolled to the side and she gazed at him through tear-spiked lashes. "That was you cheating again, displaying your fine sense of fair play."

"*Buaidh no bas,*" he snorted through a grin.

"Meaning?"

"Victory or death. No room for surrender . . . or fair play."

Catherine smiled wistfully and curled up against his body. No, he was not a man given to surrendering . . . in matters of love or war. But with the one it did not matter if there was a clear winner or a clear loser; both parties benefited immeasurably from the other's stubbornness. In war, however, the rules were more clearly defined. Someone won, someone lost. The more stubborn the contenders, the more bloody the defeat.

Victory or death? Dear God, was there to be no other compromise?

Three rooms away, Aluinn MacKail and Deirdre were snuggled together before the blazing hearth, their hands laced together, their bodies huddled one against the other beneath a cozy quilt. They were putting the time they had left together to similar use; they were naked and flushed with the afterglow of their lovemaking, relaxed and pensive as they studied the leaping flames in the hearth.

"You think there will be a battle, then?" Deirdre asked, breaking the silence for the first time in many minutes.

"The Prince is determined. He says he is tired of tucking his tail between his legs and running away like a frightened puppy."

"What do you think?"

Aluinn sighed and twined his fingers tighter around hers as he lifted her hand and brushed it with his lips. "What do I think? I think I am one of the luckiest men alive at the moment. Good friends, good food, a beautiful wife curled on my lap like a kitten—" his mouth reached for hers and found it supple, willing, and pleasantly aggressive. "What more could a humble man ask for?"

"A cause he still believed in?" Deirdre suggested gently, her hand combing through the sand-coloured locks of his hair. Watching his smile fade, her heart throbbed painfully in her chest. She felt so close to him, in mind and spirit, that she could feel his pain and sadness no matter how hard he tried to conceal it behind smiles and off-handed bravado.

"We mustn't start any rash rumours here," he chided. "It wouldn't do for morale."

"But you no longer believe Charles Stuart can win, do you?"

He sighed and turned his gaze back to the fire. "To be honest, I haven't believed it since the day he led the army across the River Esk into England. Up until then, he had a chance. A damned good chance, too; all he had to do was listen to the wind and hear which way it was blowing."

Deirdre frowned and bit her lip. She loved this man with all her heart and soul, but sometimes he forgot she was just a gameskeeper's daughter who spoke and thought in plain terms.

"Which way is it blowing now?"

"Well . . . the Prince's purse is empty, and has been for weeks. He cannot pay his army, he cannot buy it food, he cannot replace guns and ammunition—of which he had precious little to begin with. Clans have had to forage for food and supplies, and some of the humblies have been without shirts, shoes or coats since the campaign began. Council meetings are hardly more than glorified verbal brawls; the chiefs cannot even agree among themselves anymore. The men are tired. Lord knows, they're half-starved with that imbecile Murray of Broughton in charge of provisions. Lochiel and Keppoch returned to camp today, after pressing their men into a forced march from Fort William. They were issued a biscuit each and a mug of sour ale and told it would have to suffice until stores could be replenished."

"I did not know things were so bad," Deirdre said, feeling guilty as she glanced over at the remains of the huge meal she had prepared for Aluinn. He had scarcely tasted the mutton or touched the boiled fowl, and had only forced himself to pick at the cheese and fresh baked bread at her insistence. "Why does he not end it? Can he not see his men are suffering, his cause is losing?"

"End it? You mean surrender? Charles Edward Stuart? He still thinks the French are on their way to assist him. He is convinced they will land in force, any day, despite the fact that the French ambassador got down on his knees and begged the Prince to retreat and use what few resources he has left to save himself. Even if he could be persuaded, though, where could we retreat to? The northern Highlands cannot support an army living off the land, there is nothing but rock and heather and miles of moorland. We cannot go south, we cannot go east or west without Cumberland snapping at our flanks."

"And if you stand and fight?"

Aluinn stared at the flames, watching two yellow fingers dart back and forth along the top of the burning log before colliding midway and bursting into a fountain of sparks.

"We're still short of men. MacPherson is on the way with eight hundred, but God knows where he is right now, or how long it will take him to get here. We've sent messengers after Fraser and his men to recall them; the same with Cromarty and his fifteen hundred fighters. At the moment, if pressed, we could muster about five thousand if we had to, but I suspect that is a very generous guess."

"How many men does Cumberland have?"

"Ahh, now that depends on whose report you would care to believe. O'Sullivan's man—he who still swears the English are trapped by floodwaters at the River Spey—numbers the Duke's forces around seven thousand. The report we received this evening suggests it is closer to ten."

"What has Lord George Murray recommended?" Deirdre asked, astonished by the disparities and the confusion.

Aluinn smiled wryly. "Lord George, with his usual aplomb, has recommended to O'Sullivan, that the next time he has a surgeon bleed him for migraines, he should present his jugular to the knife for more wide-spread relief."

"Oh dear, they are not squabbling again, are they?"

"Again? They've never stopped. And unfortunately, the Prince's desperation makes him more inclined to listen to O'Sullivan's cloying flattery than Lord George's bare facts. He's allowed himself to be convinced it was his military genius that took Inverness and Lord George's incompetence that lost us the advantage after Falkirk. He has also been pursuaded to relieve Lord George of his command and lead the army into battle himself."

Deirdre straightened in surprise. "But he cannot do that, can he? He has never actually led the men into a real battle before, has he?"

"Lord George has always given him a wing to command—usually somewhere in the second line, in the rear, well out of harm's way. But he is, in essence, the supreme commander. It is his army to command and lead."

"What will Lord George do?"

"He won't roll over and play dead, that's for sure. Not after he has brought us this far. And certainly not after he heard O'Sullivan's proposed choice of battlefields." Aluinn's hands moved restlessly beneath the quilt and he snorted derisively. "The stupid Irish bastard has the Prince believing the moor below Culloden is the ideal field on which to win victory and glory. Lord George rode out and took a look at it today and came back white as a ghost. It's flat and treeless—perfect for Cumberland's artillery, among other things. The alternative Lord George has suggested—has pleaded for, in fact—is a glen just this side of Nairn, where the land is gorged and hilly, broken by swamp and bogland—ideally suited to the way our men fight, and with ample protection from the bloody artillery."

"The second choice sounds more logical by far, even to me," Deirdre said. "And I know as much about soldiering as I do about . . . flying. Why is the Prince being so obstinate?"

Aluinn averted his gaze from the fire and studied his wife's solemn, heart-shaped face. He hadn't realized how much he had been rambling on, and quite frankly did not want to continue. He was suddenly very much aware of Deirdre's naked bottom resting on his lap, and of the small, but perfectly shaped breasts peeping over the edge of the crumpled quilt.

"Because," he murmured, nudging aside the quilt to caress the velvety soft cap of her nipple, "if the Prince is here, occupying the high ground above Nairn, and Cumberland is here—" he traced an imaginary line from the plumpness of her breast up into the seductive little hollow at the base of her throat. "In theory, Cumberland could easily split his forces, sending half to keep the Prince's army preoccupied here—" he retraced his line to her nipple "—while the other half—" his finger touched the hollow again and began a slow descent downward, bypassing the swell of her breast to follow the deep cleft down beneath the quilt "—could march right past him and take Inverness."

"I see," she whispered, her eyes widening as his fingers probed the spot designated as his hypothetical Inverness. "And he would not be able to do so if the Prince's army stands at Culloden?"

"Culloden," he mused, his fingers rising again and trailing a slow circle around the delicate indent of her navel, "lies directly in the way of any army marching upon Inverness. Cumberland would have to take the moor first, or, if it looked as if he might be successful, we would have the option of falling back to Inverness, in which case, it would then depend upon how much resistance he encountered . . . and if Inverness was willing to be occupied."

Deirdre's soft brown eyes were glowing as she adjusted her position slightly to allow easier access to the invading army.

"I do not know about your Inverness," she murmured against his lips, "but mine is downright anxious to be occupied."

Aluinn's free hand moved up into the froth of glossy chestnut curls at the nape of her neck, holding her fast while his mouth earnestly accepted the capitulation.

Chapter Twenty-One

Despite the presence of twenty heavily-armed clansmen who looked as though they chewed trees for amusement, and despite the presence of Deirdre, Damien, and the surly familiarity of Struan MacSorley, a cold and deplorably lonely sense of isolation had settled heavily upon Catherine's shoulders since leaving Moy Hall at dawn. Alex and Aluinn had escorted their wives as far as the junction of the military roads outside of Inverness. In stark contrast to the cheerful displays of bravado fronted by all parties, Catherine's heart had remained lodged firmly in her throat; Deirdre had hardly spoken two words all morning.

MacSorley was not happy at having been assigned the duty of escorting the women to Achnacarry. He could smell a battle brewing and had five weeks of stored-up anger and frustration that needed venting. Lauren's betrayal and treachery had struck him hard; her death had been necessary and justified, but as the days passed into weeks, he shifted the blame for her actions squarely onto the shoulders of the English bastards, who had obviously corrupted her with visions of wealth and luxury. Struan had no intentions of obeying Alexander Cameron's orders to remain at Achnacarry after delivering his charges safely. His one good hand and sword arm were still worth ten of any other men, and he had a deal of vengeance to wreak upon his enemy.

Physically, only Struan's left hand bore the ugly reminders of what had transpired at Moy Hall. Archibald had mended the outer layers of skin as best he could, but the tendons had all been severed and consequently, as the fingers healed, they curled into a stiff, frozen claw. To compensate for the loss of articulation, he had fashioned a rigid leather gauntlet that fit snugly over the hand, wrist and forearm, turning the damaged limb into a fearsome club. The back of the glove was studded with inch-long metal spikes that could rake away a man's face with a single, vicious swipe—not that anyone had dared aggravate him to the point of testing it.

Damien Ashbrooke was also less than thrilled to be on the road to Lochaber. He had argued for two solid hours against his banishment, but Alex, as usual, had had the final word. Damien would be of more use at Achnacarry, he had been told, especially since it was a foregone conclusion that Struan MacSorley would be returning and, undoubtedly, bringing most of the castle guards with him. Furthermore, if there was a battle and if the English gained the ground, the rebel army would most likely fall back along the shores of Loch Ness, and it would be prudent to have someone positioned at their backs to warn of any threat from the south.

Dawn had arrived drenched in mist and rain, and the morning had not seen much improvement. The ground was slippery with mud, the air pungent with damp and woodmusk. MacSorley rode in the lead like a drowned, shaggy bear, his hair glued to his face in wet shanks, his breath steaming out in vapourous curses to convey each order and observation. The mist distorted heights and distances, gave shadows movement, and colours a disturbing lack of density. Frequent halts were called in order for scouts to ride ahead to ensure against any unpleasant surprises on the road, although for the entire morning, they had not seen another living soul.

Had they been able to imitate the gold-breasted eagles which often soared by overhead, Achnacarry was less than forty miles along the chasm of the Great Glen. Without wings, however, they were forced to follow the rough trails and tracts that snaked up, down, along and around the rolling hills and dark forests flanking Loch Ness, and they would end up travelling closer to sixty.

The loch itself was deep and cold. At times, the black water lapped against the horses' hooves as they descended a steep turn in the trail; at others, it loomed stygian blue, dozens of feet below a sheer, razor-backed fall of rock. On such a dreary day, there were patches of mist floating out across the surface of the water on which ghostly galleons seemed to echo with the eerie laughter of their phantom crews. Wet and thick, the mist never lifted out of the hollows and thickets. Passing through a bank of fog was like passing through a curtain of fine rain, after which a myriad of tiny droplets clung to clothes and skin in a layer of glistening dew.

Catherine took no notice of the rain, the mist, or the breathtaking scenery. She and Deirdre rode side by side in silence, alone with their private thoughts and miseries.

It was late afternoon when Catherine's sides began to cramp from the long hours in the saddle. While Struan sent out his scouts, Damien helped the girls dismount, his concern for his sister's delicate condition breaking through his own brooding lethargy.

"How are you feeling?" he asked, noting how gratefully she clung to his arm for support. "Are you alright?"

"No. I am not at all well. I should not be travelling in my condition, nevermind on horseback and in the abominable cold."

Damien glanced at Deirdre—whose face remained carefully blank—before scowling back at Catherine. "You are as healthy as a mule, young lady, and just as singular in character. I am no more pleased at being here than you are, but since I am, I intend to see you safely to Achnacarry if it is the last thing I do."

The slump disappeared magically from Catherine's shoulders and she squared off before her brother, her eyes threatening mutiny. "I shall inform Harriet of how hateful you have become in the past few months. A veritable tyrant. I shall also advise her to seek a divorce with all due haste."

"You do that," he agreed dryly. "I have no doubt you, of all people, can be very convincing when it comes to counselling marriages."

The defiant gleam persisted for a moment then was lost to a deep sigh. "I'm sorry. You must miss her terribly."

Damien's gaze drifted south as if he could see through the impeding barrier of mountains and endless miles. "I do," he murmured. "It was a wretched thing I did, leaving her alone like that, yet she was so wonderful about it. She knew it was tearing me apart to just stand by and do nothing while so many others were willing to risk everything they had."

"Well, you needn't feel deprived any longer," Catherine insisted. "Not after singlehandedly saving Charles Stuart's life. Lately, though, I find myself almost wishing you had failed. Perhaps, if the Prince had died that night, the rebellion might have died with him. The clans would have gone peacefully home, their pride intact, their honour upheld. Alex would have taken me home to Achnacarry; you would be back with Harriet right now. We all could have resumed normal lives."

Damien regarded her strangely for a moment, noting the use of the words home and Achnacarry said in conjunction with Alexander Cameron. He smiled his old secret smile, the one he reserved specially for Catherine, and took her gloved hands into his.

"Alex has made you happy, hasn't he Kitty? I mean . . . you don't still hold it against me that I more or less tricked you into accompanying him to Scotland all those months ago?"

"It was cowardly and low of you not to confess your involvement with the Jacobites," she protested. "Even worse, that you did not trust me enough to confide."

"I'm sorry. I just did not know how you would react. You were, after all, engaged to Hamilton Garner, and had just suffered the indignity of watching him bested in a duel."

Catherine chewed thoughfully on her lower lip. "Actually, if we are making a clean breast of things, brother dear, I suppose it is only honourable that I make a minor confession of my own. Hamilton and I were never actually engaged. He never *actually* proposed to me—although I am sure he would have, given the proper incentive."

Damien's blue eyes crinkled at the corners. "Which you sought to provide by flirting with Alexander Cameron?"

"I did not know he was Alexander Cameron, did I? Or that either one of them would display such a poor sense of humour."

Damien shook his head. "For a girl who had no idea she was playing with fire, you have managed to come through all this relatively unscathed."

"On the contrary, I have come out of it very scathed," she objected, fidgeting absently with the huge amethyst ring she wore over her gloved finger. "You need only look at me to see the proof. Here I am, standing on a road in the middle of nowhere, several hundred miles from civilized society, in the midst of a raging rebellion. I am better than four months pregnant, wed to an enemy of the crown. I am scarred with bullet holes, wanted for the murder of an English officer . . . How much more scathed could I become."

"Anyone else reciting such an enviable litany could have easily become harsh and cynical. You could have become hard and ugly and unforgiving—" he raised her hand to his lips and smiled again. "Instead, you've become softer and more beautiful than any other woman I know—with the obvious exception of my own lovely wife, of course."

"Of course," she demurred.

"You've blossomed into a woman, a wife, a mother. You make my own paltry efforts at growing up and accepting responsibility seem pale by comparison."

"Damien—you are a lawyer, not a soldier. You excel in fighting your enemies with words, not swords. You will be important to Scotland after this rebellion is over to help pick up the pieces and make the country strong again. Soldiers certainly don't know how to make laws and run governments fairly. Cromwell tried and failed miserably. So did Caesar and . . . and . . . "

Laughing, Damien pulled her abruptly into his arms for a huge, affectionate bear-hug. "Is this what it has come down to—my little sister lecturing me on history and politics?"

"By the same logic, you would dare to lecture me on motherhood," she retorted.

"Ahh, Kitty. Don't ever change." His voice had grown softer and he was still holding her close, but his gaze was fixed on Struan MacSorley. The Highlander stood a dozen paces away, frozen into a pillar of stone. His head was cocked to one side and he seemed to be sniffing the wind like a wild forest animal scenting danger.

Damien scanned the silent ring of trees but could see nothing amiss. They had stopped in one of the few barren patches of grass and rock that bordered the red sandstone road. Ahead and behind was forest, to the left the silvered sheen of Loch Ness was reflecting the slate gray sky.

Leaving his sister with Deirdre, Damien strolled casually over to where Struan was standing.

"What is it? Do you see something?"

MacSorley held up his gloved hand, unsure himself as to exactly what had raised the cold crawl of flesh along his spine. When he finally did answer, it was in a low growl, his expression as calm as if they were discussing the weather.

"Mayhap ye should take the lassies intae the wood ahind us. Slow like. An' keep them talkin' as if they hadn't a care in the world."

"Are you expecting trouble?"

"Take the lassies intae the trees. Take the ponies as well, an' if there is trouble—"

The sharp retort of a musket cracked the silence, abruptly ending whatever advice Struan was about to deliver. Almost at the same time, two of the three scouts MacSorley had dispatched forward on the road returned at a gallop, their tartans flying, their shouts raising an alarm above the pounding beat of the horses hooves.

"*Sassenachs!*" they screamed. There was more, shouted in Gaelic, but the clansmen were already in motion, shrugging off their easy stances and drawing their weapons even as Struan roared to draw their attention to the ring of scarlet-clad soldiers swelling to the edge of the forest.

Damien ran back to where Catherine and Deirdre stood, reaching their side just as a volley of gunfire erupted from the border of trees. Musketballs stung the air like a swarm of bees, thudding into the bark of trees, spitting into knolls of sand and grass. Responding to Damien's shout, the women threw themselves flat on the ground and crawled frantically for the protection of a large cairn of rocks.

The answering volley of gunfire from the Cameron clansmen sent a hot wave of acrid smoke into the misty air. Following Highland tradition, they threw the spent weapons aside, and drew their broadswords, rushing the line of soldiers before they could reload and redirect a second volley. MacSorley streaked across the narrow clearing and threw himself into the line of militiamen, scattering them like a row of scarlet pins. With an enraged bellow, he slashed his broadsword across the throat of one startled soldier, the force of the stroke carrying it through to the chest of the man who stood alongside.

Huddled behind the rocks, Deirdre and Catherine watched in shock as swords bit into flesh and hacked at bone and sinew. Men were flung to the ground in a tangle of bloodied arms and legs, pistols were drawn and fired point blank into faces, chests, bellies and thighs, some crippling the enemy, some crippling the Highlanders.

Damien lunged into the fighting, his sabre dancing and flashing in the dull gray light. More shots were being fired from beyond the trees and he felt something hot and slick tear into his shoulder, but he kept charging, kept slashing at the encroaching wave of scarlet tunics. A searing bite of steel ripped through his thigh and he whirled to meet the threat, but MacSorley was there, his huge broadsword flashing down and across, slicing through tunic and belts, bone and muscle, all but severing the man clean through at the waist.

Damien grinned his thanks and shook off the annoying sting of his wounds as more soldiers poured out of the woods. The Camerons willingly braced themselves for the onslaught, screaming their age-old battle-cry as steel clanged resoundingly against steel. Damien ran forward with the others, blinded by the smoke and confusion, but eagerly throwing himself to the aid of a clansman who had drawn the attention of three soldiers. Before he could affect a rescue, a musketball ploughed through the

Highlander's chest, jerking him backwards off his feet, freeing all three of his attackers to hunt fresh game.

Turning on Damien, they drove him back across the road toward the steep drop into the loch. He felt a juddering blow to his lower body and knew he had been hit again. A bayonet was thrust at him from nowhere, and he felt the blade punch into his ribs. Two more slashes saw his cheek opened to the bone; his sabre was torn from his fingers and sent twisting away in a graceful, silver spiral. One of the soldiers crowded in for the kill and, cursing his persistence, Damien reached for the pistol he wore tucked into his waist.

Deirdre, risking a peek above the jagged edge of the cairn, screamed as a militiaman grabbed a fistful of hair and cloak and dragged her out into the open. He drew back his sword, his ugly face splitting into a grin, and was about to strike when Catherine launched herself at his back with a scream of fury. Her weight was sufficient to throw the aim of his arm off before he could complete the fatal stroke, and in a rage, he spun around, his elbow catching Catherine squarely in the belly, sending her sprawling painfully onto the wet ground. With Deirdre flailing and kicking at the end of one long arm, he raised his sword again, taking aim on the tumbled spill of bright yellow hair at his feet.

Damien saw the sword beginning its slash downward and had just enough time to correct his aim, jerk back on the trigger, and see his shot tear away half the soldier's face.

Struan MacSorley was by Catherine's side in the next instant, kicking the twitching redcoat irreverently to one side as he dropped to his knee beside her, his hands as gentle as if he were handling a newborn babe.

"Are ye hairt, ma lady? Did the bastard hairt ye?"

Catherine clung to his arm, her eyes wide, her lungs gasping for breath as she sought to control the blazing shafts of pain in her abdomen.

"I'll . . . I'll be alright. Where is Deirdre?"

"Here. She's right here," MacSorley reached over, hauling the badly shaken Irish girl into the protective circle of his arm. "Are ye hairt, lass?"

"N-no. Just frightened."

"Aye, well, we're all that, are we na?" His grin belied the comment, and in the next breath, he was all business again, shouting for a head count among his men. The soldiers were fleeing back to the woods, but there was no way of knowing if they were in full retreat, or simply regrouping to launch another attack. Of his own men, almost half were dead or wounded.

"Christ, but, we've got tae get ye out o' here, lassies," MacSorley said, all too aware of their vulnerable position. Most of the horses had scattered in the eruption of noise and confusion; a few had remained, trembling and wall-eyed on the road, their fine senses rebelling against the scent of blood and death.

"I'll set the men after catchin' one or three o' the beasties," he declared, starting to push himself upright. Catherine's sharp cry stopped him. Her horrified stare sent his hand to his sword and his gaze to the nearby slope.

"Damien!" she cried, pushing out of Struan's restraining grasp. "Oh God . . . Damien!"

She ran to the small hillock of green and slate where Damien lay, his clothes torn and bloodied, his hand clawing into the grass. His face was turned to the side, his mouth gaped open and a long, glistening thread of pink-tinged spittle hung from his lip.

"Damien?" she whispered.

The soft blue eyes were wide and staring, but at the sound of her voice they flinched ever so slightly and rolled toward her.

"Oh thank God," she sobbed. "Thank God! Just lie still, Damien. Lie perfectly still and we'll help you."

The pale blue eyes flickered again. They managed to find hers, to hold steady for as long as it took the blood-smeared lips to form the faintest shadow of a smile. A sigh—the deepest, saddest sound Catherine had ever heard, rattled from the bleeding chest, taking with it the last glimmer of light from the glazing blue eyes.

"Oh no," she cried softly. "No, Damien. No!"

MacSorley thrust his hand beneath the collar of Damien's shirt, searching for signs of a pulse. The hand came away slowly and he shook his head in answer to Catherine's silent plea.

Her whole body tautened, and it took every last vestige of her strength to hold herself together. She was aware of the ground swaying unsteadily beneath her and the choked cry that brought Deirdre's hands shooting out to catch her as she pitched forward.

Deirdre's cry to MacSorley went unanswered, however. He was staring back over his shoulder at the low green verge of trees where an unbroken line of thirty, forty uniformed soldiers were crouching and taking aim at the battered circle of Highlanders.

"Dae ye believe it?" Archibald Cameron grumbled, spitting noisily into a clump of nearby gorse. "Callin' off a battle on account o' it's the bluidy bastard's bairthday."

Alex and Aluinn exchanged a private glance, both of them grateful for small mercies, regardless of the source. They had been on their way back from seeing Catherine and Deirdre out of Inverness, when a local farmer had inquired why they were not on Drummossie Moor with the rest of the Prince's army.

Lashing their horses almost to the point of ruin, they had arrived at Culloden House—the Prince's headquarters and now the main encampment for his army—shortly after eleven in the morning, only to have the report confirmed: The Prince had indeed ordered his army to gather on the barren sweep of plain near Culloden. He had assumed command of the army and, under no circumstances, would he appear hesitant about meeting his enemy in combat.

Fully prepared to engage Cumberland's troops, Charles Stuart had led his army onto the moor just after nine o'clock in the morning, their swords sharpened and gleaming, their kilts throwing splashes of vibrant colour against the sullen gray sky. To their right, lay a panorama of sprawling green glen and behind it, the hills of Cawdor, bare and treeless, splotched with wide patches of brown heather. To their left was the Firth and beyond it, the penninsula of the Black Isle; dotted in between were the ships of the Royal Navy standing silent guard over the exit to the open sea lanes. Crouched on the western horizon were the mountains that formed the Great Glen, their walls and peaks etched with late snow, their valleys and gorges black pits of mystery and superstition.

As Alexander and MacKail galloped up the slope flanking the position of the Jacobite army, it had been obvious that they were not the only ones who had failed to be informed of the impending battle. The opposite slopes of Drummossie were bare. Cumberland's army had not yet arrived to take up their positions.

Donald Cameron, on one of the few occasions in recent memory, had been barely able to retain the calm demeanor that had earned him the respectful title of 'Gentle Lochiel.' His men were exhausted after hurrying away from one bitter disappointment only to stand in the dismal rain and cold to face another. His brother and a senior officer had arrived on the battlefield four hours late, not even aware they had been called up for a battle, much less that they should have to scramble for equipment and excuses. Making matters worse, the Prince rode up and down the field, presenting a dazzling and heroic figure in his royal scarlet-and-blue tunic. Carrying a jewelled broadsword in one hand, and a leather *targe* studded with silver in the other, he had kept hurling insults at the invisible army lined up across the wide moor.

"Has naebody pointed out tae His Highness there's naebody wantin' tae play at war today?" Donald scowled irreverently.

"Ach, he's havin' a rare time, leave him tae it," Archibald replied, blithely avoiding the cold glare his comment earned.

But it had been true, as far as it went. The men were cheering and roaring ferociously each time their prince pranced by. Even Count Fanducci, in command of his puny battery of ten mismatched cannons, doffed his plumed tricorn and added his own colourful Italian praises to the bonnie young prince who sought to lead them into history.

By noon, however, the men were hoarse, their nerves stretched and ragged, and their energy waning under lowering temperatures and a steady, chilling drizzle. By three, it became apparent to even the most diehard individuals, that Cumberland's army had no intention of answering their challenge this day. Adding insult to injury, in honour of the occasion of his birthday on this 15th day of April, the Duke had generously ordered extra rations of meat, cheese and rum for his men, and relaxed his standing orders banning the presence of women in the camp. While the Highlanders were contemplating the mist and mud on the sodden field at Drummossie, the Duke of Cumberland was contemplating a very delightful set of bosoms seated beside him in the banquet hall of Balblair House in Nairn.

Hearing of the birthday celebrations, the clan chiefs ordered their men to stand down. Many of them, after waiting in the cold rain for more than nine hours, were too disgusted and too hungry to linger and wait for further orders. They spread out and foraged for what meat and bread they could find in local farms and villages, then sought the closest warm stack of hay on which to sleep.

Most of the soldiers returned to Culloden House, awaiting a formal dismissal from the hastily called war council. They were hungry and weary as well, however, and began drifting away when it became obvious the meeting would be long and heated.

"Hopefully, the cooler heads will prevail for once," Aluinn said, scratching his back against the rough stone facing of the stable wall. "If Lord George can just hold his temper and refrain from calling O'Sullivan an idiot—"

"O'Sullivan *is* an idiot," Alex countered, going over Shadow's coat for the third time with a handful of crushed hay. In his own silent way, he had apologized profusely for the way he had abused the stallion's loyalty and stamina earlier in the day. He had fed the proud beast his ration of oatcakes Aluinn had managed to scrounge in lieu of their own lunch or dinner, and had rewarded the enterprising Laughlan MacKintosh with a gold sovereign for stealing two apples from a farmer's cold cellar. Hardly king's fare, but the stallion seemed humbly grateful. He had almost refused the oatcakes, as if sensing he was taking his master's food.

Being only human, Alex was as cold and hungry as the rest of the men who were dragging themselves away from Culloden House to find food and a warm bed. More than food, he found himself craving one of his small black cigars, but a diligent search of his saddlebags produced nothing more than a fingerful of shredded tobacco.

Adding to his discomforts, he had a nagging ache in his temples, and a vague sense of disquiet about something he could not quite put his finger to.

"How far do you suppose they've gone?" Aluinn asked absently, kicking at a tuft of grass.

Alex shrugged and resumed currying Shadow. "If Struan has kept to the schedule, they should be near

Urquhart Castle by now, if not there already and bedded in for the night."

Aluinn studied the hard features of his companion through the late afternoon shadows. "Deirdre and Damien will both see she doesn't try to do too much, in spite of Struan's belligerence."

Alex's faint excuse for a smile was the only reply, and Aluinn sighed inwardly, wondering how he could possibly comfort Alex while his own emotions were in such turmoil. He was tired of playing the wandering nomad, weary of jousting at windmills. He wanted more evenings like the one he had spent last night with Deirdre—making love before a roaring fire, making plans for their future together. He wanted a home and children—God, but they would make beautiful children together—he wanted peace, and the grace and wisdom that came with old age. He wanted to reach back to his roots. A farm, perhaps. Something he could take pride in and call his own.

"Alex," he laughed softly, "I believe I may just have arrived at a portentous moment in my wastrel life."

"You don't appear to be the only one," Alex mused, his nod indicating the sudden flux of activity spilling from the front and rear doors of Culloden House.

Aluinn's smile was still intact as he turned and saw Lochiel rushing toward them.

"Lord George has finally convinced the Prince we mustna stand an' wait f'ae Cumberland tae attack, but take the offensive an' surprise his camp under cover o' darkness."

Alex straightened to attention. "Tonight?"

"Aye, brither," Donald said excitedly. "They'll be drunk wi' celebratin' an' their heids'll be wide as barn doors. We caught them at Preston an' we caught them at Falkirk. By Christ if we can catch them nappin' now, it'll be the end o' it once an' f'ae all."

"But the clans have dispersed," Aluinn pointed out cautiously. "We'll never be able to call them all together again by tonight. Furthermore, it's a ten-mile march over fields and marshes. Some of the men haven't eaten since dawn—"

"Aye, aye. I ken what ye're sayin' MacKail, but the truth o' it is, we either march tonight or we freeze our cockles on that bluidy moor in the mornin' again. It was all Lord George could do tae win this much o' a concession frae the Prince. We canna throw it away because a few bellies might be grumblin', an' a few tempers might be sour frae lack o' sleep. Besides, that bluidy Irishman stuck his nose in the air an' as much as said as how we Highlanders are only good until a crisis comes upon us, then we duck our heids an' plead f'ae retreat."

"That would do it," Aluinn remarked under his breath, and for his troubles, earned a scathing look from Lochiel's burning blue eyes.

"A man's honour is the one thing he canna simply lose an' find again at will. Once it's gaun, it's lost forever, an' the loss suffered by the sons an' the sons o' the sons. A man who would save his life over his honour is a man only God might take pity on."

"God and the Duke of Cumberland," Alex said grimly, throwing away the thatch of hay and reaching for Shadow's saddle. "May they both have pity on us tonight."

At that moment, William, Duke of Cumberland was pacing the creaking floorboards of the library at Balblair House, his hands clasped behind his back in a stance that made his belly more prominent than usual. His face was red above the white lace collar of his tunic. His wig was slightly over-powdered and had left a film of rice dust on the bullish shoulders. The eyes were dark and bulged like gull's eggs on either side of his nose, and the lips, hardly more than slashes on the rare occasion they indulged in a smile, were all but invisible as he threw his head back and laughed.

"Stood on the bloody moor all day long, you say? I'll warrant that played havoc with the kidneys, not to mention the tempers of our fine skirted warlords."

"Indeed, Your Grace." Hamilton Garner shared the Duke's humour. "Thankfully, the rain will cleanse away much of the stench before the morning."

The Duke harrumphed and wiped at a tear on his lashes. "I dare say it will. Was there something else, Major? You still have the look of the proverbial cat with feathers clinging to its lips."

"We are told the Prince himself was in command of the operation today, that he has relegated Lord George Murray to the task of commanding a minor regiment of Athollmen."

The Duke frowned and peered at Hamilton. "Are you absolutely certain? Why would he dismiss the only man who has managed to give us second thoughts?"

"Glory-seeking, perhaps?"

"Foolish move on his part, if it is. Superb advantage to us, however, and one I'll not refuse, you can be assured."

"We are nearly double their number, Your Grace. Our latest intelligence confirms they have between a quarter and a third of their total men dispersed on various operations throughout the Highlands."

"Numbers, or the lack of them, have never stopped them before, Major. As I recall, the odds were two to one at Prestonpans, and nearly three to one at Falkirk."

"They also used the element of surprise to their advantage."

"Yes, they seem to have an affinity for crawling through swamps in the middle of the night, appearing from nowhere, descending upon the unaware like ladies from hell."

"I have already ordered the sentries trebled and the passwords changed every hour on the half hour. They'll not come within five miles without us knowing it within minutes."

"Your initiative is commendable, Major. I like that in my officers," he added, with the barest suggestion of a smile. On the other hand, he was not fond of officers who were too clever, too ambitious, or too handsome; it made him more aware of his own inadequacies.

"Tell me, Major: How do you judge the character of the men in our army? Your honest opinion."

Wary of the verbal traps the Duke liked to bait, Hamilton chose his words carefully. "Our men are understandably nervous, Sire. Perhaps even a little anxious. They seem to have this unshakeable fear of the Highlanders, even though they have been drilled and re-drilled in new ways of countering the wild charges that have unnerved them in the past."

"An understandable fear, wouldn't you agree? I shouldn't like to see my comrades-in-arms have their limbs hacked from their bodies, or split on the blade of a broadsword. I'm told there are still some men who waken screaming, drowning in the sweat of the nightmares they have taken away from Preston and Falkirk." The Duke paused and pursed his lips thoughtfully. "You would think it would make for greater incentive, not greater misgivings. Perhaps we should hang a few of them for inspiration; a coward left hanging in full view makes for half a dozen stouter hearts in the ranks. I would not like to see my army running from the field, Major."

"Perhaps they simply require the proper motivation, Your Grace."

Cumberland looked over. "How so? Would you flog them *all* before they took to the field? Preventative discipline, what?"

"I do not believe we have to resort to anything quite so drastic, Sire," Hamilton said, reaching to an inside pocket of his scarlet frockcoat. "The fact is, something fell into our possession this afternoon which might allow the rebels themselves to provoke our men beyond any efforts we might undertake. May I?"

Cumberland waved a hand in assent as Garner produced two sheets of folded paper.

"This one—" he lifted the top sheet "—is a copy of Lord George Murray's battle orders. We intercepted two of their spies sent out this morning to scout the road between here and the moor. In essence, it reads:

> *It is His Royal Highness's positive orders that every person attach himself to some corps of the army, and remain with that corps night and day, until the battle and pursuit be finally over. This regards the Foot as well as the Horse. The order of battle is to be given to every general officer*—etcetera, etcetera, so on and so forth."

Cumberland accepted the offered document, scanning it briefly, noting the neatly slanted script, Lord George Murray's signature, and the date, April 14th.

"Standard orders, what of it?"

Garner offered a smile. "I took the liberty of engaging the somewhat dubious talents of one of our scriveners, and came up with . . . this, Your Grace."

Cumberland took the second sheet, scanning the contents as he had the first. It was written in the same bold script, signed by the same neat flourish, duplicating the original orders but for the addition of one small phrase.

"It is His Royal Highness's positive orders," Cumberland read aloud, "that every person attach himself to some corps of the army, and remain with that corps night and day, until the battle and pursuit be finally over, and—" he stopped and looked up at Hamilton Garner before continuing "*—and to give no quarter to the Elector's* *troops on any account whatsoever.* This regards the Foot as well as the Horse."

"I took the further liberty of showing the second document to Colonel John Campbell, of the Argyle militia," Hamilton said quietly.

"And?"

"The phrase *no quarter* seemed to trigger the desired effect. As you know, the Campbells, in particular, seem most eager to come face to face with certain of the opposing clans—most notably, the Camerons and MacDonalds. They have some sort of blood vendetta to settle, I gather, and would not hesitate to slaughter them to the last man if the opportunity presented itself."

"I see," said Cumberland, and he did. A common soldier reading these orders, already primed by stories and rumours of the terror a Highland fighter inflicted upon his enemies, would interpret them to mean no mercy, no leniency, even to those wounded honourably on the battlefield. The order, with its added phrase, condoned slaughter, and would lend credence to the belief that the rebels were not men at all, but bloody savages who offered live sacrifices to the druids and drank the blood of their slain enemies. It wasn't true of course, and there were many more stories centering around Charles Stuart's compassionate and honourable treatment toward the captured and the wounded . . . but a man walking into battle believing he will face only disgrace and defeat if he should throw down his sword, fights with far less conviction than a man who believes he faces certain slaughter.

"I have vowed to end this damned Jacobite curse once and for all," Cumberland muttered, almost to himself. "I have vowed to end it if it means killing every man, woman, and child in the process."

Hamilton Garner waited in silence for his commander's decision.

Cumberland looked at both copies of the order again. He took one and held the corner of it over a candle. The edge of the paper charred and curled in upon itself, then burst suddenly into flames that quickly devoured their way across the inked script until the words were consumed in a sheet of bright yellow and flickering orange. Cumberland dropped the burning document and waited until the fire had almost expired before crushing the ash to a smoky powder beneath the heel of his boot.

The second, forged copy he handed back to Hamilton Garner.

"I trust you will see this gets into the right hands, Major?"

The jade green eyes burned almost as brightly as the expired flame. "You may count on me, General. As always."

CULLODEN

Chapter Twenty-Two

Lord George Murray had started the men marching at eight o'clock, as soon as it was dark enough to move them out unobserved. He took his Athollmen in the lead, with Lochiel's Camerons by his side. Lord John Drummond and his contingents were in the centre of the column, the Prince and the Duke of Perth brought up the rear.

Colonel Anne Moy marched proudly at the head of a small party of MacKintoshes acting as guides over the rough tracts of moorland. As eager as they were to finally meet the English and defeat them on their own home land, the vanguard moved swiftly and silently through the deep basin of a glen—so swiftly, they had to call for frequent stops in order for the straggling rearguard to catch up.

The rain that had fallen all day had turned the paths and marshes into treacherously slippery mud traces. The men had to expend twice as much energy to travel half as far over rough weed-tangled ground. The columns slowed, the gap between the front and rear became almost half a mile and Lord George began to fear he would not have enough troops with him to launch any kind of an attack, nevermind the two-pronged pincer movement that gave them their best chance for success. Moreover, while the Prince's column was still dragging its way through the marsh, Lord George's forerunners were bringing back reports of unusual activity in Cumberland's camp. There were pickets and patrols marching the camp's perimeter—too many and too close to ever hope to surprise. Something, or someone, had already put them on the alert and to go ahead with the attack might mean walking into an ambush.

Lord George, conferring with chiefs and officers who rode with him, decided they had no option but to turn quickly and quietly back, before daylight arrived and caught them on the open marsh.

Charles Stuart could hardly believe his eyes when he saw the men from Lord George's column doubling back toward the coast road. He stood silhouetted against the rim of pale blue light that smeared the sky, saying nothing while O'Sullivan ranted and hurled accusations charging Lord George with everything from cowardice to outright betrayal.

It was all Alexander could do to keep himself from drawing his pistol and shooting the Irishman outright. As it was, it took the calmer, persuasive powers of Lochiel, Colonel Anne and The MacGillivray to convince Charles Stuart that Lord George had made the only sane decision. But the harm was done. Lord George, rigid with pride, angered that his loyalty and courage had been questioned openly before the staring ranks of men, strode back to Culloden in stony silence. The Prince, confused by the turn of events, was forced to accept yet another humiliation over which he had no control, and retreated behind a wall of sullen petulance and would speak to no one, least of all his chiefs and council members.

The men, exhausted by hunger and fatigue, staggered back to Culloden. Some wandered farther, into Inverness; some spread into the neighbouring farms. Almost a thousand collapsed on the sheltered parkland surrounding Culloden House, sleeping the sleep of the dead, too weary to think about their hunger, too weary to rouse themselves even when, a short time later, the message was delivered alerting them that Cumberland's army was on the road, less than two hours march away.

"Keep ye're heids doon, lassies," Struan warned, a fiery hazel eye touching on both Catherine and Deirdre, in turn. "We've come too far tae let the bastards take us now."

Catherine nodded, calmly moistening her lips and tightening the grip she had on the loaded pistol. Since the attack the previous afternoon, she had moved without thinking, obeyed without questioning any order or instruction. In return, she had won the unqualified admiration of Struan MacSorley—not given lightly under any circumstances.

"I don't know how he can see them or hear them," Deirdre whispered. "I don't know how he knows they're even out there. I have not seen or heard anything for hours."

"Struan has lived in mountains and forests all his life," Catherine reasoned. "It must be instinct . . . or some such thing."

Deirdre glanced sidelong at her former mistress, wondering how she could sound so calm and matter-of-fact. For the past twenty hours, MacSorley and the handful of men who had survived the ambush had led them on a twisted, convoluted retreat back over the mountains toward Inverness. Early in the chase, Deirdre had feared for Catherine's state of mind as well as her health—she had, after all, just seen her beloved brother killed before her eyes. Since then, she had been bounced and jostled along the treacherous paths in an attempt to elude their scarlet-clad pursuers, yet not once had the former debutante and socialite shown any sign of faltering or succumbing to the weakness Deirdre knew had to have invaded her every bone and fibre. Deirdre knew because she could feel it within herself—the cold, chilling terror of the unknown.

Catherine had not balked when Struan ordered them to conceal themselves in the foul-smelling lair of some wild mountain beast. She had blatantly refused to eat what meager foodstuffs they had salvaged from the knapsacks unless it be shared equally among them all. She had helped Deirdre with the wounded and relinquished her seat on one of the few horses they had managed to recapture, declaring she was perfectly able to walk while some of the severely wounded men could not.

It was because of the sheer strength and persistence of Catherine's courage that Deirdre was able to shore up her own. She also bolstered herself with the knowledge that when and if they ever made it back to Moy Hall alive, and when she was returned to Aluinn MacKail's side, she was never going to leave him again. Not *ever.* It was a promise she made herself in the mist-steeped blackness of the night and it was a promise she vowed to keep with all the stubbornness and determination of her Irish ancestors.

"There," Catherine hissed suddenly. "Up on those rocks. Something moved."

Deirdre squinted upward, the chilling rain making visibility a game of guesswork. MacSorley had taken advantage of the long night to push up and over the mountain and it had not seemed possible the English soldiers would have the courage or perseverence to follow so closely. Twice already, MacSorley had become annoyed with their diligence and had doubled back, demonstrating how, with the proper use of darkness, mist, and shadow, he could leave half a dozen bodies in his wake. But dawn had come upon them and so had the English, and with little more than a few minutes of sleep snatched against a niche of a rock, they were moving again, legs and arms and backs cramping in protest.

Struan had tried to suggest the women ride on ahead—Inverness was only a handful of miles along the road—but once again, Catherine had stubbornly refused to take the easy way out.

"We have come this far together, Mr. MacSorley," she had said with quiet determination. "We shall go the rest of the way together, or not at all."

"Ye dinna ken what ye're sayin', lassie."

"I *ken* very well," Catherine insisted. "You estimate there are forty soldiers following us, another forty or so circling around to cut us off somewhere up ahead. You have ten good men, including those not wounded too badly to prop a muket on their shoulders and pull the trigger. The way I see it, Deirdre and I can make ourselves count by loading those muskets and readying them for the men to fire."

"Ye ken what will happen tae ye if ye're caught?" he exclaimed.

"They killed my brother, Struan," she replied evenly. "They will kill you and me and all of us if they have the opportunity. But we're not going to give them the opportunity. We're Camerons, by God, and they're . . . they're only a pack of . . . of squint-eyed, *Sassenach* lobsterbacks."

MacSorley stared at her for a moment and then grinned. "Aye, lass. Aye, that they are."

Listening to their conversation, Deirdre was thoroughly convinced Catherine had lost her faculties.

But here they were, crouched in a dense copse of weed and tangled briar, wadding, shot, and powder laid out before them, guns clasped nervously in their hands. There was indeed movement up on the hillside; Deirdre saw splashes of crimson darting amongst the sparse trees—far too many of them for ten courageous Highlanders and two frightened women to deal with effectively. This could well be the end of it all.

"I love you Aluinn MacKail," she whispered soundlessly. "And I thank you with all my heart for loving me."

A roar, loud and bloodcurdling, split the air and sent the girls' hearts catapulting into their throats. Ahead of them on the path, they saw MacSorley leap up from the cover of the bushes, his arms raised and thrashing the air, his shaggy mane of hair whipping to and fro in his frenzy. One by one, the rest of Struan's men bounded out from under cover, unsheathing their swords and waving them overhead, spinning in a swirl of tartan, bending back their heads and shouting curses up the side of the mountain.

Deirdre gripped the pistol tightly between her clenched hands and gaped at the sight in total bewilderment. She was on the verge of screaming herself, when Catherine suddenly laughed and clutched at her arm.

"Look! Down there!"

In the basin of the glen, emerging from between two domes of green and brown-tinged rock was a column of tartan-clad Highlanders; scores of them, hundreds of them, marching out of the fog and mist behind their chief, Cluny of MacPherson.

Struan fetched one of the horses and thundered down the slope to intercept the startled party of MacPhersons. A few hastily exchanged sentences and an outthrust hand sent fully half the armed contingent streaming eagerly up the side of the slope. Catherine and Deirdre, hugging each other with relief, waited until the surge of roaring Highlanders swept past them before they descended, weary but happy, to join the welcomed troop of rebels.

As exhausted as they were, there was no desire on anyone's part to linger any longer in the glen than was necessary to see to the wounded men and settle them comfortably on horse-drawn litters. A sharp, easterly wind had begun to gust into the mouth of the valley, bringing sprays of icy sleet and driving rain.

It brought something else as well: the low, distant rumble of cannonfire.

William, Duke of Cumberland rode along the neatly formed lines of men, oblivious to the rain and wind at his back, his tricorn pulled well down over an ominous glower. His scarlet frockcoat was edged in thick bands of gold, the lapels faced in dark royal blue. Even his saddle housing was scarlet, heavily ornamented in gold tassels that flipped and danced as the animal stalked imperiously past the formed battalions. Cumberland's face below the brim of the tricorn was red and sullen, the eyes black and protruding as they inspected his army. Three months younger than Charles Stuart, he was decades older in experience, and no stranger to battlefields. His men respected and feared him, and there were few among them who doubted "Billy's" pledge to personally shoot the first man he saw turn and run from the field today.

On the government side, there were twelve battalions of infantry formed into square blocks of unbroken red. Five batteries of artillery commanded the centre and either flank, supported by eight companies of kilted militia from the glens of Argyle. In all, close to nine thousand government troops lined the gray and windswept moor below Culloden. They stood in units of military precision ten across and five deep, divided and squared into companies and platoons, each with their own flags and pennants fluttering forward in the wind. The men wore wide-skirted tunics and breeches of heavy scarlet wool, the coats cuffed and faced with the colours of their regiment, the breeches covered to mid-thigh with spatterdash gaiters of white or gray. Each man carried, as standard issue, a Brown Bess musket equipped with a bayonet of fluted steel sixteen inches long. Until the order was given to load and fire, the guns were held close to the body to shield the firing pins from the rain and sleet. Their heads, beneath the black beaver tricorns were held tautly upright by tight leather stocks which prevented them from looking in any direction but straight ahead.

What they saw, half a mile away across the rolling moor, was a writhing, turbulent sea of plaid and steel. What they felt, despite the fact they were well-rested, well-fed, and well-drilled in the methods of fighting and withstanding a Highland charge, was pure, unadulterated terror. More than one man suffered an acute shortage of confidence and turned to glance at his comrades on either side, hoping he was not alone in suffering tremors and fits of cold sweat. The depth of their fear angered them, enraged them, for it made them feel helpless even before any fighting had begun. Those who had been at Prestonpans and Falkirk knew all too well that the Highlanders were not the normal breed of soldier who quaked and fell back in the face of volley after volley of precision fire. Instead, the Scots had shown not only their willingness, but their eagerness to climb, fight, and crawl over their own dead to reach the line of arrogant redcoats, and once there, to inflict bloody, hellish slaughter with the greatest enthusiasm.

Drummers stood to the rear and flank of each battalion, their arms moving in a blur to beat courage into the spines of the waiting soldiers. Before each corps of drums was the standard-bearer, his square of embroidered silk snapping to and fro, colourfully emblazoned with the device of each batallion. There was a dragon for Howard's, a lion for Barrell's, a white horse for Wolfe's, a castle for Blakeney, a thistle for the Scots regiments. The latter, instead of the drag, roll, drag of the drums to encourage them, had two stout lines of pipers who were red-faced and sweating in their efforts to respond to the cacophony of wailed challenges railing at them from across the field.

Hamilton Garner, looking resplendent in his scarlet tunic and gold braid, rode before his assigned regiment of King's Horse, prancing up and down the line to fix each man in turn with a stare, defying any of them to repeat their cowardly performances of the past. His nostrils flared eagerly at the acrid scent of the slow burning fuses the nearby gunners held aloft, and his green eyes peered through the sheeting rain and haze at their target. The wind was driving straight into the faces of the

Highlanders, adding yet another misery to their host of misfortunes. The stupid bastards had to be exhausted, Garner exulted, what with waiting on the field all the previous day, then attempting an abortive night march only to have to drag themselves back onto the field again today.

His smile broadened.

"I hope you are there with them, Cameron. I hope you have the wit and luck to remain out of cannon range, however, because I want the pleasure of killing you myself."

Alexander Cameron turned his face to the side to avoid a gust of raw wind, cursing inwardly when he saw a dozen other men beside him doing the same thing. He was feeling the chill more than he cared to admit. Having barely snatched an hour of sleep before being wakened with the news that Cumberland was marching onto Drummossie Moor, he was irritable and his head felt as if it was stuffed with cotton wool. He was tired and hungry, and for the first time in many months, he cursed the absence of warm woolen breeches. The icy wind, it seemed, was determined to remind him he had spent the past fifteen years enjoying a more civilized and practical mode of battledress.

The moor itself offered little protection from the elements. A sea of grass in the summer, in the fall and winter months it was a bleak wasteland with nothing but a few bent, skeletal trees to break the howling breath of the north wind. Visible on the fringe of the distant slope to the north was Duncan Forbes' estate, Culloden, its parks and fields stretching from the firth to well beyond the moor. The estate supported three farms, the largest being Culwhiniac, where the enterprising owners had erected a stone enclosure eight hundred paces wide, one thousand in length. Alex was not comfortable about the Prince using the wall to protect their right flank, knowing that it gave Cumberland's gunners a range and position to sight upon. An even worse thought was that the English could send a regiment circling around to use the wall as cover while they fired into the backs of the advancing rebels.

Lord George Murray, bowing to Charles Stuart's insistence upon leading the battle himself, had assumed command of the right wing, clans consisting of his Athol Brigade, the Camerons, The Stewarts of Appin, and Lord Lovat's Frasers—about thirteen hundred men in all. The centre was under the command of Lord John Drummond, who rode proudly before the Edinburgh Regiment—the only front line unit with no clan ties—the Chisholms, the Farqharsons, and Lady MacKintosh's Clan Chattan. Colonel Anne was present on the field, dressed in a riding habit of tartan, a man's blue wool bonnet on her head. She rode before her clan on her huge, gray gelding, tears of pride in her eyes as she returned the smile of her tall and brave Colonel MacGillivray.

On the left wing, grumbling because they had dispersed to Inverness following the night march and had returned in answer to the Prince's summons too late to assume their traditional place of honour on the right, were the MacDonalds—Glengarry, Keppoch, and Clanranald. They were under the command of the Duke of Perth and were, because of the lie of the land, formed on an angle away from Cumberland's geometrically straight front lines, giving them almost three hundred extra yards of ground to cover when the order came to charge.

Each clan had its own piper, its own standards, flags, and proudly displayed shields and mottos. The moor throbbed with colour, bright and vivid, even though the sky was gray and seemed to press down upon them like a sodden blanket. The clansmen were restless, impatient to begin. They shouted jeers and insults at the stolid red mass across the field but there was no response to their baiting, no answer to their pipes aside from the steady staccato of battalion drums.

Lining the upper slopes and crowded along the road to Inverness were the townspeople and local farmers who had come to watch. Boys were playing truant from school to watch their fathers and older brothers whip the English in battle. Women gathered on the brae, chattering amongst themselves like excited magpies; even the beggars had come to watch the proceeds, hoping to loot the dead, whoever won or lost.

Great rousing cheers rose from all quarters whenever the Prince rode by. Few noticed that beneath all the bravado, his face was pale, his palms clammy, and his stomach tied in knots. It had seemed like such a brave and bold idea to lead his men into battle, to prove once and for all that he was worthy of their trust and respect. Only now, he wished he had Lord George's axe-like features by his side. Lord George could glare the enemy into shrivelling submission with one cold stare, could spur the men into glorious acts of courage with one wave of his broadsword.

Charles drew his light sabre and windmilled it over his head, scorning the thickening red wall of soldiers on the opposite side of the moor. He was gratified to hear the Highlanders' voices swell behind him and for a moment he forgot his apprehension as he enjoyed the sound of their approval.

One man, startled from an exhausted drowse, thought the roaring voices and the Prince's bright, waving sabre was the long-awaited signal for the battle to commence. He was the one regular gunner Count Giovanni Fanducci had managed to find and rouse from the death-like slumber most of his men had fallen into after the abortive trek during the night. They had dragged the heavy cannons back and forth through the marshes, expending almost superhuman effort to keep them from becoming mired in the knee-deep muck. Most of them had fallen asleep in the parks surrounding Culloden House and had not yet appeared on the field.

His feathers drooping over the rim of his tricorn, his satins flashing out from beneath the folds of a vast, multi-collared great coat, Count Fanducci had called upon his alternative gunners—men and boys who had watched enough drills to have some inkling of how the monsters worked. He had led his flock from one gun to the next, showing the men how to shore up the wheels with heather to prevent slippage on the wet grass. They had watched as he ladled black powder into each gun, packed it into the breech with a wooden plunger, then fed the three-pound iron shot into the snout. A dribble of powder was measured into the touch hole and, while the make-shift crews stood nervously by, Fanducci fixed the aim of each cannon with a quadrant, pronounced the efforts "*bene*", and moved off in a flurry of satin, wool, and Italian invectives to the next position.

The dozing gunner who had been left with the meager battery of three guns that divided the centre and left wing, was so bleary-eyed, it had taken all his concentration just to keep his smoldering linstock—the fuse soaked in saltpetre used to fire the cannons—out of the rain. He heard the roar of voices and jerked himself awake. He saw the Prince's sabre waving, saw the arm lowered in a grand sweeping motion, and, adding his own voice to the Gaelic roar around him, lowered the glowing fuse to the nearest cannon.

Catherine and Deirdre both knew there could be no mistaking the cause of the distant rolls of thunder. It was the sound of guns, firing steadily, volley upon volley until each echo blended into the next with the quaking impact of a volcano. Struan MacSorley, honouring his oath to Alexander to see to Catherine's safety, rode with them as far as Moy Hall, setting such a fast and furious pace across the fields that the girls were too weak and out of breath to protest when he left them unceremoniously at the door and streaked off like a demon toward the sound of the guns.

Lady Anne was not in residence, they were told. With complexions as pale and waxy as sheep tallow, the servants relayed the events of the past twenty-four hours—ending with the fact that only moments before Catherine and Deirdre had arrived back at Moy, the last of the clansmen who had been seeking food and respite had departed for the battlefield.

Aye, there was a battle underway. Five miles to the north-east, near as they could guess, on a moor adjacent to the Lord President's estates at Culloden. The cannons had been roaring steadily for nigh on half an hour. Nearly all the servants from the house and stables had gone to watch. Lady Anne was there . . .

Dizzy and weak in the knees, Catherine clung to Deirdre for support but would not leave the great hall either to change out of her wet clothes or to retire to a warm bedchamber. She sat by the fire, her eyes dark and haunted as she stared into the flames. Her hands were like ice, her feet and toes had no feeling left in them at all. She drank the hot broth someone pushed into her hands but there was no taste to it. She moved her arms and legs dutifully as Deirdre and another maid peeled away the soaked layers of her clothing and bundled her into a plain but warm woolen gown.

At one point she stood listening, uncaring of the cup she had dropped that crashed and shattered against the hearth. She ran to the front door and flung it open, straining now to hear and identify the cause of yet another shocking sound: the sound of absolute, deathly silence.

The battle lasted under an hour. Although the rebels had fired the first round of shot, neither their guns nor their gunners were an adequate match for Cumberland's disciplined artillery. The Prince, after unwittingly giving the signal to commence firing, retired to a position of safety behind the front lines, where he remained, so rattled by the swift and sudden eruption of violence all around him, that he neglected to issue the command to his generals to charge—not even when the Hanover artillery began pounding in deadly earnest—not even when the men in the front lines began screaming and dying, as shot after shot raked through their ranks.

Count Fanducci was like a wild man, running from gun to smoking gun in an attempt to keep the men swabbing, loading, ramming and firing, but Cumberland's aim was better, his Master of Ordnance more skilled and determined, and in less than nine minutes, the last Jacobite cannon was silenced.

The clans screamed for the order to charge, but Charles Stuart had moved again in search of the best vantage point and murderous time was wasted in locating him. If he was waiting, as it seemed, for Cumberland's infantry to attack, he was waiting in vain. The Hanover general was too canny a soldier to hasten his men forward while his guns were tearing the rebel ranks apart where they stood.

Lord George Murray, appalled by the disaster unfolding before him, did not wait for the Prince to give the order, but released his Athollmen on a cry of *claymore!* His men broke out of the line, only to find they were not the first; The MacKintoshes of Clan Chattan, being closest to the nest of now-silent artillery and having suffered the worst of the bloody cannonading, had broken away under MacGillivray's command and streamed across the moor only steps ahead of the Athol Brigade, the Camerons, and the Stewarts of Appin.

The charge was not the wild, bowel-clenching rush of bloodthirsty humanity it should have been. The MacDonalds, with the furthest to go to reach the enemy line, were the last to realize the Prince's order was taking too long in coming. With wind and hail and smoke from the enemy guns blinding them, the MacDonalds finally gave the order to charge, but by then Cumberland's seven regiments of front-line infantry—each consisting of four hundred men—had been ordered into position.

"*Make ready!*" the majors screamed, and in a wave, the first of four ranks went down on their right knees.

"*Pree-zent!*" Muskets snapped up to red-clad shoulders, right cheeks pressed close to wooden stocks, right eyes sighting along hammer to muzzle. As the first of the leaping, kilted clansmen came pouring through the smoke and haze . . .

"*Fire!*"

Donald Cameron of Lochiel, running at the head of his clan, felt a sheering hot wave of powder and shot slash through his men. A second wave, not of musket fire but of human agony, rippled through his contingent as men went down in a thrash of bloodied arms and legs. Donald's voice, already strained to the limit of its reach and power, altered in pitch as he felt the ground give way beneath him. Pain, unlike anything he had experienced before, flared throughout his body, stunning him so that he was not even aware of the second, added crush of agony as he sprawled broken and bloodied on the grass.

Behind him, Aluinn MacKail swerved to avoid the staggering, reeling mass of dying humanity and fell to his knees beside Lochiel.

"Go!" Donald screamed. "Go, f'ae the love o' God!"

Aluinn took a last, despairing look at the shattered mass of bone and torn flesh at the end of Lochiel's legs and launched himself furiously to his feet, firing both of his pistols as he ran, charging headlong into the red, unmoving wall of soldiers.

Cumberland's gunners, seeing the charge had begun, acted smoothly and calmly on the orders of their commander and changed from ball shot to paper cases containing powder, lead mini balls, nails and jagged scraps of iron—partridge shot, the English called it. After each volley, the Highlanders went down in waves, fathers stumbling over sons, brothers over brothers, their wounds more raw and terrible than could be envisioned in any nightmare.

Screaming their clan battle-cries, the Highlanders still drove forward, their broadswords, axes, scythes, and sometimes only fists waving in determined fury. With fifty yards still to go, Alexander was deafened by the roar of guns and musketfire, sickened by the screams and shouts of the men who fell and died on either side of him. A volley from Cumberland's centre line forced the men of Clan Chattan to veer to their right, and Alex found himself running alongside the equally tall, equally fearsome MacGillivray. Their combined force of men struck the government lines, the sheer impact of their rage causing Cumberland's ranks to break and fall back toward their second line of defence.

Alex hacked and slashed his way into the midst of the soldiers, his face, arms and legs becoming instantly splattered in bloody gore. On all sides, his men put forth a valiant effort, but no sooner had they carved their way through one phalanx of soldiers than another rushed forward to take its place. Moreover, it soon became appallingly evident that someone had reschooled the English soldiers in their methods of bracing themselves for a Highland charge. They no longer cringed from the sword-wielding Highlander directly in front of them, but angled their bayonets at the clansman attacking their comrade on the right. That Highlander would have his arm raised for the killing stroke, leaving his entire right side unprotected.

Alex, stunned to see how the simple change in stance and tactics was succeeding in obliterating the Highlander's power, tried to scream a warning to his men. Even as he shouted, however, Cumberland's second line was advancing, forming a deadly pocket around the Camerons, MacKintoshes, and Athollmen, trapping them in a fatal crossfire. The clansmen had no choice but to abandon the ground they had gained—and might have held, had the entire Jacobite front line charged simultaneously. Lord George Murray, his horse shot out from beneath him, hatless, wigless, covered with blood and filth, was one of the last to fall back, guarding the retreat of his men and somehow surviving the renewed and galling storm of fire from the closing ranks of the English.

Driven back, but too proud to retreat, his men stood and screamed curses, waving bloodied and broken swords in the empty air. They were shot down where they stood, and trampled underfoot as the columns of infantry advanced.

The Appin Stewarts lost nearly a hundred men in an enraged charge to win back their standard, captured by a group of infantry, and in the end, it was torn off the halberd and carried off the field wrapped securely around the waist of one of its staunchest defenders.

The ground over which the clans retreated was covered with the bodies of their dead and wounded. Among them, his sword still gripped tightly in his hands, was Donald Cameron, weeping openly as he dragged himself between the heaps of the slain in an attempt to locate any among them who still breathed. He was picked up and carried off the field by his brother, Dr. Archibald, and another clansman, who had had his hand severed from his wrist.

Far on the left flank, where a gust of wind had briefly pulled away the curtain of smoke, the crusty old curmudgeon, MacDonald of Keppoch saw that the remnants of their brave army were now in danger of being run down by the regiments of mounted dragoons Cumberland had just unleashed. Keppoch ordered his clan forward in a gallant effort to block the Duke's cavalry, but they were too few to stem the tide. Wounded twice by musketfire, the Chief of the MacDonalds continued to charge and fight until he was finally crushed beneath the churning hooves of the dragoons.

The rain and sleet had stopped, and with nothing to wash away the smoke, the air became a thick, sulphurous yellow. The moor itself appeared to be in motion as the wounded writhed and thrashed in agony. Here and there, where an injured man managed to crawl to one side or drag himself to his feet, he became easy game for the dragoons who rode him down and gleefully hacked him to pieces.

Lord George Murray, bleeding from half a dozen wounds, took advantage of the fact that Cumberland could use neither his artillery nor his infantry without risk to his own pursuing cavalry and organized the shattered clans into a defensive retreat along the road to Inverness. The Prince, disoriented and in shock over the carnage he had witnessed, rode among the men crying for their forgiveness. A bare-armed, blood-streaked clansman, responding to a sharp command from Lord George, seized the Prince's horse by the reins and led it off the field before its sobbing rider came to harm.

There were still sporadic pockets of action taking place on some parts of the moor, but the battle was over. The government soldiers, having been so recently terrified for their own lives, took out their revenge in a frenzy of bloodlust. They did not allow the Jacobites to withdraw peaceably with their wounded, but followed the express orders of their commanding officers to pursue and slaughter not only the fleeing rebels, but those who lay wounded and defenseless on the field.

Clansmen who could still stand and fight did so; a hundred or more spread themselves across the road, their swords raised toward off the advancing flood of dragoons. Alexander Cameron and The MacGillivray were among them, bloodied almost beyond recognition, but too maddened by rage and despair to worry if the blood was their own or belonged to their slain enemies.

The first wave of dragoons was repelled with shocking ferocity. They persisted, however, and, one by one, the Jacobites fell or were driven back. Wounded, cornered against a low stone wall and surrounded by a score of grinning redcoats, the fair-haired MacGillivray seized up the broken axle of one of the ammunition carts and managed to break the heads of seven of his attackers before they brought him down. Encouraged by their senior officer, the remaining cavalrymen proceeded to stab and mutilate the valiant captain of Clan Chattan, so bloodying themselves in the process they looked more like butchers than soldiers.

Alex, seeing what had happened to the brave MacGillivray, launched himself at the circle of dragoons, severing the head cleanly off the shoulders of the first man he encountered, then swinging his broadsword back to split into the chest of another.

Major Hamilton Garner was slow to recognize the bloodied and powder-blackened features of the sword-wielding madman who carved a swath into the ring of dragoons. Two more of his men lay writhing and limbless on the ground before Garner screamed the order for his men to put up their weapons and stand aside.

Alex whirled around, the hilt of his sword grasped in both crimson fists, his eyes black and wild with hatred. Sweat and blood streamed from his brow in torrents; he was cut and bleeding from his arms, legs, chest and back. His ears still rang with the insanity of battle, but Garner's shout had somehow penetrated the murderous rage and scratched along his spine like a shard of broken glass.

"Cameron . . . you bastard." Garner circled slowly, his sabre gleaming dully against the gray sky. "I told you we would meet again one day. I told you we would fight again . . . to the death this time."

The Major lunged suddenly, his sabre slashing in a blur. Alex deflected it to one side in a ringing shriek of steel, spinning with the lethal grace of a dancer to easily avoid a second deadly thrust.

"You haven't lost your touch, I see," Garner rasped pleased to find there was still enough fight left in his adversary to make for an interesting rematch.

"And you are still the same pompous, strutting peacock you were in Derby, Major," Alex snarled, wary of the nine dragoons who were fanning out behind their major and moving stealthily to encircle the two adversaries. "You have trained your animals well. Taking no chances on another loss, I see?"

"*No one touches this man!*" Garner screamed, stopping cold the action of the dragoons. "The bastard is all mine."

He launched a vicious attack, the strength and fury of it driving Alexander back more than a dozen broad paces The steel of their blades clashed sharply again and again and although he was holding his own, the muscles in Cameron's arms and legs were quivering visibly under the strain. Garner, on the other hand, was relatively fresh and vigorous, having neither soiled his snow-white gaiters nor bloodied his sword until the clans had been routed from the battlefield.

The jade-green eyes were keen enough to pick up the signs of fatigue in his enemy—the tremors in the taut bulging muscles, the brief shadows of distraction that clouded the focus of the dark gaze. Cameron was near the edge of his endurance, there was no question—no one could sustain such an intense outpouring of energy and concentration, regardless of how superbly conditioned he was. And yet, Garner knew that a cornered dog was also the wiliest and most dangerous; the will to survive could make it almost invincible.

The black eyes flickered again, lured away by the movement of the dragoons, and Hamilton's sword took advantage of the lapse to etch a deep ribbon of red across the whiteness of Alex's shirtfront. Before he could gloat over the strike, he felt a painfully sharp rebuttal slice unexpectedly through the wool of his breeches, and had to quickly refocus his attention to the defense. He lunged back before the blade could do much more than part the upper layer of flesh over his thigh, but his scream of rage was instinctive, and it brought one of the dragoons leaping forward, his sabre thrusting for the Highlander's heart.

Alex saw it coming and raised his arm to block the stroke. At any other time, he would have had speed and strength enough to parry the thrust with ease; as it was, it was incredible that he still had the ability to shake off his fatigue and react, nevermind that he could swing around and hack the flat of his blade against the dragoon's wrist, splintering the bones like kindling. Not before the soldier's blade had done its own damage, however. The tip of the military sabre had caught the flesh of Alex's forearm, gouging a deep furrow into muscle and sinew that ran the full length to his elbow.

The dragoon fell away screaming, cradling his shattered wrist and hand, and another ran forward to take his place, dying for his efforts, spitted on the end of Alex's sword like a stuck pig. Something hot slivered into Cameron's shoulder and he pivoted again, fighting the agony and the exhaustion as he gored the man who had cut him. His foot slipped on the blood-soaked grass, costing him several precious seconds and two more cuts to rib and thigh as the remaining dragoons closed the deadly circle. Staggering, he went down on one knee. His left arm was opened to the bone and useless, his body was a sheet of burning pain, but he struggled to his feet again, his lips drawn back in a snarl, his eyes flashing fire. He had the presence of mind to sense the moment the dragoons were about to rush him and he lunged first, an unholy roar carrying him forward with all the savagery of his Highland ancestry.

A second, fiendish roar caused the air to shrink in horror as a giant spectre of a man rose up out of the heather and hurled himself at the circle of dragoons like a grim reaper, his broadsword scything through arms and legs, cracking through spines and ribs before the startled soldiers even knew he was upon them. When they did, a horrifying image of a studded leather claw was the last sight two of them had, before most of their faces and throats were torn away.

Another pair also tasted a sample of Struan MacSorley's fury, finally limping away from the scene with broken or bleeding parts. With their numbers drastically and grotesquely reduced, the three remaining cavalrymen scrambled back down the slope toward their horses, scattering the already jittery beasts in all different directions. Struan ran the first dragoon to ground and sent him arching through the air in a fountain of blood. The second had his skull cleaved in two; the third had already thrown his sword down and was fumbling to reload his pistol, calling on every saint and martyr whose name he knew to protect him . . . but too few, too late. MacSorley snatched him up by the starched white band of his collar and lifted him to eye level. Putting all of his formidable power into the blow, he sent the clawed and studded fist forward, driving it with the force of a sledgehammer into the spreading yellow stain at the crux of the dragoon's thighs.

The scream reverberated down the slope and across the moor. The agony of it caused even the distant faces that were bent over their ghoulish work on the killing field to look up to where the giant Highlander stood silhouetted against the metallic gray sky.

Struan tossed the twitching, jerking body aside and retraced his steps up the slope to where Alexander Cameron lay face-down on the grass. Before he could do much more than assure himself the *Camshroinaich Dubh* was still breathing, he caught sight of the officer Alex had been fighting with dart out from behind an overturned peat cart, favouring a bleeding leg as he waved his arms and hailed a group of tartan-clad riders. Wheeling fully around, MacSorley narrowed his eyes against the distinctly carnivorous *caith ghairm* of the Clan Campbell.

Baring his teeth in a wolfish smile, Struan MacSorley threw his lion-maned head back and responded with the Cameron battle-cry. He leaped to his feet and braced himself to meet the first challenger as a score of kilted Argyle Campbells bore gleefully down on their centuries-old blood rivals.

Chapter Twenty-Three

"Defeated," Catherine whispered, the shock rippling through her body like an arctic wind. "The army routed? Scattered?"

Deirdre moved closer to her side and circled a trembling arm around Catherine's waist. They both stared at the ragged, bloody clansman who stood before them, unable, unwilling to believe the horror he was describing.

"Our husbands," Deirdre asked calmly. "Do you know what has become of our husbands?"

The man's head shook as if in the grips of a palsy. "I only ken what I saw," he sobbed. "Men . . . guid men . . . brave men . . . hundreds o' them, thou'sans mayhap . . . gaun. All gaun. Fled tae the woods, fled tae Inverness. Chased doon the roads an' o'er the muirs by the sojers. Cut tae pieces, they were. Run doon by horses, left by the wayside tae die a horrible death where they fell. An' nae just the lads," he added in a shocked, sickened whisper. "But any man, lassie, or child wha' happened across their murtherin' path."

"Oh dear God," Deirdre cried softly. "What of the wounded? What is being done to help the wounded?"

The clansman, Donald MacIntosh, looked at Deirdre with eyes as flat and dead as glass. "Nae help f'ae the wounded, lass. Horse sojers an' infantry both are takin' their pleasure killin' anyone wha' moves. Even them wha' throw doon their weepons an' surrender—I seen them kill't where they stood."

"Is no one doing anything to stop them?" Deirdre gasped, horrified.

"Only one could stop them be Cumberland, an' he be walkin' his horse slow an' easy roun the field, smilin' an' noddin' while his butchers dae their work."

"What can we do?" Catherine asked, speaking for the first time since the clansman had come pounding at the door, seeking refuge. "We must do something."

"There's naught ye can dae, lass," Donald MacIntosh insisted. "Mayhap when it's dark an' the frenzy's left them." He shook his head. "But no' now. They're makin' us pay the price f'ae Prestonpans an' Falkirk; f'ae the fear they felt on the muir this mornin'."

Compared to what she felt now Catherine realized she had never known real fear. She had known something was dreadfully wrong, had sensed it the moment she'd heard the sound of the guns. And when the clansman had begun relating the horrific details, she had visualized the battle as clearly as she had seen it, time and again, in her nightmare. It was true. It had all come true: the sea of blood, the hundreds of dead and dying men. And if that part of the nightmare had come to pass, then what of Alexander . . . the ring of soldiers . . . the raised swords . . .

"I must go to him," she said hollowly. "I must find out if he's . . . if he's hurt. If he needs help."

"Nae! Nae lass, dinna even think on it!" MacIntosh cried, turning to Deirdre for support. Instead, what he saw reflected in the cool brown eyes was total agreement. What he heard was complete insanity.

"Yes," she said. "We must go. At once!"

"I canna let ye go—"

"You can and you will," Catherine insisted harshly. "And if you won't take us there yourself, we'll find our own way."

"Take ye!" the Highlander's hair stood on end at the very notion. "Ye want me tae *take* ye there? Nae! Nae, I'll nae go back. I'll nae go back there till hell freezes!"

"Then you will stand aside," Catherine ordered, squaring her narrow shoulders. "And so help me God if you try to stop us, I'll kill you myself."

MacIntosh gaped at one determined face, then the other. Having barely escaped with his life the first time, he could think of nothing more terrifying than the prospect of returning to the scene of carnage near Culloden. By the same token, how could he live with himself if he allowed the two women to return to the moor alone?

Mind, it was doubtful they would make it further than the first mutilated body they found by the roadside. Neither one of them looked strong enough to withstand a good stiff breeze, nevermind the sight of . . . well . . .

"Christ, but," he whispered, feeling the sweat break out anew across his forehead. "I knew I should hae stayed in Glasg'y. Aye, well, I'll take ye . . . but ye'll heed ma orders an' dae exactly as I tell ye. Ye'll run when I say run an' ye'll hide when I say hide, an' if I say ye canna go any further, ye'll nae go any further. Agreed?"

"We'll need horses," Catherine said crisply, sidestepping the need to answer. "And a cart or a wagon of some sort to bring back the wounded. And guns!"

The clansman rolled his eyes. Guns, wagons, horses!

"Lady Anne," Deirdre said on a start. "What happened to Lady Anne?"

"I only ken she were wi' the Prince when the fightin' started, an' only because The MacGillivray sent her there tae be safe. But, well, Colonel Anne werena one tae obey any man's orders—*like as some ithers I could mention.*"

Deirdre brushed aside the sarcasm. "And you are certain you know nothing of our husbands, nothing of Aluinn MacKail or Alexander Cameron?"

The watery eyes flicked to one side. "Nae. I'm shamed tae say I were too busy seein' after my ain hide tae take heed o' too many ithers."

"You have nothing to feel ashamed about," Deirdre assured him softly, knowing by the number of bruises, cuts and patches of blood on the clansman's body he had given a good account of himself on the battlefield.

"Blankets," Catherine snapped, reminding them of the urgency of their mission. "And whisky. We'll take as much as we can carry."

Deirdre nodded. "I'll see to it."

When she was gone, Catherine delayed the clansman a moment longer and laid a gentle hand on his arm.

"You do know something else, don't you? Please, I beg you, sir. If you can tell me anything at all . . . "

The clansman looked down at his hands. "Aye. Aye, it's about the lassie's husband . . . "

Aluinn MacKail stared up at the dull, heavy cotton clouds that rolled across the sky. A pale, faintly luminous circle suggested there was indeed a sun up there somewhere, but just where it was or how far it had progressed toward the rim of mountains was anyone's guess. Aluinn, personally, would have sworn it had not moved so much as an inch in the past few hours. But then neither had he.

It was just as well; four . . . or was it five times now, groups of soldiers had tramped past and because of his lack of movement, had assumed him to be as dead as the body of the redcoat he was pinned beneath. They would discover their oversight soon enough, he supposed. As soon as they began collecting their dead for burial, they would come to fetch this one and . . . well, perhaps they would be merciful after all.

Aluinn ran a thick and sourly furred tongue across his lips, wishing he could somehow turn his head just enough to lick at the dew coating the long deergrass. He had tried once already, but although he felt as if he should be able to stand up and walk away with a shrug and a mocking salute, he had heard the distinct crack of his spine when he had fallen, and he had not been able to rouse so much as a twitch since.

At least the pain had faded. Initially, he had been left with some sensation in his arms and hands, but it had slowly receded and the chilling numbness had spread, inch by insidious inch. With any luck, the chill would reach his heart before the dragoons came and then he would not care what the butchers did when they found him. He just did not want to die like the others. He had heard them screaming, begging for mercy, shrieking with pain and humiliation as the soldiers cut into their living flesh. Men who had fought so valiantly and defended their honour so bravely—whether their cause was wrong or right, just or unjust, should at least be allowed the dignity of dying like men. They should not have to plead for mercy on a field of honour. They should not have to suffer the degradation of being stripped naked and left to bleed to death in agony, untended.

And the English called us barbarians and savages, Aluinn mused wryly.

He parted his lips slightly, trying to suck in a deep lungful of air, but found he could barely manage a small gasp.

Good. It was a good sign . . . although he had thought the end was near an eternity ago and he was still here. Still breathing. Still able to think and see and hear and smell with remarkable clarity. If only he could move. Just a hand, Lord. A finger. He still held a loaded pistol, wrested from the bastard lying on top of him seconds before an obliging broadsword had ended the struggle in Aluinn's favour. Unfortunately, the son of a bitch had had a healthy appetite, and had pitched forward with the thrust of the blade, taking Aluinn down with him. The damned rock had been sticking up just so, and . . .

By God's grace, if he could just move his hand, turn the gun around, and ease back on the trigger!

Where is Alex when I need him? Alex would know what to do; he would never let me die like this, slowly, inch by inch. Certainly not skewered helplessly on the end of some grinning bastard's bayonet.

Maybe if he shouted, someone would hear him and come over to investigate. He had been aware of men and women creeping among the dead for some time now, local farmers in some cases, who had come to search for friends and relatives. The soldiers kept driving them away, but they always came back.

He had to be careful, however. There were scavengers out as well, some of them no better than the soldiers when it came to slitting a throat or stripping loot from the wounded. Some of them, in exchange for being allowed to continue searching among the dead, drew attention to the living so that the soldiers could amuse themselves while the thieves continued looting. And the women were no better than the men.

"Deirdre," he whispered, the sweet, soft torture of her name bringing the sting of tears to his eyes. How cruel the fates were not to have given them more time together. Such dreams he'd had. Such plans for their future together . . .

Oh Christ! Christ, no! he thought, squeezing his eyes shut against an agony worse than any physical pain he could have imagined. *Now I'm hearing things! I'm hearing her voice!*

If nothing else, dear God, I thank You for letting her be safe. I thank You for letting her be far, far away, and I curse You for not letting me see her sweet face one last time before I die.

The soldier regarded the two women before him with an equal measure of suspicion and curiosity. He had strict orders not to let anyone onto the field—especially not the dog-faced women who wailed and clawed at him in an unintelligible brogue. These two were different, however.

The spoke the King's English better than he did, and one of them—the yellow-haired beauty—carried herself with the unmistakable air of nobility. But if she was English and she was of the nobility, why was she dressed like a peasant in homespun and a tartan shawl?

"I'm not supposed to let anyone near the bodies until a proper tally's been done," he said.

"I am looking for my brother, sergeant," Catherine said clearly. "Captain Damien Ashbrooke of the Kingston's Light Horse."

The guard shrugged noncommittally, the name meaning nothing to him.

"Surely you cannot mean to stop us from searching among the wounded?" Deirdre asked. "The battle has been over for hours and Captain Ashbrooke has not yet reported back to his regiment."

"What's it to you?" he demanded, raking an eye along Deirdre's slender form.

"You may be sure we haven't come for our pleasure," she retorted sharply. "Nor have we come all this way to be stopped and questioned by an insensitive blunderhead. If you prefer, we can take our appeal directly to Major Hamilton Garner, but I shouldn't think he would be too pleased with the disturbance."

The soldier stiffened, reacting to the major's name with suitable approbation. It was none of his business who they were and what they wanted: Ghouls came in all shapes and sizes. If they wanted to go traipsing ankle deep in blood, who was he to deny them the pleasure.

Deirdre relaxed the grip she had on the pistol, but kept it handy beneath the folds of her shawl as the guard waved them past. Having been told that most of the Highland women were being driven away from the moor, it had been Catherine's idea to use their obvious assets to advantage. After all, it was not so preposterous to suppose some of the English women travelling with

Cumberland's baggage train would be anxious to learn the fate of their men.

Believing herself to be innured to the sights and smells of the carnage that awaited them, Deirdre was only capable of taking a few halting steps before the appalling horror of their surroundings forced her to stop. There were bodies everywhere—clansmen, redcoats, even horses lay piled one upon the other in a ghastly tableau of war. The ground was pitted and charred from the barrage of cannonballs. Fires smoldered everywhere, sending twisting columns of smoke upward to blend with the mist.

The moor was half a mile square and every inch was steeped in gore. The slope they stood on was a gentle one and the road on which they walked cut diagonally through the field. To the right, separated by a neat stone wall, was a farmer's field, already cleared for spring planting. On their left, the hazed vista of the Firth with its dull lead-coloured water and black isles beyond. Incredible beauty and unbelievable horror in the same picture: It was almost too much to absorb.

"My God," Deirdre whispered. "My dear sweet God."

Catherine was numb with shock. It could only be hell they had walked into. Nightmares could be sweated and screamed away; this was not a dream, it was real, and it would surely affect the way she lived and breathed for the rest of her days.

There was no rain, no wind, no air moving at all, it seemed. The mist was thin and coated everything in a shiny wetness. Some of the bodies, still warm and bleeding sluggishly into the grass, steamed faintly where their wounds met the cool air. The first such sight they had encountered had caused both women to instantly and violently empty their stomachs and Donald MacIntosh had thankfully begun to wheel the tiny cart around and head back for Moy Hall.

Catherine would have been only too happy to flee if not for the thought of Alex possibly lying somewhere wounded and helpless. There were other women staggering along the road, dazed and weeping as they went from one bloodied splash of tartan to the next, hoping against hope they would find a husband or relative alive.

The Prince, they had been told, had managed to escape the moor with about a third of his army. Another third had scattered into the surrounding forests and glens, running for their lives; a final third would never leave the battlefield.

MacIntosh had dared to venture no closer than the edge of the forest, for there were still dragoons and laughing infantrymen prowling the roads, drunk on blood and victory, scouring the area for more victims. They eyed the groups of women and spat crude insults into their stricken faces. Some of the more loathsome creatures offered money or looted trinkets for a quick tumble in the grass; some just took what they wanted if they found a girl who was young and pretty and foolish enough to be on the road alone.

Catherine and Deirdre remained with a large group, keeping their heads bowed and their shawls low over their brows whenever the soldiers came into view. They both hoped and dreaded to see a familiar face among the dead. Once, when Deirdre glimpsed a tawny blond cap of hair by the side of the road she had cried out and stumbled over to the body, but it had not been Aluinn. Thankfully, it had not been Aluinn.

The little cart they had brought from Moy Hall had been filled with wounded long before they had ever reached the main road. MacIntosh had driven it away and come back with another, but it was useless to hope they could help everyone they found. Of the wounded who still clung to life, many did so by a thread so slender they were, for the most part, beyond pain, beyond awareness. The effort it took to pull at a last sip of strong *uisque* exacted the ultimate price and they died without even swallowing it.

And the wounds . . .

"My God," Deirdre said again. "How can men do this to one another? How can they sleep at night, or—"

Her face blanched and her sorrowful brown eyes froze on a bright ripple of tartan farther along the slope. She knew that tartan. She knew it by the distinctive stripe of ochre that had been added to the Cameron colours of crimson and black.

Deirdre pushed away from Catherine's side and ran toward the two entangled bodies. Catherine raised ice cold fingers to her lips as she heard Deirdre's cry of anguish and saw her drop to her knees and begin to pull frantically at the body of the dead government soldier that was draped across her husband. Catherine had hoped MacIntosh had been mistaken when he'd told her he thought he had seen Aluinn MacKail go down. Poor Deirdre. Poor, sweet, gentle Deirdre.

Catherine dashed away the hot tears that flooded over her lashes, surprised there were any left to shed, and started to follow after Deirdre down the slope. Somehow they would find a way to move the body off this desolate field. It was the least they could do . . .

Catherine stopped again, a gasp torn from her throat. Fear, as pure and raw as anything she had ever felt, gave strength to her limbs as she veered away from the course she was on and stumbled back along the slope, weaving her way around bodies, her feet sucking into the mud at each slippery step. She fell once, twice, and each time struggling to her feet again, hauling sodden blood- and dew-soaked skirts behind her. Just as in her dream, she ran and ran, but seemed to make little headway. Her tears blinded her, sobs burned in her throat, and her heart pounded so loudly she could hear nothing else.

When she reached the far side of what had been the Jacobite's front line she slowed, and a fresh onslaught of tears streamed down her cheeks, drawn from a bottomless, unending well of pity as she stared down at the gleaming black body.

There was no mistaking Shadow from any other horse in Britain. The regal, tapered head, the sleek coat, and powerful beauty of Alexander's faithful stallion was as recognizable in death as he was in life.

Catherine sank to her knees beside the noble stallion and her heart swelled with such a mixture of rage, sorrow, and senseless waste she did not know if her body could bear it. She reached out and stroked a gentle hand along the fine black coat. His mane and tail were flung out across the grass as if he was running, his head was arched high and proud; only the glaring obscenity of the shattered forelegs screamed out the reality of his death. She knew it would have broken Alex's heart to see Shadow lying like this. It broke hers thinking she would have to leave the magnificent beast to the carrion and scavengers. Helpless to know what else to do, she removed her shawl and draped it over the torn stumps—a foolish gesture, since there were far more hideous wounds that should have been graced with the dignity of a shield.

It was also a reckless gesture, in that it drew attention to the glowing luminosity of her long blonde hair. One pair of jade-green eyes, in particular, noticed the incongruity, doubly exaggerated against the murky brown of the moor and the black of the stallion's coat.

The major halted dead in his tracks and stared up the slope, his pulse beginning to hammer in triumph for the second time that day.

"Deirdre?" Aluinn gasped. "Deirdre . . . *is that you?*"

"Aluinn," she sobbed, her hands, her lips, her tears caressing his face. "Oh Aluinn . . . Aluinn . . . Thank God you are alive! I was so afraid. We heard so many stories, saw so many terrible things on the road!"

"Deirdre—" he blinked hard several times, convinced he was hallucinating, knowing she could not possibly be real, knowing she was half a hundred miles away in Lochaber!

"Hush," she commanded, her trembling lips pressed against his. "You mustn't try to talk. You must lie still and let us help you. We'll get you safely away from this dreadful place and—"

"We? Who is *we*?"

"Catherine and I. Oh Aluinn, I have so much to tell you, I don't know where to start. We did not get twenty miles down the road when we were ambushed by soldiers. Master Damien was killed and if it hadn't been for Mr. MacSorley, we would have died there too. But he got us away and brought us back to Moy Hall, and . . . and then we heard the cannons and . . . and . . . " She faltered, her voice quailing and her heart filling with a new dread as she saw the tears swimming in her husband's smoky gray eyes.

"Dear God, you should not have come here," he said with difficulty. "And I should burn in eternal hellfire for being glad that you did, but . . . I am. I prayed so hard to see your face one last time before I died—"

"You mustn't talk like that!" Deirdre cried. "You are not going to die! We can help you. We can help you get up and then we can—"

"Deirdre . . . I can't move—"

"Then we'll carry you!" she insisted frantically. "*I'll* carry you myself if I have to!"

"Deirdre . . . listen to me. It's my back. I cannot feel anything, I cannot move anything. I haven't been able to for a long time. I was wondering why it was taking so long to die, what I had done so terribly wrong in my life to be punished this way, but now I know I wasn't being punished at all. I must have done something terribly right in loving and marrying you."

All the blood and warmth drained from Deirdre's face, her fear growing and spreading as she noted how truly still he was lying, how oddly angled his legs were to the rest of his body.

"Archibald," she whispered desperately. "He will be able to help you. He will know what to do."

"Archie cannot help me," he said, smiling sadly. "No one can help me, Deirdre. Only you."

"Me? What can I do? Tell me what to do, Aluinn. Anything. *Anything!* Just tell me what to do!"

"You can set my mind at ease. You can get away from here and run as far and as fast as you can."

"I am not leaving you!" she cried, horrified at the thought, shocked that he would ask it of her.

"Yes you are, and you are going to take Catherine with you. Has she . . . have you seen anything of Alex?"

Deirdre shook her head. "No, but we've only seen what is here, and on the road."

"If he isn't here, then there is a chance he made it. The last time I saw him, he was . . . we were both blocking the road against the charge by the dragoons. Aye . . . if he isn't here, he might have made it, pray God. And the Prince?"

"The Devil take the Prince, Aluinn MacKail, it is you I care about! You I love!"

"Then if you love me," he said gently, "you will go now, before the soldiers notice you and—"

"*You there! What are you doing?*"

Deirdre gasped and twisted around. There were three soldiers standing within hailing distance, their hands and arms red to the elbows as they systematically searched the bodies for loot.

"Deirdre . . . please . . . !"

She looked back down at Aluinn, stricken by the pain and helplessness she saw in his eyes.

"Run," he gasped. "Take Catherine and run. Save yourself!"

"I am not leaving you! Not like this!"

Aluinn closed his eyes briefly, bracing himself. "The gun. In my hand. I promise, I will not feel a thing, and the soldiers will think you are one of them. Do it, Deirdre. Use the gun. Save yourself."

"No!" she cried aghast. "No . . . never!"

"Then do it for me," he pleaded. "Don't let me die without knowing you are safe. And don't let me die like the others—" he choked briefly on the words. "Don't let the bastards find me alive. Do it, my love. Save yourself, and save me."

Deirdre stared, remembering the hacked and mutilated bodies they had passed on the road.

"Well now." The soldiers were moving closer. "What do we have here? One of them hot little rebel wenches, maybe? How d'ya suppose she got past ol' Hornie up there on the road? Mayhap she done something nice for him. Mayhap she'll do something nice for us too."

Deirdre was drowning in Aluinn's eyes. Between his tears and her tears there was a world of love and happiness, a place filled with sunshine and laughter and gentle loving peace. It was inconceivable to think she could look away and survive. Inconceivable to think she would want to look away, ever.

"I love you," she whispered, leaning forward to press her lips to his. "I have loved you, Aluinn MacKail, from the first moment I saw you . . . and every moment since."

"Every moment since," he echoed. "My only love."

With the movement of her hands concealed from the soldier's view, she took the pistol from the cool, lifeless fingers and turned it inward, firing it into his heart while his lips still moved against hers. As soon as she heard the muffled explosion and knew there had been no misfire, she held the barrel of her own gun against her breast and squeezed the trigger.

Catherine heard two shots fired so closely together they sounded like one. Startled by the noise and the immediate shouts that followed, she pushed to her feet, a worried frown erasing all thoughts of Shadow as she saw the three soldiers running toward the spot where she had last seen Deirdre.

Deirdre!

A cry already in her throat was rammed back into her lungs as she took a step, then drew up short again, a fourth menacing presence nearby earning all of her attention. At first, she did not recognize the chiselled, patrician features staring out at her from under the brim of the black beaver tricorn; she only saw the red tunic, the gleam of a sabre, and the flaring nostrils of the horse he spurred into a quick gallop in her direction. Something about the eyes, however, the piercing, jade-green frost of them lanced through her shock and numbness and she knew who it was: Major Hamilton Garner.

She staggered back several steps as the full horror of this new threat superceded all others, and spurred her into a desperate run for the nearby verge of trees. The ground was treacherously uncertain and she slipped with every skidding footstep, stumbling, running in a half-crouch as she clawed for a hold at tufts of grass and exposed knots of stone.

She dared not stop or look back, even though behind her, the sound of angry hoofbeats drew irrepressibly closer. If she kept running, kept climbing up the slope, there was a chance she could reach the forest, a chance she could escape the animal's gusting breath as it ran her down.

Blinded by panic, Catherine tripped and sprawled painfully onto her knees. She used her hands to break the fall, and when she lifted them from the rough ground, the palms were red and skinless, embedded with bits of stinging pebbles. Sobbing, she pushed herself to her feet and forced herself to keep running, her legs tangled in her long skirts, her knees wobbling violently now, as her strength began to falter and fail. She gasped at mouthfuls of air, sucking it into lungs that burned with fear. She cried out Alex's name, soft and low, over and over, as if she could somehow will him to appear, braced to defend her against the swiftly closing threat.

Hamilton Garner leaned forward over the saddle, his arm stretched out, his gloved hand swiping at a streaming wave of bright blonde hair as he came within range. He jerked his horse to one side at the same time, causing Catherine to scream in terror as she was pulled off her feet and thrown to the ground. Hamilton's speed carried him past the spot where she fell and he wheeled his horse around, seeing her roll and struggle frantically to regain her footing.

But there was nowhere for her to run, no stamina left in her legs to carry her. She stood swaying unsteadily only half a dozen yards shy of the trees, her eyes wide, her mouth gaping as stabs of searing hot pain speared through her sides. Her hands fell protectively to cover her belly, but they were no match for the cramps, spiked with the agony of defeat. She crumpled onto her knees again, gasping for breath, struggling now to hold fast to the realm of consciousness.

Garner dismounted, wincing as his weight jarred the freshly bandaged wound in his thigh. He walked over to where Catherine knelt and, curling his hand around her upper arm, dragged her unceremoniously to her feet, his grip as ruthless and unrelenting as the look in his eyes.

"What have we here?" he hissed, forcing her to look up into his face. "Can it truly be the elusive and long-suffering Mrs. Montgomery?"

"Hamilton," she gasped. "Hamilton . . . thank God it's you."

He arched a brow. "Happy to see me, are you?"

"I . . . I'm happy to see anyone I know . . . alive."

"But you ran away from me," he chided softly.

"I . . . did not recognize you," she lied, shuddering as his fingers pinched cruelly into her arm. "I . . . did not expect to see you here."

"Did you expect I would still be waiting back in Derby?"

"N-no. No, I didn't mean that, I—"

"As I recall, that was your plan . . . and your promise, was it not?" His eyes sparkled malevolently. "I was to wait in Derby and you were to leave your new husband at the first posting inn, there to fly back into my arms and set the world to rights again."

His gaze moved slowly down the front of her labouring breasts and came to rest on her hands, which were still cradling the gentle roundness of her belly. This further proof of her disloyalty churned black and vicious through his veins, slowing his pulse, causing his heart to throb sluggishly in his chest.

"So . . . the gossips' predictions were correct, after all. The daughter of a whore surprises no one in proving herself to be a whore as well. At least Lady Caroline's affairs had a certain honesty about them; there were no pretenses in bedding her, just lust. And she found enough willing young studs in the immediate vicinity without having to roam farther afield with her deceptions. Really, Catherine—a Scotsman? A filthy rebel spy? Were there not enough ape-faced stablehands and iron-mongers in Derby to satisfy your cravings?"

Later, Catherine would never be able to say where she found the strength, let alone the audacity, to strike the leering smirk from Hamilton Garner's face. Her hand cracked sharply across his jaw, and it was with intense pleasure, she saw the shock and surprise flare in his eyes. She paid dearly for the pleasure, however, for he slapped her back, hard and fast, and with such malicious force she spun out of his grasp and sprawled on the grass at his feet. His rage unleashed, he kicked out once, twice, the polished leather toe of his boot sinking solidly into ribs and stomach with enough fury to send her jerking into a tight, fetal curl.

He might have continued, might have kicked her unresisting body into a bloody pulp if not for the three dragoons who came running up the slope to investigate the screams. The last to arrive, lagging behind the others because he was favouring a limp in one leg, joined them in staring down at the curled body. He frowned and leaned over, pushing aside the heavy veil of scattered yellow hair to have a closer look at her face.

"Well, well," he murmured. "Mrs. Cameron. We meet again."

Catherine could hardly see through the wall of pain, could barely register the added shock of recognizing Corporal Jeffrey Peters before the swarming, sickening clouds of darkness descended and smothered her sense of reality.

"Where the devil did she come from?" Peters asked, straightening. "I thought I recognized the other one, Mrs. MacKail, back there, but it was hard to be sure through all the blood."

"Shall we finish this'un off too, sar?" one of the other men inquired casually, his eyes moving hungrily over the slender, shapely body.

"No," Garner rasped, pulling himself together with a mighty effort. "No, by God, she may be of some use to me yet."

The dragoon, misinterpreting the major's meaning, grinned and dragged the tip of his bloodied sabre along the curve of Catherine's buttocks. "Aye, she looks a ripe enough one at that, Major. I've heard tell these Highland wenches are sum'mit rare hot when they're breeding, an' this'un looks like the pick of the crop."

At this ribald presumption, Garner's green eyes cut into the soldier with the sharpness of a meat cleaver. "You will take the prisoner back to the bat-wagons and see that she is placed under heavy guard. You will not touch her or vilify her in any way . . . not until I tell you you are free to do so. Is that clearly understood? As for your opinions to her worth or abilities—when I want or need either, I will ask for them."

He strode back to where his horse stood and with a final, cool glance down at Catherine's limp form, swung himself into the saddle and dug his heels into the gleaming flanks. His cheeks still stung from the bite of her hand and his indignation still rankled with the hard proof of her betrayal. But he had her in his hands now, and with her, a way of getting to Alexander Cameron, once and for all. The bastard had slipped through his net again today, but his freedom would not be long-lived, not if he evei wanted to see his Catherine alive again.

Chapter Twenty-Four

News of the manner and substance of the Jacobites' defeat on Drummossie Moor swept across the stunned Highlands like a firestorm. Word of his son's astounding victory took five days to reach King George in London, but less than twenty-four hours to reach ears on the remotest isles of Scotland. Clans loyal to the Hanovers, or those with the wit and cunning to appear to be so, quickly took up the black cockade and did not bother to wait for Cumberland's orders before descending upon any territories held by Jacobite clans. The Campbells, in particular, released their men like a flood across the borders of their age-old enemies: the MacLarens, the MacLeans, the MacDonalds, and with particular zeal, the wealthy holdings of the Camerons.

Any rebels attempting to escape the murderous rampage of Cumberland's soldiers were forced to travel mainly by night, avoiding roads and open fields where bands of militia roamed on wild killing sprees. They begged food and lodging at their own peril, often suffering the final degradation of finding themselves betrayed to the soldiers by their greedy hosts.

Lochiel, both his ankles smashed by grapeshot, had been carried from the field and taken by his clansmen to a pitiful rendezvous with the remainder of the Jacobite army. With what dignity he could muster, Charles Stuart told his loyal soldiers to run for their lives and seek what safety they could, until such time as they could recruit a new army and avenge their fallen comrades at Culloden.

Carried in a tartan sling, Lochiel and his men turned toward the shores of Loch Ness, following the inky shoreline south into Lochaber. Some five hundred Camerons and MacDonalds travelled by this route, still formidable enough in numbers and temperament to discourage any interference from marauding clans. In groups of ten and twenty, however, they broke away at intervals along the route, exchanging solemn prayers for good luck with those they left on the road. Each man was desperate to know how his family was faring. Some had been away from their homes nine months or more, since before the Prince's standard was raised at Glenfinnan. Others, like Donald and Archibald Cameron had been lucky enough to have found occasion to return to their homes in the interim, and felt relatively content that the walls of their castle had been strong and tall enough to have shielded the ones they loved from the horror and consequences of Culloden.

Still others, like Alexander Cameron, stumbled wearily alongside the litter carrying his wounded brother, oblivious to the pain and fever induced by his own injuries, numbed by all that had transpired behind him and concentrating only on what lay ahead. He thought only of Catherine. She was at Achnacarry, and he needed the calm, sane assurance of her presence more than he had ever needed anyone or anything in his life before.

Lady Maura Cameron was the first to detect movement far out beyond the avenue of elm trees Donald had planted along the road leading to the castle gates. She had been taking a late stroll around the catwalk that hugged the stone ramparts high on the castle walls, and had paused to gaze out over the smothered flush of twilight.

As always, the lowering of the sun had caused the air to haze and the blues of the sky and the surrounding mountains to deepen almost to black. By contrast, the snow-capped, regal crown of Ben Nevis was painted with pale golds and pinks, its majesty towering above the heads of the lesser, gloomier gods of the Gray Corries.

Lochaber was a world of lochs and heather, of high, impenetrable hills and dark gorges, brown moors and wild forests, splendid solitudes where the air was so still, a visitor could hear a blade of grass sighing against its neighbour. Rowanberries, red as blood, carpeted the glens in springtime, quarrelling for supremacy with beds of heather, sweet and lush, that blanketed the cragged hillsides.

Achnacarry presided over this heather splendor, a fortress of vaulting walls and stacked abutments rising in places to one hundred feet above the ground. The castle sat perched at the end of a spur of land, with orchards, parks and gardens on three sides, a sheer and breathless drop into the black waters of Loch Lochy on the fourth. Sections of the castle dated back six centuries and since then, every laird and chief had added, renovated, and rebuilt to suit the clan's growing needs and prominence. Four great towers were silhouetted against the forests and mountains, instead of a single square keep. Within the twelve-foot-thick stone walls there were two courtyards housing stables and a smithy, millroom, guardhouses, chapel, two huge kitchens, warehouses, storerooms, laundries—not to mention the vast block of family apartments, ranging from the elegance of the three-storey great hall to the libraries, parlours, and tiers of well-appointed sleeping chambers.

Maura had lived within Achnacarry's walls for sixteen years. She knew every stone and rosebush, every twisting pathway through the gardens and along the jagged shoreline. She knew enough not to trust the early evening shadows; mists that crept through the bordering forests looking like white-clad figures, a fallen tree resembling a crouched man. For several days she had felt as if the castle was being watched, as if invisible threats were closing in around them, and, as a result, she had doubled the sentries posted high atop the walls and kept the twin black oak gates closed and barred at all times. At her sister-in-law Jeannie Cameron's suggestion, she had even put the castle smithy to work cleaning the rusted fittings that had rendered the heavy, iron portcullis inoperable for decades. Some of the other family members gave her odd looks, but she did not care. Achnacarry was her home and she would take every measure to protect it in Donald's absence, regardless of how drastic those steps seemed.

Despite the fact she was born a Campbell and was niece to the powerful Duke of Argyle, she was loved and respected by every member of the Cameron clan. Her marriage to Donald Cameron had been violently opposed on both sides of the territorial boundaries, but in the end, her courage, her determination, her fierce and passionate love for Lochiel had won the hearts of her most adamant detractors. Few, if asked, would volunteer the origins of her bloodlines without a scowl, but all, to a man, would sooner part a man's head from his neck as endure any slur or insult to their beloved Lady Cameron.

"Can you make anything out?" she asked in a low voice, aware of the tense sentry who stood by her side at the ramparts. He had seen something too. Or sensed it. Even the quality of the air had altered slightly, no longer soft and melodic, but taut and secretive with hidden threats.

"Pass the alarm," Maura decided. "Make certain everyone is—"

They both heard it then. The breeze had been against their backs, a current of air humming down the throat of the Great Glen and swirling south toward the mountains. Its whisper faded now and then, calming the trees, permitting a backwash of foreign sounds to drift up to the roof of the castle. One of those sounds was the thin skirl of a lone piper, and the strained, valiantly boastful chords of the *piob rach'd* being played was that of the *Spaid-searachd*: the March of Lochiel.

"Dear God," Maura whispered. "Dear God in heaven . . . it's Donald. It's *Donald!*"

Whirling into a crush of her own deep burgundy, velvet skirts, Maura flew along the catwalk to the east tower, barely pausing to adjust her eyes to the torchlit gloom as she ran down the spiral stone staircase. She flung herself around and around the twisting corkscrew, bypassing several landings as she descended into the heart of the castle. Bursting onto the corridor of the principal apartments, she did not waste the time to detour into the main parlour, but shouted with enough exuberance to bring heads popping out of doorways all along the vaulted hallway.

Rose Cameron, nearing eighty but as spry and crisp in character as her thatch of snow-white hair, awoke from her nap with a startled curse. Jeannie Cameron, Dr. Archibald's wife, veered toward the door, her hand balancing a full glass of freshly poured *uisque baugh.*

"What the bluidy hell," she muttered. "Have the walls come bluidy tumblin' doon, then?"

"What is it?" Rose demanded, struggling up from her chair. "I thought I haird someone scream."

"Only Maura," Jeannie said dryly. "Mayhap she's seen a wee ghostie in the tower room."

"Aye, I've tald her nae tae go wanderin' roun up there in the cald air," Rose nodded sagely. "Nae wi' her lungs filled and rattlin' like coins in a purse. She'll catch the rot again, mark ma words."

"Whisht, Rose!" Jeannie frowned and held up a leathery, work-worn hand. "What's that? Sounds like as if the whole blessit castle's gaun daft."

Rose hobbled to the doorway, cursing the further need to exercise muscles that had been quite content to sleep.

She cocked an ear into the hallway for a moment, and when she straightened, she thumped Jeannie's arm with enough force to send the preciously guarded contents of the glass leaping halfway across the carpet.

"Christ, but! Ye must be the one wha's daft, hen. Daft or deef!" she declared, launching herself out into the hall. "They're hame! It's the men come hame!"

Jeannie stared after her for two full seconds until, with a whoop of excitement, she sent the glass smashing after the whisky and began running nimbly down the corridor.

As Alexander walked through the polished black-oak gates, the familiarity of the sights and smells of the outer courtyard brought a rush of hot tears into his eyes. He was not alone in his reaction. The weary, filth-encrusted men who stumbled through the gates after him all stood stock-still for several moments, swaying on unsteady limbs as if they could not believe they had come to the end of their journey. Some still had several miles to go to reach their farms and *clachans*, but to them Achnacarry represented home and sanctuary. Stoically silent throughout the furtive trek along the shores of Loch Ness and Loch Oich, many of them fell onto their knees and wept openly. The piper, who had played Lochiel's march despite the pain of a wounded leg and a torn eye, sobbed a final breath into the chanter and let it fall, the remaining air escaping in a low, tuneless wail.

Maura was first to greet them at the gates. Aglow with relief and happiness, her wide, soft eyes searched the ragged faces and finally came to rest on the first of many, many stretched tartan litters. Donald's head was bare, his hair flown this way and that as his head lolled with the motion of the stretcher-bearers. Maura's smile faded, her face blanched and her hands crushed against her breast as she moved haltingly forward.

Braced for the worst, her relief was almost palpable when she saw that he still breathed, that he was only asleep. She touched a hand to his cheek, her eyes skimming down to where the thick, blood-stained bandages encased his feet and ankles.

"He's alright," Alex said, resting a hand on her shoulder. "He's been unconscious for the past mile or so. We should have stopped to rest, but—"

Maura looked up at Alexander Cameron and felt a deeper tearing in her heart. His tartan was crusted with blood, pierced by bayonet, sword, and musket shot. His left arm was bound in foul-smelling rags, the fingers protruding stiff and blue with cold. There was a week's growth of beard on his cheeks and circles so deep and black under his eyes it looked as if he hadn't slept in a month. His teeth were clenched tightly together in a futile attempt to control the tremors that wracked his body, but a blind man could see he was flushed and burning up with fever.

"We must get you inside where it's warm," Maura said, taking command at once. "We must get you all inside where there is hot food and proper medicines."

"Catherine—?" Alex asked, shuddering as yet another racking bout of nausea threatened to topple him. He fought it, conquered it, but when he opened his dark eyes again, Maura had obviously not heard him and had turned her attention to the flock of servants who were suddenly clamouring to be of help. He shook off a concerned pair of hands and forced himself to place one foot before the other, determined to walk into the castle under his own power. Catherine was there, waiting. Catherine would take the pain away. Catherine would hold him and soothe the heartache; she would understand and share the sense of overwhelming loss he felt. She was his life, his sanity.

God . . . how he needed her.

ACHNACARRY, May 1746

Chapter Twenty-Five

Alex paced most of the morning away in a deep, black rage. Three weeks! He had been laid up with fever and illness for three weeks and as yet had heard no word of Catherine or Deirdre or the fate of the small party he had dispatched to Achnacarry in Struan MacSorley's care. At first, he had not believed his ears when Maura told him his wife had never arrived. The shock had pushed him over the edge and he had tried to run back out the gates of the castle—intending what? To run all the way back to Inverness to look for her? At the time, it had seemed the only possible thing to do.

The combined effects of his wounds, the raging fever, and the arms of four burly clansmen had finally brought him crashing to the ground. He had lain unconscious for a full week afterwards, and then had been so pitifully weak he could barely manage to relieve himself without the indignity of helping hands or soiled bedsheets. Maura had placed him in the chamber adjacent to Donald's so she would have easy access to both brothers. Archibald—miraculously unscathed even though he had been in the thickest of fighting—divided his time between Donald, Alex, and the scores of wounded men who passed through Achnacarry's gates on their way home.

When Maura was not with her husband or her brother, she was with Jeannie and Rose in the kitchens baking bread and ensuring there was a steady supply of hot food on hand at all times. The men who came to Achnacarry were starving, and not one was turned away without clean, warm clothes, full bellies, and stout words of encouragement from Lochiel. They had fought well. They had worn the Cameron badge of oak proudly and upheld the honour of the clan despite the defeat of the army at Culloden. The Prince was safe. Friends had taken him high into the mountains and would guard him until a ship could carry him away to France. He could ask nothing more of his loyal Scots.

When Alex was strong enough to walk ten paces without bringing the tapestries and wall hangings he was clenching down around his head, he informed Donald he was going back to find Catherine. He swore he had seen Struan MacSorley appear on the field at Culloden, and that Struan had saved him from certain death at the hands of the dragoons. Struan had not been seen since. No one knew or had seen anything of the giant Scot either before or after the battle.

"I know MacSorley," Alex said. "He wouldn't have left Catherine anywhere that was unfamiliar or unprotected. He wouldn't have returned to the battle unless he knew she was safe—knew they were all safe."

"If he was there at all, brither," Lochiel said quietly.

"What is that supposed to mean? You think I imagined him there on the battlefield?"

"Men have imagined stranger things."

"Not this time," Alex insisted quietly. "And if Struan was with me there, it can only mean Catherine and the others are somewhere between here and Inverness."

Or it could mean something else more terrible, Lochiel thought, unwilling to put the alternative into words. He knew it would do no good to argue with Alexander. Undoubtedly, he would do the same thing if it were Maura out there somewhere, and all the reasoning, rationalizing, and cautioning in the world would not stop him from going after her.

"Pray God they did not return to Moy Hall," he said aloud, and instantly regretted his slip. Not only had the MacKintosh estate been among the first visited and searched by Cumberland's dragoons, but they'd had word that Lady Anne had been arrested and taken to prison in Inverness. Moy Hall had been ransacked and any servants who had foolishly stayed behind had either been shot or thrown into jail with their mistress. Both Lochiel and Alex had admired Colonel Anne's courage, and to think of her behind bars in some fetid stone cell was an affront to every Scot, whether he be Jacobite or Hanover.

So many names, so many stories of horror and atrocities—from the nine-year-old lad and his father who were run down by dragoons and slain on the field they were plowing, to the woman who had given shelter to several wounded clansmen, only to have the government soldiers come and drag them into the yard where they were shot before her eyes. Two thousand already dead, more killed every day as Cumberland sent companies of soldiers into the glens and villages to search out anyone still boasting loyalty to King James, The Stuart. Naturally, the lands, holdings, and titles of the Jacobite leaders were all forfeit, meaning that looting, raping, and theft had more or less been sanctioned by the victorious general. The Duke was sending out companies of soldiers to clear the land systematically, to search for rebels and confiscate any property or livestock of value to the crown. It would only be a matter of time before they came to Achnacarry.

"I wish there was something I could do tae help, Alex," Lochiel said, staring glumly at the bulky bandages around his legs. Archibald had worked day and night to fit the splintered bones together and keep the ravaged flesh from becoming poisoned with gangrene. It would be weeks before Donald would be able to walk again—if ever.

"You'll have enough to do here, if the soldiers come."

"Aye. *When* they come, but. We're no' that remote a few guid Campbell bloodhounds couldna point the way."

"Will you fight?"

Lochiel lay back against the pillows and raised his eyes to the ornate, scrolled plasterwork that had only come to grace the ceiling of his bedchamber within the past ten years. Like the many chiefs before him, he had added personal touches here and there, tried to modernize the cold stone fortification into a warm and elegant home. He had lived at Achnacarry all his life, and it had been his and Maura's home for sixteen years. His brother Archibald and his family—uncles, aunts, nieces, nephews—and nearly a hundred men and women lived and worked within the stone walls. It was their home, too.

"I had a dream the ither night," Donald said, his blue eyes filming over with tears. "I dreamt I were walkin' in the garden, out tae where Maura was waitin' f'ae me in the gazebo. All the beds o' roses she planted over the years . . . they all looked different somehow. Changed. It wisna till I bent over tae pick some that I saw what was wrong. They were all red. No' a yellow or pink or white one among the lot. They were red, Alex. Red wi' blood. An' where I picked it, the stem were bleedin'. The blood o' the roses fell on ma hands an' I couldna rub it off. I dinna think it will ever come off, whether we fight again or na."

His eyes lowered to hide his tears, and Alex turned slowly away from the bed. Back in his own room again, he pulled a leather knapsack out of the wardrobe and threw it onto the bed.

"Going somewhere?"

Alexander glanced over his shoulder and saw Count Fanducci lounging easily against the opened doorframe. Having come away from Culloden with only the torn remnants of the clothes on his back, he looked somewhat subdued in a borrowed shirt and plain breeches. Standing there, with the muted light from the hall behind him and the blurred beams of daylight washing over him from the window, there was something about his face that jogged Alex's memory, but the moment passed as the count pushed away from the door and strode over to the bed.

"Ahh . . . shirt, coat, boots and-a breeches," he mused, inspecting the assorted garments Alex had collected and laid out on the bed. "Inglaz-y clothes and the Inglaz-y accent will only take you so far, *signore*."

"I have to try."

"*Sí, sí*. You worry after you beautiful wife. But what-a good can you do her in-a prison?"

"I'm aware of the risks, my friend," Alex replied evenly, thrusting an extra shirt into the knapsack. He winced as a sudden jab of pain shot up his bandaged left arm, reminding him he had only minimal strength in his hand, and then only at a tremendous premium in pain. The rest would come back in time, or so Archibald claimed. The trouble was, of course, he didn't have any more time. If Catherine was in trouble. If she was alone or afraid. If she needed help . . .

He stopped and squeezed his eyes shut to block out any further intruding "ifs," but was only partially successful.

If only Aluinn were here with him, the two of them could have set everything to rights again. Aluinn would not have attempted to delay him or talk him out of going. He would have been just as eager to be out looking for his wife. Good God, Deirdre was out there somewhere with Catherine. So was Damien Ashbrooke. So were twenty good clansmen. Surely, they hadn't just disappeared off the face of the earth; not if Struan had managed to make it back to Culloden.

"He was-a the good man, *signore*," Fanducci said quietly. "I'm-a sure she's safe."

Alex looked up, unaware that he had been gripping the shirt so tightly a seam had given way. And unaware his thoughts had been stamped so clearly on his face.

"I liked them both: *Signore* Struan and-a *Signore* MacKail. They were the very brave men. They would have died very well."

Alex said nothing. There was nothing he could say, without admitting to either man's death.

"The soldiers, *signore*," Fanducci said, clearing his throat and twisting at the end of his moustache with a thumb and forefinger. "They might-a not believe one crazy Inglaz-y on the road, but say if they meet one-a crazy Inglaz-y and-a one . . . mmm . . . only slightly crazy *Italiano*?"

Alex glanced up. "You truly would be crazy, Fanducci, if you volunteered to come with me."

The count shrugged. "Back home, in-a Italy, they think the Fanduccis are all a little crazy. Besides, I'm-a counted fourteen holes in my clothes when I come-a here. Fourteen chances they had to kill me and-a still they missed. I'm-a don't think either one of us is fated to die by the Inglaz-y hand, do you *signore*?"

"Not until I've finished my business with them, at any rate," Alex agreed. "Very well, if you are fool enough to risk it, I welcome your company."

"*Bene*!" Fanducci rubbed his hands together gleefully. "You give-a me ten minutes?"

Alex smiled faintly. "I'll give you ten minutes," he said.

Unfortunately, no more than three minutes passed before the guards on top of the tower walls were sounding the alarm.

The English had come to Achnacarry.

Alexander approached the clearing with caution. He held up his right hand to halt his group, and sat perfectly still on the back of a handsome chestnut stallion—a horse much smaller and compact in form than his much-missed Shadow, but one that was made more imposing by mere association with the Dark Cameron. .

Alex's men fanned out on either side of him—thirty, in all—looking as gloweringly ominous as if they had never tasted the bitter gall of defeat. Count Giovanni Fanducci reined in by Alex's side, his shoulders caped against the late afternoon chill, but the copious folds of cloth thrown back at his waist to pointedly display the gleaming snaphaunces tucked into his belt.

The clearing was no more than a hundred yards across at its widest place, ringed in thick-trunked oak trees that made the forest seem dark and oppressive, despite the trickles of sunlight filtering through the hazed gloom. Hamilton Garner and his men lined the opposite side of the glade, their leathers polished to a gloss, their peaked tricorns level as a row of pickets on a fence. Their scarlet-and-blue uniforms, starched white neck stocks, and chinking brass scabbards made an impressive show as they sat across the quiet fogged clearing, but for the first time since charging the battlefield at Culloden, they felt a distinct sense of unease. This was Cameron land and these were Cameron clansmen they faced, arguably some of the fiercest fighters they had encountered throughout the rebellion. The forest around them at once felt too dark with shadows, too close with dampness. To a man, the dragoons longed to run their fingers along the constricting edge of their collars to facilitate their breathing.

Several Argyle Campbells, travelling as guides to the English soldiers, sucked in their breaths and fingered the triggers of their muskets as they watched the Camerons file into the clearing. They remembered the old vendettas still not settled with Alexander Cameron and each member of the Campbell clan considered it a personal affront that he still lived.

Hamilton Garner measured his enemy carefully. The Highlander had taken a sabre wound to his left arm that should have disabled any other mortal, yet he held the reins easily, casually, as if he were none the worse for wear. Perhaps there was something in the Highland air, Hamilton surmised, that bred such resilience and arrogance. It had taken nearly twenty men to finally bring down the leonine giant who had come to Cameron's rescue at Culloden. Even then, the brute hadn't died, but had crawled up the slope under cover of darkness and managed to drag himself as far as a small barn some distance along the road to Inverness. The dragoons had found the body the next morning, stone cold, bled almost dry from the countless crippling wounds.

Garner dismounted and handed off his reins to an aide. He crooked an amused brow in Alexander Cameron's direction and began walking slowly into the centre of the clearing.

Alex swung himself off the chestnut's back. The strain of his weight was concentrated briefly on his damaged left arm, but if he felt the stabbing pain, he gave no outward sign of it. He tossed the reins to Fanducci, clamped his teeth securely around the butt of a small black cigar and strode to where the dragoon major waited.

"You are like a cat with nine lives," Garner commented dryly. "You keep landing on your feet, re-appearing where you are least expected."

"You wanted a meeting," Alex said brusquely. "Say what you have to say and be done with it."

"I was under the assumption I would be negotiating with your chief, Lochiel."

"My brother is indisposed. Whatever negotiating you have come to do, you can do it with me."

Garner took his time replying, absorbing the undercurrents of tension, relishing the feeling of power.

"As you may already have guessed, I have come on instructions to arrest your brother, Lochiel, and return him to Inverness to trial. As well, the name of Dr. Archibald Cameron appears high on my list, along with those of a dozen lesser officers of the clan. Having come to know the way you people think, I have no doubt you believe it is your duty to resist unto death. For my part, I could care less if the bodies I transport back are alive or not, but you might want to take this opportunity—the only one I am prepared to offer, by the way—to end it peaceably. There is no possible way you can avoid the inevitable. I have three hundred men with me, cannon and shot enough to blow the walls of your impregnable castle to kingdom come. However, as much as I should enjoy seeing you crushed slowly under the exploding rubble, I am under orders to be as expedient as possible in concluding our business here in the Highlands."

"Expedient?" Alex's white teeth flashed in a grin. "A quaint word for slaughter, theft, and destruction."

"It is the General's wish to be able to return to London with a solid guarantee that your countrymen will have neither the heart nor the means to rebel against the crown in the future."

"So you burn the cottages, kill the crofters who work the land, and rape the farms of their livestock and crops? An admirable plan for restoring peace and winning confidence for the throne."

"You invited retribution when you sought to rebel against the crown."

"Your crown, not ours."

"A matter of semantics."

"A matter of freedom, and of the right to choose our own king, make our own laws, not obey those of England's making."

"As you say, admirable sentiments, but misplaced. In war, there can be no place for sentiment, and freedom is the natural forfeit of the defeated. Give it up, Cameron. Surrender now and I can promise leniency for your men. Prolong it, and I will guarantee a corpse swinging from every bough in the forest. The officers and leaders, naturally, will be taken back to the proper authorities, regardless of whether they succumb to force or surrender willingly, but for someone who professes to hold such concern for the common masses, I should think you would be anxious to place their welfare before your own."

Alex removed the cigar from between his lips and inspected the glowing tip of red ash for a long moment. "And is that all you want? The surrender of the castle, the submission of the chief and his officers . . . nothing else, Major? I notice you did not mention my name on your lists. Does that mean I am free to go?"

Garner's eyes sparkled coldly. "It means there might be a way you could *win* your freedom."

"Ahh. You have a codicile to the terms of your . . . *generous offer*, I presume?"

"One you should not find too taxing on the imagination, Cameron. Shall we call it a chance to settle our own personal differences? No interference from any quarter this time. No saviours, no avenging angels."

"No bullets in the back if it looks like you are about to lose again?" Alex added silkily.

Hamilton's lips pinched at the insult. "The man acted against my direct order. I wanted you to myself then, and I still do now, by God. You can even pick the time and place, if it makes you feel more secure."

Alex's eyes narrowed thoughtfully. "And if I refuse?"

"If you refuse . . . you will give me the satisfaction of *knowing* you are a coward and a braggart, all talk and little substance—something *I* have known all these months, but for some unknown reason, still eludes your *wife*."

Alexander's impeccable control did him credit now, although it took every straining nerve to keep the motion of his hand steady as he lowered the cigar from his lips again.

"You have seen Catherine?" he asked quietly.

Garner crooked an eyebrow. "Haven't you? Not very observant of you, old boy."

He half-turned his head and lifted a gloved hand, the signal to someone behind him. He kept his attention on Alex's face and saw the eager, almost desperate widening of the indigo eyes as they searched along the row of sober-faced dragoons. He saw them snap back to the front of the line, saw the blood drain from the rigid countenance as two Argyleshire Campbells stepped around from behind the closed ranks of horses, half-leading, half-dragging a bound and gagged figure between them.

Catherine saw Alex, froze a moment in complete shock, then surged forward against the restraint of her guards, almost breaking free before they were able to tighten their grip on her arms and jerk her back.

Alex took an involuntary step forward as well, but pulled himself up short when he sensed the look of complete triumph on Garner's face. His hand had also dropped instinctively to the sword strapped to his waist, but the corresponding clicks of thirty flintlocks being cocked on thirty Brown Besses deterred him. Not so the alert and itching trigger fingers resting on thirty Highland muskets, and Alex felt a bubble of panic rise in his chest as he saw his men raise their guns in response to the threat from the Brown Besses.

"No!" Alex barked, knowing his men would account for a good many stiff-backed dragoons in an explosive confrontation of power. But Catherine was in the middle, an easy target for any one of the soldiers or guards who held her.

"I would call it an impasse, wouldn't you?" Garner drawled, looking casually from the levelled guns of his men to the levelled guns of the Highlanders. "Except for one glaring advantage, of course."

"If you have touched so much as a hair on her head, Major, I'll tear your heart out of your throat with my bare hands."

Garner smiled and shook his head. "I hardly think you are in a position to threaten me, Cameron. A twitch of my little finger and she is dead."

"You do that and your men get to draw maybe one breath," Alex snarled, throwing his cigar onto the ground. Instantly, from behind every tree, bush and shadow that ringed the clearing, a Highlander emerged, pistols drawn, broadswords poised against the murky haze. There had to be a hundred of them, sealing off all avenues of escape.

Garner stiffened, his composure taking a sharp plunge downward. "Is this your idea of fair play?"

"I agreed to meet with you, Garner. I never agreed to let you walk away alive."

Tiny emerald flecks of rage burned to life in Hamilton's eyes. "I trust you have left room for compromise?"

"That depends on how badly you want our *personal differences* settled, Garner."

Hamilton glared disdainfully. "The woman remains with me, *regardless*, until the matter is settled one way or another."

Alex had to fight hard to suppress a cold wave of fury. His gaze flicked past the major's shoulder to where Catherine stood, trembling and pale against the shadows. Aside from the fear shining in the huge violet eyes, she looked well enough; there were no outward signs she had been abused or mistreated in any way. Garner was on edge and it was doubtful he could be pushed much harder, yet he had introduced the word compromise first, and was obviously prepared to go to any extremes to get what he wanted.

"There is a field about a mile from here," Alex said. "Wide open. Neither one of us could hide a flea if we wanted to. If you agree to certain terms, we can have your rematch there, in plain sight of God and man."

"Terms?" Garner queried warily.

"I have two. If you won't agree to either one, I give the signal and it ends here and now, and to hell with the consequences."

Garner studied the rugged features, but there was nothing in Cameron's expression or his demeanour to suggest he would hesitate to carry through with the command.

"Name them."

"First, I want your personal guarantee the women and children will go free and unharmed whatever the outcome."

The major considered the condition, weighed it against his orders, the manpower he had at his call, and decided he could afford to be generous . . . for the time being. "Agreed. Secondly?"

"Secondly, you will bring Catherine to the field at dawn, and you will give me time—an hour, no more—to get her to safety."

Garner's mouth curved into a smile. "You must be joking."

"I'm deadly serious. Those are my conditions; meet them and you'll have your rematch."

"How do I know you will not use the time to simply find a safe place for the two of you to hide?" he scoffed. "In an hour you could be halfway to the coast."

It was Alex's turn to smile sardonically. "I would expect a question like that from a pissant drummerboy, Garner. You have my word of honour I will be back on the field within the hour. By the same token, I will want your word—as an *officer* and a *gentleman*—" he spat the words scornfully "—that you will still be there to meet me."

Hamilton quivered visibly at the insult. "I'll give you more, Cameron," he grated. "I'll give you my word as an officer in His Majesty's Royal Dragoons that if you fail to return within the allotted time, I shall personally oversee the destruction of your precious Achnacarry Castle.

Every brick, every stone, every inch of mortar, and every living soul inside will be levelled to dust."

"Agreed."

"And agreed."

Alexander cast one final glance toward Catherine, hoping she had indeed learned to read him well enough to see the message of promise and encouragement in his eyes. Then he turned and strode back to his men, knowing he had seventy-two hours worth of work to cram into the next twelve.

Chapter Twenty-Six

Dawn came early, yawning across the horizon, stretching fingers of gold, pink, and palest blue into the night sky to chase away the last few stars that hung over the mountains.

Hamilton Garner had marched his men to the appointed field well before dawn, but he was still not early enough to outflank the Highlanders. The Cameron men stood silhouetted against the mist like so many silent sentinels; only the occasional flutter of tartan or shifting of an arm or leg indicated they were hewn from anything but solid stone. They had taken the high ground and watched patiently while the dragoons filed into the lower rim of the meadow with their usual showy display of military precision.

Behind and above the Highlanders, the side of the mountain rose steeply up into the sky, blanketed under a dense forest of oak, yew, and pine trees, little of which could be seen through the clinging shroud of morning mist. The field itself shimmered under waves of dew-laden grass and silvered stalks of withered heather. Overnight, colonies of spiders had encased the weeds and low-lying shrubs in filaments that coated the branches and broken stems in gauze. Birds quarreled somewhere in the distance—impartial observers who seemed to be wagering excitedly on the outcome of the confrontation about to take place.

Garner broke away from his troop of men, cantering to a point midway across the field. In his hands he held the reins of a second pony, and, as Alex watched, wary of treachery even at this late hour, Catherine was set free and left to ride the rest of the way alone. She rode slowly, her head held high, wondering also if this was another of Hamilton's cruel mockeries. He had not said one word to her through the night, and had left her bound and gagged until shortly before taking to their horses.

As she rode toward Alex, she braced herself to feel the hail of bullets that would surely cut her from the saddle within inches of her goal. Her eyes did not waver from her husband's face. If fate had decreed she was to die within the next few moments, she wanted to die with the image of the love in his eyes emblazoned on her senses. He was alive and unhurt. Nothing else mattered.

Twenty feet, ten feet . . . five feet and her heart pounded like a triphammer in her chest. She had vowed not to cry, but her cheeks were wet, her eyes streaming, and before the horse had even stopped completely she was falling down into Alexander's outstretched arms, flinging her own around his neck, her face pressed into his neck, her body so depleted of its last reserves of strength she could not even muster a sob. Warm arms crushed her into an embrace. The low, trembling murmur of his voice was against her ear, but the words were unintelligible because of the roaring tumult of emotions rising within her.

Lips, desperate and loving, brushed her temple, her cheek. Hands that had not touched anything half so soft or silky in weeks twined into the tumble of her hair and tilted her head back so that mouths could come together, cling together, move together in tenderness, hunger, and relief.

"One hour, Cameron," Garner shouted. "Beginning now."

Alex tore his lips from hers and raised his head, his chest heaving, his eyes two beads of ebony, blacker than anything Catherine had ever seen, soulless, shot with sparks of pure, murderous hatred as he stared at Hamilton Garner.

Yet, they softened to deepest, darkest blue as he looked back down into her pale face again, and he even managed a smile of sorts as he lifted her into his arms and settled her onto the back of his chestnut stallion. He swung himself up behind her and, with Fanducci half-twisted around in his saddle to watch their backs, he led the way off the field, the rest of the Highlanders withdrawing in a slower guard behind them.

"I was so frightened," she began in a whisper.

"Hush. It's all over now. I'm taking you where you will be perfectly safe."

"Safe?" she echoed the word as if it was new to her vocabulary.

"These mountains are riddled with gorges, caves, and passes too numerous and too well hidden for the English to search in a dozen lifetimes. Lochiel is there already; we moved him up the mountain during the night. Maura, Jeannie, Rose, Archibald . . . they're all there."

"You've abandoned Achnacarry?"

"Let's just say we're not taking any chances. I told you once, a castle is only as strong as the men who guard her walls. I should have amended that to: only as strong as her walls. Ours have always been strong enough to hold off arrows and pikes, but Garner has artillery with him, and enough iron to bring down the walls of Jericho if he had to."

Catherine thought of the rugged beauty of Achnacarry, the sheer towering strength of the battlements that had seemed to personify the indomitable spirit of the Highlands. If Achnacarry could fall . . .

"Oh Alex," she cried, burying her face against the warmth of his chest. "How could it have happened? Where did it all go wrong?"

"Man's dreams are never wrong, Catherine. Only their methods of realizing them."

She raised her head and fought the lurching angle of the horse's gait to reach up and rest a small white hand on her husband's bronzed cheek. There were so many new lines on his face, so many new scars.

"Aluinn is dead," she whispered. "Deirdre is gone as well. So is Damien."

He drew back sharply on the reins, staring at her for several moments before he could gather the strength to speak.

"Aluinn . . . are you absolutely sure? How—?"

In short, bitten phrases she told him, starting with the ambush by the shores of Loch Ness, and their return to Moy Hall. Her voice was choked with tears long before she finished describing their horror at hearing about the defeat of Charles Stuart's army, the fate of the wounded.

Count Fanducci had drawn up alongside and both men listened intently, their expressions grim and unmoving, as her words took them back onto the battlefield, and they witnessed Aluinn and Deirdre's last few moments together.

"She loved him so very much," Catherine concluded shakily. "I guess . . . she simply couldn't bear the thought of living on without him."

Looking down into his wife's face, Alex stared at her hard for a long moment, then without warning, dismounted and brought her roughly down out of the saddle to stand before him.

"If you even think of doing something as stupid and senseless as that, I'll kill you myself," he snarled, gripping her arms so tightly she gasped with the pain. "*You* have everything to live for: You have your life, and the life of our child. Promise me . . . swear to me, Catherine, you'll do nothing to jeopardize either."

"But I . . . "

"*Swear it, goddammit*, or I'll wash my hands of you here and now."

"I swear it," she whispered. "I swear it, Alex, I—"

He pulled her into his arms and held her as if he meant to mold her into becoming a part of him. In the next instant, he was gasping, releasing her as a jolt of pain shot through his damaged arm and exploded unexpectedly throughout his body. He stumbled back a pace, cradling his hand and forearm against his chest.

"What is it?" Catherine cried. "What's wrong?"

"It's nothing," Alex muttered, his teeth grinding against the shock. "A souvenir of the major's good will."

Catherine stared at the injured arm, at the bright dots of crimson she could see staining through the layer of bandages, before Alex adjusted the sleeve of his shirt and hid them from view.

The Count had dismounted alongside Catherine and Alexander, but he was no longer watching them. He was focussing intently on the forest path up ahead, on the crack of a twig and the shuffle of a hide-bound foot.

Walking toward them, picking their way carefully down the steep grade of the path, were six armed clansmen and, in their midst, looking even more serene and aristocratic than Catherine remembered, was Lady Maura Cameron.

"Catherine!" There were tears in Maura's eyes as she rushed forward, her arms outstretched in welcome. Catherine went into them willingly, needing very much to feel the comfort and reassurance of another woman's compassion.

"How dreadful this must all have been for you, child," Maura said, her lips pressed to Catherine's brow, her hand trembling as it smoothed over the long golden twists of hair. "And how well you look, despite everything. You are well, are you not? You and your child?"

Catherine nodded, smiling through fresh tears.

"You are safe now. You are with us—your family—where you belong." Maura's soft brown eyes met Alexander's, and she added, "We'll take good care of her, you may be sure."

Catherine turned in time to see a signal pass between Count Fanducci and her husband. He unfastened his heavy cloak and shrugged it from his shoulders, then withdrew the steel blade of his sword a few inches from his leather scabbard and tested the sharpness of the edge against his thumb.

Catherine turned slowly, fully around. "What are you doing?"

When there was no answer, she looked frantically toward the Count. "Giovanni—what is he doing?"

"*Signora*—" Fanducci spread his hands in a gesture of helplessness.

"Alex?" She left Maura's side and ran back to him. "You're not going back there! You're not actually going back there to fight him!"

"Catherine . . . I have no choice."

"No choice!" she gasped. "We're *free*! You said yourself we can hide in these mountains forever and not be found. Please, Alex, *please*! There is no earthly reason why you should go back there and fight him!"

"I gave my word, Catherine," he said quietly. "The bastard actually honoured his half of the agreement; you can hardly expect me to do less."

"Honour! Is that what this is about—honour?" She whirled away, then rounded on him again, her face twisted with despair. "If honour is so important to you, why can't you honour me or your son? You made us a promise too, or have you forgotten?"

"I haven't forgotten."

"But playing at swords and games of male supremacy are more important?"

"Catherine—"

"I won't let you do it!" she declared fiercely. "I won't let you die because of me!"

Alex reached out a hand and touched her shoulder. "If it was only for you, my love, I would gladly spit in Garner's face and take my chances in the hills. But it isn't just for you or for me. If I don't go back, he'll destroy Achnacarry."

"He'll destroy it anyway!" she cried. "Whether you win or lose, whether he lives or dies, they'll destroy Achnacarry! Cumberland has given them specific orders to do so, and if nothing else, these bastards know how to obey orders! Alex! Are you listening to me? Do you understand what I'm telling you?"

He was looking at her, his expression calm, his eyes studying and committing every curve and contour to memory.

"*Alex*?"

"I'm listening. And I hear what you're telling me. I just . . . don't want to argue with you. Not now. Not when there is so little time left."

Catherine's lips trembled apart and she flung herself into his arms with a sob. "Please Alex. Please don't go through with this."

He cradled her face between his hands and kissed her. "I love you, Catherine. Whatever happens, I want you to remember that."

"Alex . . . *please!*"

"I want you to stay with Maura and Giovanni and do exactly what they say."

"No. Oh no, Alex. No . . . please . . . "

"Catherine, listen to me. *Listen* to me—" he angled her head up, forcing her to look into his eyes. "You are all I have. You are the singlemost important thing in my life and I want to know you are safe. Do that much for me,

Catherine. Live for me, live for our son. I'll always be with you, whatever happens, and you will always be with me. Nothing can change that. Nothing."

Catherine's eyes flooded with tears. She kissed him, urgently, desperately, and clung all the more tightly when she heard Maura come quietly up behind them. He was going. He was leaving and there was nothing she could say or do to stop him!

"*Alasdair na Camshroinaich.*" It was Maura's voice, calm and assured, in a world that, for Catherine, held only madness. "Rose told me where to find this. She thought I should bring it to you, that if ever the old *gaisgach liath's* hand should reach out from the grave and help you, it should be now."

Catherine felt her husband's body tense. Through her tears she saw Maura accept something wrapped in a dirt-encrusted length of tartan from one of the accompanying bodyguards. The folds were loosened and the polished, dazzling brilliance of a sword was introduced into the murky light of the forest.

The *clai' mór* was ancient, the hilt wrought in gold, protected by a basket-shaped guard of filagreed silver studded with topazes. With the point of the blade touching the ground, the cap of the hilt rose well above Maura's shoulder and was almost too heavy for her slender arms to balance as she held it out to him.

"Take your grandfather's sword, Alex. Use it as it was meant to be used."

Memories long buried burned in the depths of Alex's eyes as he took the sword. Memories of Annie MacSorley, the Campbell brothers—Dughall, Colin, and Malcolm. Memories of Aluinn MacKail and their shared fifteen-year-long exile; of Struan MacSorley's grinning face, and Damien Ashbrooke's reluctant but determined foray into soldiering. The memories all flashed before him as his grip tightened on the gold hilt, but none of them was stronger at the moment than the memory of the wizened, crinkled features of the sage old Highlander who had been the first to earn the title, *Camshroinaich Dubh.*

Then the dark eyes fastened on Catherine and she felt a clutch of fear squeeze around her heart, pushing all other thoughts from her mind but one.

"I love you, Alex," she whispered, barely able to stand her ground through a final embrace. Her knees wavered and her body swayed, but Maura's arms were there to support her as she watched her husband mount his horse and ride away alone down the forest path.

"What will I do?" she gasped. "What will I do if he does not come back to me?"

"You will do exactly what he asked you to do; exactly what he expects you to do," Maura said firmly. "You will live for him."

"But . . . if he does not come back—"

"You must believe he *will* come back. You must believe it with your whole heart and soul so Alex feels it and believes in the power of Sir Ewen's sword."

Catherine looked at Lady Cameron in astonishment. "Surely you do not believe there is any magical power in that sword? It's only a piece of steel!"

"I agree completely. Undoubtedly, Ewen found it when he was trekking in the mountains and concocted a wondrous story about it to inspire his men before going on raids. The real magic of it, Catherine, is in here—" she laid a hand gently over her breast. "It was Alex's love for Annie that gave him the strength to overpower the Campbell brothers, and it will be his love for you that carries him down this hill to meet his adversary."

"But . . . he's wounded. He's hurt . . . "

"And he knows you are waiting here for him to return; you and your son. That would be magic enough for any man."

Catherine glanced back along the empty forest path. Thin, lazy fingers of mist were resettling around the bases of the trees again, closing in the gap briefly caused by the passage of Alex's horse.

"*Signora Camerone*, please," the Count said, moving to her side and indicating the path back up the mountain. "We do as-a you husband wish, no? We go back up to the caves and-a wait."

Catherine squared her shoulders. Maura, ever practical, especially now when future provisioning was so uncertain, bent to retrieve the tartan the sword had been wrapped in. The Count was signalling to the other clansmen to retreat back up the hill and Catherine, on impulse, was able to reach across and withdraw one of the fancy snaphaunces from his belt. Fanducci's reflexes were lightning quick, but Catherine's, driven by fear and desperation, were quicker. She stepped back and had both serpentine flintlocks cocked before he could make any move to disarm her.

"Don't!" she warned, levelling the gun at his chest. "Please. You have been a good friend to Alex and I don't want to have to hurt you, but believe me, I will."

"Catherine!" Maura gasped.

"I'm not going to hide away in any cave to wait for news of my husband. I'm going back down the mountain and if anyone tries to stop me, or stand in my way, I'll shoot. I swear to God, I will."

"What are you going to do when you get down the mountain?" the Count asked calmly.

"I don't know. I just know I can't walk away and leave him all alone down there."

"*Signora*—"

"Catherine, they'll kill you if you go back," Maura cried, trying to reason with her, but Catherine shook her head vehemently.

"They won't kill me, I'm much more valuable to them alive. I'm the daughter of Sir Alfred Ashbrooke, a prominent member of parliament. My mother is Caroline Penrith, the King's own cousin. They wouldn't *dare* kill me."

Lady Cameron clasped her hands together, wringing them in frustration.

"Maura . . . I must go back. If I can't stop this terrible thing from happening, I can at least be there to see they do not go back on their word. I know Hamilton Garner. He'll only declare himself the winner if Alex is dead at his feet. But if he loses, I don't think his word is enough to bind the rest of his men. They know full well there is still a price on Alex's head, and it's good to any man who brings him back dead or alive. Alex is prepared to die for his honour and his family name—I can accept that. But he could never bear to be thrown into chains and put on display like some wild, caged animal. You of all people, Maura, should understand that."

Lady Cameron's face was completely bloodless, the knuckles of her hands white with strain where they were laced together.

The Count, studying Catherine's face intently, extended his hand slowly. "Give me the gun."

Catherine grasped the butt tighter in both hands, raising the barrel so that she was aiming between the two crystal clear blue eyes. For a long, breathless moment, Damien's face swam before her, but she shook away the unexpected image and backed away another determined pace.

"Catherine . . . give me the gun," he commanded. "You cannot go down there alone."

She bit down on the corner of her lip until she tasted blood, but her aim did not waver.

"You are a very brave, very resolute young lady . . . but also very foolish, no?" The handsome face relaxed into a wry smile. "Together, we would not-a be so foolish."

"T-together?"

He raised his hands, palms out. "Please, *signora*. The gun, she is-a very temperamental. A shiver, no more, and she goes off like-a the whore in-a the boy's school. Please."

Catherine lowered the barrel a fraction. "No tricks?"

"No tricks, *signora*. Your husband has-a been my good friend too. Together we make sure he's-a no cheated."

Catherine's arms fell down to her sides. The Count leaned over and eased the snaphaunce from her ice cold fingers and, with his piercingly sharp gaze still scrutinizing every minute detail of her face, he smiled. "I think, *signora*, you have the little blood of larceny in-a you veins, no?"

"More than you know," she agreed, thinking of Lady Caroline's confession.

"*Sí*. More than you know." He straightened and uncocked the hammers before replacing the gun in his belt. He crooked a finger at one of the nearby clansmen, noting the instant flash of suspicion in the violet eyes. It faded as soon as she realized he was only calling for horses.

Maura's shock trebled. "You cannot be serious! You are not really taking her back down there!"

Fanducci assisted Catherine into the saddle then doffed his tricorn in a sweepingly graceful bow to Lady Cameron. "Giovanni Alphonso Fanducci never goes-a back on his word, *signora*—something you Scots teach-a me very well. Don't worry. I won't-a let anything happen to *Signora* Catherine." He snapped his fingers and pointed collectively to the closest group of clansmen. "You, come-a with us. The rest, take Lady Cameron back to her husband. In-a one hour, if-a we don't come back, you bring-a down the mountain!"

Hamilton Garner paced the carpet of silvery, flattened heather, pausing now and then to scowl toward the upper end of the meadow. He wasn't coming back. The black-hearted, conniving bastard wasn't coming back! What in God's name had made him believe the Highlander was good for his word?

"Sir?"

"What is it, Corporal?" Garner snapped, turning to see Corporal Jeffrey Peters looking past him, staring at something higher up on the slope.

Hamilton spun around and felt a gratifying spurt of pleasure ripple through his loins. A lone figure stood poised against the distended wisps of mist, his wild, black hair flung forward against his cheeks and throat, his long, powerful legs braced wide apart. The cloak he had worn earlier had disappeared. He was dressed in black breeches and a white linen shirt, the latter fitting loosely across the massive shoulders and left open at the throat to reveal a wealth of curling black hair on his chest. Held in front of him, his hands draped almost leisurely across the hilt, was a sword that looked as if it had been forged in Dante's inferno. Tall—almost as tall as its owner, polished to a mirror brightness, it seemed to identify the warrior of legend, The Dark Cameron, and commanded the attention of every man present on the field.

Even Hamilton Garner was forced to admire the effect. The combination of black hair, black eyes, black boots and breeches, made a startling contrast against the dazzling white shirt, the gold and silver sword, and the drifting banks of mist behind him. It was enough to give a stout-hearted man pause, nevermind the low-life rabble Garner had collected in his troop. They were brave enough when it came to terrorizing a few unarmed farmers and killing the odd cornered clansman, but put them onto a field with a rogue warlord, surround them with mountains steeped in mist and superstition, and he could well imagine himself with a mutiny on his hands.

Even the Argyle Campbells, bestial brutes throughout the campaign, full of boasts on what they would do if ever turned loose in Lochaber, were standing wooden and silent, their ugly faces shining under a patina of clammy sweat.

Garner inflated his chest with a lungful of crisp, pungent air. When he was finished with Cameron, they would all be looking at him with the same awe and respect. They would cheer him as they would cheer any man who would dare slay a dragon, and there would be no limit to the heights to which he could rise. Cumberland had been the hero of the hour at Culloden, but he was bulbous and grotesque, and commanded his popularity through military discipline. He, Hamilton Garner, was the golden-haired saviour, walking alone onto a field of honour to do battle with the envoy of the Prince of Darkness.

A man with an army behind him could go far. As far as a throne.

Peters muttered something in Hamilton's ear, but the major brushed aside the interruption, wanting nothing to detract from the lush sense of anticipation surging through his veins. His smile curved into an avaricious grin as he unbuckled the scabbard housing his own slim rapier and called instead for one of the five-foot-long broadswords he had familiarized himself with over the months. If Cameron preferred Highland steel for this, his final battle, then Hamilton Garner had no objections. The hours he had spent re-training his army in their methods of countering the awesome weapons had turned his arms to the hardness of marble, increased his prowess and stamina tenfold. And indeed, if truth be known, he would prefer the bloody savagery of the double-edged blade to the swift, clean efficiency of a duelling rapier. This would be his finest performance to date, and he had no desire to end it quickly or compassionately.

Unbuttoning his tunic, Garner tossed the garment aside in a dramatic swirl of scarlet. As an afterthought, he removed the neatly powdered and curled periwig so that his pale gold hair was bare to the morning light. He adjusted the froth of lace at his throat and smoothed the white quilted satin of his long-skirted waistcoat.

"Corporal Peters, you will temper the enthusiasm of ıe men; I want no repeat of what happened at Culloden, o interference from any quarter. Is that clearly undertood?"

"Perfectly, sir. But in the event . . . er, in the event the ebel should gain an advantage—"

Hamilton glared at the younger officer. The boyish face ad suffered hideous scarring from the fall he had taken everal weeks before at Moy Hall, and his desire to evenge himself upon those he blamed for the disfiguraıon was nearly as great at Hamilton's, but it was equally bvious to Garner that the man was not stable enough to ıake cool, rational decisions.

"Corporal, if I am not able to deal with an exhausted, alf-crippled adversary, then he deserves every advanage he can win. As long as I am on my feet, however, you ill refrain from interfering."

Peters' persistence was not daunted by the glint in arner's eyes. "But if you are no longer on your feet, if he Scotsman—"

"If he wins, Corporal," the major interrupted blackly, I will expect you to carry through with your orders. his—" he pointed the tip of his sword across the field —is a private matter and has nothing whatsoever to do ith General Cumberland's specific directives."

A second officer, standing alongside Peters, snapped to ttention and saluted. "The destruction of Achnacarry astle, aye sir. The orders will be carried out."

"Your enthusiasm is commendable, Wellesley. As for he rebel—" Garner's gaze shifted back to Peters. "*Should* he inconceivable happen, Corporal, I would expect to ave his soul join mine in hell within a matter of moaents following my demise."

Peters smiled slowly. "Aye, sir. Thank you, sir."

Hamilton Garner fixed his attention once more on the igure standing before the encroaching mists. He was nildly disappointed that Cameron was not at his peak

form, for he would not want stories of his victory to b
clouded by any hint of unfair advantage. Then, clearin
his mind to concentrate on the task ahead, he forgo
everything, everyone, and as he began to walk across th
meadow, he primed himself by reliving the duel they ha
fought in the courtyard of Rosewood Hall, as well as th
confrontation at Culloden. With a fencer's instinct, h
identified and isolated all of Cameron's distinctiv
moves, knowing that the way a man fought was as idio
syncratic and personalized as the way he made love. Hav
ing replayed the humiliating moments leading up to an
including the stunning coup when Cameron's blade ha
sliced through his ribs, he was confident that this time
there could be no such unexpected surprises.

Nor was he intimidated by the size of the ancien
clai' mór Cameron had brought to the field. Hamilton sus
pected the sheer weight of the weapon would tear what
ever shreds of muscle still remained intact in the dam
aged arm; the pain alone would be monstrous and debili
tating, not to mention draining on the power of the goo
right arm. The Scot could boast a deservedly respectfu
reputation with a rapier and all things considered, h
might have been better off choosing the lighter weapon

Garner halted a sword's length from his adversary.

"It is refreshing, if not surprising, to see you are a ma
of your word."

Alexander smiled lazily as he gazed past Hamilton'
shoulders to drink in the vast, panoramic beauty of Loch
aber's mountains and glens. "Shall we skip the pleasan
tries, Major? My wife is most anxious for me to rejoi
her."

Garner parried the verbal thrust with an equally slow
insolent smile. "I will be most happy to convey you
regrets when I see her, Highlander."

In a move so quick Alex almost missed it, Hamilton'
sword came up and across in a swooshing arc that woul
have severed Cameron through the belly if he had been

heartbeat slower to react. The resounding clash of metal striking metal startled the wooded silence, scraping it raw with the shrill slide of the two blades biting into each other's metallic spines for traction. Although Garner had not been foolish enough to underestimate the determination Cameron would bring onto the field, he was still astounded at the power he felt behind the driving retaliation.

Steel slashed steel, both weapons so heavy to wield and recover that the swordsmen appeared to be moving in slow motion. Metal clanged and the echoes reverberated off the rocks, the sounds smashing one against the other until it created a wall of shrieking vibrations. Curses were barked from between clenched teeth and, at the bottom of the rolling slope, the dragoons became a rapt audience as the adversaries attacked, retreated, circled, lunged, and gored the air with sweeping rushes of destruction.

Alexander's arm screamed with pain. He could feel Archibald's meticulous stitchwork tearing apart, the blood swelling warmly against the tight bandages. Garner had targeted the weakness from the first stroke of his blade and was wearing away at it again and again, aiming each cut so that Alex's left arm and wrist bore most of the pressure.

A gentle trough in the ground briefly swallowed the two men from view and the watchers below nudged one another and broke formation, surging up the field, shouting and wagering among themselves as to which man would go down first. The major's skill was legion among the ranks of the dragoons and the exploits of the Dark Cameron had been whispered around the campfires for months. No one wanted to have to say he had missed a single detail of the final encounter, and for the time being, at any rate, no one let politics or loyalties cloud their avid sense of gamesmanship. Both combatants were championed equally, both carried the wagers of several months pay on their shoulders.

They were not faring equally, however. Alex's face poured sweat, and his hair and shirt were soaked with it. His shirtsleeve was now a shiny splotch of gore and each two-fisted swing of the mighty *clai' mór* sent a thin spray of blood droplets fanning off the ridge of his knuckles. He was tiring. The tremendous muscles in his thighs and calves bulged with the strain of absorbing shock after shock, strike upon strike, and he knew if he did not find an opening soon, he would not have to trouble himself over the pain or the fatigue much longer.

Hamilton, bloodied at hip and shoulder, had had his astonishment fueled to fury as Cameron not only continued to return as good as he was given, but initiated several attacks, the strength and savagery of which had resulted in unseemly defensive scrambles. The man was not human! He should have gone down a dozen strokes ago, not returned again and again with devastating ripostes! Garner was forced to draw on his reserves sooner than he had anticipated, even to retreat once or twice to regroup his nerve and his concentration.

The blades crossed again, the impact shuddering along both sets of arms, the concussion sending an exchange of blood and sweat across the narrow gap. The ringing thrusts of steel and explosions of power from both swordsmen carried the fight over the crest of a knoll and down into a sunken depression in the ground. Alex, backing into it, slid on the mushy earth, his ankle twisting out from under him and sending him crashing heavily onto the wet grass. He rolled, as much out of agony as out of an instinctive command for self-preservation, and regained his stance, but the stumble had cost him. Garner was waiting, and Alex felt the flat of the blade strike his shoulder and the point slash down, ripping through the previously wounded flesh of his forearm.

Somehow he managed to retain his grip on the *clai' mór* long enough to deflect Garner's blade upward. Garner, stepping into the same swampy depression that Alex had lipped on, had his attention momentarily split between voiding a similar fall and holding onto the precarious alance of the heavy sword. He heard a soft whistle of ushing air and the jade-green eyes flicked upward. A tray beam of morning light was flaring along the length f Cameron's broadsword, causing the burnished metal o glow like a fiery beacon. The blade descended toward im, the motion clean and elegant, almost beautiful to ehold as it struck the side of Garner's neck and severed, vith fiery grace, through flesh, bone, and cartilege.

It also cut through the scream that rose from Garner's hest, ending it abruptly in a gouting hiss of hot blood. There was a look of utter disbelief and horror in his eyes, nd a groping movement by his hands as if he could not ccept the fact that his head was no longer attached to is shoulders. The body crashed forward, the head jumping free and rolling to a halt against a hillock of moss-overed stones. The neatly queued blond hair came free f its velvet ribbon and lay scattered across the gray-white pallor of the face, the tips streaking spidery threads f blood across the gaping lips.

Alex swayed unsteadily on his feet, most of his weight agging against the support of the red-streaked *clai' mór.* He bent his head and leaned his brow on the cool metal f the basket hilt, his chest heaving, his legs trembling rom the massive exertion. It had happened so quickly —the opening, the strike, the cut—he half expected Garner to stand up and resume the attack.

Of the men who formed the now-silent ring of spectators, some stared at the twitching, headless corpse of heir commanding officer, most gaped at the bleeding Scotsman.

Only one of the dragoons who had had the presence of mind to carry his musket along as he followed the duelists, raised it now, carefully thumbing back the hammer to full cock. Corporal Jeffrey Peters took deliberate aim at the Highlander's chest, curled his finger around the trigger and squeezed.

The delay between the flint sparking against the powder and the powder exploding to release the lead shot was filled by a second blast of gunpowder. Peters was lifted and flung back off his feet, the action causing his weapon to discharge harmlessly into the empty air. When the smoke cleared, there was a neat round hole in the centre of his forehead, a Cyclops' eye with a rim of bright red around the edges.

Count Giovanni Fanducci lowered his snaphaunce as a dozen other armed clansmen appeared out of the mist behind him, their muskets primed and levelled on the stunned circle of redcoats.

"*Scusa, signor.* I'm-a sure you could have handled these *bastardos* on-a you own, but, eh . . . why should you have all-a the fun?"

Alex smiled weakly. "Why indeed."

"You can walk?"

Alex swallowed hard and nodded. "I can walk."

"*Bene.*" Fanducci waved the snaphaunce, indicating to the soldiers who held muskets dragging down by their sides that they would be wise to lower them all the way down to the ground. As soon as they complied, the clansmen gathered up the weapons and powderhorns and carried them to the edge of the forest. The soldiers were herded into a nervous group and driven back down the field to where their horses were tethered, while Alex, his good arm draped gratefully over Fanducci's shoulders, was led in the opposite direction into the safety of the trees.

Bleary with pain and exhaustion, Alex had no idea how far they walked before Fanducci called a halt and lowered him gently onto an overturned tree stump.

"So much blood," he muttered, tearing strips from his shirt to bind the wound on Alex's arm. "It's a wonder you do not melt into the ground, my friend."

"I would have been part of the ground if you hadn't come along when you did. Saying a mere thank you hardly seems adequate."

"Do not thank me yet, Cameron," came the quiet rejoinder . . . so quiet and so low it took several seconds for the alarm bells to penetrate Alexander's fogged brain. Other vague stirrings in what was left of his battered instincts sent his hand moving to his waist only to find that his dirk had somehow vanished from its sheath.

"I took the liberty of removing it while we were walking," the Count said in perfect English. "Unlike your friend back there, I have come to appreciate the fact that one should never underestimate your limits or your talents."

Alex stared up at the handsome face for a long moment before answering.

"You seem to have acquired a new talent of your own," he noted calmly.

The blue eyes glanced up. "A compliment from the Dark Cameron? I'm flattered."

"Don't be. Who the hell are you? And why the elaborate charade?"

"Elaborate, yes. I was told I had to be wilier than the fox himself to get close to you, and I must say, in all humility, Count Giovanni has always ranked among my best and most favorite personas."

"You have others?"

"A chameleon must be able to change his colours to adapt to his surroundings—you of all people should appreciate that, *Monsieur* Montgomery."

The use of the name set off another, louder chorus of alarm bells and Alex peered closely at the Count's face. He had shed his plumed tricorn and abandoned his wig somewhere along the way; his own sable brown hair was curled forward at the temples, liberally shot through with streaks of gray. Something about him looked damned familiar. Alex wracked his tired brain trying to dredge up some distant memory, some incident or event in his past to explain the nagging feeling he should know who this man was. *Monsieur* Montgomery, he had said. A slip . . . or a deliberate clue?

A clue, chimed the ghostly whisper of Aluinn's voice through the hushed stillness. *And if he gave you a much bigger one, he would have to hit you over the head with it. I warned you, goddammit. I warned you, but you wouldn't take me seriously, and now it's too late.*

Warned me? Warned me about what? About who?

Think, you stupid bastard! Think back—

Alex stiffened through an ice cold shudder of apprehension. The Frenchman! Aluinn had told him months ago about a man . . . an assassin hired by the Duke of Argyle to hunt him down and accomplish what his scores of brute-fisted henchmen had been so far unable to do for sixteen years. But it wasn't possible! It couldn't be possible, not after all they had gone through together—the weeks, months of camaraderie in camp, the advance into Derby, the retreat . . . *Culloden*!

"You could have killed me a hundred times over," Alex said in a shocked murmur. "Why the hell have you waited until now?"

The Frenchman smiled benignly. "A good question, *monsieur.* One I have asked myself many times over the past weeks."

"And? Any answers?"

"None I would be able to explain. None I was able to explain to myself until just a short while ago." He finished tying off the strips of bandaging around Alex's arm and straightened, moving a prudent distance away as he detected the subtle increase of tension in the Highlander's body. A truly remarkable man, he marvelled. An admirable adversary; one who would resist to the last gasp. Even now, he was calculating the distance, the obstacles, the weapons at hand. To set his mind at ease, the Frenchman withdrew one of his snaphaunces and held it casually balanced across his folded forearm.

"One of the hazards of our profession, *monsieur*: friendship. I have always prided myself in being able to resist such mundane entanglements—especially those involving the female persuasion. There too, alas, I once committed a major *faux pas*, which I now find has come back to haunt me with a vengeance."

Alex was only partially listening. He had already arrived at the conclusion that the Frenchman could kill him before he'd even struggled upright onto his feet; he was not particularly interested in hearing the bastard gloat.

Sighing, he adjusted the angle of his injured arm, cradling it higher on his chest. "So what happens now, Fanducci . . . or whatever the hell your name is."

"St. Cloud. Jacques St. Cloud."

Alex's face remained impassive. He thought he detected more than the normal degree of intensity behind the piercing blue eyes, but if the name was supposed to dislodge some of the mortar sealing his recollections, his captor was disappointed.

"So," St. Cloud mused. "There are still some secrets left in the world."

"I'm afraid I'm not following you."

"You are not required to follow me, *monsieur*, only to listen." He paused and looked down at the blood staining his fingers. "Your wife is a very beautiful woman. There could not be two faces so alike in this world, yet I did not see it—or perhaps I did, but was unwilling to resurrect the pain of old wounds. You see, I was once very much in love myself, with a woman as vibrant as the sun itself, who heated within me a passion I had never experienced, before or since. Unfortunately, there were circumstances neither one of us could control that intervened and separated us, dispatching her back into her world, and me into mine."

"St. Cloud—"

The Frenchman held up a hand. "Please. This is difficult enough to do without having to go into lengthy and involved explanations, which neither one of us have the time or inclination to waste at the moment. Suffice it to say, those questions and explanations which have been plaguing me for the past five months were finally resolved an hour ago, when your wife mentioned a name—a name I whisper to myself each night before I close my eyes, and each morning before I draw my first breath of air."

"Catherine? *Where is she?*"

"Quite safe, I assure you. I left her some distance back in the forest—very angry to be sure, and feeling doubly betrayed after I had promised she could be there to help rescue you. An incredible young woman, *monsieur.* I feel a true father's pride in knowing each of you deserves the other. I could not have chosen a better match myself."

Alex felt another shock ripple through him. He remembered! There had been a whispered confession made many months ago, muffled by fear and shadows, when Catherine and Deirdre had first joined the retreating army outside of Derby. In her need to exorcise the demons surrounding the death of the British lieutenant, Catherine had also poured out the story her mother had told her, including the revelation that Sir Alfred Ashbrooke had not sired either her or Damien.

Was this not the ultimate irony? Alexander thought as he regarded the man before him. The highwayman turned assassin come to hunt down the husband of the daughter he did not know he had?

"Dear God," Alex murmured. "Does Catherine know you are her father?"

"Catherine?" St. Cloud smiled faintly. "No, *monsieur.* This shall remain between you and me, unto the grave."

"But she already knows Ashbrooke wasn't her real father. Dammit, man, she likes you. She deserves to be told."

"No," said St. Cloud adamantly, aligning the aim of the snaphaunce for emphasis. "And if I cannot carry away your word of honour that you will hold your silence in this matter, then I shall indeed carry away your head so that I might collect my well-earned reward from *Monsieur le Duke*."

"But—"

A thumb coolly and pointedly cocked a hammer. "I will carry the tragedy of my son's death burned forever on my mind, Alexander, please . . . do not make me carry yours as well."

"You knew about Damien?"

"I knew there had been a child . . . a male child, conceived out of wedlock, and instrumental in forcing my beloved Caroline into a marriage of convenience. I did not learn this for many, many years, and, by then, there were *too* many years of bitter feelings to keep me from searching too deeply into what had become of them. Too many hard decisions made, as well, to complicate my life or compromise the lives of any others."

Alex nodded slowly. An assassin with a family? As unlikely and unhealthy as lighting a cigar in a roomful of powder.

Alex agreed reluctantly. "You have my word. Catherine will not hear the truth from me—but it won't stop me from appealing to you to tell her yourself."

"Perhaps I will, some day. For now, however, I think it best we go our separate ways. You will need time to get your family out of the country," St. Cloud said pensively. "And a fresh start, I think, without jackals sniffing after you at every turn."

"There are five thousand Campbell jackals out there, St. Cloud. You're good, but you're not that good."

"*Monsieur*! A little imagination, please. There is a perfectly good head lying back there on the field, cut to order. Some black dye, a little creativity with a knife, and *voilà*: The Duke's failing eyesight should keep my reputation unsullied."

Alex thought for a moment, then reached with painful difficulty to unclasp the silver and topaz brooch he wore fastened to his belt.

"Give this to The Campbell of Argyle. He will know there is only one way you could have taken it from me."

St. Cloud inspected the brooch's studded gems and embossed family crest. "*Bien.* It will be enough, I think."

He tucked the brooch safely into a pocket of his waistcoat and resheathed the pistol in its leather sling. Alex caught at his arm as he was about to walk past.

"You do have friends, St. Cloud. Good friends who would judge you for the man you are, not the man you were."

St. Cloud levelled his gaze on the handsome features of his son-in-law and smiled with genuine appreciation. "Unfortunately, I also have many enemies, who, as you are undoubtedly aware from your own experiences, would gain great satisfaction in discovering I had formed any . . . lasting ties. Take care of yourself, Alexander Cameron. Take care of my daughter and grandchild as well."

A faintly self-mocking salute carried St. Cloud back down the path and within seconds, he seemed to have vanished behind a wall of impenetrable shadows. Alex sat a few moments longer, lost in thought, and then, with the help of the *clai' mór,* struggled to his feet, took his bearings from the muted rill of a startled ptarmigan somewhere in the gloom of the forest, and began his own weary climb to safety.

Epilogue

Catherine walked up behind the tall, brooding figure who stood at the mouth of the cave and slipped her arms around his waist.

"Why are you torturing yourself, Alex? There is nothing you can do about it. You can't stop them."

There was no response, no movement from the rigid body as yet another series of muffled explosions reverberated off the cliffs and corries surrounding them. Cumberland's troops were destroying Achnacarry. For nearly a week, the Camerons had remained hidden in the caves high above the castle, hardly daring to hope the soldiers might move on and spare their home from demolition, but it was a wasted hope. The delay had only provided the soldiers ample time to strip the castle of anything of value and to set nearly five hundred kegs of black powder in and around the walls and apartments. The initial explosions had caused the ground to shudder and dirt to crumble from the walls and ceiling of the caves, and, since then, day in and day out, what remained of the centuries-old fortification was systematically bombarded and reduced to rubble.

Alex stood for hours at the mouth of the cave, staring at the twisting, writhing pillars of black smoke that rose from the shore of the loch. Respect for his brother's wishes had been the only thing that kept him from going down the mountain again. Lochiel had said, and rightfully so, that it was better to remember Achnacarry as it had been, not as the smoldering, skeletal mass of broken beams and smashed wreckage the soldiers would make of it.

Moreover, the mountains were crawling with patrols. A clansman had brought them word that Cumberland believed the Prince was hiding somewhere in the Western Highlands, and as determined as the Duke had been to break the rebel army at Culloden, he was obsessed with seeing Charles Stuart caught and taken back to London for trial.

Under the auspices of searching for the fugitive prince, the soldiers were sweeping through the glens like locusts; burning, looting, raping, killing, stealing everything that might provide sustenance or comfort to the cowering farmers. They were leaving a wasteland in their wake, one which would take years, if not decades, for the people to restore.

Anyone suspected of having fought with the rebels or of having supported their cause in any way was arrested and sent either to Fort William or Fort George to await trial. Deciding to save the authorities the time and bother of legal proceedings, the soldiers often took their captives no further than the first sturdy oak tree. A list containing the names of forty of the most prominent Jacobite leaders was circulated throughout the Highlands and impressive rewards for their capture were turning many a hungry eye up into the mountains. High on the list were Lord George Murray, James Drummond, Lochiel and his brothers Dr. Archibald and Alexander Cameron, Ardshiel, MacDonald of Glencoe . . . From being leaders of a glorious rebellion, they had been reduced to penniless fugitives; once chiefs and lawmakers, the voices of absolute authority, they were now solely dependent upon the loyalty and generosity of former tenants.

No one among the fugitive Jacobites knew for certain the whereabouts of Prince Charles. Lochiel seemed to think he had headed for the coast, hoping to catch a ship for France, but rumours placed him as far north as Caithness, or south in the Lowlands of Ayr.

"As soon as Donald is able to travel, we'll have to leave this place," Alex said, taking Catherine's hands and removing them from his waist, so he could draw her forward and bring her into his arms. "As long as Charles Stuart is on the loose, the soldiers will keep policing the area, searching the hills, the towns, the villages. Once again, as ever, it appears I am failing you. A hell of a husband and provider you chose for yourself, madam."

Catherine nestled deeper into his embrace, careful of his wounded arm. "This is all I want, Alexander Cameron. Just this. Just you."

Alex bowed his head and buried his lips in the crown of golden hair. "You have me. You also have my most solemn word of honour, I will never let you out of my sight again. No more conspiracies, no more intrigues, no more jousting at windmills. No more—" his voice faltered, and Catherine's arms tightened around him. She felt helpless to say or do anything to ease the pain and bitterness in his heart. It was bottomless and endless; there was an eternity of agony in his eyes, a loss he would carry with him the rest of his days.

"I keep expecting to see him walk up the hill, a smile on his face, an easy solution to all the world's problems in the palms of his hands. God, I took him for granted. I never realized how much I'd miss him, how much of a friend and brother he was to me."

"I loved Aluinn too," Catherine whispered. "He was a good friend to me—and Deirdre loved him so very much . . . ."

"I can almost accept everything else—the fighting, the killing, the stupid, senseless waste . . . But not Aluinn's death. I don't want to believe it, and I can't accept it. It never should have happened. Neither one of them should have died like that. One of the last things he said to me was how much he was looking forward to settling down to the life of an ordinary farmer, getting back to his roots, strolling into old age with a wife and children by his side . . ."

"Alex don't. Don't do this to yourself. Aluinn MacKail would not have wanted you to torment yourself this way, just as you would not have wanted him to dwell on the tragedy, had it been the other way around."

"But it wasn't me who died," he replied bitterly. "It should have been, but it wasn't. Aluinn died because he was doing what he always did—guarding my back. I'm sure he never wanted to trail over half the world with me. He loved this place. He loved Scotland; he never wanted to leave. He only went into exile with me out of a sense of duty, and later, when he'd adapted to a life in Europe, he only came away again because I decided it was time to come back. I never asked him what he wanted to do. I never once asked him if he wanted to get involved in this bloody rebellion. He just came and fought and died."

"Oh Alex, you're so wrong! He stayed with you because he was your friend and he wanted to stay with you." She reached up and laid her trembling hands on his cheeks, sharing his despair. "You once told me, the only regrets we should have in life are for the things we have never done. I do not think Aluinn MacKail had any regrets. It was his choice to make to follow you into exile, his choice to return with you when you came back. As much as you might like to fancy yourself a tyrant and overlord, Aluinn was not afraid of you. If he had not wanted to spend all those years chasing ghosts with you, he wouldn't have, and if he had not wanted to fight for what was fine and honourable about Scotland, he would not have walked onto the field at Culloden. Grieve for him, Alex, because he was a gentle and loving man, a compassionate man, a man who could find something to laugh about in the blackest hours. Cry for the loss, my love, because there will never be another Aluinn MacKail in our lives, or another Deirdre, or Damien, or Struan MacSorely. But as long as we can cry for them, and laugh with the memories, and share the gifts they left us with others, then they will always be a part of us. And in a way, so will Achnacarry." She turned to watch the spiralling black clouds of smoke. "If we remember it as it was, tall and proud and strong, then it will always be there, just like the mist and the mountains and the heather on the moors."

It was Alex's turn to feel inadequate. She had expressed it so clearly and the sentiments were so pure, there was nothing he could do but cling to her and thank whatever fates had conspired to bring them together. A chance meeting in a clearing. An impulsive, last-minute detour through Derby by a man who rarely acted on impulse. A golden-haired English beauty and a roguish Highland soldier of forture. Who would have thought it could work?

"Aluinn," he murmured. "Aluinn predicted you would be the one to tame me, as far back as the inn at Wakefield."

"Our Aluinn was a clever man," Catherine agreed, not altogether certain what had inspired the statement, but happy, nonetheless, to see a faint gleam of amusement return to her husband's eyes. He was going to be alright. Everything was going to be alright.

"Oh!" She gasped and pulled suddenly out of his arms.

"What is it? What's wrong?"

Catherine waited for the spasm to pass, then took his hand and pressed it over the hard swell of her belly.

"There. Can you feel him? Your son is reminding us not to leave him out of the conversation entirely."

Alex tilted her mouth up to his. "In that case, if it is not too premature, I would like to put forth a name for his approval."

"Too late, my lord," she said, shaking her head. "I have already chosen all three names."

"Three?"

"Aye, my lord. *Aluinn Ewen mhac Alasdair.* I warrant that should be a powerful enough charm for the son of the *Camshroinaich Dubh* to carry on down through history. One not even Aunt Rose's dark gods could ignore."

* * * *

Author's Notes

Both *The Pride of Lions* and *The Blood of Roses* are works of fiction, but it was impossible not to succumb to the temptation to use some of the actual people involved in the Jacobite uprising for not even the most fertile of imaginations could improve upon their stories. The politics, policies and conflicts are as accurately represented as the limits of the genre will allow. The Jacobite victories at Prestonpans and Falkirk were astonishing, as was the later disgrace perpetrated by Cumberland's troops in the aftermath of Culloden: I could not, in all conscience, downplay, alter, or "soften" either representation.

One of the more prominent real characters I used was Donald Cameron, The Cameron of Lochiel. He played a crucial role in the decision of the clans as to whether to "come out" in the Forty-Five—as the rebellion later came to be known—or to abstain. His involvement in the rebellion and his active participation in the Prince's councils of war were very real, as were the heroic charges led by his Cameron clansmen at Prestonpans and Culloden. Lochiel survived the terrible wounds he received at Culloden that infamous day and did, indeed, witness the destruction of his magnificent castle at Achnacarry from a hiding place in the hills. He escaped Scotland on the same ship that carried Prince Charles to safety some months later, but he never quite recovered his health and died in France in 1748.

Dr. Archibald Cameron escaped with his brother, but against all advice, jeopardized his safety by repeatedly undertaking risky ventures back to Scotland on Jacobite business. In 1753, he won the dubious distinction of being the last prominent Jacobite to be arrested and hung for his activities during the rebellion.

One of the more startling coincidences—and there were many—that seemed to come to me straight out of the twilight zone in the three years I spent researching and writing these two books concerned the creation of my hero, Alexander Cameron. Normally a matter of whimsy to choose the hero's name—the task became a massive headache very early on when I discovered that one could not merely pluck a Scottish name out of the air and use it at will. Being distinctly territorial and violently feudal in nature, the clans of the Highlands were divided and contained within definite and incontrovertable borders. A man could be hung on the spot, no questions asked, if he happened to erringly stumble onto the land of a rival clan. Therefore, for example, one could not use the name Campbell where any one of the twenty or so affiliated branches of the Clan MacDonald resided. Add to this the political turmoil—heaven save the unknowing author who plunks a Jacobite MacBean in the land of Hanover Munroes (the width of a river apart). Factor in, as well, the religious dissention at the time and the open hostilities between Highlanders and Lowlanders, and you begin to see the maze I found myself in—also, the relief I felt when I located the Camerons, Donald and Archibald, and knew they belonged to exactly the clan I needed. The name Alexander came, well, trippingly off the tongue, and my imagination was free to provide him with a mysterious past, a long forced exile on the Continent, a return to Scotland after fifteen years . . .

Imagine my shock when, some months deeper into the research, I discovered the existence of an actual Alexander Cameron, the younger brother of Donald and Archibald. So shadowy a figure was he that he was only mentioned once, but given to be a rogue and an exile with a mysterious past who had been absent on the Continent for *fifteen years*! I was not able to discover his fate; I can only hope it ran parallel to that of my Alexander, and that he escaped and found happiness elsewhere.

Lord George Murray was able to smuggle himself out of Scotland some months after Culloden and arrived in Holland in December of 1746. Although he repeatedly appealed to the Prince for an audience, Charles Stuart irrationally blamed his general for all his defeats and Lord George was never again permitted to come within the Prince's sight. Despite Charles' unjustified and adamant bitterness toward him, Lord George remained loyal to the Stuarts, refusing to seek a pardon from the Hanover government when such was offered, and never again returned to his beloved Scotland. He died in Holland in 1760.

William O'Sullivan managed to escape on the first ship out of Scotland and, being first to recount his version of the events before the court of the exiled King James, he was lauded as a hero, knighted, and later rewarded with a baronetcy. Another of O'Sullivan's cohorts, John Murray of Broughton, loudest in trumpeting his suspicions of Lord George's ulterior motives toward the Prince, was, ironically, the quickest to turn king's evidence after his arrest and imprisonment. He informed on many of the chiefs and lords he had served with during the nine months of the rebellion and caused their subsequent arrest and hanging.

Struan MacSorley was a composite of several real characters, most notably Gilles MacBean—a giant of a man who fought valiantly and heroically to his last drop of blood. Colonel Anne Moy was a real person who led her men onto the field at Culloden; her captain, the brave MacGillivray, died in the manner I have described, defending the retreat of the Jacobites.

A host of what might have seemed like incredible events actually happened, and—like the Rout of Moy, where a dozen screaming men frightened away fifteen hundred soldiers—were too good to ignore in unfolding the story of the rebellion. Others, like the forging of Lord George Murray's battle orders, which contributed to the bloody and unconscionable slaughter of hundreds of helpless men on the field at Culloden, were too important to omit. Following the barbaric behavior of the government army on that day, King George's son was known, thereafter, as "Butcher Cumberland." In 1747, he returned to the Continent to resume the war in Flanders and was soundly defeated by the French. He died in 1765, obese and dissipated, and severely out of favour with King George III.

As for Charles Stuart, I found him to be anything but the romantic "bonnie prince" I had expected. He was young and impulsive, prone to throwing tantrums, a man ripe for disillusionment in that he knew how to dream but not how to accept reality. He did not recognize the stunning accomplishment of leading his rag-tag army to within one hundred and fifty miles of London; he saw only treachery and betrayal behind the move by his loyal generals and chiefs to try to salvage what remained of their credibility as a fighting force. Could they have taken London? Given the brilliance of Lord George Murray and the audacity of the men at his command, coupled with the arrogant short-sightedness of the English at the time, it might just have been possible. That they could have held the city or the throne against Cumberland's combined forces and the blockade of the Royal Navy is pure fanciful thinking. Still, if they had tried and succeeded, even for a short occupation, one cannot help but speculate about the number of lives that would have been saved in a quick surrender in London, rather than the agonized retreat and debacle at Culloden.

Following his escape from that battle, Charles Stuart was forced to hide in the hills and glens of the Highlands for several months, often only hours ahead of the diligent and determined government troops sent to hunt him down. It is to the enormous credit of the defeated, persecuted, hounded, and brutalized Highlanders that not one of them sought to collect the thirty-thousand-pound reward offered for the Prince's capture. Yet, again, Charles never fully appreciated their loyalty. He drank heavily to compensate for the discomforts suffered during his months of hiding and later decried the Highlanders' lack of courage for not immediately re-forming an army after Culloden. In succeeding years, he wandered through Europe appealing for help from monarchs and nobles, but was never able to win any further support for his claim to the English throne. He became fat and morose from his drinking and debauchery, and died of a stroke in 1788.

One Final Note:

The Battle of Culloden was fought April 16th, 1746.

Negotiations for *The Pride of Lions* were begun over lunch, April 16th, 1986.

'The End' was typed on the final manuscript page of *The Blood of Roses* on April 16th, 1988. Neither of the latter two occurences were planned; they were, in fact, brought to the author's attention by third parties.

KNIGHTSBRIDGE
PUBLISHING